Ford M

FORD MADOX FORD (the name he adopted in 1919: he was originally Ford Hermann Hueffer) was born in Merton, Surrey, in 1873. His mother, Catherine, was the daughter of the Pre-Raphaelite painter Ford Madox Brown. His father, Francis Hueffer, was a German emigré, a musicologist and music critic for *The Times*. Christina and Dante Gabriel Rossetti were his aunt and uncle by marriage. Ford published his first book, a children's fairytale, when he was seventeen. He collaborated with Joseph Conrad from 1898 to 1908, and also befriended many of the best writers of his time, including Henry James, H.G. Wells, Stephen Crane, John Galsworthy and Thomas Hardy. He is best known for his novels, especially *The Fifth Queen* (1906–8), *The Good Soldier* (1915) and *Parade's End* (1924–8). He was also an influential poet and critic, and a brilliant magazine editor. He founded the *English Review* in 1908, discovering D.H. Lawrence, Wyndham Lewis and Ezra Pound, who became another close friend. Ford served as an officer in the Welch Regiment 1915–19. After the war he moved to France. In Paris he founded the *transatlantic review*, taking on Ernest Hemingway as a sub-editor, discovering Jean Rhys and Basil Bunting, and publishing James Joyce and Gertrude Stein. In the 1920s and 1930s he moved between Paris, New York, and Provence. He died in Deauville in June 1939. The author of over eighty books, Ford is a major presence in twentieth-century writing.

MAX SAUNDERS is Professor of English and Co-Director of the Centre for Life-Writing Research at King's College London, where he teaches modern English, European, and American literature. He studied at the universities of Cambridge and Harvard, and was a Research Fellow and then College Lecturer at Selwyn College, Cambridge. He is the author of *Ford Madox Ford: A Dual Life* (2 vols, Oxford University Press, 1996) and *Self Impression: Life-Writing, Autobiografiction, and the Forms of Modern Literature* (Oxford University Press, 2010); the editor of Ford's *Selected Poems*, *War Prose*, and (with Richard Stang) *Critical Essays* (Carcanet, 1997, 1999, 2002). He has published essays on Life-writing, on Impressionism, and on Ford, Conrad, James, Forster, Eliot, Joyce, Rosamond Lehmann, Richard Aldington, May Sinclair, Lawrence, Freud, Pound, Ruskin, Anthony Burgess and others.

## Also by Ford Madox Ford from Carcanet Press

*A Man Could Stand Up*
*Critical Essays*
*England and the English*
*The English Novel*
*The Ford Madox Ford Reader*
*The Good Soldier*
*It Was the Nightingale*
*Ladies Whose Bright Eyes*
*The Last Post*
*No Enemy*
*No More Parades*
*Provence*
*The Rash Act*
*Return to Yesterday*
*Selected Poems*
*War Prose*

FORD MADOX FORD

*Parade's End*

VOLUME I

# Some Do Not ...
*A Novel*

**Edited by Max Saunders**

**CARCANET**

*Some Do Not ...* was first published in Great Britain in 1924
by Duckworth & Co.

This edition first published in Great Britain in 2010 by
Carcanet Press Limited
Alliance House
Cross Street
Manchester M2 7AQ

A CIP catalogue record for this book is available from the British Library

ISBN 978 1 84777 012 7 (*Some Do Not ...*)
ISBN 978 1 84777 021 9 (*Parade's End* volumes I–IV)

The publisher acknowledges financial assistance from Arts Council England

Typeset by XL Publishing Services, Tiverton
Printed and bound in England by SRP Ltd, Exeter

# CONTENTS

# ACKNOWLEDGEMENTS

This edition was conceived from the outset as a collaborative project, and my greatest debt is to my fellow-editors and exemplary collaborators, Joseph Wiesenfarth, Sara Haslam, and Paul Skinner. Working with them has made the editorial task a constant pleasure and fascination, and I'm extremely grateful for their friendship, their help and wisdom in formulating the principles and conventions for the edition, and for their patience and tirelessness throughout our reading of each others' work, checking it, and contributing extra material towards it. For the preparation of *Some Do Not . . .*, I would particularly like to thank Paul Skinner for his generosity in sharing his astonishing expertise not only on the entire range of Ford's work but on its literary and historical context. He provided much of the material for the footnotes.

Ashley Chantler also deserves our special thanks for his editorial advice, especially on the comparability of work across all four volumes. I am also very grateful to other friends who helped by providing information and discussing editorial issues, including Jason Andrew, Anna Aslanyan, John Attridge, Pete Clasen, Valentina Golysheva, Warwick Gould, Kate Kennedy, Gavin Selerie, Martin Stannard, Ann-Marie Vinde and Angus Wrenn.

I am especially grateful to Don Skemer and the staff of Princeton University Library for providing a microfilm copy of the manuscript of *Some Do Not . . .* and for granting permission to publish those parts of it not published previously in the book versions. I'd particularly like to thank Charles E. Greene there for his detailed answers to my questions about the manuscript and the library's other Ford holdings. Katherine Reagan and the staff at the Carl A. Kroch Library, Cornell University, and Gayle M. Richardson, at the Huntington Library, have also been extremely helpful. I'd like to thank Cornell University, Michael Schmidt, and the estate of Janice Biala for permission to quote from Ford's and Biala's letters.

Our editor at Carcanet, Judith Willson, deserves special thanks for all her valuable advice. Finally, I'd like to thank Michael Schmidt, as director of Carcanet Press, for his confidence in the project; and, as Ford's executor, for giving himself (and us) permission to publish it.

# LIST OF ILLUSTRATIONS

# LIST OF SHORT TITLES

| | |
|---|---|
| *Ancient Lights* | *Ancient Lights and Certain New Reflections: Being the Memories of a Young Man* (London: Chapman & Hall, 1911) |
| *Country* | *The Heart of the Country* (London: Alston Rivers, 1906) |
| *England* | *England and the English*, ed. Sara Haslam (Manchester: Carcanet, 2003) (collecting Ford's trilogy on Englishness: see also under *Country* and *People*) |
| *Fifth Queen* | trilogy consisting of *The Fifth Queen* (London: Alston Rivers, 1906), *Privy Seal* (London: Alston Rivers, 1907) and *The Fifth Queen Crowned* (London: Eveleigh Nash, 1908) |
| *Ford/Bowen* | *The Correspondence of Ford Madox Ford and Stella Bowen*, ed. Sondra Stang and Karen Cochran (Bloomington and Indianapolis: Indiana University Press, 1994) |
| *Joseph Conrad* | *Joseph Conrad: A Personal Remembrance* (London: Duckworth, 1924; Boston: Little, Brown, 1924) |
| *Letters* | *Letters of Ford Madox Ford*, ed. Richard M. Ludwig (Princeton, NJ: Princeton University Press, 1965) |
| *March* | *The March of Literature* (London: Allen & Unwin, 1939) |
| *Mightier* | *Mightier Than the Sword* (London: Allen & Unwin, 1938) |
| *Mister Bosphorus* | *Mister Bosphorus and the Muses or a Short History of Poetry in Britain. Variety Entertainment in Four Acts... with Harlequinade, Transformation Scene, Cinematograph Effects,* |

# FORD MADOX FORD
## (F. M. HUEFFER)
# SOME DO NOT

## DUCKWORTH

# INTRODUCTION

## Biographical

The major books of the First World War – according to a truism of literary history – didn't appear until a decade after the Armistice. True of the most famous of the memoirs: Edmund Blunden's *Undertones of War* (1928), Robert Graves's *Goodbye to All That* (1929), or Siegfried Sassoon's *Memoirs of an Infantry Officer* (1930). True, too, of the best-known of the autobiographical novels, such as Erich Maria Remarque's *All Quiet on the Western Front* (1928–9), Richard Aldington's *Death of a Hero* (1929), or Frederic Manning's *The Middle Parts of Fortune* (1929; expurgated as *Her Privates We* in 1930); and also of R. C. Sherriff's play of 1928, *Journey's End*.

Yet the accuracy of this account fails in two fatal respects. First, much of the best-known writing of all coming from the war is its poetry, either written by men such as Wilfred Owen and Isaac Rosenberg, who didn't survive it, or by men such as Siegfried Sassoon and Ivor Gurney, who did, but who wrote powerfully and hauntingly during and immediately after it. Second, there were important war books appearing earlier: as early as 1922 in the case of C. E. Montague's *Disenchantment*, and as early as 1924 for the first volumes of two major novel-sequences about the war: R. H. Mottram's *The Spanish Farm Trilogy* (1924–6) and Ford Madox Ford's tetralogy, *Parade's End* (1924–8). These complex, ambitious, and ironic works may not have had the mass appeal of Remarque's or Sherriff's impassioned condemnations of modern total war's brutality and degradation. Or it may be that a mass readership – many members of which had themselves borne witness to the horror – simply wasn't ready to see war as aesthetic subject-matter. But it may also be that complex novelists take longer to mature than lyric poets, or cynically anti-lyric poets.

Ford Madox Hueffer (as he then was) enlisted in July 1915 and
was given a commission in the Welch Regiment.[1] His father was
the German émigré Francis Hueffer, his mother the English
daughter of the painter Ford Madox Brown. Ford went through
the whole war with his father's German name, only changing it
in 1919. He was an unlikely Welshman: perhaps someone had
associated 'Madox' with the Welsh folklore prince Madoc. Ford
was an even less likely soldier: forty-one, not particularly fit, with
a history of agoraphobic nervous breakdown and 'dyspepsia', and
an extreme sensitivity to impressions and sensations. In his twen-
ties, when he had lived on the Romney Marsh – where the
Wannops and Duchemins live in Part I of *Some Do Not . . .* – he
had gone for long walks, kept livestock, and grown vegetables.
But those were recreations – however necessary to him from time
to time – from his only true calling, which was to write. Since the
breakdown of his marriage to Elsie Hueffer, he had lived an urban,
sedentary London life. He joined up in the wave of patriotic
recruitment, one of the two-and-a-half million men who volunteered for service before conscription had to be introduced when
the numbers of volunteers fell away in 1916. But Ford had additional motives. His private life became increasingly troubled after
he began an affair with the socialite and fashionably shocking
novelist Violet Hunt from 1908–9. Elsie refused to divorce him
(paradoxically, since he was the Catholic but wanted to divorce
her). Ford went to live in Germany, having been led to believe
he could get German citizenship and then a German divorce. He
and Hunt returned to England claiming to be married, which
seemed to satisfy her need for respectability. While it's possible
they went through a ceremony of sorts on the continent, it would
probably have been deemed bigamous under British law. When
in 1912, a newspaper, the *Throne*, referred to Violet as Mrs
Hueffer, Elsie sued it and won. Violet later claimed that she and
Ford hadn't been able to document their wedding for fear of his
being jailed. But most people – including most of their friends –
thought the marriage a foolish fiction. Ford, like Christopher

---

1  For a fuller account of Ford's war-service, see Saunders, *Ford Madox Ford: A Dual Life*,
   2 vols (Oxford: Oxford University Press, 1996), II.

Tietjens, the male protagonist of *Parade's End*, said nothing to defend himself. Violet's less bohemian friends ostracised them. The scandal put an intolerable strain on their relationship. Ford felt bound to stand by her because of his part in their disgrace. But life with her had become unbearable to him. The army, and even the possibility of death, offered an escape.

Ford had published his greatest pre-war novel, *The Good Soldier*, in 1915, only four months before he took his commission. Looking back at that book in 1927, he described himself as having felt like a great Auk, who had laid his one egg 'and might as well die'; a feeling intensified by his sense of the generation of young writers – *les Jeunes* – whose work he had encouraged and published, but who in return regarded him as out of date. 'Those were the passionate days of the literary Cubists, Vorticists, *Imagistes*', he said, and recalled the Vorticist Wyndham Lewis denouncing him as 'Finished! Exploded! Done for! Blasted in fact!' and telling him: 'Your generation has gone. What is the sense of you and Conrad and Impressionism?'[2]

Ford need not have volunteered. He was old for active service and could without shame have continued his writing for 'Wellington House', the secret propaganda department run by his and Violet's friend, the Liberal Cabinet minister Charles Masterman, for whom Ford had already written two books of propaganda, *When Blood is Their Argument* and *Between St. Dennis and St. George* (both 1915), as well as numerous articles. But he appeared to want to go, and not to expect to return. When he was posted to France in the middle of July 1916, two weeks into the bloodiest battle in British military history, the Somme, it must have seemed very unlikely that he would return. He very nearly did not. At the base camp in Rouen, Ford and his fellow members of the Welch Regiment were attached to the 9th Battalion, and left Rouen on 18 July to join their units. Though he was anxious to experience the front line, his Commanding Officer thought he was too old, and Ford was stationed with the

---

2 'Dedicatory Letter to Stella Ford', first published in the 'Avignon edition' of the novel (New York: Albert and Charles Boni, 1927); reprinted in *The Good Soldier*, ed. Martin Stannard (New York and London: W. W. Norton & Company, 1995), 4. Ford, *Mightier Than the Sword* (London: Allen and Unwin, 1938), 282.

battalion transport near Bécourt Wood, just behind the Front near Albert, close to where the 9th Welch had seen heavy losses during the grisly battle of Mametz Wood and the Allied attempts to advance up 'Sausage Valley' to La Boisselle. On 28 or 29 July he was 'blown into the air' by a high-explosive shell and landed on his face, concussed, with a damaged mouth and loosened teeth. The concussion erased whole patches of his knowledge. He even forgot his own name for thirty-six hours. He was shuttled between Field Ambulances and Casualty Clearing Stations, none of which had the equipment to treat him.

About three weeks later Ford left the Casualty Clearing Station at Corbie to rejoin the 9th Battalion of the Welch Regiment, which was now stationed in the Ypres Salient near Kemmel Hill. His experiences on the Western Front are discussed in more detail in the introductions and notes to the later novels, in which Tietjens' war experiences are represented directly. But Ford's time in the Salient needs mentioning here, for two reasons: because it provided the basis for what happens to Tietjens between Parts I and II of *Some Do Not . . .*, which casts its shadow over the whole volume, though it is barely described; and because it was when Ford first started imagining writing about the war. He later said that it was while returning to the Front that he realised he was the only novelist of his age to be in the fighting. This made it all the more necessary that he should bear witness, and he recalled: 'I began to take a literary view of the war from that time.'[3] He also actually started to write about it while there, first in three extraordinary letters he sent to Conrad in the first week of September 1916, rendering his impressions of the war – including some striking 'notes upon sound'. 'I wrote these rather hurried notes yesterday because we were being shelled to hell & I did not expect to get thro' the night', he explained. 'I wonder if it is just vanity that in these cataclysmic moments makes one desire to *record*.'[4] Ford hoped Conrad might be able to use these

3   F[anny] B[utcher], 'Ford Madox Ford a Visitor Here Tells of His Work', *Chicago Tribune* (22 Jan. 1927), 8. Ford to Stella Bowen, 20 Jan. [1927], identifies 'F. B.': *The Correspondence of Ford Madox Ford and Stella Bowen*, ed. Sondra J. Stang and Karen Cochran (Bloomington and Indianapolis: Indiana University Press, 1994), 302.
4   Ford to Conrad, 7 Sept. 1916: *The Presence of Ford Madox Ford*, ed. Sondra J. Stang (Philadelphia: University of Pennsylvania Press, 1981), 176.

impressions because he did not expect to live to be able to do so.

Margaret Atwood has written on how 'all writing of the narrative kind, and perhaps all writing, is motivated, deep down, by a
fear of and a fascination with mortality – by a desire to make the
risky trip to the Underworld, and to bring something or someone
back from the dead.'[5] War writing above all is motivated by that
fear and fascination. For many participants, trench war seemed
uncannily like a trip to the underworld – as imagined, for
example, by Wilfred Owen in his poem 'Strange Meeting', in
which the trenchscape leads into a nightmare vision of the dead
speaking in an underworld no-man's land. One of Ford's first
literary efforts after the war was to translate Euripides' *Alcestis*, in
which the heroine volunteers to die in her husband's place, and
is then in turn rescued from death by the demigod Hercules.[6] Ford
said that in working on it he had 'recovered some shadow of
power over words. But not much.'[7] What struck him in the Ypres
Salient was how little power he seemed to have over words, or
how little power words had, to record the cataclysm. That was
the motive for the piece he wrote dated 15 September 1916,
which was signed 'Miles Ignotus' ('the unknown soldier') and
headed 'A Day of Battle'. Extended prose written at the Front is
relatively rare compared to letters or even poems. Trench conditions scarcely conduced to novel-writing. This is an important
document not only for what it tells of the experience, but for what
it foretells about *Parade's End*. After the war he wrote of his 'first
sight of the German lines from a down behind Albert in 1916' –
it was almost certainly while he was stationed near Bécourt in
July, before his concussion – that it was 'about the most unfor-
gettable of my own experiences in the flesh ....'[8] The literary
impressionism Ford had developed with Conrad was always
intensely visual. He often echoed Conrad's dictum that the
writer's task is 'before all, to make you *see*'.[9] But 'A Day of Battle'

5  Atwood, *Negotiating with the Dead: A Writer on Writing* (London: Virago 2003), 140.
6  'The Alcestis of Euripides: freely adapted for the Modern Stage', 1918–19; typescripts
   at Cornell. Discussed further by the editors of *A Man Could Stand Up – and Last Post*.
7  Saunders, *A Dual Life* II 78.
8  Ford, *Thus to Revisit* (London: Chapman and Hall, 1921), 77–8.
9  Conrad, Preface to *The Nigger of the 'Narcissus'*: first printed as an 'Author's Note' after
   the serialisation of the novel in the *New Review*, 17 (Dec. 1897), 628–31.

begins by asking why it is that he cannot write about the war:

> With the pen, I used to be able to 'visualize things' – as it used
> to be called [...] Now I could not make you see Messines,
> Wijtschate, St Eloi; or La Boiselle, the Bois de Bécourt or de
> Mametz – although I have sat looking at them for hours, for
> days, for weeks on end. Today, when I look at a mere coarse
> map of the Line, simply to read 'Ploegsteert' or 'Armentières'
> seems to bring up extraordinarily coloured and exact pictures
> behind my eyeballs – little pictures having all the brilliant
> minuteness that medieval illuminations had – of towers, and
> roofs, and belts of trees and sunlight; or, for the matter of these,
> of men, burst into mere showers of blood and dissolving into
> muddy ooze; or of aeroplanes and shells against the translucent
> blue. – But, as for putting them – into words! No: the mind stops
> dead, and something in the brain stops and shuts down [...][10]

It is a deeply paradoxical piece, vividly recreating the predica-
ment of someone who feels he can no longer create vivid
representations: 'As far as I am concerned an invisible barrier in
my brain seems to lie between the profession of Arms and the
mind that put things into words.'[11] This is partly because of the
predominant feeling of anxiety:

> I used to think that being out in France would be like being in
> a magic ring that would cut me off from all private troubles:
> but nothing is further from the truth. I have gone down to the
> front line at night, worried, worried, worried beyond belief
> about happenings at home in a Blighty that I did not much
> expect to see again – so worried that all sense of personal
> danger disappeared and I forgot to duck when shells went close
> overhead.[12]

Doubtless Ford did worry about 'happenings at home' while he
was in the army. The separation from friends and family, and the
enforced inactivity of much of army life, must have opened up

10 Ford, *War Prose*, ed. Max Saunders (Manchester: Carcanet, 1999), 36–7.
11 *War Prose* 37.
12 *War Prose* 41.

new spaces for anxiety. In *No Enemy* he wrote of 'that eternal "waiting to report" that takes up 112/113ths of one's time during war'.[13] Yet this account of Home Front worries pursuing the soldier even to the battlefield (as Sylvia pursues Tietjens to France in *No More Parades*) could equally be read the other way around: as fear about death and physical harm being displaced somewhere as far away as possible. Either way, it became an integral part of his aim for the series to convey the sensation of this anxiety: 'it seemed to me that, if I could present, not merely fear, not merely horror, not merely death, not merely even self-sacrifice ... but just worry; that might strike a note of which the world would not so readily tire'.[14]

## Shell-shock

Anxiety is one of Ford's major themes, and in *Parade's End* it takes different forms in each novel. *Some Do Not* ... details Tietjens' anxieties over his tortured marriage to Sylvia, then his love for Valentine, and then his amnesia; and it details Valentine's worry over their relationship, and then over whether he will survive the war. But the forms of anxiety in *Parade's End* are all suffused with the anxiety of 'shell-shock' and Ford's subsequent amnesia. *Parade's End* is not the first novel of shell-shock (now clinically termed 'post-traumatic stress disorder'). Rebecca West's *The Return of the Soldier* had appeared in 1918. But it is an early rendering of trauma produced by the First World War, written at a time when trauma was still only beginning to be understood. As Tietjens thinks later in the series: 'There was no knowing what shell shock was or what it did to you.'[15] *Some Do Not* ... preceded by a year Woolf's *Mrs Dalloway*, with its suicidal visionary veteran Septimus Warren Smith. The greatest war literature is concerned with what war does not just to bodies, but

13 Ford, *No Enemy*, ed. Paul Skinner (Manchester: Carcanet, 2002), 33.
14 Ford, *It Was the Nightingale*, ed. John Coyle (Manchester: Carcanet, 2007), 206.
15 Ford, *A Man Could Stand Up –*, ed. Sara Haslam (Manchester: Carcanet, 2011), II.vi.
   C. S. Myers is credited with having coined the term 'shell shock' in the *Lancet* in 1915 (i: 316–20). So the name was still novel at the time Sylvia's friends cynically consider it a 'purely nominal disease' (207).

also to minds. *Some Do Not . . .* is the first and greatest novel of shell-shock written by a combatant, who had not only witnessed some of the appalling facts of trench warfare, but who had also had the experience of blast-concussion, and the resulting amnesia and terror.

## Marwood

To recover more of his power over words, Ford needed to revisit the shades of his own war anxieties in *Parade's End*. But he found an oblique method for doing it, and for solving the problem of visualisation. He characteristically gave several different accounts of the gestation of the sequence. First, he described a moment while still at the Front:

> it must have been in September, 1916, when I was in a region called the Salient, and I remember the very spot where the idea came to me – I said to myself: How would all this look in the eyes of X ... – already dead, along with all English Tories?[16]

'X' was Arthur Marwood, Ford's much-admired close friend, and in many ways the prototype for Christopher Tietjens. Tietjens has Marwood's family history. The Marwoods' family seat was Busby Hall, which Ford reinvented as Groby Hall in *Parade's End*. Busby is near Stokesley in Yorkshire, not far from Redcar, where Ford had been stationed in the summer of 1917 after being invalided home. Tietjens has Marwood's mathematical prowess and education, his mannerisms, his thought-style. It was, said Ford, 'as if I "set" my mind by his':

> If I had personal problems I would go and talk to him about anything else. Then the clarity of the working of his mind had an effect on mine that *made me see*, if not what was best to do then, what would be most true to myself.[17]

---

16 Ford, 'To William Bird', Dedicatory Letter to *No More Parades: War Prose* 198.
17 Ford, *Return to Yesterday* (1931), ed. Bill Hutchings (Manchester: Carcanet, 1999), 281 (italics added).

He imagined a series of Marwoodian fictional characters before and after the war. In *Parade's End*, the reimagining of Marwood enabled him to see the war from another point of view – from a lofty, Tory perspective – to see the Western Front under another's eyes. 'A Day of Battle' is the first half of a two-part piece called 'War and the Mind'. In the person of Tietjens, Ford sends Marwood's mind to the war. In actuality Marwood, who was five years older than Ford, had been ill with tuberculosis and had died in May 1916.[18]

In 1931, in his reminiscences of the pre-war years, *Return to Yesterday*, Ford identified Tietjens explicitly with Marwood. But, surprisingly, considering his memory of 'the very spot where the idea came' to him, the scene is now set in Menton, during Ford's convalescence on the Riviera in the spring of 1917. He tells how he had been experimenting with Marwood's 'system' for gambling at Monte Carlo:

> It was whilst I was thus passing my time that it occurred to me to wonder what Marwood would have thought about the War and the way it was conducted. In the attempt to realise that problem for myself I wrote several novels with a projection of him as a central character. Of course they were no sort of biography of Marwood. He died several years before the War, though, as I have said, that is a fact that I never realise.[19]

The back-dating of Marwood's death is surprising, though such inconsistencies are characteristic of Ford's impressionism. Perhaps he was thinking of the death of their friendship (when

18 Thomas Moser, *The Life in the Fiction of Ford Madox Ford* (Princeton, NJ: Princeton University Press, 1980), 212. Ford's unusual step of making his protagonist a mathematician was thus more than an *hommage* to his friend. It was also a way of questioning how modernity has changed our modes of thinking about life, its complexity fostering ever-greater specialisation. 'Practical politics', said Ford, 'have become so much a matter of sheer figures that the average man, dreading mathematics almost as much as he dreads an open mind, is reduced, nevertheless, to a state of mind so open that he has abandoned thinking – that he has abandoned even feeling about any public matter at all': *The Critical Attitude* (London: Duckworth, 1911), 114–15. He saw art as countering such specialisation. Only 'the imaginative writer' can represent our lives, he argued, 'because no collection of facts, and no tabulation of figures, can give us any sense of proportion': *Ibid.*, 33.
19 *Return* 281.

*Some Do Not . . .*

Marwood got drawn into Ford's estrangement from Elsie); or
perhaps it is an impressionistic way of saying that Ford had heard
of Marwood's death before going to the war. Similarly, there is
doubtless some truth in both accounts of where and when Ford
had the idea of using Marwood's mind to focalise a war novel: as
he said, he already had the habit of wondering what Marwood
would think about things.

It is in *It Was the Nightingale* (1934), his reminiscences about
his post-war life, that Ford says most about the genesis and the
writing of *Parade's End*. Here, too, Marwood is involved, but this
time for a story he tells about someone else. Ford recalls a conversation in a railway carriage in 1908 or 1909:

> I said to Marwood:
> 'What really became of Waring?'
> He said:
> 'The poor devil, he picked up a bitch on a train between
> Calais and Paris. She persuaded him that he had got her with
> child.... He felt he had to marry her.... Then he found out
> that the child might be another man's, just as well as his....
> There was no real knowing.... It was the hardest luck I ever
> heard of.... She was as unfaithful to him as a street-walker....'
> I said:
> 'Couldn't he divorce?'
> – But he couldn't divorce. He held that a decent man could
> never divorce a woman. The woman, on the other hand, would
> not divorce him because she was a Roman Catholic.[20]

This provides the story-line of Tietjens' marriage to Sylvia. (It
also suggests how in both *The Good Soldier* and *Parade's End* Ford
came to reverse the religious contrast between himself as the
Catholic and Elsie Hueffer or Violet Hunt as nominal Protes-
tants.) But it includes nothing yet of the complications ensuing
from Tietjens' adulterous love for Valentine Wannop. In *It Was
the Nightingale* this second stage comes when Ford was staying in
Harold Monro's villa at St Jean Cap Ferrat during the winter of

20 *Nightingale* 189–90.

1922–3, having found the cold and mud of Sussex winters
unbearable. Nearby lived 'a poor fellow who had had almost
Waring's fate'. He does not name the man, but one reason why
his story must have stuck in Ford's mind is its similarities to the
stories of Dowell and Ashburnham in *The Good Soldier*:

> He was a wealthy American who had married a wrong 'un. She
> had been unfaithful to him before and after marriage. He had
> supported these wrongs because of his passion for the woman.
> At last she had eloped with a ship steward and had gone sailing
> around the world. The husband being an American of good
> tradition considered himself precluded from himself taking
> proceedings for divorce, but he would gladly have let the
> woman divorce him and would have provided liberally for her.
> She, however, was sailing around the world and he had no
> means of communicating with her. Almost simultaneously,
> after a year or so, he had conceived an overwhelming passion
> for another woman and the wife had returned.... What passed
> between them one had no means of knowing. Presumably she
> had announced her intention of settling down again with him
> and had flatly refused to divorce him. So he committed
> suicide....
>     The dim sight of the roof of his villa below me over the bay
> gave me then another stage of my intrigue [...] It suddenly
> occurred to me to wonder what Marwood himself would have
> thought of the story – and then what he would have thought
> of the war [...] I imagined his mind going all over the misty
> and torrential happenings of the Western Front [...] I seemed,
> even as I walked in that garden, to see him stand in some high
> place in France during the period of hostilities taking in not
> only what was visible, but all the causes and all the motive
> powers of distant places. And I seemed to hear his infinitely
> scornful comment on those places. It was as if he lived again.[21]

One way that Ford could continue not to realise Marwood's
death was to realise him as a living character. Recovering
Marwood, through a Herculean descent into the Western Front's

21 *Nightingale* 201–2.

underworld of shadows, enabled Ford to recover his own powers of visualisation. Yet to say that is to acknowledge that Tietjens' experiences in the novels are Ford's rather than Marwood's. His marital problems and his war service closely reflect Ford's own life before and during the war. Ford is also summoning back the shade of his own past self. If he felt before enlisting that he might as well die, when he came back, having come through a near-death experience, he sometimes wrote as if he had died: as when he titled his 1921 volume of reminiscences *Thus to Revisit*, casting himself as the ghost of Hamlet's father returning to the pre-war past. 'In the end', he said later, 'if one is a writer, one is a writer, and if one was in that hell, it was a major motive that one should be able to write of it [...].'[22] By combining Marwood's mind with his own experiences in the character of Tietjens, Ford had found the way to do that.

In which case, indeed, the stories of Marwood, Waring, and the 'wealthy American' might be strategically deployed to draw attention away from the autobiographical dimension of the novels. In particular, the female characters have been seen as drawing closely on Ford's partners. The haughty and vindictive Sylvia Tietjens, Christopher's estranged wife, has been identified with Violet Hunt (by her biographers as well as by Ford's). Valentine Wannop owes much to the woman for whom Ford left Hunt, the young Australian painter Stella Bowen – though she also draws upon Stella's friend Margaret Postgate, who had Valentine's classical education. And the hypocritical Edith Ethel Duchemin has been seen as an unflattering portrait of Ford's estranged wife Elsie. After the *Throne* scandal, it was in Ford's interest for these parallels not to figure in the reviews of the books. His question 'What really became of Waring?' alludes to Browning's poem, which begins: 'What's become of Waring / Since he gave us all the slip.' Wrapping the question up in an allusion suggests that the name is a pseudonym, or that the story has already begun to turn into a fiction.

As the multiplicity of these stories indicates, the gestation of *Parade's End* was a slow, oblique process. Ford said of his earlier masterpiece, *The Good Soldier*, that 'though I wrote it with comparative rapidity, I had it hatching within myself for fully another decade'.[23] This was written in 1927, by which time he had completed the first three novels of *Parade's End*. And once again, a long process of conception and development had produced his best work. This time, it was seven years since he first had the idea while in the Salient in 1916 before he finished *Some Do Not* ... in 1923, and more than a decade before he had completed all four novels in 1928. In the meantime, there had been several false starts. He had begun writing a more autobiographical novel, 'True Love & a GCM.' ('General Court Martial') in 1918–19, but left it unfinished. Also in 1919 he wrote most of the fictionalised book of reminiscences about the war that was published a decade later as *No Enemy*. He did complete a novel about the literary life and the war, but didn't publish it.[24] He wrote criticism, reminiscences, and some of his best poetry. But it was 1923 before he published his first post-war novel: *The Marsden Case*. This too is oblique about the war, though eloquent about why it needs to be:

> This is not a war novel. Heaven knows I, who saw something of that struggle, would willingly wipe out of my mind every sight that I saw, every sound that I heard, every memory in my brain. But it is impossible, though there are non-participants who demand it, to write the lives of people to-day aged thirty or so, and leave out all mention of the fact that whilst those young people were aged, say, twenty-two to twenty-eight, there existed – Armageddon. For the matter of that, it would be wicked to attempt it, since the eyes, the ears, the brain and the fibres of every soul to-day adult have been profoundly seared by those dreadful wickednesses of embattled humanity.[25]

That is very much the project of *Parade's End* too: to show how the war affected the generations of Ford and *les Jeunes*. The

---

23 'Dedicatory Letter to Stella Ford', *The Good Soldier* 5.
24 'True Love & a GCM' was published for the first time in *War Prose*. The completed novel, 'Mr Croyd', was revised and re-titled as 'The Wheels of the Plough' then 'That Same Poor Man'. The typescripts are at the Carl A. Kroch Library, Cornell University. Extracts were published in *War Prose*.
25 Ford, *The Marsden Case* (London: Duckworth, 1923), 143–4.

*Marsden Case* provided a structural model for *Some Do Not . . .* as well, since both are diptych forms, with a pre-war first half and a second after the main characters have been to the war. In both, the war itself is a disturbing absence between the two halves, though constantly suggested everywhere – as, in *Some Do Not . . .*, in the subtly connected outbreaks of violence in the regulated Edwardian civilisation of Part I.

Ford remembered another episode – this time an encounter in Paris – that heightened the urgency of writing about the war. In front of Notre Dame he met a man called Evans from his regiment. They went into the cathedral 'and looked at the bright little tablet that commemorates the death of over a million men'.[26] Inevitably, they began to reminisce about the war. They had met when Ford was on his way to rejoin his battalion from Corbie after his shell-blast and terrifying amnesia. Evans was in the same wagon, returning from England where he had been recovering from a wound in the thigh. 'The wagon had jolted more abominably than ever', recalled Ford, 'and I could, in Notre Dame, remember that I had felt beside my right thigh for the brake. The beginnings of panic came over me. I had forgotten whether I found the brake!' Panic because this small amnesia made him worry that it might herald a reprise of the larger, battle-induced one: 'The memory that had chosen to return after Corbie must be forsaking me again.' As often with him, such fear, and the ensuing urge to write novels, was associated with thoughts of death: 'I thought Evans had been killed the day after we had got back to the line – but he obviously hadn't.' Ostensibly Ford was anxious that he would not be able to write a convincing war novel if his grasp of factual detail was weakening. The significance of such detail was more personal, however (he could, after all, have rediscovered factual details with some research). If he could not recall the matter of his past, it was as if he were becoming what he referred to as 'the stuff to fill graveyards'; might himself be mistaken for dead.[27]

---

26 *Nightingale* 174–7 (174).
27 See note on 281 below. The Dedication to Ford's first volume of reminiscences, *Ancient Lights* (London: Chapman and Hall, 1911), vii–viii, x, describes a comparable impulse to 'rescue' memories 'before they go out of my mind altogether'.

There were specifically literary motives for Ford's decision to start writing about the war in the early 1920s, in addition to these more personal and psychological ones. His close involvement with fellow-Modernists, and especially with Ezra Pound, meant that he was well aware of the epoch-making work then being written. He would have known Pound's poem-sequences *Hugh Selwyn Mauberley* and *Homage to Sextus Propertius*, as well as the early stages of his epic sequence *The Cantos*. In January 1922 Pound sent Ford a draft of what was then Canto VIII, but would later be revised and incorporated into Canto II, asking Ford in his 'infinite patience' if he could 'go through the enclosed with a red, blood-red, green, blue, or other pencil and scratch what is too awful'.[28] Ford had already begun his magnificent experimental verse-satire *Mister Bosphorus and the Muses* when 'The Waste Land' was published in October 1922. Pound's vivid evocation of Mediterranean gods may have influenced Bosphorus's longing for the Southern muse; Ford's use of music-hall and cinema in the poem may signal a debt to Eliot, though Ford had written about both media before he knew of Eliot.[29] Then in July 1922 Ford wrote one of the important early reviews of Joyce's *Ulysses*, which had appeared in book form that February.[30] It was immediately apparent to him that, for all its baffling complexity, *Ulysses* had altered the literary landscape:

> One can't arrive at one's valuation of a volume so loaded as *Ulysses* after a week of reading and two or three weeks of thought about it. Next year, or in twenty years, one may. For it is as if a new continent with new traditions had appeared, and demanded to be run through in a month. *Ulysses* contains the undiscovered mind of man; it is human consciousness analyzed as it has never before been analyzed. Certain books change the world. This, success or failure, *Ulysses* does: for no

28 Pound to Ford [13 Jan. 1922]: *Pound/Ford: the Story of a Literary Friendship: the Correspondence between Ezra Pound and Ford Madox Ford and Their Writings About Each Other*, ed. Brita Lindberg-Seyersted (London: Faber & Faber, 1982), 63. See 62–7.
29 See Saunders, *A Dual Life* II 124 for a fuller discussion of the relation between Ford's and Eliot's poems.
30 Ford may have seen some of 'Ulysses' in serial form in the *Little Review*, where it appeared from 1918–20, since his own work 'Women and Men' was serialised there in 1918, though Ford was still in the army then.

novelist with serious aims can henceforth set out upon a task
of writing before he has at least formed his own private estimate as to the rightness or wrongness of the methods of the
author of *Ulysses*. If it does not make an epoch – and it well
may! – it will at least mark the ending of a period.[31]

The 'ending of a period' is, of course, also the subject of
*Parade's End* – Period's End, perhaps... When Ford and Stella
Bowen arrived in Paris in December 1922 they found themselves
witness to another epochal ending: the mourning and funeral of
Marcel Proust. Ford said that 'even at that date I still dreaded the
weakness in myself that I knew I should find if I made my
prolonged effort'. But with the example of *A la recherche du temps
perdu* added to those of Pound, Joyce, and Eliot, he now felt it was
time he began his own prolonged effort. 'I think I am incapable
of any thoughts of rivalry', he wrote. But he wanted to see some
literary work done: 'something on an immense scale': 'I wanted
the Novelist in fact to appear in his really proud position as historian of his own time. Proust being dead I could see no one who
was doing that.' *Parade's End* thus originated in multiple acts of
elegy: for Marwood; for the war-dead, or presumed-dead; for
Ford's pre-war Hueffer-self; for Proust; and for what he called 'the
world before the war'.[32] Though the war is at its heart, its scope
is much more ambitious: to trace the changes to individuals,
society, and culture wrought by the war; and to do that, Ford had
to start (as the stories of Marwood and 'Waring' indicate) with
pre-war Edwardian society, and finish with post-war regeneration
and reconstruction.

31 Ford, 'A Haughty and Proud Generation', *Yale Review*, 11 (July 1922), 703–17: in
Ford, *Critical Essays*, ed. Max Saunders and Richard Stang (Manchester: Carcanet,
2002), 208–17 (217).
32 *Nightingale* 177–80. See also 270–1. Ford to T. R. Smith, 27 July 1931: Cornell. Quoted
Saunders, *A Dual Life* II [iii].

## Plot Summary

*Some Do Not . . .* begins with the two young friends, Christopher
Tietjens and Vincent Macmaster, on the train to Rye for a golfing
weekend in the country. The year, probably 1912, is only indicated later.[33] They both work in London as government
statisticians, though Macmaster aspires to be a critic and has just
written a short book on Dante Gabriel Rossetti. He plans to call
on a parson who knew Rossetti and who lives near Rye. The first
of the novel's two parts covers the ensuing weekend, which
changes both their lives. Tietjens is preoccupied with his disastrous marriage. The second chapter switches to his elegant
socialite wife, Sylvia, who is staying with her mother at
Lobscheid, a quiet German resort, with their priest, Father
Consett. Sylvia had left Tietjens for a lover, Major Perowne, but
became bored with him. She's bored in Lobscheid too, but needs
the alibi of being there to look after her mother to account for
her absence when she returns to London. Consett probes the
state of her marriage, and senses that her anger towards Tietjens
is far from indifference. Back in England, Macmaster has called
on the Rev. Duchemin, but was received by his wife and is
instantly infatuated by her Pre-Raphaelite ambience and
elegance. He rejoins Tietjens for a round of golf with General
Campion and his brother-in-law. At the clubhouse they meet a
Liberal Cabinet minister. While they are playing, the game is
interrupted by two Suffragettes haranguing the minister. Some of
the men start chasing them, and the chase threatens to become
violent, but Tietjens manages to trip up a policeman as if by accident and the women escape. The next morning Macmaster takes
Tietjens back to the Duchemins, where he has been invited for

---

33 In *No More Parades* III.ii. and *A Man Could Stand Up* – I.ii. (In the last chapter of *Some
Do Not . . .*, II.vi, Tietjens recalls his conversation with Macmaster in the opening
chapter, thinking of it as 'Ten years' before. II.vi is probably set in 1917, which would
push the opening back to 1907; but presumably Ford's point is that the pre-war years
seem much further back in the past than they were, and that at moments of extreme
stress or excitement the experience of time distorts. As Valentine thinks in *A Man
Could Stand Up* – I.ii: 'Later she realised that that was what thought was. In ten
minutes [. . .] you found you thought out more than in two years. Or it was not as long
ago as that.') See Moser, *The Life in the Fiction of Ford Madox Ford*, 318–20, for further
discussion of these and other possible inconsistencies in the tetralogy.

one of their celebrated breakfasts. Mrs Duchemin is apprehensive about her husband, who is prone to fits of lunacy. He becomes paranoid that the two guests are doctors coming to take him to an asylum, and destroys the decorum of the occasion, first ranting about sex in Latin, then starting to describe his wedding night. Macmaster saves the day by telling Duchemin's minder how to neutralise him, and Mrs Duchemin is soon holding his hand and admiring his tact. One of the other guests is Valentine Wannop, who lives nearby with her mother, a novelist. Valentine turns out to be one of the Suffragette protesters. Mrs Wannop is also there, and is delighted to meet Tietjens, since his father had helped her when she became widowed. She is one of the few writers he admires. She insists that Tietjens come back with them for lunch. He and Valentine walk back through the countryside. When they're overtaken by Mrs Wannop on her dog-cart, he notices that the horse's strap is about to break, and potentially saves her life by fixing it. The Wannops are sheltering the other Suffragette, Gertie, and worry that the police might be looking for them. So Tietjens agrees to drive with Valentine in the cart to hide Gertie with some of the Wannops' relations. They leave at ten on Midsummer night, so as not to be seen, and drive all night. On the way back, Tietjens and Valentine are alone, conversing, arguing, and falling in love, until, in the dawn mist, General Campion crashes his car into them and injures the horse.

Part I ends on that scene of carnage. Part II begins several years later, in the middle of the war, probably in 1917. Tietjens is back in London, lunching with Sylvia. He has been fighting in France, where he was shell-shocked, and much of his memory has been obliterated. He is reduced to reading the *Encyclopaedia Britannica* to restock it. He sees Mrs Wannop regularly – she has moved to London, near his office – and has been helping her write propaganda articles. Sylvia thus suspects he has been having an affair with Valentine, though he has hardly seen her since she is working as a gym instructor in a girls' school. Macmaster has married Mrs Duchemin (Mr Duchemin having died). He holds literary parties that have become celebrated, but they have kept their marriage secret, and Valentine always accompanies her to the parties to keep up appearances. Sylvia tells Tietjens that the cause of his father's death was the rumours he heard that Tietjens

lived on women and had got Valentine pregnant. The banker,
Lord Port Scatho, arrives. His nephew, Brownlie, who is infatuated with Sylvia, has unfairly and humiliatingly dishonoured
Tietjens' cheques to his army Mess and his club. Tietjens reveals
that he has been ordered to return to France the following day,
and is determined to resign from the club. Tietjens' elder brother,
Mark, arrives, and the two brothers walk from Gray's Inn to
Whitehall, speaking candidly, as Tietjens disabuses Mark about
the rumours defaming him and Valentine. It turns out that Mark,
asked by his father to find out about Tietjens (in case he needed
money), had asked his flatmate Ruggles to discover what people
were saying about Tietjens, and that it was Ruggles who relayed
the malicious gossip to their father. As they get to the War Office
they run into Valentine, who has come to say goodbye to Tietjens. Mark talks to Valentine while they wait for Tietjens to come
out of a meeting, and she recalls a rare conversation she had with
Tietjens five or six weeks earlier, at one of Macmaster's parties,
during which she had realised he would return to the war. He told
her how his memory was improving, and how he had been able
to help Macmaster with one of his calculations. Macmaster has
taken the credit for the work, and been awarded a knighthood on
the strength of it. Mrs Duchemin/Macmaster, who has always
disliked Tietjens (despite, or rather because of, all the help and
money he has given Macmaster) has been trying to get him out
of their lives, and tries to befriend Sylvia, inviting her to one of
the parties. Valentine is shocked, and realises her friendship with
Mrs Macmaster is finished. Outside the War Office, Valentine
persuades the brothers to shake hands despite Tietjens' anger.
She and Tietjens agree to meet later that night – his last before
returning to a likely death – and she agrees to become his
mistress, after escorting her drunken brother home. But in the
event, they … do not. The novel ends with Tietjens returning to
his dark flat, recalling the events and non-events of the day and
night, including his farewell to Macmaster, and especially his last
conversations with Valentine.

## War and the Mind

The technical challenge Ford had set himself in *The Good Soldier* was to find a form to wring every drop of interest and emotion out of the story of a man, Edward Ashburnham, too stupid to be able to articulate what was happening to him, told by a narrator, John Dowell, too different, and probably too obtuse, to be able to understand the story he was telling. The challenge *Parade's End* represents is comparable but inverse: in it, supremely intelligent characters undergo experiences that threaten to destroy their minds. Though Ford had not gone to university, he had nevertheless had an extraordinarily bohemian education, surrounded by writers and artists, and he had an unusually capacious and quick mind. The writer Marie Belloc Lowndes, for instance – Violet Hunt's friend, and Hilaire Belloc's sister – said he was 'brilliantly clever'.[34] In *Parade's End* Tietjens' intellect is matched by Valentine's – deriving perhaps less from Stella Bowen, who was an accomplished painter and wrote beautifully, but was not an intellectual, than from Margaret Postgate and perhaps other 'bright young things' such as Rebecca West. Sylvia Tietjens, though not an intellectual either, has Violet Hunt's rapier mind and wit. But then, how could Tietjens have married anyone whom he couldn't respect intellectually?

Ford is not usually thought of as a philosophical novelist. He doesn't proceed, certainly, with the rigorous analytical clarity of a Thomas Mann. Nor does he write 'novels of ideas' in which characters exist as mouthpieces for debating positions. But he often wrote about thought, which he tended to couple with the arts; as when, in the closing chapter of *A Mirror to France* (which was probably the chapter written first, while at Cap Ferrat), he writes of looking from the rocks above the Mediterranean and asks: 'Let us attempt to consider the world solely from the point of view of pure thought – and the Arts [...].'[35] Or when, in an essay from 1927, he wrote: 'For militarism is the antithesis of

---

34 'Marie Belloc Lowndes on Ford and Violet Hunt', ed. Susan Lowndes Marques, *Ford Madox Ford's Literary Contacts*, ed. Paul Skinner, International Ford Madox Ford Studies, 6 (Amsterdam and New York: Rodopi, 2007), 95–100 (96).
35 Ford, *A Mirror to France* (London: Duckworth, 1926), 263.

Thought and the Arts, and it is by Thought and the Arts alone that the world can be saved.'[36] Or, in his later book about Provence, when he says: 'What I – and civilisation – most need is a place where, Truth having no divine right to glamour, experiments in thought abound.'[37] *Parade's End* might be understood as such a thought-experiment. In it, Ford attempts to take stock of the impact the war had on the nature of thinking and consciousness. But it is also an art-experiment: investigating what literary forms and styles can best represent such processes.

## Speech

It's in the conversations that the characters' qualities of mind especially flash. *Some Do Not . . .* contains some of the most brilliant dialogue in English fiction. Not the cleverness of Peacock's conversation novels, nor the epigrammatic brilliance of Wilde, but rather, as in the dialogue of Shakespeare or Lawrence, speeches alive with a sense of the full complexity of the characters' tangled lives behind them, felt through implication, association, hesitation, as the conversation jumps from one topic to another and they think with lightning speed. Some early critics were quick to grasp the nature of the achievement: 'Mr. Ford manages, with quite extraordinary ingenuity, to dovetail into his admirable dialogue long passages of reflection which reveal the essentials of an extremely complicated tissue of events', said one review; 'Mr. Ford is one of the small band of novelists who can write dialogue that rings natural, though it is infused with wit and ideas', said another.[38] Bonamy Dobrée, who said that in *Parade's End* 'Mr. Ford proved himself a great novelist', included a long excerpt from *Some Do Not . . .* in his 1934 book *Modern Prose Style* – from the extraordinary scene at the end of Part I, in which Christopher and Valentine argue as

36 'Preparedness', *New York Herald Tribune Books* (6 Nov. 1927), 7, 18: *War Prose* 69–74 (73).
37 Ford, *Provence*, ed. John Coyle (Manchester: Carcanet, 2009), 65–6.
38 [Orlo Williams] *Times Literary Supplement* (24 Apr. 1924), 252. 'Books of the Week', *Weekly Dispatch* (27 Apr. 1924), 2.

they ride through the silvery mist and begin to fall in love – as an
example of a contemporary technique in which characterisation
'is usually shown by small touches in conversation, sometimes
directly revealing by the comments of another person', and
arguing that 'This art of building up character entirely by conversation' was taken to its limit by Ivy Compton Burnett.[39] Some
later critics have thought the dialogue parodic ('Oh, *no*, Christopher ... not from the *club!*' etc.); but Ford's contemporaries
evidently considered he had a good ear for Edwardian idioms.

Ford had indeed long worried at how to represent conversation, and devotes some space to the problem in the section of his
important memoir of Conrad discussing the techniques they
developed:

> One unalterable rule that we had for the rendering of conver-
> sations – for genuine conversations that are an exchange of
> thought, not interrogatories or statements of fact – was that no
> speech of one character should ever answer the speech that
> goes before it. This is almost invariably the case in real life
> where few people listen, because they are always preparing
> their own next speeches.[40]

The expressive problem he confronted in his pre-war fiction
was the inexpressiveness of the English. Recalling one of his
collaborative novels with Conrad, Ford wrote:

> We both desired to get into situations, at any rate when anyone
> was speaking, the sort of indefiniteness that is characteristic of
> all human conversations, and particularly of English conver-
> sations that are almost always conducted entirely by means of
> allusions and unfinished sentences. If you listen to two
> Englishmen communicating by means of words, for you can

39 Dobrée, review of Ford's *The Rash Act*, *Spectator*, 151 (8 Sept. 1933), 321. Dobrée was
   perhaps put onto Ford by their mutual friend Herbert Read, with whom he had edited
   *The London Book of English Prose* (London: Eyre and Spottiswoode, 1932), which
   includes an excerpt from *A Man Could Stand Up –*. Dobrée, *Modern Prose Style*
   (Oxford: Clarendon Press, 1934), 167–9, 55–8 (55).
40 Ford, *Joseph Conrad: A Personal Remembrance* (London: Duckworth, 1924), 184–9
   (188).

hardly call it conversing, you will find that their speeches are little more than this: A. says: "What sort of a fellow is ... *you* know!" B. replies: "Oh, he's a sort of a ..." and A. exclaims: "Ah, I always thought so ...." This is caused partly by sheer lack of vocabulary, partly by dislike for uttering any definite statement at all [...].

The writer used to try to get that effect by almost directly rendering speeches that, practically, never ended so that the original draft of the *Inheritors* consisted of a series of vague scenes in which nothing definite was ever said. These scenes melted one into the other until the whole book, in the end, came to be nothing but a series of the very vaguest hints.[41]

Ford had written that first draft of *The Inheritors* (1901). Conrad's role, he said, was 'to give to each scene a final tap; these, in a great many cases, brought the whole meaning of the scene to the reader's mind'.[42] *Some Do Not* ... has moments of such indefiniteness, reminiscent of Ford's earlier work such as *A Call* (1910), when the influence of Henry James was at its strongest. ('Macmaster had answered only: "Ah!"') In *The Good Soldier* Ford's technical solution to the problem of English vagueness was – in a move that anticipates his use of Marwood's perspective in *Parade's End* – to use as a narrator the loquacious American Dowell puzzling over the reticences of his English friends. In *Some Do Not* ..., by contrast, the characters are hyper-articulate. Outstanding minds like Tietjens' and Valentine's have plenty to say, as do the dilettante literati Macmaster and Mrs Duchemin. From the first chapter, in which Tietjens and Macmaster argue over Rossetti, the novel is full of discussion about 'pure thought and the arts'. Soon after *Some Do Not* ... was published, Ford sent his former collaborator a copy, saying: 'I'm pretty sure it's the best thing I've done. You'll notice I've abandoned attempts at indirect reporting of speech – as an experiment. How late in life does one go on experimenting?'[43] Behind this experiment in dramatic presenta-

41 *Joseph Conrad* 135–6.
42 *Ibid.* 136.
43 Ford to Conrad [n. d., but written on the verso of a letter from Victor Llona to Ford, 16 Apr. 1924]: Saunders, *A Dual Life* II 152.

tion lay not only his *Alcestis* adaptation and recent verse-dramas – *A House* (1921) and *Mister Bosphorus* (1923) – but also the discipline of writing a full-length play in 1923 about Madame Récamier, since lost. But in *Parade's End* Ford elaborates a technique particular to the printed page rather than the performed script, continuing his experiments in the use of suspension dots in the rendering of speech – something he had developed early, but uses concentratedly in the tetralogy. As he explained:

> The man of letters is continually troubled by the problem that, – in cold print, the inflections and the tempi of the human voice are as impossible of rendering as are scents and the tones of musical instruments. It is to be doubted if there is anyone who ever used a pen who has not from time to time tried by underlinings, capitals and queerly spacing his words to get something more on the paper than normal paper can bear [...] For ourselves we limit ourselves to the use of..... to indicate the pauses by which the Briton – and the American now and then – recovers himself in order to continue a sentence. The typographical device is inadequate but how in the world..... how in the whole world else? – is one to render the normal English conversation?[44]

He found a way of describing it, at least, in a marvellous image, saying that 'the noise that is English conversation' resembles 'the sound put forth by a slug eating lettuce [...]'.[45] In *Some Do Not . . .* – where the dots are even raised up into the title, as if to indicate the importance of the processes of suppression and implication for the whole novel – the pauses marked by the dots are less a matter of people swallowing their words, or mumbling with embarrassment or indecision, nor of the Pinteresque pause of menace and power-play, but rather of the characters letting their minds race around and beyond the words they have heard or said or are about to say. By the same token, Ford is concerned with how people express more than their words say, or can say. Rather than giving the eloquent dramatic speech of George Bernard

44  Ford, 'Communications', *transatlantic review*, 1:1 (Jan. 1924), 97.
45  Ford, 'Preface' to *Transatlantic Stories* (London: Duckworth [1926]), vii–xxxi (xxv).

Shaw, in which characters express themselves perfectly, saying everything they mean, Ford conveys the sense of powerful intellects through rich subtexts. The probing conversation between Sylvia, her mother, and the shrewd priest in the second chapter is another particularly fine example. If Ibsen and Chekhov were models for such techniques, so were Flaubert and Turgenev, whom Ford admired above all among writers.

There are brilliant set-pieces of hallucinatory dialogue in the later volumes, especially in *No More Parades*, as Tietjens composes poetry with McKechnie during a bombardment, and as he argues with Levin. But over the sequence as a whole, dialogue recedes and interior monologue becomes more prominent. Admittedly there are compelling interior monologues in *Some Do Not ...* too, as when Tietjens walks with Valentine through the marshes in I.vi, or when she goes to meet him in Whitehall in II.v. But even these monologues partake of the dialogic, as when Tietjens imagines the kinds of comment people would make about the countryside, or when he remembers his earlier words coming back to him 'as if from the other end of a long-distance telephone. A damn long-distance one! Ten years ...' In the 'Preface' to his *Poems* (1853), Matthew Arnold famously declared: 'the dialogue of the mind with itself has commenced'.[46] *Parade's End* traces the continuation of this process, in which an eighteenth-century-style public sphere of rational exchange gives way to an alienated modernity. It is as if the war, in taking people out of their normal social contexts, forces them in on themselves, making them confront their inner lives – emotional, moral, sexual – as never before. The tetralogy that begins with the dialogue experiments of *Some Do Not ...* ends with *Last Post's* series of internal monologues, Christopher's absence, and Mark's mutism.


## Principles

*Some Do Not ...* doesn't explore intelligence for its own sake, though, but in its ethical dimension. Tietjens stands not just for

---

46 Arnold, 'Preface to First Edition of *Poems*, 1853', *Selected Criticism of Matthew Arnold*, ed. Christopher Ricks (New York: Signet, 1972), 27–8.

mind, but for ethical principle. 'Principles are like a skeleton map
of a country—you know whether you're going east or north', he
says. They can only be a rough guide, because, as Ford had written
in the period the novel is set: 'Modern life is so extraordinary, so
hazy, so tenuous with, still, such definite and concrete spots in it
[…].'[47] Tietjens is often described as an anachronistic figure: an
eighteenth-century throwback; the last Tory or last English
gentleman. The reality is more conflicted. In *The Spirit of the
People*, Ford sees Englishness as the product of sustained immi-
gration, writing of 'that odd mixture of every kind of foreigner
that is called the Anglo-Saxon race'.[48] Tietjens' name indicates
that he is no exception. Sylvia speaks of how 'The first Tietjens
who came over with Dutch William, the swine, was pretty bad to
the Papist owners.…' of the Groby estate. *The Spirit of the People*
discusses Ford's surprise at his grandfather Madox Brown writing
of the unpicturesque king 'I love Dutch William!'[49] Yet, Ford
argues, William III 'stands for principles the most vital to the
evolution of modern England', and goes on to imagine Brown,
'inspired by the Victorian canons, by principles of Protestantism,
commercial stability, political economies, Carlylism, individualism and liberty', evolving a picture of 'a strong, silent,
hard-featured, dominant personality'. The 'Glorious Revolution'
is one of the moments Ford picks out in British history (like the
Reformation and the Great War) as a turning-point at which the
world enters a new phase of modernity. 'Philosophically
speaking', he wrote, 'it began that divorce of principle from life
which, carried as far as it has been carried in England, has earned
for the English the title of a nation of hypocrites.'[50] Tietjens thus
paradoxically inherits and represents this legacy, and exemplifies
its qualities; but he is intellectually and morally opposed to its

47  Ford, *Collected Poems* (London: Max Goschen [1913]), 15.
48  Ford, *The Spirit of the People* (London: Alston Rivers, 1907), xii. In Ford, *England and
    the English*, ed. Sara Haslam (Manchester: Carcanet, 2003), 232.
49  *England* 273. Ford had quoted the sentiment from Madox Brown's diary in his biog-
    raphy of his grandfather: *Ford Madox Brown* (London: Longmans Green, 1896), 126.
50  *England* 276. Cf. 'Literary Portraits – XX. Mr. Gilbert Cannan and "Old Mole"',
    *Outlook*, 33 (24 Jan. 1914), 110: 'sentimentality, Puritanism, and everything that is
    most beastly came into England together with Dutch William'. Cf. C. E. M. Joad,
    *Thrasymachus, or the Future of Morals* (London: Kegan Paul, Trench and Trubner,
    1925), 84, on 'the gulf which separates public profession and private practice, a gulf
    which has made England a byword for hypocrisy […]'.

values and represents its fiercest critique. He is the subtlest of Ford's many portrayals of embattled altruists. However, *Some Do Not ...* is more nuanced than the earlier historical analysis. If Tietjens and Valentine stand for principles as against hypocrisy, Macmaster and Mrs Duchemin don't so much represent pure hypocrisy as principles sliding into hypocrisy, under the banner of being 'circumspect'. The ethical dimension of the novel is constructed through a series of such contrasts: Tietjens/Macmaster, Christopher/Sylvia, the Tietjens/Duchemin marriages, and so on. Certainly the more hypocritical don't come out of the contrasts well. Yet Ford is not without sympathy for the forces pushing them towards their hypocrisies. Macmaster's modest background means he can't afford Tietjens' seigneurial outspokenness (though the novel also shows how ill Tietjens can himself afford it, given the trouble it keeps landing him in). He has to be circumspect if he's to work his own way up into 'Society'.

The Spirit of the People is illuminating, too, about the contrast between Tietjens' Protestantism and the Catholicism of his wife, mother-in-law, and Father Consett. 'Catholicism, which is a religion of action and of frames of mind, is a religion that men can live up to', Ford writes. Whereas 'Protestantism no man can live up to, since it is a religion of ideals and of reason'. Thus as the Revolution 'riveted Protestantism for good and evil upon the nation's dominant types' it stands as the defining moment of the divorce of principle from life.[51] In fact Tietjens has little to say about Protestantism or the established church as such, though he does view it in such ideal terms: 'His private ambition had always been for saintliness' we are told: 'his desire was to be a saint of the Anglican variety ... as his mother had been'. His quest, which could be described as actually trying to live up to the Protestant ideal, is what incites Society at once to accuse him of delusional identification with Christ, and to assume he is in fact an adulterous hypocrite. His Marwoodian sweeping statements, many of which sound like cynical rationalism rather than Christianity, don't help. One such is that which frames the novel, appearing

51 *England* 276.

in the first and last chapters: 'I stand for monogamy and chastity. And for no talking about it. Of course, if a man who's a man wants to have a woman he has her.' At such moments he sounds more like a Fordian Catholic, seeing religion as freedom from abstract ideals rather than adherence to dogma – though the point is that he refuses to countenance hypocrisy. To that extent Tietjens represents a fusion of ethical viewpoints, whether religious or political. Ford wrote of 'the true Toryism which is Socialism'.[52] That's the sense in which Tietjens is a Tory. Rather than representing an eccentric and anachronistic position, he is really a compendium of aspects of Englishness through history. Such complexities appealed to Ford as a novelist because he viewed the novel as a form that should rise above Victorian moralism, which in turn mattered to him because he saw individuals as themselves too contradictory and conflicting to be explicable in moralistic terms. In a novel with so intricate an architecture, pure thought and the arts are not just discussed but embodied by the characters, and by the patterns the novelist makes out of them.

### 'Some Do Not': Marriage, Adultery, and Divorce

The novel's title-phrase, which echoes through it, is richly suggestive. One set of connotations is this kind of ethical discrimination, between those who do have principles, or adhere to the principles they advocate, and those who do not. The Shakespearean scholar A. C. Bradley had defined Hegel's view of tragedy as consisting in 'the self-division and intestinal warfare of the ethical substance' – the clash of equally unanswerable moral imperatives, as when Antigone is torn between the obligations of family piety and the demands of civil law.[53] Novels are

52 *England* 277. While working on *Parade's End* Ford wrote 'The Passing of Toryism', *McNaught's Monthly*, 5:6 (June 1926), 174–6, arguing that Toryism was 'a frame of mind – the frame of mind that produced, say, Dr. Samuel Johnson'; its profound individualism and scepticism a necessity to save the world from destructive crazes; its demise rendering individualism 'almost impossible and standardization almost inevitable'; and its sense of class responsibility tending towards 'an extraordinary solicitude and indeed a deep love'. 'Of that,' said Ford, 'the fields of Flanders, I assure you, gave evidence enough.'
53 Bradley, *Oxford Lectures on Poetry* (London: Macmillan and Company, 1909), 71.

more often driven by a sense of a division between the ethical and the social – what Ford calls the divorce of principle from life. *Some Do Not . . .* depicts a world in which social convention has become so hypocritical that if you use the conventional moral skeleton maps you get lost. The title-phrase acquires this resonance, suggesting social codes ('Gentlemen don't', etc.) as well as the ways in which some (like Sylvia) get away with transgression and others do not. Part of Tietjens' oddity stems from the way his personal code of honour seems in conflict with that of his society. Ford subtly suggests that his principles are at once a sign of intense personal integrity, but also sound perverse – especially to a society whose integrity is compromised: as for example his argument that Sylvia's action in tricking him into marriage because she feared she was pregnant by another man was right; or his refusal to initiate a divorce despite her subsequent infidelity. Divorce law was newly topical as Ford was writing the novel: in 1923 the law was amended so that a wife no longer needed to prove 'aggravated adultery' (that is, adultery plus incest, cruelty, bigamy, sodomy or desertion), but needed only to prove adultery without collusion – the same grounds that applied to husbands. Sylvia has not only committed adultery, but has absconded with Perowne and stayed with him in a French hotel, though she has ensured that only Tietjens, her mother, and their priest know of it. Her defamation of her husband's character is equally shameless but humiliatingly public. Yet such is her social cachet that it's as if she can do no wrong; she is still treated as a goddess in polite society. Whereas her husband, struggling not to commit adultery for most of this novel, is treated as the sinner, partly because Sylvia's denunciations spread the idea that he already has a mistress and a child by her, but also because Tietjens' outsider status, his sheer oddity, make people only too quick to believe the false rumours about him and to condemn him. Sylvia does the things society says it condemns – committing adultery, bearing false witness, and so on – whereas Tietjens does not. Yet he gets punished, ostracised; she does not.

In the first chapter, Macmaster quotes a couplet that includes the phrase, and that is almost a quotation from Ford's own poem *Mister Bosphorus*. In that poem, the phrase connotes fortune and fate. That's the sense in which Macmaster uses it, to consider who gets chosen to enjoy privilege or rewards. In *Some Do Not . . .* it's about these things too, as well as social and personal codes of behaviour. By suspending the verb, and just leaving the auxiliary 'do', the phrase becomes not only multivalent but also a powerful innuendo. Some do, or do not, what? Ah, I thought so! Through its echo of Grant Allen's notorious 'New Woman' novel, *The Woman Who Did* (1895) and also of the novel that answered it in the same year, *The Woman Who Didn't*, by 'Victoria Crosse', it is sexuality and 'free love' that the elision especially implies. As the novel progresses, the phrase comes to stand increasingly for the central contrast that unfolds between the relationships of the two pairs of lovers: some do commit adultery (but pretend not to), like Macmaster and Mrs Duchemin; some do not, like Tietjens and Valentine (though their lack of subterfuge gives their enemies ammunition to say they do).

'Some do not ...' doesn't just hint at the things the some do not do, but also foregrounds the process of repression. 'As Tietjens saw the world, you didn't "talk."' *The Spirit of the People* includes a story of how as a boy Ford was taken aside by the mother of a friend and forbidden to talk to her about 'things'. He explains how he has since discovered that these 'things' include:

> religious topics, questions of the relations of the sexes, the conditions of poverty-stricken districts – every subject from which one can digress into anything moving. That, in fact, is the crux, the Rubicon that one must never cross. And that is what makes English conversation so profoundly, so portentously, troublesome to maintain. It is a question of a very fine game, the rules of which you must observe.[54]

Trying to represent this form of society in which none of the major human interests and challenges can be expressed is a finer game for a novelist, who has to convey not only the repressed surface, but what it is that is being repressed. This introduces a central idea of the tetralogy, of the pros and cons of British upper-class repression of feelings and language. This code of conduct already looked outmoded before the war, at least to those of more

54 *England* 312.

advanced outlooks; 'a sort of parade of circumspection and rightness', as Valentine thinks of Mrs Duchemin's attempts to conceal
her liaison with Macmaster. From a post-war perspective of new
sexual and verbal freedoms, it began to look alien and incomprehensible, as when the travel writer Archibald Lyall titled his
contribution to the excellent To-Day and To-Morrow series to
suggest a piece of reverse-anthropology: *It isn't done; or, the future
of taboo among the British islanders.*[55]

## Taciturnity in Love

Ford was fascinated by the expressive possibilities of this
linguistic taboo. The climaxes to both parts of *Some Do Not . . .*
are such extreme versions of 'stiff-upper-lip' English reserve as to
verge on parody: the two love scenes between Tietjens and
Valentine, towards which the narrative has been building, but in
which they are fantastically articulate about everything but their
feelings for each other, which they don't so much as mention
directly.[56] (The novel includes a bitter-sweet comic counterpart
to these scenes, when Tietjens and his brother Mark are brutally
honest about how they view each other, in a caricature of Yorkshire taciturnity.) It isn't just that the characters have
internalised the social taciturnity around them, but that that
taciturnity is what enables them to carry on in a world in which
violence, war, and death irrupt and threaten to destroy them, and
their hopes:

> She knew she was crying out like that because her dread had
> come true. When he had said: "I'd have liked you to have said
> it," using the past, he had said his valedictory. Her man, too,
> was going.
>     And she knew too: she had always known under her mind
> and now she confessed it: her agony had been, half of it,

---

55 Lyall, *It isn't done* (London: Kegan Paul, Trench and Trubner, 1930).
56 The scene in I.vii in which Tietjens and Valentine ride through the mist recalls a
   comparable moment of climactically suppressed passion at the end of *The Good Soldier*,
   when Ashburnham takes Nancy, also in a dog-cart, to the station to be sent off to
   India.

because one day he would say farewell to her: like that, with the inflexion of a verb. As, just occasionally, using the word "we"—and perhaps without intention—he had let her know that he loved her.[57]

It draws on, but goes beyond, a Flaubertian technique. In *Madame Bovary* Flaubert had written apropos Emma's entrapment within romantic clichés that 'human speech is like a cracked cauldron on which we knock out tunes for dancing-bears when we wish to conjure pity from the stars'.[58] Ford's characters are too self-aware to fall back on sentimental cliché. And the novelist is too aware of the limits of language, whether in fiction or in conversations: 'Words passed, but words could no more prove an established innocence than words can enhance a love that exists.' This is followed by the Flaubertian touch of bathos: 'He might as well have recited the names of railway stations.' In Flaubert the clichés are seen as ridiculous, yet acquire pathos and even beauty through their failure to move the stars. Ford inverts the technique, turning the bathetic itself into an expressive resource. It is precisely when the characters suppress emotion to the point that they might as well be reciting the names of railway stations that they do manage to express their depth of feeling:

> The greatest love speech he [...] could ever make her was when, harshly and angrily, he said something like:
> "Certainly not. I imagined you knew me better"—brushing her aside as if she had been a midge.

Thus the love scenes in *Some Do Not* ... are the opposite of Emma's romantic outpourings:

> From that she knew what a love scene was. It passed without any mention of the word "love"; it passed in impulses; warmths; rigors of the skin. Yet with every word they had said to each other they had confessed their love: in that way, when you

57 See 285.
58 Flaubert, *Madame Bovary*, trans. Geoffrey Wall (Harmondsworth: Penguin, 2003), 177.

listen to the nightingale you hear the expressed craving of your lover beating upon your heart.[59]

In an earlier version of this passage, Valentine thinks:

> The day of her long interview – for she named to herself the occasions of all their intercourse: The Walk; the Drive; the Long Interview; the Short Talk – that day then, she marked as the day of her great love scene. From that she knew – and she knew that she knew it better than any of the Poets – what a love scene was.

Ford cancelled this version in the manuscript – perhaps because the capitalised episodes sound too much like the 'strong scenes' he criticised in less artful fiction.[60] Yet it offers a clue to how he may have conceived of the structure of *Some Do Not ...* as a sequence of love scenes in which love isn't actually voiced. Of course taciturnity wouldn't be especially interesting in itself; what makes it so is when the characters have something to be taciturn about. Tietjens is the almost immovable object trying to stand up to the almost irresistible forces of love and war. Ford appears to have taken particular care in revision at these moments of great intensity, such as Tietjens' parting from Valentine and then from Macmaster. As in his reminiscence about *The Inheritors*, the first version was even more elided, and he evidently felt a 'final tap' was needed to make it more specific.

After Tietjens has escorted Valentine home, and her drunken brother begins to snore (in another Flaubertian touch), making 'enormous, grotesque sounds', the seduction they both expected turns instead into an unbearably intense farewell, mostly conducted in broken, choking fragments:

> He said, he remembered:
> "But ... for ever ..."
> She said, in a great hurry:

---

59 See 322.
60 See for example *Critical Essays* 128 (on Dostoevsky); and *Thus to Revisit* 43 on serialisation and the need for suspense.

"But when you come back ... Permanently. And ... oh, as
if it were in public ... I don't know," she had added.[61]

But the point is, for all their reticence and obliqueness, these *are*
love scenes (as Tietjens recalls this parting in *No More Parades*:
'We never finished a sentence. Yet it was a passionate scene');
and Tietjens and Valentine are, eventually, able to recognise and
act upon their love. Tietjens becomes more critical of the social
codes throughout the tetralogy, musing that 'Gentlemen, as a
matter of fact, don't do anything. They exist. Perfuming the air
like Madonna lilies.'[62] Which isn't to say that he is passive in
*Some Do Not* .... He does act decisively in several key scenes:
intervening on the golf course to enable the Suffragettes to
escape; saving Mrs Wannop's life by noticing her horse's girth-
strap was about to break and tip up her cart; then saving the horse
when Campion crashes into the cart when he's driving it. But
these are all efforts to save others. In the war he learns the necessity of acting on his own impulses as well, and cuts loose from the
social world that relentlessly misprises him.

### Sexuality

Graham Greene called the Tietjens books 'almost the only adult
novels dealing with the sexual life that have been written in
English'.[63] Several crucial moments in *Some Do Not* ... reveal the
power of sexuality to disturb social life. Tietjens recalls a Groby
neighbour whose wife was 'habitually unfaithful to him', and that
this led to 'All sorts of awkwardnesses'. Reflecting on his own situation too, Tietjens muses: 'that's why society distrusts the cuckold,
really. It never knows when it mayn't be driven into something
irrational and unjust.' In the golf clubhouse the two lower-middle-
class city men talking lasciviously about their mistresses enrage

61 See 343.
62 *No More Parades* I.iii. *A Man Could Stand Up* – II.iii.
63 Greene, quoted in Strauss, *Ford Madox Ford, Parade's End*, inside front cover; Kenneth
   Young, *Ford Madox Ford* (Harlow: The British Council and Longmans Green, 1970),
   30.

General Campion's party, and this sexual rage then flares up when the golf is interrupted by Valentine's Suffragette protest. Later, when Campion crashes his car into Tietjens' and Valentine's dog-cart, his outrage is as much because he feels his suspicion confirmed that they are already having an affair (and that Tietjens was lying when he reassured him they weren't), and because at some level he feels jealous and frustrated, as it is the result of the accident itself. The connection between sex and violence was topical, as psycho-analytic ideas became pervasive amongst intellectuals. *Some Do Not . . .* mentions the notion of sadism twice, and Sylvia's sexual feelings tend to express themselves in violent actions or fantasies.[64] Influenced by her brother's radical friends, Valentine develops 'an automatic feeling that all manly men were lust-filled devils, desiring nothing better than to stride over battlefields, stabbing the wounded with long daggers in frenzies of sadism'. Just as her pacifist views on militarism (like Stella Bowen's) have to accommodate the fact that a man like Tietjens can go to war for other, more honourable, motives, so her primness about sexuality is challenged as she comes to understand that sexual feeling can express love and need not imply sadism or degradation. But *Parade's End* not only presents the world war and the sex war as parallel, but wonders whether they might not mutually incite each other.

## Mind, Body, Passion, and 'the impossible complication'

'A Tale of Passion': Ford's subtitle for *The Good Soldier* could also describe *Some Do Not . . . .* Like many of the greatest novels, *Parade's End* is focused on what it is to be an embodied mind, a consciousness with a body, and stresses Tietjens' bulky corporeality as much as his intelligence. 'One is either a body or a brain in these affairs. I suppose I'm more brain than body. I suppose so.

---

64 There is a third instance in MS, II.v, which reads 'the sadic lusts of certain novelists'; however, 'sadic' has become 'cruder' in UK, whether through the compositor's misreading or a revision to minimise repetition. For comparable examples later in the series see *No More Parades* II.i: 'It was like whipping a dying bulldog. . . .' Also *Last Post* I.iii: 'He had seen the old General whimper like a whipped dog and mumble in his poor white moustache. . . . Mother was splendid. But wasn't sex a terrible thing. . . .'

Perhaps I'm not.' He and Valentine both start by assuming they
are more brain than body. Their love is intensely cerebral, verbal.
Yet the book is about how an intellectual passion disconcerts
them as it turns into a physical one. First, they try not to acknowledge the intellectual attraction; then they try not to acknowledge
the physical. But 'she had felt the impulse of his whole body
towards her and the impulse of her whole body towards him'.

Or (Ford's subtitle for *A Call*) 'The Tale of Two Passions'?
Sylvia Tietjens, for all her insolent hauteur, only has to think of
Drake, the man with whom she had been having an affair, and
'she would stop dead, speaking or walking, drive her nails into her
palms and groan slightly....' She is haunted by a masochistic
vision of how he came to her hotel on the eve of her wedding to
Tietjens and, 'mad with grief and jealousy', assaulted her; she
becomes transfixed by 'the mental agony that there she had felt:
the longing for the brute who had mangled her: the dreadful pain
of the mind'. She too is a mistress of suppression. She has to
invent a pain of the body – 'a chronic stitch in her heart' – to
account for the involuntary groan. Yet when she actually sees
Drake again in the flesh she feels nothing for him. She realises
that the longing she experiences 'was longing merely to experience again that dreadful feeling. And not with Drake....' The
suppression dots imply she knows who she does want to experience it with. And there are several hints in the text that despite
giving the appearance of indifference or even contempt for Tietjens, she has developed a passion for him – perhaps fanned by his
indifference towards her. This is the aspect of the story brought
out by Ford's reminiscence about the 'wealthy American', though
it is one rarely commented on in accounts of *Parade's End*,
perhaps because Tietjens tries to avoid entertaining it explicitly:
'An appalling shadow of a thought went through Tietjens' mind:
he would not let it come into words.'[65] But his brother Mark puts
it into words for him. And later that afternoon, when at the War
Office Tietjens is offered a chance of service in Britain rather
than in combat, the force of the problem hits him:

65 See 242.

For the moment he had felt temptation to stay. But it came into his discouraged mind that Mark had said that Sylvia was in love with him. It had been underneath his thoughts all the while: it had struck him at the time like a kick from the hind leg of a mule in his subliminal consciousness. It was the impossible complication. It might not be true; but whether or no the best thing for him was to go and get wiped out as soon as possible. He meant, nevertheless, fiercely, to have his night with the girl who was crying downstairs....

As long as he and Sylvia are locked into a loveless marriage, adultery might be a social or even a religious problem, but it doesn't seem to Tietjens an ethical one. As long as his actions don't shame Sylvia publicly, she wouldn't be hurt by his having an affair with Valentine. But if she loved him, it would be the 'impossible complication' because he would feel honour-bound not to hurt her. This possibility gives Sylvia's character a powerful motivation for her furious pursuit of her husband, as well as making her a more sympathetic character than the wicked witch-figure she is sometimes presented as being. Given Tietjens' love for Valentine, Sylvia's belated longing for him is an unrequitable love, which would make it another version of 'The Saddest Story', as Ford had originally wanted to call *The Good Soldier*.

Such uncertainties are deeply characteristic of *Parade's End*, and of Ford's method of impressionism. Many of the crucial facts tantalise us, and the characters, with uncertainties as to whether they are facts. Rumours breed doubts, which are reasoned away but keep returning. Is Tietjens the father of Sylvia's son or not? Could it be possible that Valentine is his half-sister? Did his father die by suicide or accident? And if suicide, was it because Ruggles had just reported to him all the malicious rumours about Tietjens as if they were facts? – including the rumour that he had already had a child by Valentine. And if so, would that lend credence to the possibility of his having been Valentine's father too? Was incest the 'impossible complication' for him? The first novel Ford published after *Parade's End* was a historical romance turning on incestuous love, *A Little Less Than Gods* (1928). While planning it, he also wrote that Conrad had desired to write about incest: not 'the consummation of forbidden desires', but 'the emotions of a shared passion that by its nature must be most hopeless of all'.[66] Tietjens' and Valentine's passion doesn't tell this saddest of stories, but it is heightened by such possibilities of hopelessness flickering around the peripheries.

There's a psychological realism behind Ford's uncertainty principle. We must all live and speak and act despite there being so much we don't know or can't be sure of. The love scenes work through these uncertainties, not just because the characters have to read between the lines of each other's words, but because they aren't always sure what those words were. Indeed, the strain of excitement and hope means that where they are most uncertain is over whether anything has actually been declared: 'He wasn't certain she hadn't said: "Dear!" or "My Dear!"'; 'In the tumult of her emotions she was almost certain that he had said "dear"'.[67]

Though Tietjens begins as a stickler for accuracy – a statistical genius with an encyclopaedic memory – error is part of the novel's texture. Tietjens devotes time to correcting the errors of others – such as General Campion or the pathologically inaccurate novelist Mrs Wannop – but he is the cause of errors himself: not only the rumours he inspires, but even his telegram to Sylvia in Germany, which Father Consett reads out, saying: 'What's this: *esoecially*; it ought to be a "p"'. Names are regularly mixed up.[68] As Edith Ethel Duchemin becomes more vindictive towards Tietjens, Valentine for a time convinces herself – wrongly – that he must have been having an affair with her.

There is a peculiar form of uncertainty where one might expect a more conventional writer to be especially definite: quotation, allusion, attribution. Verse is regularly misquoted. Sometimes the deviations are attributable to a character's faulty memory, as when Tietjens is struggling to remember the words of Christina Rossetti's 'Somewhere or Other'. Macmaster's misquotation of Ford's *Mister Bosphorus* might pass for authorial modesty or, conversely, for an author claiming the right to rewrite his own

---

66 Ford, 'Tiger, Tiger: Being a Commentary on Conrad's *The Sisters*', *Bookman*, 66:5 (Jan. 1928), 495–8 (497).
67 175 and 286.
68 See 41; and 'A Note on the Text of *Some Do Not* . . .' lxxxvii.

words if he wishes. So far, so realist. In life, most quotations are misquotations. Other examples are more baffling. Macmaster argues with Duchemin over how to translate a phrase from Petronius's *Satyricon* that isn't in it. He also quotes a poem, supposedly by D. G. Rossetti, on whom he's writing a monograph (as Ford had done), but the poem is in fact by a lesser-known poet, E. B. Williams; and yet Tietjens also knows it, and quotes from it as if it were by Rossetti. This is an especially complex example, and is discussed further in the notes. Readers will have to decide whether they think the errors are the sign of a careless author, or of a cunning one using them for characterisation, or to show how (in Tietjens' phrase) 'all these useless anodynes for thought, quotations, imbecile epithets' are indicative of an intellectually bankrupt society. Are they fictional facts, supposed to be taken as true within the world of the novel (as if to say the poem by Williams is the sort of thing Rossetti might well have written)? Or, allied to the last but more mercurial, did Ford simply enjoy creating just such a sense of impressionist uncertainty in his readers?

The feature that generates most uncertainty in readers of *Some Do Not . . .* is probably the handling of time. Ford saw the 'time-shift' as central to the techniques he developed with Conrad during their collaboration. As he wrote in the year *Some Do Not . . .* was published:

> it became very early evident to us that what was the matter with the Novel, and the British novel in particular, was that it went straight forward, whereas in your gradual making acquaintance with your fellows you never do go straight forward.[69]

To render a complex character, he continues, 'you could not begin at his beginning and work his life chronologically to the end. You must first get him in with a strong impression, and then

---

69 *Joseph Conrad* 129. On the 'time-shift' see 'Autocriticism: *The Rash Act*', in *The Ford Madox Ford Reader*, ed. Sondra J. Stang (Manchester: Carcanet, 1986), 267; and *Mightier* 282.

work backwards and forwards over his past.'[70] As Malcolm Bradbury wrote of *Parade's End*:

> Ford's novel shares with Proust's deeply organic work a number
> of plain modern elements: a method of indirection, the story
> not told in conventional chronological sequences but by means
> of lines of association, dislocated memory and time-shift.[71]

This can make for a disorientating read, as the narrative flashes backwards and forwards so often (sometimes, as Valentine has it, with merely 'the inflexion of a verb') that we can lose a sense of when we are, of what the present moment of the narrative is from which these shifts are being made, and we encounter the after-effects of an event before we quite realise what the event was. The plot summary above is misleading in putting the events into a more chronological order, but probably all the more necessary for that.

In *Time and Western Man* Wyndham Lewis launched a swingeing attack on what he defined as the 'Time-mind'.[72] His arch-villains are the time-philosophies of Bergson and Einstein, but he sees the preoccupation with time and process as pervasive, and damaging to novelists like Proust. *Parade's End* is certainly a time-book, but it is one that sheds light both on the general preoccupation and on Lewis's unease with it. In taking the time-mind to the war, it diagnoses a crisis in the experience of time as a result of the war. As Ford was to put it later in the series: 'When you thought of Time in those days your mind wavered impotently like eyes tired by reading too small print....'[73] Tietjens' sense of time is in a specific crisis due to his amnesia: there are passages of his past he can no longer call to mind. Shell-shock produces new relations to time, makes it seem both fractured and recurrent: some traumatic memories won't come back; others won't stop coming back. But the war struck many as an event that appeared so cataclysmic as to be out of time; to signal the end of time, as

---

70 *Joseph Conrad* 130.
71 Malcom Bradbury, 'Introduction', *Parade's End* (London: Everyman, 1992), xvi
72 Wyndham Lewis, *Time and Western Man* (London: Chatto & Windus, 1927), 3.
73 *A Man Could Stand Up* – I.ii.

in the last battle, Armageddon. From our retrospect we know it wasn't the end of time or of history. But it certainly felt like a seismic fault in time to many witnesses (as it may have done to Lewis, who fought as an artilleryman). Valentine later thinks of it as a 'crack across the table of History'.[74] Ford's friend, and later successful war-novelist, Richard Aldington, wrote that:

> Adult lives were cut sharply into three sections – pre-war, war, and post-war. It is curious – perhaps not so curious – but many people will tell you that whole areas of their pre-war lives have become obliterated from their memories.[75]

People's experience of time during the war also changed, as they were lifted out of familiar routines and subjected to new modes of waiting, anticipating (what Ford called 'the process of the eternal waiting that is War'),[76] and new modes of anxiety about possible futures. This can produce the hyper-reality, or sometimes even the unreality, of Fordian impressions: the wavering of the mind trying to think out of time or trying to think time itself, as when Tietjens and Valentine wonder whether they couldn't erase the moment when their restraint faltered and they agreed to become lovers, and Tietjens insists they can 'Cut it out; and join time up'.

*Some Do Not ...* is structured around a larger time-gap, from about 1912 to about 1917, and ends on the eve of Tietjens' return to the Front. He tells Sylvia a little about the experience of losing his memory. Otherwise, his war experience remains a disturbingly felt blank. Though the second and third volumes show him at war during his second tour in France, the full story of his first tour is never filled in.[77] Otherwise the proliferation of time-shifts means

---

74 *A Man Could Stand Up* – I.i.

75 Aldington, *Death of a Hero* (London: Chatto & Windus, 1929), 224.

76 *A Man Could Stand Up* – II.ii.

77 The only information we get comes in *No More Parades*, when Tietjens thinks: 'This was practically his first day in the open during a *strafe*. His first whole day for quite a time. Since Noircourt! ... How long ago? ... Two years? ... Maybe! ... Then he had nothing to go on to tell him how long he would be inconvenienced!' This takes place during the spring of 1918, so 'Two years' before would be early 1916, between Parts I and II of *Some Do Not ....* Noircourt is about 60 km east of St Quentin, which was incorporated into the Hindenburg Line in 1916, and the scene of heavy fighting throughout the war.

that *Some Do Not . . .* proceeds largely by missing out events, then filling in in fragmentary and sometimes uncertain retrospect.

These kinds of formal difficulty are what makes *Parade's End* something far more modern than the anachronistic, panoramic Realist novel it has sometimes been mistaken for.[78] Its occasional old-fashioned quality is usually a signal of free indirect style, in which the narrator remains in the third person but echoes the vocabulary and cadences of the focalising character. This is usually Tietjens, whose eighteenth-century-isms thus colour the narrative. But when it is another character – some of the narrative is seen from Macmaster's point of view, more of it from Valentine's – it can sound equally quaint. Take Macmaster's thoughts about women:

> His life had necessarily been starved of women, and, arrived at a stage when the female element might, even with due respect to caution, be considered as a legitimate feature of his life, he had to fear a rashness of choice due to that very starvation. The type of woman he needed he knew to exactitude: tall, graceful, dark, loose-gowned, passionate yet circumspect, oval-featured, deliberative, gracious to everyone around her.

Ford, who himself had little respect for caution, nor for the conventionality that prescribes where respect is due (he thought it due to artists, who rarely received it), would never have written a phrase like 'even with due respect to caution' as his own. What makes it an example of a Flaubertian stylistic technique is the way it imagines Macmaster's way of imagining. Ditto 'passionate yet circumspect'. It becomes clear, as the extent of the Macmasters' hypocrisy is revealed, that circumspection is but another name for it.

One way *Parade's End* traces the massive changes through its period is that its styles and techniques evolve from volume to volume. In some ways this follows from the use of free indirect style, since in the second and third volumes, where the characters are from a broader social range, and are at war, their language

---

78 As for example by Vincent Sherry, in *The Great War and the Language of Modernism* (Oxford: Oxford University Press, 2004), 226–32.

is less formal and more slangy than Macmaster's. The changing techniques also reflect the changes coming into Modernist writing through the period, from the experiments in point of view, selection, and the time-shift of Edwardian modernists such as James and Conrad, to the Joycean stream of consciousness monologues in the last two volumes. Ford's terms for literary techniques often seem chosen for their rapport with his material: as when he describes a subject as 'an affair', or an experience as an 'impression'. The crucial term 'parade' that resounds through the series is one that had for him a similar technical valency. He wrote to Herbert Read: 'You may say that Conrad's prose is always a Ceremonial Parade of words, with a General Salute and a March Past twice in every chapter [...].'[79] 'But you *must* have gallant and splendid shots at Prose with a Panache', he told Read, another Yorkshireman like the Tietjenses, continuing: 'Yorkshire needs them more than anything else in the world! More than anything! Because we can always do the "A-Oh!," reticence stunt. Nothing, nothing is easier.... And then we call it selection.' *Parade's End* combines the two, moving between the 'reticence stunts' of Tietjens and Valentine in *Some Do Not ...*, and Mark's silence in *Last Post*, on the one hand, and a ceremonial parade-prose that owes much to writers such as James and Conrad on the other. The friction between these two modes causes sparks to fly, which takes the writing beyond both reticence and panache, giving the series a rare intimacy and depth.

*Some Do Not ...* experiments even more strikingly with point of view, and in a way that relates to its experiments in time and style, and constitutes another strong claim to its technical modernity. In Part II, the same crucial scene, in which Tietjens and Valentine meet outside the War Office, is told twice: first from his point of view, as he arrives there walking with his brother (II.iii) then from hers, as we trace her steps there (II.v) and learn what has impelled her to go and find him. The effect is extraordinary. First the meeting appears a coincidence, as it seems to

---

79 Ford to Herbert Read, 19 Sept. 1920: *Letters of Ford Madox Ford*, ed. Richard M. Ludwig (Princeton, NJ: Princeton University Press, 1965), 127–8. Ford said most of his work was 'based on historic contemplations and comparisons', and worried that younger writers desired 'to forget the standards of pomps and parades that used to sway us': 'Preface', *Transatlantic Stories* (London: Duckworth, 1926), xxx.

him. Then we learn it wasn't, because Sylvia has told her he is
going to be there, as if perversely to set the meeting up (or, as
later emerges in *No More Parades*, to try to seduce him herself
afterwards, to upstage Valentine). In an ingenious development
of his impressionism, Ford conveys how an episode can mean
different things to different participants, and thus appears
unstable in retrospect as we have to keep assimilating others'
views.[80] Tietjens himself finds a startlingly contemporary image
for this perspectival relativism:

> "Do you know those soap advertisement signs that read differ-
> ently from several angles? As you come up to them you read
> 'Monkey's Soap'; if you look back when you've passed it's
> 'Needs no Rinsing.' ... You and I are standing at different
> angles and though we both look at the same thing we read
> different messages. Perhaps if we stood side by side we should
> see yet a third [...]."

In a sense, the story the novel tells is of how they do gradually
come to stand side by side – at least mentally, since the society
that has relentlessly brought them together no less relentlessly
obstructs their attempts to spend time with each other. It's characteristic of Ford's art to suggest that third perspective, beyond
even these clairvoyant characters' perceptiveness, through the
novelist's sense of form, as Tietjens' words echo the poem
Macmaster had quoted years before, purportedly by Rossetti:
'Since, when we stand side by side'.[81]

## History of Composition

Ford said he began *Some Do Not . . .* while at Harold Monro's villa
on Cap Ferrat.[82] The manuscript has no start date, but we know

---

80 Another example is the scene in which Macmaster disturbs Tietjens playing patience:
   first, seen externally, almost as if from Macmaster's point of view, at the start of I.iii;
   then replayed from Tietjens' perspective at the end of I.iv, by which time we understand why his nerves are so fraught.
81 See 22 and note; also 232 and 341.
82 *Nightingale* 207.

Ford and Stella Bowen had arrived at Cap Ferrat on 20 December
1922 and remained till late April 1923. *It Was the Nightingale* says
at one point: 'I have used this digression about the mechanics of
writing to indicate the lapse of time that I spent at St. Jean Cap
Ferrat, writing away at the first part of my book.'[83] While this
suggests he may have written all or most of the first part there, it
doesn't entirely say that, nor that by 'first part' he means Part I –
the entire first half – rather than just the opening chapter or
chapters. However, the recollection that he only wrote part of
the novel there must be correct, given the difficulties in getting
back to work, and then the other demands on his time. In January
he told Anthony Bertam: 'I can't write at all.'[84] He did begin to
write again in the first half of 1923, but he was working on several
other books. He finished the long verse-drama *Mister Bosphorus
and the Muses*.[85] He began *A Mirror to France*.[86] And he also
completed the play about Madame Récamier, the progress of
which was regularly reported to Stella Bowen in the letters Ford
wrote to her while she was touring Italy to study paintings with
Dorothy and Ezra Pound.[87] Ford was looking after his and Stella's
daughter, Julie, while Stella was away. The play was finished on
11 May 1923, by which time he and Julie had moved to one of
his favourite Provençale towns, Tarascon, where he recalled
writing 'in a great dim old room [...] the jalousies tight-closed
against the sun and the nightingales singing like furies....'[88]
Much of the work on *Some Do Not ...* was thus probably done
between then and 22 September 1923, the completion date given
on the manuscript. From the middle of June to the end of August
Ford was staying at the Grand Hôtel Veuve Porte, St Agrève, in

83 *Nightingale* 223.
84 Ford to Bertram, 20 Jan. 1923: *Letters* 147–8.
85 The poem was drafted before they left for France. See Saunders, *A Dual Life* II 577
   n.10. But the composition dates in the published book are 'Sussex: *October* 1922 –
   Tarascon: *May* 1923'; though it's possible Ford wanted the process of composition to
   match the poem's story of abandoning the north for the south.
86 Not published till 1926, though the composition dates have it begin in March 1923,
   which is probable since the last chapter, 'From the Grey Stone', was published in
   Eliot's *Criterion* in October 1923.
87 See *Ford/Bowen* 173–200 *passim*.
88 *Nightingale* 225.

the Ardèche, where Stella rejoined them. They probably got back to Paris on 3 September.[89]

It was the writing of *Some Do Not . . .* that made Ford feel he was finally beginning to recover his form as a writer. Working on it, he could say: 'I have only quite lately got back the faculty of being able to write at all well or regularly.' When he finished it, he told H. G. Wells: 'I've got over the nerve tangle of the war and feel able at last really to write again – which I never thought I should do.' He also wrote to Conrad: 'I think I'm doing better work as the strain of the war wears off.'[90] Pound thought his renewed sense of his powers justified when Ford read to him from the manuscript: 'best he has done since *Good Soldier*, or *A Call*', he told his father.[91]

## Reception

Ford had had some success before the war, especially with his trilogy of books about England and the English and his *Fifth Queen* trilogy of historical novels about Henry VIII and Katharine Howard. *The Good Soldier* didn't get the recognition it deserved because it came out during the war, when populist reviewers attacked it as denigrating the moral fibre of the military. It was only in the 1920s, with *Parade's End*, that critics began to acknowledge his significance as a major modern novelist, though the correspondingly large sales didn't come until the later volumes. Ford said *Some Do Not . . .* sold 'like hot cakes, in England', as opposed to the later volumes, which did better in America.[92] D. D. Harvey's bibliography doesn't give sales figures for the UK edition, but notes that it was reprinted twice in 1924, and again in 1929 and 1935.[93]

89 Pound told his mother on [Thursday] 30 Aug. 1923 (Yale) that Ford was expected back the following Monday: see Saunders, *A Dual Life* II 579 n.4.
90 Ford to Monro, 20 Feb. 1923: Texas; quoted Saunders, *A Dual Life* II 133–4. Ford to Wells, 14 Oct. 1923: *Letters* 154. Ford to Conrad, 7 Oct. 1923: Yale. See Saunders, *A Dual Life* II 126–8.
91 Pound to Homer Pound, 12 Sept. 1923: *Pound/Ford* 71.
92 *Nightingale* 326.
93 David Dow Harvey, *Ford Madox Ford: 1873–1939: A Bibliography of Works and Criticism* (Princeton, NJ: Princeton University Press, 1962), 58–9.

The Duckworth edition of *Some Do Not ...* came out in Britain around 23 April 1924. Most of the British reviews were enthusiastic, and some included the highest praise Ford had ever received. The *Daily Mail* called it 'one of his cleverest and grimmest studies of mankind' (but paused to complain: 'why is it that the post-war novelist must always covertly discredit the marriage tie?' – a rather bizarre objection given that the hero and heroine do not commit adultery in this volume). 'There is no need to worry about the state of the English novel while books like this are being produced', said the *Manchester Guardian*. The *Yorkshire Post* made the striking connexion that 'What Mr. Ford does is to rewrite "The Idiot" in terms of the immediate pre-war and war years in England', adding: 'it is a piece of unusually great realistic art'. The *Observer* found it more modern than that:

> There are several chapters in this book—the scene on the golf-links with the Suffragettes and the politician; the terrible breakfast party at the Duchemins; the discussion between Christopher Tietjens, home on leave, his wife Sylvia, and the great banker, and the heart-rending, bitter controversy between Sylvia, her mother, and the priest—which are not only better than anything Mr. Ford has yet given us, but must be ranked with the best work in modern fiction.[94]

Several reviews agreed with the *Daily News*, which called it: 'one of the best novels that have appeared for a long time'.[95] The *Bystander* reviewer found it 'one of the most stimulating works of fiction' he had read in some time – perhaps because: 'In places it is amazingly, almost shockingly, outspoken.' '[H]ere is something big and startling and new', he said, urging his public: 'read it'. The *English Review* called it 'the biggest novel of the century [...] the twentieth century *Vanity Fair*'. Even the *Times Literary Supplement*, which had doubts about whether the methods of *The Marsden Case* were as suitable to a serious story like Tietjens', recognised 'a novel of unusual power and art'. The few dissentient

---

94 Quoted from the dust-jacket to the first US edition (New York: Seltzer, 1924).
95 Quoted in the end-matter of *Last Post* (London: Duckworth, 1928), [293].

voices worried about the inconclusiveness of the structure, the
fact that 'it points no noteworthy moral', and the book's strange-
ness. But even these praised the gifts they felt Ford was wasting.
The *Weekly Dispatch* thought 'The worst thing about this novel
is its title, which needs a poetical quotation to explain it'; but
went on to say: 'Otherwise Mr. Ford's new book is a brilliant piece
of work, erratic though it be in parts. It presents a satirical picture
of society just before and during the war, and the satire empha-
sises rather than exaggerates truth.' The *Nation and Athenaeum*
felt this satire edged close to caricature, claiming Ford presented
'an England that Englishmen generally will have some difficulty
in recognizing; a strange, erotic land inhabited principally by
sexual monomaniacs', yet being won over by the vision:

> This country and people [...] are made astonishingly real to
> the reader [...] It is really a triumph of mind over matter. The
> mind is always there, acutely observing even when most
> grotesquely misunderstanding; a distinguished mind that
> moulds everything to its will [...] given its premises its argu-
> ment is almost flawless.

L. P. Hartley was more ambivalent, writing in the *Spectator* that
he found it:

> hard to believe that the War and the years before the War
> produced the colours and patterns Mr. Ford's kaleidoscope
> gives them; that they were as wicked or as witty or as wrong-
> headed. But we are sorry when the pageant comes to an end.

He called it 'a bewildering book', but one which 'fascinates while
it baffles'; 'no writer was ever more self-conscious', he adds,
acknowledging that 'It is a triumph of Mr. Ford's method to have
made his portrayal of Tietjens moving and organic.' *Punch* agreed,
praising it as 'a portrait gallery of living persons', and also finding
that 'the dialogue is often astonishingly clever'. But it warned
that, despite its virtues, 'like the electric eel, it gives the reader a
number of unnecessary shocks': 'some of the characters are also
extremely unpleasant'; and it voiced the objection made by
several reviews to the strong language – a response that perhaps

affected the handling of army swearing in the later volumes.[96]

The book was less widely reviewed when it was published in America by Thomas Seltzer around 18 October 1924, bearing out Ford's later comment that the American edition sold 'relatively little'.[97] The sales figures for the Seltzer first American edition aren't known. But the A. & C. Boni royalty statements (at Cornell) show that after they took it over, they had sold 926 copies by 30 June 1928. However, the book was reissued as a cheaper reprint by Grosset and Dunlap in 1927 – on the strength of the stronger reception of the second and third novels. By the end of June 1928 *Some Do Not ...* had sold 6,000 copies in this edition, perhaps also boosted by the much larger circulation of *The Last Post*, which was chosen by the Literary Guild of America and thus benefited from the highest print run of any book of Ford's during his lifetime.

The American reviews of *Some Do Not ...* were also very positive. One from the *New York Evening Post* said it 'dwarfed most current fiction to negligibility'.[98] The *New York Times Book Review* praised 'a technique and a prose that have gone through the fires of a large knowledge and a deep experience', judging that 'Mr. Ford achieves not only what is probably his own best work but what is certainly one of the ablest of recent English novels'.[99] The *New York Herald Tribune Books* ran a long review entitled 'Vanity Fair in 1924' (again noting the parallel with Thackeray's war novel).[100] It thought 'the narrative movement [...] leaves

96  *Daily Mail* (25 Apr. 1924); 'C. M.', *Manchester Guardian* (25 Apr. 1924), 7; 'Pages in Waiting', *Yorkshire Post* (23 Apr. 1924), 4; Ralph Strauss, *Bystander*, 82 (7 May 1924), 409; *English Review*, 39 (July 1924), 148–9; *T. L. S.* (24 Apr. 1924), 252; *Daily Express* (3 May 1924) (on inconclusiveness and lack of a moral); Gerald Gould, *Saturday Review*, 137 (17 May 1924), 512 ('I have had a nightmare. I have been lost in a strange country, full of fantastic emotion and desperate incident [...] I have conversed with people whose conversation seemed as incoherent as their motives seemed incredible [...] His gifts amazing: but he insists upon wasting them'); 'Books of the Week', *Weekly Dispatch* (27 Apr. 1924), 2; *Nation and Athenaeum*, 35 (24 May 1924), 258; L. P. Hartley, 'An Elusive Allegory' (the title refers to David Garnett's *A Man at the Zoo*, reviewed here with *Some Do Not ...*), *Spectator*, 132 (3 May 1924), 720; *Punch*, 167 (2 July 1924), 26.
97  *Nightingale* 326.
98  The *New York Evening Post* review is quoted from the dust-jacket of the first American edition of *No More Parades* (New York: Boni, 1925).
99  Henry J. Forman, *New York Times Book Review* (2 Nov. 1924), 9.
100  Stuart P. Sherman, *New York Herald Tribune Books* (16 Nov. 1924), 1–2.

something to be desired, being rather choppy', but conceded: 'it contains three or four chapters of extraordinarily brilliant writing'. It commented astutely on the relation between past and present: 'His most daring artistic innovation is in assigning the chief male role in a modern novel, up to the minute in every other respect, to a man with inhibitions, which he doesn't desire to be rid of, any more than Conrad's officers desire to be rid of the code of an officer.' The judgement that 'The conclusion of the tale is, I think, of a most devastating cynicism' is curious. The ending seems now rather to risk sentimentality, but such a comment shows how finely Ford had balanced the love scenes between Tietjens and Valentine against the more critical portraits of the Macmasters, Sylvia's social world, and the conduct of the war. Understandably, to American readers the novel seemed especially concerned with Englishness (as indicated here by inhibitions and the officer code); and equally understandably, they seemed readier to accept Ford's heightened, partially satiric presentation of English society. Louis Bromfield wrote in the New York *Bookman* that 'If it were buried now, to be dug up three hundred years hence, the men who dug it up would have an extraordinarily sound picture of the England of the past quarter century.'[101] But he added, in a comment that captures its more experimental qualities as well, that it was:

> a book that is built with a sense of form, one that tells a story admirably, one in which the characterization is excellent, and one which has that quality of all great novels – a sublimation of reality, and an inherent glamor that is quite beyond such labels as realism or romanticism.

### To be continued ...?

The last page of *Some Do Not* ... bears the words 'The End'; perhaps teasingly in a work that was to have three sequels. (The only other volume to close thus was the truly final one.) It wasn't advertised as to be continued, though on the dust-jacket of the

---

101  Bromfield, *Bookman* (New York), 60 (Feb. 1925), 739.

Duckworth edition, with a design by Stella Bowen, the front flap blurb's description of it as 'inconclusive in the sense that it is no tragedy of the approved pattern' was perhaps what incited some of the comments about narrative movement and inconclusiveness. So much subsequent discussion of the tetralogy has turned on the relation of the last volume to the whole that it is hard to recover the sense of what it would have been like for contemporary readers to read the first as a free-standing novel. One surprising feature of its reception in retrospect is that it wasn't viewed as the beginning of a sequence (at least until the appearance of a sequel a year and a half later), despite the fact that its ending leaves so many questions hanging – will Tietjens survive the war? Will he and Valentine ever be united? Would they ever be free from Sylvia's harassment? How would they live after the war? That it could be read as satisfying and complete in itself says much about how readers of Modernist fiction were already attaching much less importance to conventional plotting.

This raises the question of whether Ford had written *Some Do Not . . .* intending to write sequels, or whether it was the success of the novel that encouraged him to continue it. His reminiscences about wondering what Marwood would have made of the Western Front suggest that showing Tietjens there had always been part of the plan. The dedicatory letter prefacing the next volume, *No More Parades*, describes the plan for a 'series' as formulated from the start:

> To this determination – to use my friend's eyes as a medium – I am adhering in this series of books. *Some Do Not* – of which this one is not so much a continuation as a reinforcement – showed you the Tory at home during war-time; this shows you the Tory going up the line. If I am vouchsafed health and intelligence for long enough I propose to show you the same man in the line and in process of being re-constructed.

Presumably the disavowal that *No More Parades* is a continuation is designed not to deter potential readers by making them feel they won't understand this novel if they haven't read the last, rather than denying that *No More Parades* continues the characters and story of *Some Do Not . . .*, which it certainly does.

*Some Do Not . . .* carefully plants some seeds for future plot-complications for Tietjens, in ways that support the idea that Ford had always intended to take the story further. As Macmaster and Mrs Duchemin begin to get involved, she doubly resents Tietjens, not just for his influence over his friend, but because his insight into her puts her at his mercy. Her enmity becomes crucial to Tietjens' social ostracism, not only towards the end of this novel, but in *A Man Could Stand Up* – as well. It is paralleled by General Campion's increasing anger towards Tietjens. It becomes clear that in part this is motivated by the General's infatuation with Sylvia. But Tietjens' outspokenness becomes increasingly irritating to a man unused to people standing up to him. He gets annoyed that Tietjens also stood up to his Civil Service boss, asking 'What would become of the services if everyone did as you did?' This anticipates the way the second and third volumes put Tietjens in the army and also directly under Campion's command. This argument over principle then becomes something he has to live through in the subsequent volumes. Tietjens also deliberately picks a quarrel with Campion after their car-crash. He tells Valentine it'll give her an alibi for no longer being invited to Campion's grand sister's house. But it only heightens Campion's anger, contributing to his putting Tietjens in mortal danger in the third volume.

Ford's plotting in *Some Do Not . . .* is superbly intricate – comparable to the Machiavellian intrigues of *The Fifth Queen* and the temporal and moral involutions of *The Good Soldier*. If he began his 'prolonged effort' in trepidation, he soon found his form. These anticipations of further, future complexities, together with his revision of the ending (a variant version is printed in an appendix, and discussed in the Note on the Text below), indicate that by the time he had finished drafting *Some Do Not . . .* he had indeed already thought out how the story would continue.

By the end of *Some Do Not . . .* Tietjens and Valentine know their love is mutual, but their scruples stop them from consummating it. As he puts it, 'We're the sort that ... *do not!*' Their parting is shot through with hopes for a future reunion. This too has to be suppressed. As we have seen, the closest Valentine comes to articulating it is to say 'But when you come back ...' Yet now she has another, more sombre reason for suppression: the anxiety over whether he *will* come back, alive, uninjured, sane. Thus Ford's decision to leave his readers uncertain as to whether the story will continue is more than a suspense-device to arouse a desire for future instalments; it also leaves us in a similar position to Valentine's, who, now she knows how much she wants a continuation, can't know whether there can be one.

As a structure of suspense *Some Do Not . . .* is innovative too. It is a sustained intensification of the question 'will they/won't they?', which builds up to a final crisis in which the answer is again deferred. This final prolongation of the uncertainty sheds light back and forth over the whole tetralogy's preoccupation with uncertainties over what characters said or didn't say, what they did or didn't do. The Spanish novelist Javier Marias – one of many modern writers who admire Ford's fiction – has argued, in a lecture called 'What Does and Doesn't Happen' (1995), that what we do not do is as constitutive of our life as what we do:

> We all have at bottom the same tendency ... to go on seeing the different stages of our life as the result and compendium of what has happened to us and what we have achieved and what we've realised, as if it were only this that made up our existence. And we almost always forget that ... every path also consists of our losses and farewells, of our omissions and unachieved desires, of what we one day set aside or didn't choose or didn't finish, of numerous possibilities most of which – all but one in the end – weren't realised, of our vacillations and our daydreams, of our frustrated projects and false or lukewarm longings, of the fears that paralysed us, of what we left behind or what we were left behind by. We perhaps consist, in sum, as much of what we have not been as of what we are, as much of the uncertain, indecisive or diffuse as of the shareable and quantifiable and memorable; perhaps we are made in equal measure of what could have been and what is.[102]

---

102  Marias, 'What Does and Doesn't Happen'; quoted from Benjamin Kunkel, 'Lingering and Loitering', *London Review of Books*, 31:23 (3 Dec. 2009), 18, 20–1 (18).

That 'equal measure of what could have been and what is' could stand as a definition of all successful fiction, which stands in just such a relation to our own reality, imagining possible but non-existent situations. More specifically, though, it can also describe the kind of fiction Ford attempted in this novel, in which the characters feel the weight of 'what could have been' as forcefully as that of 'what is'. William Empson – who had much in common with Tietjens: a Yorkshire squirearchical background, mathematical training, pithy irony, subversive unconventional brilliance – put much the same idea with characteristic piercing lucidity, just two years after Ford completed *Parade's End*, and in terms that bear even more sharply on *Some Do Not . . .*:

> people, often, cannot have done both of two things, but they must have been in some way prepared to have done either; whichever they did, they will have still lingering in their minds the way they would have preserved their self-respect if they had acted differently; they are only to be understood by bearing both possibilities in mind.[103]

That was very much Ford's view of how novels needed to work too: by bearing different, often contradictory, possibilities in mind about individual characters, so as to capture the complexities and nuances of their experience. While it would matter to a coroner whether Tietjens' father died by shooting accident or suicide, and to a divorce lawyer whether Tietjens were the biological father of Sylvia's son, or whether or not he and Valentine became lovers on his last night in London, what matters to the – Impressionist – novelist is that it's in the nature of our experience that we keep being forced to worry about such questions and to recognise that we might so easily not have done what we did, or have done what we did not.

103  Empson, *Seven Types of Ambiguity* (Harmondsworth: Penguin, 1977), 66.

# A NOTE ON THIS EDITION OF
## *PARADE'S END*

This edition takes as its copy-text the British first editions of the four novels. It is not a critical edition of the manuscripts, nor is it a variorum edition comparing the different editions exhaustively. The available manuscripts and other pre-publication materials have been studied and taken into account, and have informed any emendations, all of which are recorded in the textual notes.

The British first editions were the first publication of the complete texts for at least the first three volumes. The case of *Last Post* is more complicated, and is discussed by Paul Skinner in that volume; but in short, if the British edition was not the first published, the US edition was so close in date as to make them effectively simultaneous (especially in terms of Ford's involvement), so there is no case for not using the British text there too, whereas there are strong reasons in favour of using it for the sake of consistency (with the publisher's practices, and habits of British as opposed to American usage).

Complete manuscripts have survived for all four volumes. That for *Some Do Not* . . . is an autograph, the other three are typescripts. All four have autograph corrections and revisions in Ford's hand, as well as deletions (which there is no reason to believe are not also authorial). The typescripts also have typed corrections and revisions. As Ford inscribed two of them to say the typing was his own, there is no reason to think these typed second thoughts were not also his. The manuscripts also all have various forms of compositor's mark-up, confirming what Ford inscribed on the last two, that the UK editions were set from them.

Our edition is primarily intended for general readers and

students of Ford. Recording every minor change from manuscript to first book edition would be of interest to only a small number of textual scholars, who would need to consult the original manuscripts themselves. However, many of the revisions and deletions are highly illuminating about Ford's method of composition, and the changes of conception of the novels. While we have normally followed his decisions in our text, we have annotated the changes we judge to be significant (and of course such selection implies editorial judgement) in the textual notes.

There is only a limited amount of other pre-publication material, perhaps as a result of Duckworth & Co. suffering fires in 1929 and 1950, and being bombed in 1942. There are some pages of an episode originally intended as the ending of *Some Do Not . . .* but later recast for *No More Parades*, and some pages omitted from *Last Post*. Unlike the other volumes, *Last Post* also underwent widespread revisions differentiating the first UK and US editions. Corrected proofs of the first chapter only of *Some Do Not . . .* were discovered in a batch of materials from Ford's *transatlantic review*. An uncorrected proof copy of *A Man Could Stand Up –* has also been studied. There are comparably patchy examples of previous partial publication of two of the volumes. Part I of *Some Do Not . . .* was serialised in the *transatlantic review*, of which at most only the first four-and-a-half chapters preceded the Duckworth edition.[104] More significant is the part of the first chapter of *No More Parades* that appeared in the *Contact Collection of Contemporary Writers* in 1925, with surprising differences from the book versions. All of this material has been studied closely, and informs our editing of the Duckworth texts. But – not least because of its fragmentary nature – it didn't warrant variorum treatment.

The only comparable editing of Ford's work as we have prepared this edition has been Martin Stannard's admirable Norton edition of *The Good Soldier*. Stannard took the interesting decision to use the text of the British first edition, but emend the punctuation throughout to follow that of the manuscript. He makes a convincing case for the punctuation being an editorial imposition, and that even if Ford tacitly assented to it (assuming

104  See xc–xciii.

he had a choice), it alters the nature of his manuscript. A similar argument could be made about *Parade's End* too. Ford's punctuation is certainly distinctive: much lighter than in the published versions, and with an eccentrically variable number of suspension dots (between three and eight). However, there seem to us four major reasons for retaining the Duckworth punctuation in the case of *Parade's End*:[105]

1) The paucity of pre-publication material. The existence of an autograph manuscript for *Some Do Not* ... as opposed to typescripts for the other three raises the question of whether there might not have existed a typescript for *Some Do Not* ... or autographs for the others. Ford inscribed the typescripts of *A Man Could Stand Up* – and *Last Post* to say the typing was his own (though there is some evidence of dictation in both). The typescript of *No More Parades* has a label attached saying 'M.S. The property of / F. M. Ford'; although there is nothing that says the typing is his own, the typing errors make it unlikely that it was the work of a professional typist, and we have no reason to believe Ford didn't also type this novel. So we assume for these three volumes that the punctuation in the typescripts was his (and not imposed by another typist), and, including his autograph corrections, would represent his final thoughts before receiving the proofs. However, without full surviving corrected proofs of any volume it is impossible to be certain which of the numerous changes were or were not authorial. (Janice Biala told Arthur Mizener that 'Ford did his real revisions on the proofs – and only the publishers have those. The page proofs in Julies' [*sic*] and my possession are the English ones – no American publisher had those that I know

---

105  In general Duckworth seems to have attempted to standardise Ford's punctuation in *Some Do Not* . . . by using three dots (with a preceding space) when they occur in mid-sentence or end an incomplete sentence; and four dots (with no preceding space) when they follow a completed sentence. However, it isn't always clear that a sentence has been completed even if it isn't grammatically incomplete. Nor is the convention always applied consistently. Occasionally the Duckworth text uses four dots after an incomplete sentence trails off, in a way that suggests an extra pause. Sometimes the syntax is completed by a separate sentence following the four dots. I have thus not tried to standardise the ellipses rigidly, only emending what seem to be clear inconsistencies.

of.'[106] However, no page proofs for any of the four novels are among her or Ford's daughter Julia Loewe's papers now at Cornell, nor does the Biala estate hold any.)

2) Ford was an older, more experienced author in 1924–8 than in 1915. Though arguably he would have known even before the war how his editors were likely to regularise his punctuation, and had already published with John Lane, the first publisher of *The Good Soldier*, nevertheless by 1924 he certainly knew Duckworth's house style (Duckworth had published another novel, *The Marsden Case*, the previous year). More tellingly, perhaps, Ford's cordial relations with Duckworth would surely have made it possible to voice any concern, which his correspondence does not record his having done.

3) On the evidence of the errors that remained uncorrected in the first editions, the single chapter proofs for *Some Do Not . . .*, and Ford's comments in his letters on the speed at which he had to correct proofs, he does not appear to have been very thorough in his proofreading. Janice Biala commented apropos *Parade's End*:

> Ford was the worst proof reader on earth and knew it. Most of the time, the proofs were corrected in an atmosphere of [...] nervous exhaustion & exaperation [sic] with the publisher who after dallying around for months, would suddenly need the corrected proofs 2 hours after their arrival at the house etc, etc, you know.[107]

At the least, he was more concerned with style than with punctuation, as his revisions annotated here demonstrate.

4) Such questions may be revisited should further pre-publication material be discovered. In the meantime, we took the

106  Biala to Arthur Mizener, 29 May 1964, Carl A. Kroch Library, Cornell University; quoted with the kind permission of the estate of Janice Biala and Cornell University.
107  *Ibid.*

decision to retain the first edition text as our copy-text, rather than conflate manuscript and published texts, on the grounds that this was the form in which the novels went through several impressions and editions in the UK and the US during Ford's lifetime, and in which they were read by his contemporaries and (bar some minor changes) have continued to be read until now.

The emendations this edition has made to the copy-text fall into two categories:

1) The majority of cases are errors that were not corrected at proof stage. With compositors' errors the manuscripts provide the authority for the emendations, sometimes also supported by previous publication where available. We have corrected any of Ford's rare spelling and punctuation errors that were replicated in the UK text (the UK and US editors didn't always spot the same errors). We have also very occasionally emended factual and historical details where we are confident that the error is not part of the texture of the fiction. All such emendations of the UK text, whether substantive or accidental, are noted in the textual endnotes.

2) The other cases are where the manuscript and copy-text vary; where there is no self-evident error, but the editors judge the manuscript better reflects authorial intention. Such judgements are of course debatable. We have only made such emendations to the UK text when they are supported by evidence from the partial pre-publications (as in the case of expletives); or when they make better sense in context; or (in a very small number of cases) when the change between manuscript and UK loses a degree of specificity Ford elsewhere is careful to attain. Otherwise, where a manuscript reading differs from the published version, we have recorded it (if significant), but not restored it, on the grounds that Ford at least tacitly assented to the change in proof, and may indeed have made it himself – a possibility that can't be ruled out in the absence of the evidence of corrected proofs.

Our edition differs from previous ones in four main respects. First, it offers a thoroughly edited text of the series for the first time, one more reliable than any published previously. The location of one of the manuscripts, that of *No More Parades*, was unknown to Ford's bibliographer David Harvey. It was brought to the attention of Joseph Wiesenfarth (who edits it for this edition) among Hemingway's papers in the John Fitzgerald Kennedy Library (Columbia Point, Boston, Massachusetts). Its rediscovery finally made a critical edition of the entire tetralogy possible. Besides the corrections and emendations described above, the editors have made the decision to restore the expletives that are frequent in the typescript of *No More Parades*, set at the Front, but which were replaced with dashes in the UK and US book editions. While this decision may be a controversial one, we believe it is justified by the previous publication of part of *No More Parades* in Paris, in which Ford determined that the expletives should stand as accurately representing the way that soldiers talk. In *A Man Could Stand Up* – the expletives are censored with dashes in the TS, which, while it may suggest Ford's internalising of the publisher's decisions from one volume to the next, may also reflect the officers' self-censorship, so there they have been allowed to stand.[108]

Second, it presents each novel separately. They were published separately, and reprinted separately, during Ford's lifetime. The volumes had been increasingly successful. He planned an omnibus edition, and in 1930 proposed the title *Parade's End* for it (though possibly without the apostrophe).[109] But the Depression intervened and prevented this sensible strategy for

---

108  If the decision to censor the expletives in *No More Parades* is what led Ford to use euphemistic dashes in the typescript of *A Man Could Stand Up* –, that of *Last Post* complicates the story, containing two instances of 'bloody' and two instances of 'b—y'.

109  Ford wrote to his agent: 'I do not like the title *Tietjens Saga* – because in the first place "Tietjens" is a name difficult for purchasers to pronounce and booksellers would almost inevitably persuade readers that they mean the Forsyte Sage with great damage to my sales. I recognize the value of Messrs Duckworth's publicity and see no reason why they should not get the advantage of it by using those words as a subtitle beneath another general title, which I am inclined to suggest should be *Parades End* so that Messrs Duckworth could advertise it as PARADES END [TIET-JENS' SAGA]'. Ford to Eric Pinker, 17 Aug. 1930: *Letters* 197. However, the copy at Cornell is Janice Biala's transcription of Ford's original. The reply from Pinkers is

consolidating his reputation. After Ford's death, and another world war, Penguin reissued the four novels as separate paperbacks.

The first omnibus edition was produced in 1950 by Knopf. This edition, based on the US first editions, has been reprinted exactly in almost all subsequent omnibus editions (by Vintage, Penguin, and Carcanet; the exception is the new Everyman edition, for which the text was reset, but again using the US edition texts). Thus the tetralogy is familiar to the majority of its readers, on both sides of the Atlantic, through texts based on the US editions. There were two exceptions in the 1960s. When Graham Greene edited the Bodley Head Ford Madox Ford in 1963, he included *Some Do Not . . .* as volume 3, and *No More Parades* and *A Man Could Stand Up* – together as volume 4, choosing to exclude *Last Post*. This text is thus not only incomplete but also varies extensively from the first editions. Some of the variants are simply errors. Others are clearly editorial attempts to clarify obscurities or to 'correct' usage, sometimes to emend corruptions in the first edition, but clearly without knowledge of the manuscript. While it is an intriguing possibility that some of the emendations may have been Greene's, they are distractions from what Ford actually wrote. Arthur Mizener edited *Parade's End* for Signet Classics in 1964, combining the first two books in one volume, and the last two in another. Both these editions used the UK texts. Thus readers outside the US have not had a text of the complete work based on the UK text for over sixty years; those in the US, for forty-five years. Our edition restores the UK text, which has significant differences in each volume, and especially in the case of *Last Post* – for which even the title differed in the US editions, acquiring a definite article. This restoration of the UK text is the third innovation here.

---

signed 'Barton' (20 Aug. 1930: Cornell), who says they have spoken to Messrs Duckworth who agree with Ford's suggested title; but he quotes it back as 'Parade's End' with the apostrophe (suggesting Biala's transcription may have omitted it), then gives the subtitle as the 'Tietjen's Saga' (casting his marksmanship with the apostrophe equally in doubt). These uncertainties make it even less advisable than it would anyway have been to alter the title by which the series has been known for sixty years.

With the exception of paperback reissues of the Bodley Head texts by Sphere in 1969 (again excluding *Last Post*), the volumes have not been in print separately since 1948. While there is no doubt Ford intended the books as a sequence (there *is* some doubt about how many volumes he projected, as the introduction to *Last Post* discusses), the original UK editions appeared at intervals of more than a year. They were read separately, with many readers beginning with the later volumes. Like any writer of novel sequences, Ford was careful to ensure that each book was intelligible alone. Moreover, there are marked differences between each of the novels. Though all tell the story of the same group of characters, each focuses on a different selection of people. The locations and times are also different. In addition, and more strikingly, the styles and techniques develop and alter from novel to novel. Returning the novels to their original separate publication enables these differences to be more clearly visible.

*Parade's End* in its entirety is a massive work. Omnibus editions of it are too large to be able to accommodate extra material. A further advantage of separate publication is to allow room for the annotations the series now needs. This is the fourth advantage of our edition. Though *Parade's End* isn't as difficult or obscure a text as *Ulysses* or *The Waste Land*, it is dense with period references, literary allusions, and military terminology unfamiliar to readers a century later. This edition is the first to annotate these difficulties. One feature revealed by the annotations to *Some Do Not . . .* is how steeped it is in the literary culture of Englishness. One might not have expected Ford, the apostle of Flaubert and Turgenev and international literary experiment, to refer so frequently to R. S. Surtees, Rudyard Kipling, George Borrow, Gilbert White, and even George Herbert. While some of these recur in the later volumes, the density of reference to them here, alongside Pre-Raphaelites and the obligatory Shakespearean allusions, show Ford thinking himself back, from the perspective of post-war France, into the pre-war English literary world.[110]

To keep the pages of text as uncluttered as possible, we have

---

110 See *Ford Madox Ford and Englishness*, ed. Dennis Brown and Jenny Plastow, International Ford Madox Ford Studies, 5 (Amsterdam and New York: Rodopi, 2006).

normally restricted footnotes to information rather than inter-
pretation, annotating obscurities that are not easily traceable in
standard reference works. English words have only been glossed
if they are misleadingly ambiguous, or if they cannot be found in
the *Concise Oxford Dictionary*, in which case the *Oxford English
Dictionary* (or occasionally Partridge's *Dictionary of Slang*) has
been used. *Parade's End* is, like Ford's account of *The Good Soldier*,
an 'intricate tangle of references and cross-references'.[111] We
have annotated references to works by other writers, as well as
relevant biographical references that are not covered in the introductions. We have also included cross-references to Ford's other
works where they shed light on *Parade's End*. To avoid duplica-
tion, we have restricted cross-references to other volumes of the
tetralogy to those to preceding volumes. These are given by Part-
and chapter-number: i.e. 'I.iv' for Part I, chapter IV. We have,
however, generally not noted the wealth of cross-references
within the individual volumes.

Works cited in the footnotes are given a full citation on first
appearance. Subsequent citations of often-cited works are by
short titles, and a list of these is provided at the beginning of the
volume. A key to the conventions used in the textual endnotes
appears on pp. 351–2.

111 'Dedicatory Letter to Stella Ford', *The Good Soldier* 5.

154.

chin. He felt himself slipping down.

"If Tiller takes you there....", he began

"Ah, but you never will", she said

The child wasn't his. The heir to Grooby! all his brother's
were childless.... There was a deep well in the stable yard.
He had meant to tell the child how, if you dropped
a pebble in, you waited to count sixty three. And there
comes up a whispering roar... But not his child!
Perhaps he hadn't even the power to beget children. It's
married brothers hadn't.... Uneasyness shook him.
Miss Wannop had her arms over his shoulder:

"My dear!" she said. "You won't ever take me to
Grooby... It's perhaps... oh... short acquaintance: but
I feel, coming to... the...
the... he thought. "It is rather short acquaintance."
But He felt a great deal of pain, over which there presided
the still, sad skin, Monna figure of his wife...

The girl said:
"There's a fly coming" and removed her arm.

A fly drew up before them with a blear eyed material
driver. He said General Campion had kicked him out of
bid, from beside his old woman. He wanted a pound to
take them to Mrs Wannop's, waked out of his beauty
sleep + all. The knacker's cart was following.

"You'll take Miss Wannop home at once, + she's
got her mother's breakfast to see to... I shall leave the
horse till the knacker's van comes."

The fly driver touched his eye green hot with his
whip;

"Aye." he said thickly, putting a sovereign into
his waistcoat pocket, "always the gentleman... a
merciful man is merciful also to his beast... But I

It was the beautiful inquiry of the horse which had
pricked him. The fact on, if not unpardonably over him. The
more brute he treated him or the best available it up

# A NOTE ON THE TEXT OF
## *SOME DO NOT* ...

### The Status of the Manuscript

*Some Do Not* ... is the only extant manuscript of the four *Parade's End* volumes written entirely by hand (the other three being typescripts with autograph or typed revisions and corrections). The discrepancy raises a question: did Ford simply switch from writing one volume by hand to typing the rest, or do manuscript and typescript represent different stages of the compositional process (as when an author drafts by hand, then types the draft up or has it typed up professionally)? This latter possibility is worrying to textual editors, since it would imply the existence of missing manuscripts giving Ford's earlier versions of the last three novels, and of a missing typescript of *Some Do Not* ... giving authorial revisions and corrections. However, there are several reasons for believing this unlikely. First, the manuscript of *Some Do Not* ... ('MS') is so close to the text of the Duckworth first edition ('UK') version as to make an intermediate, typed state very unlikely. Such revisions as have occurred between MS and UK are much more likely to have been made in proof. Such errors that occur between MS and UK are often explicable in terms of the compositor misreading Ford's handwriting. Second, Ford asked Stella Bowen to find 'the m.s. of <u>Some Do Not</u>'; 'a great part is amongst the papers still at the Quai d'Anjou – in among the proofs of the <u>T.R.</u>'.[112] In the same letter he says that 'The typed m.s. of <u>A M.Cd.S.U.</u> is in my escritoire – or was when I left'.

---

112  Ford to Bowen, 6 Dec. 1926: *Ford/Bowen* 252–3. William Bird had taken a great domed wine-vault at 29 quai d'Anjou, on the Ile St Louis, for his Three Mountains Press; it subsequently became the editorial office for the *transatlantic review*.

The distinction between 'the m.s.' and 'The typed m.s.' implies that the manuscript in question of *Some Do Not . . .* was the surviving autograph. The sentences in between say that 'now is the time', because his 'first edns etc. are booming' but that he is worried about a slump in sales. In other words, he is concerned about the manuscripts because they are, for the moment, valuable properties; and if he wasn't considering selling them, he may have worried that someone else would try to. This in turn suggests that both the autograph *Some Do Not . . .* manuscript and the typescript of *A Man Could Stand Up* – were both the valuable authorial original drafts (and that the autograph manuscript was not, as sometimes happened, a case of an author copying out a novel by hand after publication to sell as a manuscript to a collector). Ford later described beginning *Some Do Not . . .* with a pen, and said of his gradual progress north later in the spring and summer from Provence to Paris: 'as I drifted I continued to write furiously on great sheets of foolscap', again supporting the claim of the autograph manuscript to be the original draft of *Some Do Not . . . .*[113]

Third, the evidence of other surviving manuscripts throughout Ford's career indicates that he frequently switched between handwriting some and typing others. This was probably sometimes to do with where he was writing (on boats and trains, in cafés and hotels), but also to do with his recurrent writer's cramp. Ford later mentioned this apropos *Some Do Not . . .*, saying: 'After the volume I began at St. Jean Cap Ferrat the cramp became so severe that I could not hold a pen at all. I took to writing with a machine and then, worst of all, to dictating!'[114] This seems a clear explanation of the shift to typescripts after the first volume, and is supported by the fourth kind of evidence. Ford annotated the typescripts of both *A Man Could Stand Up* – and *Last Post*, saying that they were his own typing, and the first editions were set from them. (The typescript of *No More Parades* doesn't bear such an annotation, but the typing is erratic enough to indicate it was Ford's rather than a professional typist's. The inscriptions were

113 *Nightingale* 207, 225.
114 *Nightingale* 218.

probably made later; both typescripts were left with Stella, and presumably inscribed to try to increase their value should she need to sell them – though in the event she kept them for their daughter Julie. It was perhaps because the typescript of *No More Parades* remained in Hemingway's possession that it didn't get so inscribed.) Finally, when working on the second volume, *No More Parades*, Ford wrote to his friend and agent, William Bradley: 'I usually get Duckworth to print a set or two of proofs off right away and thus save myself the bother and expense of typing.'[115] This practice makes the existence of additional manuscripts even less likely.

For these reasons the present editors assume that these only known manuscripts are not only the versions sent to the publisher, but almost certainly for the most part the first drafts. 'For the most part' because there is evidence in all of them for some substitutions of runs of pages, indicating that certain passages were revised.

An especially challenging example in *Some Do Not* ... is presented by the fragmentary variant ending – reproduced in the Appendix to this volume. The ending in MS is the one used for the published book. So the variant isn't a case of a later, revised ending sent to the publisher to replace an earlier one. Its status remained puzzling for many years. Did it represent an earlier state? And if so, did that raise the question again of whether there might have been an earlier state of the rest of MS? Or did Ford just revise the ending, after this version had been copied for the dummy copy of the *transatlantic review*, and substitute new autograph pages for the last chapter of MS? Or did the variant represent a revision of the ending of the original manuscript which he then discarded, deciding to revert to the original? Or did he write it specifically as copy for the dummy of the review, as simply a sample of the *kind* of work it would serialise, but with no intention that this version would actually be incorporated into the published novel?

One possible clue is offered by the differences in the handwriting between the end of the last two chapters, II.v and II.vi.

---

115  Ford to Bradley, 25 Jan. 1925: *Reader* 487.

The hand becomes progressively larger and shakier throughout II.v, probably indicating the writer's cramp that Ford mentioned. II.vi is written in a much smaller, more compact hand, suggesting a lapse of time between the two. The only change in the paper occurs not after this chapter break, but just before it. The last two leaves of II.v are the only ones on different paper from the rest of MS: leaf 274 is written on the verso of stationery from the Hôtel Porte in St Agrève on which he had already jotted some train times. Leaf 275 is written on the verso of a brief cover letter on Edward G. Barclay's stationery.[116] That suggests Ford ran out of fresh paper (perhaps while en route to Paris), but it doesn't shed light on whether or not the variant ending preceded the published text. These changes in handwriting and paper may just indicate a brief pause between chapters, or they may suggest that the whole of Chapter VI was redrafted later, and appended to the rest of MS. (There is also a slight glitch in the page sequence at this point. II.vi begins with an unnumbered leaf. The leaf before is 275, that after, 276. Yet the unnumbered page appears an error – one that Ford had already made three times in Part II (see below). There is no evidence of its having been inserted later, and consequently the mis-numbering seems not to shed any light on the question of the variant ending.) On the other hand, the existence of the typed portion of the variant may indicate that the shift from autograph to typescript that Ford attributed to writer's cramp actually occurred as he was finishing *Some Do Not ...*, instead of just after he finished it, and that the typed portion of the variant was the first version of the ending – the only part of MS to be typed; in which case he could have later revised the conclusion, removing any typescript.

None of these possibilities could be ruled out on the basis of the typed ending alone, which was the only known manuscript variant from *Some Do Not ....* However, some new evidence emerged during the preparation of this edition, when the editors consulted a damaged autograph leaf at Cornell, where it had been catalogued as from *No More Parades*. In fact it turned out to

116  I'm grateful to Charles Greene of Princeton University Library's Department of Rare Books and Special Collections for his description of this part of MS.

pertain to *Some Do Not* .... At first, this discovery seemed to provide evidence confirming the hypothesis of an earlier auto-graph manuscript of the last chapter (from which the *transatlantic* dummy material had been typed), which was then replaced with a revised ending corresponding to the published version. However, as explained in the Appendix, further study of it shows it almost certainly to be the 'missing link' between MS and the typescript used for the *transatlantic* dummy issue proofs, following on from the end of MS, and leading into the typed fragment. That is, rather than being pieces of writing that had been replaced by subsequent passages, these fragments derive from the original ending, continuing the story for a few pages, which Ford simply removed. The Appendix reveals how, when combined, these fragments in fact complete the jigsaw, and enable us to see Ford's entire original ending, probably in its original version, recon-structed here for the first time.

The existence of some of the manuscript in typescript may also shed some light on the history of its composition. Ford arrived back in Paris on or near 3 September 1923. MS is inscribed as having been completed in 'Paris 22.9.23.' which corroborates his memory of finishing it 'in the studio in the Boulevard Arago – or rather in the pavilion in the garden where the white blackbirds lived....'[117] It may be that once in Paris he had access to a type-writer again, after his peripatetic summer. He was writing to potential contributors to the review only six days after the 22nd.[118] The precise chronology leading up to the launch of the review is unclear. But events evidently moved fast. Soon after arriving in Paris, Ford met his brother Oliver Hueffer, who proposed the idea, and also lent him the studio. There were fraught negotiations with potential backers, involving a race-horse owner and a paranoid White Russian colonel, before the American lawyer and patron John Quinn met with Ford, Joyce, and Pound on 12 October, and offered to back the magazine.[119] The dummy issue was presumably set either just before or just

117 *Nightingale* 232.
118 Ford to Coppard, 28 Sept. 1923: *Letters* 152–3.
119 See Bernard Poli, *Ford Madox Ford and the Transatlantic Review* (Syracuse, NY: Syracuse University Press, 1967), 11–44; and Saunders, *A Dual Life* II 134–7.

after that meeting. It's possible that it was set afterwards, and that the typescript it was set from was copied (and perhaps revised) from an autograph version (which hasn't survived) of the cancelled ending. But it seems more likely it was set before the meeting, in order to encourage Quinn to invest in the review. In which case, it would have been in preparation around the time Ford was finishing MS on 23 September; and the typed fragment of the cancelled ending would be more likely to be the first draft, Ford having switched from handwriting to typewriter for the last few pages of the original manuscript – perhaps because of his writer's cramp. This supposition is broadly supported by the page numbering on the typescript, as demonstrated in the Appendix. Either way, the chronology suggests that MS must have been finished by October (especially given that the first number of the review was assembled in December), further corroborating Ford's dating of the ending.

### Description of Manuscript

The autograph manuscript of *Some Do Not . . .*, in the Naumburg Collection at Princeton University Library, consists of a title-page and 290 closely written leaves, towards the neater end of the scale of Ford's variable handwriting, though, as noted above, just before the last chapter it becomes shakier and less legible, probably due to writer's cramp. There are numerous deletions and revisions of individual words, clauses, sentences, and occasionally paragraphs. The last leaf is numbered 281, and there is essentially one single sequence of leaf numbers running through it.[120] On five occasions an extra leaf has been inserted later (as described in the textual notes), containing a revision of a cancelled passage. Four of them (after 85, 99, 100, 273) are given the same number as the preceding leaf, followed by an 'a'; the exception, leaf 263, was inserted before an existing leaf 263,

---

120  There is also a sequence of larger numbers in a different hand, not numbering pages but inscribed at the start of a new paragraph, one every 3–4 pages; presumably a printer's mark-up, perhaps related to the production of galley proofs. I'm grateful to Warwick Gould for this suggestion.

which received the 'a'-suffix to its number instead. (But then the following leaf was renumbered from 264 to 265, indicating that '263a' was then being counted as 264.) Otherwise there are five errors in the number sequence. In the first, Ford numbered two consecutive leaves '68', adding an 'a' to the second (since the syntax continues from the previous leaf, and also on to the next, there is no evidence of 68a being a later insertion). The other four all involve the omission of a number on the first leaf of new chapters in Part II (II.i, II.ii, II.iv, and II.vi); in all these cases the following leaf receives the number the chapter's first leaf should have had. With the possible exception of the last chapter (as discussed above), there is no indication that any more extensive sections or whole chapters have had revised versions substituted (as appears to be the case with the typescripts of the later novels in the series).

MS tends to use more capitalisation than UK, notably at the start of Chapter I and for social institutions such as 'Club', 'Society', or 'First Class Public Offices'. As mentioned in the 'Note on this Edition of *Parade's End*', MS's punctuation has been systematically altered for UK. MS uses fewer commas to separate clauses (and prefers them in non-standard places, such as after instead of before 'and'), but more colons and semi-colons, which UK and US tend to convert into commas.

## The Nature of the Revisions

For a handful of longer deletions Ford has drawn a box around the passage in question, then scored it out with several vertical lines, a process that leaves the passage almost entirely legible. For shorter deletions the words are themselves scored through, making their legibility depend on how heavily they have been crossed out. I haven't recorded occasional illegible minor deletions, which are most often apparently only part-words (presumably where a character was ill-formed, or when the author changed his mind mid-word), or entirely illegible short words or marks. I have occasionally recorded the presence of illegible deleted passages, when they seem as though they might be important. Such recording, as well as all conjectural readings, are given in editorial square brackets.

Insertions of individual words, phrases, and sometimes sentences are made usually above the line, occasionally below. Longer insertions are made usually in the left-hand margin, though sometimes at the foot or top of the leaf. Some changes appear to have been made while writing a word (as when Ford writes part of the wrong name, realises, and deletes it). Some deletions and substitutions are made after the sentence was completed. Sometimes this was done immediately after it was completed (as when a sentence is deleted and immediately followed by an alternative version). At other times it may have been done later, though it is usually impossible to tell. Occasionally a later insertion appears to have been squeezed into the space at the end of a paragraph, in smaller writing. However, the insertion of the occasional additional leaves (given the number of the preceding leaf with an 'A' added) indicates – as one would expect – that some of the revising was done when the manuscript was re-read later, either whole or in part. In short, the manuscript reveals different stages of revision, involving both deletions and additions.

Part of the pleasure of studying a manuscript is the light it can shed on such processes of composition. When particular revisions seemed important and illuminating in this sense, I have tried to capture the process in a textual note. Those revisions that might seem slight have been recorded if they reveal the particular attention Ford was paying to key issues in the novel.

## Examples of Revisions

Several of the small revisions involve adjustments to the time-markers – adding pluperfect 'had's, for example. In a novel where the time-shifts become so important, this seems worth remarking. When Macmaster first meets Mrs Duchemin, UK reads:

> Of Mrs. Duchemin's drawing-room itself, contrary to his habit, for he was sensitive and observant in such things, he could afterwards remember little except that it was perfectly sympathetic.

The word 'afterwards' was inserted later. Though a minor addition, it indicates Ford's care about time-markers: this whole account of his meeting with Mrs Duchemin is staged as Macmaster's retrospective reconstruction of the day's events, so whereas 'remembered afterwards' might initially seem tautological, the distinction between what he could remember at the time and what he is remembering later reminds us of this time-shift.

Some of Ford's cuts work to intensify the use of point of view. In MS he first wrote, after Valentine's first appearance: 'Mr. Waterhouse thought that girl was a ripping girl: the others found her just ordinary.' Then he deleted 'thought', and replaced it with 'said'. This apparently minor change shows Ford's attentiveness to Tietjens' point of view – an omniscient narrator could tell us Waterhouse thought it; the revision makes his words part of Tietjens' experience. It's important that he notices Waterhouse's comment, even if he hasn't yet noticed that he shares his opinion, or hasn't yet come to form it.

In another example, when Tietjens is talking to Campion, the passage in UK reads: 'But Tietjens was not listening. He was considering that it was natural for an unborn fellow like Sandbach to betray the solidarity that should exist between men.' MS had originally included the following sentences in between these two: 'The General was off on a long tale of military grievances against an indifferent public and a government of traitors. On Tietjens the [cloud] had settled down again.' The 'cloud' (if that's what it is) that had settled on Tietjens is presumably his gloomy sense of inevitable betrayal. The narrator doesn't need to tell us that, because it's evident from Tietjens' bitter thoughts. Ford appears to have decided he shouldn't tell us what the General's 'long tale' was about either, since if Tietjens is not listening, he can't know what the General is saying. Thus again the narrative is aligned with Tietjens' point of view, excluding details of which he's not aware.

UK frequently runs together clauses that MS has as separate sentences. When Sylvia says 'And I'll be bored stiff for the rest of my life. Except for one thing. I can torment that man', MS has a full-stop after 'stiff', and capitalises 'For' to start a new sentence. Without the evidence of corrected proofs, we can't know if this was an authorial change, but it seems more likely to be evidence of a copy-editor doing what copy-editors do: improving grammar, standardising, and obeying house rules. Though this edition's rules preclude restoring MS's reading here, such differences are noted, since readers may be interested in Ford's attention to Sylvia's cadences. The fractured rhythm in MS as here seems frequently to attempt to capture a breathless and impulsive rapidity of talk.

One curious cluster of revisions in Part II deletes references to 'the French', replacing them with less specific terms such as 'our allies' or 'they'. In the case of Mrs Duchemin/Macmaster, it signals a hatred of the French such that she can't bear to name them (except as 'those beastly people', etc.). Ford may have made the alterations to register an increasing anti-French hostility as British casualties increased after years of war – but which as a life-long Francophile he didn't share. It may have been a Home Front idiom he hadn't been aware of in the army, and which was pointed out by a non-combatant (such as Bowen). Or he may simply have wanted to minimise any potential offence to the French, especially when he was living in Paris and editing the *transatlantic* there.

Many of the revisions eliminate repetitions. For the most part the minor instances haven't been noted, unless they seem significant in other ways. In general, given the extreme complexity of the plot and structure, the manuscript is surprisingly fluent and the revision remarkably light – perhaps supporting Ford's account of having been planning the book ever since 1916. MS demonstrates Ford's sure sense of how the intricate narrative was to unfold. There are long stretches with hardly any revisions; punctuated by only occasional re-positionings of sentences and re-directing of attention. Yet there is also evidence in MS that (as he said) he didn't always feel he had recovered his powers; and that, like Tietjens, he was worrying about his memory and mental agility after shell-shock. The minor deletions and revisions provide one such indication of uncertainty (though they may also be a sign of the writer's cramp – indicating that he composed less relaxedly with a pen than at the typewriter). There are also indications that he didn't catch all the repetitions and awkwardnesses. Looking at it with fresh eyes Ford might have removed one of the 'great's from 'The great lady had said, with a great deal of energy, that she could not do anything at all', for example.[121] Similarly, the repeat of 'in it' is a little awkward in the sentence 'Every woman in it was counting the pleats of Sylvia's skirt and the amount of material in it', and perhaps distracted attention from the fact that you can't count an amount of material.[122] It would have been better if Valentine's thoughts about 'The greatest love speech he had ever and could ever make her' hadn't been introduced with that slight syntactic glitch ('had ever ... make').[123] In the seven months between completing the manuscript and the publication of the book there was time for revisions, certainly, and a chance to look again at the early parts of the novel as it was serialised. But Ford's life was often hectic and peripatetic. The years 1923–4 were particularly fraught, with the setting up and editing of the *transatlantic review*. It isn't surprising that he appears not to have read the proofs very carefully. And doubtless, if it had been possible to produce an omnibus edition during his lifetime, he would have wished to iron out not only some of the inconsistencies but also such occasional infelicities.

One kind of persistent problem – mixing up names – deserves mention here because it relates not only to Tietjens' amnesia and difficulty in remembering his own and other names in *Some Do Not* . . . , but also to *No More Parades*, where it is thematised in the confusion over whether Tietjens' fellow officer is McKechnie or McKenzie. That Ford too had forgotten his own name while shell-shocked, then changed it after the war, is not irrelevant to this discussion. Many of the names in *Some Do Not* . . . (and in the subsequent volumes too) get revised – multiply in the case here of Waterman/field/house. Some of the mixing up can be put down to realism, as when the odd name Tietjens is oddly associated with tea-trays. Some can be ascribed to psychological insight, as when the repeated slips between Tietjens and Macmaster might indicate that at some level they operate as alter egos. On the other hand, in some cases the confusion seems to be merely mechanical. In the passage 'It was, no doubt, however,

121  See 254.
122  See 301.
123  See 332.

Brownlie who had upset them: he wasn't very civil to Macmaster', for example, Ford had originally written 'Brownlie' again instead of 'Macmaster', which doesn't seem a genuine confusion but, rather, an indication of a tendency simply to repeat the last name mentioned.

## Application of Editorial Principles

As stated in the 'Note on this Edition', our aim is to produce an edition based on the first UK edition, informed by a reading of the manuscript and any other witnesses where appropriate. However, the handwritten nature of the manuscript in the case of *Some Do Not . . .* introduces difficulties – of legibility, spacing, ambiguity about whether letters are capitalised etc. – that rarely apply to typescript and that sometimes complicate the application of editorial principles. Such difficulties generated more errors in the first edition of this novel than the other three – most of which have been retained in all subsequent editions. And where errors were due to difficulties in reading the manuscript, recourse to the manuscript alone cannot always solve them. Thus some of the editorial decisions require longer, more speculative textual notes than are normally given in the other volumes; and the notes have more frequent recourse to the other witnesses (including subsequent publications) than is usually necessary in the other volumes.

The absence of surviving proofs (except for those for the first chapter) means that the only other witnesses available besides UK and MS are the serialisation of the first half of the novel in the *transatlantic review* ('TR') and the first US edition ('US'). Ford later wrote to George Keating: 'the American edition is so badly proofread as in many places to be almost incomprehensible'.[124] But US was published in October 1924, six months after the appearance in April of UK, making it likely that it was set from UK (which would have been much easier than deciphering Ford's hand). The differences between them are so slight as make

---

124  Ford to George Keating, 23 Jan. 1937; quoted with the kind permission of Michael Schmidt and the Carl. A. Kroch Library, Cornell University.

this almost certain. Ford doesn't say who proofread US so badly; but his remark appears to acknowledge that he hadn't proofread it carefully himself. Yet many of the errors in US were simply copied from UK, which suggests both that he wouldn't have thought any more highly of the accuracy of UK, and that he had not proofread UK any more closely. The letter to Keating suggests that he only proofread cursorily but was dismayed by the number of errors he found when looking into the novels later on.

Comparison of the various witnesses has thus warranted significant revision to the text of UK for this edition, which emends well over a hundred substantives and many more accidentals. Instances when UK and US share a reading that differs from MS can be accounted for by the assumption that US was set from UK. However, such instances could have two explanations. Ford may have made a revision on the (absent) proofs; or the compositor may have misread his handwriting, and introduced an error that was incorporated into UK and thus into US. If we think the reading resulted from a compositor's error, we have two choices. We can emend it to the MS reading, or we can leave it, on the grounds that Ford assented to it tacitly in proof. His correspondence suggests that Duckworth's practice was to supply galley proofs then page proofs. If he read both of these, and at least one set of US proofs, he would have had at least three occasions to emend an error. However, some of the errors that survived into UK – the garbled Latin on 119; the mis-spelling of Tietjens on 176 – which he would have seen to be errors if he had been proofreading carefully, confirm Janice Biala's comment that he was not a careful proofreader (quoted on p. lxx); or at least, that if he was using the slip proofs instead of a typewriter to get a first glimpse of what the prose looked like in print, he may have been attending more closely to stylistic effects than to compositor's errors. However, that he let pass details such as the phrase 'your tiny pet things' in both UK and US, when he had written 'your tin pot things' in MS (as confirmed by TR) rather weighs in on the side of carelessness.

On these grounds the main principle adopted here has been to try to distinguish between misreadings and revisions. Where the UK reading differs from MS, and the word in MS resembles the UK reading but makes better sense, the text has been emended according to MS. For example, where UK and US both read: 'Tietjens looked at her attentively, as if with magpie anguish', MS reads 'myopic' instead of 'magpie'. Ford uses the word 'magpie' several times in the novel, and describes earlier in the same chapter how Sylvia 'magpied' Tietjens' conversation. One could attempt to make sense of the phrase 'magpie anguish' along such lines. But looking at the handwriting, though the word is clearly 'myopic' rather than 'magpie', it's nonetheless understandable how it might have been so misread. If we accept this hypothesis, we need to explain why the misreading was retained. It's possible that an in-house proofreader might have put it down to a stylistic idiosyncrasy, or thought that if it weren't that, the author would correct it. But as Ford didn't, does that mean he missed it, at least three times, or that he liked it and accepted it as an improvement? It doesn't introduce a grammatical error. It does introduce an obscurity, though one that might be defended on thematic grounds. My view is that it wasn't problematic enough to attract attention as an error, but that 'myopic anguish' makes much better sense (connoting a strained, pained look which is precise for the context of their fraught discussion) and should be restored as what Ford wrote and meant. This instance seems to me fairly uncontentious, but I acknowledge that all such emendations are matters of editorial judgement, and all can be contested. Thus, in line with our general editorial principles, all such emendations of the UK text have been recorded in the endnotes.

The situation is more complex for Part I of *Some Do Not . . .*, for which we have a further witness: the partial serialisation in TR. TR has variants from US and UK, and also from MS. TR ran from January to November 1924, but with no instalments in August (because Hemingway acted as editor while Ford was in America in June, and pulled Ford's serial) or October. The November issue would probably have been published in late October, about the same time US was published. This, and the fact that it concludes the first half of the novel, were grounds for discontinuing the serial.

UK was published around 23 April 1924.[125] The issues of TR

---

125  The earliest review mentioned in Harvey's *Bibliography* is 24 April; there is at least one earlier one: 'Pages in Waiting', *Yorkshire Post* (23 Ap. 1924), 4.

were generally published in Europe a few days ahead of their month.[126] Thus the first four instalments of TR would have been published before UK. The fifth (May) instalment might just have preceded UK, or come out at about the same time in late April. On the other hand, UK would also have been printed and available to reviewers slightly ahead of its publication date, and any involvement of Ford's in the editorial process must precede that. This suggests that (though the evidence is inconclusive) he is more likely to have finalised the UK proofs before the May TR ones, and that the April TR instalment was the last to count as a 'previous publication'. In the following notes the May instalment has been considered as potentially having the status of first publication. The April instalment concludes Chapter III and takes Chapter IV up to UK p. 97. The May instalment concludes Chapter IV and takes Chapter V up to UK p. 118. Thus at most the TR version constitutes first publication of one third of the novel. As Martin Stannard has argued, publication is a complex process, especially where multiple publication is concerned, and it can be arbitrary to privilege one point in the process as having absolute authority.[127] But it is implicit in choosing UK as the copy-text that we grant it primary authority, as first complete publication, and especially as first book publication, to which the author might be expected to give particular care. Without a set of authorially corrected page proofs, the text of UK is the closest indication available of Ford's intentions at the point of first book publication. Thus prior publication in TR doesn't give a variant a *prima facie* right to overrule UK; but given Ford's involvement in TR as editor of the magazine as well as author of the serial, it can indicate what he may have intended in cases where UK seems corrupt. In practice all TR instalments have been consulted for any light they might shed on such cruces.

The only known *Some Do Not . . .* proof material surviving, the complete first chapter, is a set of UK page proofs, corrected by hand. These proofs were also found with the *transatlantic review* material that included the typescript variant ending of the novel

126  Poli, *Ford Madox Ford and the Transatlantic Review* 42, says the January issue came out in December in Europe and January in the US.
127  *The Good Soldier* 190–1.

(and are also now located at Princeton); and they appear to have been used to set TR, rather than to correct UK: they are headed 'TRANSATLANTIC REVIEW', and are marked with Ford's signed instruction to the printer to set them for the review; and several of the corrections are implemented in TR but not in UK. Since the January 1924 issue of TR was probably set in December 1923, it might seem surprising that Ford would have page proofs from Duckworth some four months before UK's April publication. But it is by no means impossible. If Ford had done with *Some Do Not . . .* what he told Bradley (just over a year later) that he usually did – 'get Duckworth to print a set or two of proofs off right away' to save 'the bother and expense of typing' – then 'right away' could have been as early as the end of September, when he finished the manuscript – or even earlier, if he was sending it off in batches. Though the surviving chapter is in page proofs rather than the galleys one might expect for the first set, there would still have been time for Ford to have received revised proofs by December. Harvey says the corrections to these proofs are 'said to be by Ernest Hemingway'. While they are not immediately identifiable as Ford's, this may be because they were being written more deliberately and clearly than usual. They seem to me ultimately too minimal to be confidently attributable. But it is possible that Ford delegated the correcting, asking Hemingway or another assistant editor to check the proofs against the manuscript. It is also surprising that, given that the proofs were being corrected for TR, the corrections were not recorded for UK as well. But it is also the case that they were not the only corrections made before UK was printed. There are errors in these proofs that were left uncorrected here, but that were corrected for UK; though again (without the evidence of Ford's surviving proofs for the whole of the novel, or at least the rest of it) we can't be sure whether such corrections were authorial (or delegated by him), or made by Duckworth's proofreader. It may be that Ford thought he could catch the errors again later when he read the proofs for the book, but instead missed some, and found others.

Lacking the evidence of other authorial proofs, it has not been possible to determine whether further chapters were set for TR from Duckworth proofs. Since about half the novel was published in TR, Ford's comment that 'a great part' of MS was 'amongst the papers still at the Quai d'Anjou – in among the proofs of the T.R.' could mean that the entire serial was set from MS, though it doesn't prove it.[128] It could just mean that MS was there for whoever was reading the Duckworth proofs to refer to at any errors or cruces, and thus that even in cases where TR and MS agree, as against UK, a set of the Duckworth proofs may still have been being used, and may have continued being corrected for TR but not for UK (until the publication of UK approached). As early as I.ii the evidence begins to conflict. There, in more cases TR agrees with UK and not MS (suggesting TR was set from UK proofs), such as in the misreading of 'Yssingeux' as 'Gosingeux'. By I.iii, conversely, in more cases TR agrees with MS and not UK (suggesting TR was set from MS) as when 'epithet' was misread for UK as 'epethet'. The evidence that I.i in TR was set from UK shows that UK proofs were ready before any of the TR serial went to press, which rules out the other possibility – that UK was set from TR – at the start, making it unlikely thereafter too. After UK was published in April, Ford would presumably have wanted the serial set from this text incorporating his proof revisions. In which case UK would be the source not just for all of US but also for TR for the remainder of Part I; meaning that cases there where TR and US seem to support UK against MS would in fact add no extra authority to UK's readings. Since we know that some of the proofs and much of MS were in the TR office, it is perhaps most likely that the process was often a hybrid, at least for the first four or five instalments, with TR being set with both MS and UK proofs (if available) beside the compositor. Without further proofs it's usually impossible to decide whether variants between UK and TR arose because TR's compositor was using corrected UK proofs, or was setting direct from MS. In such cases an editor can only base decisions on speculations about the process, and aesthetic judgments about the results.

128  *Ford/Bowen* 252: 6 Dec. 1926.

# SOME DO NOT ...
# A NOVEL

By
FORD MADOX FORD[1]

# PART I[1]

## I

THE two young men—they were of the English public official class—sat in the perfectly appointed[2] railway carriage.[*] The leather straps to the windows were of virgin newness; the mirrors beneath the new luggage racks immaculate as if they had reflected very little; the bulging upholstery in its luxuriant, regulated curves was scarlet and yellow in an intricate, minute dragon pattern, the design of a geometrician in[3] Cologne.[†] The compartment[4] smelt faintly, hygienically of admirable varnish; the train ran as smoothly—Tietjens[‡] remembered thinking—as British gilt-edged securities. It travelled fast; yet had it swayed or jolted over the rail joints, except at the curve before Tonbridge or over the points at Ashford[§] where these eccentricities are expected

---

[*] *Nightingale* 227 describes how the opening of *Some Do Not* ... 'took the shape it did out of remembrance of how Marwood and I had conversed in the railway carriage between Ashford Junction and Rye where they play golf'.

[†] When Virginia Woolf expanded her essay 'Mr Bennett and Mrs Brown' into a paper for the Heretics Society on 18 May 1924 – nearly four weeks after the UK publication of *Some Do Not* ... – she added a passage describing how Edwardian writers 'have looked very powerfully, searchingly, and sympathetically out of the window; at factories, at Utopias, even at the decoration and upholstery of the railway carriage; but never at her [Mrs Brown], never at life, never at human nature'. See *The Essays of Virginia Woolf*, vol. 3, ed. Andrew McNeillie (London: The Hogarth Press, 1988), 502–17 (512).

[‡] See Rudyard Kipling, 'The Return of Imray', in *Life's Handicap* (London: Macmillan, 1891) for one possible source for this name; and 282 and n. below. Ford would also have known of the soprano Therese Tietjens who died in London in 1877. And the poet Eunice Tietjens was on the Advisory Committee of *Poetry* – where Ford would have seen her name listed in the same issue as his poem 'A House' in 1921. However, they didn't meet until she came to Paris in October 1923, after Ford had finished *Some Do Not* ...: Eunice Tietjens, *The World at my Shoulder* (New York: The Macmillan Company, 1938), p. 199.

[§] Market town in Kent, mentioned several times in Ford's work. He lived near Ashford in the 1890s with his wife, Elsie Martindale; it was at Ashford station that he would meet or bid farewell to guests, Olive Garnett, John Galsworthy, and others.

and allowed for, Macmaster, Tietjens felt certain, would have written to the company. Perhaps he would even have written to the *Times*.*

Their class administered the world, not merely the newly-created Imperial Department of Statistics† under Sir Reginald Ingleby.‡ If they saw policemen misbehave, railway porters lack civility, an insufficiency of street lamps, defects in public services or in foreign countries, they saw to it, either with nonchalant Balliol§ voices, or with letters to the *Times*, asking in regretful indignation: "Has the British This or That come to *this!*" Or they wrote, in the serious reviews of which so many still survived,** articles taking under their care, manners, the Arts, diplomacy, inter-Imperial trade or the personal reputations of deceased statesmen and men of letters.

Macmaster, that is to say, would do all that: of himself Tietjens was not so certain. There sat Macmaster; smallish; Whig;††

*    Ford's father Francis Hueffer (né Franz Hüffer) was music critic for the *Times*. See *Provence* 121: 'In my day in London one – if you will pardon the expression – bloody well knew that London was the bloody world and if anything went wrong anywhere one said that something must be done about it. And one wrote to the *Times* and something was done about it. That at least was the frame of mind.' Dowell in *The Good Soldier* 37–8 does write to the paper, but his letters aren't printed.

†    There was a Royal Commission Report on Imperial Statistics in 1917. The British Civil Service included a Revenue, Statistics and Commerce Department from 1879. In 1921 it was replaced by two new departments, Industries and Overseas, and Commerce and Revenue. Though Ford appears to have invented a name for Ingleby's department, it is in line with other imperial powers' terms in the years before WWI: the Japanese had an Imperial Statistical Office in 1902, and the German Foreign Office had one in 1905 (the year after Ford's extended visit of 1904). See the National Archives website.

‡    The village of Ingleby Greenhow in the North York moors lies about five miles east of Busby, where the Marwood family seat, Busby Hall, is located.

§    One of the three thirteenth-century colleges of the University of Oxford (with Merton and University colleges).

**   Ironic, given Ford's role in setting up the serious literary reviews, the *English Review* in London in 1908 and the *transatlantic review* in Paris in 1924, in which Part I of *Some Do Not . . .* made its first appearance. However, 'serious' (as in Ford's frequent contrasts between the novel and the 'serious book') is ambivalent. It was characteristic of Ford's magazines that they inverted the priorities of the Victorian monthlies, placing imaginative literature at the centre and political and social commentary as ancillary.

††   The Whigs and Tories were the two main political groupings, and later political parties, dividing Britain from the seventeenth to the nineteenth centuries. Whigs tended to support constitutional monarchy as opposed to absolutism, and religious dissent, and were associated with the powerful aristocratic families, though later with industrialists and businessmen. Tories supported Anglicanism and the landowning gentry. Whiggism associated itself with free trade, the abolition of slavery, and the expansion of the franchise, and evolved into the Liberal Party in the mid-nineteenth century. Sir Robert Peel's Tamworth Manifesto initiated the evolution of the Tories into the Conservative Party.

with a trimmed, pointed black beard, such as a smallish man might wear to enhance his already germinated distinction; black hair of a stubborn fibre, drilled down with hard metal brushes; a sharp nose; strong, level teeth; a white, butterfly collar of the smoothness of porcelain; a tie confined by a gold ring, steel-blue speckled with black—to match his eyes, as Tietjens knew.[*]

Tietjens, on the other hand, could not remember what coloured tie he had on. He had taken a cab[5][†] from the office to their rooms, had got himself into a loose, tweed[6] coat and trousers, and a soft shirt, had packed, quickly, but still methodically, a great number of things in an immense two-handled kit-bag, which you could throw into a guard's van if need be. He disliked letting their[7] "man" touch his things; he had disliked letting his wife's maid pack for him. He even disliked letting porters carry his kit-bag. He was a Tory[‡]—and as he disliked changing his clothes, there he sat, on the journey, already in large, brown, hugely-welted and nailed golf boots, leaning forward on the edge of the cushion, his legs apart, on each knee an immense white hand—and thinking vaguely.

Macmaster, on the other hand, was leaning back, reading some small, unbound printed sheets, rather stiff, frowning a little. Tietjens knew that this was, for Macmaster, an impressive moment. He was correcting the proofs of his first book.

To this affair, as Tietjens knew, there attached themselves many fine shades. If, for instance, you had asked Macmaster whether he were a writer, he would have replied with the merest suggestion of a deprecatory shrug.

"No, dear lady!" for of course no man would ask the question of anyone so obviously a man of the world. And he would continue with a smile: "Nothing so fine! A mere trifler at odd moments. A critic, perhaps. Yes! A little of a critic."[§]

[*]  It has been suggested that Macmaster shares some background and characteristics with the writer John Buchan (1875–1940). See Christopher Harvie's introduction to Buchan's *The Thirty-Nine Steps* (1915; Oxford: Oxford University Press, 1993), xii.

[†]  In 1904 there were 11,000 licensed hansom cabs and just two motorised taxis in London; by 1910 there were 5,000 hansoms and 6,300 taxis.

[‡]  Ford often identified himself as a 'Tory', though like Tietjens, he associated himself with a Toryism long extinct by the Edwardian period in which *Some Do Not . . .* is set; more of an abstract standard according to which other positions can be judged, rather than a programme identifiable with an actual political party.

[§]  In *Mister Bosphorus and the Muses* (London: Duckworth, 1923), 42–3, when Bosphorus asks Bulfin 'You are a critic?', he replies: 'I never', as if it were an offensive occupation.

Nevertheless Macmaster moved in drawing-rooms that, with long curtains, blue china plates, large-patterned wallpapers and large, quiet mirrors, sheltered the long-haired of the Arts. And, as near as possible to the dear ladies who gave the At Homes, Macmaster could[8] keep up the talk—a little magisterially. He liked to be listened to with respect when he spoke of Botticelli, Rossetti, and those early Italian artists whom he called "The Primitives."[*] Tietjens had seen him there. And he didn't disapprove.

For, if they weren't, these gatherings, Society; they formed a stage on the long and careful road to a career in a first-class Government office. And, utterly careless as Tietjens imagined himself of careers or offices, he was, if sardonically, quite sympathetic towards his friend's ambitiousnesses. It was an odd friendship, but the oddnesses of friendships are a frequent guarantee of their lasting texture.

The youngest son of a Yorkshire country gentleman, Tietjens himself was entitled to the best—the best that first-class public offices and first-class people could afford. He was without ambition, but these things would come to him as they do in England. So he could afford to be negligent of his attire, of the company he kept, of the opinions he uttered. He had a little private income under his mother's settlement;[†] a little income from the Imperial Department of Statistics; he had married[9] a woman of means, and he was, in the Tory manner, sufficiently a master of flouts and jeers[‡] to be listened to when he spoke. He was twenty-six; but, very big, in a fair, untidy, Yorkshire way, he carried more weight than his age warranted. His chief, Sir Reginald Ingleby, when Tietjens chose to talk of public tendencies which influenced statistics, would listen with attention. Sometimes Sir Reginald would say: "You're a perfect encyclopædia of exact material

---

* The painters of the early Italian Renaissance, such as Giotto, admired by the Pre-Raphaelites.
† A marriage settlement allowed a parent to settle money on a daughter that would remain hers but under the control of trustees, and would thus be protected from her husband. The practice was widespread before the passing of the Married Women's Property Acts of 1882 and 1893.
‡ Disraeli had denounced Lord Salisbury as 'a great master of gibes and flouts and jeers'. See K. Theodore Hoppen, *The Mid-Victorian Generation, 1846–1886* (Oxford: Oxford University Press, 1998), 613.

knowledge, Tietjens," and Tietjens thought that that was his due, and he would accept the tribute in silence.

At a word from Sir Reginald, Macmaster, on the other hand, would murmur:[10] "You're very good, Sir Reginald!" and Tietjens thought that perfectly proper.

Macmaster was a little the senior in the service, as he was probably a little the senior in age. For, as to his room-mate's years, or as to his exact origins, there was a certain blank in Tietjens' knowledge. Macmaster was obviously Scotch by birth, and you accepted him as what was called a son of the manse.* No doubt he was really the son of a grocer in Cupar† or a railway porter in Edinburgh. It does not matter with the Scotch, and as he was very properly reticent as to his ancestry, having accepted him, you didn't, even mentally, make any enquiries.

Tietjens always had accepted Macmaster—at Clifton,‡ at Cambridge, in Chancery Lane and in their rooms at Gray's Inn.§ So for Macmaster he had a very deep affection[11]—even a gratitude. And Macmaster might be considered as returning these feelings. Certainly he had always done his best to be of service to Tietjens. Already at the Treasury and attached as private secretary to Sir Reginald Ingleby, whilst Tietjens was still at Cambridge, Macmaster had brought to the notice of Sir Reginald Tietjens' many[12] great natural gifts, and Sir Reginald, being on the look-out for young men for his ewe lamb, his newly-founded department, had very readily accepted Tietjens as his third in command. On the other hand, it had been Tietjens' father who had recommended Macmaster to the notice of Sir Thomas Block at the Treasury itself. And, indeed, the Tietjens[13] family had provided a little money—that was Tietjens' mother really—to

---

* Son of a Protestant minister, especially in the Church of Scotland, as Buchan actually was: Andrew Lownie, *John Buchan: The Presbyterian Cavalier* (London: Constable, 1995), 21.

† Cupar is a market town in the Howe of Fife, near St Andrews and between Dundee and Edinburgh.

‡ Clifton College in Bristol has included among its pupils Arthur Quiller-Couch, Robert Hichens, Henry Newbolt, and Joyce Cary. It was also attended by Arthur Marwood.

§ Chancery Lane and Gray's Inn are both in London WC2, in the predominantly legal part of Bloomsbury. Gray's Inn is one of the Inns of Court, though neither Tietjens nor Macmaster appear to have studied law or been called to the bar.

get Macmaster through Cambridge and install him in Town. He had repaid the small sum—paying it partly by finding room in his chambers for Tietjens when in turn he came to Town.

With a Scots young man such a position had been perfectly possible. Tietjens had been able to go to his fair, ample, saintly mother in her morning-room and say:

"Look here, mother, that fellow[14] Macmaster! He'll need a little money to get through the University," and his mother could[15] answer:

"Yes, my dear. How much?"[16]

With an English young man of the lower orders[17] that would have left a sense of class obligation. With Macmaster it just didn't.[18]

During Tietjens' late trouble—for four months before Tietjens' wife had left him to go abroad with another man —Macmaster had filled a place[19] that no other man could have filled. For the basis of Christopher Tietjens' emotional existence was a complete taciturnity—at any rate as to his emotions.[20] As Tietjens saw the world, you didn't "talk." Perhaps you didn't even think about how you felt.

And, indeed, his wife's flight had left him almost completely without emotions that he could realise, and he had not spoken more than twenty words at most about the event. Those had been mostly to his father, who, very tall, very largely built, silver-haired and erect, had drifted, as it were, into Macmaster's drawing-room in Gray's Inn, and after five minutes of silence had said:

"You will divorce?"

Christopher had answered:

"No! No one but a blackguard would ever submit a woman to the ordeal of divorce."

Mr. Tietjens had digested[21] that, and after an interval had asked:

"You will permit her to divorce you?"

He had answered:

"If she wishes it. There's the child to be considered."

Mr. Tietjens said:

"You will get her settlement transferred to the child?"

Christopher answered:

"If it can be done without friction."

Mr. Tietjens had commented only:

"Ah!" Some minutes later he had said:

"Your mother's very well." Then: "That motor-plough *didn't* answer,"* and then: "I shall be dining at the club."

Christopher said:

"May I bring Macmaster in, sir? You said you would put him up."†

Mr. Tietjens answered:

"Yes, do. Old General ffolliott[22] will be there. He'll second him.[23] He'd better make his acquaintance." He had gone away.

Tietjens considered that his relationship with his father was an almost perfect one. They were like two men in the club—the *only* club; thinking so alike that there was no need to talk. His father had spent a great deal of time abroad before succeeding to the estate. When, over the moors, he went into the industrial town that he owned, he drove always in a coach-and-four.‡ Tobacco smoke had never been known inside Groby Hall:§ Mr. Tietjens had twelve pipes filled every morning by his head gardener and placed in rose bushes down the drive.** These he smoked during the day. He farmed a good deal of his own land; had sat for Holdernesse†† from 1876 to 1881, but had not presented himself for election after the re-distribution of seats;‡‡ he was patron of eleven livings;§§ rode to hounds every now and then, and shot fairly regularly. He had three[24] other sons and two daughters, and was now sixty-one.

To his sister Effie, on the day after his wife's elopement, Christopher had said over the telephone:

---

\*  This presumably picks up the conversation of an earlier meeting; the motor-plough proved not to live up to expectations.

†  Propose him for membership.

‡  A carriage drawn by four horses. 'To drive a coach and four through' is to find a way of evading a law or rule, thus making it an absurdity; often used with reference to an Act of Parliament.

§  Groby is perhaps based on Arthur Marwood's family seat (since 1587) of Busby Hall, near Stokesley, Yorkshire. Ford was based at Redcar nearby in 1918, though there is no evidence he had visited the house.

**  Thackeray's daughter Anne remembered how, in Thomas Carlyle's garden in Cheyne Row, 'at intervals in the brickwork lay the tobacco-pipes all ready for use': Anne Thackeray Ritchie, *Chapters from Some Memoirs* (London: Macmillan, 1894), 134.

††  Area on the Yorkshire coast.

‡‡  The Reform and Redistribution Acts of 1884–5 redistributed 138 seats and nearly doubled the size of the electorate.

§§  Positions as vicars or rectors, with income or property attached.

"Will you take Tommie for an indefinite period? Marchant will come with him. She offers to take charge of your two youngest as well, so you'll save a maid, and I'll pay their board and a bit over."

The voice of his sister—from Yorkshire—had answered:

"Certainly, Christopher." She was the wife of a vicar, near Groby, and she had several children.

To Macmaster Tietjens had said:

"Sylvia has left me with that fellow Perowne."*

Macmaster had answered only: "Ah!"

Tietjens had continued:

"I'm letting the house and warehousing the furniture. Tommie is going to my sister Effie. Marchant is going with him."

Macmaster had said:

"Then you'll be wanting your old rooms." Macmaster occupied a very large storey of the Gray's Inn buildings. After Tietjens had left him on his marriage he had continued to enjoy solitude, except that his man had moved down from the attic to the bedroom formerly occupied by Tietjens.

Tietjens said:

"I'll come in to-morrow night if I may. That will give Ferens time to get back into his attic."[25]

That morning, at breakfast, four months having passed, Tietjens had received a letter from his wife. She asked, without any contrition at all, to be taken back. She was fed-up with Perowne and Brittany.

Tietjens looked up at Macmaster. Macmaster was already half out of his chair, looking[26] at him with enlarged, steel-blue eyes, his beard quivering. By the time Tietjens spoke Macmaster had his hand on the neck of the cut-glass brandy decanter in the brown wood tantalus.†

Tietjens said:

"Sylvia asks me to take her back."

---

* In *Mightier* 19, Ford writes of a prospective housekeeper of Henry James's having spent thirty years with 'Sir Ponsonby Peregrine Perowne'.

† Named after the Titan punished by Zeus by being condemned never to be able to reach the food and drink he craved, a tantalus is a lockable stand to stop unauthorised drinking (as for example by servants).

Macmaster said:

"Have a little of this!"

Tietjens was about to say: "No," automatically. He changed that to:

"Yes. Perhaps. A liqueur glass."

He noticed that the lip of the decanter crepitated,[27] tinkling on the[28] glass. Macmaster must be trembling.

Macmaster, with his back still turned, said:

"Shall you take her back?"

Tietjens answered:

"I imagine so." The brandy warmed his chest in its descent. Macmaster said:

"Better have another."

Tietjens answered:

"Yes. Thanks."

Macmaster went on with his breakfast and his letters. So did Tietjens. Ferens came in, removed the bacon plates and set on the table a silver water-heated dish that contained poached eggs and haddock. A long time afterwards Tietjens said:

"Yes, in principle I'm determined to. But I shall take three days to think out the details."

He seemed to have no feelings about the matter. Certain insolent phrases in Sylvia's letter hung in his mind. He preferred a letter like that. The brandy made no difference to his mentality, but it seemed to keep him from shivering.

Macmaster said:

"Suppose we go down to Rye by the 11.40. We could get a round after tea now the days are long. I want to call on a parson near there. He has helped me with my book."

Tietjens said:

"Did your poet know parsons? But of course he did. Duchemin[29]* is the name, isn't it?"

Macmaster said:

"We could call about two-thirty. That will be all right in the country. We stay till four with a cab outside. We can be on the first tee at five. If we like the course we'll stay next day: then

---

* Among the list of names of those cured by 'Our Lady of Deliverance' in Chapter 9 of Flaubert's *Bouvard et Pécuchet* is 'Marie Duchemin'.

Tuesday at Hythe and Wednesday at Sandwich.* Or we could stay
at Rye all your three days."

"It will probably suit me better to keep moving," Tietjens said.
"There are those British Columbia figures of yours.[30] If we took a
cab now I could finish them for you in an hour and twelve
minutes. Then British North America can go to the printers.[31]
It's only 8.30 now."

Macmaster said, with some concern:

"Oh, but you *couldn't*. I can make our going all right with Sir
Reginald."[32]

Tietjens said:

"Oh, yes I can. Ingleby will be pleased[33] if you tell him they're
finished.[34] I'll have them ready for you to give him when he comes
at ten."[35]

Macmaster said:

"What an extraordinary fellow you are, Chrissie. Almost a
genius!"

"Oh," Tietjens answered: "I was looking at your papers
yesterday after you'd left and I've got most of the totals in my
head. I was thinking about them before I went to sleep. I think
you make a mistake in over-estimating the pull of Klondyke† this
year on the population. The passes are open, but relatively no one
is going through. I'll add a note to that effect."[36]

In the cab he said:

"I'm sorry to bother you with my beastly affairs. But how will
it affect you and the office?"

"The office," Macmaster said, "not at all. It is supposed that
Sylvia is nursing Mrs. Satterthwaite abroad. As for me, I wish
. . . ."[37]—he closed his small, strong teeth—"I wish you would
drag the woman through the mud. By God I do! Why should she
mangle you for the rest of your life? She's done enough!"

Tietjens gazed out over the flap of the cab.‡

---

* Ford was himself a keen golfer, and had been a member of the golf club at Hythe.
† The Klondike River in Canada's Yukon Territory was the scene of the turn-of-the-century gold rush.
‡ The flaps on hansom cabs were raked-back doors at the front of the cabin that closed to shield passengers' legs from the elements.

That explained a question. Some days before, a young man, a
friend of his wife's rather than of his own, had approached him
in the club and had said that he hoped Mrs. Satterthwaite—his
wife's mother—was better. He said now:

"I see. Mrs. Satterthwaite has probably gone abroad to cover
up Sylvia's retreat.[38] She's a sensible woman, if a bitch."

The hansom ran through nearly empty streets, it being very
early for the public official quarters. The hoofs of the horse clattered precipitately. Tietjens preferred a hansom, horses being
made for gentlefolk. He had known nothing of how his fellows
had viewed his affairs. It was breaking up a great, numb inertia to
enquire.

During the last four[39] months he had employed himself in
tabulating from memory[40] the errors in the *Encyclopædia Britannica*, of which a new edition had lately appeared.[*] He had even
written an article for a dull monthly on the subject. It had been

---

[*] Cf. Arthur Marwood's similar feat in *Return* 280; and see *Nightingale* 208. Cf. also *An
English Girl* (London: Methuen, 1907), 37, where Mr Greville's reviewing activities
are devoted to a journal 'chiefly distinguished for its staff of reviewers, who were
unequalled in discovering minute errors in works of encyclopaedic length'.
Commenting on Conan Doyle's use of the *Encyclopaedia* in 'The Red-Headed League',
Ed Glinert suggests that this plot device was inspired by Oliver Wendell Holmes, in
'The Autocrat of the Breakfast-Table', in which a man memorises the first volume:
*The Adventures and the Memoirs of Sherlock Holmes* (Harmondsworth: Penguin, 2001),
514 n.13. In Edgar Lee Masters' *Spoon River Anthology* (New York: Macmillan, 1915),
29, 'Frank Drummer' has been driven on (and possibly mad) by 'trying to memorize /
The Encyclopedia Britannica!', dying in a cell (presumably of an asylum) at twenty-
five. Ford had reviewed Masters' book during the war, in 'The Characters of Spoon
River', *Outlook*, 36 (7 Aug. 1915), 174–6. *Britannica* was first published in Edinburgh
in 1771. Ford's father, Francis Hueffer, had written entries for the ninth edition
(1875–89) on composers such as Bach, Handel, Beethoven, and Chopin, as well as on
writers such as Boccaccio. The eleventh edition appeared from 1910–11, and has been
celebrated as the finest. Ford's uncle, William Michael Rossetti, wanting to help him
to earn some money, had asked Ford in 1905 to help him revise his articles for the
eleventh edition, mainly on Italian painters. *Nightingale* 188 recalls Marwood going
through 'the whole of the Ninth Edition of the *Encyclopædia Britannica* wagering that,
out of his own head, he would find seven times as many errors and misstatements as
there were pages in that compilation. And he did. . . .' The ninth edition had appeared
from 1875–89; the tenth from 1902–03, just before the time Ford probably met
Marwood, which makes it a likelier candidate. In the 'Dedication' to *Ancient Lights*,
Ford wrote, addressing his daughters: 'To the one of you who succeeds in finding the
greatest number [of errors] I will cheerfully present a copy of the ninth edition of the
*Encyclopaedia Britannica*, so that you may still further perfect yourself in the hunting
out of errors' (xv). As the eleventh edition was then appearing, could that 'ninth
edition' be a joke example of such an error?

so caustic as to miss its mark, rather. He despised people who used works of reference;* but the point of view had been so unfamiliar that his article had galled no one's withers, except possibly Macmaster's. Actually it had pleased Sir Reginald Ingleby, who had been glad to think that he had under him a young man with a memory so tenacious and so encyclopædic a knowledge....

That had been a congenial occupation, like a long drowse. Now he had to make enquiries. He said:

"And my breaking up the establishment at twenty-nine?† How's that viewed? I'm not going to have a house again."

"It's considered," Macmaster answered, "that Lowndes Street did not agree with Mrs. Satterthwaite. That accounted for her illness. Drains wrong. I may say that Sir Reginald entirely— expressly—approves. He does not think that young married men in Government offices should keep up expensive establishments in the S.W. district."‡

Tietjens said:

"Damn him." He added: "He's probably right though." He then said: "Thanks. That's all I want to know. A certain discredit has always attached to cuckolds. Very properly. A man ought to be able to keep his wife."

Macmaster exclaimed anxiously:

"No! No! Chrissie."

Tietjens continued:

"And a first-class public office is very like a public school. It might very well object to having a man whose wife had bolted amongst its members. I remember Clifton[41] hated it when the Governors decided to admit the first Jew and the first nigger."

Macmaster said:

"I wish you wouldn't go on."

"There was a fellow," Tietjens continued, "whose land was

---

*   Cf. *Provence* 149: 'if, for your private occasions, you need a memory you should never, never, never, load it with any details that you can find in an address book or work of reference or calendar or dictionary of dates'.

†   The Tietjens' marital home at 29 Lowndes St, London SW1, just south of Knights-bridge.

‡   The London postal district is subdivided into areas. Until 1917 these were identified by letters only: WC and EC for Western and Eastern Central; otherwise points of the compass. SW was the fashionable South Western area.

next to ours. Conder[42] his name was. His wife was habitually unfaithful to him. She used to retire with some fellow for three months out of every year. Conder never moved a finger. But we felt Groby and the neighbourhood were unsafe.[43] It was awkward introducing him—not to mention her—in your drawing-room. All sorts of awkwardnesses. Everyone knew the younger children weren't Conder's. A fellow married the youngest daughter and took over the hounds. And not a soul called on her. It wasn't rational or just. But that's why society distrusts the cuckold, really. It never knows when it mayn't be driven into something irrational and unjust."

"But you *aren't*," Macmaster said with real anguish, "going to let Sylvia behave like that."

"I don't know," Tietjens said. "How am I to stop it? Mind you, I think Conder[44] was quite right. Such calamities are the will of God. A gentleman accepts them. If the woman won't divorce, he *must* accept them,[45] and it gets[46] talked about. You seem to have made it all right this time. You and, I suppose, Mrs. Satterthwaite between you. But you won't be always there. Or I might come across another woman."

Macmaster said:

"Ah!" and after a moment:

"What then?"

Tietjens said:

"God knows . . . There's that poor little beggar to be considered. Marchant says he's beginning to talk broad Yorkshire already."

Macmaster said:

"If it wasn't for that. . . . That would be a solution."*

Tietjens said: "Ah!"

When he paid the cabman, in front of a grey cement portal with a gabled arch, reaching up, he said:

"You've been giving the mare less licorice in her mash. I told you she'd go better."

---

* Presumably Macmaster thinks Tietjens should punish Sylvia by committing adultery himself, but is reminded of Christopher and Sylvia's son, and how a public sexual scandal might damage him.

The cabman, with a scarlet, varnished face, a shiny hat, a drab box-cloth* coat and a gardenia in his buttonhole, said:

"Ah! Trust you to remember, sir."[47]

In the train, from beneath his pile of polished dressing and despatch cases—Tietjens[48] had thrown his immense kit-bag with his own hands into the guard's van—Macmaster looked across at his friend. It was, for him, a great day. Across his face were the proof-sheets of his first, small, delicate-looking volume. . . . A small page, the type black and still odorous! He had the agreeable smell of the printer's ink in his nostrils; the fresh paper was still a little damp. In his white, rather spatulate, always slightly cold fingers, was the pressure of the small, flat, gold pencil he had purchased especially for these corrections. He had found none to make.

He had expected a wallowing of pleasure—almost the only sensuous pleasure he had allowed himself for many months. Keeping up the appearances of an English gentleman on an exiguous income was no mean task. But to wallow in your own phrases, to be rejoiced by the savour of your own shrewd pawkinesses, to feel your rhythm balanced and yet sober—that is a pleasure beyond most, and an inexpensive one at that. He had had it from mere "articles"—on the philosophies and domestic lives of such great figures as Carlyle and Mill, or on the expansion of inter-colonial trade. This was a book.

He relied upon it to consolidate his position.[49] In the office they were mostly "born,"† and not vastly sympathetic. There was a sprinkling, too—it was beginning to be a large one—of young men who had obtained their entry by merit or by sheer industry. These watched promotions jealously, discerning nepotic increases of increment and clamouring amongst themselves at favouritisms.

To these he had been able to turn a cold shoulder. His intimacy with Tietjens permitted him to be rather on the "born" side

---

*    A heavy cloth used particularly for riding garments.
†    This usage isn't attested by the *OED*, which requires a noun, adjective, or complementary phrase (as when ex-Sergeant-Major Cowley speaks of 'your born gentleman' in *No More Parades* II.ii). But it appears from the context to mean men who have been given their positions because of their upper-class connexions.

of the institution, his agreeableness—he knew he was agreeable and useful!—to Sir Reginald Ingleby, protecting him in the main from unpleasantness. His "articles" had given him a certain right to an austerity of demeanour; his book he trusted to let him adopt an almost judicial attitude. He would then be *the* Mr. Macmaster, the critic, the authority. And the first-class departments are not averse[50] from having distinguished men as ornaments to their company; at any rate the promotions[51] of the distinguished are not objected to. So Macmaster saw—almost physically—Sir Reginald[52] Ingleby perceiving the empressement* with which his valued subordinate was treated in the drawing-rooms of Mrs. Leamington, Mrs. Cressy, the Hon. Mrs. de Limoux; Sir Reginald would perceive that, for he was not a reader himself of much else than Government publications, and he would feel fairly safe in making easy the path of his critically-gifted and austere young helper. The son of a very poor shipping clerk in an obscure Scotch harbour town, Macmaster had very early decided on the career that he would make. As between the heroes of Mr. Smiles,† an author enormously popular in Macmaster's boyhood, and the more distinctly intellectual achievements open to the very poor Scot, Macmaster had had no difficulty in choosing. A pit lad *may* rise to be a mine owner; a hard, gifted, unsleeping Scots youth, pursuing unobtrusively and unobjectionably a course of study and of public usefulness, *will* certainly achieve distinction, security and the quiet admiration of those around him. It was the difference between the *may* and the *will*, and Macmaster had had no difficulty in making his choice. He saw himself by now almost certain of a career that should give him at fifty a knighthood, and long before that a competence, a drawing-room of his own and a lady who should contribute to his unobtrusive fame, she moving about, in that room, amongst the best of the intellects of the day, gracious, devoted, a tribute at once to his discernment and his achievements. Without some disaster he was sure of himself. Disasters come to men through drink, bankruptcy and women. Against the first two he knew himself immune,[53] though his expenses had a tendency to outrun his income, and he was always

---

* 'Animated display of cordiality' (French): OED.
† As in Samuel Smiles's *Self-Help* (1859) and *Lives of the Engineers* (1861–2).

a little in debt to Tietjens. Tietjens fortunately had means. As to the third, he was not so certain. His life had necessarily been starved of women, and, arrived at a stage when the female element might, even with due respect to caution, be considered as a legitimate feature of his life, he had to fear a rashness of choice due to that very starvation. The type of woman he needed he knew to exactitude: tall, graceful, dark, loose-gowned, passionate yet circumspect, oval-featured, deliberative, gracious to everyone[54] around her. He could almost hear the very rustle of her garments.

And yet ... He had had passages when a sort of blind unreason had attracted him almost to speechlessness towards girls of the most giggling, behind-the-counter order, big-bosomed, scarlet-cheeked. It was only Tietjens who had saved him from the most questionable entanglements.

"Hang it," Tietjens would say, "don't get messing round that trollop. All you could do with her would be to set her up in a tobacco[55] shop, and she would be tearing your beard out inside the quarter. Let alone you can't afford it."

And Macmaster, who would have sentimentalised the plump girl to the tune of *Highland Mary*,* would for a day damn Tietjens up and down for a coarse brute. But at the moment he thanked God for Tietjens. There he sat, near to thirty, without an entanglement, a blemish on his health, or a worry with regard to any woman.

With deep affection and concern he looked across at his brilliant junior, who hadn't saved himself.† Tietjens had fallen into the most barefaced snare, into the cruellest snare, of the worst woman that could be imagined.

And Macmaster suddenly realised that he wasn't wallowing, as he had imagined that he would, in the sensuous current of his prose. He had begun spiritedly with the first neat square of a paragraph. ... Certainly his publishers had done well by him in the matter of print:

---

* Song setting of a Robert Burns poem; many of Burns's poems were addressed to Mary, said to have been a daughter of Archibald Campbell, a Clyde sailor, and to have died young in about 1784–6.
† Cf. *Matthew* 27.41–2: 'Likewise also the chief priests mocking *him*, with the scribes and elders, said, / He saved others; himself he cannot save'; the second line of which is alluded to more directly on 329 below, and later in the tetralogy.

"Whether we consider him as the imaginer of mysterious, sensuous and exact plastic beauty; as the manipulator of sonorous,[56] rolling and full-mouthed lines; of words as full of colour as were his canvases; or whether we regard him as the deep philosopher, elucidating and drawing his illumination from the arcana of a mystic hardly greater than himself, to Gabriel Charles Dante Rossetti,* the subject of this little monograph, must be accorded the name of one who has profoundly influenced the[57] outward aspects, the human contacts, and all those things that go to make up the life of our higher civilisation as we live it to-day...."†

Macmaster realised that he had only got thus far with his prose, and had got thus far without any of the relish that he had expected, and that then he had turned to the middle paragraph of page three—after the end of his exordium. His eyes wandered desultorily along the line:

"The subject of these pages was born in the western central district of the metropolis in the year ..."

The words conveyed nothing to him at all. He understood that that was because he hadn't got over that morning. He had looked up from his coffee-cup—over the rim—and had taken in a blue-grey sheet of notepaper in Tietjens' fingers, shaking, inscribed in the large, broad-nibbed writing of that detestable harridan. And Tietjens had been staring—staring with the intentness of a maddened horse—at his, Macmaster's, face! And grey! Shapeless! The nose like a pallid triangle on a bladder of lard! That was Tietjens' face....[58]
He could still feel the blow, physical, in the pit of his stomach!

---

*   This is the correct form of the artist's given names, though he is better known as Dante Gabriel Rossetti, the form he used for publication.
†   There is self-mockery here. Ford had himself published a small monograph, *Rossetti: A Critical Essay on his Art* (London: Duckworth, 1902). Unlike Macmaster he was already an established author at the time – it was his tenth book. But it was his first book of criticism, written when Ford – the grandson of the painter Ford Madox Brown – was trying to make his name as an authority on the Pre-Raphaelites. And it invokes Macmaster's tone of the 'serious reviews' (beginning, for example: 'We may call Rossetti a genius; we cannot call him a master').

He had thought Tietjens was going mad: that he *was* mad. It had passed. Tietjens had assumed the mask of his indolent, insolent self. At the office, but later,[59] he had delivered an extraordinarily forceful—and quite rude—lecture to Sir Reginald on his reasons for differing from the official figures of population movements in the western territories.* Sir Reginald had been much impressed. The figures were wanted for a speech of the Colonial Minister— or an answer to a question[†]—and Sir Reginald had promised to put Tietjens' views before the great man. That was the sort of thing to do a young fellow good—because it got kudos for the office. They had to work on figures provided by the Colonial Governments, and if they could correct those fellows[60] by sheer brain work—that scored.

But there sat Tietjens, in his grey tweeds, his legs apart, lumpish,[61] clumsy, his tallowy, intelligent-looking hands drooping inert between his legs, his eyes gazing at a coloured photograph of the port of Boulogne beside the mirror beneath the luggage rack. Blonde, high-coloured, vacant apparently, you couldn't tell what in the world he was thinking of. The mathematical theory of waves, very likely, or slips in some one's article on Arminianism.[‡] For absurd as it seemed, Macmaster knew that he knew next to nothing of his friend's feelings. As to them, practically no confidences had passed between them. Just two:

On the night before his starting for his wedding in Paris Tietjens had said to him:

"Vinny, old fellow, it's a back door way out of it. She's bitched *me*."

And once, rather lately, he had said:

"Damn it! I don't even know if the child's my own!"

This last confidence had shocked Macmaster so irremedi-

---

* Of Canada.
† A question asked in Parliament (orally or written in advance).
‡ James Arminius or Harmensen (1560–1609), a Dutch Protestant theologian, denied the Calvinist doctrine of absolute predestination. Tietjens explains to Sylvia in II.i that he has been trying to write on Arminianism: see 208–9. Seen from Macmaster's point of view here, Tietjens appears to be thinking in terms of encyclopædia articles. However, though Boulogne is in the *département* of Pas-de-Calais, Ford may have meant the view of the French coast to remind him of his wife's adultery in another coastal region of northern France, Brittany.

ably—the child had been a seven months' child, rather ailing, and Tietjens' clumsy tenderness towards it had been so marked that, even without this nightmare, Macmaster had been affected by the sight of them together—that confidence then had pained Macmaster so frightfully, it was so appalling, that Macmaster had regarded it almost as an insult. It was the sort of confidence a man didn't make to his equal, but only to solicitors, doctors, or the clergy who are not quite men.* Or, at any rate, such confidences are not made between men without[62] appeals for sympathy, and Tietjens had made no appeal for sympathy. He had just added sardonically:

"She gives me the benefit of the agreeable doubt. And she's as good as said as much to Marchant"—Marchant had been Tietjens' old nurse.

Suddenly—and as if in a sort of unconscious losing of his head—Macmaster remarked:

"You can't say the man wasn't a poet!"

The remark had been, as it were, torn from him, because he had observed, in the strong light of the compartment, that half of Tietjens' forelock and a roundish patch behind it was[63] silvery white. That might have been going on for weeks: you live beside a man and notice his changes very little.[64] Yorkshire men of fresh colour and blondish often go speckled with white very young; Tietjens had had a white hair or two at the age of fourteen, very noticeable in the sunlight when he had taken his cap off to bowl.

But Macmaster's mind, taking appalled charge,[65] had felt assured that Tietjens had gone white with the shock of his wife's letter: in four hours! That meant that terrible things must be going on within him; his thoughts, at all costs, must be distracted. The mental process in Macmaster had been quite subconscious. He would not, advisedly, have introduced[66] the painter-poet as a topic.

Tietjens said:

"I haven't said anything at all that I can remember."

The obstinacy of his hard race awakened in Macmaster:

---

* Cf. *The Good Soldier* 26: 'You see, I suppose he regarded me not so much as a man. I had to be regarded as a woman or a solicitor.' Also 158.

"'Since,'" he quoted, "'when we stand side by side

> Only hands may meet,
> Better half this weary world
> Lay between us, sweet!
> Better far tho' hearts may break
> Bid farewell for aye!
> Lest thy sad eyes, meeting mine,
> Tempt my soul away!'[67]*

"You can't," he continued, "say that that isn't poetry! Great poetry."

"I can't say," Tietjens answered contemptuously. "I don't read poetry except Byron. But it's a filthy picture. ..."

Macmaster said uncertainly:

"I don't know that I know the picture. Is it in Chicago?"

"It isn't painted!" Tietjens said. "But it's there!"

He continued with sudden fury:

"Damn it. What's the sense of all these attempts to justify fornication? England's mad about it. Well, you've got your John Stuart Mill's[68] and your George Eliot's[69] for the high-class thing. Leave the furniture out![†] Or leave me out at least. I tell you it revolts me to think of that obese, oily[70] man who never took a bath, in a[71] grease-spotted dressing-gown and the underclothes he's slept in, standing beside a five-shilling model with crimped

---

* 'Better far'. Song, written in 1883 by E. B. Williams. No. 1, of *Six Songs*, set by Frederic Hymen Cowen. Cowen's *Scandinavian Symphony* was written in 1880 and dedicated to Ford's father, Francis Hueffer, who wrote the libretto for Cowen's *Sleeping Beauty* (1885). Macmaster quotes this poem as an example of Rossetti's gifts. It's possible that Ford (who was writing the novel in France, almost certainly without access to the score) misremembered it as by Rossetti. But it is also possible that he meant Macmaster to be testing the limits of Tietjens' knowledge by trying to catch him out. Yet later in the chapter (28 below) Tietjens demonstrates that he does know it, completing the lyric to Macmaster's chagrin (whether because Tietjens has caught out Macmaster trying to catch him out, or because it is supposed – in the world of the book – to be by Rossetti, and Macmaster is humiliated that Tietjens knows better than he does himself the subject on which he wants to set himself up as an authority).

† This cryptic phrase probably means something like 'no need to go into details: you get the picture'; though it might be equivalent to 'Let alone the furniture!' implying that the 'respectability' of Victorian bourgeois domesticity seemed hypocritically to license such earnest justifications of adultery (thus leading into Tietjens' excoriation of showy decor later in the paragraph).

hair, or some Mrs. W. Three Stars,* gazing into a mirror that reflects their fetid selves and gilt sunfish and drop chandeliers and plates sickening with cold bacon fat and gurgling about passion."†

Macmaster had gone chalk white, his short beard bristling:

"You daren't … you daren't talk like that," he stuttered.

"I *dare!*" Tietjens answered; 'but I oughtn't to … to you! I admit that. But you oughtn't, almost as much, to talk about that stuff to me, either. It's an insult to my intelligence."

"Certainly," Macmaster said stiffly, "the moment was not opportune."

"I don't understand what you mean," Tietjens answered. "The moment can never be opportune. Let's agree that making a career is a dirty business—for me as for you! But decent augurs grin behind their masks.‡ They never preach to each other."

"You're getting esoteric," Macmaster said faintly.

"I'll underline," Tietjens went on. "I quite understand that the favour of Mrs. Cressy and Mrs. de Limoux is essential to you! They have the ear of that old don Ingleby."

Macmaster said:

"Damn!"

"I quite agree," Tietjens continued, "I quite approve. It's the game as it has always been played. It's the tradition, so it's right. It's been sanctioned since the days of the *Précieuses Ridicules*."72§

"You've a way of putting things," Macmaster said.

"I haven't," Tietjens answered. "It's just because I haven't that

---

* i.e. 'Mrs. W***', the identity circumspectly concealed. Also see D. G. Rossetti's 'The Blessed Damozel' (1850/1870): 'She had three lilies in her hand, / And the stars in her hair were seven'; ll. 5–6 (www.rossettiarchive.org).

† In 'True Love & a GCM' Gabriel is taken (as young Ford would have been) to Rossetti's studio: 'an immense, gloomy, coloured and dusty room, where gilded sunfishes hung from the ceiling, and immense pictures of ladies stood on easels, so that whole spaces of the room were hidden, and the big dark man stood there wearing what Gabriel took to be an overcoat': *War Prose* 94–5. In *Return* 17 Ford recalled Henry James's disapproval of Rossetti's receiving him in what James took to be a dressing-gown, and deducing from that 'that he was disgusting in his habits, never took baths, and was insupportably lecherous. He repeated George Meredith's account of the masses of greasy ham and bleeding eggs which Rossetti devoured at breakfast.'

‡ The smile of the Roman augurs became a byword for hypocrisy: 'To the sophisticates in the Roman upper class the rituals lost any meaning and were duly considered a hoax perpetrated on the masses. Hence, the adage of the "smile of the augurs"': Karl Loewenstein, *The Governance of Rome* (The Hague: Nijhoff, 1973), 47. If Tietjens' iambic pentameter is a quotation, it remains to be traced. But cf. Shakespeare's Sonnet 107: 'And the sad augurs mock their own presage'.

§ Molière's play. Title: apers of distinguished persons.

what I *do* say sticks out in the minds of fellows like you who are always fiddling about after literary expression. But what I do say is this: I stand for monogamy."

Macmaster uttered a "*You!*" of amazement.

Tietjens answered with a negligent "*I!*" He continued:

"I stand for monogamy and chastity. And for no talking about it. Of course, if a man who's a man wants to have a woman he has her. And again, no talking about it. He'd no doubt be in the end better, and better off, if he didn't. Just as it would probably be better for him if he didn't have the second glass of whisky and soda...."

"You call that monogamy and chastity!" Macmaster interjected.

"I do," Tietjens answered. "And it probably is, at any rate it's clean. What is loathesome is all your fumbling in placket-holes* and polysyllabic Justification by Love. You stand for lachrymose polygamy. That's all right if you can get your club to change its rules."

"You're out of my depth," Macmaster said. "And being very disagreeable. You appear to be justifying promiscuity. I don't like it."

"I'm probably being disagreeable," Tietjens said. "Jeremiahs† usually are. But there ought to be a twenty years' close time‡ for discussions of sham sexual morality. Your Paolo and Francesca[73]—and Dante's—went, very properly, to Hell, and no bones about it. You don't get Dante justifying them. But your fellow whines about creeping into Heaven."

"He *doesn't!*" Macmaster exclaimed. Tietjens continued with equanimity:

"Now your novelist who writes a book to justify his every tenth or fifth seduction of a commonplace young woman in the name[74] of the rights of shop boys ... "

---

*   Cf. *Mightier* 27–8: 'the almost universal proneness of Anglo-Saxon writers to indulge in their works in a continually intrusive fumbling in placket-holes as Sterne called it, or in the lugubrious occupation of composing libidinous Limericks'.
†   The Old Testament prophet Jeremiah is noted for his lamentations at moral corruption and denunciatory warnings of catastrophe. Cf. the opening sentence of *Ancient Lights'* last chapter, 'Where We Stand': '[...] I find that I have written a jeremiad' (287).
‡   Period during which killing game or specific fish is forbidden.

"I'll admit," Macmaster conceded,[75] "that Briggs* is going too far. I told him only last Thursday at Mrs. Limoux's...."

"I'm not talking of anyone in particular," Tietjens said. "I don't read novels. I'm supposing a case. And it's a cleaner case than that of your pre-Raphaelite horrors! No! I don't read novels, but I follow tendencies. And if a fellow chooses to justify his seductions of uninteresting and viewy young females along the lines of freedom and the rights of man, it's relatively respectable. It would be better just to boast about his conquests in a straightforward and exultant way. But ..."

"You carry joking too far sometimes," Macmaster said. "I've warned you about it."

"I'm as solemn as an owl!" Tietjens rejoined. "The lower classes are becoming vocal. Why shouldn't they? They're the only people in this country who are sound in wind and limb. They'll save the country if the country's to be saved."

"And you call yourself a Tory!" Macmaster said.

"The lower classes," Tietjens continued equably, "such of them as get through the secondary schools, want irregular and very transitory unions. During holidays they go together on personally-conducted tours to Switzerland and such places. Wet afternoons they pass in their tiled bathrooms, slapping each other hilariously on the backs and splashing white enamel paint about."

"You say you don't read novels," Macmaster said, "but I recognise the quotation."[†]

"I don't *read* novels," Tietjens answered. "I know what's in 'em.[‡] There has been nothing worth *reading* written in England since the eighteenth century except by a woman[76][§].... But it's

---

\*   Possibly based on H. G. Wells, with whom Ford had a long-running humorously prickly friendship.

†   Possibly an allusion to *The Diary of a Nobody* (1888–9), by George and Weedon Grossmith, which involves plenty of hilarity and enamel paint (though no tours to Switzerland).

‡   Stella Bowen, *Drawn From Life* (London: Virago, 1984), 114, remembered Ford saying while editing the *transatlantic review*: 'I don't read manuscripts [...] I know what's in 'em'.

§   The first of Tietjens' several comments praising Mrs Wannop. She is thought to have been based on Lucy Clifford (1846–1929), who published as Mrs W. K. Clifford, and was a friend of Henry James as well as of Ford and Violet Hunt. She is best known now for *Mrs Keith's Crime* (1885), *Aunt Anne* (1892), and the stories she wrote for her children, *The Anyhow Stories, Moral and Otherwise* (1882). Also see *Nightingale* 73 on another possible inspiration for the character of Mrs Wannop, Miss Braddon, the

natural for your enamel splashers to want to see themselves in a
bright and variegated literature. Why shouldn't they? It's a[77]
healthy, human desire, and now that printing and paper are
cheap they get it satisfied. It's healthy, I tell you. Infinitely
healthier than ..." He paused.

"Than what?" Macmaster asked.

"I'm thinking," Tietjens said, "thinking how not to be too
rude."

"You want to be rude," Macmaster said bitterly, "to people
who lead the contemplative ... the circumspect life."[*]

"It's precisely that," Tietjens said. He quoted:

> "'She walks the lady of my delight,
>    A shepherdess of sheep;
> She is so circumspect and right:
>    She has her thoughts to keep.'"[†]

Macmaster said:

"Confound you, Chrissie. You know everything."

"Well, yes," Tietjens said musingly, "I think I should want to
be rude to her. I don't say I should be. Certainly I shouldn't if she
were good looking. Or if she were your soul's affinity. You can rely
on that."

Macmaster had a sudden vision of Tietjens' large and clumsy
form walking beside the lady of his, Macmaster's, delight, when
ultimately she was found—walking along the top of a cliff
amongst tall grass and poppies and making himself extremely

author of *Lady Audley's Secret*: 'I had always had the greatest possible respect for this
literary figure. Few novelists of her day had her workmanlike knowledge or could write
such sound English – like Cobbett's.' Ezra Pound in Canto LXXX recalled Ford taking
him 'to Miss Braddon's' in Richmond: *The Cantos* (London: Faber & Faber, 1975), 508.

[*]   In 'Towards a History of English Literature', written the year before *Some Do Not . . .*,
Ford repeatedly cites circumspection as a stifling demand made by established critics.
This book-length manuscript was eventually partly-published in Ford's *transatlantic
review* in 1924 as 'Stocktaking: Towards a Revaluation of English Literature': see *Critical Essays* 243, 253, 267.

[†]   Alice Meynell (1847–1922), 'The Shepherdess'. One of her best-known lyrics; originally published in *Later Poems* (1901), and set to music by several composers, it was
reissued in *The Shepherdess and Other Verses* (London: Burns and Oates [1914]), as well
as in various collected *Poems*, including the first posthumous 'Complete Edition' in
the year Ford was working on *Some Do Not . . .* (London: Burns and Oates, 1923), 51.

agreeable[78] with talk of Tasso* and Cimabue.† All the same, Macmaster imagined, the lady wouldn't like Tietjens. Women didn't as a rule. His looks and his silences alarmed them. Or they hated him.... Or they liked him very much indeed. And Macmaster said conciliatorily:

"Yes, I think I could rely on that!" He added: "All the same I don't wonder that ... "

He had been about to say:

"I don't wonder that Sylvia calls you immoral." For Tietjens' wife alleged that Tietjens was detestable. He bored her, she said, by his silences; when he did speak she hated him for the immorality of his views.... But he did not finish his sentence, and Tietjens went on:

"All the same when the war comes it will be these little snobs who will save England, because they've the courage to know what they want and to say so."

Macmaster said loftily:

"You're extraordinarily old-fashioned at times, Chrissie. You ought to know as well as I do that a war is impossible—at any rate with this country in it. Simply because ... " He hesitated and then emboldened himself: "We—the circumspect—yes, the circum-spect classes, will pilot the nation through the tight places."

"War, my good fellow," Tietjens said—the train was slowing down preparatorily to running into Ashford—"is inevitable, and with this country plumb centre in the middle of it. Simply because you fellows are such damn hypocrites.‡ There's not a country in the world that trusts us. We're always, as it were, committing adultery—like your fellow!—with the name of Heaven on our lips." He was jibing again at the subject of Macmaster's monograph.

---

\* Torquato Tasso (1544–95), best known for his epic of the First Crusade, *La Gerusalemme liberata* (*Jerusalem Delivered*).

† Thirteenth-century Italian painter, teacher of Giotto.

‡ Like other veterans and fellow-Modernists (such as his friends Richard Aldington and Ezra Pound) Ford developed the view that a failure of sincerity in language was a cause of the war. See *Mightier* 265; and Joseph Wiesenfarth, 'Ford Madox Ford and the Pre-Raphaelite Horrors: Or How Dante Gabriel Rossetti Started the First World War', *Modernism and the Individual Talent: Moderne und besondere Begabung*, ed. J. W. Rademacher (Münster: Lit, 2002), 30–6. Wyndham Lewis recalled Ford himself in 1914 prophesying war in comparably omniscient terms: *Blasting and Bombardiering*, revised edition (London: John Calder, 1982), 58–9.

"He never!" Macmaster said in almost a stutter. "He never whined about Heaven."

"He did," Tietjens said. "The beastly poem you quoted ends:

"'Better far though hearts may break,
        Since we dare not love,
    Part till we once more may meet
        In a Heaven above.'"

And Macmaster, who had been dreading that shot—for he never knew how much or how little of any given poem his friend would have by heart—Macmaster collapsed, as it were, into fussily getting down his dressing-cases and clubs from the rack, a task he usually left to a porter. Tietjens who, however much a train might be running into a station he was bound for, sat like a rock until it was dead-still, said:

"Yes, a war is inevitable. Firstly, there's you fellows who can't be trusted. And then there's the multitude who mean to have[79] bathrooms and white enamel. Millions of them; all over the world. Not merely here. And there aren't enough bathrooms and white enamel in the world to go round. It's like you polygamists with women.* There aren't enough women in the world to go round[80] to satisfy your insatiable appetites. And there aren't enough men in the world to give each woman one. And most women want several. So you have divorce cases. I suppose you won't say that because you're so circumspect and right there shall be no more divorce? Well, war is as inevitable as divorce...."

Macmaster had his head out of the carriage window and was calling for a porter.

On the platform a number of women in lovely sable cloaks, with purple or red jewel cases, with diaphanous silky scarves flying from motor hoods,† were drifting towards the branch train

---

* Ford described *The Good Soldier* as 'an analysis of the polygamous desires that underlie all men': *Reader* 477–8.
† 'In the early years of the twentieth century women dressed in motoring hoods and veils startled onlookers as they drove their new steam, electric and gas engine automobiles': Julie Wosk, *Women and the Machine* (Baltimore and London: Johns Hopkins University Press, 2001), x. Ford would often visit Henry James in Rye; James's friend Edith Wharton would take him driving when motor-cars were still a rarity in Edwardian Britain. *Return* 11–12 recalls James telling an elaborate story about Kipling's expensive car breaking down. Ford never owned a car. To get around in Kent and Sussex,

for Rye, under the shepherding of erect, burdened footmen. Two of them nodded to Tietjens.[81]

Macmaster considered that he was perfectly right to be tidy in his dress; you never knew whom you mightn't meet on a railway journey. This confirmed him as against Tietjens, who preferred to look like a navvy.

A tall, white-haired, white-moustached, red-cheeked fellow limped after Tietjens, who was getting his immense bag out of the guard's van. He clapped the young man on the shoulder and said:

"Hullo! How's your mother-in-law? Lady Claude wants to know. She says come up and pick a bone tonight[82] if you're going to Rye." He had extraordinarily blue, innocent eyes.

Tietjens said:

"Hullo, general," and added: "I believe she's much better. Quite restored. This is Macmaster. I think I shall be going over to bring my wife back in a day or two. They're both at Lobscheid[83*] . . . a German spa."

The general said:

"Quite right. It isn't good for a young man to be alone. Kiss Sylvia's finger-tips for me. She's the real thing, you lucky beggar." He added, a little anxiously: "What about a foursome to-morrow? Paul Sandbach is down.[84] He's as crooked as me. We can't do a full round at singles."[†]

"It's your own fault," Tietjens said. "You ought to have gone to my bone-setter. Settle it with Macmaster, will you?"[85] He jumped into the twilight of the guard's van.

The general looked at Macmaster, a quick, penetrating scrutiny:

"You're *the* Macmaster," he said. "You would be if you're with Chrissie."

A high voice called:

"General! General!"

"I want a word with you," the general said, "about the figures

or to get to the station for trains to London, he had to walk or use a horse and cart. Hence his (and Tietjens') knowledge about horses.
* Town in Nordrhein-Westfalen, Germany, about 50 km from Cologne.
† A singles match is played between two people. In a foursome, each team of two only use one ball, teeing off alternately, and taking alternate shots on each hole.

in that article you wrote about Pondoland.* Figures are all right. But we shall lose the beastly country if . . . But we'll talk about it after dinner to-night.[86] You'll come up to Lady Claudine's. . . ."

Macmaster congratulated himself again on his appearance. It was all very well for Tietjens to look like a sweep; he was of these people. He, Macmaster, wasn't. He had, if anything, to be an authority, and authorities wear gold tie-rings and broadcloth. General Lord Edward Campion had a son, a permanent head of the Treasury department that regulated increases of salaries and promotions in all the public offices. Tietjens[87] only caught the Rye train by running alongside it, pitching his enormous kit-bag through the carriage window and swinging on the footboard. Macmaster reflected that if he had done that half the station would have been yelling, "Stand away there."

As it was Tietjens a stationmaster was galloping after him to open the carriage door and grinningly to pant:[88]

"Well caught, sir!" for it was a cricketing county.

"Truly," Macmaster quoted[89] to himself.

> "'The gods to each ascribe a differing lot:
> Some enter at the portal. Some do not!'"[90]‡

---

* Region along the coast of the Eastern Cape province of South Africa.
† Ford's *Mister Bosphorus* includes a refrain of couplets beginning thus, such as: 'The Gods to each ascribe their various fates: / Some entering in; some baffled at the gates!' (56); or: 'The Gods to each ascribe a differing lot! / Some rest on snowy bosoms! Some do not!' (57). But Macmaster's version does not appear in the poem (which of course had not been written by the time in which the novel is set).

# II

MRS. SATTERTHWAITE with her French maid, her priest, and her disreputable young man, Mr. Bayliss, were at Lobscheid, an unknown and little-frequented air resort amongst the pinewoods of the Taunus.* Mrs. Satterthwaite was ultra-fashionable and consummately indifferent—she only really lost her temper if at her table and under her nose you consumed her famous Black Hamburg grapes without taking them[1] skin and all. Father Consett was out to have an uproarious good time during his three weeks' holiday from the slums of Liverpool; Mr. Bayliss, thin like a skeleton in tight blue serge, golden haired and pink, was so nearly dead of tuberculosis,[2] was so dead penniless, and of tastes so costly that he was ready to keep stone quiet, drink six pints of milk a day and behave himself. On the face of it he was there to write the letters of Mrs. Satterthwaite, but the lady never let him enter her private rooms for fear of infection. He had to content himself with nursing a growing adoration for Father Consett. This priest, with an enormous mouth, high cheek bones, untidy black hair, a broad face that never looked too clean and waving hands that always looked too dirty, never kept still for a moment, and had a brogue such as is seldom heard outside old-fashioned English novels of Irish life. He had a perpetual laugh,[3] like the noise made by a steam roundabout. He was, in short, a saint, and Mr. Bayliss knew it, though he didn't know how. Ultimately, and with the financial[4] assistance of Mrs. Satterthwaite, Mr. Bayliss became almoner to Father Consett, adopted the rule of St. Vincent de Paul† and wrote some very admirable, if decorative, devotional verse.

---

* The forest of the Taunus Wald. Cf. *The Good Soldier* 12: 'It wasn't a minuet that we stepped; it was a prison – a prison full of screaming hysterics, tied down so that they might not outsound the rolling of our carriage wheels as we went along the shaded avenues of the Taunus Wald.'
† The St Vincent de Paul Society was founded as a Catholic charitable organisation in 1833 and named after the priest who gave up an ecclesiastical career at Court to work with the poor.

They proved thus a very happy, innocent party. For Mrs. Satterthwaite interested herself—it was the only interest she had—in handsome, thin and horribly disreputable young men. She would wait for them, or send her car to wait for them, at the gaol gates. She would bring their usually admirable wardrobes up to date and give them enough money to have a good time. When contrary to all expectations—but it happened more often than not!—they turned out well, she was lazily pleased. Sometimes she sent them away to a gay spot with a priest who needed a holiday; sometimes she had them down to her place in the west of England.

So they were a pleasant company and all very happy. Lobscheid contained one empty hotel with large verandahs and several square farmhouses, white with grey beams, painted in the gables with bouquets of blue and yellow flowers or with scarlet huntsmen shooting at purple stags. They were like gay cardboard boxes set down in fields of long grass; then the pinewoods commenced and ran, solemn, brown and geometric for miles up and down hill. The peasant girls wore black velvet waistcoats, white bodices, innumerable petticoats and absurd parti-coloured headdresses of the shape and size of halfpenny buns. They walked about in rows of four to six abreast; with a slow step, protruding white-stockinged feet in dancing pumps, their headdresses nodding solemnly; young men in blue blouses, knee-breeches and, on Sundays, in three-cornered hats, followed behind singing part-songs.

The French maid—whom Mrs. Satterthwaite had borrowed from the Duchesse de Carbon Châteaulherault in exchange for her own maid—was at first inclined to find the place *maussade*.* But getting up a tremendous love affair[5] with a fine, tall, blonde young fellow, who included[6] a gun, a gold-mounted hunting knife as long as his arm, a light, grey-green uniform, with gilt badges and buttons, she was reconciled to her lot. When the young[7] Förster† tried to shoot her—"*et pour cause*,"‡ as she said—she was ravished and Mrs. Satterthwaite lazily amused.

---

\*   Disagreeable, dull (French).
†   Forest ranger (German).
‡   And with good reason (French).

They were sitting playing bridge in the large, shadowy dining-hall of the hotel: Mrs. Satterthwaite, Father Consett, Mr. Bayliss. A young blonde[8] sub-lieutenant of great obsequiousness who was there as a last chance for his right lung and his career, and the bearded Kur*-doctor cut in.† Father Consett, breathing heavily[9] and looking frequently at his watch, played very fast, exclaiming: "Hurry up now; it's nearly twelve. Hurry up wid ye." Mr. Bayliss being dummy,‡ the Father exclaimed: "Three no trumps; I've to make. Get me a whisky and soda quick, and don't drown it as ye did the last." He played his hand with extreme rapidity, threw down his last three cards, exclaimed: "Ach! Botheranouns an' all; I'm two down and I've revoked§ on the top av it," swallowed down his whisky and soda, looked at his watch and exclaimed: "Done it to the minute! Here, doctor, take my hand and finish the rubber."** He was to take the mass next day for the local priest, and mass must be said fasting from midnight, and without cards played. Bridge was his only passion; a fortnight every year was what, in his worn-out life, he got of it. On his holiday he rose at ten. At eleven it was: "A four for the Father." From two to four they walked in the forest. At five it was: "A four for the Father." At nine it was: "Father, aren't you coming to your bridge?" And Father Consett grinned all over his face and said: "It's good ye are to a poor ould soggart.†† It will be paid back to you in Heaven."

The other four played on solemnly. The Father sat himself down behind Mrs. Satterthwaite, his chin in the nape of her neck. At excruciating moments he gripped her shoulders, exclaimed: "Play the *queen*, woman!" and breathed hard down her back. Mrs. Satterthwaite would play the two of diamonds, and the Father, throwing himself back, would groan. She said over her shoulder:

---

* *Kur*: the 'cure' (German) offered by the resort, here described as an 'air' resort suitable for lung patients, but described by Tietjens in I.i as a spa. Much of the action of *The Good Soldier* takes place in the spa resort of Nauheim.
† 'To join in a game [...] by taking the place of a player *cutting out*': OED; thus enabling more than four players to participate.
‡ In contract bridge, the dummy is the player whose hand is turned face up, and who then leaves most of the play to his or her partner, the declarer.
§ Failed to follow suit as required when he was able to.
** In bridge, the set of successive deals ending when one pair wins two games.
†† Irish term for priest: OED.

"I want to talk to you to-night, Father," took the last trick of the rubber, collected 17 marks 50 from the doctor and 8 marks from the unter-leutnant. The doctor exclaimed:

"You gan't dake that immense sum from us and then ko off. Now we shall pe ropped py Herr Payliss at gutt-throat!"

She drifted, all shadowy black silk, across the shadows of the dining-hall, dropping her winnings into her black satin vanity bag and attended by the priest. Outside the door, beneath the antlers of a royal stag, in an atmosphere of paraffin lamps and varnished pitch-pine, she said:

"Come up to my sitting-room. The prodigal's returned. Sylvia's here."

The Father said:

"I thought I saw her out of the corner of my eye in the 'bus after dinner. She'll be going back to her husband. It's a poor world."

"She's a wicked devil!" Mrs. Satterthwaite said.

"I've known her myself since she was nine," Father Consett said, "and it's little I've seen in her to hold up to the commendation of my flock." He added: "But maybe I'm made unjust by the shock of it."

They climbed the stairs slowly.

Mrs. Satterthwaite sat herself on the edge of a cane chair. She said:

"Well!"

She[10] wore a black hat like a cart-wheel and her dresses appeared always to consist of a great many squares of silk that might[11] have been thrown on to her. Since she considered that her complexion, which was mat[12] white, had gone slightly violet from twenty years of make-up, when she was not made up—as she never was at Lobscheid—she wore bits of puce-coloured satin ribbon stuck[13] here and there, partly to counteract the violet of her complexion, partly to show[14] she was not in mourning. She was very tall and extremely emaciated; her dark eyes that had beneath them dark brown thumb-marks were very tired or very indifferent by turns.

Father Consett walked backwards and forwards, his hands behind his back, his head bent, over the not too well polished floor. There were two candles, lit but dim, in imitation pewter *nouvel art* candlesticks, rather dingy; a sofa of cheap mahogany with red plush cushions and rests,[15] a table covered with a cheap carpet, and an American roll-top desk that had thrown into it a great many papers in scrolls or flat. Mrs. Satterthwaite was extremely indifferent to her surroundings, but she insisted on having a piece of furniture for her papers. She liked also to have a profusion of hot-house, not garden, flowers, but as there were none of these at Lobscheid she did without them. She insisted also, as a rule, on a comfortable chaise longue which she rarely, if ever, used; but the German Empire of those days did not contain a comfortable chair, so she did without it, lying down on her bed when she was really tired. The walls of the large room were completely covered with pictures of animals in death agonies: capercailzies* giving up the ghost with gouts of scarlet blood on the snow; deer dying with their heads back and eyes glazing, gouts of red blood on their necks; foxes dying with scarlet blood on green grass. These pictures were frame to frame, representing sport, the hotel having been a former Grand Ducal hunting-box, freshened to suit the taste of the day with varnished pitch-pine, bath-rooms, verandahs,[16] and excessively modern but noisy lavatory arrangements which had been put in for the delight of possible English guests.

Mrs. Satterthwaite sat on the edge of her chair; she had always the air of being just about to go out somewhere or of having just come in and being on the point of going to take her things off. She said:

"There's been a telegram waiting for her all the afternoon. I knew she was coming."

Father Consett said:

"I saw it in the rack myself. I misdoubted it." He added: "Oh dear, oh dear! After all we've talked about it; now it's come."

Mrs. Satterthwaite said:

"I've been a wicked woman myself as these things are measured; but ..."

Father Consett said:

"Ye have! It's no doubt from you she gets it, for your husband was a good man. But one wicked woman is enough for my

---

*  Wood-grouse.

contemplation[17] at a time. I'm no St. Anthony*.... The young man says he will take her back?"

"On conditions," Mrs. Satterthwaite said. "He[18] is coming here to have an interview."

The priest said:

"Heaven knows, Mrs. Satterthwaite, there are times when to a poor priest the rule of the Church as regards marriage seems bitter hard and he almost doubts her inscrutable wisdom. He doesn't mind you. But at times I wish that that young man would take what advantage—it's all there is!—that he can of being a Protestant and divorce Sylvia. For I tell you, there are bitter things to see amongst my flock over there . . ." He made a vague gesture towards the infinite.... "And bitter things I've seen, for the heart of man is a wicked place.[19]† But never a bitterer than this young man's lot."

"As you say," Mrs. Satterthwaite said, "my husband was a good man. I hated him, but that was as much my fault as his. More! And the only reason I don't wish Christopher to divorce Sylvia is that it would bring disgrace on my husband's name. At the same time, Father . . ."

The priest said:

"I've heard near enough."

"There's this to be said for Sylvia," Mrs. Satterthwaite went on. "There are times when a woman hates a man—as Sylvia hates her husband.... I tell you I've walked behind a man's back and nearly screamed because of the desire to put my nails into the veins of his neck.[20] It was a fascination. And it's worse with Sylvia. It's a natural antipathy."

"Woman!" Father Consett fulminated, "I've no patience wid

---

* St Antony the Great of Thebes (c. 251–356). Founder of Christian Monachism, or monasticism. Famously tempted by devils, as in the novel Flaubert thought of as his masterpiece, *La Tentation de Saint Antoine*, and wrote in three versions before publishing the last in 1874.

† Ford often quotes the Russian proverb 'the heart of another is a dark forest' (*chuzhaia dusha – potemki*): see Anat Vernitski, 'The Complexity of Truth: Ford and the Russians', *Ford Madox Ford's Literary Contacts*, ed. Paul Skinner, International Ford Madox Ford Studies, 6 (Amsterdam and New York: Rodopi, 2007), 109, which he takes from Turgenev's *Liza*. See *Critical Essays* 40, 177; *Ancient Lights* xi; 'Women and Men – II' *Little Review*, 2 (Mar. 1918), 36–51 (49). 'The Dark Forest' was his working title for the novel *The New Humpty-Dumpty* (1912); eventually he used the proverb in a quotation attributed to 'Tambov', though that is in fact a province in Russia.

ye! If the woman, as the Church directs, would have children by her husband and live decent, she would have no such[21] feelings. It's unnatural living and unnatural practices[22] that cause these complexes. Don't think I'm an ignoramus, priest if I am."

Mrs. Satterthwaite said:

"But Sylvia's had a child."

Father Consett swung round like a man that has been shot at.

"Whose?" he asked, and he pointed a dirty finger at his interlocutress.[23] "It was that blackguard Drake's, wasn't it? I've long suspected that."

"It was probably[24] Drake's," Mrs. Satterthwaite said.

"Then," the priest said, "in the face of the pains of the hereafter how could you let that decent lad in the hotness of his sin? ..."

"Indeed," Mrs. Satterthwaite said, "I shiver sometimes when I think of it. Don't believe that I had anything to do with trepanning* him. But I couldn't hinder it. Sylvia's my daughter, and dog doesn't eat dog."

"There are times when it should," Father Consett said contemptuously.

"You don't seriously," Mrs. Satterthwaite said, "say that I, a mother, if an indifferent one, with my daughter appearing[25] in trouble, as the kitchenmaids say, by a married man—that I should step in and stop a marriage that was a Godsend. ...."

"Don't," the priest said, "introduce the sacred name into an affair of Piccadilly bad girls. ...." He stopped. "Heaven help me," he said again, "don't ask me to answer the question of what you should or shouldn't have done. You know I loved your husband like a brother, and you know I've loved you and Sylvia ever since she was a tiny.[26] And I thank God that I am not your spiritual adviser, but only your friend in God. For if I had to answer your question I could answer it only in one way." He broke off to ask: "Where is that woman?"

Mrs. Satterthwaite called:

"Sylvia! Sylvia! Come here!"

A door in the shadows opened and light shone from another

* Entrapping, ensnaring, beguiling (archaic or obscure): *OED*.

room behind a tall figure leaning one hand on the handle of the door. A very deep voice said:

"I can't understand, mother, why you live in rooms like a sergeants' mess." And Sylvia Tietjens wavered into the room. She added: "I suppose it doesn't matter. I'm bored."

Father Consett groaned:

"Heaven help us, she's like a picture of Our Lady by Fra Angelico."

Immensely tall, slight and slow in her movements, Sylvia Tietjens wore her reddish, very fair hair in great bandeaux right down over her ears. Her very oval, regular face had an expression of virginal lack of interest such as used to be worn by fashionable Paris courtesans a decade before that time. Sylvia Tietjens considered that, being privileged to go everywhere where one went and to have all men[27] at her feet, she had no need to change her expression or to infuse into it the greater animation that marked the more common beauties of the early twentieth century. She moved slowly from the door and sat languidly on the sofa against the wall.

"There you are, Father," she said. "I'll not ask you to shake hands with me. You probably wouldn't."

"As I am a priest," Father Consett answered, "I could not refuse. But I'd rather not."

"This," Sylvia repeated, "appears to be a boring place."

"You won't say so to-morrow," the priest said. "There's two young fellows. . . . And a sort of policeman to trepan away from your mother's maid!"

"That," Sylvia answered, "is meant to be bitter. But it doesn't hurt. I am done with men." She added suddenly: "Mother, didn't you one day, while you were still young, say that you had done with men? Firmly! And mean it?"

Mrs. Satterthwaite said:

"I did."

"And did you keep to it?" Sylvia asked.

Mrs. Satterthwaite said:

"I did."

"And shall I, do you imagine?"

Mrs. Satterthwaite said:

"I imagine you will."

Sylvia said:

"Oh dear!"

The priest said:

"I'd be willing to see your husband's telegram. It makes a difference to see the words on paper."

Sylvia rose effortlessly.

"I don't see why you shouldn't," she said. "It will give you no pleasure." She drifted towards the door.

"If it would give me pleasure," the priest said, "you would not show it me."

"I would not," she said.

A silhouette in the doorway, she halted, drooping, and looked over her shoulder.

"Both you and mother," she said, "sit there scheming to make life bearable for the Ox. I call my husband the Ox. He's repulsive: like a swollen animal. Well ... you can't do it." The lighted doorway was vacant. Father Consett sighed.

"I told you this was an evil place," he said. "In the deep forests. She'd not have such evil thoughts in another place."

Mrs. Satterthwaite said:

"I'd rather you didn't say that, Father. Sylvia would have evil thoughts in any place."

"Sometimes," the priest said, "at night I think I hear the claws of evil things scratching on the shutters.* This was the last place in Europe to be christianised. Perhaps it wasn't ever even christianised and they're here yet."

Mrs. Satterthwaite said:

"It's all very well to talk like that in the day-time. It makes the place seem romantic. But it must be near one at night.† And things are bad enough as it is."

"They are," Father Consett said. "The devil's at work."

Sylvia drifted back into the room with a telegram of several sheets. Father Consett held it close to one of the candles to read, for he was short-sighted.

---

*   Cf. Ford, *The Young Lovell* (London: Chatto and Windus, 1913), 234: 'He [the monk Francis] imagined devils with twisted snouts and long claws scraping and scratching at the leads of the painted glass and at the stones of the mortar.'
†   i.e. nearly one o'clock in the morning.

"All men are repulsive," Sylvia said; "don't you think so, mother?"

Mrs. Satterthwaite said:

"I do not. Only a heartless woman would say so."

"Mrs. Vanderdecken," Sylvia went on, "says all men are repulsive and it's woman's disgusting task to live beside them."

"You've been seeing that foul creature?" Mrs. Satterthwaite said. "She's a Russian agent. And worse!"

"She was at Yssingeux[28]* all the time we were," Sylvia said. "You needn't groan. She won't split on us. She's the soul of honour."

"It wasn't because of that I groaned, if I did," Mrs. Satterthwaite answered.

The priest, from over his telegram, exclaimed: "Mrs. Vanderdecken! God forbid."

Sylvia's face, as she sat on the sofa, expressed languid and incredulous amusement.

"What do you know of her?" she asked the Father.

"I know what you know," he answered, "and that's enough."

"Father Consett," Sylvia said to her mother, "has been renewing[29] his social circle."

"It's not," Father Consett said, "amongst the dregs of the people that you must live if you don't want to hear of the dregs of society."

Sylvia stood up. She said:

"You'll keep your tongue off my best friends if you want me to stop and be lectured. But for Mrs. Vanderdecken I should not be here, returned to the fold!"

Father Consett exclaimed:

"Don't say it, child. I'd rather, heaven help me, you had gone on living in open sin."

Sylvia sat down again, her hands listlessly in her lap.

"Have it your own way," she said, and the Father returned to the fourth sheet of the telegram.

"What does this mean?" he asked. He had returned to the first

---

\*  The place Sylvia has been staying adulterously with Perowne in Brittany; named as Yssingeux-les-Pervenches in *No More Parades*. No town exists in Brittany with this name, but there is an Yssingeaux in the Auvergne.

sheet. "This here: 'accept[30] resumption yoke'?" he read, breathlessly.

"Sylvia," Mrs. Satterthwaite said, "go and light the spirit lamp for some tea. We shall want it."

"You'd think I was a district messenger boy," Sylvia said as she rose. "Why don't you keep your maid up? . . . It's a way we had of referring to our . . . union," she explained to the Father.

"There was sympathy enough between you and him then," he said, "to have bywords for things. It was that I wanted to know. I understood the words."

"They were pretty bitter bywords, as you call them," Sylvia said. "More like curses than kisses."

"It was you that used them then," Mrs. Satterthwaite said. "Christopher never said a bitter thing to you."

An expression like a grin came slowly over Sylvia's face as she turned back to the priest.

"That's mother's tragedy," she said. "My husband's one of her best boys. She adores him. And he can't bear *her*." She drifted behind the wall of the next room and they heard her tinkling the tea-things as the Father read on again beside the candle. His immense shadow began at the centre and ran along the pitch-pine ceiling, down the wall and across the floor to join his splay feet in their clumsy boots.

"It's bad," he muttered. He made a sound like[31] "Umbleumbleumble.... Worse than I feared ... umbleumble.... '*accept resumption yoke but on rigid conditions.*' What's this: *esoecially*; it ought to be a 'p,' '*especially regards child reduce establishment ridiculous our position remake settlements in child's sole interests flat not house entertaining minimum am prepared resign office settle Yorkshire but imagine this not suit you child remain sister Effie open visits both wire if this rough outline provisionally acceptable in that case will express draft general position Monday for you*[32] *and mother reflect upon follow self Tuesday arrive Thursday Lobscheid go Wiesbaden fortnight on social tack*[33] *discussion Thursday limited solely*[34] *comma emphasised comma to affairs.*'"[35]

"That means," Mrs. Satterthwaite said, "that he doesn't mean to reproach her. *Emphasised* applies to the word *solely*...."

"Why d'you take it ..."[36] Father Consett asked, "did he spend an immense lot of money on this telegram? Did he imagine you were in such trepidation. ... " He broke off.[37] Walking slowly, her long arms extended to carry the tea-tray, over which her wonderfully moving face had a rapt expression of indescribable mystery, Sylvia was coming through the door.

"Oh, child," the Father exclaimed, "whether it's St. Martha or that Mary that made the better[38] choice, not one of them ever looked more virtuous[39] than you. Why aren't ye born to be a good man's help-meet?"

A little tinkle sounded from the tea-tray and three pieces of sugar fell on to the floor. Mrs. Tietjens hissed with vexation.

"I *knew* that damned thing would slide off the teacups," she said. She dropped the tray from an inch or so of height on to the carpeted table.* "I'd made it a matter of luck between myself and myself," she said. Then she faced the priest.

"I'll tell you,"[40] she said, "why he sent the telegram. It's because of that[41] dull display of the English gentleman that I detested. He gives himself the solemn airs of the Foreign Minister, but he's only a youngest son at the best. That is why I loathe him."

Mrs. Satterthwaite said:

"That isn't the reason why he sent the telegram."

Her daughter had a gesture of amused, lazy tolerance.

"Of course it isn't," she said. "He sent it[42] out of consideration: the lordly, full dress consideration that drives me distracted. As he would say: 'He'd imagine I'd find it convenient to have ample

---

* When Ford took Violet Hunt to visit Joseph Conrad in 1911, she recalled 'a noise and a clatter' when, during 'a discussion over the divine right of kings', she irritated Conrad with a quip that 'Marie Antoinette had been guilty of treason to France': 'Conrad brought his fist down on the tin tea-tray, and the cups danced horribly, but not one was broken [ . . . ]'. In his memoir of Conrad, Ford also recalled the scene, saying that 'With a hypersensitiveness to impressions the writer, too, remembers Conrad throwing teacups into the fireplace'; though he later acknowledges that Conrad cannot actually 'have thrown the tea-cups into the fire since on going away the lady said: "What a *charming* man Mr. Conrad is! I must see him often"': Ford, *Joseph Conrad* 19; Hunt, *The Flurried Years* (London: Hurst and Blackett, 1926), 204–5. We have not seen the last of this surreal conjunction of tea-trays, Tietjens, and violence. Ford wrote to Conrad from the Ypres Salient describing how 'Shells falling on a church [ . . . ] make a huge "*corrump*" sound, followed by a noise like crockery falling off a tray – as the roof tiles fall off': *Letters* 73; Stang, *Presence* 173. R. H. Mottram, too, juxtaposed the war with teatime civilities. In his *Spanish Farm Trilogy 1914–18*, Dormer thinks about the Germans: 'in 1914 they had finally kicked over the tea-table of the old quiet comfortable life' (London: Chatto & Windus 1930), 732. The term 'tea-table' also occurs seven times in *Some Do Not . . .*.

time for reflection.'[43] It's like being addressed as if one were a monument and by a herald according to protocol. And partly because he's the soul of truth like a stiff Dutch doll. He wouldn't write a letter because he couldn't without beginning it 'Dear Sylvia' and ending it 'Yours sincerely' or 'truly' or 'affectionately.' ... He's that sort of precise imbecile. I tell you he's so formal he can't do without all the conventions there are and so truthful he can't use half of them."

"Then," Father Consett said, "if ye know him so well, Sylvia Satterthwaite, how is it ye can't get on with him better? They say: *Tout savoir c'est tout pardonner.*"[*]

"It isn't," Sylvia said. "To know everything about a person is to be bored ... bored ... bored!"

"And how are ye going to answer this telegram of his?" the Father asked. "Or have ye answered it already?"

"I shall wait until Monday night to keep him as bothered as I can to know whether he's to start on Tuesday. He fusses like a hen over his packings and the exact hours of his movements. On Monday I shall telegraph: 'Righto' and nothing else."

"And why," the Father asked, "will ye telegraph him a vulgar word that you never use, for your language is the one thing about you that isn't vulgar?"

Sylvia said:

"Thanks!" She curled her legs up under her on the sofa and laid her head back against the wall so that her Gothic arch of a chinbone pointed at the ceiling. She admired her own neck, which was very long and white.

"I know!" Father Consett said. "You're a beautiful woman. Some men would say it was a lucky fellow that lived with you. I don't ignore the fact in my cogitation.[44] He'd imagine all sorts of delights to lurk[45] in the shadow of your beautiful hair.[†] And they wouldn't."

Sylvia brought her gaze down from the ceiling and fixed her brown eyes for a moment on the priest, speculatively.

"It's great handicaps[46] we suffer from," he said.

---

[*] 'To know everything is to forgive everything' (French: Mme de Staël (1766–1817)).

[†] Perhaps an anticipation of Dante Gabriel Rossetti's 'Three Shadows', lines 1–2, alluded to on 69 below.

"I don't know why I selected that word," Sylvia said, "it's one word, so it costs only fifty pfennigs. I couldn't hope really to give a jerk to his pompous self-sufficiency."

"It's great handicaps we priests suffer from," the Father repeated. "However much a priest may be a man of the world— and he has to be to fight the world . . . "

Mrs. Satterthwaite said:

"Have a cup of tea, Father, while it's just right. I believe Sylvia is the only person in Germany who knows how to make tea."

"There's always behind him the Roman collar and the silk bib, and you don't believe in him," Father Consett went on,[47] "yet he knows ten—a thousand times!—more of human nature than ever you can."

"I don't see," Sylvia said placably, "how you can learn in your slums anything about the nature of Eunice Vanderdecken, or Elizabeth B. or Queenie James, or any of my set." She was on her feet pouring cream into the Father's tea. "I'll admit for the moment that you aren't giving me pi-jaw."*

"I'm glad," the priest said, "that ye remember enough of yer schooldays to use the old term."

Sylvia wavered backwards to her sofa and sank down again.

"There you are," she said, "you can't really get away from preachments. Me for the pyore† young girl is always at the back of it."

"It isn't," the Father said. "I'm not one to cry for the moon."

"You don't want me to be a pure young girl," Sylvia asked with lazy incredulity.

"I do not!" the Father said, "but I'd wish that at times ye'd remember you once were."

"I don't believe I ever was," Sylvia said.[48] "If the nuns had known I'd have been expelled from the Holy Child."‡

"You would not," the Father said. "Do stop your boasting. The nuns have too much sense. . . . Anyhow, it isn't a pure young girl I'd have you or behaving like a Protestant deaconess for the craven fear of hell. I'd have ye be a physically healthy, decently

* Pious lecturing from teachers or parents.
† 'pure' – presumably with a satirical accent.
‡ Her convent school.

honest-with-yourself young devil of a married woman. It's them that are the plague and the salvation of the world."

"You admire mother?" Mrs. Tietjens asked suddenly. She added in parenthesis: "You see you can't get away from salvation."

"I mean keeping bread and butter in their husbands'[49] stomachs," the priest said. "Of course I admire your mother."

Mrs. Satterthwaite moved a hand slightly.

"You're at any rate in league with[50] her against me," Sylvia said. She asked with more interest: "Then would you have me model myself on her and do good works to escape hell fire? She wears a hair shirt in Lent."

Mrs. Satterthwaite started from her doze on the edge of her chair. She had been trusting the Father's wit to[51] give her daughter's insolence a run for its money, and she imagined that if the priest hit hard enough he might, at least, make Sylvia think a little about some of her ways.

"Hang it, no, Sylvia," she exclaimed now[52] suddenly. "I may not be much, but I'm a sportsman. I'm afraid of hell fire; horribly, I'll admit. But I don't bargain with the Almighty. I hope He'll let me through; but I'd go on trying to pick men out of the dirt—I suppose that's what you and Father Consett mean—if I were as certain of going to hell as I am of going to bed to-night. So that's that!"

"'And lo! Ben Adhem's name led all the rest!'"* Sylvia jeered softly. "All the same I bet you wouldn't bother to reclaim men if you could not find[53] the young, good-looking, interestingly vicious sort."

"I wouldn't," Mrs. Satterthwaite said. "If they didn't interest me, why should I?"

Sylvia looked at Father Consett.

"If you're going to trounce me any more," she said, "get a move on. It's late, I've been travelling for thirty-six hours."

"I will," Father Consett said. "It's a good maxim that if you swat flies enough some of them stick to the wall. I'm only trying

---

* Last line of Leigh Hunt's 'Abou Ben Adhem'. He dreams of an angel writing in a golden book the names of those who 'loved the Lord', but is told he isn't among them. He tells the angel to inscribe his instead 'as one who loves his fellow men'. The next night the angel shows him 'the names whom love of God had blessed', and that's the list he heads.

to make a little mark on your common sense. Don't you see what you're going to?"

"What?" Sylvia said indifferently. "Hell?"

"No," the Father said, "I'm talking of this life. Your confessor must talk to you about the next. But I'll not tell you what you're going to. I've changed my mind. I'll tell your mother after you're gone."

"Tell me," Sylvia said.

"I'll not," Father Consett answered. "Go to the fortune-tellers at the Earl's Court exhibition;[*] they'll tell ye all about the fair woman you're to beware of."

"There's one[54] of them said to be rather good," Sylvia said. "Di Wilson's told me about her. She said she was going to have a baby.... You don't mean that, Father? For I swear I never will...."[55]

"I daresay not," the priest said. "But let's talk about men."

"There's nothing you can tell me I don't know," Sylvia said.

"I daresay not," the priest answered. "But let's rehearse what you do know. Now suppose you could elope with a new man every week and no questions asked? Or how often would you want to?"

Sylvia said:

"Just a moment, Father," and she addressed Mrs. Satterthwaite: "I suppose I shall have to put myself to bed."

"You will," Mrs. Satterthwaite said. "I'll not have my[56] maid kept up after ten in a holiday resort. What's she to do in a place like this? Except listen for the bogies it's full of?"

"Always considerate!" Mrs. Tietjens gibed. "And perhaps it's just as well. I'd probably beat that Marie of yours'[57] arms to pieces with a hair-brush if she came near me." She added: "You were talking about men, Father...." And then began with sudden animation to her mother:

"I've changed my mind about that telegram. The first thing to-morrow I shall wire: '*Agreed entirely but arrange bring Hullo Central with you.*'"

She addressed the priest again.

---

[*]  Earls Court in West London is usually spelled without an apostrophe. The exhibitions were an annual fixture, but in 1911 there was a Coronation Exhibition. Ford was in London for the Coronation, so may well have seen it.

"I call my maid Hullo Central* because she's got a tinny voice like a telephone. I say: 'Hullo Central'—when she answers 'Yes, modd'm,'† you'd swear it was the Exchange speaking. . . . But you were telling me about men."

"I was reminding you!" the Father said. "But I needn't go on. You've caught the drift of my remarks. That is why you are pretending not to listen."

"I assure you, no," Mrs. Tietjens said. "It is simply that if a thing comes into my head I have to say it. . . . You were saying that if one went away with a different man for every week-end . . ."

"You've shortened the period already," the priest said. "I gave a full week to every man."

"But, of course, one would have to have a home," Sylvia said, "an address. One would have to fill one's mid-week engagements. Really it comes to it that one has to have a husband and a place to store one's maid in. Hullo Central's been on board-wages‡ all the time. But I don't believe she likes it. . . . Let's agree that if I had a different man every week I'd be bored with the arrangement. That's what you're getting at, isn't it?"

"You'd find," the priest said, "that it whittled down until the only divvy§ moment was when you stood waiting in the booking-office for the young man to take the tickets. . . . And then

---

* When telephone calls had to be connected manually by an operator, a caller would call the Central Exchange. 'Hullo Central' was how the caller would address the operator or how the operator would answer. The operators (usually female) were sometimes known as 'Hello Girls'. Hank Morgan's wife Sandy names their child 'Hello Central' because she has heard Hank call the name out longingly in his sleep, in Mark Twain's *A Connecticut Yankee at King Arthur's Court*, a novel Ford satirised in his 1911 historical romance *Ladies Whose Bright Eyes*. There was a mawkish 1901 popular song 'Hello Central, Give Me Heaven', by Charles Kassell and Joseph Clauder, in which a child tries to telephone her dead mother. But perhaps more relevant to *Parade's End* is Al Jolson's 1918 hit updating the trope, 'Hello, Central, Give Me No Man's Land' (w. Sam M. Lewis & Joe Young, m. Jean Schwartz) in which a child tries to telephone her father having been told he's in No Man's Land, when in fact he has been killed.
† Madam.
‡ Board wages can be food and lodging offered in lieu of (or on top of) a salary; but in this context it probably means that the maid has been given an allowance for food and lodging while Sylvia has been abroad with Perowne (perhaps because she couldn't stay at the Tietjens' marital home under the circumstances, or because Sylvia wanted to give the impression she wasn't planning to return).
§ 'Extremely pleasant, "divine", "heavenly"': *OED* (this instance being one of the dictionary's two citations). Close to 'deevy' (equally deevie, deevy, deevie, devey, or devy), which the dictionary glosses as '"Divine"; delightful, sweet, charming'.

gradually that wouldn't be divvy any more.... And you'd yawn and long to go back to your husband."

"Look here," Mrs. Tietjens said, "you're abusing the secrets of the confessional. That's exactly what Tottie* Charles said. She tried it for three months while Freddie Charles was in Madeira. It's *exactly* what she said down to the yawn and the booking-office. *And* the 'divvy.' It's only Tottie Charles who uses it every two words. Most of us prefer ripping! It *is* more sensible."

"Of course I haven't been abusing the secrets of the confessional," Father Consett said mildly.

"Of course you haven't," Sylvia said with affection. "You're a good old stick and no end of a mimic, and you know us all to the bottom of our hearts."

"Not all that much," the priest said, "there's probably a good deal of good at the bottom of your hearts."[58]

Sylvia said:

"Thanks." She asked suddenly: "Look here. *Was* it what you saw of us—the future[59] mothers of England, you know, and all—at Miss Lampeter's—that made you take to the slums? Out of disgust and despair?"

"Oh, let's not make melodrama out of it," the priest answered. "Let's say I wanted a change. I couldn't see that I was doing any good."

"You did us all the good there was done," Sylvia said. "What with Miss Lampeter always drugged to the world, and all the French mistresses as wicked as hell."

"I've heard you say all this before," Mrs. Satterthwaite said. "But it was supposed to be the best finishing school in England. I know it cost enough!"

"Well, say it was we who were a rotten lot," Sylvia concluded; and then to the Father: "We *were* a lot of rotters, weren't we?"

The priest answered:

"I don't know. I don't suppose you were—or are—any worse than your mothers or grandmothers,[60] or the patricianesses of Rome or the worshippers of Ashtaroth. It seems we have to have a governing class and governing classes are subject to special temptations."

---

\* Diminutive of Charlotte.

"Who's Ashtaroth?" Sylvia asked. "Astarte?"* and then: "Now, Father, after your experiences would you say the factory girls of Liverpool, or any other slum, are any better women than us that you used to look after?"

"Astarte Syriaca," the Father said, "was a very powerful devil. There's some that hold she's not dead yet. I don't know that I do myself."

"Well, I've done with her," Sylvia said.

The Father nodded:

"You've had dealings with Mrs. Profumo?" he asked. "And that loathsome fellow.... What's his name?"†

"Does it shock you?" Sylvia asked. "I'll admit it was a bit thick‡.... But I've done with it. I prefer to pin my faith to Mrs. Vanderdecken.⁶¹ And, of course, Freud."

The priest nodded his head and said:

"Of course! Of course...."

But Mrs. Satterthwaite exclaimed, with sudden energy:

"Sylvia Tietjens, I don't care what you do or what you read, but if you ever speak another word to that woman, you never do to me!"

Sylvia stretched herself on her sofa. She opened her brown eyes wide and let the lids slowly drop again.

"I've said once," she said, "that I don't like to hear my friends miscalled. Eunice Vanderdecken is a bitterly misjudged woman. She's a real good pal."

"She's a Russian spy," Mrs. Satterthwaite said.

---

*  Ashtaroth or Astaroth is a powerful demon, a 'Prince of Hell', and thus male. Astarte is an ancient Semitic goddess, the equivalent of the Greek Aphrodite, and of Ashtoreth, who in Jewish mythology is considered a female demon of lust. In Book I of *Paradise Lost*, Milton writes: 'Came *Astoreth*, whom the *Phœnicians* call'd / *Astarte*, Queen of Heav'n, with crescent Horns'. D. G. Rossetti painted *Astarte Syriaca* or *Venus Astarte* in 1877. In *The March of Literature* (London: Allen & Unwin, 1939), 26, Ford writes of how, once Egypt became a Roman province after the fall of Cleopatra, 'the Graeco-Roman gods became confounded with the deities of the Nile – Astarte being confounded at once with the Venus of the Romans and Aphrodite of the Greeks [...]'.

†  From 54 below it becomes clear that Mrs Profumo and her circle dabble in black magic. The 'loathsome fellow' whose name escapes him (twice) might be a dig at the notorious Satanist Aleister Crowley. Hemingway, in *A Moveable Feast* (London: Jonathan Cape, 1964), 78–9, tells a Fordian anecdote about Ford 'cutting' a man he believes to be Hilaire Belloc, but who is in fact Crowley.

‡  Excessive, unreasonable.

"Russian grandmother," Sylvia answered. "And if she is, who cares? She's welcome for me.... Listen now, you two. I said to myself when I came in: 'I daresay I've given them both a rotten time.' I know you're both more nuts on me than I deserve. And I said I'd sit and listen to all the pi-jaw you wanted to give me if I sat till dawn. And I will. As a return. But I'd rather you let my friends alone."

Both the elder people were silent. There came from the shuttered windows of the dark room a low, scratching rustle.

"You hear!" the priest said to Mrs. Satterthwaite.

"It's the branches," Mrs. Satterthwaite answered.[62]

The Father answered: "There's no tree within ten yards! Try bats as an explanation."

"I've said I wish you wouldn't, once," Mrs. Satterthwaite shivered.[63]

Sylvia said:

"I don't know what you two are talking about. It sounds like superstition. Mother's rotten with it."

"I don't say that it's devils trying to get in," the Father said. "But it's just as well to remember that devils *are* always trying to get in. And there are especial spots. These deep forests are noted among others." He suddenly turned his back and pointed at the shadowy wall. "Who," he asked, "but a savage possessed by a devil could have conceived of *that* as a decoration?" He was pointing at a life-sized, coarsely daubed picture of a wild boar dying, its throat cut, and gouts of scarlet blood. Other agonies of animals went away into all the shadows.

"*Sport!*" he hissed. "It's devilry!"

"That's perhaps true," Sylvia said. Mrs. Satterthwaite was crossing herself with great rapidity. The silence remained.

Sylvia said:

"Then if you're both done talking I'll say what I have to say. To begin with . . . " She stopped and sat rather erect, listening to the rustling from the shutters.

"To begin with," she began again with impetus, "you spared me the catalogue of the defects of age; I know them. One grows skinny—my sort—the complexion fades, the teeth stick out. And then there is the[64] boredom. I know it; one is bored . . . bored . . . bored! You can't tell me anything I don't know about that. I'm thirty.* I know what to expect. You'd like to have told me, Father, only you were afraid of taking away from your famous man of the world effect—you'd like to have told me that one can insure against the boredom and the long, skinny teeth by love of husband and child. The home stunt! I believe it! I do quite believe it. Only I hate my husband . . . and I hate . . . I hate[65] my child."

She paused, waiting for exclamations of dismay or disapprobation from the priest. These did not come.

"Think," she said, "of all the ruin that child has meant for me; the pain in bearing him and the fear of death."

"Of course," the priest said, "child-bearing is for women a very terrible thing."

"I can't say," Mrs. Tietjens went on, "that this has been a very decent conversation. You get a girl . . . fresh from open sin, and make her talk about it. Of course you're a priest and mother's mother;[66] we're en famille. But Sister Mary of the Cross at the convent had a maxim: 'Wear velvet gloves in family life.' We seem to be going at it with the gloves off."

Father Consett still didn't say anything.

"You're trying, of course, to draw me," Sylvia said. "I can see that with half an eye. . . . Very well then, you shall. . . ."

She drew a breath.

"You want to know why I hate my husband. I'll tell you; it's because of his simple, sheer immorality. I don't mean his actions; his views! Every speech he utters[67] about everything makes me—I swear it makes me—in spite of myself, want to stick a knife into him, and I can't prove he's wrong, not ever, about the simplest thing. But I can pain him. And I will. . . . He sits about in chairs that fit his back, clumsy, like a rock, not moving for hours. . . . And I can make him wince. Oh, without showing it. . . . He's what you call . . . oh, loyal. . . . There's an absurd little chit of a fellow. . . . oh, Macmaster . . . and his mother . . . whom he persists in a silly, mystical way in calling a saint . . . a Protestant saint! . . . And his old nurse, who looks after the child . . . and the child itself. . . . I tell you I've only got to raise an eyelid . . .

---

* Tietjens' age is given as 26 in I.i. Though it was less common then for men to marry older women, Violet Hunt was ten years older than Ford.

yes, cock an eyelid up a little when anyone of them is mentioned
. . . and it hurts him dreadfully. His eyes roll in a sort of mute
anguish. . . . Of course he doesn't say anything. He's an English
country gentleman."

Father Consett said:

"This immorality you talk about in your husband. . . . I've
never noticed it. I saw a good deal of him when I stayed with you
for the week before your child was born. I talked with him a great
deal. Except in matters of the two communions—and even in
these[68] I don't know that we differed so much—I found him
perfectly sound."

"Sound!" Mrs. Satterthwaite said with sudden emphasis; "of
course he's sound. It isn't even the word. He's the best ever. There
was your father, for a good man . . . and him. That's[69] an end of
it."[70]

"Ah," Sylvia said, "you don't know. . . . Look here. Try and be
just. Suppose I'm looking at the *Times* at breakfast and say, not
having spoken to him for a week: 'It's wonderful what the doctors
are doing. Have you seen the latest?'[71] And at once he'll be on
his high-horse—he knows *everything*![72]—and he'll prove . . .
*prove* . . . that all unhealthy children must be lethal-chambered
or the world will go to pieces.* And it's like being hypnotised; you
can't think of what to answer him. Or he'll reduce you to speech-
less rage by proving that murderers ought not to be executed. And
then I'll ask, casually, if children ought to be lethal-chambered
for being constipated. Because Marchant—that's the nurse—is
always whining that the child's bowels aren't regular and the
dreadful diseases that leads to. Of course *that* hurts him. For he's
perfectly soppy about that[73] child, though he half knows it isn't
his own. . . . But that's what I mean by immorality. He'll profess
that murderers ought to be preserved in order to breed from
because they're bold fellows, and innocent little children
executed because they're sick. . . .[74] And he'll almost make you
believe it, though you're on the point of retching at the ideas."

"You wouldn't now," Father Consett began, and almost coax-
ingly, "think of going into retreat for a month[75] or two."

---

\*    Ford's *The Critical Attitude* (London: Duckworth, 1911), 119 discusses a newspaper
column advocating the use of a 'lethal chamber for the feeble-minded'.

"I wouldn't," Sylvia said. "How could I?"

"There's a convent of female Premonstratensians* near Birkenhead, many ladies go there,"[76] the Father went on. "They cook very well, and you can have your own furniture and your own maid if ye don't like nuns to wait on you."

"It can't be done," Sylvia said, "you can see for yourself. It would make people smell a rat at once. Christopher wouldn't hear of it. ..."

"No, I'm afraid it can't be done, Father," Mrs. Satterthwaite interrupted finally. "I've hidden here for four months to cover Sylvia's tracks. I've got Wateman's† to look after. My new land steward's coming in next week."

"Still," the Father urged, with a sort of tremulous eagerness, "if only for a[77] month.... If only for a fortnight.... So many Catholic ladies do it.... Ye might think of it."

"I see what you're aiming at," Sylvia said with sudden anger; "you're revolted at the idea of my going straight from one man's arms to another."

"I'd be better pleased if there could be an interval," the Father said. "It's what's called bad form."

Sylvia became electrically rigid on her sofa.

"Bad form!" she exclaimed. "You accuse me of bad form."

The Father slightly bowed his head like a man facing a wind.

"I do," he said. "It's disgraceful. It's unnatural. I'd travel a bit at least."

She placed her hand on her long throat.

"I know what you mean," she said, "you want to spare Christopher ... the humiliation. The ... the nausea. No doubt he'll feel nauseated.[78] I've reckoned on that. It will give me a little of my own back."

The Father said:

"That's enough, woman. I'll hear no more."

Sylvia said:

"You will then. Listen here.... I've always got this to look

---

\* Austere order of canons known also as the Norbertines (after their founder St Norbert) and in England as the 'White Canons' due to the colour of their habit.

† Presumably her country estate: 'her place in the west of England' mentioned in the second paragraph of this chapter, the name perhaps echoing that of Kipling's house, Bateman's, in Burwash, East Sussex.

forward to: I'll settle down by that man's side. I'll be as virtuous as any woman. I've made up my mind to it and I'll be it. And I'll be bored stiff for the rest of my life. Except for one thing. I can torment that man. And I'll do it. Do you understand how I'll do it? There are many ways. But if the worst comes to the worst I can always drive him silly . . . by corrupting the child!"[79] She was panting a little, and round her brown eyes the whites showed. "I'll get even with him. I can. I know how, you see. And with you, through him, for tormenting me. I've come all the way from Brittany without stopping. I haven't slept. . . . But I can. . ."

Father Consett put his hand beneath the tail of his coat.

"Sylvia Tietjens," he said, "in my pistol[80] pocket I've a little bottle of holy water which I carry for such occasions. What if[81] I was to throw two drops of it over you and cry: *Exorciso te Ashtaroth in nomine?*\* . . ."[82]

She erected her body above her skirts on the sofa, stiffened like a snake's neck above its coils. Her face was quite pallid, her eyes staring out.

"You . . . you *daren't*," she said. "To me . . . an outrage!" Her feet[83] slid slowly to the floor; she measured the distance to the doorway with her eyes. "You *daren't*," she said again; "I'd denounce you to the Bishop. . . ."

"It's little the Bishop would help you with them burning into your skin," the priest said. "Go away, I bid you, and say a Hail Mary or two. Ye need them. Ye'll not talk of corrupting a little child before me again."

"I won't," Sylvia said. "I shouldn't have . . ."[84]

Her black figure showed in silhouette against the open doorway.

When the door was closed upon them, Mrs. Satterthwaite said:

"Was it necessary to threaten her with that? You know best, of course. It seems rather strong to me."

"It's a hair from the dog that's bit her," the priest said. "She's a silly girl. She's been playing at black masses along with that Mrs. Profumo and the fellow whose[85] name I can't remember. You

---

\*    Father Consett is threatening Sylvia with ritual exorcism.

could tell that. They cut the throat of a white kid and splash its blood about. . . . That was at the back of her mind. . . . It's not very serious. A parcel of silly, idle girls. It's not much more than palmistry or fortune-telling to them if one has to weigh it, for all its[86] ugliness, as a sin. As far as their volition goes, and it's voli- tion that's the essence of prayer, black or white. . . . But it was at the back of her mind, and she won't forget to-night."[87]

"Of course, that's your affair, Father," Mrs. Satterthwaite said lazily. "You hit her pretty hard. I don't suppose she's ever been hit so hard. What was it you wouldn't tell her?"

"Only," the priest said, "I wouldn't tell her because the thought's best not put in her head. . . . But her hell on earth will come when her husband goes running, blind, head down, mad after another woman."

Mrs. Satterthwaite looked at nothing; then she nodded.

"Yes," she said; "I hadn't thought of it. . . . But will he? He *is* a very sound fellow, isn't he?"

"What's to stop it?" the priest asked. "*What* in the world but the grace of our blessed Lord, which he hasn't got and doesn't ask for?* And then ... He's a young man, full-blooded, and they won't be living ... *maritalement.*† Not if I know him. And then. . . . *Then* she'll tear the house down. The world will echo with her wrongs."

"Do you mean to say," Mrs. Satterthwaite said, "that Sylvia would do anything vulgar?"

"Doesn't every woman who's had a man to torture for years when she loses him?" the priest asked. "The more she's made an occupation of torturing him the less right she thinks she has to lose him."

Mrs. Satterthwaite looked gloomily into the dusk.

"That poor devil. . . ." she said. "Will he get any peace anywhere? . . . What's the matter, Father?"

The Father said:

"I've just remembered she gave me tea and cream and I drank it. Now I can't take mass for Father Reinhardt. I'll have to go and knock up his curate, who lives away in the forest."[88]

---

* i.e. because Christopher is not a Roman Catholic like Sylvia and her mother.
† As man and wife (French).

At the door, holding the candle, he said:

"I'd have you not get up to-day nor yet to-morrow, if ye can stand it. Have a headache and let Sylvia nurse you . . . You'll have to tell how she nursed you when you get back to London. And I'd rather ye didn't lie more out and out than ye need, if it's to please me. . . . Besides, if ye watch Sylvia nursing you, you might hit on a characteristic touch to make it seem more truthful*. . . . How her sleeves brushed the medicine bottles and irritated you, maybe . . . or—*you'll* know! If we can save scandal to the congregation, we may as well."

He ran downstairs.

---

*   Father Consett's advice on how to make a fiction seem more truthful parallels Ford's accounts of literary Impressionism, such as the section in *Joseph Conrad* headed 'It is Above All to Make You See . . .': 165–215.

# III

AT the slight creaking made by Macmaster in pushing open his door, Tietjens[1] started violently. He was sitting in a smoking-jacket, playing patience engrossedly in a sort of garret bedroom. It had a sloping roof outlined by black oak beams, which cut into[2] squares the cream coloured patent distemper of the walls. The room contained also a four-post bedstead, a corner cupboard in black oak, and many rush mats on a polished oak floor of very irregular planking. Tietjens,[3] who hated these disinterred and waxed relics of the past, sat in the centre of the room at a flimsy card-table beneath a white-shaded electric light of a brilliance that, in those surroundings, appeared unreasonable. This was[4] one of those restored old groups of cottages that it was at that date the fashion to convert into hostelries. To it Macmaster, who was in search of the[5] inspiration of the past, had preferred to come. Tietjens, not desiring to interfere with his friend's culture, had accepted the quarters, though he would have preferred to go to a comfortable modern hotel as being less affected and cheaper. Accustomed to what he called the grown oldnesses of a morose, rambling Yorkshire manor house, he disliked being among collected and rather pitiful bits which, he said, made him feel ridiculous, as if he were trying to behave seriously at a fancy-dress ball. Macmaster, on the other hand, with gratification and a serious air, would run his finger tips along the bevellings of a darkened piece of furniture, and would declare it genuine "Chippendale" or "Jacobean oak," as the case might be. And he seemed to gain an added seriousness and weight of manner with each piece of ancient furniture that down the years he thus touched. But Tietjens would declare that you could tell the beastly thing was a fake by just cocking an eye at it and, if the matter happened to fall under the test of professional[6] dealers in old furniture, Tietjens was the more often in the right of it, and Macmaster, sighing slightly, would prepare to proceed still further along the difficult road to

connoisseurship.* Eventually, by conscientious study, he got so
far as[7] at times to be called in by Somerset House[†] to value[8] great
properties for probate—an occupation at once distinguished and
highly profitable.

Tietjens swore with the extreme vehemence of a man who has
been made, but who much dislikes being seen, to start.

Macmaster—in evening dress he looked extremely miniature!—said:

"I'm sorry, old man, I know how much you dislike being interrupted. But the General is in a terrible temper."

Tietjens rose stiffly, lurched over to an eighteenth century
rosewood folding washstand, took from its top a glass of flat
whisky and soda, and gulped down a large quantity. He looked
about uncertainly, perceived a notebook on a "Chippendale"
bureau, made a short calculation in pencil and looked at his
friend momentarily.

Macmaster said again:

"I'm sorry, old man. I must have interrupted one of your
immense calculations."

Tietjens said:

"You haven't. I was only thinking. I'm just as glad you've
come. What did you say?"

Macmaster repeated:

"I said, the[9] General is in a terrible temper. It's just as well you
didn't come up to dinner."

Tietjens said:

"He isn't . . . He isn't in a temper. He's as pleased as punch at
not having to have these women up before him."[‡]

---

* Tietjens' expertise about furniture becomes especially important in *Last Post*, where it
   provides his living. But it also indicates his good judgment in telling the genuine from
   the sham. Ford had been sparring with Ezra Pound on the subject in the early 1920s,
   rebuking him over his 'objection to renderings of the mania for FURNITURE', saying:
   'having no taste for bric a brac you hate to have to read about this passion. . . . But it
   is one of the main passions of humanity [. . .] You might really, just as legitimately,
   object to renderings of the passion of LOVE, with which indeed the FURNITURE
   passion is strangely bound up. . . .': 19 Sept. 1920: *Pound/Ford* 44–5.

† Neoclassical Palladian palace between the Thames and Strand, next to Waterloo
   Bridge and King's College London. Ford's uncle, William Michael Rossetti, had
   worked there in the offices of the Inland Revenue.

‡ As emerges later, Campion is a magistrate.

Macmaster said:

"He says he's got the police scouring the whole county for them, and that you'd better leave by the first train to-morrow."

Tietjens said:

"I won't. I can't. I've got to wait here for a wire from Sylvia."

Macmaster groaned:

"Oh dear! Oh dear!" Then he said hopefully: "But we could have it forwarded to Hythe."

Tietjens said with some vehemence:

"I tell you I won't leave here. I tell you I've settled it with the police and that swine of a Cabinet Minister.[10] I've mended the leg of the canary of the wife of the police-constable. Sit down and be reasonable. The police don't touch people like us."

Macmaster said:

"I don't believe you realise the public feeling there is . . ."

"Of course I do, amongst people like Sandbach," Tietjens said. "Sit down I tell you. . . . Have some whisky. . . ." He filled himself out another long tumbler and, holding it, dropped into a too low-seated, reddish wicker armchair that had cretonne* fixings. Beneath his weight the chair sagged a good deal and his dress-shirt front bulged up to his chin.

Macmaster said:

"What's the matter with you?" Tietjens' eyes were bloodshot.

"I tell you," Tietjens said, "I'm waiting for a wire from Sylvia."

Macmaster said:

"Oh!" And then: "It can't come to-night, it's getting on for one."

"It can," Tietjens said, "I've fixed it up with the postmaster—all the way up to Town! It probably[11] won't come because Sylvia won't send it until the last moment, to bother me. None the less, I'm waiting for a wire from Sylvia, and this is what I look like."

Macmaster said:

"That woman's the cruellest beast . . ."

"You might," Tietjens interrupted, "remember that you're talking about my wife."

"I don't see," Macmaster said, "how one can talk about Sylvia without . . ."

---

* Cotton cloth with printed pattern.

"The line is a perfectly simple one to draw," Tietjens said. "You can relate a lady's actions if you know them and are asked to. You mustn't comment. In this case you don't know the lady's actions even, so you may as well hold your tongue." He sat looking straight in front of him.

Macmaster sighed from deep in his chest. He asked himself if this was what sixteen hours waiting had done for his friend, what were all the remaining hours going to do?

Tietjens[12] said:

"I shall be fit to talk about Sylvia after two more whiskies. . . . Let's settle your other perturbations first. . . . The fair girl is called Wannop: Valentine Wannop."

"That's the Professor's name," Macmaster said.

"She's the late[13] Professor Wannop's daughter," Tietjens said. "She's also the daughter of the novelist."

Macmaster interjected:

"But . . ."

"She supported herself for a year after the Professor's death as a domestic servant," Tietjens said. "Now she's housemaid[14] for her mother, the novelist, in an inexpensive cottage. I should imagine the two experiences would make her desire to better the lot of her sex."

Macmaster again interjected a "But . . ."

"I got that information from the policeman whilst I was putting his wife's canary's leg in splints."

Macmaster said:

"The policeman you knocked down?" His eyes expressed unreasoning surprise. He added: "He knew Miss . . . eh . . . Wannop then!"

"You would not expect much intelligence from the police of Sussex," Tietjens said. "But you would be wrong.* P.C. Finn is

---

* At the beginning of 1915 Ford had been ordered to leave the county by the Chief Constable of West Sussex. He was staying at Selsey, and had irritated a neighbour, Edward Heron Allen, by satirising him in a story, 'The Scaremonger', published in November. He suspected Allen had denounced him to the authorities. The order was withdrawn four days later. Ford's friend Ezra Pound also had interesting times with the Sussex police in February 1916 when he was staying with Yeats at Stone Cottage: see A. D. Moody, *Ezra Pound: Poet*, vol. 1 (Oxford: Oxford University Press, 2007), 294; Longenbach, *Stone Cottage* (New York: Oxford University Press, 1988), 260; remembered in the *Cantos*, 'aliens in a prohibited area': 'LXXXIII', 534. Ford, though serving

clever enough to recognise the young lady who for several years past has managed the constabulary's wives and children's annual tea and sports. He says Miss Wannop holds the quarter-mile, half-mile, high jump, long jump and putting the weight records for East Sussex. That explains how she went over that dyke in such tidy style. . . . And precious glad the good, simple man was when I told him he was to leave the girl alone. He didn't know, he said, how he'd ever a had the face to serve the warrant on Miss Wannop. The other girl—the one that squeaked and fell in[15]— is a stranger, a Londoner probably."

Macmaster said:

"*You* told the policeman . . ."

"I gave him," Tietjens said, "the Rt. Hon. Stephen Fenwick[16] Waterhouse's[17*] compliments, and he'd be much obliged if the P.C. would hand in a 'No Can Do' report in the matter of those ladies every morning to his inspector. I gave him also a brand new fi' pun note—from the Cabinet Minister—and a couple of quid and the price of a new pair of trousers from myself. So he's the happiest constable in Sussex. A very decent fellow; he told me how to know a dog otter's spoor from a gravid bitch's. . . . But that wouldn't interest you."

He began again:

"Don't look so inexpressibly foolish. I told you I'd been dining with that swine. . . . No, I oughtn't to call him a swine after eating his dinner. Besides, he's a very decent fellow. . . ."

"You *didn't*[18] tell me you'd been dining with Mr. Water-house,"[19] Macmaster said. "I hope you remembered that, as he's amongst other things the President of the Funded Debt[†] Commission he's the power of life and death over the department and us."[20]

---

by then, would have known of it not least because Pound asked Lucy Masterman if her husband Charles Masterman (see next note) could intervene.

* Ford and Violet Hunt were close friends with the Liberal Cabinet Minister, Charles F. G. Masterman (1873–1927) and his wife Lucy. Masterman became an MP in the Liberal landslide of 1906, and joined the Cabinet as Chancellor of the Duchy of Lancaster in 1914.

† Funded Debt is that part of the national debt 'which has been converted into a fund or stock of which the government no longer seeks to pay off the principal, but to provide the annual interest': *OED*.

"You didn't think," Tietjens[21] answered, "that you are the only one to dine with the great ones of the earth![22] I wanted to talk to that fellow ... about those figures their cursed crowd made me fake. I meant to give him a bit of my mind."

"You *didn't!*" Macmaster said with an expression of panic. "Besides, they didn't ask you to fake the calculation.[23] They only asked you to work it out on the basis of given figures."

"Anyhow," Tietjens said, "I gave him a bit of my mind. I told him that, at threepence, it must run the country—and certainly himself as a politician!—to absolute ruin."

Macmaster uttered a deep "Good Lord!" and then: "But won't you ever remember you're a Government servant? He could ..."

"Mr. Waterhouse,"[24] Tietjens said, "asked me if I wouldn't consent to be transferred to his secretary's department. And when I said: 'Go to hell!'[25] he walked round the streets with me for two hours arguing.... I was working out the chances on a 4½d. basis for him when you interrupted me. I've promised to let him have the figures when he goes up by[26] the 1.30 on Monday."

Macmaster said:

"You haven't.... But by Jove you're the only man in England that could do it."

"That was what Mr. Waterhouse[27] said," Tietjens commented. "He said old Ingleby had told him so."

"I do hope," Macmaster said, "that you answered him politely!"

"I told him," Tietjens answered, "that there were a dozen men who could do it as well as I, and I mentioned your name in particular."

"But I *couldn't*," Macmaster answered. "Of course I could convert a 3d. rate into 4½d. But there are the actuarial[28]* variations; they're infinite. I couldn't touch them."[29]

Tietjens said negligently: "I don't want my name mixed up in the unspeakable affair. When I give him the papers on Monday I shall tell him you did most of the work."

---

\* Marwood wrote an article, published in the first two numbers of Ford's *English Review*, outlining 'A Complete Actuarial Scheme for Insuring John Doe against all the Vicissitudes of Life', which advocates a state system of old age pensions and pensions for widows and dependants, as well as sickness and unemployment benefits: *English Review*, 1 (Dec. 1908), 171–5 and 2 (Jan. 1909), 363–9.

Again Macmaster groaned.[30]

Nor was this distress mere altruism. Immensely ambitious for his brilliant friend, Macmaster's ambition was one ingredient of his strong desire for security. At Cambridge he had been perfectly content with a moderate, quite respectable place on the list of mathematical postulants. He knew that that made him safe, and he had still more satisfaction in the thought that it would warrant him in never being brilliant in after life. But when Tietjens, two years after, had come out as a mere Second Wrangler,* Macmaster had been bitterly and loudly disappointed. He knew perfectly well that Tietjens simply hadn't taken trouble; and, ten chances to one, it was on purpose that Tietjens hadn't taken trouble. For the matter of that, for Tietjens it wouldn't have been trouble.

And, indeed, to Macmaster's upbraidings, which Macmaster hadn't spared him, Tietjens had answered that he hadn't been able to think of going through the rest of his life with a beastly[31] placard like Senior Wrangler hung round his neck.

But Macmaster had early made up his mind that life for him would be safest if he could go about, not very much observed but still an authority, in the midst of a body of men all labelled. He wanted to walk down Pall Mall on the arm, precisely, of a largely-lettered Senior Wrangler; to return eastward on the arm of the youngest Lord Chancellor England had ever seen; to stroll down Whitehall in familiar converse with a world-famous novelist, saluting on the way a majority of My Lords Commissioners of the Treasury. And, after tea, for an hour at the club all these,[32] in a little group, should treat him with the courtesy of men who respected him for his soundness. Then he would be safe.

And[33] he had no doubt that Tietjens was the most brilliant man in England of that day, so that nothing caused him more anguish than the thought that Tietjens might not make a brilliant and rapid career towards some illustrious position in the public services. He would very willingly—he desired, indeed,

---

* Students awarded first-class honours in Part II of the Mathematics Tripos at the University of Cambridge are known as 'Wranglers'. The top-scorer is the Senior Wrangler, the next highest, Second Wrangler. In *Thus to Revisit* 59, Ford describes Marwood as a distinguished mathematician and the Fellow of some Cambridge college – 'Trinity, I think'. But later he's determined not to be a Senior Wrangler and deliberately sets down 'five ciphers wrong': *Return* 280.

nothing better!—have seen Tietjens pass over his own head! It did not seem to him a condemnation of the public services that this appeared to be unlikely.

Yet Macmaster was still not without hope. He was quite aware that there are other techniques of careers than that which he had prescribed for himself. He could not imagine himself, even in the most deferential way, correcting a superior; yet he could see that, though Tietjens treated almost every hierarch as if he were a born fool, no one very much resented it. Of course Tietjens was a Tietjens of Groby; but was that going to be enough to live on for ever? Times were changing, and Macmaster imagined this to be a democratic age.

But Tietjens went on, with both hands as it were, throwing away opportunity and committing outrage. . . .

That day Macmaster could only consider to be one of disaster. He got up from his chair and filled himself another drink; he felt himself to be distressed and to need it. Slouching amongst his cretonnes, Tietjens was gazing in front of him. He said:

"Here!" without looking at Macmaster, and held out his long glass. Into it Macmaster poured whisky with a hesitating hand. Tietjens said: "Go on!"

Macmaster said:

"It's late; we're breakfasting at the Duchemins'³⁴ at ten." Tietjens answered:

"Don't worry, sonny. We'll be there for your pretty lady." He added: "Wait another quarter of an hour. I want to talk to you."

Macmaster sat down again and deliberately began to review the day. It had begun with disaster, and in disaster it had continued.

And, with something like a bitter irony, Macmaster remembered and brought up now for digestion the parting words of General Campion to himself. The General had limped with him to the hall door up at Mountby³⁵ and, standing patting him on the shoulder, tall, slightly bent and very friendly, had said:

"Look here. Christopher Tietjens is a splendid fellow. But he needs a good woman to look after him. Get him back to Sylvia as quick as you can.³⁶ Had a little tiff, haven't they? Nothing serious?³⁷ Chrissie hasn't been running after the skirts? No? I daresay a little. No? Well then . . ."

Macmaster had stood like a gate-post, so appalled. He had stuttered:

"No! No!"

"We've known them both so long," the General went on. "Lady Claudine in particular. And, believe me, Sylvia is a splendid girl. Straight as a die; the soul of loyalty to her friends. And fearless . . .[38] She'd face the devil in his rage. You should have seen[39] her out with the Belvoir!* Of course you know her. . . . Well then!"

Macmaster had just managed to say that he knew Sylvia, of course.

"Well then . . ." the General had continued . . . "you'll agree with me that if there *is* anything wrong between them he's to blame. And it will be resented. Very bitterly. He wouldn't set foot in this house again. But he says he's going out to her and Mrs. Satterthwaite. . . ."

"I believe . . ." Macmaster had begun . . . "I believe he is . . ."

"Well then!" the General had said: "It's all right. . . . But Christopher Tietjens needs a good woman's backing. . . . He's a splendid fellow. There are few young fellows for whom I have more . . . I could almost say respect. . . . But he needs that. To ballast him."

In the car, running down the hill from Mountby,[40] Macmaster had exhausted himself in the effort to restrain his execrations of the General. He wanted to shout that he was a pig-headed old fool: a meddlesome ass. But he was in the car with the two secretaries of the Cabinet Minister: the Rt. Hon. Edward Fenwick Waterhouse,[41] who, being himself an advanced Liberal down for a week-end of golf,[42] preferred not to dine at the house of the Conservative member. At that date there was, in politics, a phase of bitter social feud between the parties: a condition that had not till lately been characteristic of English political life. The prohibition had not extended itself to the two younger men.[43]

Macmaster was not unpleasurably aware that these two fellows treated him with a certain deference. They had seen Macmaster being talked to familiarly by General Lord Edward

---

* The Belvoir (pronounced 'Beaver') Hunt, at Belvoir Castle, the seat of the dukes of Rutland near Grantham in Lincolnshire, remained one of the premier foxhunts, beloved by royalty.

Campion. Indeed, they and the car had been kept waiting whilst the General patted their fellow guest on the shoulder; held his upper arm and spoke in a low voice into his ear. . . .

But that was the only pleasure that Macmaster got out of it.

Yes, the day had begun disastrously with Sylvia's letter; it ended—if it was ended!—almost more disastrously with the General's eulogy of that woman. During the day he had nerved himself to having an immensely disagreeable[44] scene with Tietjens. Tietjens *must* divorce the woman; it was necessary for the peace of mind of himself, of his friends, of his family; for the sake of his career; in the very name of decency!

In the meantime Tietjens had rather forced his hand. It had been a most disagreeable affair. They had arrived at Rye in time for lunch—at which Tietjens had consumed the best part of a bottle of Burgundy. During lunch Tietjens had given Macmaster Sylvia's letter to read, saying that, as he should later consult his friend, his friend had better be made acquainted with the document.

The letter had appeared extraordinary in its effrontery, for it said nothing. Beyond the bare statement, "I am now ready to return to you," it occupied itself simply with the fact that Mrs. Tietjens wanted—could no longer get on without—the services of her maid, whom she called Hullo Central. If Tietjens wanted her, Mrs. Tietjens, to return to him he was to see that Hullo Central was waiting on the doorstep for her, and so on. She added the detail that there was *no one* else, underlined, she could bear round her while she was retiring for the night. On reflection Macmaster could see that this was the best letter the woman could have written if she wanted to be taken back;[45] for, had she extended herself into either excuses or explanations, it was ten chances to one Tietjens would have taken the line that he couldn't go on living with a woman capable of such a lapse in taste. But Macmaster had never thought of Sylvia as wanting in *savoir faire*.

It had none the less hardened him in his determination to urge his friend to divorce. He had intended to begin this campaign in the fly,* driving to pay his call on the Rev. Mr. Duchemin, who,

* A light horse-drawn carriage for hire.

in early life, had been a personal disciple of Mr. Ruskin* and a patron and acquaintance of the poet-painter, the subject of Macmaster's monograph. On this drive Tietjens preferred not to come. He said that he would loaf about the town and meet Macmaster at the golf club towards four-thirty. He was not in the mood for making new acquaintances. Macmaster, who knew the pressure under which his friend must be suffering, thought this reasonable enough, and drove off up Iden Hill† by himself.

Few women had ever made so much impression on Macmaster as Mrs. Duchemin. He knew himself to be in a mood to be impressed by almost any woman, but he considered that that was not enough to account for the very strong influence she at once exercised over him. There had been two young girls in the drawing-room when he had been ushered in, but they had disappeared almost simultaneously, and although he had noticed them immediately afterwards riding past the window on bicycles, he was aware that he would not have recognised them again. From her first words on rising to greet him: "Not *the* Mr. Macmaster!" he had had eyes for no one else.

It was obvious that the Rev. Mr. Duchemin must be one of those clergymen of considerable wealth and cultured taste who not infrequently adorn the Church of England. The rectory itself, a great, warm-looking manor house of very old red brick,[46] was abutted on to by one of the largest tithe barns that Macmaster had ever seen; the church itself, with a primitive roof of oak shingles, nestled in the corner formed by the ends of rectory and tithe barn, and was by so much the smallest of the three and so undecorated that but for its little belfry it might have been a good cow-byre. All three buildings stood on the very edge of the little row of hills that looks down on the Romney Marsh;‡ they were sheltered from the north wind by a great symmetrical fan of elms

*   John Ruskin (1819–1900), the greatest of Victorian critics on art and architecture, and champion of the Pre-Raphaelites.
†   The village of Iden is about two miles north of Rye, with a hill at the beginning of Iden Road.
‡   Ford lived on the Romney Marsh from 1894 to 1907, and wrote about it especially in *The Cinque Ports* (Edinburgh and London: William Blackwood and Sons, 1900); *The Heart of the Country* (London: Alston Rivers, 1906), and *Return*.

and from the south-west by a very tall hedge and shrubbery, all of remarkable yews. It was, in short, an ideal cure of souls for a wealthy clergyman of cultured tastes, for there was not so much as a[47] peasant's cottage within a mile of it.

To Macmaster, in short, this was the ideal English home. Of Mrs. Duchemin's drawing-room itself, contrary to his habit, for he was sensitive and observant in such things, he could afterwards[48] remember little except that it was perfectly sympathetic. Three long windows gave on to a perfect lawn, on which, isolated and grouped, stood standard rose trees, symmetrical half globes of green foliage picked out with flowers like bits of carved pink marble. Beyond the lawn was a low stone wall; beyond that the[49] quiet expanse of the marsh shimmered in the sunlight.

The furniture of the room was, as to its woodwork, brown, old, with the rich softnesses of much polishing with beeswax. What pictures there were Macmaster recognised at once as being by Simeon Solomon, one of the weaker and more frail æsthetes— aureoled, palish heads of ladies carrying lilies that were not very like lilies. They were in the tradition—but not the best of the tradition. Macmaster understood—and later Mrs. Duchemin confirmed him in the idea—that Mr. Duchemin kept his more precious specimens of work in a sanctum, leaving to the relatively public room, good-humouredly and with slight contempt, these weaker specimens. That seemed to stamp Mr. Duchemin[50] at once as being of the elect.

Mr. Duchemin in person was, however, not present; and there seemed to be a good deal of difficulty in arranging a meeting between the two men. Mr. Duchemin, his wife said, was much occupied at the week-ends. She added, with a faint and rather absent smile, the word, "Naturally." Macmaster at once saw that it was natural for a clergyman to be much occupied during the week-ends. With a little hesitation Mrs. Duchemin suggested that Mr. Macmaster and his friend might come to lunch on the next day—Saturday. But Macmaster had made an engagement to play the foursome with General Campion—half the round from twelve till one-thirty: half the round from three to half-past four. And, as their then present arrangements stood, Macmaster and Tietjens were to take the 6.30 train to Hythe; that ruled out either tea or dinner next day.

With sufficient, but not too extravagant regret, Mrs. Duchemin raised her voice to say:

"Oh dear! Oh dear! But you must see my husband and the pictures after you have come so far."

A rather considerable volume of harsh sound was coming through the end wall of the room—the barking of dogs, apparently the hurried removal of pieces of furniture or perhaps of packing cases, guttural ejaculations. Mrs. Duchemin said, with her far away air and deep voice:

"They are making a good deal of noise. Let us go into the garden and look at my husband's roses, if you've a moment more to give us."

Macmaster quoted to himself:

"'I looked and saw your eyes in the shadow of your hair....'"*

There was no doubt that Mrs. Duchemin's eyes, which were of a dark, pebble blue, were actually in the shadow of her blue-black, very regularly waved hair. The hair came[51] down on the square, low forehead. It was a phenomenon that Macmaster had never before really seen, and, he congratulated himself, this was one more confirmation—if confirmation were needed!—of the powers of observation of the subject of his monograph!

Mrs. Duchemin bore the sunlight! Her dark complexion was clear; there was, over the cheekbones, a delicate suffusion of light carmine. Her jawbone was singularly clear-cut, to the pointed chin—like an alabaster, mediæval[52] saint's.

She said:

"Of course you're Scotch. I'm from Auld Reekie† myself."

Macmaster would have known it. He said he was from the Port of Leith. He could not imagine hiding anything from Mrs. Duchemin.[53] Mrs. Duchemin said with renewed insistence:

"Oh, but of *course* you must see my husband and the pictures. Let me see.... We must think.... Would breakfast now? ..."

Macmaster said that he and his friend were Government servants and up to rising early. He had a great desire to breakfast in that house. She said:

"At a quarter to ten, then, our car will be at the bottom of your

---

*   Dante Gabriel Rossetti, 'Three Shadows', lines 1–2.
†   Edinburgh: Scots 'old', and 'reek' referring to the pall of smoke usual before the clean-air legislation of the nineteenth century.

street. It's a matter of ten minutes only, so you won't go hungry long!"

She said, gradually gaining animation, that of course Macmaster would bring his friend. He could tell Tietjens that he should meet a very charming girl. She stopped and added suddenly: "Probably, at any rate." She said the name which Macmaster caught as "Wanstead." And possibly another girl. And Mr. Horsted, or something like it, her husband's junior curate. She said reflectively:

"Yes, we might try quite a party ..." and added, "quite noisy and gay. I hope your friend's talkative!"

Macmaster said something about trouble.

"Oh, it can't be too much trouble," she said. "Besides it might do my husband good." She went on: "Mr. Duchemin is apt to brood. It's perhaps too lonely here." And added the rather astonishing words: "After all."

And, driving back in the fly, Macmaster said to himself that you couldn't call Mrs. Duchemin ordinary, at least. Yet meeting her was like going into a room that you had long left and never ceased to love. It felt good. It was perhaps partly her Edinburghness. Macmaster allowed himself to coin that word.[54] There was in Edinburgh a society—he himself had never been privileged to move in it, but its annals are part of the literature of Scotland!—where the ladies are all great ladies in tall drawing-rooms; circumspect yet shrewd: still yet with a sense of the comic: frugal yet warmly hospitable. It was perhaps just Edinburgh-ness that was wanting in the drawing-rooms of his friends in London. Mrs. Cressy, the Hon. Mrs. Limoux and Mrs. Delaunay[55] were all almost perfection in manner, in speech, in composure. But, then, they were not young, they weren't Edinburgh—and they weren't strikingly elegant!

Mrs. Duchemin was all three! Her[56] assured, tranquil manner she would retain to any age: it betokened the enigmatic soul of her sex, but, physically, she couldn't be more than thirty. That was unimportant, for she would never want to do anything in which physical youth counted. She would never, for instance, have occasion to run: she would always just "move"—floatingly! He tried to remember the details of her dress.

It had certainly been dark blue—and certainly of silk: that

rather coarsely-woven, exquisite material that has on its folds as if[57] a silvery shimmer with minute knots. But very dark blue. And it contrived to be at once[58] artistic—absolutely in the tradition! And yet well cut! Very large sleeves, of course, but still with a certain fit.[59] She had worn an immense necklace of yellow polished amber: on the dark blue! And Mrs. Duchemin had said, over her husband's roses, that the blossoms always reminded her of little mouldings of pink cloud come down for the cooling of the earth…. A charming thought![60]

Suddenly he said to himself:

"What a mate for Tietjens!" And his mind added: "Why should she not become an Influence!"[61]

A vista opened before him, in time! He imagined Tietjens, in some way proprietarily responsible for Mrs. Duchemin: quite *pour le bon*, tranquilly passionate and accepted, *motif*,* and "immensely improved" by the association. And himself, in a year or two, bringing the at last found Lady of his Delight to sit at the feet of Mrs. Duchemin—the Lady of his Delight whilst circumspect would be also young and impressionable!—to learn the mysterious assuredness of manner, the gift of dressing, the knack of wearing amber and bending over standard roses—and the Edinburgh-ness!

Macmaster was thus not a little excited, and finding Tietjens at tea amid the green-stained furnishings and illustrated papers of the large, corrugated iron golf-house, he could not help exclaiming:

"I've accepted[62] the invitation to breakfast with the Duchemins to-morrow for us both. I hope you won't mind," although Tietjens was sitting at a little table with General Campion and his brother-in-law, the Hon. Paul Sandbach, Conservative member for the division and husband of Lady Claudine.[63] The General said pleasantly to Tietjens:

"Breakfast! With Duchemin! You go, my boy! You'll get the best breakfast you ever had in your life."

He added to his brother-in-law: "Not the eternal mock kedgeree[64] Claudine gives us every morning."

Sandbach grunted:

---

* An archaic French term for 'moving'.

"It's not for want of trying to steal their cook.[65] Claudine has a shy at it every time we come down here."

The General said pleasantly to Macmaster—he spoke always pleasantly, with a half smile and a slight sibilance:

"My brother-in-law isn't serious, you understand. My sister wouldn't think of stealing a cook. Let alone from Duchemin. She'd be frightened to."

Sandbach grunted:

"Who wouldn't?"

Both these gentlemen were very lame: Mr. Sandbach from birth and the General as the result of a slight but neglected motor accident.[66] He had practically only one vanity, the belief that he was qualified to act as his own chauffeur, and since he was both inexpert and very careless, he met with frequent accidents. Mr. Sandbach had a dark, round, bull-dog face and a violent manner. He had twice been suspended from[67] his Parliamentary duties for applying to the then Chancellor of the Exchequer the epithet[68] "lying attorney,"[69] and he was at that moment still suspended.

Macmaster then became unpleasantly perturbed. With his sensitiveness he was perfectly aware of an unpleasant chill in the air. There was also a stiffness about Tietjens' eyes. He was looking straight before him; there was a silence too. Behind Tietjens' back were two men with bright green coats, red knitted waistcoats and florid faces. One was bald and blonde, the other had black hair, remarkably oiled and shiny; both were forty-fivish. They were regarding the occupants of the Tietjens[70] table with both their mouths slightly open. They were undisguisedly listening. In front of each were three empty sloe-gin glasses and one half-filled tumbler of brandy and soda. Macmaster understood why the General had explained that his sister had not tried to steal Mrs. Duchemin's cook.

Tietjens said:

"Drink up your tea quickly and let's get started." He was drawing from his pocket a number of telegraph forms which he began arranging. The General said:

"Don't burn your mouth. We can't start off before all ... all these other gentlemen. We're too slow."[71]

"No; we're beastly well stuck," Sandbach said.

Tietjens handed the telegraph forms over to Macmaster.

"You'd better take a look at these," he said. "I mayn't see you again to-day after the match. You're dining up at Mountby.[72] The General will run you up. Lady Claude will excuse me. I've got work to do."

This was already matter for dismay for Macmaster. He was aware that Tietjens would have disliked dining up at Mountby with the Sandbachs, who would have a crowd, extremely smart but more than usually unintelligent. Tietjens called this crowd, indeed, the plague-spot of the party—meaning of Toryism. But Macmaster couldn't help thinking that a disagreeable dinner would be better for his friend than brooding in solitude in the black shadows of the huddled town. Then Tietjens said:

"I'm going to have a word with that swine!" He pointed his square chin rather rigidly before him, and looking past the two brandy drinkers, Macmaster saw one of those faces that frequent caricature made familiar and yet strange. Macmaster couldn't, at the moment, put a name to it. It must be a politician, probably a Minister. But which? His mind was already in a dreadful state. In the glimpse he had caught of the telegraph form now in his hand, he had perceived that it was addressed to Sylvia Tietjens and began with the word "agreed." He said swiftly:

"Has that been sent or is it only a draft?"

Tietjens said:

"That fellow is the Rt. Hon. Stephen Fenwick Waterhouse. He's chairman of the Funded Debt Commission. He's the swine who made us fake that return in the office."

That moment was the worst Macmaster had ever known. A worse came. Tietjens said:

"I'm going to have a word with him. That's why I'm not dining at Mountby. It's a duty to the country."

Macmaster's mind simply stopped. He was in a space, all windows. There was sunlight outside. And clouds. Pink and white. Woolly! Some ships. And two men: one dark and oily, the other rather blotchy on a blonde baldness. They were talking, but their words made no impression on Macmaster. The dark, oily man said that he was not going to take Gertie to Budapest.[*] Not

---

[*] In *The Good Soldier*, Dowell predicts that Leonora's second husband, Rodney Bayham, 'will keep a separate establishment, secretly, in Portsmouth, and make occasional trips to Paris and to Buda-Pesth': 153.

half! He winked like a nightmare. Beyond were two young men
and a preposterous face. . . . It was all so like a nightmare that the
Cabinet Minister's[73] features were distorted for Macmaster. Like
an enormous mask of pantomime: shiny, with an immense nose
and elongated, Chinese eyes.*

Yet not unpleasant! Macmaster was a Whig by conviction, by
nation, by temperament. He thought that public servants should
abstain from political activity. Nevertheless, he couldn't be
expected to think a Liberal Cabinet Minister ugly. On the
contrary, Mr. Waterhouse appeared to have a frank, humorous,
kindly expression. He listened deferentially to one of his secretaries, resting his hand on the young man's shoulder, smiling a
little, rather sleepily. No doubt he was overworked. And then,
letting himself go in a side-shaking laugh. Putting on flesh!

What a pity! What a *pity!* Macmaster was reading a string of
incomprehensible words[74] in Tietjens' heavily scored writing.[75]
*Not entertain . . . flat not house . . . child remain at sister*[76]. . . . His
eyes went backwards and forwards over the phrases. He could not
connect the words without stops. The man with the oily hair said
in a sickly voice that Gertie was hot stuff, but not the one for
Budapest with all the Gitana† girls you were telling me of! Why,
he'd kept Gertie for five years now. More like the real thing! His
friend's voice was like a result of indigestion. Tietjens, Sandbach
and the General were stiff, like pokers.

What a pity![77] Macmaster thought.

He ought to have been sitting . . . It would have been pleasant
and right to be sitting with the pleasant Minister. In the ordinary
course he, Macmaster, would have been. The best golfer in the
place was usually set to play with distinguished visitors, and[78]
there was next to no one in the south of England who ordinarily
could beat him. He had begun at four, playing with a miniature
cleek and a found shilling ball over the municipal links. Going
to the poor school every morning and back to[79] dinner; and back
to school and back to bed! Over the cold, rushy, sandy links,
beside the grey sea. Both shoes full of sand. The found shilling
ball had lasted him three years. . . .

* Recognisably a sketch of C. F. G. Masterman.
† Gypsy.

Macmaster exclaimed: "Good God!" He had just gathered from the telegram that Tietjens meant to go to Germany on Tuesday. As if at Macmaster's ejaculation Tietjens said:

"Yes. It *is* unbearable. If you don't stop those swine, General, I shall."

The General sibilated low, between his teeth:

"Wait a minute.... Wait a minute.... Perhaps that other fellow will."

The man with the black oily hair said:

"If Budapest's the place for the girls you say it is, old pal, with the Turkish baths and all, we'll paint the old town red all right, next month," and he winked at Tietjens. His friend, with his head down, seemed to make internal rumblings, looking apprehensively beneath his blotched forehead at the General.

"Not," the other continued argumentatively, "that I don't love my old woman. She's all right. And then there's Gertie. 'Ot stuff, but the real thing. But I say a man wants ..." He ejaculated, "Oo!"[80]

The General, his hands in his pockets, very tall, thin, red-cheeked, his white hair combed forward in a fringe, sauntered towards the other table. It was not two yards, but it seemed a long saunter. He stood right over them, they looking up, open-eyed, like schoolboys at a balloon. He said:

"I'm glad you're enjoying our links, gentlemen."

The bald man said: "We are! We are! First-class. A treat!"

"But," the General said, "it isn't wise[81] to discuss one's ... eh ... domestic[82] circumstances ... at ... at mess, you know, or in a golf house. People might hear."

The gentleman with the oily[83] hair half rose and exclaimed:

"Oo, the..." The other man mumbled: "Shut up, Briggs."

The General said:

"I'm the president of the club, you know. It's my duty to see that the *majority* of the club and its visitors are pleased. I hope you don't mind."

The General came back to his seat. He was trembling with vexation.

"It makes one as beastly a bounder as themselves," he said. "But what the devil else was one to do?" The two city men had ambled hastily into the dressing-rooms; the dire silence fell.

Macmaster realised that, for these Tories at least, this was really the end of the world. The Last[84] of England!* He returned, with panic in his heart, to Tietjens' telegram. . . . Tietjens was going to Germany on Tuesday. He offered to throw over the department. . . . These were unthinkable things. You couldn't imagine them!

He began to read the telegram all over again. A shadow fell upon the flimsy sheets. The Rt. Hon. Mr. Waterhouse was between the head of the table and the windows. He said:

"We're much obliged, General. It was impossible to hear ourselves speak for those obscene fellows' smut. It's fellows like that that make our friends the suffragettes! That warrants them. . . ." He added: "Hullo! Sandbach! Enjoying your rest?"

The General said:

"I was hoping you'd take on the job of telling those[85] fellows off."

Mr. Sandbach, his bull-dog jaw sticking out, the short black

* *The Last of England* is the title of a major oil painting by Ford's grandfather, Ford Madox Brown, using himself and his wife Emma as models for a couple forced by hardship to emigrate to Australia: 1855, Birmingham Museums and Art Gallery. (There is also a later watercolour replica (1864–6) in Tate Britain.) The phrase recurs in *Parade's End*, and connotes ways in which the war and its end seem to signal the end of the idea of England and Englishness. See below 266 and *Last Post* I.iv. In *Nightingale* 86, recounting his own decision to leave England, Ford uses the phrase in connexion with the oppressive bureaucracy of 'Dora' (the Defence of the Realm Act) to invoke an opposite emotion. Instead of the class snobbery Macmaster is sensitive to here, Ford laments the decline of an ideal of liberty: 'No political fugitives, no martyrs for whatever faith were ever any more to land on those shores – because of an order in Council – an Order in Council evolved by some unknown member of the most suspect government the realm had ever suffered from! What then was to become of England of the glorious traditions? It had been political fugitives and martyrs that had given England her place among the nations. It had been the Flemish weavers, the Anabaptists, the Huguenots, the ceaseless tide of the discontented from every nation that had given England, not alone her tradition of freedom but her crafts, her system of merchanting, her sense of probity, her very security. . . . This then was the last of England, the last of London. . . .' (This probably refers to the 1914 Aliens Restriction Act, which gave 'powers for imposing restrictions upon aliens, and prohibiting the residence of aliens in any area certified by Order in Council': *Hansard*; House of Lords, 10 September 1914 vol 17 cc589–602). Later in *Nightingale* 137, the phrase recurs to describe his image of the country as he left: 'On the 11th November, 1922, Authority granted me a passport that permitted me to proceed to France. There was, as I passed through Trafalgar Square, a dense fog and the results of a general election coming in . . . an immense shouting mob in a muffled and vast obscurity. The roars made the fog sway in vast curtains over the baffled light-standard. That for me was the last of England.'

hair on his scalp appearing to rise, barked: "Hullo, Waterslops![86] Enjoying your plunder?"

Mr. Waterhouse, tall, slouching and untidy-haired, lifted the flaps of his coat. It was so ragged that it appeared as if straws stuck out of the elbows.

"All that the suffragettes have left of me," he said laughingly. "Isn't one of you fellows a genius called Tietjens?" He was looking at Macmaster. The General said:

"Tietjens ... Macmaster ..." The Minister went on very friendly:[87]

"Oh, it's you? ... I just wanted to take the opportunity of thanking you."

Tietjens said:

"Good God! What for?"

` "*You* know!" the Minister said, "we couldn't have got the Bill before the House till next session without your figures...." He said slily: "Could we, Sandbach?" and added to Tietjens: "Ingleby told me...."

Tietjens was chalk-white and stiffened. He stuttered:

"I can't take any credit.... I consider ..."

Macmaster exclaimed:

"Tietjens ... you ..." he didn't know what he was going to say.

"Oh, you're too modest," Mr. Waterhouse overwhelmed Tietjens. "We know whom we've to thank ..." His eyes drifted to Sandbach a little absently. Then his face lit up.

"Oh! Look here, Sandbach," he said.... "Come here, will you?" He walked a pace or two away, calling to one of his young men: "Oh, Sanderson, give the bobbie a drink. A good stiff one." Sandbach jerked himself awkwardly out of his chair and limped to the Minister.

Tietjens burst out:

"Me too modest! *Me!* ... The swine.... The unspeakable swine!"

The General said:

"What's it all about, Chrissie? You probably are too modest."

Tietjens said:

"Damn it. It's a serious matter. It's driving me out of the unspeakable office I'm in."

Macmaster said:

"No! No! You're wrong. It's a wrong view you take." And with a good deal of real passion he began to explain to the General. It was an affair that had already given him a great deal of pain. The Government had asked the statistical department for figures illuminating a number of schedules that they desired to use in presenting their new Bill to the Commons. Mr. Waterhouse was to present it.

Mr. Waterhouse at the moment was slapping Mr. Sandbach on the back, tossing the hair out of his eyes and laughing like a hysterical schoolgirl. He looked suddenly tired.[88] A police constable, his buttons shining, appeared, drinking from a pewter-pot outside the glazed door. The two city men ran across the angle from the dressing-room to the same door, buttoning their clothes. The Minister said loudly:

"Make it guineas!"

It seemed to Macmaster painfully wrong that Tietjens should call anyone so genial and unaffected an unspeakable swine. It was unjust. He went on with his explanation to the General.

The Government had wanted a set of figures based on a calculation called B7. Tietjens, who had been working on one called H19—for his own instruction—had persuaded himself that H19 was the lowest figure that was actuarially[89] sound.

The General said pleasantly:[90]

"All this is Greek to me."

"Oh no, it needn't be," Macmaster heard himself say. "It amounts to this. Chrissie was asked by the Government—by Sir Reginald Ingleby—to work out what 3 x 3 comes to: it was that sort of thing in principle.[91] He said that the only figure that would not ruin the country was nine times nine..."

"The Government wanted to shovel money into the working man's pockets, in fact," the General said. "Money for nothing.... or votes, I suppose."

"But that isn't the point, sir,"[92] Macmaster ventured to say. "All that Chrissie was asked to do was to say what 3 x 3 was."

"Well, he appears to have done it and earned no end of kudos," the General said. "That's all right. We've all, always, believed in Chrissie's ability. But he's a strong-tempered beggar."

"He was extraordinarily rude to Sir Reginald over it,"

Macmaster went on.

The General said:

"Oh dear! Oh dear!" He shook his head at Tietjens and assumed with care the blank, slightly disapproving[93] air of the regular officer. "I don't like to hear of rudeness to a superior. In *any* service."

"I don't think," Tietjens said with extreme mildness, "that Macmaster is quite fair to me. Of course he's a right to his opinion as to what the discipline of a service demands. I certainly told Ingleby that I'd rather resign than do that beastly job...."

"You shouldn't have," the General said. "What would become of the services if everyone did as you did?"[94]

Sandbach came back laughing and dropped painfully into his low arm-chair.

"That fellow ..." he began.

The General slightly raised his hand.

"A minute!" he said. "I was about to tell Chrissie, here, that if I am offered the job—of course it's an order really—of suppressing the Ulster Volunteers* ... I'd rather cut my throat than do it...."

Sandbach said:

"Of course you would, old chap. They're our brothers. You'd see the beastly, lying Government damned first."

"I was going to say that I should accept," the General said, "I shouldn't resign my commission."

Sandbach said:

"Good *God!*"

Tietjens said:

"Well, I didn't."

Sandbach exclaimed:

"General! You! After all Claudine and I have said...."

Tietjens interrupted:

---

* Unionist militia, which had just been formed (in 1912) to oppose Irish Home Rule. The Conservative Party had, also in 1912, completed a merger with the Liberal Unionist Party (Liberals who had seceded in 1886 to oppose any dismantling of the United Kingdom). Campion as a Tory would naturally support the Unionist cause. In the pseudonymous article 'A Declaration of Faith', Ford had expressed pronounced anti-Tory views: 'I desire Home Rule for Ireland with as much fervour as I desire to see the vote given to women': *English Review*, 4 (Feb. 1910), 543–51 (548).

"Excuse me, Sandbach. I'm receiving[95] this reprimand for the moment. I wasn't, then, rude to Ingleby. If I'd expressed contempt for what he said or for himself, that would have been rude. I didn't. He wasn't in the least offended. He looked like a cockatoo, but he wasn't offended. And I let him over-persuade me. He was right, really. He pointed out that, if I didn't do the job, those swine would put on one of our little competition[96] wallah head clerks* and get all the schedules faked, as well as starting off with false premises!"

"That's the view I take," the General said, "if I don't take the Ulster job the Government will put on a fellow who'll burn all the farm-houses and rape all the women in the three counties.† They've got him up their sleeve. He only asks for the Connaught Rangers‡ to go through the north with. And you

---

\* 'Wallah' is an Anglo-Indian suffix for 'man' or 'fellow'. 'Competition-wallah' is defined in *Hobson-Jobson*, ed. Henry Yule and Arthur Coke Burnell (London: Murray, 1886) as 'A hybrid of English and Hindustani, applied in modern Anglo-Indian colloquial to members of the Civil Service who have entered it by the competitive system first introduced in 1856. The phrase was probably the invention of one of the older or Haileybury members of the same service. These latter, whose nominations were due to interest, and who were bound together by the intimacies and *esprit de corps* of a common college, looked with some disfavour upon the children of Innovation. The name was readily taken up in India, but its familiarity in England is probably due in great part to the "Letters of a Competition-wala", written by one who had no real claim to the title, Mr G. O. Trevelyan', who later wrote a *Life* of his uncle, Lord Macaulay. The 'Letters' appeared in *Macmillan's* magazine and were republished as *The Competition Wallah* in 1864.

The phrase exemplifies Ford's subtle ear for minute class gradations – the rough herding of competitors rather than the smooth glide of hereditary privilege and unbothered inheritance of position – in its hint of patronising and contempt. The irony is that Macmaster sees himself as separated from Campion and Sandbach and, to some extent, from Tietjens himself, by just that gulf. Patronage, quite literally, since Tietjens' family eased his passage through university financially.

After his father's premature death in 1889, when Ford was 15, he prepared himself 'very strenuously for the Indian Civil Service': *Ancient Lights* 156–7. 'Ford Hueffer came round to me from Brown's', noted his uncle, William Michael Rossetti (himself a civil servant), 'bringing a letter which he proposes to send to the Civil Service Commissioners, asking when the next examination for Boy Clerkships would be held; as he thinks (and I consider it a reasonable idea) of competing at such an examination.' A month later he reported: 'Ford is attending, for 3 months, a Civil Service College in Chancery Lane' (Rossetti, diary for 4 February and 4 March 1889: *Selected Letters of William Michael Rossetti*, ed. Roger W. Peattie (University Park and London: Pennsylvania State University Press, 1990), 529 n.2). He didn't become a civil servant, of course; in part, perhaps, because the idea of his grandson becoming a 'cursed clerk' was 'a real grief' to Madox Brown: *Ancient Lights* 156–7.

† The three counties historically part of the province of Ulster but with Catholic majorities, and now in the Republic of Ireland, not Northern Ireland.

‡ Irish regiment of the British Army, known as 'The Devil's Own'.

know what *that* means. All the same . . ." He looked at Tietjens: "One should not be rude to one's superiors."

"I tell you I wasn't rude," Tietjens exclaimed. "Damn your nice, paternal old eyes. Get that into your[97] mind!"

The General shook his head:

"You brilliant fellows!" he said. "The country, or the army, or anything, could not be run by you. It takes stupid fools like me and Sandbach, along with sound moderate heads like our friend here." He indicated Macmaster and, rising, went on: "Come along. You're playing me, Macmaster. They say you're hot stuff. Chrissie's no good. He can take Sandbach on."

He walked off with Macmaster towards the dressing-room.

Sandbach, wriggling awkwardly out of his chair, shouted:

"Save the country. . . . Damn it. . . ." He stood on his feet. "I and Campion . . . Look at what the country's come to. . . . What with swine like those[98] two in our club houses! And policemen to go round the links with Ministers to protect them from the wild women. . . . By God! I'd like to have the flaying of the skin off some of their backs. I would. By God I would."

He added:

"That fellow Waterslops is a bit of a sportsman. I haven't been able to tell you about our bet, you've been making such a noise. . . . Is your friend really plus one[99] at North Berwick? What are you like?"

"Macmaster is a good plus two[100*] anywhere when he's in practice."

Sandbach said:

"Good Lord. . . . A stout fellow. . . ."

"As for me," Tietjens said, "I loathe the beastly game."

"So do I," Sandbach answered. "We'll just lollop along behind them."

---

* Most golfers need to take more strokes than are considered 'par' for a course, and are assigned a 'handicap' – the number of strokes above par they can achieve at their best. Macmaster is so good that he has a negative handicap, referred to (confusingly) as a 'plus' number. Thus 'plus two' means he can normally complete the course two under par.

# IV

THEY came out into the bright open where all the distances under the tall sky showed with distinct prismatic[1] outlines. They made a little group of seven—for Tietjens would not have a caddy—waiting on the flat, first teeing ground. Macmaster walked up to Tietjens and said under his voice:

"You've really *sent* that wire? . . ."

Tietjens said:

"It'll be in Germany by now!"

Mr. Sandbach hobbled from one to the other explaining the terms of his wager with Mr. Waterhouse. Mr. Waterhouse had backed one of the young men playing with him to drive into and hit twice in the eighteen holes the two city men who would be playing ahead of them. As the Minister had taken rather short odds, Mr. Sandbach considered him a good sport.

A long way down the first hole Mr. Waterhouse and his two companions were approaching the first green. They had high sandhills to the right and, to their left, a road that[2] was fringed with rushes and a narrow dyke. Ahead of the Cabinet Minister the two city men and their two caddies stood on the edge of the dyke or poked downwards into the rushes. Two girls appeared and disappeared on the tops of the sandhills. The policeman was strolling along the road, level with Mr. Waterhouse. The General said:

"I think we could go now."

Sandbach said:

"Waterslops will get a hit at them from the next tee. They're in the dyke."

The General drove a straight, goodish ball. Just as Macmaster was in his swing Sandbach shouted:

"By God! He nearly did it. See that fellow jump!"

Macmaster looked round over his shoulder and hissed with vexation between his teeth:

"Don't you know that you don't shout while a man is driving?

Or haven't you played golf?" He hurried fussily after his ball.

Sandbach said to Tietjens:

"Golly! That chap's got a temper!"

Tietjens said:

"Only over this game. You deserved what you got."

Sandbach said:

"I did. . . . But I didn't spoil his shot. He's outdriven the General twenty yards."

Tietjens said:

"It would have been sixty but for you."

They loitered about on the tee waiting for the others to get their distance. Sandbach said:

"By Jove, your friend is on with his second . . . You wouldn't believe it of such a *little* beggar!" He added: "He's not much class, is he?"

Tietjens looked down his nose.

"Oh, about *our* class!" he said. "He wouldn't take a bet about driving into the couple ahead."

Sandbach hated Tietjens for being a Tietjens of Groby: Tietjens was enraged by the existence of Sandbach, who was the son of an ennobled mayor of Middlesbrough,[3] seven miles or so from Groby. The feuds between the Cleveland landowners and the Cleveland plutocrats are very bitter. Sandbach said:

"Ah, I suppose he gets you out of scrapes with girls and the Treasury, and you take him about in return. It's a practical combination."

"Like Pottle Mills and Stanton," Tietjens said. The financial operations connected with the[4] amalgamating of these two steel-works had earned Sandbach's father a good deal of odium[5] in the Cleveland district. . . . Sandbach said:

"Look here, Tietjens. . . ." But he changed his mind and said:

"We'd better go now." He drove off with an awkward action but not without skill. He certainly outplayed Tietjens.

Playing very slowly, for both were desultory and Sandbach very lame, they lost sight of the others behind some coastguard cottages and dunes before they had left the third tee. Because of his game leg Sandbach sliced a good deal. On this occasion he sliced right into the gardens of the cottages and went with his boy to look for his ball among potato-haulms, beyond a low wall. Tiet-

jens patted his own ball lazily up the fairway and, dragging his bag
behind him by the strap, he sauntered on.

Although Tietjens hated golf as he hated any occupation that
was of a competitive nature he could engross himself in the mathematics of trajectories when he accompanied Macmaster in one
of his expeditions for practice. He accompanied Macmaster
because he liked there to be one pursuit at which his friend indisputably[6] excelled himself, for it was a bore always brow-beating
the fellow. But he stipulated that they should visit three different
and, if possible, unknown courses every week-end when they
golfed.[7] He interested himself then in the way the courses were
laid out, acquiring thus an extraordinary connoisseurship in golf
architecture, and he made abstruse calculations[8] as to the flight
of balls off sloped club-faces, as to the foot-poundals of energy
exercised by one muscle or the other, and as to theories of spin.
As often as not he palmed Macmaster off as a fair, average player
on some other unfortunate fair, average stranger. Then he passed
the afternoon in the club-house studying the pedigrees and forms
of racehorses, for every club-house contained a copy of Ruff's
Guide.* In the spring he would hunt for and examine the nests of
soft-billed birds, for he was interested in the domestic affairs of
the cuckoo, though he hated natural history and field botany.

On this occasion he had just examined some notes of other
mashie shots, had put the notebook back in his pocket, and had
addressed his ball with a niblick that had an unusually roughened
face and a head like a hatchet. Meticulously, when he had taken
his grip he removed his little and third fingers from the leather of
the shaft. He was thanking heaven that Sandbach seemed to be
accounted for[9] for ten minutes at least, for Sandbach was miserly
over lost balls and, very slowly, he was raising his mashie to half
cock for a sighting shot.

He was aware that someone, breathing a little heavily from
small lungs, was standing close to him and watching him: he
could indeed, beneath his cap-rim, perceive the tips of a pair of
boy's white sand-shoes. It in no way perturbed him to be watched

---

\*    *Ruff's Guide to the Turf*, a complete record of racing under Jockey Club and National
     Hunt Rules in Great Britain and Ireland, was published from 1842. In *Provence* 38
     Ford recalls some of Arthur Marwood's racing tips.

since he was avid of no personal glory when making his shots. A voice said:

"I say . . ." He continued to look at his ball.

"Sorry to spoil your shot," the voice said. "But . . ."

Tietjens dropped his club altogether and straightened his back. A fair young woman with a fixed scowl[10] was looking at him intently. She had a short skirt and was panting a little.

"I say," she said, "go and see they don't hurt Gertie. I've lost her . . ." She pointed back to the sandhills. "There looked to be some beasts among them."

She seemed a perfectly negligible girl except for the frown: her eyes blue, her hair no doubt fair under a white canvas hat. She had a striped cotton[11] blouse, but her fawn tweed skirt was well hung.

Tietjens said:

"You've been demonstrating."

She said:

"Of course we have, and of course you object on principle. But you won't let a girl be man-handled. Don't wait to tell me:[12] I know it . . . ."

Noises existed. Sandbach, from beyond the low garden wall fifty yards away, was yelping, just like a dog: "Hi! Hi! Hi! Hi!" and gesticulating.[13] His little caddy, entangled in his golf-bag, was trying to scramble over the wall. On top of a high sandhill stood the policeman: he waved his arms like a windmill and shouted. Beside him and behind, slowly rising, were the heads of the General, Macmaster and their two boys. Further along, in completion were appearing the figures of Mr. Waterhouse, his two companions and *their* three boys. The Minister was waving his driver and shouting. They all shouted.

"A regular rat-hunt," the girl said; she was counting. "Eleven and two more caddies!" She exhibited satisfaction. "I headed them all off except two beasts. They couldn't run. But neither can Gertie . . ."

She said urgently:

"Come along! You aren't going to leave Gertie to those beasts! They're drunk. . . ."

Tietjens said:

"Cut away then. I'll look after Gertie." He picked up his bag.

"No, I'll come with you," the girl said.

Tietjens answered: "Oh, you don't want to go to gaol. Clear out!"

She said:

"Nonsense. I've put up with worse than that. Nine months as a slavey. . . . Come *along!*"

Tietjens started to run—rather like a rhinoceros seeing purple. He had been violently spurred, for he had been pierced by a shrill, faint scream. The girl ran beside him.

"You . . . can . . . run!" she panted, "put on a spurt."

Screams protesting against physical violence were at that date rare things in England. Tietjens had never heard the like. It upset him frightfully, though he was aware only of an expanse of open country. The policeman, whose buttons made him noteworthy, was descending his conical sandhill, diagonally, with caution. There is something grotesque about a town policeman, silvered helmet and all, in the open country.[14] It was so clear and still in the air; Tietjens felt as if he were in a light museum looking at specimens. . . .

A little young woman, engrossed, like a hunted rat, came round the corner of a green mound. "This is an assaulted female!" the mind of Tietjens said to him. She had a black skirt covered with sand, for she had just rolled down the sandhill; she had a striped grey and black silk blouse, one shoulder torn completely off, so that a white camisole showed. Over the shoulder of the sandhill came the two city men, flushed with triumph and panting; their red knitted waistcoats moved like bellows. The black-haired one, his eyes lurid and obscene, brandished aloft a fragment of black and grey stuff. He shouted hilariously:

"Strip the bitch naked! . . . Ugh . . . Strip the bitch stark naked!" and jumped down the little hill. He cannoned into Tietjens, who roared at the top of his voice:

"You infernal swine. I'll knock your head off if you move!"

Behind Tietjens' back the girl said:

"Come along, Gertie. . . . It's only to there . . ."

A voice panted in answer:

"I . . . can't. . . . My heart . . ."

Tietjens kept his eye upon the city man. His jaw had fallen

down, his eyes stared! It was as if the bottom of his assured world, where all men desire in their hearts to bash women, had fallen out. He panted:

"Ergle! Ergle!"

Another scream, a little farther than the last voices from behind his back, caused in Tietjens a feeling of intense weariness. What did beastly women want to scream for? He swung round, bag and all. The policeman, his face scarlet like a lobster just boiled, was lumbering unenthusiastically towards the two girls who were trotting towards the dyke. One of his hands, scarlet also, was extended. He was not a yard from Tietjens.

Tietjens was exhausted, beyond thinking or shouting. He slipped his clubs[15] off his shoulder and, as if he were pitching his kit-bag into a luggage van, threw the whole lot between the policeman's running legs. The man, who had no impetus to speak of, pitched forward on to his hands and knees. His helmet over his eyes, he seemed to reflect for a moment; then he removed his helmet and with great deliberation rolled round and sat on the turf. His face was completely without emotion, long, sandy-moustached and rather shrewd. He mopped his brow with a carmine handkerchief that had white spots.

Tietjens walked up to him.

"Clumsy of me!" he said. "I hope you're not hurt." He drew from his breast pocket a curved silver flask. The policeman said nothing. His world, too, contained uncertainties and he was profoundly glad to be able to sit still without discredit. He muttered:

"Shaken. A bit! Anybody would be!"

That let him out and he fell to examining with attention the bayonet catch of the flask top. Tietjens opened it for him. The two girls, advancing at a fatigued trot, were near the dyke side. The fair girl, as they trotted, was trying to adjust her companion's hat;[16] attached by pins to the back of her hair it flapped on her shoulder.

All the rest of the posse were advancing at a very slow walk, in a converging semi-circle. Two little caddies were running, but Tietjens saw them check, hesitate and stop. And there floated to Tietjens' ears the words:

"Stop, you little devils. She'll knock your heads off."

The[17] Rt. Hon. Mr. Waterhouse must have found an admirable voice trainer somewhere. The drab girl was balancing tremulously over a plank on the dyke; the other took it at a jump:[18] up in the air—down on her feet; perfectly business-like. And, as soon as the other girl was off the plank, she was down on her knees before it, pulling it towards her, the other girl trotting away over the vast marsh field.

The girl dropped the plank on the grass. Then she looked up and faced the men and boys who stood in a row on the road. She called in a shrill, high voice, like a young cockerel's:

"Seventeen to two! The usual male odds! You'll *have* to go round by Camber railway bridge, and we'll be in Folkestone by then. We've got bicycles!" She was half going when she checked and, searching out Tietjens to address, exclaimed: "I'm sorry I said that. Because some of you didn't want to catch us. But some of you *did*. And you *were* seventeen to two." She addressed Mr. Waterhouse:

"Why *don't* you give women the vote?" she said. "You'll find it will interfere a good deal with your indispensable golf if you don't. Then what becomes of the nation's health?"

Mr. Waterhouse said:

"If you'll come and discuss it quietly . . ."

She said:

"Oh, tell that to the marines," and turned away, the men in a row watching her figure disappear into the distance of the flat land.[19] Not one of them was inclined to risk that jump: there was nine foot of mud in the bottom of the dyke. It was quite true that, the plank being removed, to go after the women they would have had to go several miles round. It had been a well thought out raid. Mr. Waterhouse said that girl was a ripping girl: the others found her just ordinary. Mr. Sandbach, who had only lately ceased to shout: "Hi!" wanted to know what they were going to do about catching the women, but Mr. Waterhouse said: "Oh, chuck it, Sandy," and went off.

Mr. Sandbach refused to continue his match with Tietjens. He said that Tietjens was the sort of fellow who was the ruin of England. He said he had a good mind to issue a warrant for the arrest of Tietjens—for obstructing the course of justice. Tietjens pointed out that Sandbach wasn't a borough magistrate and so couldn't. And Sandbach went off, dot and carry one,\* and began a furious row with the two city men who had retreated to a distance. He said they were the sort of men who were the ruin of England. They bleated like rams. . . .

Tietjens wandered slowly up the course, found his ball, made his shot with care and found that the ball deviated[20] several feet less to the right of a straight line than he had expected. He tried the shot again, obtained the same result and tabulated his observations in his notebook. He sauntered slowly back towards the club-house. He was content.

He felt himself to be content for the first time in four months. His pulse beat calmly;[21] the heat of the sun all over him appeared to be a beneficent flood. On the flanks of the older and larger sandhills he observed the minute herbage, mixed with little purple aromatic plants. To these the constant nibbling of sheep had imparted a protective tininess. He wandered, content, round the sandhills to the small, silted harbour mouth. After reflecting for some time on the wave-curves in the sloping mud of the water sides he had a long conversation, mostly in signs, with a Finn who hung over the side of a tarred, stump-masted, battered vessel that had a gaping, splintered hole where the anchor should have hung. She came from Archangel; was of several hundred tons burthen, was knocked together anyhow, of soft wood, for about ninety pounds, and launched, sink or swim, in the timber trade. Beside her, taut, glistening with brasswork, was a new fishing boat, just built there for the Lowestoft fleet.[22] Ascertaining her price from a man who was finishing her painting, Tietjens reckoned that you

---

\* 'Dot and carry one' was a mnemonic used by children doing addition requiring a '1' to be carried left to the next column. It also became used to mimic the gait of someone with a limp or an artificial leg, as in Kipling's 'Gunga Din', in *Barrack-Room Ballads* (London: Methuen, 1892), 23–6 (24):

> It was 'Din! Din! Din!
> You 'eathen, where the mischief 'ave you been?
> You put some *juldee* in it
> Or I'll *marrow* you this minute
> If you don't fill up my helmet, Gunga Din!'

> 'E would dot an' carry one
> Till the longest day was done;
> An' 'e didn't seem to know the use o' fear.

Also see *Treasure Island* (1883), Part IV, Chapter XVI: 'I know my pulse went dot and carry one.'

could have built three of the Archangel timber ships for the cost
of that boat, and that the Archangel vessel[23] would earn about
twice as much per hour per ton. . . .

It was in that way his mind worked when he was fit: it picked
up little pieces of definite, workmanlike information. When it
had enough it classified them: not for any purpose, but because
to know things was agreeable and gave a feeling of strength, of
having in reserve something that the other fellow would not
suspect. . . . He passed a long, quiet, abstracted afternoon.

In the dressing-room he found the General, among lockers,
old coats, and stoneware[24] washing-basins set in scrubbed wood.
The General leaned back against a row of these things.

"You are the ruddy *limit!*" he exclaimed.

Tietjens said:

"Where's Macmaster?"

The General said he had sent Macmaster off with Sandbach
in the two-seater. Macmaster had to dress before going up to
Mountby.[25] He added: "The *ruddy* limit!" again.

"Because I knocked the bobbie over?" Tietjens asked. "He
liked it."

The General said:

"Knocked the bobbie over . . . I didn't see that."

"He didn't want to catch the girls," Tietjens said, "you could
see him—oh, yearning not to."

"I don't want to know anything about that," the General said.
"I shall hear enough about it from Paul Sandbach. Give the
bobbie a quid and let's hear no more of it. I'm a magistrate."

"Then what have I done?" Tietjens said. "I helped those girls
to get off. *You* didn't want to catch them; Waterhouse didn't, the
policeman didn't. No one did except the swine. Then what's the
matter?"

"Damn it all!" the General said, "don't you remember that
you're a young married man?"

With the respect for the General's superior age[26] and achievements, Tietjens[27] stopped himself laughing.

"If you're really serious, sir," he said, "I always remember it
very carefully. I don't suppose you're suggesting that I've ever
shown want of respect for Sylvia."

The General shook his head.

"I don't know," he said. "And damn it all I'm worried. I'm ...
Hang it all, I'm your father's oldest friend." The General looked
indeed worn and saddened in the light of the sand-drifted,
ground-glass windows. He said: "Was that skirt a ... a friend of
yours? Had you arranged it with her?"

Tietjens said:

"Wouldn't it be better, sir, if you said what you had on your
mind? ..."

The old General blushed a little.

"I don't like to," he said straightforwardly. "You brilliant
fellows.... [28] I only want, my dear boy, to hint that ..."

Tietjens said, a little more stiffly:

"I'd prefer you to get it out, sir.... I acknowledge your right
as my father's oldest friend."[29]

"Then," the General burst out, "who was the skirt you were
lolloping up Pall Mall with? On the last day they trooped the
colour? ... I didn't see her myself.... Was it this same one? Paul
said she looked like a cook maid."

Tietjens made himself a little more rigid.

"She was, as a matter of fact, a bookmaker's secretary,"[30] Tietjens said. "I imagine I have the right to walk where I like, with
whom I like. And no one has the right to question it.... I don't
mean you, sir. But no one else."

The General said puzzledly:

"It's you *brilliant* fellows.... They all say you're brilliant...."

Tietjens said:

"You might let your rooted distrust of intelligence ... It's
natural of course; but you might let it allow you to be just to me.
I assure you there was nothing discreditable ..."[31]

The General interrupted:

"If you were a stupid young subaltern and told me you were
showing your mother's new cook the way to the Piccadilly tube
I'd believe you[32].... But, then, no young subaltern would do such
a damn, blasted, tomfool thing! Paul said you walked beside her
like the king in his glory![33] Through the crush outside the
Haymarket,[34] of all places in the world!'"*

---

\* The Haymarket theatres had been drawing fashionable crowds for two centuries.

"I'm obliged to Sandbach for his commendation. . . ." Tietjens said. He thought a moment. Then he said:[35]

"I was trying to get that young woman. . . . I was taking her out to lunch from her office at the bottom of the Haymarket. . . . To get her off a friend's back. That is, of course, between ourselves."

He said this with great reluctance because he didn't want to cast reflection on Macmaster's taste, for the young lady had been by no means[36] one to be seen walking with a really circumspect public official. But he had said nothing to indicate Macmaster, and he had other friends.

The General choked.

"Upon my soul," he said, "what do you take me for?" He repeated the words as if he were amazed. "If," he said, "my G.S.O. II*—who's the stupidest ass I know—told me such a damn-fool lie as that I'd have him broke† to-morrow." He went on expostulatorily: "Damn it all, it's the first duty of a soldier—it's the first duty of all Englishmen—to be able to tell a good lie in answer to a charge. But a lie like that . . ."

He broke off breathless, then he began again:

"Hang it all, I told that lie to my grandmother and my grandfather told it to *his* grandfather. And they call you brilliant! . . ." He paused and then asked reproachfully: "Or do you think I'm in a state of senile decay?"

Tietjens said:

"I know you, sir, to be the smartest general of division in the British Army.[37] I leave you to draw your own conclusions as to why I said what I did. . . ." He had told the exact truth, but he was[38] not sorry to be disbelieved.

The General said:

"Then I'll take it that you tell me a lie meaning me to know that it's a lie. That's quite proper. I take it you mean to keep the woman officially out of it. But look here, Chrissie"—his tone took a deeper seriousness—"if the woman that's come between you and Sylvia—that's broken up your home, damn it, for that's what it is!—is little Miss Wannop . . ."

---

\* General Staff Officer, Grade 2.
† Demoted.

"Her name was Julia Mandelstein," Tietjens said.

The General said:

"Yes! Yes! Of course! . . . But if it *is* the little Wannop girl and it's not gone too far . . . Put her back . . . Put her back, as you used to be a good boy![39] It would be too hard on the mother. . . . "

Tietjens, said:

"General! I give you my word . . . "

The General said:

"I'm not asking any questions, my boy; I'm talking now.[40] You've told me the story you want told and it's the story I'll tell for you! But that little piece is . . . she used to be! . . . as straight as a die. I daresay you know better than I. Of course when they get among the wild women there's no knowing what happens to them. They say they're all whores. . . . I beg your pardon, if you like the girl . . . "

"Is Miss Wannop," Tietjens asked, "the girl who demonstrates?"[41]

"Sandbach said," the General went on, "that he couldn't see from where he was whether that girl was the same as the one in the Haymarket. But he thought it was . . . He was pretty certain."

"As he's married your sister," Tietjens said, "one can't impugn his taste in women."[42]

"I say again, I'm not asking," the General said. "But I do say again too: put her back. Her father was a great friend of your father's: or your father was a great admirer of his. They say he was the most brilliant brain of the party."

"Of course I know who Professor Wannop was," Tietjens said. "There's nothing you could tell me about him."

"I daresay not," the General said drily. "Then you know that he didn't leave a farthing when he died and the rotten Liberal Government wouldn't put his wife and children on the Civil List[*] because he'd sometimes written for a Tory paper. And you know that the mother has had a deuced hard row to hoe and has only just turned the corner. If she can be said to have turned it. I know

---

[*]  The Civil List is the budget approved by Parliament to cover the expenses of sovereigns and their households. Under Queen Victoria it was extended to grant pensions, on the advice of the government, to those distinguishing themselves in the arts, literature, or science, or who had served the Crown.

Claudine takes them all the peaches she can cadge out of Paul's gardener."

Tietjens was about to say that Mrs. Wannop, the mother, had written the only novel worth reading since the eighteenth century....[43] But the General went on:

"Listen to me, my boy.... If you can't get on without women ... I should have thought Sylvia was good enough. But I know what we men are.... I don't set up to be a saint. I heard a woman in the promenade of the Empire say once that it was the likes of them that saved the lives and figures of all the virtuous women of the country. And I daresay it's true.... But choose a girl that you can set up in a tobacco shop and do your courting in the back parlour.[44] Not in the Haymarket.... Heaven knows if you can afford it. That's your affair. You appear to have been sold up. And from what Sylvia's let drop to Claudine ..."

"I don't believe," Tietjens said, "that Sylvia's said anything to Lady Claudine[45] ... She's too straight."

"I didn't say 'said,'" the General exclaimed, "I particularly said 'let drop.' And perhaps I oughtn't to have said as much as that, but[46] you know what devils for ferreting out women are. And Claudine's worse than any woman I ever knew...."

"And, of course, she's had Sandbach to help," Tietjens said.

"Oh, that fellow's worse than any woman," the General exclaimed.

"Then what does the whole indictment amount to?" Tietjens asked.

"Oh, hang it," the General brought out, "I'm not a beastly detective, I only want a plausible story to tell Claudine. Or not even plausible. An obvious lie as long as it shows you're not flying in the face of society—as walking up the Haymarket with the little Wannop when your wife's left you because of her would be."[47]

"What does it amount to?" Tietjens said patiently: "What Sylvia 'let drop'?"

"Only," the General answered, "that you are—that your views are—immoral. Of course they often puzzle me. And, of course, if you have views that aren't the same as other people's, and don't keep them to yourself, other people will suspect you of immorality. That's what put Paul Sandbach on your track! ...[48]

and that you're extravagant.... Oh, hang it.... Eternal
hansoms, and taxis and telegrams.... You know, my boy, times
aren't what they were when your father and I married. We used
to say you could do it on five hundred a year as a younger son....
And then this girl too...." His voice took on a more agitated
note of shyness and pain....[49] "It probably hadn't occurred to
you.... But, of course, Sylvia has an income of her own.... And,
don't you see ... if you outrun the constable and ... In short,
you're spending Sylvia's money on the other girl, and that's what
people can't stand." He added quickly: "I'm bound to say that
Mrs. Satterthwaite backs you through thick and thin. Thick and
thin! Claudine wrote to her. But you know what women are with
a handsome son-in-law that's always polite to them. But I may
tell you that but for your[50] mother-in-law, Claudine would have
cut you out of her visiting list months ago. And you'd have been
cut out of some others too...."

Tietjens said:

"Thanks. I think that's enough to go on with.... Give me a
couple of minutes to reflect on what you've said ..."[51]

"I'll wash my hands and change my coat," the General said
with intense relief.

At the end of two minutes Tietjens said:

"No; I don't see that there is anything I want to say."

The General exclaimed with enthusiasm:

"That's my good lad! Open confession is next to reform....
And ... and try to be more respectful to your superiors.... Damn
it; they say you're brilliant. But I thank heaven I haven't got you
in my command.... Though I believe you're a good lad. But
you're the sort of fellow to set a whole division by the ears.... A
regular ... what's 'is name? A regular Dreyfus!"*

"Did you think Dreyfus was guilty?" Tietjens asked.

"Hang it," the General said, "he was worse than guilty—the
sort of fellow you couldn't believe in and yet couldn't prove
anything against. The curse of the world...."

---

* The wrongful conviction for treason of the young French Jewish officer Alfred Dreyfus
  in 1894 caused a national political scandal. Dreyfus is mentioned in *The Good Soldier*
  105, and *Between St. Dennis and St. George* (London: Hodder and Stoughton, 1915),
  77; see also *A Mirror to France* (London: Duckworth, 1926), 26–8, 102.

Tietjens said:

"Ah."

"Well, they are," the General said: "fellows like that *unsettle* society.* You don't know where you are. You can't judge. They make you uncomfortable. . . . A brilliant fellow too! I believe he's a brigadier-general by now. . . ." He put his arm round Tietjens' shoulders.

"There, there, my dear boy," he said, "come and have a sloe gin. That's the real answer to all beastly problems."[52]

It was some time before Tietjens could get to think of his own problems.[53] The fly that took them back went with the slow pomp of a procession over the winding marsh road in front of the absurdly picturesque red pyramid of the very old town. Tietjens had to listen to the General suggesting that it would be better if he didn't come to the golf-club till Monday. He would get Macmaster some good games. A good, sound fellow that Macmaster now. It was a pity Tietjens hadn't some of his soundness!

The[54] two city men had approached the General on the course and had used some violent invectives against Tietjens: they had objected to being called ruddy swine to their faces: they were going to the police.[55] The General said that he had told them himself, slowly and quietly,[56] that they *were* ruddy swine and that they would never get another ticket at that club after Monday. But till Monday, apparently, they had the right to be there and the club wouldn't want scenes. Sandbach, too, was infuriated about Tietjens.[57]

Tietjens said that[58] the fault lay with the times that permitted the introduction into gentlemen's company of such social[59] swipes[†] as Sandbach. One acted perfectly correctly and then a dirty little beggar like that put dirty little constructions on it and

---

* Cf. 'The Fun of Genius', *English Review*, 13 (Dec. 1912), 52–63: 'That sort of chap ought to be shot neatly through the head. They disturb the world' (56). Cf. also Dowell's sentiment at the end of *The Good Soldier* 291: 'society can only exist if the normal, if the virtuous, and the slightly-deceitful flourish, and if the passionate, the headstrong, and the too-truthful are condemned to suicide and to madness'.

† 'An objectionable person; also, such persons considered *collect*[ively]. *slang*': OED, citing D. H. Lawrence's *Pansies* of 1929 (138) 'And do you think it's my business to be handing out money to a lot of inferior swipe?'

ran about and bleated. He added that he knew Sandbach was the
General's brother-in-law, but he couldn't help it. That was the
truth.... The General said: "I know, my boy: I know...." But
one had to take society as one found it. Claudine had to be
provided for and Sandbach made a very good husband, careful,
sober, and on the right side in politics.[60] A bit of a rip; but they
couldn't ask for everything![61] And Claudine was using all the
influence she had with the other side*—which was not a little,
women were so wonderful!—to get him a diplomatic job in
Turkey, so as to get him out of the way of Mrs. Crundall! Mrs.
Crundall was the leading Anti-Suffragette of the little town.
That was what made Sandbach so bitter against Tietjens. He told
Tietjens so that Tietjens might understand.

Tietjens had hitherto flattered himself that he could examine
a subject swiftly and put it away in his mind.[62] To the General he
hardly listened.[63] The allegations against himself were beastly;
but he could usually ignore allegations against himself and[64] he
imagined that if he said no more about them he would himself
hear no more.[65] And, if there were, in clubs and places where men
talk, unpleasant rumours as to himself he preferred it to be
thought that he was the rip, not his wife the strumpet.[66] That was
normal, male vanity: the preference of the English gentleman!
Had it been a matter of Sylvia spotless and himself as spotless as
he was—for in all these things he knew himself to be spotless!—
he would certainly have defended himself, at least, to the
General. But[67] he had acted practically in not defending himself[68]
more vigorously. For he imagined that, had he really tried, he
could have made the General believe him. But he had behaved
rightly! It was not mere vanity. There was the child up at his sister
Effie's. It was better for a boy to have a rip of a father than a whore
for mother![69]

The General was expatiating on the solidity of a squat castle,
like a pile of draughts, away to the left, in the sun, on the flat-
ness. He was saying that we didn't build like that nowadays.

Tietjens said:

"You're perfectly wrong, General. All the castles that Henry

---

* The general and his brother-in-law, like Tietjens, are Tories. The 'other side' is
  Asquith's Liberal government.

VIII[70] built in 1543 along this coast are mere monuments of jerry-building.... 'In 1543 *jactat castra Delis, Sandgatto, Reia, Hastingas Henricus Rex*' ... That means he chucked them down ..."*

The General laughed:

"You are an incorrigible fellow.... If ever there's any known, certain fact ..."

"But go and *look* at the beastly things," Tietjens said. "You'll see they've got just a facing of Caen stone that he tide-floated[71] here, and the fillings-up are just rubble, any rubbish.... Look here! It's a known certain fact, isn't it, that your eighteen-pounders are better than the French seventy-fives. They tell us so in the House, on the hustings, in the papers: the public believes it.... But would you put one of your tin-pot[72] things firing—what is it?—four shells a minute?—with the little bent pins in their tails to stop the recoil—against their seventy-fives with the compressed-air cylinders...."

The General sat stiffly upon his cushions:

"That's different," he said. "How the devil do you get to know these things?"

"It isn't different," Tietjens said, "it's the same muddle-headed frame of mind that sees good building in Henry VIII[73] as lets us into wars with hopelessly antiquated field guns and rottenly inferior ammunition. You'd fire any fellow on your staff who said we could stand up for a minute against the French."

"Well, anyhow," the General said, "I thank heaven you're not on my staff for you'd talk my hind leg off in a week. It's perfectly true that the public ..."

But Tietjens was not listening.[74] He was considering that it was natural for an unborn† fellow like Sandbach to betray the solidarity that should exist between men. And it was natural for a childless woman like Lady Claudine Sandbach, with a notoriously, a flagrantly unfaithful husband to believe in the unfaithfulness of the husbands of other women!

The General was saying:

---

* 'In 1543 King Henry built the castles of Deal, Sandwich, Rye, and Hastings' (the Latin verb *jacere* also means 'to throw'). Cf. *Cinque Ports* 44 on William the Conqueror's castle at Hastings, which 'in comparison with Henry VIII's castle at Camber[,] ... seems jerry-built'.

† See note on 16.

"Who did you hear that stuff from about the French field gun?"
Tietjens said:

"From you. Three weeks ago!"

And all the other society women[75] with unfaithful
husbands.... They must do their best to down and out a man.
They would cut him off their visiting lists! Let them. The barren
harlots mated to faithless eunuchs! ... Suddenly he thought that
he didn't know for certain that he was the father of his child and
he groaned.

"Well, what have I said wrong now?" the General asked.
"Surely you don't maintain that pheasants do eat mangolds...."

Tietjen proved his reputation for sanity with:

"No! I was just groaning at the thought of[76] the Chancellor!
That's sound enough for you, isn't it?" But it gave him a nasty
turn. He hadn't been able to pigeon-hole and padlock his
disagreeable reflections. He had been as good as talking to
himself....[77]

In the bow-window of another hostelry than his own he
caught the eye of Mr. Waterhouse, who was looking at the view
over the marshes. The great man beckoned to him and he went
in. Mr. Waterhouse was anxious[78] that Tietjens—whom he
assumed to be a man of sense—should get any pursuit of the two
girls stopped off. He couldn't move in the matter himself, but[79] a
five pound note and possibly a police promotion or so might be
handed round if no advertisement were given to the mad women
on account of their raid of that afternoon.

It was not a very difficult matter: for where the great man was
to be found in the club lounge, there, in the bar, the mayor, the
town clerk, the local head of the police, the doctors and solicitors would be found drinking together. And after it was arranged
the great man himself came into the bar, had a drink and pleased
them all immensely by his affability....

Tietjens himself, dining alone with the Minister to whom he
wanted to talk about his Labour Finance Act,* didn't find him a
disagreeable fellow: not really foolish, not sly except in his

---

*   The Liberals applied minimum wages to the 'sweated trades' and passed the redistrib-
    utive 'people's budget' in 1909; they went on to introduce labour exchanges and pass
    the National Insurance Act of 1911.

humour, tired obviously, but livening up after a couple of whiskies, and certainly not as yet plutocratic; with tastes for apple-pie and cream[80] of a fourteen-year-old boy. And, even as regards his famous Act, which was then shaking the country to its political foundations, once you accepted its fundamental unsuitedness to the temperament and needs of the English working-class, you could see that Mr. Waterhouse didn't want to be dishonest. He accepted with[81] gratitude several of Tietjens' emendations in the actuarial schedules. . . . And over their port they agreed on two fundamental legislative ideals: every working man to have a minimum of four hundred a year and every beastly manufacturer who wanted to pay less to be hung.* That, it appeared, was the High Toryism of Tietjens as it was the extreme Radicalism of the extreme Left of the Left. . . .

And Tietjens, who hated no man, in face of this simple-minded and agreeable schoolboy type of fellow, fell to wondering why it was that humanity that was next to always agreeable in its units was, as a mass, a phenomenon so hideous. You took[82] a dozen men, each of them not by any means detestable and not uninteresting: for each of them would have technical details of their affairs to impart: you formed them into a Government or a club, and at once, with oppressions, inaccuracies, gossip, back-biting, lying, corruptions and vileness, you had the combination of wolf, tiger, weasel and louse-covered ape that was human society. And he remembered the words of some Russian:[83] "Cats and monkeys. Monkeys and cats. All humanity is there."†

Tietjens and Mr. Waterhouse spent the rest of the evening together.

Whilst Tietjens was interviewing the policeman, the Minister sat on the front steps of the cottage and smoked cheap cigarettes, and when Tietjens went to bed Mr. Waterhouse insisted on sending by him kindly messages to Miss Wannop, asking her to come and discuss female suffrage any afternoon she liked in his

---

* In *People* 83 (*England* 277) Ford writes of 'the true Toryism which is Socialism'; and in *Return* 64, he gives the 'Tory view' that every workman should be 'assured of four hundred a year' as his own.
† See Henry James, 'The Madonna of the Future' (1873), which repeats the sentence: 'Cats and monkeys, monkeys and cats; all human life is there!': *The Tales of Henry James*, ed. Maqbool Aziz, vol. II (Oxford: Clarendon Press, 1978), 202–32 (226, 232).

private room at the House of Commons. Mr. Waterhouse flatly
refused to believe that Tietjens hadn't arranged the raid with
Miss Wannop. He said it had been too neatly planned for any
woman, and he said Tietjens was a lucky fellow, for she was a
ripping girl.

Back in his room under the rafters, Tietjens fell, nevertheless,
at once a prey to real agitation. For a long time he pounded from
wall to wall and, since he could not shake off the train of thought,
he got out at last his patience cards, and devoted himself seriously
to thinking out the conditions of his life with Sylvia. He wanted
to stop scandal if he could; he wanted them to live within his
income, he wanted to subtract that child from the influence of
its mother. These were all definite but difficult things. . . . Then
one half of his mind lost itself in the rearrangement of schedules,
and on his brilliant table his hands set queens on kings and
checked their recurrences.

In that way the sudden entrance of Macmaster gave him a
really terrible physical shock. He nearly vomited: his brain reeled
and the room fell about. He drank a great quantity of whisky in
front of Macmaster's goggling eyes; but even at that he couldn't
talk, and he dropped into his bed faintly aware of his friend's
efforts to loosen his clothes. He had, he knew, carried the
suppression of thought in his conscious mind so far that his
unconscious self had taken command and had, for the time, paral-
ysed both his body and his mind.[84]

# V

"It doesn't seem quite fair, Valentine," Mrs. Duchemin said. She was rearranging in a glass bowl some minute flowers that floated on water. They made there, on the breakfast-table, a patch, as it were, of mosaic amongst silver chafing dishes, silver épergnes piled with peaches in pyramids, and great silver rose-bowls filled with roses, that drooped to the damask cloth, a congeries of silver largenesses made as if a fortification for the head of the table; two huge silver urns, a great silver kettle on a tripod and a couple of silver vases filled with the extremely tall blue spikes of delphiniums that, spreading out, made as if a fan. The eighteenth century room was very tall and long; panelled in darkish wood. In the centre of each of four of the panels, facing the light, hung pictures, a mellowed orange in tone, representing mists and the cordage of ships in mists at sunrise. On the bottom of each large gold frame was a tablet bearing the ascription: "J. M. W. Turner." The chairs, arranged along the long table that was set for eight people, had the delicate, spidery, mahogany backs of Chippendale; on the golden mahogany sideboard that had behind it green silk curtains on a brass-rail were displayed an immense, crumbed ham, more peaches on an épergne, a large meat-pie with a varnished crust, another épergne that supported the large pale globes of grape-fruit; a galantine, a cube of inlaid meats, encased in thick jelly.

"Oh, women have to back each other up in these days," Valentine Wannop said. "I couldn't let you go through this alone after breakfasting with you every Saturday since I don't know when."

"I do feel," Mrs. Duchemin said, "immensely grateful to you for your moral support. I ought not, perhaps, to have risked this morning. But I've told Parry to keep him out till 10.15."

"It's, at any rate, tremendously sporting of you," the girl said. "I think it was worth trying."

Mrs. Duchemin, wavering round the table, slightly changed the position of the delphiniums.

"I think they make a good screen," Mrs. Duchemin said.

"Oh, nobody will be able to see him," the girl answered reassuringly. She added with a sudden resolution, "Look here, Edie. Stop worrying about my mind. If you think that anything I hear at your table after nine months as an ash-cat* at Ealing, with three men in the house, an invalid wife and a drunken cook, can corrupt my mind, you're simply mistaken. You can let your conscience be at rest, and let's say no more about it."

Mrs. Duchemin said, "Oh, Valentine! How could your mother let you?"

"She didn't know," the girl said. "She was out of her mind for grief. She sat for most of the whole nine months with her hands folded before her in a board and lodging house at twenty-five shillings a week, and it took the five shillings a week that I earned to make up the money." She added, "Gilbert had to be kept at school[1] of course. And in the holidays, too."

"I don't understand!" Mrs. Duchemin said. "I simply don't understand."

"Of course you wouldn't," the girl answered. "You're like the kindly people who subscribed at the sale to buy my father's library back and present it to my mother. That cost us five shillings a week for warehousing, and at Ealing they were always nagging at me for the state of my print dresses...."

She broke off and said:[2]

"Let's not talk about it any more if you don't mind. You have me in your house, so I suppose you've a right to references, as the mistresses call them. But you've been very good to me and never asked. Still, it's come up; do you know I told a man on the links yesterday that I'd been a slavey for nine months.[3] I was trying to explain why I was a suffragette; and, as I was asking him a favour, I suppose I felt I needed to give *him* references too."

Mrs. Duchemin, beginning to advance towards the girl impulsively, exclaimed:

"You darling!"

Miss Wannop said:

---

* Clearly meant as 'slavey', though Eric Partridge and Paul Beale, *A Dictionary of Slang* (London: Routledge, 2002) give: 'A fireman in the M[erchant] N[avy]: nautical; esp. R[oyal] N[avy]: late C.19–20.'

"Wait a minute. I haven't finished. I want to say this: I never talk about that stage of my career because I'm ashamed of it. I'm ashamed because I think I did the wrong thing, not for any other reason. I did it on impulse and I stuck to it out of obstinacy. I mean it would probably have been more sensible to go round with the hat to benevolent people, for the keep of mother and to complete my education. But if we've inherited the Wannop ill-luck, we've inherited the Wannop pride.[4] And I *couldn't* do it. Besides I was only seventeen, and I gave out we were going into the country after the sale. I'm not educated at all, as you know, or only half, because father, being a brilliant man, had ideas. And one of them was that I was to be an athlete,[5] not a classical don at Cambridge, or I might have been, I believe. I don't know why he had that tic[6] ... But I'd like you to understand two things. One I've said already: what I hear in this house won't ever shock or corrupt me;[7] that it's said in Latin is neither here nor there. I understand Latin almost as well as English because father used to talk it to me and Gilbert as soon as we talked at all.[8*] ... And, oh yes: I'm a suffragette because I've been a slavey. But I'd like you to understand that, though I was a slavey and am a suffragette—you're an old-fashioned woman and queer things are thought about these two things—then I'd like you to understand that in spite of it all I'm pure! Chaste, you know.... Perfectly virtuous."[9]

Mrs. Duchemin said:

"Oh, Valentine! Did you wear a cap and apron? You! In a cap and apron."

Miss Wannop replied:

"Yes! I wore a cap and apron and sniffled 'M'm' to the mistress; and slept under the stairs, too.[10] Because I would not sleep with the beast of a cook."

Mrs. Duchemin now ran forward and catching Miss Wannop by both hands kissed her first on the left and then on the right cheek.

"Oh, Valentine," she said, "you're a heroine. And you only twenty-two![11] ... Isn't that the motor coming?"

---

*   Cf. Ford's *The Fifth Queen* (London: Alston Rivers, 1906), 64: Katherine: 'I was brought up in the Latin tongue or ever I had the English.'

But it wasn't the motor coming and Miss Wannop said:

"Oh, no! I'm not a heroine. When I tried to speak to that Minister yesterday, I just couldn't. It was Gertie who went for him. As for me, I just hopped from one leg to the other and stuttered: 'V ... V ... Votes for W .. W ... W ... omen!' ... If I'd been decently brave I shouldn't have been too shy to speak to a strange man.... For that was what it really came to."

"But that surely," Mrs. Duchemin said—she continued to hold both the girl's hands—"makes you all the braver.... It's the person who does the thing he's afraid of who's the real hero, isn't it?"

"Oh, we used to argue that old thing over with father when we were ten. You can't tell. You've got to define the term brave. I was just abject.... I could harangue the whole crowd when I got them together. But speak to one man in cold blood I couldn't.... Of course I *did* speak to a fat golfing idiot with bulging eyes, to get him to save Gertie. But that was different."

Mrs. Duchemin moved both the girl's hands up and down in her own.

"As you know, Valentine," she said, "I'm an old-fashioned woman. I believe that woman's true place is at her husband's side. At the same time ..."

Miss Wannop moved away.

"Now, don't, Edie, don't!" she said. "If you believe that, you're an anti.[12]* Don't run with the hare and hunt with the hounds. It's your defect really.... I tell you I'm *not* a heroine. I *dread* prison: I *hate* rows. I'm thankful to goodness that it's my duty to stop and housemaid-typewrite for mother, so that I can't really *do* things.... Look at that miserable, adenoidy little Gertie, hiding upstairs in our garret. She was crying all last night—but that's just nerves. Yet she's been in prison five times, stomach-pumped and all. Not a moment of funk about her! ... But as for me, a girl as hard as a rock that prison wouldn't touch.... Why, I'm all of a jump now. That's why I'm talking nonsense like a pert schoolgirl. I just dread that every sound may be the police coming for me."

Mrs. Duchemin stroked the girl's fair hair and tucked a loose strand behind her ear.

---

*   i.e. an anti-Suffragette.

"I wish you'd let me show you how to do your hair," she said. "The right man might come along at any moment."

"Oh, the right man!" Miss Wannop said. "Thanks for tactfully changing the subject. The right man for me, when he comes along, will be a married man. That's the Wannop luck!"

Mrs. Duchemin said, with deep concern:

"Don't talk like that. . . . Why should you regard yourself as being less lucky than other people? Surely your mother's done well. She has a position; she makes money. . . ."

"Ah, but mother isn't a Wannop," the girl said, "only by marriage. The real Wannops . . . they've been executed, and attaindered, and falsely accused and killed in carriage accidents and married adventurers or died penniless like father. Ever since the dawn of history. And then, mother's got her mascot . . ."

"Oh, what's that?" Mrs. Duchemin asked, almost with animation, "a relic . . ."

"Don't you know mother's mascot?" the girl asked. "She tells everybody. . . . Don't you know the story of the man with the champagne? How mother was sitting contemplating suicide in her bed-sitting-room and there came in a man with a name like Tea-tray; she always calls him the mascot and asks us to remember him as such in our prayers. . . . He was a man who'd been at a German university with father years before and loved him very dearly, but had not kept touch with him. And he'd been out of England for nine months when father died and round about it. And he said: 'Now, Mrs. Wannop, what's this?' And she told him. And he said, 'What you want is champagne!' And he sent the slavey out with a sovereign for a bottle of Veuve Clicquot.[13] And he broke the neck of the bottle off against the mantelpiece because they were slow in bringing an opener.* And he stood over her while she drank half the bottle out of her tooth-glass. And he took her out to lunch . . . o . . . o . . . oh, it's cold! . . . And lectured her . . . And got her a job to write leaders on a paper he had shares in . . ."

Mrs. Duchemin said:

"You're shivering!"

---

* Various tools for opening champagne bottles were available: knives, wire-cutters, and corkscrews with integral taps that enabled the bottle to function like a soda siphon.

"I know I am," the girl said. She went on very fast. "And of course, mother always *wrote* father's articles for him. He found the ideas, but couldn't write, and she's a splendid style.... And, since then, he—the mascot—Tea-tray—has always turned up when she's been in tight places. Then[14] the paper blew her up and threatened to dismiss her for inaccuracies! She's frightfully inaccurate. And he wrote her out a table of things every leader writer must know, such as that 'A. Ebor' is the Archbishop of York, and that the Government is Liberal. And one day he turned up and said: 'Why don't you write a novel on that story you told me?' And he lent her the money to buy the cottage we're in now to be quiet and write in ... Oh, I can't go on!"

Miss Wannop burst into tears.

"It's thinking of those beastly days," she said. "And that beastly, *beastly* yesterday!" She ran the knuckles of both her hands fiercely into her eyes, and determinedly eluded Mrs. Duchemin's handkerchief and embraces. She said almost contemptuously:

"A nice, considerate person I am. And you with this ordeal hanging over you! Do you suppose I don't appreciate all your silent heroism of the home, while we're marching about with flags and shouting? But it's just to stop women like you being tortured,[15] body and soul, week in, week out, that we ..."

Mrs. Duchemin had sat down on a chair near one of the windows; she had her handkerchief hiding her face.

"Why women in your position don't take lovers ..." the girl said hotly. "Or that women in your position *do* take lovers..."

Mrs. Duchemin looked up; in spite of its tears her white face had an air of serious dignity:

"Oh, *no*, Valentine," she said, using her deeper tones. "There's something beautiful, there's something *thrilling* about chastity. I'm not narrow-minded. Censorious![16] I don't *condemn!*\* But to preserve in word, thought and action a lifelong fidelity.... It's no mean achievement...."

"You mean like an egg and spoon race," Miss Wannop said.[17]

"It isn't," Mrs. Duchemin replied gently, "the way I should

---

\* In *John* 8.11 Jesus tells the woman taken in adultery: 'Neither do I condemn thee.' See 213 below.

have put it. Isn't the real symbol Atalanta, running fast and not[18] turning aside for the golden apple?* That always seemed to me the real[19] truth hidden in the beautiful old legend. . . . "

"I don't know," Miss Wannop said, "when I read what Ruskin says about it in the *Crown of Wild Olive*. Or no! It's the *Queen of the Air*.† That's his Greek rubbish, isn't it? I always think it seems like an egg-race in which the young woman didn't keep her eyes in the boat. But I suppose it comes to the same thing."

Mrs. Duchemin said:

"My *dear!* Not a word against John Ruskin in *this* house!"

Miss Wannop screamed.

An immense voice had shouted:

"This way! This way! . . . The ladies will be here!"

Of Mr. Duchemin's curates—he had three of them,[20] for he had three marshland parishes almost without stipend, so that no one but a very rich clergyman could have held them—it was observed that they were all very large men with the physiques rather of prize-fighters than of clergy. So that when by any chance at dusk, Mr. Duchemin, who himself was of exceptional stature, and his three assistants went together along a road the hearts of any malefactors whom in the mist they chanced to encounter went pit-a-pat.

Mr. Horsley—the number two—had in addition an enormous voice.[21] He shouted four or five words, interjected tee-hee, shouted four or five words more and again interjected tee-hee. He had enormous wrist-bones that protruded from his clerical cuffs, an enormous Adam's apple, a large, thin, close-cropped, colourless face like a skull, with very sunken eyes, and when he was once started speaking it was impossible to stop him,[22] because his own voice in his ears drowned every possible form of interruption.

---

* Atalanta said she would only marry a suitor who could win a running race against her; suitors who lost were put to death. Milanion (or Hippomenes) sought Venus' help, and the goddess gave him three golden apples which he rolled in front of Atalanta during their race, and thus won.

† Atalanta isn't mentioned in either book, but *The Queen of the Air* (1869) is about Greek myth (especially that of Athena); and Ruskin defines myth in words that Mrs Duchemin echoes here: 'in all the most beautiful and enduring myths, we shall find, not only a literal story of a real person, – not only a parallel imagery of moral principle, but an underlying worship of natural phenomena': *The Complete Works of John Ruskin*, ed. E. T. Cook and Alexander Wedderburn, vol. XIX (London: Allen, 1905), 300.

This morning, as an inmate of the house, introducing to the breakfast-room Messrs. Tietjens and Macmaster, who had driven up to the steps just as he was mounting them, he had a story to tell. The introduction was, therefore, not, as such, a success. . . . [23]

"A STATE OF SIEGE, LADIES! Tee-hee!" he alternately roared and giggled. "We're living in a regular state of siege. . . . What with . . ." It appeared that the night before, after dinner, Mr. Sandbach and rather more than half-a-dozen of the young bloods who had dined at Mountby,[24] had gone scouring the country lanes, mounted on motor bicycles and armed with loaded canes* . . . for suffragettes! Every woman they had come across in the darkness they had stopped, abused, threatened with their loaded canes and subjected to cross-examination. The country-side was up in arms.[25]

As a story this took, with the appropriate reflections and repetitions, a long time in telling, and[26] afforded Tietjens and Miss Wannop the opportunity of gazing at each other.[27] Miss Wannop was frankly afraid that this large, clumsy, unusual-looking man, now that he had found her again, might hand her over to the police whom she imagined to be searching for herself and her friend Gertie,[28] Miss Wilson, at that moment in bed, under the care, as she also imagined, of Mrs. Wannop. On the links he had seemed to her natural and in place; here, with his loosely hung clothes and immense hands, the white patch on the side of his rather cropped head and his marked,[29] rather shapeless features, he affected her queerly as being both in and out of place. He seemed to go with the ham, the meat-pie, the galantine and even at a pinch with the roses; but the Turner pictures, the æsthetic curtain and Mrs. Duchemin's flowing robes, amber and rose in the hair did not go with him at all. Even the Chippendale chairs hardly did. And she felt herself thinking oddly, beneath her perturbations[30] of a criminal and the voice of the Rev. Horsley that *his* Harris tweeds went all right with her skirt, and she was glad that she had on a clean, cream-coloured silk blouse, not a striped pink cotton.

She was right as to that.[31]

---

* Walking sticks weighted with lead at one end to make them effective combat weapons.

In every man there are two minds that work side by side,[32] the one checking the other; thus emotion stands against reason, intellect corrects passion and first impressions act just a little, but very little, before quick reflection. Yet first impressions have always a bias in their favour, and even quiet reflection has often a job to efface them.

The night before Tietjens had given several thoughts to this young woman. General Campion had assigned her to him as *maîtresse en titre*.[33]* He was said to have ruined himself, broken up his home and spent his wife's money on her. Those were lies. On the other hand they were not inherent impossibilities. Upon occasion and given the right woman, quite sound men have done such things. He might, heaven knows, himself be so caught. But that he should have ruined himself over an unnoticeable young female who had announced herself as having been a domestic servant, and wore a pink cotton blouse . . . that had seemed to go beyond the bounds of even the unreason of club gossip!

That was the strong, first impression! It was all very well for his surface mind to say that the girl was not by birth a tweeny maid; she was the daughter of Professor Wannop and she could jump! For[34] Tietjens held very strongly the theory that what finally separated the classes was that the upper could lift its feet from the ground whilst common people couldn't. . . . But the strong impression remained. Miss Wannop was a tweeny maid. Say a lady's help, by nature. She was[35] of good family, for the Wannops were first heard of at Birdlip in Gloucestershire in the year 1417—no doubt enriched after Agincourt. But even brilliant men of good family will now and then throw daughters who are lady helps by nature. That was one of the queernesses of heredity. . . . And, though Tietjens had even got as far as to realise that Miss Wannop must be a heroine who had sacrificed her young years to her mother's gifts, and no doubt to a brother at school—for he had guessed as far as that—even then Tietjens couldn't make her out as more than a lady help. Heroines are all very well; admirable, they may even be saints; but if they let themselves get careworn in face and go shabby. . . . Well, they must wait for the gold that shall be amply stored for them in

---

* Official or favourite mistress, as Louis XV's Madame de Pompadour.

heaven. On this earth you could hardly accept them as wives for men of your own set. Certainly you wouldn't spend your own wife's money on them. That was what it really came to.[36]

But, brightened up as he now suddenly saw her, with silk for the pink cotton, shining coiled hair for the white canvas hat, a charming young neck, good shoes beneath neat ankles, a healthy flush taking the place of yesterday's pallor of fear for her comrade; an obvious equal in the surroundings of quite good people; small, but well-shaped and healthy; immense blue eyes fixed without embarrassment on his own....

"By Jove ..." he said to himself: "It's true! What a jolly little mistress she'd make!"

He blamed Campion, Sandbach and the club gossips for the form the thought had taken. For the cruel, bitter and stupid pressure of the world has yet about it something selective; if it couples male and female in its inexorable rings of talk, it will be because there is something harmonious in the union. And there exists then the pressure of suggestion!

He took a look at Mrs. Duchemin and[37] considered her infinitely commonplace and probably a bore. He disliked her large-shouldered, many-yarded style of blue dress and considered that no woman should wear clouded amber, for which the proper function was the provision of cigarette holders for bounders. He looked back at Miss Wannop, and considered that she would make a good wife for Macmaster; Macmaster liked bouncing girls and this girl was quite lady enough.

He heard Miss Wannop shout against the gale to Mrs. Duchemin: "Do I sit beside the head of the table and pour out?"

Mrs. Duchemin answered:

"No! I've asked Miss Fox to pour out. She's nearly stone deaf." Miss Fox was the penniless sister of a curate deceased. "You're to amuse Mr. Tietjens."

Tietjens noticed that Mrs. Duchemin had an agreeable throat[38] voice; it penetrated the noises of Mr. Horsley as the missel-thrush's note a gale.* It was rather agreeable. He noticed that Miss Wannop made a little grimace.

---

*    William Morris, in 'Bellerephon at Argos' writes: 'Strange the sharp crying of the missel-thrush': *The Earthly Paradise: A Poem*, Part IV (London: F. S. Ellis, 1870), 124.

Mr. Horsley, like a megaphone addressing a crowd, was turning from side to side, addressing his hearers by rotation. At the moment he was bawling at Macmaster; it would be Tietjens' turn again in a moment to hear a description of the heart attacks of old Mrs. Hogben[39] at Nobeys. But Tietjens' turn did not come. . . .

A high-complexioned, round-cheeked, forty-fivish lady, with agreeable eyes, dressed rather well in the black of the not-very-lately widowed, entered the room with precipitation. She patted Mr. Horsley on his declamatory right arm and, since he went on talking, she caught him by the hand and shook it. She exclaimed in high, commanding tones:

"Which is Mr. Macmaster, the critic?" and then, in the dead lull to Tietjens: "Are you Mr. Macmaster, the critic? No! . . . Then *you* must be."

Her turning to Macmaster[40] and the extinction of her interest in himself had been one of the rudest things Tietjens had ever experienced, but it was an affair so strictly businesslike that he took it without any offence. She was remarking to Macmaster:

"Oh, Mr. Macmaster, my new book will be out on Thursday week," and she had begun to lead him towards a window at the other end of the room.

Miss Wannop said:[41]

"What have you done with Gertie?"

"Gertie!" Mrs. Wannop exclaimed with the surprise of one coming out of a dream. "Oh yes! She's fast asleep. She'll sleep till four. I told Hannah to give a look at her now and then."

Miss Wannop's hands fell open at her side.

"Oh, *mother!*" forced itself from her.

"Oh, yes," Mrs. Wannop said, "we'd agreed to tell old Hannah we didn't want her to-day. So we had!"[42] She said to Macmaster: "Old Hannah is our charwoman," wavered a little and then went on brightly:[43] "Of course it will be of use to you to hear about my new book. To you journalists a little bit of previous explanation . . ." and she dragged off Macmaster, who seemed to bleat faintly. . . .

That had come about because just as she had got into the dog-cart to be driven to the rectory—for she herself could not drive a horse—Miss Wannop had told her mother that there would be two men at breakfast, one whose name she didn't know; the other, a Mr. Macmaster, a celebrated critic. Mrs. Wannop had called up to her:

"A critic? Of what?" her whole sleepy being electrified.

"I don't know," her daughter had answered. "Books, I daresay." . . .

A second or so after, when the horse, a large black animal that wouldn't stand, had made twenty yards or so at several bounds, the handy man who drove had said:

"Yer mother's 'owlin' after yer." But Miss Wannop had answered that it didn't matter. She was confident that she had arranged for everything. She was to be back to get lunch; her mother was to give an occasional look at Gertie[44] Wilson in the garret; Hannah, the daily help, was to be told she could go for the day. It was of the highest importance that Hannah should not know that a completely strange young woman was asleep in the garret at eleven[45] in the morning. If she did, the news[46] would be all over the neighbourhood at once, and the police instantly down on them.

But Mrs. Wannop was a woman of business. If she heard of a reviewer within driving distance she called on him with eggs as a present.[47] The moment the daily help had arrived, she had set out and walked to the rectory. No consideration of danger from the police would have stopped her; besides, she had forgotten all about the police.[48]

Her arrival[49] worried Mrs. Duchemin a good deal, because she wished all her guests to be seated and the breakfast well begun before the entrance of her husband. And this was not easy.[50] Mrs. Wannop, who was uninvited, refused to be separated from Mr. Macmaster. Mr. Macmaster had told her that he never wrote reviews in the daily papers, only articles for the heavy quarterlies, and it had occurred to Mrs. Wannop that an article on her new book in one of the quarterlies was just what was needed. She was, therefore, engaged in telling Mr. Macmaster how to write about herself, and twice after Mrs. Duchemin had succeeded in shepherding Mr. Macmaster nearly to his seat, Mrs. Wannop had conducted him back to the embrasure of the window.[51] It was only by sitting herself firmly in her chair next to Macmaster that Mrs. Duchemin was able to retain for herself this all-essential, strategic position. And it was only by calling out:

"Mr. Horsley, *do* take Mrs. Wannop to the seat beside you and feed her," that Mrs. Duchemin got Mrs. Wannop out of Mr.[52] Duchemin's own seat at the head of the table, for Mrs. Wannop, having perceived this seat to be vacant and next to Mr. Macmaster, had pulled out the Chippendale armchair and had prepared to sit down in it. This could only have spelt disaster, for it would have meant turning Mrs. Duchemin's husband loose amongst the other guests.

Mr. Horsley, however, accomplished his duty of leading away this lady[53] with such firmness that Mrs. Wannop conceived of him as a very disagreeable and awkward person. Mr. Horsley's seat was next to Miss Fox, a grey spinster, who sat, as it were, within the fortification of silver urns and deftly occupied herself with the ivory taps of these machines. This seat, too, Mrs. Wannop tried to occupy, imagining that, by moving the silver vases that upheld the tall delphiniums, she would be able to get a diagonal view of Macmaster and so to shout to him. She found, however, that she couldn't, and so resigned herself to taking the chair that had been reserved for Miss Gertie Wilson,[54] who was to have been the eighth guest. Once there she sat in distracted gloom, occasionally saying to her daughter:

"I think it's very bad management. I think this party's very badly arranged." Mr. Horsley she hardly thanked for the sole that he placed before her; Tietjens she did not even look at.

Sitting beside Macmaster,[55] her eyes fixed on a small door in the corner of a panelled wall, Mrs. Duchemin became a prey to a sudden and overwhelming fit of apprehension. It forced her to say to her guest, though she had resolved to chance it and say nothing:

"It wasn't perhaps fair to ask you to come all this way. You may get nothing out of my husband. He's apt . . . especially on Saturdays. . . ."

She trailed off into indecision. It was possible that nothing might occur. On two Saturdays out of seven nothing *did* occur. Then an admission would be wasted; this sympathetic being would go out of her life with a knowledge that he needn't have had—to be a slur on her memory in his mind. . . . But then, overwhelmingly, there came over her the feeling that, if he knew of her sufferings,[56] he might feel impelled to remain and comfort her. She cast about for words with which to finish her sentence. But Macmaster said:

"Oh, dear lady!" (And it seemed to her to be charming to be addressed thus!) "One understands ... One is surely trained and adapted to understand ... that these great scholars, these abstracted cognoscenti ..."

Mrs. Duchemin breathed a great "Ah!" of relief. Macmaster had used the exactly right words.

"And," Macmaster was going on, "merely to spend a short hour; a swallow flight ... 'As when the swallow gliding from lofty portal to lofty portal!'* ... You know the lines ... in these, your perfect surroundings ..."

Blissful waves seemed to pass from him to her. It was in this way that men should speak; in that way—steel-blue tie, true-looking gold ring, steel-blue eyes beneath black brows!—that men should look. She was half-conscious of warmth; this suggested the bliss of falling asleep, truly, in perfect surroundings. The roses on the table were lovely;[57] their scent came to her.

A voice came to her:

"You *do* do the thing in style, I must say."

The large, clumsy but otherwise unnoticeable being that this fascinating man had brought in his train was[58] setting up pretensions to her notice. He had just placed before her a small blue china plate that contained a little black caviare and a round of lemon; a small Sèvres,[59] pinkish, delicate plate that held the pinkest peach in the room. She had said to him: "Oh ... a little caviare! A peach!" a long time before, with the vague under-feeling that the names of such comestibles must convey to her person a charm in the eyes of Caliban.[60]

She buckled about her her armour of charm; Tietjens was gazing with large, fishish eyes at the caviare before her.

"How do you get *that*, for instance?" he asked.[61]

---

* Possibly a version of Virgil, *Aeneid*, XII: 473–5: 'Nigra velut magnas domini cum divitis aedes / pervolat et pennis alta atria lustrat hirundo'; quoted in Letter XIX of Gilbert White's *Natural History of Selborne*; translated by Dryden as: 'As the black swallow near the palace plies; / O'er empty courts, and under arches, flies'. Or it may not be a genuine quotation, but an example of what Mrs Duchemin thinks of as Macmaster's 'kindredly running phrases—as if out of books she had read!'; 116 below.

"Oh!" she answered: "If it wasn't my husband's doing it would look like ostentation. I'd find it ostentatious for myself." She found a smile, radiant, yet muted. "He's trained Simpkins of New Bond Street. For a telephone message overnight special messengers go to Billingsgate at dawn for salmon, red mullet, this,[62] in ice, and great blocks of ice too. It's such pretty stuff . . . and then by seven the car goes to Ashford Junction. . . . All the same, it's difficult to give a breakfast before ten."

She didn't want to waste her careful sentences[63] on this grey fellow;[64] she couldn't, however, turn back, as she yearned to do, to the kindredly running phrases—as if out of books she had read!—of the smaller man.

"Ah, but it isn't," Tietjens said, "ostentation. It's the great Tradition. You mustn't ever forget that your husband's Breakfast Duchemin of Magdalen."

He seemed to be gazing, inscrutably, deep into her eyes. But no doubt he meant to be agreeable.

"Sometimes I wish I could," she said. "He doesn't get anything out of it himself. He's ascetic to unreasonableness. On Fridays he eats nothing at all. It makes me quite anxious ... for Saturdays."

Tietjens said:

"I know."

She exclaimed—and almost with sharpness:

"You *know!*"

He continued to gaze straight into her eyes:

"Oh, of course one knows all about Breakfast Duchemin!" he said. "He was one of Ruskin's road-builders. He was said to be the most Ruskin-like of them all!"[*]

Mrs. Duchemin cried out: "Oh!" Fragments of the worst stories that in his worst moods her husband[65] had told her of his old preceptor went through her mind. She imagined that the shameful parts of her intimate life must be known to this nebulous monster. For Tietjens, turned sideways and facing her, had

---

[*] In 1874 John Ruskin had organised some of his students to help repair the road of the Oxfordshire village of Ferry Hinksey. Those who helped with the digging included Oscar Wilde, the politician Alfred – later Viscount – Milner, and the historian Arnold Toynbee. Ruskin suffered from mental illness in later life. Ford wrote in *Mightier* 267: 'Mr. Ruskin went really mad in the effort to be as moral as the *John Ruskin* of the *Stones of Venice*'; thus Duchemin is 'Ruskin-like' in his insanity too.

seemed to grow monstrous,[66] and as if with undefined outlines. He was the male, threatening, clumsily odious and external! She felt herself say to herself: "I will do you an injury, if ever ..."[67] For already she had felt herself swaying the preferences, the thoughts and the future of the man on her other side.[68] He was the male, tender, in-fitting; the complement of the harmony, the meat for consumption, like the sweet pulp of figs. . . . It was inevitable; it was essential to the nature of her relationship with her husband that Mrs. Duchemin should have these feelings. . . .[69]

She heard, almost without emotion, so great was her disturbance, from behind her back the dreaded, high, rasping tones:

"*Post coitum tristia!*[70]* Ha! Ha! That's what it is?" The voice repeated the words and added sardonically: "You know what *that* means?"[71] But the problem of her husband had become secondary; the real problem was: "What was this monstrous and hateful man going to say of her to his friend, when, for long hours, they were away?"

He was still gazing into her eyes. He said nonchalantly, rather low.

"I wouldn't look round if I were you. Vincent Macmaster is quite up to dealing with the situation."

His voice had the familiarity[72] of an elder brother's. And at once Mrs. Duchemin knew—that *he* knew that[73] already close ties were developing between herself and Macmaster. He was speaking as a man speaks in emergencies to the mistress of his dearest friend. He was then one of those formidable and to be feared males who possess the gift of right intuitions. . . .

Tietjens said: "You heard!"

To the gloating, cruel tones that had asked:[74]

"You know what *that*[75] means?" Macmaster had answered clearly, but with the snappy intonation of a reproving Don:

---

* Alludes to the Latin tag 'post coitum omne animal triste' – every animal is sad after sex. Variously attributed to Aristotle, Galen, Horace, and Petronius, though not by the *Oxford Dictionary of Quotations*, which calls it post-classical and offers it as anonymous. 'Tristia' might be Duchemin's (or Ford's) mistake, or it might allude to Ovid's *Tristia* – the poems written from exile, described by Ford as 'sad things in which without avail he prayed for his recall': *March* 243. Ford had written his own 'Tristia' sequence of poems, probably during the war, though he left them unpublished: see Harvey, *Bibliography* 123.

"Of course I know what it means. It's no discovery!" That was exactly the right note. Tietjens—and Mrs. Duchemin too— could hear Mr. Duchemin, invisible behind his rampart of blue spikes and silver, give the answering snuffle of a reproved schoolboy. A hard-faced, small man, in grey tweed that buttoned, collar-like, tight round his throat, standing behind the invisible chair, gazed straight forward into infinity.

Tietjens said to himself:

"By God! Parry! the Bermondsey light middle-weight! He's there to carry Duchemin off if he becomes violent!"[76]

During the quick look that Tietjens took round the table Mrs. Duchemin gave, sinking lower in her chair, a short gasp of utter relief. Whatever Macmaster was going to think of her, he thought now. He knew the worst![77] It was[78] settled, for good or ill. In a minute she would look round at him.

Tietjens said:[79]

"It's all right, Macmaster will be splendid. We had a friend up at Cambridge with your husband's[80] tendencies, and Macmaster could get him through *any* social occasion. . . . Besides, we're all gentlefolk here!"

He had seen the Rev. Horsley and Mrs. Wannop both interested in their plates. Of Miss Wannop he was not so certain. He had caught, bent obviously on himself, from large, blue eyes, a glance that was evidently appealing. He said to himself: "She must be in the secret. She's appealing to me not to show emotion and upset the applecart! It is a shame that she should be here: a girl!" and into his answering glance he threw the message: "It's all right as far as this end of the table is concerned."

But Mrs. Duchemin had felt come into herself a little stiffening of morale.[81] Macmaster by now knew the worst; Duchemin was quoting snufflingly[82] to him the hot licentiousness of the *Trimalchion*[83]* of Petronius; snuffling[84] into Macmaster's ear. She

* The long account of Trimalchio's feast and its drunken aftermath from Petronius Arbiter's *Satyricon*. Chapters 26–78 are usually referred to as the *Cena Trimalchionis* (or 'Trimalchio's Feast'). Some nineteenth-century editions published a selection under this title. Ford mentions a German example in *When Blood is Their Argument* (London: Hodder & Stoughton, 1915), xiii. 'Trimalchion' is the French form for Trimalchio, but here appears to be a conflation of this character's name with the name of the work. However, the quotation, which Macmaster confidently attributes to Petronius, does not appear in the *Satyricon* (nor, apparently, anywhere else). The

caught the phrase: *Festinamus, puer callide.*[85]* ... Duchemin, holding her wrist with the painful force of the maniac, had translated it to her over and over again.... No doubt, that too, this hateful man beside her would have guessed![86]

She said: "Of course we should be all gentlefolk here.[87] One naturally arranges that...."

Tietjens began to say:

"Ah! But it isn't easy to arrange nowadays. All sorts of bounders[88] get into all sorts of holies of holies!"

Mrs. Duchemin turned her back on him right in the middle of his sentence. She devoured Macmaster's face with her eyes, in an infinite sense of calm.

Macmaster four minutes before[89] had been the only one to see the entrance, from a small panelled door that had behind it another of green baize, of the Rev. Mr. Duchemin, and following him a man whom Macmaster, too, recognised at once as Parry, the ex-prize-fighter. It flashed through his mind at once that this was an extraordinary conjunction. It flashed through his mind, too, that it was extraordinary that anyone so ecstatically handsome as Mrs. Duchemin's husband should not have earned high preferment in a church always hungry for male beauty. Mr. Duchemin was extremely tall, with a slight stoop of the proper clerical type. His face was of alabaster; his grey hair, parted in the middle, fell brilliantly on his high brows; his glance was quick,

---

nearest thing in the *Satyricon* is perhaps 'the celebrated song' about homosexual passion Ford had quoted in his discussion of the *Satyricon* in *When Blood* 298–300 (299): 'Qualis nox fuit illa, di deaeque, / quam mollis torus! Haesimus calentes / et transfudimus hinc et hinc labellis / errantes animas. Valete curae / mortales.' ('What a night that was, gods and goddesses, / how soft the bed. We clung, hotly, and each to each transfused with our lips / our wandering souls. Farewell, mortal cares'). Yet only two or three years before writing *Some Do Not* ..., in *Thus to Revisit* 191, Ford had been able to quote impeccably from the work the index identifies correctly (though in an unusual spelling) as the *Satyrikon* (from Ch. 79). Thus, as so often in Ford's work, such errors may be attributable to the characters (Duchemin's madness – he might be confused, or wilfully inventing salacious passages to torment his wife) or the tenuousness of their impressions (in her distraction, the phrase Mrs Duchemin 'caught' she may have misheard) rather than the author.

* This phrase does not appear in the *Satyricon*; a literal translation of the Latin as it appears here would be 'Let us hurry, crafty boy'; or 'warm boy', if Ford had meant 'calide', as the discussion on 123 implies.

penetrating, austere; his nose very hooked and chiselled. He was the exact man to adorn a lofty and gorgeous fane, as Mrs. Duchemin was the exact woman to consecrate an episcopal drawing-room. With his great wealth, scholarship and tradition. . . . "Why then," went through Macmaster's mind in a swift pin-prick of suspicion, "isn't he at least a dean?"

Mr. Duchemin had walked swiftly to his chair which Parry, as swiftly walking behind him, drew out. His master slipped into it with a graceful, sideways motion. He shook his head at grey Miss Fox who had moved a hand[90] towards an ivory urn-tap. There was a glass of water beside his plate, and round it his long, very white fingers closed. He stole a quick glance at Macmaster, and then looked at him steadily with laughingly glittering eyes. He said: "Good morning, doctor," and then, drowning Macmaster's quiet protest: "Yes! Yes! The stethoscope meticulously packed into the top-hat and the shining hat left in the hall."

The prize-fighter, in tight box-cloth leggings, tight whipcord breeches, and a short tight jacket that buttoned up at the collar to his chin—the exact stud-groom of a man of property, gave a quick glance of recognition to Macmaster and then to Mr. Duchemin's back another quick look, raising his eyebrows. Macmaster, who knew him very well because he had given Tietjens boxing lessons at Cambridge, could almost hear him say: "A queer change this, sir! Keep your eyes on him a second!" and, with the quick, light tip-toe of the pugilist he slipped away to the sideboard. Macmaster stole a quick glance on his own account at Mrs. Duchemin. She had her back to him, being deep in conversation with Tietjens.[91] His heart jumped a little when, looking back again, he saw Mr. Duchemin half raised to his feet, peering round the fortifications of silver. But he sank down again in his chair, and surveying Macmaster with an expression of cunning singular on his ascetic features, exclaimed:

"And your friend? Another medical man! All with stethoscope complete. It takes, of course, two medical men to certify . . ."*

He stopped and with an expression of sudden, distorted rage,

---

* Ford's early novel *The Benefactor* (London: Brown, Langham, 1905), 336 also features a mad clergyman, Mr Brede.

pushed aside the arm of Parry, who was sliding a plate of sole-fillets on to the table beneath his nose.

"Take away," he was beginning to exclaim thunderously, "these conducements to the filthy lusts of . . ." But with another cunning and apprehensive look at Macmaster, he said: "Yes! yes! Parry! That's right. Yes! Sole! A touch of kidney to follow. Another! Yes! Grape-fruit! With sherry!" He had adopted an old Oxford voice, spread his napkin over his knees and hastily placed in his mouth a morsel of fish.

Macmaster with a patient and distinct intonation said that he must be permitted to introduce himself. He was Macmaster, Mr. Duchemin's correspondent on the subject of his little mono-graph. Mr. Duchemin looked at him, hard, with an awakened attention that gradually lost suspicion and became gloatingly joyful:

"Ah, yes, Macmaster!" he said. "Macmaster. A budding critic. A little of a hedonist, perhaps? And yes . . . you wired that you were coming. Two friends! Not medical men! Friends!" He moved his face closer to Macmaster and said:

"How tired you look! Worn! Worn!"

Macmaster was about to say that he was rather hard-worked when, in a harsh, high cackle close to his face there came the Latin words[92] Mrs. Duchemin—and Tietjens!—had heard. He knew then what he was up against. He took another look at the prize-fighter; moved his head to one side to catch a momentary view of the gigantic Mr. Horsley, whose size took on a new meaning. Then he settled down in his chair and ate a kidney. The physical force present was no doubt enough to suppress Mr. Duchemin should he become violent.[93] And trained! It was one of the curious, minor coincidences of life that, at Cambridge, he had once thought of hiring this very Parry to follow round his dear friend Sim.[94] Sim, the most brilliant of sardonic ironists, sane, decent, and ordinarily a little prudish on the surface, had been subject to just such temporary lapses as Mr. Duchemin. On society occasions he would stand up and shout or sit down and whisper the most unthinkable indecencies. Macmaster, who had loved him very much, had run round with Sim as often as he could, and had thus gained skill in dealing with these manifesta-tions. . . . He felt suddenly a certain pleasure! He thought he might gain prestige[95] in the eyes of Mrs. Duchemin if he dealt quietly and efficiently with this situation. It might even lead to an[96] intimacy. He asked nothing better!

He knew that Mrs. Duchemin had turned towards him: he could feel her listening and observing him; it was as if her glance was warm on his cheek. But he did not look round; he had to keep his eyes on the gloating face of her husband. Mr. Duchemin was quoting Petronius, leaning towards his guest. Macmaster consumed kidneys stiffly.

He said:

"That isn't the amended version of the iambics. Wilamowitz-Möllendorff that we used . . . "[97]*

To interrupt him Mr. Duchemin put his thin hand courteously on Macmaster's arm. It had a great cornelian seal set in red gold on the third finger. He went on, reciting in ecstasy; his head a little on one side as if he were listening to invisible choristers. Macmaster really disliked the Oxford intonation of Latin. He looked for a short moment at Mrs. Duchemin; her eyes were upon him; large, shadowy, full of gratitude. He saw, too, that they were welling over with wetness.

He looked quickly[98] back at Duchemin. And suddenly it came to him; she was suffering! She was probably suffering intensely. It had not occurred to him that she would suffer—partly because he was without nerves himself,[99] partly because he had conceived of Mrs. Duchemin as firstly feeling[100] admiration for himself. Now it seemed to him abominable that she should suffer.

Mrs. Duchemin was in an agony.[101] Macmaster had looked at her intently and looked away! She read into his glance contempt for her situation, and anger that he should have been placed in such a position.[102] In her pain she stretched out her hand and touched his arm.[103]

Macmaster was aware of her touch; his mind seemed filled with sweetness. But he kept his head obstinately averted. For her sake he did not dare to look away from the maniacal face. A crisis

---

\*  Ulrich von Wilamowitz-Moellendorff (1848–1931) was an influential professor of classical philology. The reference is probably to his *Commentariolum Metricum* (Göttingen, 1895). Ford criticises 'national self-consciousness' of his championing of German culture in *When Blood* xvi–xvii.

was coming. Mr. Duchemin had arrived at the English translation. He placed his hands on the table-cloth in preparation for
rising; he was going to stand on his feet and shout obscenities
wildly to the other guests. It was the exact moment.

Macmaster made his voice dry and penetrating to say:

"'Youth of tepid loves' is a lamentable rendering of *puer callide!*
It's lamentably antiquated . . . "

Duchemin chewed and said:

"What? What? What's that?"

"It's just like Oxford to use an eighteenth-century crib. I
suppose that's Whiston and Ditton?* Something like that . . . " He
observed Duchemin, brought out of his impulse, to be
wavering—as if he were coming awake in a strange place! He
added:

"Anyhow it's wretched schoolboy smut. Fifth form. Or not
even that. Have some galantine. I'm going to. Your sole's cold."

Mr. Duchemin looked down at his plate.

"Yes! Yes!" he muttered. "Yes! With sugar and vinegar sauce!"
The prize-fighter slipped away to the sideboard, an admirable
quiet fellow; as unobtrusive as a burying beetle. Macmaster said:

"You were about to tell me something for my little monograph. What became of Maggie . . . Maggie Simpson. The Scots
girl who was model for *Alla Finestra del Cielo?*†

Mr. Duchemin looked at Macmaster with sane, muddled,
rather exhausted eyes:

"*Alla Finestra!*" he exclaimed: "Oh yes! I've got the watercolour. I saw her sitting for it and bought it on the spot. . . . " He
looked again at his plate, started at sight of the galantine and
began to eat ravenously: "A beautiful girl!" he said. "Very long

---

* William Whiston, the former Lucasian Professor of Mathematics at Cambridge, and
  Humphrey Ditton, the mathematical master at Christ's Hospital, London, are best
  known today for petitioning parliament in 1714 to offer a reward for the discovery of
  longitude. They also published theological work, but were not classicists.
† See Pamela Bickley, 'Ford and Pre-Raphaelitism', in *Ford Madox Ford: A Reappraisal*,
  ed. Robert Hampson and Tony Davenport, International Ford Madox Ford Studies,
  1 (Amsterdam and New York: Rodopi, 2002), 70: 'This is, presumably, a reference to
  Rossetti's oil-painting *La Donna della Finestra* (1879) [. . .] the title (and medium) of
  the painting, the details here are slightly askew. Jane Morris was the model for
  Rossetti's painting, but the details Duchemin supplies – the model is now an old
  woman who has kept a number of pictures – fit better with Fanny Cornforth.'

necked ... She wasn't of course ... eh ... respectable! She's living yet, I think. Very old. I saw her two years ago. She had a lot of pictures. Relics of course! ... In the Whitechapel Road she lived.* She was naturally of that class. . . ." He went muttering on, his head over his plate. Macmaster considered that the fit was over. He was irresistibly impelled to turn to Mrs. Duchemin;[104] her face was rigid, stiff. He said swiftly:

"If he'll eat a little: get his stomach filled ... It calls the blood down from the head. . . ."

She said:

"Oh, forgive! It's dreadful for you! Myself I will never forgive!"

He said:

"No! No! ... Why it's what I'm *for!*"

A deep emotion brought her whole white face to life:

"Oh, you *good* man!" she said in her profound tones, and they remained gazing at each other.

Suddenly, from behind Macmaster's back Mr. Duchemin shouted:

"I say he made a settlement on her, *dum casta et sola,*[105†] of course. Whilst she remained chaste and alone!"

Mr. Duchemin, suddenly feeling the absence of the powerful will that had seemed to overweigh his own like a great force in the darkness, was on his feet, panting and delighted:

"Chaste!" he shouted. "Chaste, you observe! What a world of suggestion in the word ... "‡ He surveyed the opulent broadness of his tablecloth; it spread out before his eyes as if it had been a great expanse of meadow in which he could gallop, relaxing his limbs after long captivity. He shouted three obscene words and went on in his Oxford Movement voice: "But chastity ... "

Mrs. Wannop suddenly said:

"Oh!" and looked at her daughter, whose face grew slowly[106] crimson as she continued to peel a peach. Mrs. Wannop turned

* In London's traditionally working-class East End.
† The Latin phrase is used in divorce settlements when a man wants to terminate maintenance payments to an ex-wife should she re-marry.
‡ Cf. *Return* 241 on Walter Hines Page (of Doubleday Page) objecting to Ford using the sentence 'You will find a chaste whore as soon as that' in one of his historical novels. Ford suggests replacing the word 'whore' with a dash, but says Page replied: 'We certainly could not print the word "chaste". It is too suggestive.'

to Mr. Horsley beside her and said:

"You write, too, I believe, Mr. Horsley. No doubt something more learned than my poor readers would care for ..." Mr. Horsley had been preparing, according to his instructions from Mrs. Duchemin,[107] to shout a description of an article he had been writing about the *Mosella* of Ausonius,* but as he was slow in starting the lady got in first. She talked on serenely about the tastes of the large public. Tietjens leaned across to Miss Wannop and, holding in his right hand a half-peeled fig, said to her as loudly as he could:

"I've got a message for you[108] from Mr. Waterhouse. He says if you'll ..."

The completely deaf Miss Fox—who had had her training by writing—remarked diagonally to Mrs. Duchemin:

"I think we shall have thunder to-day. Have you remarked the number of minute insects...."

"When my revered preceptor," Mr. Duchemin thundered on "drove away in the carriage on his wedding day he said to his bride: 'We will live like blessed angels!'† How sublime! I, too, after my nuptials ..."

Mrs. Duchemin suddenly screamed:

"Oh ... *no!*"

As if checked for a moment in their stride all the others paused—for a breath. Then they continued talking with polite animation and listening with minute attention.[109] To Tietjens that seemed the highest achievement and justification of English manners!

Parry, the prize-fighter, had twice caught his master by the arm and shouted that breakfast was getting cold. He said now to Macmaster that he and the Rev. Horsley could get Mr. Duchemin away, but there'd be a hell of a fight. Macmaster whispered: "Wait!" and, turning to Mrs. Duchemin he said: "I can stop him. Shall I?" She said:

---

* The minor Latin author Decimus Magnus Ausonius (c. 310–95) was born in Gaul, and summoned by the emperor Valentinian to teach the heir apparent, Gratian. This poem describes the life and scenery along the river Moselle.
† Cf. *Mightier* 267: Ruskin 'told Mrs. Ruskin in the carriage when they drove away from the wedding service that they were going to live as God's blessed angels lived'.

"Yes! Yes! Anything!" He observed tears; isolated upon her cheeks, a thing he had never seen. With caution and with hot rage he whispered into the prize-fighter's hairy ear that was held down to him:

"Punch him in the kidney. With your thumb. As *hard* as you can without breaking your thumb . . ."

Mr. Duchemin had just declaimed:

"I, too, after my nuptials . . ." He began to wave his arms, pausing and looking from unlistening face to unlistening face.[110] Mrs. Duchemin had just screamed.

Mr. Duchemin thought that the arrow of God struck him.[111] He imagined himself an unworthy messenger. In such pain as he had never conceived of he fell into his chair and sat huddled up, a darkness covering his eyes.

"He won't get up again," Macmaster whispered to the appreciative pugilist. "He'll want to. But he'll be afraid to."

He said to Mrs. Duchemin:

"Dearest lady! It's all over. I assure you of that. It's a scientific nerve counter-irritant."

Mrs. Duchemin said:

"Forgive!"[112] with one deep sob: "You can never respect . . ." She felt her eyes explore his face as the wretch in a cell explores the face of his executioner for a sign of pardon. Her heart stayed still: her breath suspended itself. . . .

Then complete heaven began. Upon her left palm she felt cool fingers beneath the cloth. This man knew always the exact right action! Upon the fingers, cool, like spikenard and ambrosia, her fingers closed themselves.

In complete bliss, in a quiet room, his voice went on talking. At first with great neatness of phrase, but with what refinement! He explained that certain excesses being merely nervous cravings,[113] can be combatted if not, indeed, cured altogether, by the fear of, by the determination not to ensue,[114] sharp physical pain—which of course is a nervous matter, too! . . .

Parry, at a given moment, had said into his master's ear:

"It's time you prepared for your sermon for to-morrow, sir," and Mr. Duchemin had gone as quietly as he had arrived, gliding over the thick carpet to the small door.

Then Macmaster said to her:

"You come from Edinburgh? You'll know the Fifeshire coast then."

"Do I not?" she said. His hand remained in hers. He began to talk of the whins on the links and the sanderlings along the flats, with such a Scots voice and in phrases so vivid that she saw her childhood again, and had in her eyes a wetness of a happier order. She released his cool hand after a long gentle pressure.[115] But when it was gone it was as if much of her life went. She said: "You'll be knowing Kingussie House, just outside your town. It was there I spent my holidays as a child."

He answered:

"Maybe I played round it a barefoot lad and you in your grandeur within."

She said:

"Oh, no! Hardly! There would be the difference of our ages!* And . . . And indeed there are other things I will tell you."

She addressed herself to Tietjens, with all her heroic armour of charm buckled on again:

"Only think! I find Mr. Macmaster and I almost played together in our youths."

He looked at her, she knew, with a commiseration that she hated:

"Then you're an older friend than I," he said,[116] "though I've known him since I was fourteen, and I don't believe you could be a better. He's a good fellow. . . ."

She hated him for his condescension towards a better man and for his warning—she *knew* it was a warning—to her to spare his friend.

Mrs. Wannop[117] gave a distinct, but not an alarming scream. Mr. Horsley had been talking[118] to her about an unusual fish that used to inhabit the Moselle in Roman times. The *Mosella* of Ausonius, the subject of the essay he was writing, is mostly about fish. . . .[119]

"No," he shouted, "it's been said to be the roach. But there are

---

* Macmaster thinks of himself as 'near to thirty'; he is 'probably a little the senior in age' compared to Tietjens' twenty-six (and mathematician Tietjens' blankness 'as to his room-mate's years' suggests evasiveness on Macmaster's part). Macmaster thinks Mrs Duchemin 'couldn't be more than thirty'. The implication is that she is slightly older than Macmaster, or thinks she is, or he thinks she is.

no roach in the river now. '*Vannulis viridis, oculisque.*'[120]* No. It's
the other way round: *Red* fins ..."

Mrs. Wannop's scream and her wide gesture: her hand,
indeed, was nearly over his mouth and her trailing sleeve across
his plate!—were enough to interrupt him.

"*Tietjens!*" she again screamed. "Is it possible? ..."

She pushed her daughter out of her seat and, moving round
beside the young man, she overwhelmed him with vociferous
love. As Tietjens had turned to speak to Mrs. Duchemin she had
recognised his aquiline half-profile as exactly that of his father at
her own wedding-breakfast. To the table that knew it by heart—
though Tietjens himself didn't!—she recited the story of how his
father had saved her life, and was her mascot. And she offered the
son—for to the father she had never been allowed to make any
return—her horse,[121] her purse, her heart, her time, her all.† She
was so completely sincere that, as the party broke up, she just
nodded to Macmaster and, catching Tietjens forcibly by the arm,
said perfunctorily to the critic:

"Sorry I can't help you any more with the article. But my dear
Chrissie must have the books he wants. At once! This very minute!"

She moved off, Tietjens grappled to her, her daughter
following as a young swan follows its parents.[122] In her gracious
manner Mrs. Duchemin had received the thanks of her guests for
her wonderful breakfast and had hoped that now that they had
found their ways there.... [123]

The echoes of the dispersed festival seemed to whisper in the
room. Macmaster and Mrs. Duchemin faced each other, their
eyes wary—and longing.

He said:

"It's dreadful to have to go now. But I have an engagement."

---

* Latin; literally: 'With green fans, and eyes'. Only 'viridis' occurs in the *Mosella*, and
in different contexts. 'Vannulus' is a diminutive of 'vannus', a fan; possibly meant here
as a metaphor for delicate fins; or another sign of Horsley's unsure memory.

† Perhaps an allusion to the longer of William Cowper's two poems 'Retirement':

O'erwhelm'd at once with wonder, grief and joy,
He press'd him much to quit his base employ,
His countenance, his purse, his heart, his hand,
Influ'nce, and pow'r, were all at his command.

William Cowper, *Poems* (London: J. Johnson, 1782), 2 vols, I 258–98 (288).

She said:

"Yes! I know! With your great friends."

He answered:

"Oh, only with Mr. Waterhouse and General Campion ... and Mr. Sandbach, of course ..."

She had a moment of fierce pleasure at the thought that Tietjens was not to be of the company: *her* man would be outsoaring the vulgarian of his youth, of his past that she didn't know....[124] Almost harshly she exclaimed:

"I don't want you to be mistaken about Kingussie House. It was just a holiday school. Not a grand place."

"It was very costly," he said, and she seemed to waver on her feet.

"Yes! yes!" she said, nearly in a whisper. "But you're so grand now! I was only the child of very poor bodies. Johnstons of Midlothian. But very poor bodies.... I ... He bought me, you might say. You know.... Put me to very rich schools: when I was fourteen ... my people were glad.... But I think if my mother had known when I married ..." She writhed her whole body. "Oh, dreadful! dreadful!" she exclaimed. "I want you to know ..."

His hands were shaking as if he had been in a jolting cart....

Their lips met in a passion of pity and tears. He removed his mouth to say: "I must see you this evening.... I shall be mad with anxiety about you." She whispered: "Yes! yes! ... In the yew walk." Her eyes were closed, she pressed her body fiercely into his. "You are the ... first ... man ..." she breathed.

"I will be the only one for ever," he said.

He began to see himself: in the tall room, with the long curtains: a round, eagle mirror reflected them gleaming: like a bejewelled picture with great depths: the entwined figures.

They drew apart to gaze at each other: holding hands.... The voice of Tietjens said:

"Macmaster! You're to dine at Mrs. Wannop's to-night. Don't dress; I shan't." He was looking at them without any expression, as if he had interrupted a game of cards; large, grey, fresh-featured, the white patch glistening on the side of his grizzling hair.

Macmaster said:

"All right. It's near here, isn't it? ... I've got an engagement just after ..." Tietjens said that that would be all right: he would be working himself. All night probably. For Waterhouse ...

Mrs. Duchemin said with swift jealousy:

"You let him order you about ..." Tietjens was gone. Macmaster said absently:

"Who? Chrissie? ... Yes! Sometimes I him, sometimes he me.... We make engagements. My best friend. The most brilliant man in England, of the best stock too. Tietjens of Groby...." Feeling that she didn't appreciate his friend he was abstractedly[125] piling on commendations: "He's making calculations now.[126] For the Government. That no other man in England could make. But he's going ..."

An extreme languor had settled on him, he felt weakened but yet triumphant with the cessation of her grasp. It occurred to him numbly that he would be seeing less of Tietjens. A grief. He heard himself quote:

"'Since when we stand side by side!'"* His voice trembled.

"Ah yes!" came in her deep tones: "The beautiful lines ... They're true. We must part. In this world ..." They seemed to her lovely and mournful words to say; heavenly to have them to say, vibratingly, arousing all sorts of images. Macmaster, mournfully too, said:

"We must wait." He added fiercely: "But to-night, at dusk!" He imagined the dusk, under the yew hedge. A shining motor drew up in the sunlight under the window.

"Yes! yes!" she said. "There's a little white gate from the lane." She imagined their interview of passion and mournfulness amongst dim objects half seen. That she could allow herself of glamour.

Afterwards he must come to the house to ask after her health and they would walk side by side on the lawn, publicly, in the warm light, talking of indifferent but beautiful poetries, a little wearily, but with what currents electrifying and passing between their flesh.... And then: long, circumspect years....

Macmaster went down the tall steps to the car that gleamed in the summer sun. The roses shone over the supremely levelled turf. His heel met the stones with the hard tread of a conqueror. He could have shouted aloud!

---

* See note on 22.

# VI[1]

T IETJENS lit a pipe beside the stile, having first meticulously cleaned out the bowl and the stem with a surgical needle, in his experience the best of all pipe-cleaners, since, made of German silver, it is flexible, won't corrode and is indestructible. He wiped off methodically, with a great dock-leaf, the glutinous brown products of burnt tobacco, the young woman, as he was aware, watching him from behind his back. As soon as he had restored the surgical needle to the notebook in which it lived, and had put the notebook into its bulky pocket, Miss Wannop moved off down the path: it was only suited for Indian file, and had on the left hand a[2] ten foot, untrimmed quicken* hedge, the hawthorn blossoms just beginning to blacken at the edges and small green haws to show. On the right the grass was above knee high and bowed to those that passed. The sun was exactly vertical; the chaffinches[3] said "Pink! pink!": the young woman had an agreeable back.

This, Tietjens thought, is England! A man and a maid walk through Kentish grass fields: the grass ripe for the scythe. The man honourable, clean, upright; the maid virtuous, clean, vigorous: he of good birth; she of birth quite as good; each filled with a too good breakfast that each could yet capably digest. Each come just from an admirably appointed establishment: a table surrounded by the best people: their promenade sanctioned, as it were, by the Church—two clergy—the State: two Government officials; by mothers, friends, old maids. . . . Each knew the names of birds that piped and grasses that bowed: chaffinch, greenfinch, yellow-ammer (not, my dear, hammer! ammer[4] from the Middle High German for "finch"),† garden warbler, Dartford warbler,

---

\* Quicken (or wicken) is rowan or mountain ash, *Sorbus aucuparia*. But the following description suggests a confusion with hawthorn, *Cratægus Oxyacantha*, N.O. *Rosaceæ*, often used in 'quick' or 'quickset' hedges; see note on 172.

† The *OED* quotes Yarrell, *Brit. Birds* (1856) I 518: 'I have ventured to restore to this bird what I believe to have been its first English name, Yellow *Ammer*. The word *Ammer* is a well known German term for Bunting.'

pied-wagtail, known as "dishwasher." (These *charming* local
dialect names.) Marguerites over the grass, stretching in an infinite white blaze: grasses purple in a haze to the far distant
hedgerow: cocksfoot,[5] wild white clover, sainfoin, Italian rye
grass (all technical names that the best people must know: the
best grass mixture for permanent pasture on the Wealden* loam).
In the hedge: Our lady's bedstraw: dead-nettle: bachelor's button
(but in *Sussex* they call it ragged robin, my dear: So interesting!)[6]
cowslip (paigle,[7] you know, from the old French *pasque*, meaning
Easter): burr, burdock (farmer that thy wife may thrive, let[8] not
burr and burdock wive!);† violet leaves, the flowers of course over;
black briony; wild clematis: later it's old man's beard; purple
loose-strife. (That our young maids[9] long purples call and liberal[10]
shepherds give a grosser name.‡ So racy of the soil!) ... Walk,
then, through the field, gallant youth and fair maid, minds clut-
tered up with all these useless anodynes for thought, quotations,[11]
imbecile epithets!§ Dead silent: unable to talk: from too good
breakfast to probably extremely bad lunch.[12] The young woman,
so the young man is duly warned, to prepare it: pink india-rubber
half-cooked cold beef, no doubt: tepid potatoes, water in the
bottom of willow-pattern dish. (*No! Not* genuine willow-pattern,
of *course*, Mr. Tietjens.) Overgrown lettuce with wood-vinegar to
make the mouth scream with pain; pickles, also preserved in
wood-vinegar;[13] two bottles of public-house beer that, on
opening, squirts to the wall. A glass of invalid port ... for the
*gentleman!* ... and the jaws hardly able to open after the too enormous breakfast at 10.15. Mid-day now!

"God's England!" Tietjens exclaimed to himself in high good

---

*   The Weald is a district, once wooded, including parts of Kent, East Sussex and Surrey.
†   This 'old saying' is quoted from *Lorna Doone*, Chapter 22.
‡   A garbled redaction of *Hamlet*, IV.vii.141–3: 'long purples, / That liberal shepherds give a grosser name, / But our cold maids do dead men's fingers call them.'
§   In *Provence* 106, Ford writes: 'It was indeed only with the Cockney School of Poetry [i.e. Leigh Hunt, Keats and Hazlitt] that the Englishman became de-Latinised, a lover of "Nature", a compendium of the names and habits of the few birds or of the extremely limited fauna of his country.' And in *Nightingale* 114: 'In England, if you don't wish to be ostracised you must know – or pretend to know – the difference between a bearded tit and a crested grebe [...] and your conversation must be perpetually larded with the names of all the wearisome tits and trying finches and with anecdotes of foxes and spaniels and pointers and hares. . . .'

humour.[14] "'Land of Hope and Glory!'"*—F natural descending to tonic, C major: chord of 6-4, suspension over dominant seventh to common chord of C major.... All absolutely correct! Double basses, 'cellos, all violins: all wood wind:[15] all brass. Full grand organ: all stops: special *vox humana* and key-bugle effect.... Across the counties came the sound of bugles that his father knew.... [16†] Pipe exactly right. It must be: pipe of Englishman of good birth: ditto tobacco. Attractive young woman's back. English mid-day mid-summer. Best climate in the world! No day on which man may not go abroad!"‡ Tietjens paused and aimed with his hazel stick an immense blow at a tall spike of yellow mullein with its undecided, furry, glaucous leaves and its undecided, buttony, unripe lemon-coloured flower. The structure collapsed, gracefully, like a woman killed among crinolines!

"Now I'm a bloody murderer!" Tietjens said. "Not gory! Green-stained with vital fluid of innocent plant ... And by God! Not a woman in the country who won't let you rape her after an hour's acquaintance!" He slew two more mulleins and a sow-thistle! A shadow, but not from the sun, a gloom, lay across the sixty acres of purple grass bloom and marguerites, white: like petticoats of lace over the grass!

"By God," he said, "Church! State! Army! H.M.§ Ministry: H.M. Opposition: H.M. City Man.... All the governing class!"**

---

* 'Land of Hope and Glory!' by Edward Elgar, whom Ford had met. Words by A. C. Benson.

† T. W. H. Crosland's 'The Yeoman' (1899) includes the lines: 'Across the counties came the sound / Of war-drums that his fathers knew; / He had no heart for horse or hound. / He said, "Am I not English too?"': *The Collected Poems of T. W. H. Crosland* (London: Martin Secker, 1917), 175. In *Ancient Lights* 230 Ford wrote: 'One had such an enthusiasm for the work of Mr. Crosland in those days, and a little later.'

‡ In *Country* 174 Ford had written: 'It was, I think, Charles II. who said that, upon the whole, the British weather was the best weather in the world, for in the whole year there is no day, either for its inclemency or its heat, so unpleasant that a man may not go abroad' (*England* 203). And in *Joseph Conrad* 40 Ford wrote of Kent and Sussex: 'In that part of England the words of Charles II are most true; what with the shelter of the downs and the position near the sea, there is there scarcely any day upon which a man may not go abroad.' Stephen Switzer, in *The Nobleman, Gentleman and Gardener's Recreation* (1715) recorded Charles as saying that 'he lik'd ... that Country best, which might be enjoy'd the most Hours of the Day, and the most Days in the Year, which he was sure to be done in England more than in any country whatsoever'. Quoted by Emma Tennant, *Trees in the Landscape* (London: John Murray, 1998), 11.

§ His Majesty [the King]'s.

** Cf. *Nightingale* 39: 'Heaven knows nobody could be further from the English governing-class frame of mind than I am.'

All rotten! Thank God we've got a navy! . . . But perhaps that's rotten too! Who knows! Britannia needs no bulwarks* . . . Then thank God for the upright young man and the virtuous maiden in the summer fields: he Tory of the Tories as he should be: she suffragette of the militants: militant here on earth[†] . . . as she should be! As she should be! In the early decades of the twentieth century however[17] else can a woman keep clean and wholesome! Ranting from platforms, splendid for the lungs: bashing in policemen's helmets. . . . No! It's I do that: my part, I think, miss! . . . Carrying heavy banners in twenty-mile processions through streets of Sodom. All splendid! I bet she's virtuous. But you don't have to bet. It isn't done on certainties. You can tell it in the eye. Nice eyes! Attractive back. Virginal cockiness. . . . Yes, better occupation for mothers of empire than attending on lewd husbands year in year out till you're as hysterical as a female cat on heat. . . . You could see it in her: that woman: you can see it in most of 'em! Thank God then for the Tory, upright young married man and the suffragette kid . . . Backbone of England! . . . "

He killed another flower.

"But by God! we're both under a cloud! Both! . . . That kid and I! And General Lord Edward Campion, Lady Claudine Sandbach, and the Hon. Paul, M.P. (suspended) to spread the tale. . . . And forty toothless fogies in the club to spread it: and no end visiting books yawning to have your names cut out of them, my boy! . . . My dear boy: I so regret: your father's oldest friend. . . . By Jove, the pistachio nut of that galantine! Repeating! Breakfast gone wrong: gloomy reflections! Thought I could stand anything: digestion of an ostrich. . . . But no! Gloomy reflections: I'm hysterical: like that large-eyed whore! For same reason! Wrong diet and wrong life: diet meant for partridge shooters over the turnips consumed by the sedentary.

---

\*   A quotation from the third stanza of Thomas Campbell's poem of 1900, 'Ye Mariners of England'.

†   Ford had written an article on Suffragettes entitled 'The Critical Attitude: "Militants Here on Earth"', *English Review*, 3 (Aug. 1909), 137–42; he had also (in counter-Tory mode) contributed to *Women's Suffrage and Militancy*, ed. Huntly Carter (London: Frank Palmer, 1911), 25–8; reprinted in Stang, *Presence* 165–9; and written a pro-Suffragette pamphlet called *This Monstrous Regiment of Women* for the Women's Freedom League in 1913.

England the land of pills ... *Das Pillen-Land*, the Germans call us.[*] Very properly ... And, damn it: outdoor diet: boiled mutton, turnips: sedentary life ... and forced up against the filthiness of the world: your nose in it all day long! ...[18] Why, hang it, I'm as badly off as she. Sylvia's as bad as Duchemin! ... I'd never have thought that ... No wonder meat's turned to uric acid ... prime cause of neurasthenia.... What a beastly muddle! Poor Macmaster! He's finished. Poor devil: he'd better have ogled this kid. He could have sung 'Highland Mary',[19] a better tune than 'This is the end of every man's desire'[†] ... You can cut it on his tombstone, you can write it on his card that a young man tacked on to a paulo-post Pre-Raphaelite prostitute...."[‡]

He stopped suddenly in his walk. It had occurred to him that he ought not to be walking with this girl!

"But damn it all," he said to himself, "she makes a good screen for Sylvia ... who cares! She must chance it. She's probably struck off all their beastly visiting lists already ... as a suffragette!"

Miss Wannop, a cricket pitch or so ahead of him, hopped over a stile: left foot on the step, right on the top bar, a touch of the left on the other step,[20] and down on the white, drifted dust of a road they no doubt had to cross. She stood waiting, her back still to him.... Her nimble foot-work, her attractive back, seemed to him, now, infinitely pathetic.[21] To let scandal attach to her was like cutting the wings of a goldfinch: the bright creature, yellow, white, golden and delicate that in the sunlight makes a haze with its wings beside thistle-tops. No; damn it! it was worse; it was

---

[*]  Ford's breakdown of 1904 had been characterised by 'dyspepsia' and 'neurasthenia', and he had undergone various 'nerve cures' in Germany. See *Return* 202–17. See *Country* 8: 'This England, which is for the rest of the world, The Land of Pills' (*England* 114); also *Ancient Lights* 230–1: 'the country with its atrocious food and cooking is, in England, the home of dyspepsia. ¶ I suppose that is why England is known abroad as *das Pillenland – le pays des pilules* – the land of patent medicines.'

[†]  See 18 above on 'Highland Mary'. 'This is the end of every man's desire' is the refrain of Swinburne's 'A Ballad of Burdens'.

[‡]  Kipling, 'With any Amazement', the wedding chapter of 'The Story of the Gadbys' in *Soldiers Three*: 'you may carve it on his tombstone, you may cut it on his card, / That a young man married is a young man marred!' (adapting the last line from Shakespeare's *All's Well that Ends Well*, II.iii.291: 'A young man married is a man that's marr'd'). *Paulo-post*: Latin, 'a little after'.

worse than putting out, as the bird-fancier does, the eyes of a chaffinch. . . . Infinitely pathetic!

Above the stile, in an elm, a chaffinch said: "Pink! pink!"

The imbecile sound filled him with rage; he said to the bird: "Damn your eyes! *Have* them put out, then!" The beastly bird that made the odious noise, when it had its eyes put out, at least squealed like any other skylark or tom-tit. Damn all birds, field naturalists, botanists! In the same way he addressed the back of Miss Wannop: "Damn your eyes! *Have* your chastity impugned then![22] What do you speak to strange men in public for! You know you can't do it in this country. If it were a decent, straight land like Ireland where people cut each other's throats for clean issues: Papist versus Prot. . . . well, you could! You could walk through Ireland from east to west and speak to every man you met. . . . 'Rich and rare were the gems she wore. . .'\* To every man you met as long as he wasn't an Englishman of good birth: *that* would deflower you!" He was scrambling clumsily over the stile. "Well! *be* deflowered then: *lose* your infantile reputation. You've spoken to strange pitch: you're defiled . . . with the benefit of Clergy, Army, Cabinet, Administration,[23] Opposition, mothers and old maids of England. . . . They'd all tell you you can't talk to a strange man, in the sunlight, on the links without becoming a screen for some Sylvia or other. . . . Then *be* a screen for Sylvia: *get* struck off the visiting books! The deeper you're implicated, the more bloody villain I am![24] I'd like the whole lot to see us here: that would settle[25] it. . . . "

Nevertheless, when at the roadside he stood level with Miss Wannop who did not look at him, and saw the white road running to right and left with no stile opposite, he said gruffly to her:

"Where's the next stile? I hate walking on roads!" She pointed with her chin along the opposite hedgerow.[26] "Fifty yards!" she said.[27]

"Come along!" he exclaimed, and set off at a trot almost. It had come into his head that it would be just the beastly sort of thing that would happen if a car with General Campion and Lady Claudine and Paul Sandbach all aboard should come along that

---

\* Title and first line of a ballad by the Irish poet Thomas Moore (1779–1852).

blinding stretch of road: or one alone: perhaps the General driving the dog-cart he affected. He said to himself:

"By God! If they cut this girl I'd break their backs over my knee!" and he hastened. "Just the beastly thing that *would* happen." The road probably led straight in at the front door of Mountby![28]

Miss Wannop trotted along a little in his rear. She thought him the most extraordinary man: as mad as he was odious. Sane people, if they're going to hurry—but *why* hurry!—do it in the shade of field hedgerows, not in the white blaze of county council roads. Well, he could go ahead. In the next field she was going to have it out with him: she didn't intend to be hot with running: let him be, his hateful, but certainly noticeable eyes, protruding at her like a lobster's; but she cool and denunciatory in her pretty blouse. . . .

There was a dog-cart coming behind them!

Suddenly it came into her head: that fool had been lying when he had said that the police meant to let them alone: lying over the breakfast-table. . . . The dog-cart contained the police: after them! She didn't waste time looking round: she wasn't a fool like Atalanta in the egg race. She picked up her heels and sprinted. She beat him by a yard and a half to the kissing-gate, white in the hedge: panicked: breathing hard. He panted into it, after her: the fool hadn't the sense to let her through first. They were jammed in together: face to face, panting! An occasion on which sweethearts kiss in Kent: the gate being made in three, the inner flange of the V moving on hinges. It stops cattle getting through: but this great lout of a Yorkshireman didn't know: trying to push through like a mad[29] bullock! Now they were caught. Three weeks in Wandsworth gaol. . . . Oh hang. . . .

The voice of Mrs. Wannop—of course it was only mother! Twenty feet on high or so behind the kicking mare, with a good, round face like a peony—said:[30]

"Ah, you can jam my Val in a gate and hold her . . . but she gave you seven yards in twenty and beat you to the gate. That was her father's ambition!" She thought of them as children running races. She beamed down, round-faced and simple, on Tietjens from[31] beside the driver, who had a black, slouch hat and the grey beard of St. Peter.

"My dear boy!" she said, "my dear boy; it's such a satisfaction to have you under my roof!"

The black horse reared on end, the patriarch sawing at its mouth. Mrs. Wannop said unconcernedly: "Stop her[32] Joel! I haven't done talking."

Tietjens was gazing enragedly at the lower part of the horse's sweat-smeared stomach.

"You soon will have," he said, "with the girth in that state. Your neck will be broken."

"Oh, I don't think so," Mrs. Wannop said. "Joel only bought the turn-out* yesterday."

Tietjens addressed the driver with some ferocity:

"Here; get down, you," he said. He held, himself, the head of the horse whose nostrils were wide with emotion: it rubbed its forehead almost immediately against his chest. He said: "Yes! yes! There! there!" Its limbs lost their tautness. The aged driver scrambled down from the high seat, trying to come down at first forward and then backwards. Tietjens fired indignant orders at him:

"Lead the horse into the shade of that tree. Don't touch his[33] bit: his mouth's sore. Where did you get this job lot? Ashford market: thirty pounds: it's worth more. . . . But, blast you, don't you see you've got a thirteen hands pony's harness for a sixteen and a half hands horse. Let the bit out: three holes: it's cutting the animal's tongue in half. . . . This animal's a rig.† Do you know what a rig is? If you give it corn for a fortnight it will kick you and the cart and the stable to pieces in five minutes one day." He led the conveyance, Mrs. Wannop triumphantly complacent and all, into a patch of shade beneath elms.

"Loosen that bit, confound you," he said to the driver. "Ah! you're afraid."

He loosened the bit himself, covering his fingers with greasy harness polish which he hated. Then he said:

"Can you hold his head or are you afraid of that too? You

* A driving equipage; a carriage with its horse or horses, and other adjuncts: OED.
† The OED gives one definition as equivalent to 'ridgel' or 'riggald': 'An animal which has been imperfectly castrated (or spayed), or whose genital organs are not properly developed; esp. a male animal (ram, bull, or horse) with only one testicle'.

*deserve* to have him bite your hands off." He addressed Miss Wannop: "Can *you?*" She said: "No! I'm afraid of horses. I can drive any sort of car: but I'm afraid of horses." He said: "Very proper!" He stood back and looked at the horse: it had dropped its head and lifted its near hind foot, resting the toe on the ground: an attitude of relaxation.

"He'll stand now!" he said. He undid the girth, bending down uncomfortably, perspiring and greasy: the girth-strap parted in his hand.

"It's true," Mrs. Wannop said. "I'd have been dead in three minutes if you hadn't seen that. The cart would have gone over backwards ..."

Tietjens took out a large, complicated, horn-handled knife like a schoolboy's.[34] He selected a punch and pulled it open. He said to the driver:

"Have you got any cobbler's thread? Any string? Any copper wire? A rabbit wire, now? Come, you've got a rabbit wire or you're not a handy man."

The driver moved his slouch hat circularly in negation. This seemed to be Quality who summons you for poaching if you own to possessing rabbit wires.

Tietjens laid the girth along the shaft and punched into it with his punch.

"Woman's work!" he said to Mrs. Wannop, "but it'll take you home and last you six months as well ... But I'll sell this whole lot for you to-morrow."

Mrs. Wannop sighed:

"I suppose it'll fetch a ten pound note ..." She said: "I ought to have gone to market myself."

"No!" Tietjens answered: "I'll get you fifty for it or I'm no Yorkshireman.[35] This fellow hasn't been swindling you. He's got you deuced good[36] value for money, but he doesn't know what's suited for ladies; a white pony and a basket-work chaise is what you want."

"Oh, I like a bit of spirit," Mrs. Wannop said.

"Of course you do," Tietjens answered: "but this turn-out's too much."

He sighed a little and took out his surgical needle.

"I'm going to hold this band together with this," he said. "It's so pliant it will make two stitches and hold for ever. . . ."

But the handy man was beside him, holding out the contents of his pockets: a greasy leather pouch, a ball of beeswax, a knife, a pipe, a bit of cheese and a pale rabbit wire. He had made up his mind that *this* Quality was benevolent and he made offering of all his possessions.

Tietjens said: "Ah," and then, while he unknotted the wire:

"Well! Listen . . . you bought this turn-out of a higgler* at the back door of the Leg of Mutton Inn."†

"Saracen's 'Ed!" the driver muttered.

"You got it for thirty pounds because the higgler wanted money bad. *I* know. And dirt cheap. . . . But a rig isn't everybody's driving. All right for a vet or a horse-coper. Like the cart that's too tall! . . . But you did damn well. Only you're not what you were, are you, at thirty? And the horse looked to be a devil and the cart so high you couldn't get out once you were in. And you kept it[37] in the sun for two hours waiting for your mistress."

"There wer' a bit o' lewth‡ 'longside stable wall," the driver muttered.

"Well! He didn't like waiting," Tietjens said placably. "You can be thankful your old neck's not broken. Do this band up, one hole less for the bit I've taken in."

He prepared to climb into the driver's seat, but Mrs. Wannop was there before him, at an improbable altitude on the sloping watch-box§ with strapped cushions.

"Oh, no, you don't," she said, "no one drives me and my horse but me or my coachman when I'm about. Not even you, dear boy."

"I'll come with you then," Tietjens said.

"Oh, no, you don't," she answered. "No one's neck's to be

---

* An itinerant dealer or tinker. Ford published a story by A. E. Coppard in the May 1924 issue of the *transatlantic review* entitled 'The Higgler' – much to Pound's dismay. See Bernard Poli, *Ford Madox Ford and the 'Transatlantic Review'* (Syracuse, NY: Syracuse University Press, 1967), 83.

† Cf. *Country* 54 (*England* 140) on a carrier: 'Arrived at his market-town, that autocrat will stable his horse at the "Leg of Mutton" [. . .]'.

‡ Shelter.

§ The *OED* doesn't have this sense of 'watch-box'. It gives definitions of 'box' as 'A box under the driver's seat on a coach; hence in general the seat on which the driver sits'; and as 'A compartment or place partitioned off for the separate accommodation of people or animals'.

broken in this conveyance but mine and Joel's," she added: "perhaps to-night if I'm satisfied the horse is fit to drive."

Miss Wannop suddenly exclaimed:

"Oh, *no*, mother." But the handy man having climbed in, Mrs. Wannop flirted her whip and started the horse. She pulled up at once and leaned over to Tietjens:

"*What* a life for that poor woman," she said. "We must *all* do all we can for her.[38] She could have her husband put in a lunatic asylum to-morrow. It's sheer self-sacrifice that she doesn't."

The horse went off at a gentle, regular trot.

Tietjens addressed Miss Wannop:

"What hands your mother's got," he said, "it isn't often one sees a woman with hands like that on a horse's mouth.... Did you see how she pulled up? ..."

He was aware that, all this while, from the road-side, the girl had been watching him with shining eyes: intently even: with fascination.

"I suppose you think that a mighty fine performance," she said.

"I didn't make a very good job of the girth," he said. "Let's get off this road."

"Setting poor, weak[39] women in their places," Miss Wannop continued. "Soothing the horse like a man with a charm. I suppose you soothe women like that, too. I pity your wife.... The English country male! And making a devoted vassal at sight of the handy man. The feudal system all complete...."

Tietjens said:

"Well, you know, it'll make him all the better servant to you if he thinks you've friends in the know. The lower classes are like that. Let's get off this road."

She said:

"You're in a mighty hurry to get behind the hedge. Are the police after us or aren't they? Perhaps you were lying at breakfast: to calm the hysterical nerves of a weak woman."

"I wasn't[40] lying," he said, "but I hate roads when there are field-paths ..."

"That's a phobia, like any woman's," she exclaimed.

She almost ran through the kissing-gate and stood awaiting him:

"I suppose," she said, "if you've stopped off the police with your high and mighty male ways you think you've destroyed my romantic young dream. You haven't. I don't *want* the police after me. I believe I'd *die* if they put me in Wandsworth ... I'm a coward."

"Oh, no, you aren't," he said, but he was following his own train of thought, just as she wasn't in the least listening to him. "I daresay you're a heroine all right. *Not* because you persevere in actions the consequences of which you fear. But I daresay you can touch pitch and not be defiled."

Being too well brought up to interrupt she waited till he had said all he wanted to say, then she exclaimed:

"Let's settle the preliminaries. It's obvious mother means us to see a great deal of you. *You're* going to be a mascot too, like your father. I suppose you think you are: you saved me from the police yesterday,[41] you appear to have saved mother's neck to-day. You appear, too, to be going to make twenty pounds profit on a horse deal. You say you will and you seem to be that sort of a person ... Twenty pounds is no end in a family like ours ... Well, then, you appear to be going to be the regular *bel ami** of the Wannop family ...'"

Tietjens said:

"I hope not."

"Oh, I don't mean," she said, "that you're going to rise to fame by making love to all the women of the Wannop family. Besides, there's only me. But mother will press you into all sorts of odd jobs: and there will always be a plate for you at the table. Don't shudder! I'm a regular good cook—*cuisine bourgeoise* of course. I learned under a real professed cook, though a drunkard. That meant I used to do half the cooking and the family was particular. Ealing people are: county councillors, half of them, and the like. So I know what men are ..." She stopped and said good-naturedly: "But do, for goodness' sake, get it over. I'm sorry I was rude to you. But it *is* irritating to have to stand like a stuffed rabbit while a man is acting like a regular Admirable Crichton,[†] and

---

\*   In Maupassant's *Bel-Ami*, published in 1885, the protagonist learns to succeed in a corrupt society thanks to a series of mistresses. Valentine's familiarity with the plot of such an explicitly sexual French novel indicates her unconventionally liberal education.

†   James Crichton (1560–82), known as 'The Admirable', was a Scots adventurer and poet, who served in the French army and died in a brawl in Mantua. Ainsworth's novel, *Crichton*, appeared in 1837, J. M. Barrie's play, *The Admirable Crichton*, in 1902.

cool and collected, with the English country gentleman air and all."

Tietjens winced. The young woman had come a little too near the knuckle of his wife's frequent denunciations of himself. And she exclaimed:

"No! That's not fair! I'm an ungrateful pig! You didn't show a bit more side* really than a capable workman must who's doing his job in the midst of a crowd of incapable duffers. But just get it out, will you? Say once and for all that—you know the proper, pompous manner: you are not without sympathy with our aims: but you disapprove—oh, immensely[42] strongly—of our methods."

It struck Tietjens that the young woman was a good deal more interested in the cause—of votes for women—than he had given her credit for. He wasn't much in the mood for talking to young women, but it was with considerably more than the surface of his mind that he answered:

"I don't. I approve entirely of your methods: but your aims are idiotic."

She said:

"You don't know, I suppose, that Gertie Wilson, who's in bed at our house, is wanted by the police: not only for yesterday, but for putting explosives in a whole series of letter-boxes?"

He said:

"I didn't ... but it was a perfectly proper thing to do. She hasn't burned any of my letters or I might be annoyed; but it wouldn't interfere with my approval."

"You don't think," she asked earnestly, "that we ... mother and I ... are likely to get heavy sentences for shielding her. It would be beastly bad luck on mother. Because she's an anti[43] ... "

"I don't know about the sentence," Tietjens said, "but we'd better get her off your premises as soon as we can...."

She said:

"Oh, you'll *help?*"

He answered:

"Of course, your mother can't be incommoded. She's written the only novel that's been fit to read since the eighteenth century."

---

* 'Pretentiousness, swagger, conceit': *OED*.

She stopped and said earnestly:

"Look here. *Don't* be one of those ignoble triflers who say the vote won't do women any good. Women have a rotten time. They do, really. If you'd seen what I've seen, I'm not talking through my hat." Her voice became quite deep: she had tears in her eyes: "*Poor* women *do!*" she said, "little insignificant creatures. We've *got* to change the divorce laws. We've *got* to get better conditions. *You* couldn't stand it if you knew what I know."

Her emotion vexed him, for it seemed to establish a sort of fraternal intimacy that he didn't at the moment want.[44] Women do not show emotion except before their familiars. He said drily:

"I daresay I shouldn't. But I don't know, so I can!"

She said with deep disappointment:

"Oh, you *are* a beast! And I shall never beg your pardon for saying that. I don't believe you mean what you say, but merely to say it is heartless."

This was another of the counts of Sylvia's indictment and Tietjens winced again. She explained:[45]

"You don't know the case of the Pimlico army clothing factory workers or you wouldn't say the vote would be no use to women."*

"I know the case perfectly well," Tietjens said: "It came under my official notice, and I remember thinking that there never was a more signal instance of the uselessness of the vote to anyone."

"We can't be thinking of the same case," she said.

"We are," he answered. "The Pimlico army clothing factory is in the constituency of Westminster; the Under-Secretary for War is member for Westminster; his majority at the last election was six hundred. The clothing factory employed seven hundred men at 1s. 6d. an hour, all these men having votes in Westminster. The seven hundred men wrote to the Under-Secretary to say that if their screw wasn't raised to two bob they'd vote solid

---

\*  The Pimlico factory had become a high-profile example of gender-inequality. See *The Case for Women's Suffrage*, ed. Brougham Villiers (London: T. Fisher Unwin. 1907), 60: 'So that, in the Pimlico Clothing Factory, the skilled woman worker gets an average of 15s. a week, while no man labourer gets less than 23s. The Government mechanically gets its female labour as cheap as it can, unchecked by political considerations.' *A Suffrage Reader*, ed. Claire Eustance, Joan Ryan, and Laura Ugolini (London: Leicester University Press, 2000), 153, mentions a statement in parliament in mid-March 1911 about how women's wages for making service dress trousers were to be reduced.

against him at the next election. . . . "

Miss Wannop said: "Well then!"

"So," Tietjens said: "The Under-Secretary had the seven hundred men at eighteenpence fired and took on seven hundred women at tenpence. What good did the vote do the seven hundred men? What good did a vote ever do anyone?"

Miss Wannop checked at that and Tietjens prevented her exposure of his fallacy* by saying quickly:

"Now, if the seven hundred women, backed by all the other ill-used, sweated women of the country, had threatened the Under-Secretary, burned the pillar-boxes, and cut up all the golf greens round his country-house, they'd have had their wages raised to half-a-crown next week. That's the only straight method. It's the feudal system at work."

"Oh, but we couldn't cut up *golf* greens," Miss Wannop said. "At least the W.S.P.U.† debated it the other day, and decided that anything so unsporting would make us *too* unpopular. I was for it personally."

Tietjens groaned:

"It's maddening," he said, "to find women, as soon as they get in Council, as muddleheaded and as afraid to face straight issues as men! . . . "[46]

"You won't, by-the-by," the girl interrupted, "be able to sell our horse to-morrow. You've forgotten that it will be Sunday."

"I shall have to on Monday, then," Tietjens said. "The point about the feudal system . . . "[47]

Just after lunch—and it was an admirable lunch of the cold lamb, new potatoes and mint-sauce variety, the mint-sauce made with white wine vinegar and as soft as kisses, the claret perfectly drinkable and the port much more than that, Mrs. Wannop having gone back to the late professor's wine merchants—Miss Wannop herself went to answer the telephone. . . .

---

\*  Presumably that – since no women in Britain had the vote before 1918 – the MP would have lost the 700 men's votes and thus lost his seat anyway.

†  Women's Social and Political Union. Founded in 1903 by Emmeline and Christabel Pankhurst. Violet Hunt was a member, and gave a dinner for Christabel Pankhurst in June 1909; Hunt and Ford arranged a meeting for her the following year. Ford's mother and sister had joined a Suffrage procession ('in a small motor') in February 1907, and Ford became an active supporter. See note on 134 above.

The cottage had no doubt been a cheap one, for it was old, roomy and comfortable; but effort had no doubt, too, been lavished on its low rooms. The dining-room had windows on each side and a beam across; the dining silver had been picked up at sales, the tumblers were old cut glass; on each side of the ingle was a grandfather's chair. The garden had red brick paths, sunflowers, hollyhocks and scarlet gladioli. There was nothing to it all, but the garden-gate was well hung.

To Tietjens all this meant effort. Here was a woman who, a few[48] years ago, was penniless, in the most miserable of circumstances, supporting life with the most exiguous of all implements. What effort hadn't it meant! and what effort didn't it mean? There was a boy at Eton . . . a senseless, but a gallant effort.

Mrs. Wannop sat opposite him in the other grandfather's chair; an admirable hostess, an admirable lady. Full of spirit in dashes; but tired. As an old horse is tired that, taking three men to harness it in the stable yard, starts out like a stallion, but soon drops to a jog-trot. The face tired, really; scarlet-cheeked with the good air, but seamed downward. She could sit there at ease, the plump hands covered with a black lace shawl, and descending on each side of her lap, as much at ease as any other Victorian great lady. But at lunch she had let drop that she had written for eight hours every day for the last four years—till that day—without missing a day. To-day being Saturday, she had no leader to write:

"And, my darling boy," she had said to him. "I'm giving it to you. I'd give it to no other soul but your father's son. Not even to . . ." And she had named the name that she most respected. "And that's the truth," she had added. Nevertheless, even over lunch, she had fallen into abstractions, heavily and deeply, and made fantastic mis-statements, mostly about public affairs. . . . It all meant a tremendous record. . . .

And there he sat, his coffee and port on a little table beside him; the house belonging to him. . . .

She said:

"My dearest boy . . . you've so much to do. Do you think you ought really to drive the girls to Plimsoll tonight? They're young and inconsiderate; work comes first."

Tietjens said:

"It isn't the distance . . ."

"You'll find that it is," she answered humorously. "It's twenty miles beyond Tenterden. If you don't start till ten when the moon sets, you won't be back till five, even if you've no accidents. . . . The horse is all right, though . . . "

Tietjens said:

"Mrs. Wannop, I ought to tell you that your daughter and I are being talked about. Uglily!"

She turned her head to him; rather stiffly. But she was only coming out of an abstraction.

"Eh?" she said, and then; "Oh! About the golf-links episode. . . . It must have looked suspicious. I daresay you made a fuss, too, with the police, to head them off her." She remained pondering for a moment, heavily, like an old pope:

"Oh, you'll live it down," she said.

"I ought to tell you," he persisted, "that it's more serious than you think. I fancy I ought not to be here."

"Not here!" she exclaimed. "Why, where else in the world should you be? You don't get on with your wife; I know. She's a regular wrong 'un. Who else could look after you as well as Valentine and I."

In the acuteness[49] of that pang, for, after all, Tietjens cared more for his wife's reputation than for any other factor in a complicated world, Tietjens asked rather sharply why Mrs. Wannop had called Sylvia a wrong 'un. She said in rather a protesting, sleepy way:

"My dear boy, nothing! I've guessed that there are differences between you; give me credit for some perception. Then, as you're perfectly obviously a right 'un, she must be a wrong 'un. That's all, I assure you."

In his relief Tietjens' obstinacy revived. He liked this house; he liked this atmosphere; he liked the frugality, the choice of furniture, the way the light fell from window to window; the weariness after hard work; the affection of mother and daughter; the affection, indeed, that they both had for himself, and he was determined, if he could help it, not to damage the reputation of the daughter of the house.

Decent men, he held, don't do such things, and he recounted with some care the heads of the conversation he had had with General Campion in the dressing-room. He seemed to see the

cracked wash-bowls in their scrubbed oak settings. Mrs.
Wannop's face seemed to grow greyer, more aquiline; a little
resentful! She nodded from time to time; either to denote attention or else in sheer drowsiness:

"My dear boy," she said at last, "It's pretty damnable to have
such things said about you. I can see that. But I seem to have lived
in a bath of scandal all my life. Every woman who has reached my
age has that feeling. . . . [50] Now it doesn't seem to matter . . ." She
really nodded nearly off: then she started. "I don't see . . . I really
don't see how I can help you as to your reputation. I'd do it if I
could: believe me. . . . But I've other things to think of. . . . I've
this house to keep going and the children to keep fed and at
school. I can't give all the thought I ought to to other people's
troubles. . . ."

She started into wakefulness and right out of her chair.

"But what a beast I am!" she said, with a sudden intonation
that was exactly that of her daughter; and, drifting with a Victorian majesty of shawl and long skirt behind Tietjens'[51]
high-backed chair, she leaned over it and stroked the hair on his
right temple:

"My dear boy," she said. "Life's a bitter thing. I'm an old
novelist and know it. There you are working yourself to death to
save the nation with a wilderness of cats and monkeys* howling
and squalling your personal reputation away. . . . It was Dizzy†
himself said these words to me at one of our receptions. 'Here I
am, Mrs. Wannop,' he said. . . . [52] And . . ." She drifted for a
moment. But she made another effort: "My dear boy," she whispered, bending down her head to get it near his ear: "My dear boy;
it doesn't matter; it doesn't really matter. You'll live it down. The
only thing that matters is to do good work. Believe an old woman
that has lived very hard; 'Hard lying money'‡ as they call it in the

---

* While 'cats and monkeys' echoes the phrase noted on 100 above, the addition of
  'wilderness' here adds another echo, to *The Merchant of Venice*, III.i.112–14, when
  Shylock says to his friend: 'Thou torturest me, Tubal: it was my turquoise; I had it of
  Leah when I was a bachelor: I would not have given it for a wilderness of monkeys.'
† Benjamin Disraeli (1804–81), architect of the modern Conservative Party and twice
  Prime Minister.
‡ 'The extra allowance granted to officers and men for service in destroyers and torpedo
  boats . . . compensation for wear and tear of uniform and clothing etc.' See Partridge
  and Beale, *A Dictionary of Slang*, 531.

navy. It sounds like cant, but it's the only real truth. . . . You'll find consolation in that. And you'll live it all down. Or perhaps you won't; that's for God in His mercy to settle. But it won't matter; believe me, as thy day so shall thy strength be."* She drifted into other thoughts; she was much perturbed over the plot of a new novel and much wanted to get back to the consideration of it. She stood gazing at the photograph, very faded, of her husband in side-whiskers and an immense shirt-front, but she continued to stroke Tietjens' temple with a subliminal[53] tenderness.

This kept Tietjens sitting there. He was quite aware that he had tears in his eyes; this was almost too much tenderness to bear, and, at bottom his was a perfectly direct, simple and sentimental soul. He always had bedewed eyes at the theatre, after tender love scenes and so avoided the theatre. He asked himself twice whether he should or shouldn't make another effort, though it was almost beyond him. He wanted to sit still.

The stroking stopped; he scrambled on to his feet:

"Mrs. Wannop," he said, facing her, "It's perfectly true. I oughtn't to care what these swine say about me, but I do. I'll reflect about what you say till I get it into my system . . . "

She said:

"Yes, yes! My dear," and continued to gaze at the photograph:

"But," Tietjens said; he took her mittened hand and led her back to her chair: "What I'm concerned for at the moment is not my reputation, but your daughter Valentine's."

She sank down into the high chair, balloon-like, and came to rest:

"Val's reputation!" she said, "Oh! you mean they'll be striking *her* off their visiting lists. It hadn't struck me. So they will!" She remained lost in reflection for a long time.

Valentine was in the room, laughing a little. She had been giving the handy man his dinner, and was still amused at his commendations of Tietjens.

"You've got one admirer," she said to Tietjens. "'Punched that rotten strap,' he goes on saying, 'like a gret ol' yaffle punchin' a 'ollow log!'[54] He's had a pint of beer and said it between each

---

* 'As thy days, so shall thy strength be': *Deuteronomy* 33.25. Ford would use 'As thy Day' as a working title for his 1934 novel *Henry for Hugh*.

gasp." She continued to narrate the quaintnesses of Joel which appealed to her; informed Tietjens that "yaffle" was Kentish for great green woodpecker; and then said:

"You haven't got any friends in Germany, have you?" She was beginning to clear the table.

Tietjens said:

"Yes; my wife's in Germany; at a place called Lobscheid."

She placed a pile of plates on a black japanned tray.

"I'm so sorry," she said, without an expression of any deep regret. "It's the ingenious clever-stupidities[55] of the telephone. I've got a telegraph message for you then. I thought it was the subject for mother's leader. It always comes through with the initials of the paper which are not unlike Tietjens, and the girl[56] who always sends it is called Hopside. It seemed rather inscrutable, but I took it to have to do with German politics and I thought mother would understand it.... You're not both asleep, are you?"

Tietjens opened his eyes; the girl was standing over him, having approached from the table. She was holding out a slip of paper on which she had transcribed the message. She appeared all out of drawing and the letters of the message ran together.[*] The message was:

"Righto. But arrange for certain Hullo Central travels with you. Sylvia Hopside Germany."

Tietjens leaned back for a long time looking at the words; they seemed meaningless. The girl placed the paper on his knee, and went back to the table. He imagined the girl wrestling with these incomprehensibilities on the telephone.

"Of course if I'd had any sense," the girl said, "I should have known it couldn't have been mother's leader note; she never gets one on a Saturday."[†]

Tietjens heard himself announce clearly, loudly and with between each word a pause:

"It means I go to my wife on Tuesday and take her maid with me."

[*] 'out of drawing' is generally used of incorrectly depicted art-works. Here it indicates Tietjens' bleary vision rather than a comment on Valentine's writing.

[†] In I.ii on Saturday evening Sylvia first says she'll send the telegram on Monday, then that she'll send it first thing on Sunday.

"Lucky you!" the girl said, "I wish I was you. I've never been in the Fatherland of Goethe and Rosa Luxemburg."[57]* She went off with her great tray load, the table cloth over her forearm. He was dimly aware that she had before then removed the crumbs with a crumb-brush. It was extraordinary with what swiftness she worked, talking all the time. That was what domestic service had done for her; an ordinary young lady would have taken twice the time,[58] and would certainly have dropped half her words if she had tried to talk. Efficiency! He had only just realised that he was going back to Sylvia, and of course to Hell! Certainly it was Hell. If a malignant and skilful devil ... though the devil of course is stupid and uses toys[59] like fireworks and sulphur; it is probably only God who can, very properly, devise the long ailings of mental oppressions ... if God then desired (and one couldn't object but one hoped He would not!) to devise for him, Christopher Tietjens, a cavernous eternity of weary hopelessness.... But He had done it; no doubt as retribution. What for? Who knows what sins of his own are heavily punishable in the eyes of God, for God is just? ... Perhaps God then, after all, visits thus heavily sexual offences.

There came back into his mind, burnt in, the image of their breakfast-room, with all the brass, electrical fixings, poachers, toasters, grillers, kettle-heaters, that he detested for their imbecile inefficiency; with gross piles of hothouse flowers—that he detested for their exotic waxennesses!—with white enamelled panels that he disliked and framed, weak prints—quite genuine of course, my dear, guaranteed so by Sotheby—pinkish women in sham Gainsborough hats, selling mackerel or brooms. A wedding present that he despised. And Mrs. Satterthwaite, in negligé, but with an immense hat; reading the *Times* with an eternal rustle of leaves because she never could settle down to any one page; and Sylvia walking up and down because she could not sit still, with a piece of toast in her fingers or her hands behind her back. Very tall; fair; as graceful, as full of blood and as cruel as the usual degenerate Derby winner. In-bred for generations for one purpose: to madden men of one type.... Pacing backwards and forwards, exclaiming: "I'm bored! Bored!"; sometimes even

* German left-wing revolutionary (1871–1919).

breaking the breakfast plates . . . And talking! For ever talking; cruelly,[60] cleverly, with imbecility; with maddening inaccuracy; with wicked penetration, and clamouring to be contradicted; a gentleman has to answer his wife's questions. . . . And in his forehead the continual pressure; the determination to sit put;[61] the *décor* of the room seeming to burn into his mind. It was there, shadowy before him now. And the pressure upon his forehead. . . .

Mrs. Wannop was talking to him now; he did not know what she said; he never knew afterwards what he had answered.

"God!" he said within himself,[62] "if it's sexual sins God punishes, He indeed is just and inscrutable!" . . . Because he had had physical contact with this woman before he married her; in a railway carriage; coming down from the Dukeries.* An extravagantly beautiful girl!

Where was the physical attraction of her gone to now?[63] Irresistible; reclining back as the shires rushed past. . . . His mind said that she had lured him on. His intellect put the idea from him. No gentleman thinks such things of his wife.

No gentleman thinks. . . . By God; she must have been with child by another man. . . . He had been fighting the conviction down all the last four months. . . . He knew now that he had been fighting the conviction all the last four months, whilst, anæsthetised, he had bathed in figures and wave-theories. . . . Her last words had been: her very last words: late: all in white she had gone up to her dressing-room, and he had never seen her again; her last words had been about the child . . . "Supposing," she had begun . . . He didn't remember the rest. But he remembered her eyes. And her gesture as she peeled off her long white gloves. . . .

He was looking at Mrs. Wannop's ingle; he thought it a mistake in taste, really, to leave logs in an ingle during the summer. But then what are you to do with an ingle in summer. In Yorkshire cottages they shut the ingles up with painted doors. But that is stuffy, too!

He said to himself:

"By God! I've had a stroke!" and he got out of his chair to test his legs. . . . But he hadn't had a stroke. It must then, he thought,

---

\*   An area of northern Nottinghamshire (including the remnants of Sherwood Forest) named for its cluster of five large ducal estates.

be that the pain of his last consideration must be too great for his mind to register, as certain great physical pains go unperceived. Nerves, like weighing machines, can't register more than a certain amount, then they go out of action. A tramp who had had his leg cut off by a train had told him that he had tried to get up, feeling nothing at all. . . . The pain comes back though . . .

He said to Mrs. Wannop, who was still talking:

"I beg your pardon. I really missed what you said."

Mrs. Wannop said:

"I was saying that that's the best thing I can do for you."

He said:

"I'm really very sorry: it was that that I missed. I'm a little in trouble you know."

She said:

"I know: I know. The mind wanders; but I wish you'd listen. I've got to go to work, so have you. I said: after tea you and Valentine will walk into Rye to fetch your luggage."

Straining his intelligence, for, in his mind,[64] he felt a sudden strong pleasure: sunlight on pyramidal red roofs[65] in the distance: themselves descending in a long diagonal, a green hill: God, yes, he wanted open air:[66] Tietjens said:

"I see. You take us both under your protection. You'll bluff it out."

Mrs. Wannop said rather coolly:

"I don't know about you both. It's you I'm taking under my protection (it's *your* phrase!) As for Valentine: she's made her bed; she must lie on it. I've told you all[67] that already. I can't go over it again."

She paused, then made another effort:

"It's disagreeable," she said, "to be cut off the Mountby[68] visiting list. They give amusing parties. But I'm too old to care and they'll miss my conversation more than I do theirs. Of course, I back my daughter against the cats and monkeys. Of course, I back Valentine through thick and thin. I'd back her if she lived with a married man or had illegitimate children. But I don't approve, I don't approve of the suffragettes: I despise their aims: I detest their methods. I don't think young girls ought to talk to strange men. Valentine spoke to you and look at the worry it has caused you. I disapprove. I'm a woman: but I've made my own

way: other women could do it if they liked or had the energy. I
disapprove! But don't believe that I will ever go back on any
suffragette, individual, in gangs; my Valentine or any other.
Don't believe that I will ever say a word against them that's to be
repeated—*you* won't repeat them.[69] Or that I will ever write a
word against them. No, I'm a woman and I stand by my sex!"

She got up energetically:

"I must go and write my novel," she said. "I've Monday's
instalment to send off by train to-night. You'll go into my study:
Valentine will give you paper; ink; twelve different kinds of nibs.
You'll find Professor Wannop's books all round the room. You'll
have to put up with Valentine typing in the alcove. I've got two
serials running, one typed, the other in manuscript."

Tietjens said:

"But *you!*"

"I," she exclaimed, "I shall write in my bedroom on my knee.
I'm a woman and can. You're a man and have to have a padded
chair and sanctuary. . . . You feel fit to work? Then: you've got till
five, Valentine will get tea then. At half-past five you'll set off to
Rye. You'll be back with your luggage and your friend and your
friend's luggage at seven."

She silenced him imperiously with:

"Don't be foolish. Your friend will certainly prefer this house
and Valentine's cooking to the pub and the pub's cooking. And
he'll save on it. . . . It's *no* extra trouble. I suppose your friend
won't inform against that wretched little suffragette girl upstairs."
She paused and said: "You're *sure* you can do your work in the
time and drive Valentine and her to that place . . . Why it's
necessary is that the girl daren't travel by train and we've relations there who've never been connected with the suffragettes.
The girl can live hid there for a bit. . . . But sooner than you
shouldn't finish your work I'd drive them myself . . ."

She silenced Tietjens again: this time sharply:

"I tell you it's *no* extra trouble. Valentine and I *always* make
our own beds. We don't like servants among our intimate things.
We can get three times as much help in the neighbourhood as we
want. We're liked here. The extra work you give will be met by
extra help. We could have servants if we wanted. But Valentine
and I like to be alone in the house together at night. We're very

fond of each other."

She walked to the door and then drifted back to say:

"You know I can't get out of my head that unfortunate woman and her husband. We must *all* do what we can for them." Then she started and exclaimed: "But, good heavens, I'm keeping you from your work ... The study's in there, through that door."

She hurried through the other doorway and no doubt along a passage, calling out:

"Valentine! Valentine! Go to Christopher in the study. At once ... at ..." Her voice died away.

JUMPING down from the high step of the dog-cart[2] the girl completely disappeared[3] into the silver: she had on an otter-skin toque, dark, that should have been visible. But she was gone more completely[4] than if she had dropped into deep water, into snow— or through tissue paper. More suddenly, at least! In darkness or in deep water a moving paleness would have been visible for a second: snow or a paper hoop would have left an opening. Here there had been nothing.

The constatation[5] interested him. He had been watching her intently and with concern for fear she should miss the hidden lower step, in which case she would certainly bark her shins. But she had jumped clear of the cart: with unreasonable pluckiness, in spite of his: "Look out how you get down." He wouldn't have done it himself: he couldn't have faced jumping down into that white solidity . . .

He would have asked: "Are you all right?" but to express more concern than the "look out," which he had expended already, would have detracted from his stolidity. He was Yorkshire and stolid: she south country and soft: emotional: given to such ejaculations as "I hope you're not hurt," when the Yorkshireman only grunts.[6] But soft because she was south country. She was as good as a man—a south country man. She was ready to acknowledge the superior woodenness of the north. . . . That was their convention: so he did not call down: "I hope you're all right," though he had desired to.

Her voice came, muffled, as if from the back of the top of his head: the ventriloquial effect was startling:[7]

"Make a noise from time to time. It's ghostly down here and the lamp's no good at all. It's almost out."

He returned to his constatations[8] of the concealing effect of water vapour. He enjoyed the thought of the grotesque appearance he must present in that imbecile landscape. On his right an immense, improbably brilliant horn of a moon, sending a trail as if down the sea, straight to his neck: beside the moon a grotesquely huge star: in an extravagant position above them the Plough, the only constellation that he knew; for, though a mathematician, he despised astronomy. It was not theoretical enough for the pure mathematician and not sufficiently practical for daily life. He had of course calculated the movements of abstruse heavenly bodies: but only from given figures: he had never looked for the stars of his calculations. . . . Above his head and all over the sky were other stars: large and weeping with light, or as the dawn increased, so paling that at times, you saw them; then missed them. Then the eye picked them up again.

Opposite the moon was a smirch or two of cloud; pink below, dark purple above; on the more pallid, lower blue of the limpid sky.

But the absurd[9] thing was this mist! . . . It appeared to spread from his neck, absolutely level, absolutely silver, to infinity on each side of him.* At great distances on his right black tree-shapes, in groups—there were four of them—were exactly like coral islands on a silver sea. He couldn't escape the idiotic comparison: there wasn't any other.

Yet it didn't actually spread from his neck: when he now held his hands, nipple-high, like pallid fish they held black reins which ran downwards into nothingness. If he jerked the rein, the horse threw its head up. Two pricked ears were visible in greyness: the horse being sixteen two and a bit over, the mist might be ten foot high. Thereabouts. . . . He wished the girl would come back and jump out of the cart again. Being ready for it he would watch her disappearance more scientifically. He couldn't of course ask her to do it again: that was irritating. The phenomenon would have proved—or it might of course disprove—his idea of smoke screens. The Chinese of the Ming dynasty were said to have approached and overwhelmed their enemies under clouds of—of course, not acrid—vapour. He had read that the Patagonians, hidden by smoke, were accustomed to approach so near to birds

---

\* Cf. W. H. Hudson, on the horses amidst the thistledown, 'plunged breast-deep into this insubstantial whiteness', in the opening of *Nature in Downland* (London: Longmans, Green & Co., 1900), 2, to which passage Ford often refers.

or beasts as to be able to take them by hand. The Greeks under Paleologus* the . . .

Miss Wannop's voice said—from beneath the bottom board of the cart:

"I wish you'd make some noise. It's lonely down here, besides being possibly dangerous. There might be dicks on each side of the road."

If they were on the marsh there certainly would be dykes— why did they call ditches "dykes," and why did she pronounce it "dicks"?—on each side of the road. He could think of nothing to say that wouldn't express concern and he couldn't do that by the rules of the game. He tried to whistle "John Peel"! But he was no hand at whistling. He sang:

"D'ye ken, John Peel at[10] the break of day . . ." and felt like a fool. But he kept on at it,[11] the only tune that he knew. It was the Yorkshire Light Infantry quick-step: the regiment of his brothers in India. He wished he had been in the army; but his father hadn't approved of having more than two younger[12] sons in the army. He wondered if he would ever run with John Peel's hounds again: he had once or twice.† Or with any of the trencher-fed foot packs‡ of the Cleveland district, of which there had been still several when he had been a boy. He had been used to think of himself as being like John Peel with his coat so grey . . . Up through the heather, over Wharton's place; the pack running wild; the heather dripping; the mist rolling up . . . another kind of mist than this south country silver sheet. Silly stuff! Magical! That was the word. A silly word. . . .[13] South country. . . In the north the old grey mists rolled together, revealing black hillsides!

He didn't suppose he'd have the wind now: this rotten bureaucratic life! . . . If he had been in the army like the two brothers, Ernest and James, next above him . . . But no doubt he would not

---

* The Palaeologus dynasty was the longest-lived and the last to rule the Byzantine empire, from 1259 to 1453, producing eleven emperors.

† The John Peel immortalised in the song lived near Caldbeck in Cumbria, and died in 1854. The Blencathra Foxhounds is a foot pack kennelled in Threlkeld that still boasts hounds descended directly from some of John Peel's.

‡ Hunting dogs kept individually by farmers and only brought together to form packs for hunting, in this case with the huntsmen on foot rather than on horseback.

have liked the army. Discipline! . . . He supposed he would have put up with the discipline: a gentleman had to. Because *noblesse oblige:*\* not for fear of consequences . . . But army officers seemed to him pathetic. They spluttered and roared: to make men jump smartly: at the end of apoplectic[14] efforts the men jumped smartly. But there was the end of it. . . .

Actually, this mist was not silver, or was, perhaps, no longer silver: if you looked at it with the eye of the artist . . . With the exact eye![†] It was smirched with bars of purple; of red; of orange: delicate reflections: dark blue shadows from the upper sky where it formed drifts like snow. . . . The exact eye: exact observation: it was a man's work. The only work for a man. Why then, were artists soft: effeminate: not men at all: whilst the army officer, who had the inexact mind of the schoolteacher, was a manly man? Quite a manly man: until he became an old woman!

And the bureaucrat then? Growing fat and soft like himself, or dry and stringy like Macmaster or old Ingleby? They did men's work: exact observation: return no. 17642 with figures exact. Yet they grew hysterical: they ran about corridors or frantically rang table bells, asking with high voices of querulous eunuchs why form ninety thousand and two wasn't ready. Nevertheless men liked the bureaucratic life: his own brother, Mark, head of the family: heir to Groby. . . . Fifteen years older: a queer[15] stick: wooden: brown: always in a bowler hat,[16] as often as not with his racing glasses hung around him. Attending his first-class office when he liked: too good a man for any administration to lose by putting on the screw. . . . But heir to Groby: what would that stick make of the place? . . . Let it, no doubt, and go on pottering from the Albany to race meetings—where he never betted—to White-hall, where he was said to be indispensable. . . . Why indispensable? Why in heaven's name? That stick who had never hunted, never shot: couldn't tell coulter from plough-handle and lived in his bowler hat![17] . . . A "sound" man: the archetype of all

---

\* French: 'privilege entails responsibility'.

† Cf. *Nightingale* 129: 'perhaps an artist is not a proper man'; or 224: '[. . .] I like to be able to sit in the shade of an olive tree, on a flat rock, extremely lightly clad. And then to think. It seems to me that that is the proper occupation of a proper man.' Also see the note on *The Good Soldier* on 281 below.

sound men. Never in his life had anyone[18] shaken his head at Mark and said:

"You're *brilliant!*" Brilliant! That stick! No, he was indispensable!

"Upon my soul!" Tietjens said to himself, "that girl down there is the only intelligent living soul I've met for years.". . . A little pronounced in manner sometimes; faulty in reasoning naturally, but quite intelligent,[19] with a touch of wrong accent now and then. But if she was wanted anywhere, there she'd be![20] Of good stock, of course: on both sides! . . . But, positively, she and Sylvia were the only two human beings he had met for years whom he could respect: the one for sheer efficiency in killing: the other for having the constructive desire and knowing how to set about it. Kill or cure! The two functions of man. If you wanted something killed you'd go to Sylvia Tietjens in the sure faith that she would kill it: emotion: hope: ideal: kill it quick and sure. If you wanted something kept alive you'd go to Valentine: she'd find something to do for it . . . The two types of mind:[21] remorseless enemy: sure screen: dagger . . . sheath!

Perhaps the future of the world then was to women? Why not? He hadn't in years met a man that he hadn't to talk down to— as you talk down to a child: as he had talked down to General Campion or to Mr. Waterhouse . . . as he always talked down to Macmaster. All good fellows in their way. . . .

But why was he born to be a sort of lonely buffalo: outside the herd? Not artist: not soldier: not bureaucrat: not certainly indispensable anywhere: apparently not even sound in the eyes of these dim-minded specialists . . . An exact observer. . . .

Hardly even that for the last six and a half hours:

> "Die Sommer Nacht hat mir's[22] angethan
> Das war ein schwiegsames[23] Reiten . . ."*

he said aloud.

---

* Not by Heine, as Tietjens thinks, but from the third section of 'Der Trompeter von Säkkingen' by Joseph Victor Von Scheffel (1826–86): 'Die Sommernacht hat mir's angetan, / Das ist ein schweigsames Reiten'. See Harvey, *Bibliography* 201–2, for Ford's appreciation of Heine's language. There was a popular seting by Victor Nessler in 1884.

How could[24] you translate that: you couldn't translate it: no one could translate Heine:

> "It was the summer night came over me:
> That was silent riding ..."

A voice cut into his warm, drowsy thought:
"Oh, you *do* exist. But you've spoken too late. I've run into the horse." He must have been speaking aloud. He had felt the horse quivering at the end of the reins. The horse, too, was used to her by now.[25] It had hardly stirred ... He wondered when he had left off singing "John Peel." ... He said:
"Come along, then: have you found anything?"
The answer came:
"Something ... But you can't talk in this stuff ... I'll just ..."
The voice died away as if a door had shut. He waited: consciously waiting: as an occupation! Contritely and to make a noise he rattled the whip-stock in its bucket. The horse started and he had to check in quickly: a damn fool he was. Of course a horse would start if you rattled a whip-stock. He called out:
"Are you all right?" The cart might have knocked her down. He had, however, broken the convention. Her voice came from a great distance:
"I'm all right. Trying the other side ..."
His last thought came back to him. He had broken their convention: he had exhibited concern: like any other man.... He said to himself:
"By God! Why not take a holiday: why not break all conventions?"
They erected themselves intangibly and irrefragably. He had not known this young woman twenty-four hours: not to speak to: and already the convention existed between them that he must play stiff and cold, she warm and clinging.... Yet she was obviously as cool a hand as himself: cooler no doubt, for at bottom he was certainly a sentimentalist.
A convention of the most imbecile type ... Then break all conventions: with the young woman: with himself above all. For forty-eight hours ... almost exactly forty-eight hours till he started for Dover....

> "And I must to the greenwood go,
> Alone: a banished[26] man!'"*

Border ballad! Written not seven miles from Groby!

By the descending moon: it being then[27] just after cockcrow of midsummer night—what sentimentality!—it must be half-past four on Sunday. He had worked out that to catch the morning Ostend boat at Dover he must leave the Wannops' at 5.15 on Tuesday morning, in a motor for the junction. . . . What incredible cross-country train connections! Five hours for not forty miles.

He had then forty-eight and three-quarter hours! Let them be a holiday! A holiday from himself above all: a holiday from his standards: from his convention with himself. From clear observation: from exact thought: from knocking over all the skittles of the exactitudes of others: from the suppression of emotions. . . . From all the wearinesses that made him intolerable to himself. . . . He felt his limbs lengthen, as if they too had relaxed.

Well, already he had had six and a half hours of it. They had started at 10 and, like any other man, he had enjoyed the drive, though it had been difficult to keep the beastly cart balanced, the girl had had to sit behind with her arm round the other girl, who screamed at every oak tree. . . .

But he had—if he put himself to the question—mooned along under the absurd moon that had accompanied them down the heaven: to the scent of hay: to the sound of nightingales, hoarse by now, of course—in June he changes his tune;[28†] of corncrakes, of bats, of a heron twice, overhead. They had passed the blue-

---

\*   The refrain of alternate stanzas of most of 'The Nut-brown Maid'.

†   In *Joseph Conrad* 23–4, Ford recalled Conrad's dejection as Ford read to him the manuscript of 'Seraphina', which they were to collaborate on, and which was eventually published as *Romance*: 'The writer finished with the statement that, as it was June the nightingale sang a trifle hoarsely. This zoological observation, in spite of the cadence, gave the final touch to Conrad's dejection. The writer's voice having stopped he exclaimed: "What? What? What? What's that?" When he heard that that was the end he groaned and said: "Good God!" – for the last time. There are writers – French writers – who can keep the final revelation of a whole long novel back until the last three words. For this he had hoped.'

black shadows of corn stacks,* of heavy, rounded oaks, of hop oasts that are half church tower, half finger-post.† And the road silver grey, and the night warm.... It was midsummer night that had done that to him.... *Hat mir's angethan.*

*Das war ein schwiegsames*[29] *Reiten....*

Not absolutely silent of course: but silentish! Coming back from the parson's, where they had dropped the little London sewer rat, they had talked very little.... Not unpleasant people the parson's: an uncle of the girl's: three girl cousins, not unpleasant, like the girl but without the individuality ... A remarkably good bite of beef: a truly meritorious Stilton and a drop of whisky that proved the parson to be a man. All in candle-light. A motherly mother of the family to take the rat up some stairs ... a great deal of laughter of girls ... then a re-start an hour later than had been scheduled.... Well, it hadn't mattered: they had the whole of eternity before them: the good horse—*really* it was a good horse!—putting its shoulders into the work....

They had talked a little at first; about the safeness of the London girl from the police now; about the brickishness of the parson in taking her in. She certainly would never have reached Charing Cross by train....

There had fallen long periods of silences. A bat had whirled very near their off-lamp.

"What a large bat!" she had said. "*Noctilux major...*"

He said:

"Where do you get your absurd Latin nomenclature from? Isn't it *phalæna* ..." She had answered:

---

* Ford Madox Brown noted such effects in his *Painter's Diary*, and captured them in his paintings *Hayfield* and *Walton-on-the Naze*, a generation ahead of Monet's celebrated haystack series from 1890: 'What wonderful effects I have seen this evening in the hay fields, the warmth of the uncut grass, the greeny greyness of the unmade hay in furrows or tufts ... lovely violet shadows ... melting away one tint into another ... one moment more & cloud passes & all the magic is gone.' *The Diary of Ford Madox Brown*, ed. Virginia Surtees (New Haven and London: Yale University Press, 1981), 145, entry for 21 July 1855. See Angela Thirlwell, 'From Paint to Print – Grandfather's Legacy', in *Ford Madox Ford and Visual Culture*, ed. Laura Colombino, International Ford Madox Ford Studies, 8 (Amsterdam and New York: Rodopi, 2009), 29–38.

† 'A post set up at the parting of roads, with one or more arms, often terminating in the shape of a finger, to indicate the directions of the several roads': *OED*. Kentish oast-houses are generally circular brick kilns, with conical tiled roofs, capped by revolving white cowls with wind-vanes resembling wooden road-signs.

"From White . . .[30] The *Natural History of Selborne* is the only natural history I ever read. . . ."*

"He's the last English writer that could write," said Tietjens.

"He calls the downs 'those majestic and amusing mountains,'" she said. "Where do you get your dreadful Latin pronunciation from? Phal . . . i . . . i . . . na! To rhyme with Dinah!"

"It's '*sublime* and amusing mountains,' not 'majestic and amusing,'" Tietjens said. "I got my Latin pronunciation, like all public schoolboys of to-day, from the German."[31]

She answered:

"You would! Father used to say it made him sick."

"Cæsar equals Kaiser," Tietjens said. . . .

"Bother your Germans," she said, "they're no ethnologists; they're rotten at philology!" She added: "Father used to say so," to take away from an appearance of pedantry.

A silence then! She had right over her head a rug that her aunt had lent her; a silhouette beside him, with a cocky nose turned up straight out of the descending black mass. But for the square toque she would have had the silhouette of a Manchester cotton-hand: the toque gave it a different line; like the fillet† of Diana. It was piquant and agreeable to ride beside a quite silent lady in the darkness of the thick Weald that let next to no moon-light through. The horse's hoofs went clock, clock: a good horse. The near lamp illuminated the russet figure of a man with a sack on his back, pressed into the hedge, a blinking lurcher beside him.

"Keeper between the blankets!" Tietjens said to himself: "All these south country keepers sleep all night. . . . And then you give them a five-quid tip for the week-end shoot. . . ." He determined that, as to that too he would put his foot down. No more week-ends with Sylvia in the mansions of the Chosen People. . . .

The girl said suddenly; they had run into a clearing of the deep underwoods:

---

* Gilbert White (1720–93), English clergyman as well as naturalist. *The Natural History and Antiquities of Selborne* was published in 1789. In fact White doesn't use the term *noctilux major*, but does mention *phalaenae*. He calls the Sussex Downs 'that chain of majestic mountains' in Letter XVII, and adds: 'I think there is somewhat peculiarly sweet and amusing in the shapely figured aspect of chalk-hills in preference to those of stone.'
† Headband.

"I'm not stuffy with you over that Latin, though you were unnecessarily[32] rude. And I'm not sleepy. I'm loving it all."

He hesitated for a minute. It was a silly-girl thing to say. She didn't usually say silly-girl things. He ought to snub her for her own sake. . . .

He had said:

"I'm rather loving it too!" She was looking at him; her nose had disappeared from the silhouette. He hadn't been able to help it; the moon had been just above her head; unknown stars all round her; the night was warm. Besides, a really manly man may condescend at times! He rather owes it to himself. . . .

She said:

"That was nice of you! You might have hinted that the rotten drive was taking you away from your so important work. . . . "

"Oh, I can think as I drive," he said. She said:

"Oh!" and then: "The reason why I'm unconcerned over your rudeness about my Latin is that I know[33] I'm a much better Latinist than you. You can't quote a few lines of Ovid without sprinkling howlers in. . . . It's *vastum*, not *longum* . . . 'Terra tribus scopulis vastum procurrit'[*] . . . It's *alto*, not *coelo* . . . 'Uvidus ex alto desilientis. . . .'[†] How could Ovid have written *ex coelo*? The 'c' after the 'x' sets your teeth on edge."

Tietjens said:

"*Excogitabo!*"[‡]

"That's purely canine!"[§] she said with contempt.

---

[*]  Ovid, *Fasti* IV.416: 'It runs out in three rocky capes to the vast ocean.' The quotation, explaining how the land of Trinacris was named for its geography, is from the passage introducing the rape of Persephone. Ford writes appreciatively on the *Persephone Rapta* in *March* 243–4, and analyses the syllabics of this passage in *Mightier* 274.

[†]  Ovid, *Fasti*, IV.427–8: 'Valle sub umbrosa locus est aspergine multa / Uvidus ex alto desilientis aquae': 'In a shady vale there is a place moist with the abundant spray from a high waterfall.' Ford alludes to this passage as an example of the fruits of a 'gentlemanly-scholarly contemplation of the Classics' in an essay on Compton Mackenzie: 'Literary Portraits – I', *Outlook*, 32 (13 Sept. 1913), 353–4. See *Critical Essays* 110–14. He also quotes the lines (impeccably) in *Provence* 291, where he describes them as from 'the "Persephone Rapta" which would seem to counsel young women to live rather in Provence than in Sussex dampness. . . .'

[‡]  'I shall contrive' (i.e. to remember it; to get it right next time).

[§]  i.e. 'dog-Latin': a spurious or schoolboy variety. That Tietjens in mock-contrition also manages to find a Latin word which includes 'the "c" after the "x"' presumably adds to her irritation.

"Besides," Tietjens said, "*longum* is much better than *vastum*. I hate cant adjectives like 'vast.' ..."

"It's like your modesty to correct Ovid," she exclaimed. "Yet you say Ovid and Catullus were the only two Roman poets to *be* poets. That's because they *were* sentimental and used adjectives like *vastum*.... What's 'Sad tears mixed with kisses'[34] but the sheerest sentimentality!"

"It ought,[35] you know," Tietjens said with soft dangerousness, "to be 'Kisses mingled with sad tears'... 'Tristibus et lacrimis oscula mixta dabis.' ..."*

"I'm hanged if I ever could," she exclaimed explosively. "A man like you could die in a ditch and I'd never come near. You're desiccated even for a man who has learned his Latin[36] from the Germans."

"Oh, well, I'm a mathematician," Tietjens said. "Classics is not my line!"[37]

"It *isn't*," she answered tartly.

A long time afterwards from her black figure came the words:

"You used 'mingled' instead of 'mixed' to translate *mixta*. I shouldn't think you took English at Cambridge, either! Though they're as rotten at that as at everything else, father used to say."

"Your father was Balliol, of course," Tietjens said with the snuffy contempt of a scholar of Trinity College, Cambridge.[38†] But having lived most of her life amongst Balliol people she took this as a compliment and an olive branch.

Some time afterwards Tietjens, observing that her silhouette was still between him and the moon, remarked:

"I don't know if you know that for some minutes we've been running nearly due west. We ought to be going south-east by a bit south. I suppose you *do* know this road. ..."

"Every inch of it," she said, "I've been on it over and over again on my motor-bicycle with mother in the side-car. The next cross road is called Grandfather's Wantways.‡ We've got eleven miles and a quarter still to do. The road turns back here because of the old Sussex iron pits; it goes in and out amongst them; hundreds

---

\* Not Catullus, but Tibullus, I.62.

† Arthur Marwood had entered Trinity College, Cambridge, in 1887 to read mathematics, but had to leave in his second year due to ill health.

‡ See *The Cinque Ports* 171: '"wantways" is the local word ...'

of them. You know the exports of the town of Rye in the eighteenth century were hops, cannon, kettles, and chimney backs.
The railings round St. Paul's are made of Sussex iron."

"I knew that, of course," Tietjens said: "I come of an iron
county myself.... Why didn't you let me run the girl over in the
side-car,[39] it would have been quicker?"

"Because," she said, "three weeks ago I smashed up the side-
car on the milestone at Hog's Corner: doing forty."

"It must have been a pretty tidy smash!" Tietjens said. "Your
mother wasn't aboard?"

"No," the girl said, "suffragette literature. The side-car was
full. It *was* a pretty tidy smash. Hadn't you observed I still limp a
little?" ...

A few minutes later she said:

"I haven't the least notion where we really are. I clean forgot
to notice the road. And I don't care.... Here's a signpost though;
pull in to it...."

The lamps would not, however, shine on the arms of the post;
they were burning dim and showing low. A good deal of fog was
in the air. Tietjens gave the reins to the girl and got down. He
took out the near light and, going back a yard or two to the signpost, examined its bewildering ghostlinesses....

The girl gave a little squeak that went to his backbone; the
hoofs clattered unusually; the cart went on. Tietjens went after
it; it was astonishing; it had completely disappeared. Then he ran
into it: ghostly, reddish and befogged. It must have got much
thicker suddenly. The fog swirled all round the near lamp as he
replaced it in its socket.

"Did you do that on purpose?" he asked the girl. "Or can't you
hold a horse?"

"I can't drive a horse," the girl said; "I'm afraid of them. I can't
drive a motor-bike either. I made that up because[40] I *knew* you'd
say you'd rather have taken Gertie over in the side-car[41] than
driven with me."

"Then do you mind," Tietjens said, "telling me if you know
this road at all?"

"Not a bit!" she answered cheerfully. "I never drove it in my
life.[42] I looked it up on the map before we started because I'm sick
to death of the road we went by. There's a one-horse 'bus from

Rye to Tenterden, and I've walked from Tenterden to my uncle's over and over again...."

"We shall probably be out all night then," Tietjens said. "Do you mind? The horse may be tired...."

She said:

"Oh, the poor horse! ... I *meant* us to be out all night.... But the poor horse.... * What a brute I was not to think of it."

"We're thirteen[43] miles from a place called Brede;[†] eleven and a quarter from a place whose name I couldn't read; six and three-quarters from somewhere called something like Uddlemere...." Tietjens said. "This is the road to Uddlemere."

"Oh, that was Grandfather's Wantways all right," she declared. "I know it well. It's called 'Grandfather's' because an old gentleman used to sit there called Gran'fer Finn. Every Tenterden market day he used to sell fleed[‡] cakes from a basket to the carts that went by. Tenterden market was abolished in 1845—the effect of the repeal of the Corn Laws, you know. As a Tory you ought to be interested[44] in that."

Tietjens said patiently: He could sympathise with her mood; she had now a heavy weight off her chest; and, if long acquaintance with his wife had not made him able to put up with feminine vagaries, nothing ever would.

"Would you mind," he said then, "telling me ... "

"If," she interrupted, "that was really Gran'fer's Wantways: midland English. 'Vent' equals four crossroads: high French *carrefour*.... Or, perhaps, that isn't the right word. But it's the way your mind works...."

"You have, of course, often walked from your uncle's to Gran'fer's Wantways," Tietjens said, "with your cousins, taking brandy to the invalid in the old toll-gate house. That's how you know the story of Grandfer. You said you had never driven it; but you *have* walked it. That's the way *your* mind works, isn't it?"

She said: "*Oh!*"

---

* David Garnett recalled Ford giving a melancholy rendition of 'the Westmoreland folksong *Poor Old Horse*': *The Golden Echo* (London: Chatto & Windus, 1953), 127–8.

† Ford's friend, the American writer Stephen Crane, lived in the Tudor manor house Brede Place, discussed in *The Cinque Ports* 90–1. See also *Return* 27–9.

‡ Lard. The *OED* gives an example from 1845: 'Fleed or flead cakes [...] served as a tea-cake at the tables of the superior order of Kentish farmers.'

"Then," Tietjens went on, "would you mind telling me—for the sake of the poor horse—whether Uddlemere is or isn't on our road home. I take it you don't know just this stretch of road, but you know whether it is the right road."

"The touch of pathos,"[45] the girl said, "is a wrong note. It's you who're in mental trouble about the road.[46] The horse isn't. . . . "

Tietjens let the cart go on another fifty yards; then he said:

"It *is* the right road. The Uddlemere turning *was* the right one. You wouldn't let the horse go another five steps if it wasn't. You're as soppy about horses as . . . as I am."

"There's at least that bond of sympathy between us," she said drily. "Gran'fer's Wantways is six and three-quarter miles from Udimore; Udimore is exactly five from us; total, eleven and three-quarters; twelve and a quarter if you add half a mile for Udimore itself. The name is Udimore, not Uddlemere. Local place-name enthusiasts derive this from 'O'er the mere.' Absurd!* Legend as follows: Church builders desiring to put church with relic of St. Rumwold† in wrong place, voice wailed: 'O'er the mere.' Obviously absurd! . . . Putrid! 'O'er the' by Grimm's law impossible as 'Udi';‡ 'mere' not a Middle Low[47] German word at all. . . . "

"Why," Tietjens said, "are you giving me all this information?"

"Because," the girl said, "it's the way your mind works. . . . It picks up useless facts as silver after you've polished it picks up sulphur vapour; and tarnishes! It arranges the useless facts in obsolescent patterns and makes Toryism out of them. . . . I've never met a Cambridge Tory man before. I thought they were all in museums and you work them up again out of bones. That's what father used to say; he was an Oxford Disraelian Conservative Imperialist. . . . "

"I know of course," Tietjens said.

---

* See *The Cinque Ports* 89, footnote: 'The name is explained by legendists as meaning "O'er the mere." The church, they say, was originally commenced elsewhere, but the builders were continually alarmed by the foul fiend, who assailed their ears with cries of "O'er the mere." It is said that the builders took the hint.' See also plate facing 67.
† The church at Udimore is St Mary's. In *Mightier* 40, Ford mentions 'Saint Rumwold of Bonnington' – the Kentish village he had first lived in on the Romney Marsh from 1894–6.
‡ Hypothesis of consonantal shift between Indo-European and modern languages postulated by J. L. Grimm (1785–1863).

"Of course you know," the girl said. "You know everything. . . . And you've worked everything into absurd principles. You think father was unsound because he tried to apply tendencies to life. *You* want to be a Nenglish[48] country gentleman and spin principles out of the newspapers and the gossip of horse-fairs. And let the country go to hell, you'll never stir a finger except to say I told you so."

She touched him suddenly on the arm:

"*Don't* mind me!" she said. "It's reaction. I'm so happy. I'm so happy."

He said:

"That's all right! That's all right!" But for a minute or two it wasn't really. All feminine claws, he said to himself, are sheathed in velvet; but they can hurt a good deal if they touch you on the sore[49] places of the defects of your qualities—even merely with the velvet. He added: "Your mother works you very hard."

She exclaimed:

"How you *understand*. You're amazing: for a man who tries to be a sea-anemone!" She said:[50] "Yes, this is the first holiday I've had for four solid months; six hours a day typing; four hours a day work for the movement; three, housework and gardening; three, mother reading out her day's work for slips of the pen. . . . And on the top of it the raid and the anxiety. . . . Dreadful anxiety, you know. Suppose mother *had* gone to prison. . . . Oh, I'd have gone mad. . . . Week-days and Sundays. . . . " She stopped: "I'm apologising, really," she went on. "Of course I ought not to have talked to you like that. You a great Panjandrum;* saving the country with your statistics and all. . . . It *did* make you a rather awful figure, you know . . . and the relief to find you're . . . oh, a man like oneself with feet of clay. . . . I'd dreaded this drive. . . . I'd have dreaded it dreadfully if I hadn't been in such a dread about Gertie and the police. And, if I hadn't let off steam I should have had to jump out and run beside the cart. . . . I could still . . . "

"You couldn't," Tietjens said. "You couldn't see the cart."

They had just run into a bank of solid fog that seemed to

---

* A burlesque potentate: the phrase occurs in a 'farrago of nonsense' composed by the eighteenth-century wit and dramatist, Samuel Foote (1720–77), supposedly to test the Irish actor Charles Macklin, who claimed to have such a perfect memory that he could recall anything having read it over once.

encounter them with a soft, ubiquitous blow. It was blinding; it was deadening to sounds; it was in a sense mournful; but it was happy, too, in its romantic unusualness. They couldn't see the gleam of the lamps; they could hardly hear the step of the horse; the horse had fallen at once to a walk. They agreed that neither of them could be responsible for losing the way; in the circumstances that was impossible. Fortunately the horse would take them somewhere; it had belonged to a local higgler: a man that used the roads buying poultry for re-sale.... They agreed that they had no responsibilities; and after that went on for unmeasured hours in silence; the mist growing, but very, very gradually, more luminous.... Once or twice, at a rise in the road, they saw again the stars and the moon, but mistily. On the fourth occasion they had emerged into the silver lake; like mermen rising to the surface of a tropical sea....

Tietjens had said:

"You'd better get down and take the lamp. See if you can find a milestone; I'd get down myself, but you might not be able to hold the horse...." She had plunged in ...

And he had sat, feeling he didn't know why, like a Guy Fawkes; up in the light, thinking by no means disagreeable thoughts—intent, like Miss Wannop herself, on a complete holiday of forty-eight hours; till Tuesday morning! He had to look forward to a long and luxurious day of figures; a rest after dinner; half a night more of figures; a Monday devoted to a horse-deal in the market-town where he happened to know the horse-dealer. The horse-dealer, indeed, was known to every hunting man in England![51] A luxurious, long argument in the atmosphere of stable-hartshorn and slow wranglings couched in ostler's epigrams. You couldn't have a better day; the beer in the pub.[52] probably good, too. Or if not that, the claret.... The claret in south country inns was often quite good; there was no sale for it so it got well kept....

On Tuesday it would close in again, beginning with the meeting of his wife's maid at Dover....

He was to have, above all, a holiday from himself and to take it like other men, free of his conventions, his strait waistcoatings....

The girl said:

"I'm coming up now! I've found out something. . . ." He watched intently the place where she must appear; it would give him pointers about the impenetrability of mist to the eye.

Her otter skin cap had beads of dew: beads of dew were on her hair beneath: she scrambled up, a little awkwardly: her eyes sparkled with fun: panting a little: her cheeks bright. Her hair was darkened by the wetness of the mist, but she appeared golden in the sudden moonlight.[53]

Before she was quite up, Tietjens almost kissed her. Almost. An all but irresistible impulse! He exclaimed:

"Steady, the Buffs!"* in his surprise.

She said:

"Well, you might[54] as well have given me a hand."[55] "I found," she went on, "a stone[56] that had I.R.D.C.† on it, and there the lamp went out. We're not on the marsh because we're between quick hedges.‡ That's all I have found. . . . But I've worked out[57] what makes me so tart with you. . . ."

He couldn't believe she could be so absolutely calm: the after-wash of that impulse had been so strong in him that it was as if he had tried to catch her to him and had been foiled by her. . . . She ought to be indignant, amused, even pleased. . . . She ought to show some emotion. . . .

She said:

"It was your silencing me with that absurd non-sequitur about the Pimlico clothing factory. It was an insult to my intelligence."

"You recognised that it was a fallacy!" Tietjens said. He was looking hard at her. He didn't know what had happened to him. She took a long look at him, cool, but with immense eyes. It was as if for a moment destiny, which usually let him creep past somehow, had looked at him. "Can't," he argued with destiny, "a man want to kiss a schoolgirl in a scuffle. . . ." His own voice, a caricature of his own voice, seemed to come to him: "Gentlemen don't . . ." He exclaimed:

---

* The East Kent Regiment were called 'the Buffs' after being issued with dull yellow coats. 'Steady the Buffs!' – originally a regimental parade ground drill order – is glossed by Partridge as a catch-phrase of adjuration or of self-admonition: originally army, since mid-nineteenth century.
† Icklesham Rural District Council.
‡ Quick (or quickset) hedges, especially of thorny plants such as hawthorn, are commonly grown in the south-east to fence off fields.

"Don't gentlemen? . . ." and then stopped because he realised that he had spoken aloud.

She said:

"Oh, *gentlemen* do!" she said,[58] "use fallacies to glide over tight places in arguments. And they browbeat schoolgirls with them. It's that, that underneath, has been exasperating me with you. You regarded me at that date—three-quarters of a day ago—as a schoolgirl."

Tietjens said:

"I don't now!" He added: "Heaven knows I don't now!"

She said: "No; you don't now!"

He said:

"It didn't need your putting up all that blue stocking* erudition to convince me. . . . "

"Blue stocking!" she exclaimed contemptuously. "There's nothing of the blue stocking about me. I know Latin because father spoke it with us. It was your pompous blue socks I was pulling."[59]

Suddenly she began to laugh. Tietjens was feeling sick, physically sick. She went on laughing. He stuttered:

"What is it?"

"The sun!" she said, pointing. Above the silver horizon was the sun; not a red sun: shining, burnished.

"I don't see . . ." Tietjens said.

"What there is to laugh at?" she asked. "It's the day! . . . The longest day's begun . . . and to-morrow's as long. . . . The summer solstice, you know. . . . After to-morrow the days shorten towards winter. But to-morrow's as long. . . . I'm so glad . . . "[60]

"That we've got through the night? . . ." Tietjens asked.[61]

She looked at him for a long time. "You're not so dreadfully ugly, really," she said.

Tietjens said:

"What's that church?"

Rising out of the mist on a fantastically green knoll, a quarter

---

* The Blue Stocking Society met in the mid-eighteenth century to discuss literature, with some of the women wearing ordinary blue (rather than dress-) stockings. The phrase came to apply to women having or affecting learning: usually derogatory. Valentine plays on it, commenting on Tietjens' 'blue socks', a phrase that doesn't normally have this connotation.

of a mile away, was an unnoticeable place of worship: an oak shingle tower[62] roof that shone grey like lead: an impossibly bright weathercock, brighter than the sun. Dark elms all round it, holding wetnesses of mist.

"Icklesham!" she cried softly.* "Oh, we're nearly home. Just above Mountby[63] . . . That's the Mountby drive. . . ."

Trees existed, black and hoary with the dripping mist. Trees in the hedgerow and the avenue that led to Mountby: it made a right-angle just before coming into the road and the road went away at right-angles across the gate.[64]

"You'll have to pull to the left before you reach the avenue," the girl said. "Or as like as not the horse will walk right up to the house. The higgler who had him used to buy Lady Claudine's eggs. . . ."

Tietjens exclaimed barbarously:

"Damn Mountby. I wish we'd never come near it," and he whipped the horse into a sudden trot. The hoofs sounded suddenly loud. She placed her hand on his gloved driving hand. Had it been his flesh she wouldn't have done it.

She said:

"My dear, it couldn't have lasted for ever . . . But you're a good man. And very clever. . . . You will get through. . . ."

Not ten yards ahead Tietjens saw a tea-tray, the underneath[65] of a black-lacquered tea-tray, gliding towards them: mathematically straight, just rising from the mist. He shouted: mad: the blood in his head. His shout was drowned by the scream of the horse: he had swung it to the left. The cart turned up: the horse emerged from the mist: head and shoulders: pawing. A stone sea-horse from the fountain of Versailles! Exactly that! Hanging in air for an eternity: the girl looking at it, leaning slightly forward.[66]

The horse didn't come over backwards: he had loosened the reins. It wasn't there any more. The damndest thing that *could* happen! He had known it would happen. He said:

"We're all right now!" There was a crash and scraping: like twenty tea-trays: a prolonged sound. They must be scraping along

---

\*    Icklesham church is illustrated in *The Cinque Ports*, facing 88. On 89 Ford says 'The church is particularly picturesque when it is lit up on Sunday evenings. A sufficiently unromantic person once said that it seems at such times to be the nook nearest heaven upon the earth.'

the mud-guard of the invisible car.[67] He had the pressure of the
horse's mouth: the horse was away: going hell for leather. He
increased the pressure. The girl said:

"I know I'm all right with you."

They were suddenly in bright sunlight: cart: horse: commonplace hedgerows. They were going uphill: a steep brae. He wasn't
certain she hadn't said: "Dear!" or "My dear!" Was it possible
after so short . . . ? But it had been a long night. He was, no doubt,
saving her life too. He increased his pressure on the horse's mouth
gently:[68] up to all his twelve stone: all his strength. The hill told
too. Steep, white road between shaven grass banks![69]

Stop; damn you! Poor beast . . . The girl fell out of the cart.
No! jumped clear! Out[70] to the animal's head. It threw its head
up. Nearly off her feet: she was holding the bit. . . . She couldn't![71]
Tender mouth . . . afraid of horses. . . . He said:

"Horse cut!"[72] Her face like a little white blancmange!

"Come quick," she said.

"I must hold a minute," he said, "might go off if I let go to get
down. Badly cut?"

"Blood running down solid! Like an apron," she said.

He was at last at her side. It was true. But not so much like an
apron. More like a red, varnished stocking. He said:

"You've a white petticoat on. Get over the hedge; jump it, and
take it off . . ."

"Tear it into strips?" she asked.[73] "Yes!"

He called to her; she was suspended halfway up the bank:

"Tear one half off first.[74] The rest into strips."

She said: "All right!" She didn't go over the quickset as neatly
as he had expected. No take off. But she was over. . . .

The horse, trembling, was looking down, its nostrils
distended, at the blood pooling from its near foot. The cut was
just on the shoulder. He put his left arm right over the horse's
eyes. The horse stood it, almost with a sigh of relief. . . . A
wonderful magnetism with horses. Perhaps with women too? God
knew. He was almost certain she had said "Dear."

She said: "Here." He caught a round ball of whitish stuff. He
undid it. Thank God: what sense! A long, strong, white band. . . .
What the devil was the hissing. . . . A small, closed car with
crumpled mud-guards:[75] noiseless nearly: gleaming black . . . God

curse it: it passed them: stopped ten yards down . . . the horse
rearing back: mad! Clean mad . . . something like a scarlet and
white cockatoo, fluttering out of the small car door . . . a general.
In full tog. White feathers! Ninety medals! Scarlet coat! Black
trousers with red stripe. Spurs too, by God!

Tietjens[76] said:

"God damn you, you bloody swine. Go away!"

The apparition, past the horse's blinkers, said:

"I can, at least, hold the horse for you. I went past to get you
out of Claudine's sight."

"Damn good-natured of[77] you," Tietjens said as rudely as he
could. "You'll have to pay for the horse."

The General exclaimed:

"Damn it all! Why should I? You were driving your beastly
camel right into my drive."

"You never sounded your horn," Tietjens said.

"I was on private ground," the General shouted. "Besides
I did." An enraged, scarlet scarecrow, very thin, he was holding
the horse's bridle. Tietjens was extending[78] the half petticoat,
with a measuring eye, before the horse's chest. The General
said:

"Look here! I've got to take the escort for the Royal party at
St. Peter-in-Manor, Dover. They're laying the Buffs'[79] colours on
the altar or something."

"You never sounded your horn," Tietjens said. "Why didn't
you bring your chauffeur? He's a capable man. . . . You talk very
big about the widow and child. But when it comes to robbing
them of fifty quid by slaughtering their horse . . . "

The General said:

"What the devil were[80] you doing coming into our drive at five
in the morning?"

Tietjens, who had applied the half petticoat to the horse's
chest, exclaimed:

"Pick up that thing and give it me." A thin roll of linen was
at his feet: it had rolled down from the hedge.

"Can I leave the horse?" the General asked.

"Of course you can," Tietjens said. "If I can't quiet a horse
better than you can run a car . . . "

He bound the new linen strips over the petticoat: the horse

dropped its head, smelling his hand. The General, behind Tietjens, stood back on his heels, grasping his gold-mounted sword. Tietjens went on twisting and twisting the bandage.

"Look here," the General[81] suddenly bent forward to whisper into Tietjens' ear, "what am I to tell Claudine? I believe she saw the girl."

"Oh, tell her we came to ask what time you cast off* your beastly otter hounds," Tietjens said; "that's a matutinal job...."

The General's voice had a really pathetic intonation:

"On a Sunday!" he exclaimed. Then in a tone of relief he added: "I shall tell her you were going to early communion in Duchemin's church at Pett."[82]

"If you want to add blasphemy to horse-slaughtering as a profession, do," Tietjens said. "But you'll have to pay for the horse."

"I'm damned if I will," the General shouted. "I tell you you were driving into my drive."

"Then I *shall*," Tietjens said, "and you know the construction you'll put on *that*."

He straightened his back to look at the horse.

"Go away," he said, "say what you like. Do what you like! But as you go through Rye send up the horse-ambulance[83] from the vet.'s. Don't forget that. I'm going to save this horse...."

"You know, Chris," the General said, "you're the most wonderful hand with a horse ... There isn't another man in England ..."

"I know it," Tietjens said. "Go away. And send up that ambulance.... There's your sister getting out of your car...."

The General began:

"I've an awful lot to get explained ..." But, at a thin scream of: "General! General!" he pressed on his sword hilt to keep it from between his long, black, scarlet-striped legs, and running to the car pushed back into its door a befeathered, black bolster. He waved his hand to Tietjens:

"I'll send the ambulance," he called.

The horse, its upper leg swathed with criss-crosses of white through which a purple stain was slowly penetrating, stood

---

\* Let the hounds loose on a scent.

motionless, its head hanging down, mule-like, under the blinding sun. To ease it Tietjens began to undo the trace. The girl hopped over the hedge and, scrambling down, began to help him.

"Well. My reputation's gone," she said cheerfully. "I know what Lady Claudine is.... Why did you try to quarrel with the General?..."

"Oh, you'd better," Tietjens said wretchedly, "have a lawsuit with him. It'll account for ... for your not going to Mountby[84] ..."

"You think of everything," she said.

They wheeled the cart backwards off the motionless horse. Tietjens moved it[85] two yards forward—to get it out of sight of its own blood. Then they sat down side by side on the slope of the bank.

"Tell me about Groby," the girl said at last.

Tietjens began to tell her about his home.... There was, in front of it, an avenue that turned into the road at right angles. Just like the one at Mountby.

"My great-great-grandfather made it," Tietjens said. "He liked privacy and didn't want the house visible by vulgar people on the road ... just like the fellow who planned Mountby, no doubt.... But it's beastly dangerous with motors. We shall have to alter it ...[86] just at the bottom of a dip. We can't have horses hurt.... You'll see ..." It came suddenly into his head that he wasn't perhaps the father of the child who was actually the heir to that beloved place over which generation after generation had brooded.[87] Ever since Dutch William!* A damn Nonconformist swine!

On the bank his knees were almost level with his chin. He felt himself slipping down.

"If I ever take you there ..." he began.

"Oh, but you never will," she said.

The child wasn't his. The heir to Groby! All his brothers[88] were childless ... There was a deep well in the stable yard. He had meant to teach the child how, if you dropped a pebble in, you waited to count sixty-three. And there came up a whispering

---

\*    William of Orange.

roar.... But not his child! Perhaps he hadn't even the power to
beget children. His married brothers hadn't.... Clumsy sobs
shook him. It was the dreadful injury to the horse which had
finished him. He felt as if the responsibility were his. The poor
beast had trusted him and he had smashed it up.[89] Miss Wannop
had her arm over his shoulder.

"My dear!" she said, "you won't ever take me to Groby ... It's
perhaps ... oh ... short acquaintance; but[90] I feel you're the
splendidest ..."

He thought: "It *is* rather short acquaintance."[91]

He felt a great deal of pain, over which there presided the tall,
eel-skin, blonde figure of his wife....

The girl said:

"There's a fly coming!" and removed her arm.

A fly drew up before them with a blear-eyed[92] driver. He said
General Campion had kicked him out of bed, from beside his old
woman. He wanted a pound to take them to Mrs. Wannop's,
waked out of his beauty sleep and all. The knacker's cart was
following.[93]

"You'll take Miss Wannop home at once," Tietjens said, "she's
got her mother's breakfast to see to.... I shan't leave the horse
till the knacker's van comes."

The fly-driver touched his age-green hat with his whip.

"Aye," he said thickly, putting a sovereign into his waistcoat
pocket. "Always the gentleman ... a merciful man is merciful
also to his beast*.... But I wouldn't leave my little wooden 'ut,
nor miss my[94] breakfast, for no beast.... Some do and some ...
do not."

He drove off with the girl in the interior of his antique
conveyance.

Tietjens remained on the slope of the bank, in the strong
sunlight, beside the drooping horse. It had done nearly forty miles
and lost, at last, a lot of blood.

Tietjens said:

"I suppose I could get the governor to pay fifty quid for it. They
want the money...."

He said:

---

* Proverbial.

"But it wouldn't be playing the game!"

A long time afterwards he said:

"Damn all principles!" And then:

"But one has to keep on going. . . .* Principles are like a skeleton map of a country[95]—you know whether you're going east or north."[96]

The knacker's cart lumbered round the corner.

---

\* A phrase (sometimes given as 'keep all on gooing', to reflect the original pronunciation) that Ford took from Meary Walker of Bonnington. Cf. *The Soul of London* (London: Alston Rivers, 1905), 11, 118 (*England* 12, 72); *Return* 112; *Nightingale* 118.

# PART II[1]

## I

SYLVIA TIETJENS rose from her end of the lunch-table and swayed along it, carrying her plate. She still wore her hair in bandeaux and her skirts as long as she possibly could: she didn't, she said, with her height, intend to be taken for a girl guide. She hadn't, in complexion, in figure or in the languor of her gestures, aged by a minute. You couldn't discover in the skin of her face any deadness: in her eyes the shade more of fatigue than she intended to express, but she had purposely increased her air of scornful insolence. That was because she felt that her hold over men increased to the measure of her coldness. Someone, she knew, had once said of a dangerous woman, that when she entered the room every woman kept her husband on the leash. It was Sylvia's pleasure to think that, before she went out of that room, all the women in it realised with mortification[2]—that they needn't! For if coolly and distinctly she had said on entering: "Nothing doing!" as barmaids will to the enterprising, she couldn't more plainly have conveyed to the other women that she had no use for their treasured rubbish.

Once, on the edge of a cliff in Yorkshire, where the moors come[3] above the sea, during one of the tiresome shoots that are there the fashion, a man had bidden her observe the demeanour of the herring gulls below. They were dashing from rock to rock on the cliff face,[4] screaming, with none of the dignity of gulls. Some of them even let fall the herrings that they had caught and she saw the pieces of silver dropping into the blue motion. The man told her to look up; high, circling and continuing for a long time to circle; illuminated by the sunlight below, like a pale flame against the sky was a bird.[5] The man told her that that was some sort of fish-eagle or hawk. Its normal habit was to chase the[6] gulls which, in their terror, would drop their booty of herrings, where-upon the eagle would catch the fish before it struck the water. At the moment the eagle was not on duty, but the gulls were just as terrified as if it had been.

Sylvia stayed for a long time watching the convolutions of the eagle. It pleased her to see that, though nothing threatened the gulls, they yet screamed and dropped their herrings ... The whole affair reminded her of herself in her relationship to the ordinary women of the barnyard.... Not that there was the breath of a scandal against herself; that she very well knew, and it was her preoccupation just as turning down nice men—the "really nice men" of commerce—was her hobby.

She practiced every kind of "turning down" on these crea-tures: the really nice ones, with the Kitchener moustaches, the seal's brown eyes, the honest, thrilling voices, the clipped words, the straight backs and the admirable records—as long as you didn't enquire *too* closely. Once, in the early days of the Great Struggle, a young man—she *had* smiled at him in mistake for someone more trustable—had followed in a taxi, hard on her motor, and flushed with wine, glory and the firm conviction that all women in that lurid carnival had become common property,[7] had burst into her door from the public stairs.... She had over-topped him by the forehead and before a few minutes were up she seemed to him to have become ten foot high with a gift of words that scorched his backbone and the voice of a frozen[8] marble statue: a *chaud-froid** effect. He had come in like a stallion, red-eyed, and all his legs off the ground: he went down the stairs like a half-drowned rat, with dim eyes and really looking wet, for some reason or other.

Yet she hadn't really told him more than the way one should behave to the wives of one's brother officers then actually in the line, a point of view that, with her intimates, she daily agreed was pure bosh. But it must have seemed to him like the voice of his mother—when his mother had been much younger, of course—speaking from paradise, and his conscience had contrived the rest of his general wetness. This, however, had been melodrama and war stuff at that: it hadn't, therefore, interested her. She preferred

* French: 'hot-cold'. A cooked dish cooled before serving.

to inflict deeper and more quiet pains.

She could,[9] she flattered herself, tell the amount of empressement which a man would develop about herself at the first glance—the amount and the quality too. And from not vouchsafing a look at all, or a look of the barest and most incurious to some poor devil who even on introduction couldn't conceal his desires, to letting, after dinner, a measured glance travel from the right foot of a late dinner partner, diagonally up the ironed fold of the right trouser to the watch pocket, diagonally still, across the shirt front, pausing at the stud and so, rather more quickly away over the left shoulder, while the poor fellow stood appalled, with his dinner going wrong—from the milder note to the more pronounced she ran the whole gamut of "turnings down." The poor fellows next day would change their bootmakers, their sock merchants, their tailors, the designers of their dress-studs and shirts: they would sigh even to change the cut of their faces, communing seriously with their after-breakfast[10] mirrors. But they knew in their hearts that calamity came from the fact that she hadn't deigned to look into their eyes.... Perhaps hadn't dared was the right word!

Sylvia, herself, would have cordially acknowledged that it might have been. She knew that, like her intimates—all the Elizabeths, Alixs, and Lady Moiras of the smooth-papered, be-photographed weekly journals—she was man-mad. It was the condition, indeed, of their intimacy as of their[11] eligibilities for reproduction on hot-pressed paper. They went about in bands with, as it were, a cornfield of feather boas floating above them, though to be sure no one *wore* feather boas; they shortened their hairs and their skirts and flattened, as far as possible, their chest developments, which *does* give, oh, you know ... a *certain* ... They adopted demeanours as like as possible—and yet how unlike[12]—to those of waitresses in tea-shops frequented by city men. And one reads in police court reports of raids what *those* are! Probably they were, in action, as respectable as any body of women; *more* respectable, probably, than the great middle class of before the war, and certainly spotless by comparison with their own upper servants whose morals, merely as recorded in the divorce court statistics—*that* she had from Tietjens—would put to shame even those of Welsh or lowland Scotch villages. Her

mother was accustomed to say that she was sure her butler would
get to heaven, simply because the Recording Angel, being an
angel—and, as such, delicately minded—wouldn't have the face
to put down, much less read out, the least venial of Morgan's
offences. . . .

And, sceptical as she was by nature, Sylvia Tietjens didn't
really even believe in the capacity for immoralities of her friends.
She didn't believe that any one of them was seriously what the
French would call the *maîtresse en titre*[13] of any particular man.
Passion wasn't, at least, their strong suit: they left that to more—
or to less—august circles. The Duke of A . . . and all the little A's
. . . might be the children of the morose and passion-stricken
Duke of B . . . instead of the still more morose but less passionate
late Duke of A . . . Mr. C, the Tory statesman and late Foreign
Minister, might equally be the father of all the children of the
Tory Lord Chancellor E . . . The Whig front benches, the gloomy
and disagreeable Russells and Cavendishes trading off these—
again French—*collages sérieux*\* against the matrimonial
divagations of their own Lord F and Mr. G. . . . But those
amours[14] of heavily titled and born front benchers were matter[15]
of august politics. The hot-pressed weekly journals never got hold
of them: the parties to them didn't, for one thing, photograph
well, being old, uglyish and terribly[16] badly dressed. They were
matter rather for the memoirs of the indiscreet, already written,
but not to see the light for fifty[17] years. . . .

The affairs of her own set, female front benchers† of one side
or other as they were, were more tenuous. If they ever came to
heads, their affairs, they had rather the nature of promiscuity and
took place at the country[18] houses where bells rang at five in the
morning. Sylvia had heard of[19] such country houses, but she
didn't know of any. She imagined that they might be the baro-
nial halls of such barons of the crown as had patronymics ending
in schen . . . stein . . . and baum. There were getting to be a good

---

\*   The French *collage* (from coller, 'to stick') can be used figuratively to describe a man
     and a woman living together unmarried.
†   There were no women MPs before 1918–19, and no women members of the House of
     Lords before 1958, so these must be metaphorical 'front-benchers': either leaders of
     their social set, wives of the powerful politicians, or the women who would have been
     prominent politicians were office open to them.

many of these, but Sylvia did not visit them. She had in her that much of the papist.

Certain of her more brilliant girl friends certainly made very sudden marriages; but the averages of those were not markedly higher than in the case of the daughters of doctors, solicitors, the clergy, the lord mayors and common councilmen. They were the product usually of the more informal type of dance, of inexperience and champagne—of champagne of unaccustomed strength or of champagne taken in unusual circumstances—fasting as often as not. They were, these hasty marriages, hardly ever the result of either passion or temperamental[20] lewdness.

In her own case—years ago now—she had certainly been taken advantage of, after champagne, by a married man called Drake. A bit of a brute she acknowledged him now to be. But after the event passion had developed: intense on her side and quite intense enough on his. When, in a scare that had been as much her mother's as her own, she had led Tietjens on and married him in Paris to be out of the way—though it was fortunate that the English Catholic church of the Avenue Hoche* had been the scene of her mother's marriage also, thus establishing a precedent and an ostensible reason!—there had been dreadful scenes right up to the very night of the marriage. She had hardly to close her eyes in order to see the Paris hotel bedroom, the distorted face of Drake, who was mad with grief and jealousy, against a background of white things, flowers and the like, sent in overnight for the wedding. She knew that she had been very near death. She had wanted death.

And even now she had only to see the name of Drake in the paper—her mother's influence with the pompous front bencher of the Upper House, her cousin, had put Drake in the way of colonial promotions that were recorded in gazettes—nay, she had only involuntarily to think of that night and she would stop dead, speaking or walking, drive her nails into her palms and groan slightly.... She had to invent a chronic stitch in her heart to account for this groan which ended in a mumble and seemed to herself to degrade her....

* Ford had been received into the Catholic Church in November 1892 at the English-speaking church of St Joseph's on the Avenue Hoche. See *Provence* 136.

The miserable memory would come, ghost-like, at any time, anywhere. She would see Drake's face, dark against the white things; she would feel the thin night-gown ripping off her shoulder; but most of all she would seem, in darkness that excluded the light of any room in which she might be, to be transfused by the mental agony that there she had felt: the longing for the brute who had mangled her: the dreadful pain of the mind. The odd thing was that the sight of Drake himself, whom[21] she had seen several times since the outbreak of the war, left her completely without emotion. She had no aversion, but no longing for him. . . . She had, nevertheless, longing, but she knew it was longing merely to experience again that dreadful feeling. And not with Drake. . . .

Her "turnings down" then of the really nice men, if it were a sport, was a sport not without a spice of danger. She imagined that, after a success, she must feel much of the exhilaration that men told her they felt after bringing off a clean right and left, and no doubt she felt some of the emotions that the same young men felt when they were out shooting with beginners. Her personal chastity she now cherished much as she cherished her personal cleanliness and persevered in her Swedish exercises* after her baths before an open window, her[22] rides afterwards,[23] and her long nights of dancing which she would pursue in any room that was decently ventilated. Indeed, the two sides of life were, in her mind, intimately connected: she kept herself attractive by her skilfully selected exercises and cleanlinesses: and the same fatigues, healthful as they were, kept her in the mood for chastity of life.[24] She had done so ever since her return to her husband; and this not because of any attachment to her husband or to virtue as such, as because she had made the pact with herself out of caprice and meant to keep it. She *had* to have men at her feet: that was, as it were, the price of her—purely social—daily bread: as it was the price of the daily bread of her intimates. She was, and had been for many years, absolutely continent.[25] And so very likely were, and had been, all her Moiras, and Megs, and Lady Marjories—but she was perfectly aware that they had to have, above their assemblies as it were, a light[26] vapour of the airs and

---

* Dowell also does 'Swedish exercises' at Nauheim in *The Good Soldier* 12.

habits of the brothel. The public demanded that ... a light vapour, like the slight traces of steam that she had seen, glutinously adhering to the top of the water in the crocodile-houses of the Zoo.

It was, indeed, the price; and she was aware that she had been lucky. Not many of the hastily-married young women of her set really kept their heads above water *in* her set: for a season you would read that Lady Marjorie and Captain Hunt, after her presentation at Court on the occasion of her marriage, were to be seen at Roehampton,* at Goodwood† and the like: photographs of the young couple, striding along with the palings of the Row‡ behind them, would appear for a month or so. Then the records of their fashionable doings[27] would transfer themselves to the lists of the attendants and attachés of distant vice-regal courts in tropics bad for the complexion. "And then no more of he and she,"§ as Sylvia put it.

In her case it hadn't been so bad, but it had been nearish. She had had the advantage of being an only daughter of a very rich woman: her husband wasn't just any Captain Hunt to stick on a vice-regal staff. He was in a first-class office and when Angélique** wrote notes on the young menage she could—Angélique's ideas of these things being hazy—always refer to the husband as the future Lord Chancellor or Ambassador to Vienna. And their little, frightfully expensive establishment—to which her mother, who had lived with them had very handsomely contributed—had floated them over the first dangerous two years. They had entertained like mad, and[28] two much-canvassed scandals had had their beginnings in Sylvia's small drawing-room. She had been quite established when she had gone off with Perowne....

---

\* Roehampton was one of the three London polo clubs in 1911, with Hurlingham and Ranelagh. The Hare and Hounds running races between Oxford and Cambridge had also been held at Roehampton since 1896.

† Racecourse on the Sussex Downs.

‡ Rotten Row is a broad track for horses and carriages through the south side of Hyde Park, where fashionable Londoners would go to be seen.

§ Her allusion is to stanza 32 of Edward Fitzgerald's version of the *Rubáiyát of Omar Khayyám*: 'Some little Talk awhile of ME and THEE / There seemed—and then no more of THEE and ME' (London: Bernard Quaritch, 1859), 7.

\*\* Presumably a gossip columnist in one of the society papers.

And coming back had not been so difficult. She had expected it would be, but it hadn't. Tietjens had stipulated for large rooms in Gray's Inn. That hadn't seemed to her to be reasonable; but she imagined that he wanted to be near his friend and, though she had no gratitude to Tietjens for taking her back and nothing but repulsion from the idea of living in his house, as they were making a bargain, she owed it to herself to be fair. She had never swindled a railway company, brought dutiable[29] scent past a custom-house or represented to a second-hand dealer that her clothes were[30] less worn than they were, though with her prestige she could actually have done this. It was fair that Tietjens should live where he wished and live there they did, their very tall windows looking straight into those of Macmaster across the Georgian quadrangle.

They had[31] two floors of a great building, and that gave them a great deal of space,[32] the breakfast-room, in which during the war they also lunched, was an immense room, completely lined with books that were nearly all calf-backed, with an immense mirror over an immense, carved, yellow and white marble mantelpiece, and three windows that, in their great height, with the spideriness of their divisions and their old, bulging glass— some of the panes were faintly violet in age—gave to the room an eighteenth century distinction. It suited, she admitted, Tietjens, who was an eighteenth century figure of the Dr. Johnson type—the only eighteenth century type of which she knew, except for that of the beau something* who wore white satin and ruffles, went to Bath and must have been indescribably tiresome.

Above, she had a great white drawing-room, with fixings that she knew were eighteenth century and to be respected. For Tietjens—again she admitted—had a marvellous gift for old furniture: he despised it as such, but he knew it down to the ground. Once when her friend Lady Moira had been deploring the expense of having her new, little house furnished from top to toe under the advice of Sir John Robertson, the specialist (the Moiras had sold Arlington Street stock, lock, and barrel to some American), Tietjens, who had come in to tea and had been

---

\* Probably Beau Nash (1674–1762), the celebrated dandy, and Bath precursor of London's Regency dandy Beau Brummell.

listening without speaking, had said, with the soft good nature,
rather sentimental in tone, that once in a blue moon he would
bestow on her prettiest friends:

"You had better let me do it for you."[33]

Taking a look round Sylvia's great drawing-room, with the
white panels, the Chinese lacquer screens, the red lacquer and
ormolu cabinets and the immense blue and pink carpet (and
Sylvia knew that[34] if only for the three panels by a fellow called
Fragonard, bought just before Fragonards had been boomed by
the late King, her drawing-room was something remarkable),
Lady Moira had said to Tietjens, rather flutteringly and almost
with the voice with which she began one of her affairs:

"Oh, if only you *would*."

He had done it, and he had done it for a quarter of the estimate of Sir John Robertson. He had done it without effort, as if
with a roll or two of his elephantine shoulders, for he seemed to
know what was in every dealer's and auctioneer's catalogue by
looking at the green halfpenny[35] stamp on the wrapper. And, still
more astonishingly, he had made love to Lady Moira—they had
stopped twice with the Moiras in Gloucestershire and the Moiras
had three times week-ended with Mrs. Satterthwaite as the Tietjens' *invités*.... Tietjens had made love to Lady Moira quite
prettily and sufficiently to tide Moira over until she was ready to
begin her affair with Sir William[36] Heathly.

For the matter of that, Sir John Robertson, the specialist in
old furniture, challenged by Lady Moira to pick holes in her beautiful house, had gone there, poked his large spectacles against
cabinets, smelt the varnish of table tops and bitten the backs of
chairs in his ancient and short-sighted way, and had then told
Lady Moira that Tietjens had bought her nothing that wasn't
worth a bit more than he had given for it. This increased their
respect for the old fellow: it explained his several millions. For, if
the old fellow proposed to make out of a friend like Moira a profit
of 300 per cent.—limiting it to that out of sheer affection for a
pretty woman—what wouldn't he make out of a natural—and
national—enemy like a United States senator!

And the old man took a great fancy to Tietjens himself—
which Tietjens, to Sylvia's bewilderment, did not resent. The old
man would come in to tea and, if Tietjens were present, would

stay for hours talking about old furniture. Tietjens would listen without talking.[37] Sir John would expatiate over and over again about this to Mrs. Tietjens. It was extraordinary. Tietjens went purely by instinct: by taking a glance at a thing and chancing its price. According to Sir John one of the most remarkable feats of the furniture trade had been Tietjens' purchase of the Hemingway bureau for Lady Moira. Tietjens, in his dislikeful way, had bought this at a cottage sale for £3 10s., and had told Lady Moira it was the best piece she would ever possess: Lady Moira had gone to the sale with him. Other dealers present had hardly looked at it: Tietjens certainly hadn't opened it. But at Lady Moira's, poking his spectacles into the upper part of the glazed piece, Sir John had put his nose straight on the little bit of inserted yellow wood by a hinge, bearing signature, name and date: "Jno. Hemingway, Bath, 1784." Sylvia remembered them because Sir John told her so often. It was a lost "piece" that the furnishing world had been after for many years.

For that exploit the old man seemed to love Tietjens. That he loved Sylvia herself, she was quite aware. He fluttered round her tremulously, gave fantastic entertainments in her honour and was the only man she had never turned down. He had a harem, so it was said, in an enormous house at Brighton or somewhere. But it was another sort of love he bestowed on Tietjens: the rather pathetic love that the aged bestow on their possible successors in office.

Once Sir John came in to tea and quite formally and with a sort of portentousness announced that that was his seventy-first birthday, and that he was a broken man. He seriously proposed that Tietjens should come into partnership with him with the reversion of the business—not, of course, of his private fortune. Tietjens had listened amiably, asking a detail or two of Sir John's proposed arrangement. Then he had said, with the rather[38] caressing voice that he now and then bestowed on a pretty woman, that he didn't think it would do. There would be too much beastly money about it. As a career it would be more congenial to him than his office . . . but there was too much beastly money about it.

Once more, a little to Sylvia's surprise—but men are queer creatures!—Sir John seemed to see this objection as quite reasonable, though he heard it with regret and combated it feebly. He went away with a relieved jauntiness; for, if he couldn't have Tietjens he couldn't; and he invited Sylvia to dine with him somewhere where they were going to have something fabulous and very nasty at about two guineas the ounce on the menu. Something like that! And during dinner Sir John had entertained her by singing the praises of her husband. He said that Tietjens was much too great a gentleman to be wasted on the old-furniture trade: that was why he hadn't persisted. But he sent by Sylvia a message to the effect that if ever Tietjens *did* come to be in want of money ...

Occasionally Sylvia was worried to know why people—as they sometimes did—told her that her husband had great gifts. To her he was merely unaccountable. His actions and opinions seemed simply the products of caprice—like her own; and, since she knew that most of her own manifestations were a matter of contrariety, she[39] abandoned the habit of thinking much about him.

But gradually and dimly she began to see that Tietjens had, at least, a consistency of character and a rather unusual knowledge of life. This came to her when she had to acknowledge that their move to the Inn of Court had been a social success and had suited herself. When they had discussed the change at Lobscheid—or rather when Sylvia had unconditionally given in to every stipulation of Tietjens!—he had predicted almost exactly what would happen, though it had been the affair of her mother's cousin's opera box that had most impressed her. He had told her, at Lobscheid, that he had no intention of interfering with her social level, and he[40] was convinced that he was not going to. He had thought about it a good deal.

She hadn't[41] much listened to him. She had thought, firstly, that he was a fool and, secondly, that he *did* mean to hurt her. And she acknowledged that he had a certain right. If, after she had been off with another man, she asked this one still to extend to her the honour of his name and the shelter of his roof, she had no right to object to his terms. Her only decent revenge on him was to live afterwards with such equanimity as to let him know the mortification of failure.

But at Lobscheid he had talked a lot of nonsense, as it had seemed to her: a mixture of prophecy and politics. The Chancellor of the Exchequer of that date had been putting pressure on the great landlords: the great landlords had been replying by cutting down their establishments and closing their town houses—not to any great extent, but enough to make a very effective gesture of it, and so as to raise a considerable clamour from footmen and milliners.[42] The Tietjens—both of them—were of the great landowning class: they could adopt that gesture of shutting up their Mayfair* house and going to live in a wilderness. All the more if they made their wilderness a thoroughly comfortable affair!

He had counselled her to present this aspect of the matter to her mother's cousin, the morosely portentous Rugeley. Rugeley was a great landowner—almost the greatest of all; and he was a landowner obsessed with a sense of his duties both to his dependants and his even remote relatives. Sylvia had only, Tietjens said, to go to the Duke and tell him[43] that the Chancellor's exactions had forced them to this move, but[44] that they had done it partly as a protest, and the Duke would accept it almost as a personal tribute to himself. *He* couldn't, even as a protest, be expected to shut up Mexborough or reduce his expenses. But, if his humbler relatives spiritedly did, he would almost certainly make it up to them. And Rugeley's favours were on the portentous scale of everything about him. "I shouldn't wonder," Tietjens had said, "if he didn't lend you the Rugeley box to entertain in."

And that is exactly what had happened.

The Duke—who must have kept a register of his remotest cousins—had, shortly before their return to London, heard that this young couple had parted with every prospect of a large and disagreeable scandal. He had approached Mrs. Satterthwaite— for whom he had a gloomy affection—and he had been pleased to hear that the rumour was a gross libel. So that, when the young couple actually turned up again—from Russia!—Rugeley, who perceived that they were not only together, but to all appearances quite united, was determined not only to make it up to them, but to show, in order to abash their libellers as signal a mark of his favour as he could without inconvenience to himself. He, therefore, twice—being a widower—invited Mrs. Satterthwaite to

---

\* In I.i the Tietjenses have a house in Lowndes Street, which is between Knightsbridge and Belgravia rather than being in Mayfair.

entertain for him, Sylvia to invite the guests, and then had Mrs. Tietjens' name placed on the roll of those who could have the Rugeley box at the opera, on application at the Rugeley estate office, when it wasn't wanted. This was a very great privilege and Sylvia had known how to make the most of[45] it.

On the other hand, on the occasion of their conversation at Lobscheid, Tietjens had prophesied what at the time seemed to her a lot of tosh. It had been two or three years before, but Tietjens had said that about the time grouse-shooting began,[*] in 1914, a European conflagration would take place which would shut up half the houses in Mayfair and beggar their inhabitants. He had patiently supported his prophecy with financial statistics as to the approaching bankruptcy of various European powers and the growingly acquisitive skill and rapacity of the inhabitants of Great Britain. She had listened to that with some attention: it had seemed to her rather like the usual nonsense talked in country houses—where, irritatingly, he never talked. But she liked to be able to have a picturesque fact or two with which to support herself when she too, to hold attention, wanted to issue moving statements as to revolutions, anarchies and strife in the offing. And she had noticed that when she magpied Tietjens' conversations more serious men in responsible positions were apt to argue with her and to pay her more attention than before. . . .

And now, walking along the table with her plate in her hand, she could not but acknowledge that, triumphantly—and very comfortably for her!—Tietjens had been right! In the third year of the war it was very convenient to have a dwelling, cheap, comfortable, almost august and so easy to work that you could have, at a pinch, run it with one maid, though the faithful Hullo Central had not let it come to that yet. . . .

Being near Tietjens she lifted her plate, which contained two cold cutlets in aspic and several leaves of salad: she wavered a little to one side and, with a circular motion of her hand, let the whole contents fly at Tietjens' head. She placed the plate on the table and drifted slowly towards the enormous mirror over the fireplace.

---

[*]  The grouse-shooting season traditionally begins in Scotland and the north of England on the 'Glorious Twelfth' of August. War was declared on 4 August – the date Ford had used as the pivot for much of the action of *The Good Soldier*.

"I'm bored," she said. "Bored! Bored!"

Tietjens had moved slightly as she had thrown: the[46] cutlets and most of the salad leaves had gone over his shoulder. But one, couched, very green leaf was on his shoulder-strap, and the oil and vinegar from the plate—Sylvia *knew* that she took too much of all condiments—had splashed from the revers of his tunic to his green staff-badges. She was glad that she had hit him as much as that: it meant that her marksmanship had not been quite rotten. She was glad, too, that she had missed him. She was also supremely indifferent. It had occurred to her to do it and she had done it. Of that she was glad!

She looked at herself for some time in the mirror of bluish depths. She pressed her immense bandeaux with both hands on to her ears. She was all right: high-featured: alabaster complexion —but that was mostly the mirror's doing[47]—beautiful, long, cool hands—what man's forehead wouldn't long for them? . . . And that hair! What man wouldn't think of it, unloosed on white shoulders! . . . Well, Tietjens wouldn't! Or, perhaps, he did . . . she hoped he did, curse him, for he never saw that sight. Obviously sometimes, at night, with a little whisky taken he must want to!

She rang the bell and bade Hullo Central sweep the plateful from the carpet; Hullo Central, tall and dark, looking with wide-open eyes, motionlessly at nothing.

Sylvia[48] went along the bookshelves, pausing over a book back, "*Vitae*[49] *Hominum Notiss* . . ."* in gilt, irregular capitals pressed deep into the old leather. At the first long window she supported herself by the blind-cord. She looked out and back into the room.

"There's that veiled woman!" she said, "going into eleven. . . . It's two o'clock, of course. . . . "

She looked at her husband's back hard, the clumsy khaki back that was getting round-shouldered now. Hard! She wasn't going to miss a motion or a stiffening.

"I've found out who it is!" she said, "and who she goes to. I got it out of the porter." She waited. Then she added:

---

* 'Lives of the Most Famous Men' (Latin).

"It's the woman you travelled down from Bishop Auckland[50]*
with. On the day war was declared."

Tietjens turned solidly round in his chair. She knew he would
do that out of stiff politeness, so it meant nothing.

His face was whitish in the pale light, but it was always whitish
since he had come back from France and passed his day in a tin
hut among dust heaps. He said:

"So you saw me!" But that, too, was mere politeness.

She said:

"Of course the whole crowd of us from Claudine's[51] saw you!
It was old Campion who said she was a Mrs. . . . I've forgotten the
name."

Tietjens said:

"I imagined he would know her. I saw him looking in from the
corridor!"

She said:

"Is she your mistress, or only[52] Macmaster's, or the mistress of
both of you? It would be like you to have a[53] mistress in
common. . . . She's got a mad husband, hasn't she? A clergyman."

Tietjens[54] said:

"She hasn't!"

Sylvia[55] checked suddenly in her next questions,[56] and Tietjens, who in these discussions never manœuvred for position, said:

"She has been Mrs. Macmaster over six months."

Sylvia said:

"She married him then the day after her husband's death."

She drew a long breath and added:

"I don't care. . . . She has been coming here every Friday for
three years. . . . I tell you I shall expose her unless that little beast
pays you to-morrow the money he owes you. . . . God knows you
need it!" She said then hurriedly, for she didn't know how Tietjens might take that proposition:

"Mrs. Wannop rang up this morning to know who was . . . oh!
. . . the evil genius of the Congress of Vienna. Who, by the by, is

---

*  A market town in County Durham, in the north-east of England. Ford and Violet
   Hunt had been just across the border in Scotland, at a country house party given by
   the American novelist Mary Borden, at Duns, near Berwick-upon-Tweed, and had
   returned to London either just before or just as war was declared.

Mrs. Wannop's secretary? She wants to see you this afternoon. About war babies!"

Tietjens said:

"Mrs. Wannop hasn't got a secretary. It's her daughter who does her ringing-up."

"The girl," Sylvia said, "you were so potty about at that horrible afternoon Macmaster gave. Has she had a war baby by you? They all say she's your mistress."

Tietjens said:

"No, Miss Wannop isn't my mistress. Her mother has had a commission to write an article about war babies. I told her yesterday there weren't any war babies to speak of, and she's upset because she won't be able to make a sensational article. She wants to try and make me change my mind."

"It *was* Miss Wannop at that beastly affair of your friend's?" Sylvia asked.[57] "And I suppose the woman who received was Mrs. What's-er-name: your other mistress. An unpleasant show. I don't think much of your taste. The one where all the horrible geniuses in London were? There was a man like a rabbit talked to me about how to write poetry."

"That's no good as an identification of the party,"[58] Tietjens said. "Macmaster gives a party every Friday, not Saturday. He has for years.[59] Mrs. Macmaster goes there every Friday. To act as hostess. She has for years. Miss Wannop goes there every Friday after she has done work for her mother. To support Mrs. Macmaster. . . ."

"She has for years!" Sylvia mocked him. "And you go there every Friday![60] to croodle* over Miss Wannop. Oh, Christopher!"—she adopted a mock pathetic voice—"I never did have much opinion of your taste . . . but not *that*! Don't let it be that. Put her back.[61] She's too young for you. . . ."

"All the geniuses in London," Tietjens continued equably, "go to Macmaster's every Friday. He has been trusted with the job of giving away Royal Literary Bounty money: that's why they go. They go: that's why he was given his C.B."†

"I should not have thought they counted," Sylvia said.

"Of course they count," Tietjens said. "They write for the

---

\* 'To make a continued soft low murmuring sound; *esp.* to coo as a dove': OED.

† Companion of the Bath, an honour awarded to state servants.

Press. They can get anybody anything[62] ... except themselves!"

"Like you!" Sylvia said; "exactly like you! They're a lot of bribed squits."

"Oh, no," Tietjens said. "It isn't done obviously or[63] discreditably. Don't believe that Macmaster distributes forty-pounders yearly of bounty on condition that he gets advancement. He hasn't, himself, the least idea of how it works, except by his atmosphere."

"I never knew a beastlier atmosphere," Sylvia said. "It *reeked* of rabbit's food."

"You're quite mistaken," Tietjens said; "that is the Russian leather of the backs of the specially bound presentation copies in the *large* bookcase."

"I don't know what you're talking about," Sylvia said. "What *are* presentation copies? I should have thought you'd had enough of the beastly Russian smells Kiev stunk of."

Tietjens considered for a moment.

"No! I don't remember it," he said. "Kiev? ... Oh, it's where we were ... "

"You put half your mother's money," Sylvia said, "into the Government of Kiev 12½ per cent. City Tramways...."

At that Tietjens certainly winced, a type of wincing that Sylvia hadn't wanted.

"You're[64] not fit to go out to-morrow," she said. "I shall wire to old Campion."[65]

"Mrs. Duchemin," Tietjens said woodenly:[66] "Mrs. Macmaster that is, also used to burn a little incense in the room before the parties.... Those Chinese stinks ... what do they call them? Well, it doesn't matter"; he added that resignedly. Then he went on: "Don't you make any mistake. Mrs. Macmaster is a very superior woman. Enormously efficient! Tremendously[67] respected. I shouldn't advise even you to come up against her, now she's in the saddle."

Mrs. Tietjens said:

"*That* sort of woman!"

Tietjens said:

"I don't say you ever will come up against her. Your spheres differ. But, if you do, don't.... I say it because you seem to have got your knife into her."

"I don't like that sort of thing going on under my windows," Sylvia said.

Tietjens said:

"What sort of thing? . . . I was trying to tell you a little about Mrs. Macmaster . . . she's like the woman who was the mistress of the man who burned the other fellow's horrid book*. . . . I can't remember the names."

Sylvia said quickly:

"Don't try!" In a slower tone she added: "I don't in the least want to know. . . ."

"Well, she was an Egeria!"† Tietjens said. "An inspiration to the distinguished. Mrs. Macmaster is all that. The geniuses swarm round her, and with the really select ones she corresponds. She writes[68] superior letters, about the Higher Morality usually; very delicate in feeling. Scotch naturally. When they go abroad she sends them snatches[69] of London literary happenings; well done, mind you! And then, every now and then, she slips in something she wants Macmaster to have. But with great delicacy. . . . Say it's this C.B. . . . she transfuses into the minds of Genius One, Two and Three the idea of a C.B. for Macmaster. . . . Genius No One lunches with the Deputy Sub-Patronage Secretary, who looks after literary honours and lunches with geniuses to get the gossip. . . ."

Sylvia asked:[70]

"Why did you lend Macmaster all that money?"

"Mind you," Tietjens continued his own speech, "it's perfectly proper. That's the way patronage *is* distributed in this country; it's the way it should be. The only clean way. Mrs. Duchemin backs Macmaster because he's a first-class fellow for his job. And *she* is an influence over the geniuses because she's a first-class person for hers. . . . She represents the higher, nicer morality for really nice Scots. Before long she will be getting tickets stopped from being sent to people for the Academy soirées. She already does it for the Royal Bounty dinners. A little later, when Macmaster is knighted for bashing the French in the eye, she'll

---

\*    Possibly Madame de Maintenon (an important presence in *Last Post*), the mistress, then secret morganatic wife, of Louis XIV, who had in 1660 ordered the burning of Pascal's *Lettres Provinciales* (1656–7), part of the great Jansenist–Jesuit controversy.

†    Egeria was a water-nymph who became the second wife and counsellor of Numa Pompilius, the legendary second king of Rome.

have a tiny share in auguster assemblies.... Those people have to ask *somebody* for advice. Well, one day you'll want to present some débutante. And you won't get a ticket...."

"Then I'm glad," Sylvia exclaimed, "that I wrote to Brownie's uncle about the woman. I was a little sorry this morning because, from what Glorvina told me, you're in such a devil of a hole...."

"Who's Brownie's uncle?" Tietjens asked. "Lord ... Lord ... The banker! I know Brownie's in his uncle's bank."

"Port Scatho!"* Sylvia said. "I wish you wouldn't act forget-ting people's names. You overdo it."

Tietjens' face went a shade whiter....

"Port Scatho," he said, "is the chairman of the Inn Billeting Committees, of course. And you wrote to him? ..."

"I'm sorry," Sylvia said. "I mean I'm sorry I said that about your forgetting.... I wrote to him and said that as a resident of the Inn I objected to your mistress—he knows the relationship, of course!—creeping in every Friday under a heavy veil and creeping out every Saturday at four in the morning."

"Lord Port Scatho knows about my relationship," Tietjens began.

"He saw her in your arms in the train," Sylvia said. "It upset Brownie so much he offered to shut down your overdraft and return any cheques you had out marked R.D."†

"To please you?" Tietjens asked. "*Do* bankers do that sort of thing? It's a new light on British society." ...

"I suppose bankers try to please their women friends, like other men," Sylvia said. "I told him very emphatically it wouldn't please me ...[71] But ..." she hesitated: "I wouldn't give him a chance to get back on you. I don't want to interfere in your affairs. But Brownie doesn't like you...."

"He wants you to divorce me and marry him?" Tietjens asked.

"How did you know?" Sylvia asked indifferently. "I let him give me lunch now and then because it's convenient to have him manage my affairs, you being away.... But of course he hates you for being in the army. All the men who aren't hate all the men that are. And, of course, when there's a woman between them

---

* The fishing port on the south coast of Cornwall, near Falmouth, is generally spelt as Portscatho. *No Enemy* 63 refers to it as Port Scathow.
† 'Refer to Drawer', meaning that the cheque is effectively cancelled and the recipient must get another cheque or cash from the signatory.

the men who aren't do all they can to do the others in. When they're bankers they have a pretty good pull...."

"I suppose they have," Tietjens said, vaguely; "of course they would have...."

Sylvia abandoned the blind-cord on which[72] she had been dragging with one hand. In order that light might fall on her face and give more impressiveness to her words, for, in a minute or two, when she felt brave enough, she meant really to let him have her bad news!—she drifted to the fireplace. He followed her round, turning on his chair to give her his face.

She said:

"Look here, it's all the fault of this beastly war, isn't it? Can you deny it? ... I mean that decent, gentlemanly fellows like Brownie have turned into beastly squits!"

"I suppose it is," Tietjens said dully. "Yes, certainly it is. You're quite right. It's the incidental degeneration of the heroic impulse:[73] if the heroic impulse has too even a strain put on it the incidental degeneration gets the upper hand. That accounts for the Brownies ... all the Brownies ... turning squits...."

"Then why do you go on with it?" Sylvia said. "God knows, I could wangle you out if you'd back me in the least little way."

Tietjens said:

"Thanks! I prefer to remain in it.... How else am I to get a living? ..."

"You know then,"[74] Sylvia exclaimed almost shrilly. "You know that they won't have you back in the office if they can find a way of getting you out...."

"Oh, they'll find that!" Tietjens said.... He continued his other speech: "When we go to war with France," he said dully.... And Sylvia knew he was only now formulating his settled opinion so as not to have his active[75] brain to give to the discussion. He must be thinking hard of the Wannop girl! With her littleness: her tweed-skirtishness.... A provincial[76] miniature of herself, Sylvia Tietjens.... If she, then, had been[77] miniature, provincial.... But Tietjens' words cut her as if she had been lashed with a dog-whip. "We shall behave more creditably," he had said,[78] "because there will be less heroic impulse about it. We shall ... half of us ... be ashamed of ourselves. So there will be much less incidental degeneration."

Sylvia who, by that was listening to him, abandoned the consideration of Miss Wannop and the picture[79] that obsessed her of Tietjens saying four words, against a background of books at Macmaster's party. She exclaimed:

"Good God! What are you talking about? . . ."

Tietjens went on:

"About our next war with France. . . . We're the natural enemies of the French. We have to make our bread either by robbing them or making catspaws of them. . . ."

Sylvia said:

"We can't! We couldn't . . ."

"We've got to!" Tietjens said. "It's the condition of our existence. We're a practically bankrupt, over-populated, northern country: they're rich southerners, with a falling population. Towards 1930 we shall have to do what Prussia did in 1914. Our conditions will be exactly those of Prussia then. It's the . . . what is it called? . . ."

"But . . ." Sylvia cried out. "You're a Franco-maniac. . . . You're thought to be a French agent. . . . That's what's bitching your career!"

"I am?" Tietjens asked uninterestedly. He added: "Yes, that probably *would* bitch my career. . . ." He went on, with a little more animation and a little more of his mind:

"Ah! *that* will be a war worth seeing. . . . None of their drunken rat-fighting for imbecile boodlers. . . ."[*]

"It would drive mother mad!" Sylvia said.

"Oh, no it wouldn't," Tietjens said. "It will stimulate her if she is still alive. . . . Our heroes won't be drunk with wine and lechery: our squits[80] won't stay at home and stab the heroes in the back. Our Minister for Water-closets won't keep two and a half million men in any base in order to get the votes of their women at a General Election—that's been[81] the first evil effects of giving women the vote![†] With the French holding Ireland and

---

[*]   Boodlers are corrupt politicians, especially those involved in bribery.

[†]   The 1918 Representation of the People Act gave women aged 30 and over the right to vote. The age limit wasn't lowered to 21 (as for men) until 1928. The first election in which women were able to use the vote took place after the Armistice, on 14 December 1918, so this might seem anachronistic. But though the Bill wasn't given Royal assent till February 1918, the House of Commons passed it on 28 March 1917.

stretching in a solid line from Bristol to Whitehall, we should hang the Minister before he had time to sign the papers. And we should be decently loyal to our Prussian allies and brothers.... Our Cabinet won't hate them as they hate the French for being frugal and strong in logic and well-educated and remorselessly[82] practical. Prussians are the sort of fellows you can be hoggish with when you want to...."

Sylvia interjected violently:[83]

"For God's sake stop it. You almost make me believe what you say is true. I tell you mother would go mad. Her greatest friend is the Duchesse Tonnerre Chateaulherault...."

"Well!" Tietjens said. "Your greatest friends are the Med ... Med ... the Austrian[84] officers you take chocolates and flowers to. That there was all the row about ... we're at war with *them* and you haven't gone mad!"

"I don't know," Sylvia said. "Sometimes I think I am going mad!" She drooped. Tietjens, his face very strained, was looking at the tablecloth. He muttered: "Med ... Met ... Kos ..." Sylvia said:

"Do you know a poem called *Somewhere?* It begins: 'Somewhere or other there must surely be ...'"*

Tietjens said:

"I'm sorry. No! I haven't been able to get up my poetry again."

Sylvia said:

"*Don't!*" She added: "You've got to be at the War Office at 4.15, haven't you? What's the time now?" She extremely wanted to give him her bad news before he went; she extremely wanted to put off giving it as long as she could. She wanted to reflect on the matter first; she wanted also to keep up a desultory conversation, or he might leave the room. She didn't want to have to say to him: "Wait a minute, I've something to say to you!" for she might not, at that moment, be in the mood. He said it was not yet two. He could give her an hour and a half more.

To keep the conversation going, she said:

---

\*   The poem is 'Somewhere or Other', by Ford's aunt Christina Rossetti, the first stanza of which runs: 'Somewhere or other there must surely be / The face not seen, the voice not heard, / The heart that not yet – never yet – ah me! / Made answer to my word': *The Poetical Works of Christina Georgina Rossetti*, with Memoir and Notes &C by William Michael Rossetti (London: Macmillan, 1904), 362.

"I suppose the Wannop girl is making bandages or being a Waac.* Something forceful."

Tietjens said:

"No; she's a pacifist. As pacifist as you. Not so impulsive; but, on the other hand, she has more arguments. I should say she'll be in prison before the war's over. . . . "

"A nice time you must have between the two of us," Sylvia said. The memory of her interview with the great lady nicknamed Glorvina[†]—though it was not at all a good nickname—was coming over her forcibly.

She said:

"I suppose you're always talking it over with her? You see her every day."

She imagined that that might keep him occupied for a minute or two. He said—she caught the sense of it only—and quite indifferently that he had tea with Mrs. Wannop every day. She had moved to a place called Bedford Park,[‡] which was near his office: not three minutes' walk. The War Office had put up a lot of huts on some public green in that neighbourhood. He only saw the daughter once a week, at most. They never talked about the war; it was too disagreeable a subject for the young woman. Or rather, too painful. . . . His talk gradually drifted into unfinished sentences. . . .

They played that comedy occasionally, for it is impossible for two people to live in the same house and not have some common meeting ground. So they would each talk: sometimes talking at great length and with politeness, each thinking his or her thoughts till they drifted into silence.

And, since she had acquired the habit of going into retreat—with an Anglican sisterhood in order to annoy Tietjens, who hated convents and considered that the communions should not mix—Sylvia had acquired also the habit of losing herself almost

---

* The Women's Auxiliary Army Corps was established in January 1917, recruiting women to work in roles such as clerks, telephonists, waitresses, cooks and gas mask instructors.

† Glorvina is the beautiful Princess of Inishmore in *The Wild Irish Girl* (1806), the third novel by Sydney Owenson, Lady Morgan (1776–1859). Thackeray borrowed the name for Glorvina O'Dowd in *Vanity Fair* (1847–8).

‡ Bedford Park, in Chiswick, West London, was the first garden suburb, and associated with the Aesthetic movement.

completely in reveries. Thus she was now vaguely conscious that a greyish lump, Tietjens, sat at the head of a whitish expanse: the lunch-table.[85] There were also books . . . actually she was seeing a quite different figure and other books[86]—the books of Glorvina's husband, for the great lady had received Sylvia in that statesman's library.

Glorvina, who was the mother of two of Sylvia's absolutely most intimate friends, had sent for Sylvia. She wished, kindly and even wittily, to remonstrate with Sylvia because of her complete abstention from any patriotic activity. She offered Sylvia the address of a place in the city where she could buy wholesale and ready-made diapers for babies which Sylvia could present to some charity or other as being her own work. Sylvia said she would do nothing of the sort, and Glorvina said she would present the idea to poor Mrs. Pilsenhauser. She—Glorvina—said she spent some time every day thinking out acts of patriotism for the distressed rich with foreign names, accents[87] or antecedents. . . .

Glorvina was a fiftyish lady with a pointed, grey face and a hard aspect; but when she was inclined to be witty or to plead earnestly she had a kind manner. The room in which they were was over a Belgravia back garden. It was lit by a skylight and the shadows from above deepened the lines of her face, accentuating the rather dusty grey of the hair as well as both the hardness and the kind manner. This very much impressed Sylvia, who was used to seeing the lady by artificial light. . . .

She said, however:

"You don't suggest, Glorvina, that I'm the distressed rich with a foreign name!"

The great lady had said:

"My dear Sylvia; it isn't so much you as your husband. Your last exploit with the Esterhazys and Metternichs has pretty well done for *him*. You forget that the present powers that be are not logical. . . ."

Sylvia remembered that she had sprung up from her leather saddle-back chair, exclaiming:

"You mean to say that those unspeakable swine think that *I'm* . . ."

Glorvina said patiently:

"My dear Sylvia, I've already said it's not you. It's your

husband that suffers. He appears to be too good a fellow to suffer. Mr. Waterhouse says so. I don't know him myself, well."

Sylvia remembered that she had said:

"And who in the world is Mr. Waterhouse?" and hearing that Mr. Waterhouse was a late Liberal Minister, had lost interest. She couldn't, indeed, remember any of the further words of her hostess, as words. The sense of them had too much overwhelmed her. . . .

She stood now, looking at Tietjens and only occasionally seeing him, her mind completely occupied with the effort to recapture Glorvina's own words in the desire for exactness. Usually she remembered conversations pretty well; but on this occasion her mad fury, her feeling of nausea, the pain of her own nails in her palms, an unrecoverable sequence of emotions had overwhelmed her.

She looked at Tietjens now with a sort of gloating[88] curiosity. How was it possible that the most honourable man she knew should be so overwhelmed by foul and baseless rumours?[89] It made you suspect that honour had, in itself, a quality of the evil eye. . . .

Tietjens, his face pallid, was fingering a piece of toast. He muttered:

"Met . . . Met[90] . . . It's Met . . ." He wiped his brow with a table-napkin, looked at it with a start, threw it on the floor and pulled[91] out a handkerchief. . . . He muttered: "Mett . . . Metter . . ." His face illuminated itself like the face of a child listening at a shell.

Sylvia screamed with a passion of hatred:

"For God's sake say *Metternich* . . . you're driving me mad!"

When she looked at him again his face had cleared and he was walking quickly to the telephone in the corner of the room. He asked her to excuse him and gave a number at Ealing. He said after a moment:

"Mrs. Wannop? Oh! My wife has just reminded me that Metternich was the evil genius of the Congress of Vienna. . . ."*
He said: "Yes! Yes!" and listened. After a time he said: "Oh, you could put it stronger than that. You could put it that the Tory

---

* The Congress of Vienna (1814–15) was the peace conference held after the Napoleonic wars, chaired by the Austrian statesman Prince von Metternich. To liberal historians his name became synonymous with reactionary politics.

determination to ruin Napoleon at all costs was one of those pieces of party imbecility that, etc. . . . Yes; Castlereagh. And of course Wellington. . . .[92] I'm very sorry I must ring off. . . . Yes; to-morrow at 8.30 from Waterloo. . . . No; I *shan't* be seeing her again. . . . No; she's made a mistake. . . . Yes; give her my love . . . good-bye." He was reversing the earpiece to hang it up, but a high-pitched series of yelps from the instrument forced it back to his ear: "Oh! *War babies!*" he exclaimed. "I've already sent the statistics off to you! No! there *isn't* a marked increase of the ille-gitimacy rate, except in patches. The rate's appallingly high in the lowlands of Scotland; but it always *is* appallingly high there . . ." He laughed and said good-naturedly: "Oh, you're an old jour-nalist: you won't let fifty quid go for that . . ." He was breaking off. But: "*Or,*" he suddenly exclaimed, "here's another idea for you. The rate's about the same, probably because of this: half the fellows who go out to France are reckless because it's the last chance, as they see it. But the other half are made twice as consci-entious. A decent Tommie thinks twice about leaving his girl in trouble just before he's killed. . . . The divorce statistics are up, of course, because people will chance making new starts within the law. . . . Thanks . . . thanks . . ." He hung up the earpiece. . . .

Listening to that conversation had extraordinarily cleared Sylvia's mind. She said, almost sorrowfully:

"I suppose that that's why you don't seduce that girl." And she knew—she had known at once from the suddenly changed inflec-tion of Tietjens' voice when he had said "a decent Tommie thinks twice before leaving his girl in trouble"!—that Tietjens himself had thought twice.

She looked at him now almost incredulously, but with great coolness. Why *shouldn't* he, she asked herself, give himself a little pleasure with his girl before going to almost certain death. . . . She felt a real, sharp pain at her heart. . . . A poor wretch in such a devil of a hole. . . .

She had moved to a chair close beside the fireplace and now sat looking at him, leaning interestedly forward, as if at a garden party she had been finding—*par impossible!*—a pastoral play not so badly produced. Tietjens was a fabulous monster. . . . *

---

* Another recurrent Fordian phrase. *The Cinque Ports* 246 says that Lucius, 'the first christened British king', 'is something of a fabulous monster'. In *Return* 220–1 the jour-

He was a fabulous monster not because he was honourable and virtuous. She had known several very honourable and very virtuous men. If she had never known an honourable or virtuous woman except among her French or Austrian friends, that was, no doubt, because virtuous and honourable women did not amuse her or because, except just for the French and Austrians, they were not Roman Catholics.... But the honourable and virtuous men she had known had usually prospered and been respected. They weren't the great fortunes, but they were well-offish: well spoken of: of the country gentleman type ... Tietjens....

She arranged her thoughts. To get one point settled in her mind, she asked:

"What really happened to you in France? What is really the matter with your memory? Or your brain, is it?"

He said carefully:

"It's half of it, an irregular piece of it, dead. Or rather pale. Without a proper blood supply.... So a great portion of it, in the shape of memory, has gone."

She said:

"But *you!* ... without a brain! ..." As this was not a question he did not answer.

His going at once to the telephone, as soon as he was in the possession of the name "Metternich," had at last convinced her that he had not been, for the last four months, acting hypochondriacal or merely lying to obtain sympathy or extended sick leave. Amongst Sylvia's friends a wangle known as shell-shock was cynically[93] laughed at and quite approved of. Quite decent and, as far as she knew, quite brave menfolk of her women would openly boast that, when they had had enough of it over there, they would wangle a little leave or get a little leave extended by simulating this purely nominal disease, and in the general carnival of lying, lechery, drink and howling that this affair was, to pretend to a little shell-shock had seemed to her to be almost virtuous. At any rate if a man passed his time at garden parties— or, as for the last months Tietjens had done, passed his time in a

---

nalist and novelist Richard Whiteing so shocks Conrad by saying that 'We all write for money and nothing else' that Conrad 'stared at that old man as if he had been a fabulous monster'. *Provence* 20 calls various legendary inhabitants of Provence 'fabulous monsters'.

tin hut amongst dust heaps, going to tea every afternoon in order to help Mrs. Wannop with her newspaper articles—when men were so engaged they were, at least, not trying to kill each other.

She said now:

"Do you mind telling me what actually happened to you?"

He said:

"I don't know that I can very well.... Something burst[94]—or 'exploded' is probably the right word—near me, in the dark. I expect you'd rather not hear about it? ..."

"I want to!" Sylvia said.

He said:

"The point about it is that I *don't* know what happened and I don't remember what I did. There are three weeks of my life dead....[*] What I remember is being in a C.C.S.[†] and not being able to remember my own name."

"You *mean* that?" Sylvia asked. "It's not just a way of talking?"

"No, it's not just a way of talking," Tietjens answered. "I lay in bed in the C.C.S.... Your friends were dropping bombs on it."

"You might not call them my friends," Sylvia said.

Tietjens said:

"I beg your pardon.[95] One gets into a loose way of speaking. The poor bloody Huns then were dropping bombs from aeroplanes on the hospital huts....[‡] I'm not suggesting they knew it was a C.C.S.; it was, no doubt, just carelessness...."

"You needn't spare the Germans for me!" Sylvia said. "You needn't spare any man who has killed another man."

"I was, then, dreadfully worried," Tietjens went on. "I was composing a preface for a book on Arminianism...."

"You haven't written a book!" Sylvia exclaimed eagerly, because she thought that if Tietjens took to writing a book there

---

[*] Ford's own experiences in the Battle of the Somme are described in the Introduction. He too suffered concussion and amnesia from a nearby shell-explosion: 'I had completely lost my memory so that [...] three weeks of my life are completely dead to me': *Nightingale* 175. Like Tietjens, he even forgot his own name for thirty-six hours. See Saunders, *Dual Life* II 2.

[†] Casualty Clearing Station.

[‡] In *Mightier* 264–6 Ford recalled how: 'after I was blown up at Bécourt-Bécordel in '16 and, having lost my memory, lay in the Casualty Clearing Station in Corbie, with the enemy planes dropping bombs all over it and the dead Red Cross nurses being carried past my bed, I used to worry agonizedly about what my name could be'; see *War Prose* 222.

might be a way of his earning a living. Many people had told her that he ought to write a book.

"No, I hadn't written a book," Tietjens said, "and I didn't know what Arminianism was...."

"You know perfectly well what the Arminian heresy is," Sylvia said sharply; "you explained it all to me years ago."

"Yes," Tietjens exclaimed. "Years ago I could have, but I couldn't then. I could now, but I was a little worried about it then. It's a little awkward[96] to write a preface about a subject of which you know nothing. But it didn't seem to me to be discreditable in an army sense.[97] ... Still it worried me dreadfully not to know my own name. I lay and worried and worried and thought how discreditable it would appear if a nurse came along and asked me and I didn't know. Of course my name was on a luggage label tied to my collar; but I'd forgotten they did that to casualties.... Then a lot of people carried pieces of a nurse down the hut: the Germans'[98] bombs had done that of course. They were still drop-ping about the place."

"But good heavens," Sylvia cried out, "do you mean they carried a dead nurse past you? ..."

"The poor dear wasn't dead," Tietjens said. "I wish she had been. Her name was Beatrice Carmichael ... the first name I learned after my collapse. She's dead now of course.... That seemed to wake up a fellow on the other side of the room with a lot of blood[99] coming through the bandages on his head.... He rolled out of his bed and, without a word, walked across the hut and began to strangle me...."

"But this isn't believable," Sylvia said. "I'm sorry, but I can't believe it.... You were an officer:[100] they *couldn't* have carried a wounded nurse under your nose. They must have known your sister Caroline was a nurse and was killed...."

"Carrie!" Tietjens said, "was drowned on a hospital ship. I thank God I didn't have to connect the other girl with her.... But you don't suppose that in addition to one's name, rank, unit, and date of admission they'd put that I'd lost a sister and two brothers in action and a father—of a broken heart I dare say...."

"But you only lost one brother," Sylvia said. "I went into mourning for him and your sister...."

"No, two," Tietjens said;[101] "but the fellow who was strangling me was what I wanted to tell you about. He let out a number of ear-piercing shrieks and lots of orderlies came and pulled him off me and sat all over him. Then he began to shout 'Faith!' He shouted: 'Faith! ... Faith! ... Faith!...' at intervals of two seconds, as far as I could tell by my pulse, until four in the morning, when he died.... I don't know whether it was a religious exhortation or a woman's name, but I disliked him a good deal because he started my tortures, such as they were.... * There had been a girl I knew called Faith. Oh, not a love affair: the daughter of my father's head gardener, a Scotsman. The point is that every time he said Faith I asked myself 'Faith ... Faith what?' I couldn't remember the name of my father's head gardener."

Sylvia, who was thinking of other things, asked:

"What *was* the name?"

Tietjens answered:

"I don't know, I don't know to this day.... The point is that when I knew that I didn't know *that* name, I was as ignorant, as *uninstructed*, as a new-born babe and much more worried about it.... The Koran says—I've got as far as K in my reading of the Encyclopædia Britannica every afternoon at Mrs. Wannop's— 'The strong man when smitten is smitten in his pride!'... Of course I got King's Regs. and the M.M.L. and Infantry Field Training and all the A.C.I.s to date by heart very quickly.† And that's all a British officer is really encouraged to know...."

"Oh, Christopher!" Sylvia said. "*You* read that Encyclopædia; it's pitiful. You used to despise it so."

"That's what's meant by 'smitten in his pride,'" Tietjens said.

---

* Ford wrote to Conrad, 6 Sept. 1916: 'When I was in hospital a man three beds from me died *very* hard, blood pouring thro' bandages & he himself crying perpetually "Faith! Faith! Faith!" It was very disagreeable as long as he had a chance of life – but one lost all interest and forgot him when one heard he had none'; transcribed in Stang, *Presence* 172–6 (173). Cf. *Provence* 308: 'Faith, in short, died after the war – every sort of Faith [...]'.

† 'King's Regulations': the army's code of conduct, including topics such as discipline and military law. 'M.M.L.': Manual of Military Law. 'Infantry Field Training': possibly the manual *Infantry Training*, issued in 1914, of which Ch. 8 outlines 'Training in Field Operations'. 'A.C.I.s': Army Council Instructions. The Army Council had command of the army, and issued Orders and Instructions; the latter were more concerned with organisation, training, and logistics.

"Of course what I read or hear now I remember.... But I haven't got to M, much less V. That was why I was worried about Metternich and the Congress of Vienna. I try to remember things on my own, but I haven't yet done so. You see it's as if a certain area of my brain had been wiped white. Occasionally one name suggests another. You noticed, when I got Metternich it suggested Castlereagh and Wellington—and even other names.... But that's what the Department of Statistics will get me on. When they fire me out. The real reason will be that I've served. But they'll pretend it's because I've no more general knowledge than is to be found in the Encyclopædia: or two-thirds or more or less—according to the duration of the war.... Or, of course, the real reason will be that I won't fake statistics to dish the French with. They asked me to, the other day, as a holiday task. And when I refused you should have seen their faces."

"Have you *really*," Sylvia asked, "lost two brothers in action?"

"Yes," Tietjens answered. "Curly and Longshanks. You never saw them because they were always in India. And they weren't noticeable...."

"*Two!*" Sylvia said. "I only wrote to your father about one called Edward. And your sister Caroline. In the same letter...."

"Carrie wasn't noticeable either," Tietjens said. "She did Charity Organisation Society work.... But[102] I remember: you didn't like her. She was the born old maid...."

"Christopher!" Sylvia asked, "do you still think your mother died of a broken heart because I left you?"

Tietjens said:

"Good God; no. I never thought so and I don't think so. I *know* she didn't."

"*Then!*" Sylvia exclaimed, "she died of a broken heart because I came back.... It's no good protesting that you don't think so. I remember your face when you opened the telegram at Lobscheid. Miss Wannop forwarded it from Rye. I remember the postmark. She was born to do me ill. The moment you got it I could see you thinking that you must conceal from me that you thought it was because of me[103] she died. I could see you wondering if it wouldn't be practicable to conceal from me that she was dead. You couldn't, of course, do that because, you remember, we were to have gone to Wiesbaden and show ourselves; and we couldn't do that because we should have to be in mourning. So you took me to Russia to get out of taking me to the funeral."

"I took you to Russia," Tietjens said. "I remember it all now— because I had an order from Sir Robert* Ingleby to assist the British Consul-General in preparing a Blue Book† statistical table of the Government of Kiev. . . . It appeared to be the most industrially promising region in the world in those days. It isn't now, naturally. I shall never see back a penny of the money I[104] put into it.‡ I thought I was clever in those days. . . . And of course, yes, the money was my mother's settlement. It comes back . . . yes, of course. . . ."

"Did you," Sylvia asked, "get out of taking me to your mother's funeral because you thought I should defile your mother's corpse by my presence? Or because you were afraid that in the presence of your mother's body you wouldn't be able to conceal from me that you thought I[105] killed her? . . . Don't deny it. And don't get out of it by saying that you can't remember those days. You're remembering now: that I killed your mother: that Miss Wannop sent the telegram—why don't you score it against her that she sent the news? . . . Or, good God, why don't you score it against yourself, as the wrath of the Almighty,[106] that your mother was dying while you and that girl were croodling over each other? . . . At Rye! Whilst I was at Lobscheid. . . ."

Tietjens wiped his brow with his handkerchief.

"Well, let's drop that," Sylvia said. "God knows I've no right to put a spoke in that girl's wheel or in yours. If you love each other you've a right to happiness and I daresay she'll make you happy. I can't divorce you, being a Catholic; but I won't make it difficult for you other ways, and self-contained people like you and her will manage somehow. You'll have learned the way from Macmaster and his mistress. . . . But, oh, Christopher Tietjens, have you ever considered how foully you've used *me*!"

---

*  Tietjens' boss is named Sir Reginald Ingleby in Part I (though see endnote 52 to I.i for an occasion in the manuscript when Ford also wrote 'Robert', but then revised it to 'Reginald').
†  Blue book: 'one of the official reports of Parliament and the Privy Council, which are issued in a dark blue paper cover': *OED*.
‡  The investment would have been lost as a result of the 1917 Bolshevik Revolution.

Tietjens looked at her attentively, as if with myopic[107] anguish.

"If," Sylvia went on with her denunciation, "you had once in our lives said to me: 'You whore! You bitch! You killed my mother. May you rot in hell for it. . . .' If you'd only once said something like it . . . about the child! About Perowne! . . . you might have done something to bring us together. . . ."

Tietjens said:

"That's, of course, true!"

"I know," Sylvia said, "you can't help it. . . . But when, in your famous county family pride—though a youngest son!—you say to yourself: And I daresay if . . . Oh, Christ! . . . you're shot in the trenches you'll say it . . . oh, between the saddle and the ground! that you never did a dishonourable action. . . . And, mind you, I believe that no other man save one has ever had more right to say it than you. . . ."

Tietjens said:

"You believe that!"

"As I hope to stand before my Redeemer," Sylvia said, "I believe it. . . . But, in the name of the Almighty, how could any woman live beside you . . . and be for ever forgiven? Or no: not forgiven: ignored! . . . Well, be proud when you die because of your honour. But, God, you be humble about . . . your errors in judgment. *You* know what it is to ride a horse for miles with too tight a curb-chain and its tongue cut almost in half. . . . You remember the groom your father had who had the trick of turning the hunters out like that. . . . And you horse-whipped him, and[108] you've told me you've almost cried ever so often afterwards for thinking of that mare's mouth. . . . Well! Think of *this* mare's mouth sometimes! You've ridden me like that for seven years. . . ."

She stopped and then went on again:

"Don't you know, Christopher Tietjens, that there is only one man from whom a woman could take '*Neither do I condemn thee*'[109]* and not hate him more than she hates the fiend! . . ."

Tietjens so looked at her that he contrived to hold her attention.

* *John* 8.11: see 107 above.

"I'd like you to let me ask you," he said, "how I could throw stones at you? I have never disapproved of your actions."

Her hands dropped dispiritedly to her sides.

"Oh, Christopher," she said, "don't carry on that old play acting.[110] I shall never see you again, very likely, to speak to. You'll sleep with the Wannop girl to-night: you're going out to be killed to-morrow. *Let's* be straight for the next ten minutes or so. And give me your attention. The Wannop girl can spare that much if she's to have all the rest. . . . "

She could see that he was giving her his whole mind.

"As you said just now," he exclaimed slowly, "as I hope to meet my Redeemer I believe you to be a good woman. One that never did a dishonourable thing."

She recoiled a little in her chair.

"Then!" she said, "you're the wicked man I've always made believe to think you, though I didn't."

Tietjens said:

"No! . . . Let me try to put it to you as I see it."

She exclaimed:

"No! . . . I've been a wicked woman. I have ruined you. I am not going to listen to you."

He said:

"I daresay you have ruined me. That's nothing to me. I am completely indifferent."

She cried out:

"Oh! Oh! . . . Oh!" on a note of agony.

Tietjens said doggedly:

"I don't care. I can't help it. Those are—those *should* be—the conditions of life amongst decent people. When our next war comes I hope it will be fought out under those conditions. Let us, for God's sake, talk of the gallant enemy.* Always. We have *got* to plunder the French or millions of our people must starve: they have *got* to resist us successfully or be wiped out. . . . It's the same with you and me. . . . "

---

*   In the first month of the war Ford had written: 'I do wish that, as far as this country is concerned, this war could be fought in terms of "the gallant enemy"': 'Literary Portraits – LI: The Face of Janus', *Outlook*, 34 (29 Aug. 1914), 237–8; alluded to in *No Enemy* 47. See also 'Literary Portraits LXIX – Annus Mirabilis', *Outlook*, 35 (2 Jan. 1915), 15.

She exclaimed:

"You mean to say that you don't think I was wicked when I ... when I trepanned is what mother calls it? ..."

He said loudly:

"No! ... You had been let in for it by some brute. I have always held that a woman who has been let down by one man has the right—has the duty for the sake of her child—to let down a man. It becomes woman against man: against one man. I happened to be that one man: it was the will of God. But you were within your rights. I will never go back on that. Nothing will make me, ever!"

She said:

"And the others! And Perowne.... I know you'll say that anyone is justified[111] in doing anything as long as they are open enough about it.... But it killed your mother. Do you disapprove of my having killed your mother? Or you consider that I have corrupted the child...."

Tietjens said:

"I don't.... I want to speak to you about that."

She exclaimed:

"You *don't*...."

He said calmly:

"You know I don't ... while I was certain that I was going to be here to keep him straight and an Anglican I fought your influence over him. I'm obliged to you for having brought up of yourself the considerations that I may be killed and that I am ruined. I am. I could not raise a hundred pounds[112] between now and to-morrow. I am, therefore, obviously not the man to have sole charge of the heir of Groby."

Sylvia was saying:[113]

"Every penny I have is at your disposal...." when the maid, Hullo Central, marched up to her master and placed a card in his hand. He said:

"Tell him to wait five minutes in the drawing-room."

Sylvia said:

"Who is it?"

Tietjens answered:

"A man ... Let's get this settled. I've never thought you corrupted the boy. You tried to teach him to tell white lies. On perfectly straight Papist lines. I have no objection to Papists and no objection to white lies for Papists. You told him once to put a frog in Marchant's bath. I've no objection to a boy putting a frog in his nurse's bath, as such. But Marchant is an old woman, and the heir to Groby should respect old women always and old family servants in particular. . . . It hasn't, perhaps,[114] struck you that the boy is heir to Groby. . . . "

Sylvia said:

"If . . . if your second brother is killed. . . . But your eldest brother . . ."

"He," Tietjens said, "has got a French woman near Euston station. He's lived with her for over fifteen years, of afternoons, when there were no race meetings. She'll never let him marry and she's past the child-bearing stage. So there's no one else. . . . "

Sylvia said:

"You mean that I may bring the child up as a Catholic."

Tietjens said:

"A *Roman* Catholic. . . . You'll teach him, please, to use that term before myself if I ever see him again. . . . "

Sylvia said:

"Oh, I thank God that he has softened your heart. This will take the curse off this house."

Tietjens shook his head:

"I think not," he said, "off you, perhaps. Off Groby very likely. It was, perhaps, time that there should be a Papist owner of Groby again. You've read Spelden[115*] on sacrilege about Groby? . . . "

She said:

"Yes! The first Tietjens who came over with Dutch William, the swine, was pretty bad to the Papist owners. . . . "

"He was a tough Dutchman," Tietjens said, "but let us get on! There's enough time, but not too much. . . . I've got this man to see."

"Who is he?" Sylvia asked.

Tietjens was collecting his thoughts.

---

\* As Paul Skinner notes in his edition of *Last Post*, Henry Spelman's *The History and Fate of Sacrilege*, written in the early seventeenth century but not published until 1698, did indeed assert that those who profited from seized Catholic properties would come to a bad end. It's possible Ford was conflating him with John Selden (1584–1654), the jurist and expert on England's ancient laws and constitution. In 1618 his *History of Tithes* was published, and stirred up a controversy about sacrilege.

"My dear!" he said. "You'll permit me to call you 'my dear'? We're old enemies enough and we're talking about the future of our child."

Sylvia said:

"You said 'our' child, not 'the' child...."

Tietjens said with a great deal of concern:

"You will forgive me for bringing it up. You might prefer to think he was Drake's child. He can't be. It would be outside the course of nature.... I'm as poor as I am because ... forgive me ... I've spent a great deal of money on tracing the movements of you and Drake before our marriage. And if it's a relief to you to know ..."

"It *is*," Sylvia said. "I ... I've always been too beastly shy to put the matter before a specialist, or even before mother.... And we women are so ignorant...."

Tietjens said:

"I know ... I know you were too shy even to think about it yourself, hard." He went into months and days; then he continued: "But it would have made no difference: a child born in wedlock is by law the father's, and if a man who's a gentleman muffs[116] the begetting of his child he must, in decency, take the consequences: the woman and the child must come before the man, be he who he may. And worse-begotten children than ours have inherited statelier names. And I loved the little beggar with all my heart and with all my soul from the first minute I saw him. That may be the surest[117] clue, or it may be sheer sentimentality.... So I fought your influence because it was Papist, while I was a whole man. But I'm not a whole man any more, and the evil eye that is on me might transfer itself to him."

He stopped and said:

"For I must to the greenwood go. Alone a broken man.... But have him well protected against the evil eye...."

"Oh, Christopher," she said, "it's true I've not been a bad woman to the child. And I never will be. And I will keep Marchant with him till she dies. You'll tell her[118] not to interfere with his religious instruction, and she won't...."

Tietjens said with a friendly weariness:

"That's right ... and you'll have Father ... Father ... the priest that was with us for a fortnight before he was born to give him his teachings. He was the best man I ever met and one of the most intelligent. It's been a great comfort to me to think of the boy as in his hands. . . . "

Sylvia stood up, her eyes blazing out of a pallid face of stone:

"Father Consett," she said, "was hung on the day they shot Casement.* They dare not put it into the papers because he was a priest and all the witnesses Ulster witnesses. . . . And yet I may not say this is an accursed war."

Tietjens shook his head with the slow heaviness of an aged man.

"You may for me . . . " he said. "You might ring the bell, will you? Don't go away. . . . "

He sat with the blue gloom[119] of that enclosed space all over him, lumped heavily in his chair.

"Spelden[120] on sacrilege," he said, "may be right after all. You'd say so from the Tietjenses. There's not been a Tietjens since the first Lord Justice cheated the Papist Loundeses out of Roby,[121] but

---

*    Roger Casement had been arrested for treason, sabotage and espionage, for soliciting German support for the Easter Rising in Dublin. He was hanged rather than shot at Pentonville Prison in London on 3 August 1916. In the dedicatory letter to *No More Parades* Ford writes:

> I was roundly taken to task by the only English critic whose review of my last book I read – after he had *horribly* misrepresented the plot of the work at a crucial point for my inaccuracy in stating that poor Roger Casement was shot. As a matter of fact, I had been struck by the fact that a lady with whom I had been discussing Casement twice deliberately referred to the shooting of Casement, and stated that she did so because she could not bear to think that we had hanged him. In making therefore a lady – who had loved Casement – refer to his execution in the book in question, I let her say that Casement was shot. . . . Indeed, I should prefer to think that he had been shot, myself. . . . Or still more to think that we had allowed him to escape, or commit suicide, or be imprisoned during His Majesty's pleasure. . . . The critic preferred to rub in the hanging. It is a matter of relative patriotism.

The review in question was Gerald Gould's in the *Saturday Review*, 137 (17 May 1924), 512. (In his review of *No More Parades*, *Daily News* (28 Sept. 1925), 4, Gould identifies himself as the rebuked critic.) In *Joseph Conrad*, probably published the following month, Ford writes about Conrad's encounter with Casement (101). On 129 he says: 'It was as unspeakably painful to him when later Casement, loathing the Belgians so much for their treatment of the natives on the Congo, took up arms against his own country and was, to our eternal discredit, hanged, rather than shot in the attempt to escape. . . . ' Ottoline Morrell noted in her memoirs: 'Someone else went to Asquith the night before he was hung to entreat of him to grant a pardon, or at all events to shoot Casement instead of hanging him. Asquith got out of bed in his pyjamas, cross and obdurate. Even President Wilson and many Americans petitioned for a reprieve. It was all in vain': *Ottoline at Garsington: Memoirs of Lady Ottoline Morrell 1915–1918*, ed. Robert Gathorne-Hardy (London: Faber & Faber 1974), 114–15.

died of a broken neck or of a broken heart: for all the fifteen thousand acres of good farming land and iron land, and for all the heather on the top of it. . . . What's the quotation: 'Be ye something as something and something and ye shall not escape. . . .' What is it?"*

"Calumny!" Sylvia said. She spoke with intense bitterness.[122] . . . "Chaste as ice and cold as . . . as you are. . . . "

Tietjens said:

"Yes! Yes. . . . And mind you none of the Tietjens were ever soft. Not one! They had reason for their broken hearts. . . . Take my poor father. . . . "

Sylvia[123] said:

"*Don't!*"

"Both my brothers were killed in Indian regiments on the same day and not a mile apart. And my sister in the same week: out at sea, not so far from them. . . . Unnoticeable people. But one can be fond of unnoticeable people. . . . "

Hullo Central was at the door. Tietjens told her to ask Lord Port Scatho to step down. . . .

"You must, of course, know these details," Tietjens said, "as the mother to my father's heir. . . . My father got the three notifications on the same day. It was enough to break his heart. He only lived a month. I saw him . . . "

Sylvia screamed piercingly:

"Stop! stop! stop!" She clutched at the mantelpiece to hold herself up. "Your father died of a broken heart," she said, "because your brother's best friend, Ruggles, told him you were a squit who lived on women's money and had got the daughter of his oldest friend with child. . . . "

Tietjens said:

"Oh! Ah! Yes! . . . I suspected that. I know it, really. I suppose the poor dear knows better now. Or perhaps he doesn't. . . . It doesn't matter."

---

* It's *Hamlet*, III.i.138–9: 'be thou as chaste as ice, as pure as snow, thou shalt not escape calumny. Get thee to a nunnery, go, farewell.'

# II

IT has been remarked that the peculiarly English habit of self-suppression in matters of the emotions puts the Englishman at a great disadvantage in moments of unusual[1] stresses. In the smaller matters of the general run of life he will be impeccable and not to be moved; but in sudden confrontations of anything but physical dangers he is apt—he is, indeed, almost certain—to go to pieces very badly. This, at least, was the view of Christopher Tietjens, and he very much dreaded his interview with Lord Port Scatho—because he feared that he must be near breaking point.

In electing to be peculiarly English in habits and in as much of his temperament as he could control—for, though no man can choose the land of his birth or his ancestry, he can, if he have industry and determination, so watch over himself as materially to modify his automatic habits—Tietjens had quite advisedly and of set purpose adopted a habit of behaviour that he considered to be the best in the world for the normal life. If every day and all day long you chatter at high pitch and with the logic and lucidity of the Frenchman; if you shout in self-assertion, with your hat on your stomach, bowing from a stiff spine and by implication threaten all day long to shoot your interlocutor, like the Prussian; if you are as lachrymally emotional as the Italian, or as drily and epigrammatically imbecile over inessentials as the American, you will have a noisy, troublesome and thoughtless society without any of the surface calm that should distinguish the atmosphere of men when they are together. You will never have deep arm-chairs in which to sit for hours in clubs thinking of nothing at all—or of the off-theory in bowling.* On the other hand, in the face of death—except at sea, by fire, railway accident or accidental

---

\* In *The Soul of London* Ford wrote of how 'the course of a life becomes visible and sensible' only during leisurely moments when one can be 'unthinking, speculating on nothing' at a club window: *England*, 75. The 'off-theory' is a tactic in cricket whereby the fielders are concentrated on the off side, and the bowler aims at or outside the off stump.

drowning in rivers; in the face of madness, passion, dishonour or—and particularly—prolonged mental strain, you will have all the disadvantage of the beginner at any game and may come off very badly indeed. Fortunately death, love, public[2] dishonour and the like are rare occurrences in the life of the average man, so that the great advantage would seem to have lain with English society; at any rate before the later months of the year 1914. Death for man came but once: the danger of death so seldom as to be practically negligible: love of a distracting kind was a disease merely of the weak: public dishonour for persons of position, so great was the hushing up power of the[3] ruling class and the power of absorption of the remoter Colonies, was practically unknown.

Tietjens found himself now faced by all these things, coming upon him cumulatively and rather suddenly, and he had before him an interview that might cover them all and with a man whom he much respected and very much desired not to hurt. He had to face these, moreover, with a brain two-thirds of which felt numb. It was exactly like that.

It was not so much that he couldn't use what brain he had as trenchantly as ever: it was that there were whole regions of fact upon which he could no longer call in support of his argument. His knowledge of history was still practically negligible: he knew nothing whatever of the humaner letters and, what was far worse, nothing at all of the higher and more sensuous phases of mathematics. And the coming[4] back of these things was much slower than he had confessed to Sylvia. It was with these disadvantages that he had to face Lord Port Scatho.

Lord Port Scatho was the first man of whom Sylvia Tietjens had thought when she had been considering of men who were absolutely honourable, entirely benevolent ... and rather lacking in constructive intelligence.[5] He had inherited the management of one of the most respected of the great London banks,[6] so that his commercial and social influences were very extended: he was extremely interested in promoting Low Church interests, the reform of the divorce laws and sports for the people, and he had a great affection for Sylvia Tietjens. He was forty-five, beginning to put on weight, but by no means obese; he had a large, quite round head, very high-coloured cheeks that shone as if with frequent ablutions; an uncropped, dark moustache, dark, very cropped, smooth hair, brown eyes, a very new grey tweed suit, a very new grey Trilby hat, a black tie in a gold ring and very new patent leather boots that had white calf tops. He had a wife almost the spit of himself in face, figure, probity, kindliness and interests, except that for his interest in sports for the people she substituted that for maternity hospitals. His heir was his nephew, Mr. Brownlie, known as Brownie, who would also be physically the exact spit of his uncle, except that, not having put on flesh, he appeared to be taller and that his moustache and hair were both a little longer and more fair. This gentleman entertained for Sylvia Tietjens[7] a gloomy and deep passion that he considered to be perfectly honourable because he desired to marry her after she had divorced her husband. Tietjens he desired to ruin because he wished to marry Mrs. Tietjens and partly because he considered Tietjens to be an undesirable person of no great means. Of this passion Lord Port Scatho was ignorant.

He now came into the Tietjens' dining-room, behind the servant, holding an open letter: he walked rather stiffly because he was very much worried. He observed that Sylvia had been crying and was still wiping her eyes. He looked round the room to see if he could see in it anything to account for Sylvia's crying. Tietjens was still sitting at the head of the lunch-table: Sylvia was rising from a chair beside the fireplace.

Lord Port Scatho said:

"I want to see you, Tietjens, for a minute on business."

Tietjens said:

"I can give you ten minutes. . . ."

Lord Port Scatho said:

"Mrs. Tietjens perhaps . . ."

He waved the open letter towards Mrs. Tietjens. Tietjens said:

"No! Mrs. Tietjens will remain." He desired to say something more friendly. He said: "Sit down."

Lord Port Scatho said:

"I shan't be stopping a minute. But really . . ." and he moved the letter, but not with so wide a gesture, towards Sylvia.

"I have no secrets from Mrs. Tietjens," Tietjens said. "Absolutely none . . ."

Lord Port Scatho said:

"No . . . No, of course not . . . But . . ."

Tietjens said:

"Similarly, Mrs. Tietjens has no secrets from me. Again absolutely none."

Sylvia said:

"I don't, of course, tell Tietjens about my maid's love affairs or what the fish costs every day."

Tietjens said:

"You'd better sit down." He added on an impulse of kindness: "As a matter of fact I was just clearing up things for Sylvia to take over . . . this command." It was part of the disagreeableness of his mental disadvantages that upon occasion he could not think of other than military phrases. He felt intense annoyance. Lord Port Scatho affected him with some of the slight nausea that in those days you felt at contact with the civilian who knew none of your thoughts, phrases or preoccupations. He added, nevertheless equably:

"One has to clear up. I'm going out."

Lord Port Scatho said hastily:

"Yes; yes. I won't keep you. One has so many engagements in spite of the war. . . . " His eyes wandered in bewilderment. Tietjens could see them at last fixing themselves on the oil stains that Sylvia's salad dressing had left on his collar and green tabs.* He said to himself that he must remember to change his tunic before he went to the War Office. He must not forget. Lord Port Scatho's bewilderment at these oil stains was such that he had lost himself in the desire to account for them. . . . You could see the slow thoughts moving inside his square, polished brown forehead. Tietjens wanted very much to help him. He wanted to say: "It's about Sylvia's letter that you've got in your hand, isn't it?" But Lord Port Scatho had entered the room with the stiffness, with the odd, high-collared sort of gait that on formal and unpleasant occasions Englishmen use when they approach each other; braced up, a little like strange dogs meeting in the street. In view of that, Tietjens couldn't say "Sylvia." . . . But it would add to the formality and unpleasantness if he said again "Mrs. Tietjens!" *That* wouldn't help Port Scatho. . . .

---

*    The tabs were small patches on the lapels of officers' tunics, colour-coded to indicate specialisation. Green tabs were used by home-based Intelligence officers. See Partridge and Beale, *A Dictionary of Slang*, and note on 271–2.

Sylvia said suddenly:

"You don't understand, apparently. My husband is going out to the front line. To-morrow morning. It's for the second time."

Lord Port Scatho sat down suddenly on a chair beside the table. With his fresh face and brown eyes suddenly anguished he exclaimed:

"But, my dear fellow! You! Good God!" and then to Sylvia: "I beg your pardon!" To clear his mind he said again to Tietjens: "*You!* Going out to-morrow!" And, when the idea was really there, his face suddenly cleared. He looked with a swift, averted glance at Sylvia's face and then for a fixed moment at Tietjens' oil-stained tunic. Tietjens could see him explaining to himself with immense enlightenment that *that* explained both Sylvia's tears and the oil on the tunic. For Port Scatho might well imagine that officers went to the conflict in their oldest clothes. . . .

But, if his puzzled brain cleared, his distressed mind became suddenly distressed doubly. He had to add to the distress he had felt on entering the room[8] the distress at finding himself in the midst of what he took to be a highly emotional family parting.[9] And Tietjens knew[10] that during the whole war Port Scatho had never witnessed a family parting at all. Those that were not inevitable he would avoid like the plague, and his own nephew and all his wife's nephews were in the bank. That was quite proper for, if the ennobled family of Brownlie were not of the Ruling Class—who had to go!—they were of the Administrative Class, who were privileged to stay. So he had seen no partings.

Of his embarrassed hatred of them he gave immediate evidence. For he first began several sentences of[11] praise of Tietjens' heroism which he was unable to finish and then getting quickly out of his chair exclaimed:

"In the circumstances then . . . the little matter I came about . . . I couldn't of course think . . . "

Tietjens said:

"No; don't go. The matter you came about—I know all about it of course—had better be settled."

Port Scatho sat down again: his jaw fell slowly: under his bronzed complexion his skin became a shade paler.[12] He said at last:

"You know what I came about? But then . . . "

His ingenuous and kindly mind could be seen to be working
with reluctance: his athletic figure drooped. He pushed the letter
that he still held along the tablecloth towards Tietjens. He said,
in the voice of one awaiting a reprieve:

"But you *can't* be . . . aware . . . Not of this letter. . . ."

Tietjens left the letter on the cloth;[13] from there he could read
the large handwriting on the blue-grey paper:

"Mrs. Christopher Tietjens presents her compliments to Lord
Port Scatho and the Honourable Court of Benchers* of the
Inn. . . ." He wondered where Sylvia had got hold of that phrase-
ology: he imagined it to be fantastically wrong. He said:

"I have already told you that I know about this letter, as I have
already told you that I know—and I will add that I approve!—of
all Mrs. Tietjens' actions. . . ." With his hard blue eyes he looked
brow-beatingly into Port Scatho's soft brown orbs, knowing that
he was sending the message: "Think what you please and be
damned to you!"

The gentle brown things remained on his face; then they
filled[14] with an expression of deep pain. Port Scatho cried:[15]

"But good God! Then . . ."

He looked at Tietjens again. His mind, which took refuge
from life in the affairs of the Low Church, of Divorce Law Reform
and of Sports for the People, became a sea of pain at the contemplation of strong situations. His eyes said:

"For heaven's sake do not tell me that Mrs. Duchemin, the
mistress of your dearest friend, is the mistress of yourself, and that
you take this means of wreaking a vulgar spite on them."

Tietjens, leaning heavily forward, made his eyes as enigmatic
as he could; he said very slowly and very clearly:

"Mrs. Tietjens is, of course, not aware of *all* the circumstances."

Port Scatho threw himself back in his chair.

"I don't understand!" he said. "I do not understand. How am
I to act? You do not wish me to act on this letter? You can't!"

Tietjens, who found himself, said:

"You had better talk to Mrs. Tietjens about that. I will say
something myself later. In the meantime let me say that Mrs.

---

* Senior barristers who form the governing bodies of the Inns of Court.

Tietjens would seem to me to be quite within her rights. A lady, heavily veiled, comes here every Friday and remains until four of the Saturday morning.... If you are prepared to palliate the proceeding you had better do so to Mrs. Tietjens...."

Port Scatho turned agitatedly on Sylvia.

"I can't, of course, palliate," he said.[16] "God forbid.... But, my dear Sylvia ... my dear Mrs. Tietjens.... In the case of two people so much esteemed!... We have, of course, argued the matter of principle. It is a part of a subject I have very much at heart: the granting of divorce ... civil divorce, at least ... in cases in which one of the parties to the marriage is in a lunatic asylum. I have sent you the pamphlets of E. S. P. Haynes* that we publish. I know that as a Roman Catholic you hold strong views.... I do not, I assure you, stand for latitude...." He became then simply eloquent: he really had the matter at heart, one of his sisters having been for many years married to a lunatic. He expatiated on the agonies of this situation all the more eloquently in that it was the only form of human distress which he had personally witnessed.

Sylvia took a long look at Tietjens: he imagined for counsel. He looked at her steadily for a moment, then at Port Scatho, who was earnestly turned to her, then back at her. He was trying to say:

"Listen to Port Scatho for a minute. I need time to think of my course of action!"

He needed, for the first time in his life, time to think of his course of action.

He had been thinking with his under mind ever since Sylvia had told him that she had written her letter to the benchers denouncing Macmaster and his woman; ever since Sylvia had reminded him that Mrs. Duchemin in the Edinburgh to London express of the day before the war had been in his arms he had seen[17] with extraordinary clearness a great many north country scenes though he could not affix names to all the places. The forgetfulness of the names was abnormal: he ought to know the

---

* Lawyer and author of many books, including *Divorce as it might be* (1915) and (with Derek Walker-Smith) *Divorce and its Problems* (1935). Haynes wrote an essay on 'Divorce Law Reform' for Ford's *English Review*, 3 (Nov. 1909), 724–9. Douglas Goldring, *The Last Pre-Raphaelite* (London: Macdonald, 1948), 272, calls him an 'old friend' of Ford's.

names of places from Berwick down to the vale of York—but that he should have forgotten the incidents was normal enough. They had been of little importance: he preferred not to remember the phases of his friend's love affair; moreover, the events that happened immediately afterwards had been of a nature to make one forget quite normally what had just preceded them. That Mrs. Duchemin should be sobbing on his shoulder in a locked corridor carriage hadn't struck him as in the least important: she was the mistress of his dearest friend: she had had a very trying time for a week or so, ending in a violent, nervous quarrel with her agitated lover. She was, of course, crying off the effects of the quarrel which had been all the more shaking in that Mrs. Duchemin, like himself, had always been almost too self-contained. As a matter of fact he did not himself like Mrs. Duchemin, and he was pretty certain that she herself more than a little disliked him; so that nothing but their common feeling for Macmaster had brought them together. General Campion, however, was not to know that.... He had looked into the carriage in the way one does in a corridor just after the train had left.[18] ... He couldn't remember the name.... Doncaster ... No!... Darlington; it wasn't that. At Darlington there was a model of the Rocket ... or perhaps it isn't the Rocket.* An immense clumsy leviathan of a locomotive by ... by ... The great gloomy stations of the north-going trains ... Durham ... No! Alnwick.... No!... Wooler ... By God! Wooler! The junction for Bamborough....

It had been in one of the castles at Bamborough that he and Sylvia had been staying with the Sandbachs. Then ... a name had come into his mind spontaneously!... Two names!... It was, perhaps, the turn of the tide! For the first time ... To be marked with a red stone ... after this: some names, sometimes, on the tip of the tongue, might come over! He had, however, to get on....

The Sandbachs, then, and he and Sylvia ... others too ...

* Rocket was the early steam engine built by George Stephenson and his son Robert for a competition in 1829 to select the locomotive for the Liverpool and Manchester Railway. An earlier engine of theirs, Locomotion No. 1, hauled the first train on the Stockton and Darlington Railway in 1825. It was on display on a platform of Darlington's main station from 1892 to 1975.

had been in Bamborough since mid-July: Eton and Harrow at
Lord's, waiting for the real house parties that would come with
the 12th. . . . He repeated these names and dates[19] to himself for
the personal satisfaction of knowing that, amongst the repairs
effected in his mind, these two remained: Eton and Harrow, the
end of the London season: 12th of August, grouse shooting
begins. . . . It was pitiful. . . .

When General Campion had come up to rejoin his sister he,
Tietjens, had stopped only two days. The coolness between the
two of them remained; it was the first time they had met, except
in Court, after the accident. . . . For Mrs. Wannop, with grim
determination, had sued the General for the loss of her horse. It
had lived all right—but it was only fit to draw a lawn-mower for
cricket pitches. . . . Mrs. Wannop, then, had gone bald-headed
for the General, partly because she wanted the money, partly
because she wanted a public reason for breaking with the Sandbachs. The General had been equally obstinate and had
undoubtedly perjured himself in Court: not the best, not the most
honourable, the most benevolent man in the world would not
turn oppressor of the widow and orphan when his efficiency as a
chauffeur was impugned or the fact brought to light that at a very
dangerous turning he hadn't sounded his horn. Tietjens had
sworn that he hadn't: the General that he had. There *could* not
be any question of doubt, for the horn was a beastly thing that
made a prolonged noise like that of a terrified peacock. . . . So
Tietjens had not, till the end of that July, met the General again.
It had been quite a proper thing for gentlemen to quarrel over
and was quite convenient, though it had cost the General fifty
pounds for the horse and, of course, a good bit over for costs. Lady
Claudine had refused to interfere in the matter: she was privately
of opinion that the General *hadn't* sounded his horn, but the
General was both a passionately devoted and explosive brother.
She had remained closely intimate with Sylvia, mildly cordial
with Tietjens and had continued to ask the Wannops to such of
her garden parties as the General did not attend. She was also
very friendly with Mrs. Duchemin.

Tietjens and the General had met with the restrained
cordiality of English gentlemen who had some years before
accused each other of perjury in a motor accident. On the second

morning a violent quarrel had broken out between them on the subject of whether the General had or hadn't sounded his horn. The General had ended up by shouting ... really shouting:

"By God! If I ever get you under my command. ..."

Tietjens remembered that he had quoted and given the number of a succinct paragraph in King's Regs. dealing with the fate of general or higher field officers who gave their subordinates bad confidential reports because of private quarrels. The General had exploded into noises that ended in laughter.

"What a rag-bag of a mind you have, Chrissie!" he said. "What's King's Regs. to you? And how do you know it's paragraph 66 or whatever you say it is? I don't." He added more seriously: "*What* a fellow you are for getting into obscure rows! What in the world do you do it for?"

That afternoon Tietjens had gone to stop, a long way up in the moors, with his son, the nurse, his sister Effie and her children. They were the last days of happiness he was to know and he hadn't known so many. He was then content. He played with his boy, who, thank God, was beginning to grow healthy at last. He walked about the moors with his sister Effie, a large, plain, parson's wife, who had no conversation at all, though at times they talked of their mother. The moors were like enough to those above Groby to make them happy. They lived in a bare, grim farmhouse, drank great quantities of butter-milk and ate great quantities of Wensleydale. It was the hard, frugal life of his desire and his mind was at rest.

His mind was at rest because there was going to be a war. From the first moment of his reading the paragraph about the assassination of the Archduke Franz Ferdinand he had known that, calmly and with assurance. Had he imagined that this country would come in he would not have known a mind at rest. He loved this country for the run of its hills, the shape of its elm trees and the way the heather, running uphill to the skyline, meets the blue of the heavens. War for this country could only mean humiliation, spreading under the sunlight, an almost invisible pall, over the elms, the hills, the heather, like the vapour that spread from ... oh, Middlesbrough! We were fitted neither for defeat nor for victory: we could be true to neither friend nor foe. Not even to ourselves!

But of war for us he had no fear. He saw our Ministry sitting tight till the opportune moment and then grabbing a French channel port or a few German colonies as the price of neutrality.[20] And he was thankful to be out of it; for his back-doorway out— his second!—was the French Foreign Legion. First Sylvia: then that! Two tremendous disciplines: for the soul and for the body.

The French he admired: for their tremendous efficiency, for their frugality of life, for the logic of their minds, for their admirable achievements in the arts, for their neglect of the industrial system, for their devotion, above all, to the eighteenth century. It would be restful to serve, if only as a slave, people who saw clearly, coldly, straight: not obliquely and with hypocrisy only such things as should deviously conduce to[21] the standard of comfort of hogs and to lecheries winked at. . . . He would rather sit for hours on a bench in a barrack-room polishing a badge in preparation for the cruellest of route marches of immense lengths under the Algerian sun.

For, as to the Foreign Legion, he had had no illusion. You were treated not as a hero, but as a whipped dog: he was aware of all the *asticoteries*,* the cruelties, the weight of the rifle, the cells. You would have six months of training in the desert and then be hurtled[22] into the line to be massacred without remorse . . . as foreign dirt. But the prospect seemed to him one of deep peace: he had never asked for[23] soft living and now was done with it. . . . The boy was healthy; Sylvia, with the economies they had made, very rich . . . and even at that date he was sure that, if the friction of himself, Tietjens, were removed, she would make a good mother. . . .

Obviously he might survive; but after that tremendous physical drilling what survived would not be himself, but a man with cleaned, sand-dried bones: a clear mind. His private ambition had always been for saintliness: he must be able to touch pitch and not be defiled. That he knew marked him off as belonging to the sentimental branch of humanity. He couldn't help it: Stoic or Epicurean: Caliph in the harem or Dervish desiccating in the sand: one or the other you must be. And his desire was to be a saint of the Anglican variety . . . as his mother had been, without

* baitings, provocations (French).

convent, ritual, vows, or miracles to be performed by your relics! That sainthood, truly, the Foreign Legion might give you.... The desire of every English gentleman from Colonel Hutchinson* upwards.... A mysticism....

Remembering the clear sunlight of those naïvetés—though in his blue gloom he had abated no jot of the ambition—Tietjens sighed deeply as he came back for a moment to regard his dining-room. Really, it was to see how much time he had left in which to think out what to say to Port Scatho....[24] Port Scatho had moved his chair over to beside Sylvia and, almost touching her, was leaning over and recounting the griefs of his sister who was married to a lunatic. Tietjens gave himself again for a moment to the luxury of self-pity. He considered that he was dull-minded, heavy, ruined, and so calumniated that at times he believed in his own infamy, for it is impossible to stand up for ever against the obloquy of your kind and remain unhurt in the mind. If you hunch your shoulders too long against a storm your shoulders will grow bowed....

His mind stopped for a moment and his eyes gazed dully at Sylvia's letter which lay open on the tablecloth. His thoughts came together, converging on the loosely-written words:

"For the last nine months a woman ..."

He wondered swiftly what he had already said to Port Scatho: only that he had known of his wife's letter; not when! And that he approved! Well, on principle! He sat up. To think that one could be brought down to thinking so slowly!

He ran swiftly over what had happened in the train from Scotland and before....

Macmaster had turned up one morning beside their breakfast table in the farm house, much agitated, looking altogether too small in a cloth cap and a new grey tweed suit. He had wanted £50 to pay his bill with: at some place up the line above ... above ... Berwick suddenly flashed into Tietjens' mind....

That was the geographic position. Sylvia was at Bamborough on the coast (junction Wooler); he, himself, to the north-west, on the moors. Macmaster to the north-east of him, just over the

---

* Sir John Hutchinson (1615–64), one of the Puritan leaders during the English Civil War, is best known from the biography by his wife Lucy, *Memoirs of the Life of Colonel Hutchinson* (not published till 1806).

border: in some circumspect beauty spot where you did not meet
people. Both Macmaster and Mrs. Duchemin would know that
country and gurgle over its beastly literary associations.... The
Shirra! Maida! Pet Marjorie* ... Faugh! Macmaster would, no
doubt, turn an honest penny by writing articles about it and Mrs.
Duchemin would hold his hand....

She had become Macmaster's mistress, as far as Tietjens knew,
after a dreadful scene in the rectory, Duchemin having mauled
his wife like a savage dog, and Macmaster[25] in the house.... It
was natural: a Sadic[26] reaction as it were. But Tietjens rather
wished they hadn't. Now it appeared they had been spending a
week together ... or more. Duchemin by that time was in an
asylum....

From what Tietjens[27] had made out they had got out of bed
early one morning to take a boat and see the sunrise on some lake
and had passed an agreeable day together quoting, "Since when
we stand side by side only hands may meet" and other poems of
Gabriel Charles Dante Rossetti, no doubt to justify their sin.[†] On
coming home they had run their boat's nose into the tea-table of
the Port Scathos with Mr. Brownlie, the nephew, just getting out
of a motor to join them. The Port Scatho group were spending
the night at the Macmasters' hotel which backed on to the lake.
It was the ordinary damn sort of thing that must happen in these
islands that are only a few yards across.

The Macmasters appear to have lost their heads frightfully,
although Lady Port Scatho[28] had been as motherly as possible to
Mrs. Duchemin; so motherly, indeed, that if they had not been
unable to observe anything, they might have recognised the Port
Scathos as backers rather than spies upon themselves. It was, no
doubt, however, Brownlie who had upset them: he wasn't very
civil to Macmaster,[29] whom he knew as a friend of Tietjens. He
had dashed up from London in his motor to consult his uncle,

*  'Shirra' is Scots for 'Sheriff'. Sir Walter Scott was Sheriff of Selkirkshire from 1799 till
   his death in 1832. Maida was Scott's dog, and is portrayed with him in the Scott Monument in Edinburgh. 'Pet Marjorie' was the child prodigy Marjorie Fleming, a distant
   relation of Scott's, who wrote poetry before her death just days after her eighth
   birthday in 1811; she was written about not only by Scott but by Mark Twain and
   Leslie Stephen.
†  See 22.

who was dashing down from the west of Scotland, about the policy of the bank in that moment of crisis. . . .

Macmaster,[30] anyhow, did not spend the night in the hotel, but went to Jedburgh or Melrose or some such place, turning up again almost before it was light to have a frightful interview about five in the morning with Mrs. Duchemin, who, towards three, had come to a disastrous conclusion as to her condition.[31] They had lost their nerves for the first time in their association, and they had lost them very badly indeed, the things that Mrs. Duchemin said to Macmaster seeming almost to have passed belief. . . .

Thus, when Macmaster turned up at Tietjens' breakfast, he was almost out of his mind. He wanted Tietjens to go over in the motor he had brought, pay the bill at the hotel, and travel down to town with Mrs. Duchemin,[32] who was certainly in no condition to travel alone. Tietjens was also to make up the quarrel with Mrs. Duchemin and to lend Macmaster £50 in cash, as it was then impossible to change cheques anywhere. Tietjens got the money from his old nurse, who, because she distrusted banks, carried great sums in £5 notes in a pocket under her under-petticoat.

Macmaster, pocketing the money, had said:

"That makes exactly two thousand guineas that I owe you. I'm making arrangements to repay you next week. . . ."

Tietjens remembered that he had rather stiffened and had said: "For God's sake don't. I beg you not to. Have Duchemin properly put under trustees in lunacy,[33] and leave his capital alone. I really beg you. You don't know what you'll be letting yourselves in for. You don't owe me anything and you can always draw on me."

Tietjens never knew what Mrs. Duchemin had done about her husband's estate over which she had at that date had a power of attorney; but he had imagined that, from that time on, Macmaster had felt a certain coldness for himself and that Mrs. Duchemin had hated him. During several years Macmaster had been borrowing hundreds at a time from Tietjens. The affair with Mrs. Duchemin had cost her lover a good deal; he had week-ended almost continuously in Rye at the expensive hostel. Moreover, the famous Friday[34] parties for geniuses had been going on for several years now, and these had meant new furnishings, bindings, carpets, and loans to geniuses—at any rate before Macmaster had had the ear of the Royal Bounty. So the sum had grown to £2,000, and now to guineas. And, from that date, the Macmasters had not offered any repayment.

Macmaster had said that he dare not travel with Mrs. Duchemin because all London would be going south by that train. All London had. It pushed in at every conceivable and inconceivable station all down the line—it was the great rout of the 3-8-14.* Tietjens had got on board at Berwick, where they were adding extra coaches, and by giving a £5 note to the guard, who hadn't been able to promise isolation for any distance, had got a locked carriage. It hadn't remained locked for long enough to let Mrs. Duchemin have her cry out—but it had apparently served to make some mischief. The Sandbach party had got on, no doubt at Wooler; the Port Scatho party somewhere else. Their petrol had run out somewhere and sales were stopped, even to bankers. Macmaster, who after all had travelled by the same train, hidden beneath two bluejackets, had picked up Mrs. Duchemin at King's Cross[35] and that had seemed the end of it.

Tietjens,[36] back in his dining-room, felt relief and also anger. He said:

"Port Scatho. Time's getting short. I'd like to deal with this letter if you don't mind."

Port Scatho came as if up out of a dream. He had found the process of attempting to convert Mrs. Tietjens to divorce law reform very pleasant—as he always did. He said:

"Yes! ... Oh, yes!"

Tietjens said slowly:

"If you can listen.... Macmaster has been married to Mrs. Duchemin exactly nine months.... Have you got that? Mrs. Tietjens did not know this till this afternoon. The period Mrs. Tietjens complains of in her letter is nine months. She did perfectly right to write the letter. As such I approve of it. If she had known that the Macmasters were married she would not have written it. I didn't know she was going to write it. If I had known she was going to write it I should have requested her not to. If I

---

* A rout is a disorderly defeat; this refers to masses of people rushing home, anticipating the declaration of war the following day.

had requested her not to she would, no doubt, not[37] have done so. I did know of the letter at the moment of your coming in. I had heard of it at lunch only ten minutes before. I should, no doubt, have heard of it before, but this is the first time I have lunched at home in four months. I have to-day had a day's leave as being warned for foreign service. I have been doing duty at Ealing. To-day is the first opportunity I have had for serious business conversation with Mrs. Tietjens.... Have you got all that? ..."

Port Scatho was running towards Tietjens, his hand extended, and over his whole shining personage the air of an enraptured bridegroom. Tietjens moved his right hand a little to the right, thus eluding the pink, well-fleshed hand of Port Scatho. He went on frigidly:

"You had better, in addition, know as follows: The late Mr. Duchemin was a scatological[38]*—afterwards a homicidal—lunatic. He had recurrent fits, usually on a Saturday morning. That was because he fasted—not abstained merely—on Fridays. On Fridays he also drank. He had acquired the craving[39] for drink when fasting, from finishing the sacramental wine after communion services. That is a not unknown occurrence. He behaved latterly with great physical violence to Mrs. Duchemin. Mrs. Duchemin, on the other hand, treated him with the utmost consideration and concern: she might have had him certified much earlier, but, considering the pain that confinement must cause him during his lucid intervals, she refrained. I have been an eye-witness of the most excruciating heroisms on her part. As for the behaviour of Macmaster and Mrs. Duchemin, I am ready to certify—and I believe society accepts—that it has been most ... oh, circumspect and right!... There has been no secret of their attachment to each other. I believe that their determination to behave with decency during their period of waiting has not been questioned...."

Lord Port Scatho said:

"No! no! Never ... Most ... as you say ... circumspect and, yes ... right!"

---

* The OED cites this passage as an illustration of one of its definitions: 'characterized by a preoccupation with obscenity'.

"Mrs. Duchemin," Tietjens continued, "has presided at Macmaster's literary Fridays for a long time; of course since long before they were married. But, as you know, Macmaster's Fridays have been perfectly open: you might almost call them celebrated. . . ."

Lord Port Scatho said:

"Yes! yes! indeed . . . I sh'd be only too glad to have a ticket for Lady Port Scatho. . . ."

"She's only got to walk in," Tietjens said. "I'll warn them: they'll be pleased. . . . If, perhaps, you would look in to-night! They have a special party. . . . But Mrs. Macmaster was always attended by a young lady who saw her off by the last train to Rye. Or I very frequently saw her off myself, Macmaster being occupied by the weekly article that he wrote for one of the papers on Friday nights. . . . They were married on the day after Mr. Duchemin's funeral. . . ."

"You can't blame 'em!" Lord Port Scatho proclaimed.

"I don't propose to," Tietjens said. "The really frightful tortures Mrs. Duchemin had suffered justified—and indeed necessitated—her finding protection and sympathy at the earliest possible moment. They have deferred this announcement of their union partly out of respect for the usual period of mourning, partly because Mrs. Duchemin feels very strongly that, with all the suffering that is now abroad,[40] wedding feasts and signs of rejoicing on the part of non-participants are eminently to be deprecated. Still, the little party of to-night is by way of being an announcement that they are married. . . ." He paused to reflect for a moment.

"I perfectly understand!" Lord Port Scatho exclaimed. "I perfectly approve. Believe me, I and Lady Port Scatho will do everything. . . . Everything! Most admirable people. . . . Tietjens, my dear fellow, your behaviour . . . most handsome. . . ."

Tietjens said:

"Wait a minute. . . . There was an occasion in August, '14. In a place on the border. I can't remember the name. . . ."

Lord Port Scatho burst out:

"My dear fellow . . . I beg you won't. . . . I beseech you not to . . ."

Tietjens went on:

"Just before then Mr. Duchemin had made an attack on his wife of an unparalleled violence. It was that that caused his final incarceration. She was not only temporarily disfigured, but she suffered serious internal injuries and, of course, great mental disturbance. It was absolutely necessary that she should have change of scene.... But I think you will bear me out that, in that case too, their behaviour was ... again, circumspect and right...."

Port Scatho said:

"I know; I know ... Lady Port Scatho and I agreed—even without knowing what you have just told me—that the poor things almost exaggerated it.... He slept, of course, at Jedburgh? ..."41

Tietjens said:

"Yes! They almost exaggerated it.... I had to be called in to take Mrs. Duchemin home.... It caused, apparently, misunderstandings...."

Port Scatho—full of enthusiasm at42 the thought that at least two unhappy victims of the hateful divorce laws had, with decency and circumspectness, found the haven of their desires—burst out:

"By God, Tietjens, if I ever hear a man say a word against you.... Your splendid championship of your friend.... Your ... your unswerving devotion ..."

Tietjens said:

"Wait a minute, Port Scatho, will you?" He was unbuttoning the flap of his breast pocket.

"A man who can act so splendidly in one instance," Port Scatho said.... "And your going to France.... If any one ... if *any* one ... dares ..."

At the sight of a vellum-cornered, green-edged book in Tietjens' hand Sylvia suddenly stood up; as Tietjens took from an inner flap a cheque that had lost its freshness she made three great strides over the carpet to him.

"Oh, Chrissie! ..." she cried out. "He hasn't ... That beast hasn't ..."

Tietjens answered:

"He has ..." He handed the soiled cheque to the banker. Port Scatho looked at it with slow bewilderment.

"'Account overdrawn,'" he read. "Brownie's . . . my nephew's handwriting. . . . To the club . . . It's . . ."

"You aren't going to take it lying down?" Sylvia said. "Oh, thank goodness, you aren't going to take it lying down."

"No! I'm not going to take it lying down," Tietjens said. "Why should I?" A look of hard suspicion came over the banker's face.

"You appear," he said, "to have been overdrawing your account. People should not overdraw their accounts. For what sum are you overdrawn?"

Tietjens handed his pass-book to Port Scatho.

"I don't understand on what principle you work," Sylvia said to Tietjens. "There are things you take lying down; this you don't."

Tietjens said:

"It doesn't matter, really. Except for the child."

Sylvia said:

"I guaranteed an overdraft for you up to a thousand pounds[43] last Thursday. You can't be overdrawn over a thousand pounds."

"I'm not overdrawn at all," Tietjens said. "I was for about fifteen pounds yesterday. I didn't know it."

Port Scatho was turning over the pages of the pass-book, his face completely blank.

"I simply don't understand," he said. "You appear to be in credit. . . . You appear always to have been in credit except for a small sum now[44] and then. For a day or two."

"I was overdrawn," Tietjens said, "for fifteen pounds yesterday. I should say for three or four hours: the course of a post, from my army agent* to your head office. During these two or three hours your bank selected two out of six of my cheques to dishonour— both being under two pounds. The other one was sent back to my mess at Ealing, who won't, of course, give it back to me. That also is marked 'account overdrawn,'[45] and in the same handwriting."

"But good God," the banker said. "That means your ruin."

"It certainly means my ruin," Tietjens said. "It was meant to."

"But," the banker said—a look of relief came into his face which had begun to assume the aspect of a broken man's—"you

---

* 'Army agents kept the accounts of army regiments, distributing pay and subsistence, dealing in supplies of clothing, claims for pensions and injury, and providing a general banking business for soldiers and their families' (RBS Heritage Online).

must have other accounts with the bank ... a speculative one, perhaps, on which you are heavily down.... I don't myself attend to clients' accounts, except the very huge ones, which affect the bank's policy."

"You ought to," Tietjens said. "It's the very little ones you ought to attend to, as a gentleman making his fortune out of them. I have no other account with you. I have never speculated in anything in my life. I have lost a great deal in Russian securities—a great deal for me. But so, no doubt, have you."

"Then ... betting!" Port Scatho said.

"I never put a penny on a horse in my life," Tietjens said. "I know too much about them."

Port Scatho looked at the faces first of Sylvia, then of Tietjens. Sylvia, at least, was his very old friend. She said:[46]

"Christopher never bets and never speculates. His personal expenses are smaller than those of any man in town. You could say he had *no* personal expenses."[*]

Again the swift look of suspicion came into Port Scatho's open face.

"Oh," Sylvia said, "you couldn't suspect Christopher and me of being in a plot to blackmail you."

"No; I couldn't suspect that," the banker said. "But the other explanation is just as extraordinary.... To suspect the bank ... the *bank*.... How do *you* account? ..." He was addressing Tietjens; his round head seemed to become square, below; emotion worked on his jaws.

"I'll tell you simply this," Tietjens said. "You can then repair the matter as you think fit.[47] Ten days ago I got my marching orders. As soon as I had handed over to the officer who relieved me I drew cheques for everything I owed—to my military tailor, the mess—for one pound twelve shillings. I had also to buy a compass and a revolver, the Red Cross orderlies having annexed mine when I was in hospital...."

Port Scatho said: "Good God!"

"Don't you know they annex things?" Tietjens asked. He went on: "The total, in fact,[48] amounted to an overdraft of fifteen pounds, but I did not think of it as such because my army agents

* Cf. *The Benefactor* 52: George Moffat's personal expenses are 'of the smallest'.

ought to have paid my month's army pay over to you on the first. As you perceive, they have only paid it over this morning, the 13th. But, as you will see from my pass-book, they have always paid about the 13th, not the 1st. Two days ago I lunched at the club and drew that cheque for one pound fourteen shillings and sixpence: one ten for personal expenses and the four and six for lunch...."

"You were, however, actually overdrawn," the banker said sharply.

Tietjens said:

"Yesterday, for two hours."

"But then," Port Scatho said, "what do you want done? We'll do what we can."

Tietjens said:

"I don't know. Do what you like.[49] You'd better make what explanation you can to the military authority. If they court-martialled me it would hurt you more than me. I assure you of that. There *is* an explanation."

Port Scatho began suddenly to tremble.

"What ... what ... what explanation?" he said. "You ... damn it ... you draw this out.... Do you dare to say my bank...." He stopped, drew his hand down his face and said: "But yet ... you're a sensible, sound man.... I've heard things against you. But I don't believe them.... Your father always spoke very highly of you.... I remember he said if you wanted money you could always draw on him through us for three or four hundred.... That's what makes it so incomprehensible.... It's ... it's ..." His agitation grew on him. "It seems to strike at the very heart...."

Tietjens said:

"Look here, Port Scatho.... I've always had a respect for you. Settle it how you like. Fix the mess up for both our sakes with any formula that's not humiliating for your bank. I've already resigned from the club...."

Sylvia said: "Oh, *no*, Christopher ... not from the *club!*"

Port Scatho started back from beside the table.

"But if you're in the right!" he said. "You *couldn't* ... Not resign from the club.... I'm on the committee.... I'll explain to them, in the fullest, in the most generous ..."

"You couldn't explain," Tietjens said. "You can't get ahead of rumour.... It's half over London at this moment. You know what the toothless old fellows of your committee are.... Anderson! ffolliott ... And my brother's friend, Ruggles...."

Port Scatho said:

"Your brother's friend, Ruggles.... But look here.... He's something about the Court, isn't he? But look here...." His mind stopped. He said: "People shouldn't overdraw.... But if your father said you could draw on him I'm really much concerned.... You're a first-rate fellow.... I can tell that from your pass-book alone.... Nothing but cheques drawn to first-class tradesmen for reasonable amounts. The sort of pass-book I liked to see when I was a junior clerk in the bank...." At that early reminiscence feelings of pathos overcame him and his mind once more stopped.

Sylvia came back into the room; they had not perceived her going. She in turn held in her hand a letter.[50]

Tietjens said:

"Look here, Port Scatho, don't get into this state. Give me your word to do what you can when you've assured yourself the facts are as I say. I wouldn't bother you at all, it's not my line, except for Mrs. Tietjens. A man alone can live that sort of thing down, or die. But there's no reason why Mrs. Tietjens should live, tied to a bad hat, while he's living it down or dying."

"But that's not *right*," Port Scatho said, "it's not the right way to look at it. You can't pocket ... I'm simply bewildered...."

"You've no right to be bewildered," Sylvia said. "You're worrying your mind for expedients to save the reputation of your bank. We know your bank is more to you than a baby. You should look after it better, then."

Port Scatho, who had already fallen two paces away from the table, now fell two paces back, almost on top of it. Sylvia's nostrils were dilated.

She said:

"Tietjens shall not resign from your beastly club. He shall not! Your committee will request him formally to withdraw his resignation. You understand? He will withdraw it. Then he will resign for good. He is too good to mix with people like you...." She paused, her chest working fast. "Do you understand what you've got to do?" she asked.

An appalling shadow of a thought went through Tietjens'
mind: he would not let it come into words.

"I don't know . . ." the banker said. "I don't know that I can
get the committee . . ."

"You've got to," Sylvia answered. "I'll tell you why . . .
Christopher was never overdrawn. Last Thursday I instructed
your people to pay a thousand pounds to my husband's account.
I repeated the instruction by letter and I kept a copy of the letter
witnessed by my confidential maid. I also registered the letter and
have the receipt for it. . . . You can see them."

Port Scatho mumbled from over the letter:

"It's to Brownie . . . Yes, a receipt for a letter to Brownlie . . ."
and he[51] examined the little green slip on both sides. He said:
"Last Thursday. . . . To-day's Monday. . . . An instruction to sell
North-Western stock to the amount of one thousand pounds and
place to the account of . . . Then . . ."

Sylvia said:

"That'll do. . . . You can't angle for time any more. . . . Your
nephew has been in an affair of this sort before. . . . I'll tell you.
Last Thursday at lunch your nephew told me that Christopher's
brother's solicitors had withdrawn all the permissions for over-
drafts on the books of the Groby estate. There were several to
members of the family. Your nephew said that he intended to
catch Christopher on the hop—that's his own expression—and
dishonour the next cheque of his that came in. He said he had
been waiting for the chance ever since the war and the brother's
withdrawal had given it him.[52] I begged him not to . . ."

"But, good God," the banker said, "this is unheard of . . ."

"It isn't," Sylvia said. "Christopher has had five snotty, little,
miserable subalterns to defend at court-martials for exactly
similar cases. One was an exact reproduction of this. . . ."

"But, good God," the banker exclaimed again, "men giving
their lives for their country. . . . Do you mean to say Brownlie did
this out of revenge for Tietjens' defending at court-martials. . . .
And then . . . your thousand pounds is not shown in your
husband's pass-book. . . ."

"Of course it's not," Sylvia said. "It has never been paid in. On
Friday I had a formal letter from your people pointing out that
North-Westerns were likely to rise and asking me to reconsider

my position. The same day I sent an express telling them explic-itly to do as I said. . . . Ever since then your nephew has been on the 'phone begging me not to save my husband. He was there, just now, when I went out of the room. He was also beseeching me to fly with him."

Tietjens said:

"Isn't that enough, Sylvia? It's rather torturing."

"Let them be tortured," Sylvia said. "But it appears to be enough."

Port Scatho had covered his face with both his pink hands. He had exclaimed:

"Oh, my God! Brownlie again. . . . "

Tietjens' brother Mark was in the room. He was smaller, browner and harder than Tietjens and his blue eyes protruded more. He had in one hand a bowler hat, in the other an umbrella, wore a pepper-and-salt suit and had race-glasses slung across him.[53] He disliked Port Scatho, who detested him. He had lately been knighted. He said:

"Hullo, Port Scatho," neglecting to salute his sister-in-law. His eyes, whilst he stood motionless, rolled a look round the room and rested on a miniature bureau that stood on a writing-table, in a recess, under and between bookshelves.

"I see you've still got that cabinet," he said to Tietjens. Tiet-jens said:

"I haven't. I've sold it to Sir John Robertson. He's waiting to take it away till he has room in his collection."[54]

Port Scatho walked, rather unsteadily, round the lunch-table and stood looking down from one of the long windows. Sylvia sat down on her chair beside the fireplace. The two brothers stood facing each other, Christopher suggesting wheat-sacks, Mark, carved wood. All round them, except for the mirror that reflected bluenesses, the gilt backs of books. Hullo Central was clearing the table.

"I hear you're going out again to-morrow," Mark said.[55] "I want to settle some things with you."

"I'm going at nine from Waterloo,"* Christopher said. "I've

---

* This is slightly inconsistent with the 8.30 time Tietjens gives for his departure when speaking to Mrs Wannop (206) and to Valentine (338).

not much time. You can walk with me to the War Office if you like."

Mark's eyes followed the black and white of the maid round the table. She went out with the tray. Christopher suddenly was reminded of Valentine Wannop clearing the table in her mother's cottage. Hullo Central was no faster about it. Mark said:

"Port Scatho! As you're there we may as well finish one point. I have cancelled my father's security for my brother's overdraft."

Port Scatho said, to the window, but loud enough: "We all know it. To our cost."

"I wish you, however," Mark Tietjens went on, "to make over from my own account a thousand a year to my brother as he needs it. Not more than a thousand in any one year."

Port Scatho said:[56]

"Write a letter to the bank. I don't look after clients' accounts on social occasions."

"I don't see why you don't," Mark Tietjens said. "It's the way you make your bread and butter, isn't it?"

Tietjens said:

"You may save yourself all this trouble, Mark. I am closing my account in any case."

Port Scatho spun round on his heel.

"I beg that you won't," he exclaimed. "I beg that we ... that we may have the honour of continuing to have you draw upon us." He had the trick of convulsively working jaws: his head against the light was like the top of a rounded gate-post. He said to Mark Tietjens: "You may tell your friend, Mr. Ruggles, that your brother is empowered by me to draw on my private account ... on my personal and private account up to any amount he needs. I say that to show my estimate of your brother; because I know he will incur no obligations he cannot discharge."

Mark Tietjens stood motionless; leaning slightly on the crook of his umbrella on the one side; on the other displaying, at arm's length, the white silk lining of his bowler hat, the lining being the brightest object in the room.

"That's your affair," he said to Port Scatho. "All I'm concerned with is to have a thousand a year paid to my brother's account till further notice."

Christopher Tietjens said, with what he knew was a sentimental voice, to Port Scatho. He was very touched; it appeared to him that with the spontaneous appearance of several names in his memory, and with this estimate of himself from the banker, his tide was turning and that this day might indeed be marked by a red stone:

"Of course, Port Scatho, I won't withdraw my wretched little account from you if you want to keep it. It flatters me that you should." He stopped and added: "I only wanted to[57] avoid these ... these family complications. But I suppose you can stop my brother's money being paid into my account. I don't want his money."

He said to Sylvia:

"You had better settle the other matter with Port Scatho." To Port Scatho:

"I'm intensely obliged to you, Port Scatho.... You'll get Lady Port Scatho round to Macmaster's this evening if only for a minute; before eleven...." And to his brother:

"Come along, Mark. I'm going down to the War Office. We can talk as we walk."

Sylvia said very nearly with timidity—and again a dark thought went over Tietjens' mind:

"Do we meet again then? ... I know you're very busy...."

Tietjens said:

"Yes. I'll come and pick you out from Lady Job's, if they don't keep me too long at the War Office. I'm dining, as you know, at Macmaster's; I don't suppose I shall stop late."

"I'd come," Sylvia said, "to Macmaster's, if you thought it was appropriate. I'd bring Claudine Sandbach and General Wade. We're only going to the Russian dancers.* We'd cut off early."

Tietjens could settle that sort of thought very quickly. "Yes, do," he said hurriedly. "It would be appreciated." He got to the

---

* Probably Sergei Diaghilev's Ballets Russes, whose London seasons ran from 1911 and continued during and after the war. Though their production of *Parade*, with music by Satie, plot by Cocteau, and sets and costumes by Picasso, premiered in Paris on 18 May 1917, its London premiere wasn't till 14 November 1919; so even if Ford saw it and had it in mind while writing *Parade's End*, in a non-fictional world Sylvia couldn't have seen it in London during the war. Goldring, *South Lodge* 72, describes seeing the Ballets Russes in 1913. Though he doesn't mention Ford seeing them, he does recall Ford admiring the ballerina Adeline Genée at the Empire.

door: he came back: his brother was nearly through. He said to Sylvia, and for him the occasion was a very joyful one:

"I've worried out some of the words of that song. It runs:

'Somewhere or other there must surely be
The face not seen: the voice not heard . . .'

Probably it's 'the voice not ever heard' to make up the metre. . . . I don't know the writer's name. But I hope I'll worry it all out during the day."

Sylvia had gone absolutely white.

"Don't!" she said. "Oh . . . *don't*." She added coldly: "Don't take the trouble," and wiped her tiny handkerchief across her lips as Tietjens went away.

She had heard the song at a charity concert and had cried as she heard it. She had read, afterwards, the words in the programme and had almost cried again. But she had lost the programme and had never come across the words again. The echo of them remained with her like something terrible and alluring: like a knife she would some day take out and with which she would stab herself.

# III

THE two brothers walked twenty steps from the door along the empty Inn pavements without speaking. Each was completely expressionless. To Christopher it seemed like Yorkshire. He had a vision of Mark, standing on the lawn at Groby, in his bowler hat and with his umbrella, whilst the shooters walked over the lawn, and up the hill to the butts.* Mark probably never had done that; but it was so that his image always presented itself to his brother. Mark was considering that one of the folds of his umbrella was disarranged. He seriously debated with himself whether he should unfold it at once and refold it—which was a great deal of trouble to take!—or whether he should leave it till he got to his club, where he would tell the porter to have it done at once. That would mean that he would have to walk for a mile and a quarter through London with a disarranged umbrella, which was disagreeable.

He said:

"If I were you I wouldn't let that banker fellow go about giving you testimonials of that sort."

Christopher said:

"Ah!"

He considered that, with a third of his brain in action, he was over a match for Mark, but he was tired of discussions. He supposed that some unpleasant construction would be put by his brother's friend, Ruggles, on the friendship of Port Scatho for himself. But he had no curiosity. Mark felt a vague discomfort. He said:

"You had a cheque dishonoured at the club this morning?"

Christopher said:

"Yes."

Mark waited for explanations. Christopher was pleased at the

---

* 'In grouse-shooting, a position either sunken or on the level ground, protected by a wall or bank of earth behind which the sportsman may stand and fire unobserved by the game': OED.

speed with which the news had travelled: it confirmed what he
had said to Port Scatho. He viewed his case from outside. It was
like looking at the smooth working of a mechanical model.

Mark was more troubled. Used as he had been for thirty years
to the vociferous south he had forgotten that there were tacitur-
nities still. If at his Ministry he laconically accused a transport
clerk of remissness, or if he accused his French mistress—just as
laconically—of putting too many condiments on his nightly
mutton chop, or too much salt in the water in which she boiled
his potatoes, he was used to hearing a great many excuses or nega-
tions, uttered with energy and continued for long. So he had got
into the habit of considering himself almost the only laconic
being in the world. He suddenly remembered with discomfort—
but also with satisfaction—that his brother was his brother.

He knew nothing about Christopher, for himself. He had
seemed to look at his little brother down avenues, from a
distance, the child misbehaving himself. Not a true Tietjens:
born very late: a mother's child, therefore, rather than a father's.
The mother an admirable woman, but from the South Riding.*
Soft, therefore, and ample. The elder Tietjens' children, when
they had experienced failures, had been wont to blame their
father for not marrying a woman of their own Riding. So, for
himself, he knew nothing of this boy. He was said to be brilliant:
an un-Tietjens-like quality. Akin to talkativeness! . . . Well, he
wasn't talkative. Mark said:

"What have you done with all the brass our mother left you?
Twenty thousand, wasn't it?"

They were just passing through a narrow way between Georgian houses. In the next quadrangle Tietjens stopped and looked
at his brother. Mark stood still to be looked at. Christopher said
to himself:

"This man has the right to ask these questions!"

It was as if a queer slip had taken place in a moving-picture.
This fellow had become the head of the house: he, Christopher,

---

\* Yorkshire was divided into three sub-districts called 'Ridings' since the days of Viking
rule. But there are only three: North, West, and East Riding. There is no South Riding
(except in Winifred Holtby's 1936 novel of that title), which makes it either Mark's
(and Ford's) joke or Ford's oversight.

was the heir. At that moment, their father, in the grave four months now, was for the first time dead.

Christopher remembered a queer incident. After the funeral, when they had come back from the churchyard[1] and had lunched, Mark—and Tietjens could now see the wooden gesture—had taken out his cigar-case and, selecting one cigar for himself, had passed the rest round the table. It was as if people's hearts had stopped beating. Groby had never, till that day, been smoked in: the father had his twelve pipes filled and put in the rose-bushes in the drive. . . .

It had been regarded merely as a disagreeable incident: a piece of bad taste. . . . Christopher, himself, only just back from France, would not even have known it as such, his mind was so blank, only the parson had whispered to him: "And Groby never smoked in till this day."

But now! It appeared a symbol, and an absolutely right symbol. Whether they liked it or not, here were the head of the house and the heir. The head of the house must make his arrangements, the heir agree or disagree; but the elder brother had the right to have his enquiries answered.

Christopher said:

"Half the money was settled at once on my child. I lost seven thousand in Russian securities. The rest I spent. . . ."

Mark said:

"Ah!"

They had just passed under the arch that leads into Holborn. Mark, in turn, stopped and looked at his brother and Christopher stood still to be inspected, looking into his brother's eyes. Mark said to himself:

"The fellow isn't at least afraid to look at you!" He had been convinced that Christopher would be. He said:

"You spent it on women? Or where do you get the money that you spend on women?"

Christopher said:

"I never spent a penny on a woman in my life."

Mark said:

"Ah!"

They crossed Holborn and went by the backways towards Fleet Street.

Christopher said:

"When I say 'woman' I'm using the word in the ordinary sense. Of course I've given women of our own class tea or lunch[2] and paid for their cabs. Perhaps I'd better put it that I've never—either before or after marriage—had connection with any woman other than my wife."

Mark said:

"Ah!"

He said to himself:

"Then Ruggles must be a liar." This neither distressed nor astonished him. For twenty years he and Ruggles had shared a floor of a large and rather gloomy building in Mayfair. They were accustomed to converse whilst shaving in a joint toilet-room, otherwise they did not often meet except at the club. Ruggles was attached to the Royal Court in some capacity, possibly as sub-deputy gold-stick-in-waiting.[*] Or he might have been promoted in the twenty years. Mark Tietjens had never taken the trouble to enquire. Enormously proud and shut in on himself, he was without curiosity of any sort. He lived in London because it was immense, solitary, administrative and apparently without curiosity as to its own citizens. If he could have found, in the north, a city as vast and as distinguished by the other characteristics, he would have preferred it.

Of Ruggles he thought little or nothing. He had once heard the phrase "agreeable rattle," and he regarded Ruggles as an agreeable rattle, though he did not know what the phrase meant.[†] Whilst they shaved Ruggles gave out the scandal of the day. He never, that is to say, mentioned a woman whose virtue was not purchasable, or a man who would not sell his wife for advancement. This matched[3] with Mark's ideas of the south. When Ruggles aspersed the fame of a man of family from the north, Mark would stop him with:

"Oh, no. That's not true. He's a Craister of Wantley Fells," or

---

* The office of Gold Stick originated in Tudor times. Two officers were assigned as body-guards to the sovereign, the one on duty being referred to as Gold Stick-in-waiting. Since Victoria's reign the role has been ceremonial. Technically the deputy to Gold Stick-in-waiting is Silver Stick-in-waiting.

† 'A person who talks incessantly in a lively or inane manner; a constant chatterer': OED. The dictionary cites Rose Macaulay's *Orphan Island*, also of 1924: 'xiii. 143, I think he must have been a rather agreeable rattle'.

another name, as the case might be. Half Scotchman, half Jew, Ruggles was very tall and resembled a magpie, having his head almost always on one side. Had he been English Mark would never have shared his rooms with him: he knew indeed few Englishmen of sufficient birth and position to have that privilege, and, on the other hand, few Englishmen of birth and position would have consented to share rooms so grim and uncomfortable, so furnished with horse-hair seated mahogany, or so lit with ground-glass skylights. Coming up to town at the age of twenty-five, Mark had taken these rooms with a man called Peebles, long since dead, and he had never troubled to make any change, though Ruggles had taken the place of Peebles. The remote similarity of the names had been less disturbing to Mark Tietjens than would have been the case had the names been more different. It would have been very disagreeable, Mark often thought, to share with a man called, say, Granger. As it was he still often called Ruggles Peebles, and no harm was done. Mark knew nothing of Ruggles' origins, then—so that, in a remote way, their union resembled that of Christopher with Macmaster. But whereas Christopher would have given his satellite the shirt off his back, Mark would not have lent Ruggles more than a five pound note, and would have turned him out of their rooms if it had not been returned by the end of the quarter. But, since Ruggles never had asked to borrow anything at all, Mark considered him an entirely honourable man. Occasionally Ruggles would talk of his determination to marry some widow or other with money, or of his influence with people in exalted stations, but, when he talked like that, Mark would not listen to him and he soon returned to stories of purchasable women and venial men.

About five months ago Mark had said one morning to Ruggles:

"You might pick up what you can about my youngest brother Christopher and let me know."

The evening before that Mark's father had called Mark to him from over the other side of the smoking-room[4] and had said:

"You might find out what you can about Christopher. He may be in want of money. Has it occurred to you that he's the heir to the estate! After you, of course." Mr. Tietjens had aged a good deal after the deaths of his children. He said: "I suppose you won't marry?" and[5] Mark had answered:

"No; I shan't marry. But I suppose I'm a better life than Christopher. He appears to have been a good deal knocked about out there."

Armed then with this commission Mr. Ruggles appears to have displayed extraordinary activity in preparing a Christopher Tietjens dossier. It is not often that an inveterate gossip gets a chance at a man whilst being at the same time practically shielded against the law of libel. And Ruggles disliked Christopher Tietjens with the inveterate dislike of a man who revels in gossip for the man who never gossips. And Christopher Tietjens had displayed more than his usual insolence to Ruggles. So Ruggles' coattails flashed round an unusual[6] number of doors and his top-hat gleamed before an unusual number of tall portals during the next week.

Amongst others he had visited the lady known as Glorvina.

There is said to be a book, kept in a holy of holies, in which bad marks are set down against men of family and position in England. In this book Mark Tietjens and his father—in common with a great number of hard-headed Englishmen of county rank—implicitly believed.[*] Christopher Tietjens didn't: he imagined that the activities of gentlemen like Ruggles were sufficient to stop the careers of people whom they disliked. On the other hand, Mark and his father looked abroad upon English society and saw fellows, apparently with every qualification for successful careers in one service or the other; and these fellows got no advancements, orders,[†] titles or preferments of any kind. Just, rather mysteriously, they didn't make their marks. This they put down to the workings of the book.

* This idea perhaps draws on the Pemberton Billing case, detailed in Philip Hoare's *Wilde's Last Stand* (London: Duckworth, 1997), which cites this passage, 210. Pemberton Billing became an MP during the war. He founded a journal, *Imperialist*, and published an article in it alleging that the Germans kept a 'Black Book' of the names of 47,000 Englishmen they were luring into homosexuality and then blackmailing, thus preventing Britain from winning the war. After a second article, 'The Cult of the Clitoris', attacking lesbianism, Billing was accused of libelling the actress Maud Allan, then playing Wilde's *Salomé*. There was a sensational trial in May 1918 at which Billing defended himself and was acquitted. While the book Ford mentions appears to be kept by the English elite, and to record any conduct deemed unacceptable, it stands for the paranoid sense of the time that sexuality, conspiracy, and war were all disturbingly entangled.
† The OED gives a definition of 'order' as 'The badge or insignia representing or demonstrating membership of an order of knighthood, honour, or merit'.

Ruggles, too, not only believed in the existence of that compilation of the suspect and doomed, but believed that his hand had a considerable influence over the inscriptions in its pages. He believed that if, with more moderation and with more grounds than usual, he uttered denigrations of certain men before certain personages, it would at least do those men a great deal of harm. And, quite steadily and with, indeed, real belief in much of what he said, Ruggles had denigrated Tietjens before these personages. Ruggles could not see why Christopher had taken Sylvia back after her elopement with Perowne: he could not see why Christopher had, indeed, married Sylvia at all when she was with child by a man called Drake—just as he wasn't going to believe that Christopher could get a testimonial out of Lord Port Scatho except by the sale of Sylvia to the banker. He couldn't see anything but money or jobs at the bottom of these things: he couldn't see how Tietjens otherwise got the money to support Mrs. Wannop,[7] Miss Wannop and her child, and to maintain Mrs. Duchemin and Macmaster in the style they affected, Mrs. Duchemin being the mistress of Christopher. He simply could see no other solution.[8] It is, in fact, asking for trouble if you are more altruist than the society that surrounds you.

Ruggles, however, hadn't any pointers as to whether or no or to what degree he had really damaged his room-mate's brother. He had talked in what he considered to be the right quarters, but he hadn't any evidence that what he had said had got through. It was to ascertain that that[9] he had called on the great lady, for if anybody knew, she would.

He hadn't definitely ascertained anything, for the great lady was—and he knew it—a great deal cleverer than himself. The great lady, he was allowed to discover, had a real affection for Sylvia, her daughter's close friend, and she expressed real concern to hear that Christopher Tietjens wasn't getting on. Ruggles had gone to visit her quite openly to ask whether something better couldn't be done for the[10] brother of the man with whom he lived. Christopher had, it was admitted, great abilities; yet neither in his office—in which he would surely have remained had he been satisfied with his prospects—nor in the army did he occupy anything but a very subordinate position. Couldn't, he asked, Glorvina do anything for him? And he added: "It's almost as if he had a bad mark against him. . . . "

The great lady had said, with a great deal of energy, that she could not do anything at all. The energy was meant to show how absolutely her party had been downed, outed and jumped on by the party in power, so that she had no influence of any sort anywhere. That was an exaggeration; but it did Christopher Tietjens no good, since Ruggles chose to take it to mean that[11] Glorvina said she could do nothing because there *was* a black mark against Tietjens in the book of the inner circle to which—if anyone had—the great lady must have had access.

Glorvina, on the other hand, had been awakened to concern for Tietjens. In the existence of a book she didn't believe: she had never seen it. But that a black mark of a metaphorical nature might have been scored against him she was perfectly ready to believe and, when occasion served, during the next five months, she made enquiries about Tietjens. She came upon a Major Drake, an intelligence officer, who had access to the central depôt of confidential reports upon officers, and Major Drake showed her, with a great deal of readiness, as a specimen, the report on Tietjens. It was of a most discouraging sort and peppered over[12] with hieroglyphics, the main point being Tietjens' impecuniosity and his predilection for the French; and apparently for the French Royalists. There being at that date and with that Government a great deal of friction with our Allies, this characteristic which earlier had earned him a certain number of soft jobs had latterly done him a good deal of harm. Glorvina carried away the definite information that Tietjens had been seconded to the French artillery as a liaison officer and had remained with them for some time, but, having been shell-shocked, had been sent back. After that a mark had been added against him: "Not to be employed as liaison officer again."

On the other hand, Sylvia's visits to Austrian officer-prisoners had also been noted to Tietjens' account and a final note added: "Not to be entrusted with any confidential work."*

---

* Ford's service record at the Public Records Office, Kew, file WO 339/37369, shows that his attempt to get transferred to a staff job was blocked, both by his C.O., Lieutenant-Colonel Cooke, who wanted him out of the army, but also by MI6, on the grounds that his German ancestry made him unsuitable for intelligence work.

To what extent Major Drake himself compiled these records the great lady didn't know and didn't want to know. She was acquainted with the relationships of the parties and was aware that in certain dark, full-blooded men the passion for sexual revenge is very lasting, and she let it go at that. She discovered, however, from Mr. Waterhouse—now also in retreat—that he had a very high opinion of Tietjens' character and abilities, and that just before Waterhouse's[13] retirement he had especially recommended Tietjens for very high promotion.* That alone, in the then state of Ministerial friendships and enmities, Glorvina knew to be sufficient to ruin any man within range of Governmental influence.

She had, therefore, sent for Sylvia and had put all these matters before her, for she had too much wisdom to believe that, even supposing there should be differences between the young people of which she had no evidence at all, Sylvia could wish to do anything but promote her husband's material interests. Moreover, sincerely benevolent as the great lady was towards this couple, she also saw that here was a possibility of damaging, at least, individuals of the party in power. A[14] person in a relatively unimportant official position can sometimes make a very nasty stink if he is unjustly used, has determination and a small amount of powerful backing. This Sylvia, at least, certainly had.

And Sylvia had received the great lady's news with so much emotion that no one could have doubted that she was utterly devoted to her husband and would tell him all about it. This Sylvia had not as yet managed to do.

Ruggles in the meantime had collected a very full budget of news and inferences to present to Mark Tietjens whilst shaving. Mark had been neither surprised nor indignant. He had been accustomed to call all his father's children, except the brother immediately next him, "the whelps," and their concerns had been

---

* Under the rules of the day, when C. F. G. Masterman had been given his Cabinet post he was required to recontest his seat in a by-election. When he lost his own seat of Bethnal Green South West, he made a second attempt in Ipswich, but lost that too, so felt obliged to resign from government. He was appointed head of 'Wellington House', the War Propaganda Bureau, soliciting propaganda work from many of his writer-friends, including Ford, who wrote two books for him: *When Blood* and *Between St. Dennis* (both 1915).

no concerns of his. They would marry, beget unimportant children who would form collateral lines of Tietjens and disappear as
is the fate of sons of younger sons. And the deaths of the intermediate brothers had been so recent that Mark[15] was not yet used
to thinking of Christopher as anything but a whelp, a person
whose actions might be disagreeable but couldn't matter. He said
to Ruggles:

"You had better talk to my father about this. I don't know that
I could keep all these particulars accurately in my head."

Ruggles had been only too pleased to, and[16]—with to give him
weight, his intimacy with the eldest son, who certified to his reli-
ability in money matters and his qualifications for amassing
details as to personalities, acts and promotions—that day, at tea
at the club, in a tranquil corner, Ruggles had told Mr. Tietjens
senior that Christopher's wife had been with child when he had
married her; he[17] had hushed up her elopement with Perowne and
connived at other love affairs of hers to his own dishonour, and
was suspected in high places of being a French agent, thus being
marked down as suspect in the great book.... All this in order
to obtain money for the support of Miss Wannop, by whom he
had had a child, and to maintain Macmaster and Mrs. Duchemin
on a scale unsuited to their means, Mrs. Duchemin being his
mistress. The story that Tietjens had had a child by Miss Wannop
was first suggested, and then supported, by the fact that in Yorkshire he certainly had a son who never appeared in Gray's Inn.[18]

Mr. Tietjens was a reasonable man: not reasonable enough to
doubt Ruggles' circumstantial history. He believed implicitly in
the great book—which has been believed in by several generations of country gentlemen: he perceived that his brilliant son
had made no advancement commensurate with either his brilliance or his influence: he suspected that brilliance was
synonymous with reprehensible tendencies. Moreover, his old
friend, General ffolliott, had definitely told him some days before
that he ought to enquire into the goings on of Christopher. On
being pressed ffolliott had, also definitely, stated that Christopher
was suspected of very dishonourable dealings, both in money and
women. Ruggles' allegations came, therefore, as a definite confirmation of suspicions that appeared only too well backed up.

He bitterly regretted that, knowing Christopher to be bril-

liant, he had turned the boy—as is the usual portion of younger
sons—adrift, with what of a competence could be got together,
to sink or swim. He had, he said to himself, always wished to keep
at home and under his own eyes this boy for whom he had had
especial promptings of tenderness.[19] His wife, to whom he had
been absolutely attached by a passionate devotion, had been
unusually wrapped up in Christopher,[20] because Christopher had
been her youngest son, born very late. And, since his wife's death,
Christopher had been especially dear to him, as if he had carried
about his presence some of the radiance and illumination that
had seemed to attach to his mother. Indeed, after his wife's death,
Mr. Tietjens had very nearly[21] asked Christopher and his wife to
come and keep house for him at Groby, making, of course, special
testamentary provision for Christopher in order to atone[22] for his
giving up his career at the Department of Statistics. His sense of
justice to his other children[23] had prevented him[24] doing this.

What broke his heart was that Christopher should not only
have seduced but should have had a child by Valentine Wannop.
Very grand seigneur in his habits, Mr. Tietjens had always
believed in his duty to patronise the arts and, if he had actually
done little in this direction beyond purchasing some chocolate-
coloured pictures of the French historic school, he had for long
prided himself on what he had done for the widow and children
of his old friend, Professor Wannop. He considered, and with
justice, that he had made Mrs. Wannop a novelist, and he considered her to be a very great novelist. And his conviction of the
guilt of Christopher was strengthened by a slight tinge of jealousy
of his son: a feeling that he would not have acknowledged to
himself. For, since Christopher, he didn't know how, for he had
given his son no introduction, had become an intimate of the
Wannop household, Mrs. Wannop had completely given up
asking him, Mr. Tietjens, clamorously and constantly for advice.
In return she had sung the praises of Christopher in almost
extravagant terms. She had, indeed, said that if Christopher had
not been almost daily in the house or at any rate at the end of the
'phone she would hardly have been able to keep on working at
full pressure. This had not overpleased Mr. Tietjens.[25] Mr. Tietjens entertained for Valentine Wannop an affection of the very
deepest, the same qualities appealing to the father as appealed to

the son.[26] He had even, in spite of his sixty odd years, seriously entertained the idea of marrying the girl. She was a lady: she would have managed Groby very well; and, although the entail on the property was very strict indeed, he would, at least, have been able to put her beyond the reach of want after his death. He had thus no doubt of his son's guilt, and he had to undergo the additional humiliation of thinking that not only had his son betrayed this radiant personality, but he had done it so clumsily as to give the girl a child and let it be known. That was unpardonable want of management in the son of a gentleman. And now this boy[27] was his heir with a misbegotten brat to follow. Irrevocably!

All his four tall sons, then, were down. His eldest tied for good to—a quite admirable!—trollops:[28] his two next dead: his youngest worse than dead: his wife dead of a broken heart.[29]

A soberly but deeply religious man, Mr. Tietjens' very religion made him believe in Christopher's guilt. He knew that it is as difficult for a rich man to go to heaven as it is for a camel to go through the gate in Jerusalem called the Needle's Eye. He humbly hoped that his Maker would receive him amongst the pardoned. Then, since he was a rich—an enormously rich—man, his sufferings on this earth must be very great. . . .

From tea-time that day until it was time to catch the midnight train for Bishop[30] Auckland he had been occupied with his son Mark in the writing-room of the club. They had made many notes. He had seen his son Christopher, in uniform, looking broken and rather bloated, the result, no doubt, of debauch. Christopher had passed through the other end of the room and Mr. Tietjens had avoided his eye. He had caught the train and reached Groby, travelling alone. Towards dusk he had taken out a gun. He was found dead next morning, a couple of rabbits beside his body, just over the hedge from the little churchyard. He appeared to have crawled through the hedge, dragging his loaded gun, muzzle forwards, after him. Hundreds of men, mostly farmers, die from that cause every year in England. . . .[31]

With these things in his mind—or as much of them as he could keep at once—Mark was now investigating his brother's affairs. He would have let things go on longer, for his father's estate was by no means wound up,[32] but that morning Ruggles had told him that the club had had a cheque of his brother's returned and that his brother was going out to France next day. It was five months exactly since the death of their father. That had happened in March, it was now August: a bright, untidy day in narrow, high courts.

Mark arranged his thoughts.

"How much of an income," he said, "do you need to live in comfort? If a thousand isn't enough, how much? Two?"

Christopher said that he needed no money and didn't intend to live in comfort. Mark said:

"I am to[33] let you have three thousand, if you'll live abroad. I'm only carrying out our father's instructions. You could cut a hell of a splash on three thousand in France."

Christopher did not answer.

Mark began again:

"The remaining three thousand then: that was over from our mother's money. Did you settle it on your girl, or just spend it on her?"

Christopher repeated with patience that he hadn't got a girl. Mark said:

"The girl who had a child by you.[34] I'm instructed, if you haven't settled anything already—but father took it that you would have—I was to let her have enough to live in comfort. How much do you suppose she'll need to live in comfort? I allow Charlotte* four hundred. Would four hundred be enough? I suppose you want to go on keeping her? Three thousand isn't a great lot for her to live on with a child."

Christopher said:

"Hadn't you better mention names?"

Mark said:

"No! I never mention names. I mean a woman writer and her daughter. I suppose the girl[35] is father's daughter, isn't she?"

Christopher said:

"No. She couldn't be. I've thought of it. She's twenty-seven. We were all in Dijon for the two years before she was born. Father

---

* Mark's mistress, and later wife, is called Marie Léonie in *Last Post* I.vi, which explains that 'he had called her Charlotte for reasons of camouflage before the marriage'.

didn't come into the estate till next year.* The Wannops were
also in Canada at the time. Professor Wannop was principal of a
university there. I forget the name."

Mark said:

"So we were. In Dijon! For my French!" He added: "Then she
can't be father's daughter. It's a good thing. I thought, as he
wanted to settle money on them, they were very likely his children. There's a son, too. He's to have a thousand. What's he
doing?"

"The son," Tietjens said, "is a conscientious objector.† He's on
a mine-sweeper. A bluejacket. His idea is that picking up mines
is saving life, not taking it."

"Then he won't want the brass yet," Mark said, "it's to start
him in any business. What's the full name and address of your
girl? Where do you keep her?"

They were in an open space, dusty, with half-timber buildings
whose demolition had been interrupted. Christopher halted close
to a post that had once been a cannon; up against this he felt that
his brother could lean in order to assimilate ideas. He said slowly
and patiently:

"If you're consulting with me as to how to carry out our father's
intentions, and as there's money in it you had better make an
attempt to get hold of the facts. I wouldn't bother you if it wasn't
a matter of money. In the first place, no money is wanted at this
end. I can live on my pay. My wife is a rich woman, relatively.
Her mother is a very rich woman. . . ."

"She's Rugeley's mistress, isn't she?" Mark asked. Christopher
said:

"No, she isn't. I should certainly say she wasn't. Why should
she be? She's his cousin."

"Then it's your wife who was Rugeley's mistress?" Mark asked.
"Or why should she have the loan of his box?"

"Sylvia also is Rugeley's cousin, of course, a degree further

---

*    i.e. Mr Tietjens senior didn't inherit Groby until the year after Valentine was born.
†    When conscription was introduced in Britain in 1916, those objecting to participating
     in combat on moral grounds had to convince a Military Service Tribunal of the quality
     of their objection. They might be exempted service altogether, required to perform
     alternative civilian service, or to serve as non-combatants in roles such as stretcher-
     bearers.

removed," Tietjens said. "She isn't anyone's mistress. You can be certain of that."

"They *say* she is," Mark answered. "They say she's a regular tart. . . . I suppose you think I've insulted you." Christopher said:

"No, you haven't. . . . It's better to get all this out. We're practically strangers, but you've a right to ask."

Mark said:

"Then you haven't got a girl and don't need money to keep her. . . . You could have what you liked. There's no reason why a man shouldn't have a girl, and if he has he ought to keep her decently. . . ."

Christopher did not answer.[36] Mark leaned against the half-buried cannon and swung his umbrella by its crook.

"But," he said, "if you don't keep a girl what do you do for . . ." He was going to say "for the comforts of home," but a new idea had come into his mind. "Of course," he said, "one can see that your wife's soppily in love with you." He added: "Soppily . . . one can see that with half an eye. . . ."

Christopher felt his jaw drop. Not a second before—that very second!—he had made up his mind to ask Valentine Wannop to become his mistress that night.[37] It was no good, any more, he said to himself. She loved him, he knew, with a deep, an unshakable passion, just as his passion for her was a devouring element that covered his whole mind as the atmosphere envelopes[38] the earth. Were they, then, to go down to death separated by years, with no word ever spoken? To what end? For whose benefit? The whole world conspired to force them together! To resist became a weariness![39]

His brother Mark was talking on. "I know all about women," he had announced. Perhaps he did. He had lived with exemplary fidelity to a quite unpresentable woman, for a number of years. Perhaps the complete study of one woman gave you a map of all the rest!

Christopher said:

"Look here, Mark. You had better go through all my pass-books for the last ten years. Or ever since I had an account.[40] This discussion is no good if you don't believe what I say."

Mark said:

"I don't want to see your pass-books. I believe you."

He added, a second later:

"Why the devil shouldn't I believe you? It's either believing you're a gentleman or Ruggles a liar. It's only common sense to believe Ruggles a liar, in that case. I didn't before because I had no grounds to."

Christopher said:[41]

"I doubt if liar is the right word. He picked up things that were said against me. No doubt he reported them faithfully enough. Things *are* said against me. I don't know why."

"Because," Mark said with emphasis, "you treat these south country swine with the contempt that they deserve. They're incapable of understanding the motives of a gentleman.[42] If you live among dogs they'll think you've the motives of a dog. What other motives can they give you?" He added: "I thought you'd been buried so long under their muck that you were as mucky as they!"

Tietjens looked at his brother with the respect one has to give to a man ignorant but shrewd. It was a discovery: that his brother was shrewd.[43]

But, of course, he would be shrewd. He was the indispensable[44] head of a great department. He had to have some qualities. . . . Not cultivated, not even instructed. A savage! But penetrating!

"We must move on," he said, "or I shall have to take a cab." Mark detached himself from his half buried cannon.

"What did you do with the other three thousand?" he asked. "Three thousand is a hell of a big sum to chuck away. For a younger[45] son."

"Except for some furniture I bought for my wife's rooms," Christopher said, "it went mostly in loans."

"Loans!" Mark exclaimed. "To that fellow Macmaster?"

"Mostly to him," Christopher answered. "But about seven hundred to Dicky Swipes, of Cullercoats."

"Good God! Why to him?" Mark ejaculated.

"Oh, because he was Swipes, of Cullercoats," Christopher said, "and asked for it. He'd have had more, only that was enough for him to drink himself to death on."

Mark said:

"I suppose you don't give money to every fellow that asks for it?"

Christopher said:

"I do. It's a matter of principle."

"It's lucky," Mark said, "that a lot of fellows don't know that. You wouldn't have much brass left for long."

"I didn't have it for long," Christopher said.

"You know," Mark said, "you couldn't expect to do the princely patron on a youngest son's portion. It's a matter of taste. I never gave a ha'penny to a beggar myself. But a lot of the Tietjens were princely. One generation to addle brass:* one to keep: one to spend. That's all right.... I suppose Macmaster's wife *is* your mistress? That'll account for it not being the girl. They keep an arm-chair for you."

Christopher said:

"No. I just backed Macmaster for the sake of backing him. Father lent him money to begin with."

"So he did," Mark exclaimed.

"His wife," Christopher said, "was the widow of Breakfast Duchemin. *You* knew Breakfast Duchemin?"

"Oh, *I* knew Breakfast Duchemin," Mark said. "I suppose Macmaster's a pretty warm† man now. Done himself proud with Duchemin's money."[46]

"Pretty proud!" Christopher said. "They won't be knowing me long now."

"But damn it all!" Mark said, "You've Groby to all intents and purposes. *I'm* not going to marry and beget children to hinder you."

Christopher said:

"Thanks. I don't want it."

"Got your knife into me?" Mark asked.

"Yes. I've got my knife into you," Christopher answered. "Into the whole bloody lot of you, and Ruggles's and ffolliots[47] and our father!"

Mark said: "Ah!"

"You don't suppose I wouldn't have?" Christopher asked.

"Oh, *I* don't suppose you wouldn't have," Mark answered. "I thought you were a soft sort of bloke. I see you aren't."

---

* To gain money (Northern dialect).
† 'Comfortably off, well to do; rich, affluent. Now chiefly *colloq.*': OED. Cf. *The Bene-factor* 157: 'a warm man'; and 'True Love & a GCM', in *War Prose* 84: 'warm city men'.

"I'm as North Riding as yourself!" Christopher answered.

They were in the tide of Fleet Street, pushed apart by foot passengers and separated by traffic. With some of the imperious-ness of the officer of those days Christopher barged across through motor-buses and paper lorries. With the imperiousness of the head of a department Mark said:

"Here, policeman, stop these damn things and let me get over." But Christopher was over much the sooner and waited for his brother in the gateway of the Middle Temple. His mind was completely swallowed up in the[48] endeavour to imagine the embraces of Valentine Wannop. He said to himself that he had burnt his boats.

Mark, coming alongside him, said:

"You'd better know what our father wanted."

Christopher said:

"Be quick then. I must get on." He had to rush through his War Office interview to get to Valentine Wannop. They would have only a few hours in which to recount the loves of two life-times. He saw her golden head and her enraptured face. He wondered how her face would look, enraptured. He had seen on it humour, dismay, tenderness, in the eyes—and fierce anger and contempt for his, Christopher's, political opinions. His mili-tarism!

Nevertheless they halted by the Temple fountain. That respect was due to their dead father. Mark had been explaining. Christopher had caught some of his words and divined the links. Mr. Tietjens had left no will, confident that his desires as to the disposal of his immense fortune would be carried out meticulously by his eldest son. He would have left a will, but there was the vague case of Christopher to be considered. Whilst Christopher had been a youngest son you arranged that he had a good lump sum and went, with it, to the devil how he liked. He was no longer a youngest son: by the will of God.

"Our father's idea," Mark said by the fountain, "was that no settled sum could keep you straight. His idea was that if you were a bloody pimp living on women ... You don't mind?"

"I don't mind your putting it straightforwardly," Christopher said. He considered the base of the fountain that was half full of leaves. This civilisation had contrived a state of things in which leaves rotted by August. Well, it was doomed!

"If you were a pimp living on women," Mark repeated, "it was no good making a will. You might need uncounted thousands to keep you straight. You were to have 'em. You were to be as debauched as you wanted, but on clean money. I was to see how much in all probability that[49] would be and arrange the other legacies to scale.... Father had crowds of pensioners...."

"How much did father cut up for?" Christopher asked.

Mark said:

"God knows.... You saw we proved* the estate[50] at a million and a quarter as far as ascertained. But it might be twice that.[51] Or five times! ... With steel prices what they have been for the last three years it's impossible to say what the Middlesbrough district property won't produce.... The death duties even can't catch it up. And there are all the ways of getting round *them*."

Christopher inspected his brother with curiosity. This brown-complexioned fellow with bulging eyes, shabby on the whole, tightly buttoned into a rather old pepper-and-salt suit, with a badly rolled umbrella, old race-glasses,[52] and his bowler hat the only neat[53] thing about him, was, indeed, a prince. With a rigid outline! All real princes must look like that. He said:

"Well! You won't be a penny the poorer by me."

Mark was beginning to believe this. He said:

"You won't forgive father?"

Christopher said:

"I won't forgive father for not making a will. I won't forgive him for calling in Ruggles. I saw him and you in the writing-room the night before he died. He never spoke to me. He could have. It was clumsy stupidity. That's unforgiveable."

"The fellow shot himself," Mark said. "You usually forgive a fellow who shoots himself."

"I don't," Christopher said. "Besides, he's probably in heaven and don't need my forgiveness. Ten to one he's in heaven. He was a good man."

"One of the best," Mark said. "It was I that called in Ruggles though."

---

* Obtained 'probate', i.e. established 'the genuineness and validity' of their father's will.

"I don't forgive you either," Christopher said.

"But you *must*," Mark said—and it was a tremendous conces-
sion to sentimentality—"take enough to make you comfortable."

"By God!" Christopher exclaimed. "I loathe your whole
beastly buttered toast,* mutton-chopped, carpet-slippered, rum-
negused comfort as much as I loathe your beastly Riviera-palaced,
chauffeured, hydraulic-lifted, hot-house aired beastliness of
fornication.. . . ." He was carried away, as he seldom let himself
be, by the idea of his amours with Valentine Wannop which
should take place on the empty boards of a cottage, without
draperies, fat meats, gummy aphrodisiacs. . . . "You won't," he
repeated, "be a penny the poorer by me."

Mark said:

"Well, you needn't get shirty about it. If you won't you won't.
We'd better move on. You've only just time. We'll say that settles
it. . . . Are you, or aren't you, overdrawn at your bank? I'll make
that up, whatever you damn well do to stop it."

"I'm not overdrawn," Christopher said. "I'm over thirty
pounds in credit, and I've an immense overdraft guaranteed by
Sylvia. It was a mistake of the bank's."

Mark hesitated for a moment. It was to him almost unbeliev-
able that a bank could make a mistake. One of the great banks.
The props of England.

They were walking down towards the Embankment.[54] With
his precious umbrella Mark aimed a violent blow at the railings
above the tennis lawns, where whitish figures, bedrabbled by the
dim atmosphere, moved like marionettes practising crucifixions.

"By God!" he said, "this is the last of England. . . . There's only
my department where they never make mistakes. I tell you, if
there were any mistakes made there there would be some backs
broken!" He added: "But don't you think that I'm going to give
up comfort, I'm not. My Charlotte makes better buttered toast
than they can at the club. And she's got a tap of French rum that's

* *Nightingale* 56 describes a discussion with E. V. Lucas in which Ford attacks Charles
Lamb and the English school of essay-writing for 'buttered-toast-clean-fire-clear-
hearth-spirit-of-the-game-beery-gin-sodden sentimentalism', only to be astounded
when Lucas gently counters that Ford can't appreciate such writing because he is 'not
really English'. An earlier account is in 'Literary Portraits – XX. Mr. Gilbert Cannan
and "Old Mole"', *Outlook*, 33 (24 Jan. 1914), 110–11.

saved my life over and over again after a beastly wet day's racing. And she does it all on the five* hundred I give her and keeps herself clean and tidy on top of it. Nothing like a Frenchwoman for managing. . . . By God, I'd marry the doxy if she wasn't a Papist. It would please her and it wouldn't hurt me. But I couldn't stomach marrying a Papist. They're not to be trusted."

"You'll have to stomach a Papist coming into Groby," Christopher said. "My son's to be brought up as a Papist."

Mark stopped and dug his umbrella into the ground.

"Eh, but that's a bitter one," he said. "Whatever made ye do that? . . . I suppose the mother made you do it. She tricked you into it before you married her." He added: "I'd not like to sleep with that wife of yours. She's too athletic. It'd be like sleeping with a bundle of faggots. I suppose though you're a pair of turtle doves. . . . Eh, but I'd not have thought ye would have been so weak."

"I only decided this morning," Christopher said, "when my cheque was returned from the bank. You won't have read Spelden on Sacrilege, about Groby."

"I can't say I have," Mark answered.

"It's no good trying to explain that side of it then," Christopher said, "there isn't time. But you're wrong in thinking Sylvia made it a condition of our marriage. Nothing would have made me consent then.[55] It has made her a happy woman that I have. The poor thing thought our house was under a curse for want of a Papist heir."

"What made ye consent now?"[56] Mark asked.

"I've told you," Christopher said, "it was getting my cheque returned to the club;[57] that on the top of the rest of it. A fellow who can't do better than that had better let the mother bring up the child. . . . Besides, it won't hurt a Papist boy to have a father with dishonoured cheques as much as it would a Protestant. They're not quite English."

"That's true too," Mark said.

He stood still by the railings of the public garden near the Temple station.

"Then," he said, "if I'd let the lawyers write and tell you the

---

* Mark says four hundred on 259.

guarantee for your overdraft from the estate was stopped as they wanted to, the boy wouldn't be a Papist? You wouldn't have overdrawn."

"I didn't overdraw," Christopher said. "But if you had warned me I should have made enquiries at the bank and the mistake wouldn't have occurred. Why didn't you?"

"I meant to," Mark said. "I meant to do it myself. But I hate writing letters. I put it off.[58] I didn't much like having dealings with the fellow I thought you were. I suppose that's another thing you won't forgive me for?"

"No. I shan't forgive you for not writing to me," Christopher said. "You ought to write business letters."

"I hate writing 'em," Mark said. Christopher was moving on. "There's one thing more," Mark said. "I suppose the boy is your son?"

"Yes, he's my son," Christopher said.

"Then that's all," Mark said. "I suppose if you're killed you won't mind my keeping an eye on the youngster?"

"I'll be glad," Christopher said.[59]

They strolled along the Embankment side by side, walking rather slowly, their backs erected and their shoulders squared because of their satisfaction of walking together, desiring to lengthen the walk by going slow. Once or twice they stopped to look[60] at the dirty silver of the river, for both liked grim effects of landscape. They felt very strong, as if they owned the land!

Once Mark chuckled and said:

"It's too damn funny. To think of our both being . . . what is it? . . . monogamists? Well, it's a good thing to stick to one woman . . . you can't say it isn't. It saves trouble. And you know where you are."

Under the lugubrious arch that leads into the War Office quadrangle Christopher halted.

"No. I'm coming in," Mark said. "I want to speak to Hogarth. I haven't spoken to Hogarth for some time. About the transport waggon parks in Regent's Park. I manage all those beastly things and a lot more."

"They say you do it damn well," Christopher said. "They say you're indispensable." He was aware that his brother desired to stay with him as long as possible. He desired it himself.

"I damn well am!" Mark said. He added: "I suppose you couldn't do that sort of job in France? Look after transport and horses."

"I could," Christopher said, "but I suppose I shall go back to liaison work."

"I don't think you will," Mark said. "I could put in a word for you with the transport people."

"I wish you would," Christopher said. "I'm not fit to go back into the front line. Besides I'm no beastly hero! And I'm a rotten infantry officer. No Tietjens was ever a soldier worth talking of."

They turned the corner of the arch. Like something fitting in, exact and expected, Valentine Wannop stood looking at the lists of casualties that hung beneath a cheaply green-stained deal shelter against the wall, a tribute at once to the weaker art movements of the day and the desire to save the ratepayers' money.

With the same air of finding Christopher Tietjens fit in exactly to an expected landscape she turned on him. Her face was blue-white and distorted. She ran upon him and exclaimed:

"Look at this horror! And you in that foul uniform can support it!"

The sheets of paper beneath the[61] green roof were laterally striped with little serrated lines: each line[62] meant the death of a man, for the day.

Tietjens had fallen a step back off the kerb[63] of the pavement that ran round the quadrangle. He said:

"I support it because I have to. Just as you decry it because you have to. They're two different patterns that we see." He added: "This is my brother Mark."

She turned her head stiffly upon Mark: her face was perfectly waxen. It was as if the head of a shopkeeper's lay-figure had been turned. She said to Mark:

"I didn't know Mr. Tietjens had a brother. Or hardly. I've never heard him speak of you."

Mark grinned feebly,[64] exhibiting to the lady the brilliant lining of his hat.

"I don't suppose anyone has ever heard me speak of *him*," he said, "but he's my brother all right!"

She stepped on to the asphalte carriage-way and caught between her fingers and thumb a fold of Christopher's[65] khaki sleeve.

"I must speak to you," she said; "I'm going then."

She drew Christopher into the centre of the enclosed, hard and ungracious space, holding him still by the stuff of his tunic. She pushed him round until he was facing her. She swallowed hard, it was as if the motion of her throat took an immense time. Christopher looked round the sky-line of the buildings of sordid and besmirched stone. He had often wondered what would happen if an air-bomb of some size dropped into the mean,[66] grey stoniness of that cold heart of an embattled world.

The girl was devouring his face with her eyes: to see him flinch. Her voice was hard between her little teeth. She said:

"Were you the father of the child Ethel was going to have? Your wife says you were."

Christopher considered the dimensions of the quadrangle. He said vaguely:

"Ethel? Who's she?" In pursuance of the habits of the painter-poet Mr. and Mrs. Macmaster called each other always "Gug Gums!" Christopher had in all probability never heard Mrs. Duchemin's Christian names. Certainly he had never heard them since his disaster had swept all names out of his head.

He came to the conclusion that the quadrangle was not a space sufficiently confined to afford much bursting resistance to a bomb.

The girl said:

"Edith Ethel Duchemin! Mrs. Macmaster that is!" She was obviously waiting intensely. Christopher said with vagueness:

"No! Certainly not! . . . What was said?"

Mark Tietjens was leaning forward over the kerb in front of the green-stained shelter, like a child over a brook-side. He was obviously waiting, quite patient, swinging his umbrella by the crook.[67] He appeared to have no other means of self-expression. The girl was saying that when she had rung up Christopher that morning a voice had said, without any preparation at all: the girl repeated, without any preparation at all:

"You'd better keep off the grass if you're the Wannop girl. Mrs. Duchemin is my husband's mistress already. You keep off!"

Christopher said:

"She said that, did she?" He was wondering how Mark kept his balance, really. The girl said nothing more. She was waiting.

With an insistence that seemed to draw him: a sort of sucking in of his personality. It was unbearable. He made his last effort of that afternoon.

He said:

"Damn it all. How could you ask such a tomfool question?[68] *You!* I took you to be an intelligent person. The only intelligent person I know.[69] Don't you *know* me?"

She made an effort to retain her stiffening.

"Isn't Mrs. Tietjens a truthful person?" she asked. "I thought she looked truthful when I saw her at Vincent and Ethel's."

He said:

"What she says she believes. But she only believes what she wants to, for the moment. If you call that truthful, she's truthful. I've nothing against her." He said to himself: "I'm not going to appeal to her by damning my wife."

She seemed to go all of a piece, as the hard outline goes suddenly out of a piece of lump sugar upon which you drop water.

"Oh," she said, "it *isn't* true. I *knew* it wasn't true." She began to cry.

Christopher said:

"Come along. I've been answering tomfool questions all day. I've got another tomfool to see here, then I'm through."

She said:

"I can't come with you, crying like this."

He answered:

"Oh, yes you can. This is the place where women cry."[70] He added: "Besides there's Mark. He's a comforting ass."

He delivered her over to Mark.

"Here, look after Miss Wannop," he said. "You want to talk to her anyhow, don't you?" and he hurried ahead of them like a fussy shopwalker into the lugubrious hall. He felt that, if he didn't come soon to an unemotional ass in red, green, blue, or pink tabs,*

---

* Geoffrey Sparrow and James Ross, *On Four Fronts with the Royal Naval Division* (London: Hodder and Stoughton, 1918), 253, 255 explained: 'Practically every officer attached to formations other than a battalion, who specialises even in a small way, wraps some coloured flannel round his hat, and adorns the lapels of his immaculate tunic with material of a similar shade, surmounted by a small gold button [...] Those who wear blue tabs are too numerous to mention, and to attempt an accurate classi-fication of the many other colours of tabs is too intricate to be interesting, and too uninteresting to serve any useful purpose.' This notwithstanding, red tabs indicated

who would have fish-like eyes and would ask the sort of questions that fishes ask in tanks, he, too, must break down and cry. With relief! However, that was a place where men cried, too![71]

He got through at once by sheer weight of personality, down miles of corridors, into the presence of a quite intelligent, thin, dark person with scarlet tabs. That meant a superior staff affair: not dustbins.

The dark man said to him at once:

"Look here! What's the matter with the Command Depôts? You've been lecturing a lot of them.[*] In economy.[†] What are all these damn mutinies about? Is it the rotten[72] old colonels in command?"

Tietjens said amiably:

"Look here! I'm not a beastly spy, you know? I've had hospitality from the rotten[73] old colonels."

The dark man said:

"I daresay you have. But that's what you were sent round for. General Campion said you were the brainiest chap in his command. He's gone out now, worse luck.... What's the matter with the Command Depôts? Is it the men? Or is it the officers? You needn't mention names."

Tietjens said:

"Kind of Campion. It isn't the officers and it isn't the men. It's the foul system. You get men who think they've deserved well of their country—and they damn well have!—and you crop their heads...."

"That's the M.O.s,"[74] the dark man said. "They don't want lice."

Staff officers; green, Intelligence; blue were used for logistical support, such as Transport and Medical officers; sky blue for the Royal Flying Corps, etc.

* In April 1917 a Medical Board had refused to pass Ford as fit enough to return to France, and he was assigned to a new commanding officer, Lieutenant-Colonel G. R. Powell, with the 23rd King's Liverpool Regiment, stationed at Kinmel Park. Powell described him as 'a lecturer of the first water on several military subjects'. In early 1918 Ford was was given a new job attached to the staff, to go 'all over the N[orth]. of England inspecting training & lecturing'. See Saunders, *Dual Life* II 36.

† Ford sent Stella Bowen a notice about 'Salvage' (urging the men to save for recycling 'valuable material that used to be regarded as rubbish') as what he jokingly called 'a specimen of my prose – for tho' the signature be that of Alexander [Lieutenant-Colonel Alexander Pope, his previous C.O.], the voice is yᵗ F.M.H's': 5 Oct. 1918; letter and circular printed in *Ford/Bowen* 20–2.

"If they prefer mutinies . . ." Tietjens said. "A man wants to walk with his girl and have a properly oiled quiff. They don't like being regarded as convicts. That's how they are regarded."

The dark man said:

"All right. Go on. Why don't you sit down?"

"I'm a little in a hurry," Tietjens said. "I'm going out tomorrow and I've got a brother and people waiting below." The dark man said:

"Oh, I'm sorry. . . . But damn. You're the sort of man we want at home. Do you want to go? We can, no doubt, get you stopped if you don't."

Tietjens hesitated for a moment.

"Yes!" he said eventually. "Yes, I want to go."

For the moment he had felt temptation to stay.[75] But it came into his discouraged mind that Mark had said that Sylvia was in love with him. It had been underneath his thoughts all the while: it had struck him at the time like a kick from the hind leg of a mule in his subliminal consciousness. It was the impossible complication. It might not be true; but whether or no the best thing for him was to go and get wiped out as soon as possible. He meant, nevertheless, fiercely, to have his night with the girl who was crying downstairs. . . .

He heard in his ear, perfectly distinctly, the lines:[76]

> "The voice that never yet . . .
> Made answer to my word . . ."

He said to himself:

"That was what Sylvia wanted! I've got that much!"

The dark man had said something. Tietjens repeated:

"I'd take it very unkindly if you stopped my going . . . I want to go."

The dark man said:

"Some do. Some do not. I'll make a note of your name in case you come back . . . You won't mind going on with your cinder-sifting, if you do? . . . Get on with your story as quick as you can.[77] And get what fun you can before you go. They say it's rotten out there. Damn awful! There's a hell of a strafe on. That's why they want all you."

For a moment Tietjens saw the grey dawn at rail-head with the distant sound of a ceaselessly boiling pot, from miles away! The army feeling re-descended upon him. He began to talk about Command Depôts, at great length and with enthusiasm. He snorted with rage at the way men were treated in these gloomy places. With ingenious stupidity!

Every now and then the dark man interrupted him with:

"Don't forget that a Command Depôt is a place where sick and wounded go to get made fit. We've got to get 'em back as soon as we can."

"And do you?" Tietjens would ask.

"No, we don't," the other would answer. "That's what this enquiry[78] is about."

"You've got," Tietjens would continue, "on the north side of a beastly clay hill nine miles from Southampton three thousand men from the Highlands, North Wales, Cumberland. . . . God knows where, as long as it's three hundred miles from home to make them rather mad with nostalgia. . . . You allow 'em out for an hour a day during the pub's closing time: you shave their heads to prevent 'em appealing to local young women who don't exist, and you don't let 'em carry the[79] swagger-canes! God knows why! To prevent their poking their eyes out, if they fall down, I suppose.[80] Nine miles from anywhere, with chalk down roads to walk on and not a bush for shelter or shade . . . And, damn it, if you get two men, chums, from the Seaforths or the Argylls* you don't let them sleep in the same hut, but shove 'em in with a lot of fat Buffs or Welshmen,[81] who stink of leeks and can't speak English. . . ."

"That's the infernal medicals' orders to stop 'em talking all night."

"To make 'em conspire all night not to turn out for parade," Tietjens said. "And there's a beastly mutiny begun. . . . And, damn it, they're fine men. They're first-class fellows. Why don't you—as this is a Christian land—let 'em go home to convalesce with their girls and pubs and friends and a little bit of swank, for heroes? Why in God's name don't you? Isn't there suffering enough?"

---

* Two Scottish regiments, the Seaforth Highlanders and the Argyll and Sutherland Highlanders.

"I wish you wouldn't say 'you,'" the dark man said. "It isn't me. The only A.C.I. I've drafted was to give every Command Depôt a cinema and a theatre. But the beastly medicals got it stopped ... for fear of infection. And, of course, the parsons and Nonconformist magistrates ..."

"Well, you'll have to change it all," Tietjens said, "or you'll just have to say: thank God we've got a navy. You won't have an army. The other day three fellows—Warwicks—asked me at question time, after a lecture, why they were shut up there in Wiltshire whilst Belgian refugees were getting bastards on their wives in Birmingham. And when I asked how many men made that complaint over fifty stood up. All from Birmingham...."

The dark man said:

"I'll make a note of that.... Go on."

Tietjens went on; for as long as he stayed there he felt himself a man, doing[82] work that befitted a man, with the bitter contempt for fools that a man should have and express. It was a letting up: a real last leave.

# IV

MARK TIETJENS, his umbrella swinging sheepishly, his bowler hat pushed firmly down on to his ears to give him a sense of stability, walked beside the weeping girl in the quadrangle.

"I say," he said, "don't give it to old Christopher too beastly hard about his militarist opinions. . . . [1] Remember, he's going out to-morrow and he's one of the best."

She looked at him quickly, tears remaining upon her cheeks, and then away.

"One of the best," Mark said. "A fellow who never told a lie or did a dishonourable thing in his life. Let him down easy, there's a good girl. You ought to, you know."

The girl, her face turned away, said:

"I'd lay down my life for him!"

Mark said:

"I know you would. I know a good woman when I see one. And think! He probably considers that he *is* . . . offering his life, you know, for you. And me, too, of course! . . . It's a different way of looking at things." He gripped her awkwardly but irresistibly by the upper arm. It was very thin under her blue cloth coat.[2] He said to himself:

"By Jove! Christopher likes them skinny. It's the athletic sort that attracts him. This girl is as clean run as . . . " He couldn't think of anything as clean run as Miss Wannop, but he felt a warm satisfaction at having achieved an intimacy with her and his brother. He said:

"You aren't going away? Not without a kinder word to him. You think! He might be killed. . . . Besides. Probably he's never killed a German. He was a liaison officer. Since then he's been in charge of a dump where they sift army dustbins. To see how they can give the men less to eat. That means that the civilians get more. You don't object to his giving civilians more meat? . . . It isn't even helping to kill Germans. . . . "

He felt her arm press his hand against her warm side.

"What's he going to do now?" she asked. Her voice wavered.

"That's what I'm here about," Mark said. "I'm going in to see old Hogarth. You don't know Hogarth? Old General Hogarth? I think I can get him to give Christopher a job with the transport. A safe job. Safeish! No beastly glory business about it. No killing beastly Germans either.... I beg your pardon, if you like Germans."

She drew her arm from his hand in order to look him in the face.

"Oh!" she said, "*you* don't want him to have any beastly military glory!" The colour came back into her face: she looked at him open eyed.

He said:

"No! Why the devil should he?" He said to himself: "She's got enormous eyes: a good neck: good shoulders: good breasts: clean hips: small hands. She isn't knock-kneed: neat ankles. She stands well on her feet. Feet not too large! Five foot four, say! A real good filly!" He went on aloud: "Why in the world should he want to be a beastly soldier? He's the heir to Groby. That ought to be enough for one man."

Having stood still sufficiently long for what she knew to be his critical inspection, she put her hand in turn, precipitately, under his arm and moved him towards the entrance steps.

"Let's be quick then," she said. "Let's get him into your transport at once. Before he goes to-morrow. Then we'll know he's safe."

He was puzzled by her dress. It was very business-like, dark blue and very short. A white blouse with a black silk, man's tie. A wide-awake,* with, on the front of the band, a cipher.

"You're in uniform yourself," he said. "Does your conscience let you do war work?"

She said:

"No. We're hard up. I'm taking the gym classes in a great big school to turn an honest penny.... *Do* be quick!"

Her pressure on his elbow flattered him. He resisted it a little, hanging back, to make her more insistent. He liked being pleaded with by a pretty woman: Christopher's girl at that.

---

* A 'soft, wide-brimmed low-crowned felt hat': *OED*.

He said:

"Oh, it's not a matter of minutes. They keep 'em weeks at the base before they send 'em up.... We'll fix him up all right, I've no doubt. We'll wait in the hall till he comes down."

He told the benevolent commissionaire, one of two in a pulpit in the crowded grim hall, that he was going up to see General Hogarth in a minute or two. But not to send a bell-boy. He might be some time yet.

He sat himself beside Miss Wannop, clumsily on a wooden bench, humanity surging[3] over their toes as if they had been on a beach. She moved a little to make room for him and that, too, made him feel good. He said:

"You said just now: 'we' are hard up. Does 'we' mean you and Christopher?"

She said:

"I and Mr. Tietjens. Oh, no! I and mother! The paper she used to write for stopped. When your father died, I believe.[4] He found money for it, I think. And mother isn't suited to free-lancing. She's worked too hard in her life."

He looked at her, his round eyes protruding.

"I don't know what that is, free-lancing," he said. "But you've got to be comfortable. How much do you and your mother need to keep you comfortable? And put in a bit more so that Christopher could have a mutton-chop now and then!"

She hadn't really been listening. He said with some insistence: "Look here! I'm here on business. Not like an elderly admirer forcing himself on you. Though, by God, I do admire you too.... But my father wanted your mother to be comfortable...."

Her face, turned to him, became rigid.

"You don't mean ..." she began. He said:

"You won't get it any quicker by interrupting. I have to tell my stories in my own way. My father wanted your mother to be comfortable. He said so that she could write books, not papers. I don't know what the difference is: that's what he said. He wants you to be comfortable too.... You've not got any encumbrances! Not ... oh, say a business: a hat shop that doesn't pay? Some girls have...."

She said: "No. I just teach ... oh, *do* be quick...."

For the first time in his life he dislocated the course of his thoughts to satisfy a longing in some one else.

"You may take it to go on with," he said, "as if my father had left your mother a nice little plum." He cast about to find his scattered thoughts.

"He has! He *has!* After all!" the girl said. "Oh, thank God!"

"There'll be a bit for you, if you like," Mark said, "or perhaps Christopher won't let you. He's ratty with me. And something for your brother to buy a doctor's business with." He asked:[5] "You haven't fainted, have you?" She said:

"No. I don't faint. I cry."

"That'll be all right," he answered. He went on: "That's your side of it. Now for mine. I want Christopher to have a place where he'll be sure of a mutton-chop and an arm-chair by the fire. And someone to be good for him. *You're* good for him. I can see that. I know women!"

The girl was crying, softly and continuously. It was the first moment of the lifting of strain that she had known since[6] the day before the Germans crossed the Belgian frontier, near a place called Gemmenich.

It had begun with the return of Mrs. Duchemin from Scotland. She had sent at once for Miss Wannop to the rectory, late at night. By the light of candles in tall silver sticks,[7] against oak panelling she had seemed like a mad block of marble, with staring, dark eyes and mad hair. She had exclaimed in a voice as hard as a machine's:

"How do you get rid of a baby? You've been a servant. You ought to know!"

That had been the great shock, the turning-point, of Valentine Wannop's life. Her last years before that had been of great tranquillity, tinged of course with melancholy because she loved Christopher Tietjens. But she had early learned to do without, and the world as she saw it was a place of renunciations,[8] of high endeavour and sacrifice. Tietjens had to be a man who came to see her mother and talked wonderfully. She had been happy when he had been in the house—she in the housemaid's pantry, getting the tea-things. She had, besides, been very hard worked for her mother; the weather had been, on the whole, good, the corner of the country in which they lived had continued to seem fresh and agreeable. She had had excellent health, got an occa-

sional ride on the *qui-tamer*\* with which Tietjens had replaced
Joel's rig; and her brother had done admirably at Eton, taking
such a number of exhibitions and things that, once at Magdalen,[†]
he had been nearly off his mother's hands. An admirable, gay boy,
not unlikely to run for, as well as being a credit to, his university,
if he didn't get sent down for his political extravagances. He was
a Communist!

And at the rectory there had been the Duchemins, or rather
Mrs. Duchemin and, during most week-ends, Macmaster somewhere about.

The passion of Macmaster for Edith Ethel and of Edith Ethel
for Macmaster had seemed to her one of the beautiful things of
life. They seemed to swim in a sea of renunciations, of beautiful
quotations, and of steadfast waiting. Macmaster did not interest
her personally much, but she took him on trust because of Edith
Ethel's romantic passion and because he was Christopher Tietjens' friend. She had never heard him say anything original;[9]
when he used quotations they would be apt rather than striking.
But she took it for granted that he was the right man—much as
you take it for granted that the engine of an express train in which
you are is reliable. The right people have chosen it for you. . . .

With Mrs. Duchemin, mad before her, she had the first inti-
mation that her idolised friend, in whom she had believed as she
had believed in the firmness of the great, sunny earth, had been
the mistress of her lover—almost since the first day she had seen
him. . . . And that Mrs. Duchemin had, stored somewhere, a
character of an extreme harshness and great vulgarity of
language. She raged up and down in the candlelight, before the
dark oak panelling, screaming coarse phrases of the deepest
hatred for her lover. Didn't the oaf know his business better than
to . . . ? The dirty little Port of Leith fish-handler. . . .

What, then, were tall candles in silver sticks for? And polished
panelling in galleries?

---

\*  The term is used in *Handley Cross* (1838–9) by the classic British writer on hunting,
   R. S. Surtees (1805–64), and appears to mean a reliable and un-temperamental horse.
   See also *Tales for Sportsmen* by 'Dragon': 'We had six hunters each, and a joint-stock
   Qui-tamer that went in the brougham or dog-cart, hacked and carried us or our friends
   with hounds when wanted, doing about three times the work of any other, and always
   fit to go' (London: Simpkin, Marshall, & Co., 1885), 52.
†  Magdalen College, Oxford.

Valentine Wannop couldn't have been a little ashcat in worn cotton dresses, sleeping under the stairs, in an Ealing household with a drunken cook, an invalid mistress and three over-fed men, without acquiring[10] a considerable knowledge of the sexual necessities and excesses of humanity. But, as all the poorer helots of great cities hearten their lives by dreaming of material beauties, elegance, and suave wealth, she had always considered that, far from the world of Ealing and its county councillors who over-ate and neighed like stallions,* there were bright colonies of beings, chaste, beautiful in thought, altruist and circumspect.

And, till that moment, she had imagined herself on the skirts of such a colony. She presupposed a society of beautiful intellects centring in London round her friends. Ealing she just put out of her mind. She considered: she had, indeed once heard Tietjens say that humanity was made up of exact and constructive intellects[11] on the one hand and on the other of stuff to fill graveyards.† ... Now, what had become of the exact and constructive intellects?

Worst of all, what became of her beautiful inclination towards Tietjens, for she couldn't regard it as anything more? Couldn't her heart sing any more whilst she was in the housemaid's pantry and he in her mother's study? And what became, still more, of what she knew to be Tietjens' beautiful inclination towards her? She asked herself the eternal question—and she knew it to be the eternal question—whether no man and woman can ever leave it at the beautiful inclination. And, looking at Mrs. Duchemin, rushing backwards and forwards in the light of candles, blue-white of face and her hair flying, Valentine Wannop said: "No! no! The[12] tiger lying in the reeds will always raise its head!" But tiger ... it was more like a peacock....

---

* Cf. *The Good Soldier* 15: 'Am I no better than a eunuch or is the proper man – the man with the right to existence – a raging stallion forever neighing after his neighbour's womankind?'

† This is a favourite distinction of Ford's. He wrote 'from my earliest childhood I was brought up to believe that humanity divided itself into two classes – those who were creative artists and those who were merely the stuff to fill graveyards. In that belief I tranquilly abide': 'Not Idle', *New York Herald Tribune Books* (1 July 1928), 1, 6; see also *Nightingale* 59: 'The world divided itself for me into those who were artists and those who were merely the stuff to fill graveyards. And I used to feel in the company of those who were not artists the same sort of almost physical, slight aversion that one used, during the war, to feel for civilians'; also 69.

Tietjens, raising his head from the other side of the tea-table and looking at her with his long, meditative glance from beside her mother: ought he then, instead of blue and protruding, to have eyes divided longitudinally in the blacks of them—that should divide, closing or dilating, on a yellow ground, with green glowings of furtive light?*

She was aware that[13] Edith Ethel had done her an irreparable wrong, for you cannot suffer a great sexual shock and ever be the same. Or not for years. Nevertheless she stayed with Mrs. Duchemin until far into the small hours, when she fell, a mere parcel of bones in a peacock blue wrapper, into a deep chair and refused to move or speak; nor did she afterwards slacken in her faithful waiting on her friend. . . .[14]

On the next day came the war. That was a nightmare of pure suffering, with never a let-up, day or night. It began on the morning of the fourth with the arrival of her brother from some sort of Oxford Communist[15] Summer School on the Broads. He was wearing a German corps student's cap and was very drunk. He had been seeing German friends off from Harwich. It was the first time she had ever seen a drunken man, so that was a good present to her.

Next day, and sober, he was almost worse. A handsome, dark boy like his father, he had his mother's hooked nose and was always a little unbalanced: not mad, but always over-violent in any views he happened for the moment to hold. At the Summer School he had been under very vitriolic teachers of all sorts of notions. That hadn't hitherto mattered. Her mother had written for a Tory paper: her brother, when he had been at home, had edited some sort of Oxford organ of disruption. But her mother had only chuckled.

The war changed that. Both seemed to be filled with a desire for blood and to torture: neither paid the least attention to the other. It was as if—so for the rest of those years the remembrance of that time lived with her—in one corner of the room her mother, ageing, and on her knees, from which she only with difficulty rose, shouted[16] hoarse prayers to God, to let her, with her

---

* According to the *The New Readers' Guide to the works of Rudyard Kipling*, 'Tietjens' is Afrikaans for 'Tiger-Eyes'. See: http://www.kipling.org.uk/rg_imray_notes_p.htm

own hands, strangle, torture and flay off all his skin, a being called the Kaiser,[17] and as if, in the other corner of the room, her brother, erect, dark, scowling and vitriolic, one hand clenched above his head, called down the curse of heaven on the British soldier, so that in thousands, he might die in agony, the blood spouting from his scalded lungs. It appeared that the Communist leader whom Edward* Wannop affected had had ill-success in his attempts to cause disaffection among some units or other of the British army, and had failed rather gallingly, being laughed at or ignored rather than being ducked in a horse-pond, shot or otherwise martyrised. That made it obvious that the British man in the ranks was responsible for the war. If those ignoble hirelings had refused to fight all the other embattled and terrorised millions would have thrown down their arms!

Across that dreadful phantasmagoria went the figure of Tietjens. He was in doubt. She heard him several times voice his doubts to her mother, who grew every day more vacant. One day Mrs. Wannop had said:

"What does your wife think about it?"

Tietjens had answered:

"Oh, Mrs. Tietjens is a pro-German.... Or no, that isn't exact![18] She has German prisoner-friends and looks after them. But she spends nearly all her time in retreat in a convent reading novels of before the war. She can't bear the thought of physical suffering. I can't blame her."

Mrs. Wannop was no longer listening: her daughter was.

For Valentine Wannop the war had turned Tietjens into far more of a man and far less of an inclination—the war and Mrs. Duchemin between them. He had seemed to grow less infallible. A man with doubts is more of a man, with eyes, hands, the need for food and for buttons to be sewn on. She had actually tightened up a loose glove button for him.

One Friday afternoon at Macmaster's[19] she had had a long talk with him: the first she had had since the drive and the accident.

Ever since Macmaster had instituted his Friday afternoons—

---

* Valentine's brother has been named as Gilbert in Part I. It's conceivable that Ford's play of 'affected' / 'disaffection' here insinuates that the alternative name may be an affectation to make him sound lower-class. But it is more likely to be one of several inconsistencies in the tetralogy.

and that had been some time before the war—Valentine
Wannop had accompanied Mrs. Duchemin to town by the
morning train and back at night to the rectory. Valentine poured
out the tea, Mrs. Duchemin drifting about the large book-lined
room amongst the geniuses and superior journalists.

On this occasion—a November day of very chilly[20] wet—
there had been next to nobody present, the preceding Friday
having been unusually full. Macmaster and Mrs. Duchemin had
taken a Mr. Spong, an[21] architect, into the dining-room to inspect
an unusually fine set of Piranesi's *Views of Rome** that Tietjens
had picked up somewhere and had given to Macmaster. A Mr.
Jegg and a Mrs. Haviland were sitting close together in the far
window-seat. They were talking in low tones. From time to time
Mr. Jegg used the word "inhibition." Tietjens rose from the fire-
seat on which he had been sitting and came[22] to her. He ordered
her to bring her cup of tea over by the fire and talk to him. She
obeyed. They sat side by side on the leather fire-seat that stood
on polished brass rails, the fire warming their backs. He said:

"Well, Miss Wannop. What have you been doing?" and they
drifted into talking of the war. You couldn't not. She was astonished not to find him so loathsome[23] as she had expected, for, just
at that time, with the facts that were always being driven into her
mind by the[24] pacifist friends of her brother and with continual
brooding over the morals of Mrs. Duchemin, she had an automatic feeling that all manly men were lust-filled devils, desiring
nothing better than to stride over battlefields, stabbing the
wounded with long daggers in frenzies of sadism.[25] She knew that
this view of Tietjens was wrong, but she cherished it.

She found him—as subconsciously she knew he was—astonishingly mild. She had too often watched him whilst he listened
to her mother's tirades against the Kaiser, not to know that. He
did not raise his voice, he showed no emotion. He said at last:

"You and I are like two people . . . " He paused and began again
more quickly: "Do you know those[26] soap advertisement signs
that read differently from several angles? As you come up to them

* Series of etchings by Giovanni Battista Piranesi (1720–78). *Varie Vedute di Roma Antica e Moderna* appeared in 1745, and was followed by several selected editions. His meticulous recording of Roman remains was a powerful influence on neoclassicism.

you read 'Monkey's Soap'; if you look back when you've passed it's 'Needs no Rinsing.'.... You and I are standing at different angles and though we both look at the same thing we read different messages. Perhaps if we stood side by side* we should see yet a third.... But I hope we respect each other. We're both honest. I, at least, tremendously respect you and I hope you respect me."

She kept silent. Behind their backs the fire rustled. Mr. Jegg, across the room, said: "The failure to co-ordinate ..." and then dropped his voice.

Tietjens looked at her attentively.

"You don't respect me?" he asked. She kept obstinately silent.

"I'd have liked you to have said it," he repeated.

"Oh," she cried out, "how can I respect you when there is all this suffering? So much pain! Such torture ... I can't sleep ... Never ... I haven't slept a whole night since ... Think of the immense spaces, stretching out under the night ... I believe pain and fear must be worse at night...." She knew she was crying out like that because her dread had come true. When he had said: "I'd have liked you to have said it," using the past, he had said his valedictory. Her man, too, was going.

And she knew too: she had always known under her mind and now she confessed it: her agony had been, half of it, because one day he would say farewell to her: like that, with the inflexion of a verb.[27] As, just occasionally, using the word "we"—and perhaps without intention—he had let her know that he loved her.

Mr. Jegg drifted across from the window: Mrs. Haviland was already at the door.

"We'll leave you to have your war talk out," Mr. Jegg[28] said. He added: "For myself, I believe it's one's sole[29] duty to preserve the beauty of things that's preservable. I can't help saying that."

She was alone with Tietjens and the quiet day.† She said to herself:

"Now he must take me in his arms. He must. He *must!*" The deepest of her instincts came to the surface, from beneath layers

---

*   Perhaps Tietjens is alluding to the poem that he misattributes to Rossetti on 22, and that both he and Macmaster recall later in the novel (130, 232 and 341).
†   Cf. the closing words of Henry James's story 'The Turn of the Screw' (1898): 'We were alone with the quiet day, and his little heart, dispossessed, had stopped'; quoted by Ford in *Henry James: A Critical Study* (London: Martin Secker, 1913), 169.

of thought hardly known to her. She could feel his arms round her: she had in her nostrils the peculiar scent of his hair—like the scent of the skin of an apple, but very faint. "You must! You *must!*" she said to herself. There came back to her overpoweringly the memory of their drive together and the moment, the overwhelming moment, when, climbing out of the white fog into the blinding air, she had felt the impulse of his whole body towards her and the impulse of her whole body towards him. A sudden lapse: like the momentary dream when you fall. . . . She saw the white disk of the sun over the silver mist and behind them was the long, warm night. . . .

Tietjens sat, huddled rather together, dejectedly, the firelight playing on the silver places of his hair. It had grown nearly dark outside: they had a sense of the large room that, almost week by week, had grown, for its gleams of gilding and hand-polished dark woods, more like the great dining-room at the Duchemins. He got down from the fire-seat with a weary movement, as if the fire-seat had been very high. He said, with a little bitterness, but as if with more fatigue:

"Well, I've got the[30] business of telling Macmaster that I'm leaving the office. That, too, won't be an agreeable affair! Not that what poor Vinnie thinks matters." He added: "It's queer,[31] dear . . ." In the tumult of her emotions she was almost certain that he had said "dear." . . . "Not three hours ago my wife used to me almost the exact words you have just used. Almost the exact words. She talked of her inability to sleep at night for thinking of immense spaces full of pain that was worse at night. . . . And she, too, said that she could not respect me. . . ."

She sprang up.

"Oh," she said, "she didn't meant it. *I* didn't mean it. Almost every man who is a man must do as you are doing.[32] But don't you see it's a desperate attempt to get you to stay: an attempt on moral lines? How can we leave any stone unturned that could keep us from losing our men?" She added, and it was another stone that she didn't leave unturned: "Besides, how can you reconcile it with your sense of duty, even from your point of view? You're more useful—you know you're more useful to your country here than . . ."

He stood over her, stooping a little, somehow suggesting great gentleness and concern.

"I can't reconcile it with my conscience," he said. "In this affair there is nothing that any man can reconcile with his conscience. I don't mean that we oughtn't to be in this affair and on the side we're on. We ought. But I'll put to you things I have put to no other soul."

The simplicity of his revelation seemed to her to put to shame any of the glibnesses she had heard. It appeared to her as if a child were speaking. He described the disillusionment it had cost him personally as soon as this country had come into the war. He even described the sunlit heather landscape of the north, where naïvely he had made his tranquil resolution to join the French Foreign Legion as a common soldier and his conviction that that would give him, as he called it, clean bones again.

That, he said, had been straightforward. Now there was nothing straightforward: for him or for any man.* One could have fought with a clean heart for a civilisation: if you like for the eighteenth century against the twentieth, since that was what fighting for France against the enemy countries meant. But our coming in had changed the aspect at once. It was one part of the twentieth century using the eighteenth as a catspaw† to bash the other half of the twentieth. It was true there was nothing else for it. And as long as we did it in a decent spirit it was just bearable. One could keep at one's job—which was faking statistics against the other fellow—until you were sick and tired of faking and your brain reeled. And then some!

It was probably impolitic[33] to fake—to overstate!—a case against enemy nations. The chickens would come home to roost in one way or another, probably. Perhaps they wouldn't. That was a matter for one's superiors. Obviously! And the first gang‡ had been simple, honest fellows. Stupid, but relatively disinterested. But now! . . . What was one to do? . . . He went on, almost mumbling. . . .

She had suddenly a clear view of him as a man extraordinarily clear-sighted in the affairs of others, in great affairs, but in his own

---

* In *Joseph Conrad* 129 Ford wrote: 'it became very early evident to us that what was the matter with the Novel, and the British novel in particular, was that it went straight forward, whereas in your gradual making acquaintance with your fellows you never do go straight forward'.

† More usually 'cat's-paw': 'A person used as a tool by another to accomplish a purpose': *OED*.

‡ Asquith's Liberal government of 1910–15.

so simple as to be almost a baby. And gentle! And extraordinarily unselfish. He didn't betray one thought of self-interest . . . not one!

He was saying:

"But now! . . . with this crowd of boodlers!* . . . Supposing one's asked to manipulate the figures of millions of pairs of boots in order to force someone else to send some miserable general and his troops to, say, Salonika—when they and you and common-sense and everyone and everything else, know it's disastrous? . . . And from that to monkeying with our own forces. . . . Starving particular units for political . . ." He was talking to himself, not to her. And indeed he said:

"I can't, you see, talk really before you. For all I know your sympathies, perhaps your activities, are with the enemy nations."

She said passionately.

"They're not! They're not! How dare you say such a thing?"

He answered:

"It doesn't matter . . . No! I'm sure you're not . . . But, anyhow, these things are official. One can't, if one's scrupulous, even talk about them . . . And then . . . You see it means such infinite deaths of men, such an infinite prolongation . . . all this interference for side-ends! . . . I seem to see these fellows with[34] clouds of blood over their heads. . . . And then . . . I'm to carry out their orders because they're my superiors. . . . But helping them[35] means unnumbered deaths. . . ."

He looked at her with a faint, almost humorous smile:

"You see!" he said, "we're perhaps not so very far apart! You mustn't think you're the only one that sees all the deaths and all the sufferings. And[36] you see: I, too, am a conscientious objector. My conscience won't let me continue any longer with these fellows. . . ."

She said:

"But isn't there any other . . ."

He interrupted:

"No! There's no other course. One is either a body or a brain in these affairs. I suppose I'm more brain than body. I suppose so. Perhaps I'm not. But my conscience won't let me use my brain in this service. So I've a great, hulking body! I'll admit I'm probably

---

* From 1915 Asquith led a Coalition government, which collapsed in 1916, when another Coalition was formed, led by Lloyd George.

not much good. But I've nothing to live for: what I stand for isn't any more in this world. What I want, as you know, I can't have. So . . ."

She exclaimed bitterly:

"Oh, say it! Say it! Say that your large hulking body will stop two bullets in front of two small anæmic fellows. . . . And how can you say you'll have nothing to live for? You'll come back. You'll do your good work again. You know you did good work . . ."

He said:

"Yes! I believe I did. I used to despise it, but I've come to believe I did. . . . But no! They'll never let me back. They've got me out, with all sorts of bad marks against me. They'll pursue me, systematically. . . . You see in such a world as this, an idealist—or perhaps it's only a sentimentalist—must be stoned to death. He makes the others so uncomfortable. He haunts them at their golf. . . . No; they'll get me, one way or the other. And some fellow—Macmaster here—will do my jobs. He won't do them so well, but he'll do them more dishonestly. Or no. I oughtn't to say dishonestly. He'll do them with enthusiasm and righteousness. He'll fulfil the orders[37] of his superiors with an immense docility and unction. He'll fake figures against our allies[38] with the black enthusiasm of a Calvin and, when *that* war comes, he'll do the requisite faking with the righteous wrath of Jehovah smiting the priests of Baal.* And he'll be right. It's all we're fitted for. We ought never to have come into this war. We ought to have snaffled other peoples'[39] colonies as the price of neutrality. . . ."

"Oh!" Valentine Wannop said, "how can you so hate your country?"

He said with great earnestness:

"Don't say it! Don't believe it! Don't even for a moment think it! I love every inch of its fields and every plant in the hedgerows: comfrey, mullein, paigles, long red purples, that liberal shepherds give a grosser name . . . and all the rest of the rubbish—you remember the field between the Duchemins and your mother's—and we have always been boodlers and robbers and reivers and pirates and cattle thieves, and so we've built up the great tradi-

---

* 'Baal' is Hebrew for 'master' or 'lord', and has been applied to Jehovah and also Satan ('Beelzebub' derives from Ba'al Zebûb), as well as to many false gods. In *Kings* 1.18 Elijah challenges the 450 prophets of Baal to a competition, to see whose god could ignite their sacrificial bullocks. He wins and slaughters all the prophets.

tion that we love.... But, for the moment, it's painful. Our present crowd is not more corrupt than Walpole's. But one's too near them. One sees of Walpole that he consolidated the nation by building up the National Debt: one doesn't see his methods.... My son, or his son, will only see the glory of the boodle we make out of this show. Or rather out of the next. He won't know about the methods. They'll teach him at school that across the counties went the sound of bugles that his father knew.* ... Though that was another discreditable affair...."

"But you!" Valentine Wannop exclaimed. "*You!* what will *you* do! After the war!"

"I!" he said rather bewilderedly. "I! ... Oh, I shall go into the old furniture business. I've been offered a job...."

She didn't believe he was serious. He hadn't, she knew, ever thought about his future. But suddenly she had a vision of his white head and pale face in the back glooms of a shop full of dusty things. He would come out, get heavily on to a dusty bicycle and ride off to a cottage sale. She cried out:

"Why don't you do it at once? Why don't you take the job at once?" for in the back of the dark shop he would at least be safe.

He said:

"Oh, no! Not at this time! Besides the old furniture trade's probably not itself for the minute...." He was obviously thinking of something else.

"I've probably been a low cad," he said, "wringing your heart with my doubts. But I wanted to see where our similarities come in. We've always been—or we've seemed always to me—so alike in our thoughts. I daresay I wanted you to respect me...."

"Oh, I respect you! I respect you!" she said. 'You're as innocent as a child."

He went on:

"And I wanted to get some thinking done. It hasn't been often

---

* Tietjens echoed T. W. H. Crosland's poem 'The Yeoman' before the war (see 133) in almost identical words, with Crosland's 'war-drums' misremembered or re-imagined as bugles. If then the bugles evoked the hunt as well as the army, in this wartime context they sound the theme of the 'Last Post'. Crosland's poem was a call to arms for the Boer War (the other 'discreditable affair' in the following sentence). Tietjens' or Ford's rewriting of it reflects the discussion Tietjens and Valentine have been having (and which Ford had with Stella Bowen) about militarism and its mortal consequences.

of late that one has had a quiet room and a fire and . . . you! To think in front of. You *do* make one collect one's thoughts. I've been very muddled till to-day . . . till five minutes ago! Do you remember our drive? You analysed my character. I'd never have let another soul . . . But you see . . . Don't you see?"

She said:

"No! What am I to see? I remember . . ."

He said:

"That I'm certainly not an English country gentleman now; picking up the gossip of the horse markets and saying: let the country go to hell, for me!"

She said:

"Did I say that? . . . Yes, I said that!"

The deep waves of emotion came over her: she trembled. She stretched out her arms. . . . She thought she stretched out her arms. He was hardly visible in the firelight. But she could see nothing: she was blind for tears. She could hardly be stretching out her arms, for she had both hands to her handkerchief on her eyes. He said something: it was no word of love or she would have held it; it began with: "Well, I must be . . ." He was silent for a long time: she imagined herself to feel great waves coming from him to her. But he wasn't in the room. . . .

The rest, till that moment at the War Office, had been pure agony, and unrelenting. Her mother's paper cut down her money; no orders for serials came in: her mother, obviously, was failing. The eternal diatribes of her brother were like lashes upon her skin. He seemed to be praying Tietjens to death. Of Tietjens she saw and heard nothing. At the Macmasters she heard, once, that he had just gone out. It added to her desire to scream when she saw a newspaper. Poverty invaded them. The police raided the house in search of her brother and his friends.[40] Then her brother went to prison: somewhere in the Midlands. The friendliness of their farm-neighbours[41] turned to surly suspicion. They could get no milk. Food became almost unprocurable without going to long distances. For three days Mrs. Wannop was clean out of her mind. Then she grew better and began to write a new book. It promised to be rather good. But there was no publisher. Edward came out of prison, full of good-humour and boisterousness. They seemed to have had a great deal to drink in prison. But, hearing that his

mother had gone mad over that disgrace, after a terrible scene
with Valentine, in which he accused her of being the mistress of
Tietjens and therefore militarist, he consented to let his mother
use her influence—of which she had still some—to get him
appointed as an A.B.* on a mine-sweeper. Great winds became
an agony to Valentine Wannop in addition to the unbearable
sounds of firing that came continuously over the sea. Her mother
grew much better: she took pride in having a son in a service. She
was then the more able to appreciate the fact that her paper
stopped payment altogether. A small mob on the fifth of
November burned Mrs. Wannop in effigy in front of their cottage
and broke their lower windows. Mrs. Wannop ran out and in the
illumination of the fire knocked down two farm labourer
hobbledehoys. It was terrible to see Mrs. Wannop's grey hair in
the firelight. After that the butcher refused them meat altogether, ration card or no ration card. It was[42] imperative that they
should move to London.[43]

The marsh horizon became obscured with giant stilts:† the air
above it filled with aeroplanes: the roads covered with military
cars. There was then no getting away from the sounds of the war.

Just as they had decided to move Tietjens came back. It was
for a moment heaven to have him in this country. But when, a
month later, Valentine Wannop saw him for a minute, he seemed
very heavy, aged and dull.[44] It was then almost as bad as before,
for it seemed to Valentine as if he hardly had his reason.

On hearing that Tietjens was to be quartered—or, at any rate,
occupied—in the neighbourhood of Ealing, Mrs. Wannop at
once took a small house in Bedford Park,[45] whilst, to make ends
meet—for her mother made terribly little—Valentine Wannop
took a post as athletic mistress in a great school in a not very near
suburb. Thus, though Tietjens came in for a cup of tea almost
every afternoon with Mrs. Wannop in the dilapidated little
suburban house, Valentine Wannop hardly ever saw him. The
only free afternoon she had was the Friday, and on that day she
still regularly chaperoned Mrs. Duchemin: meeting her at

* An able seaman (not, as sometimes glossed, 'able-bodied seaman'): the middle rank
for non-commissioned personnel, between ordinary seaman and leading seaman.
† Possibly part of the coastal air-defences against Zeppelins or bombers heading to
London, including radio masts, moorings for barrage balloons, or anti-aircraft guns.

Charing Cross towards noon and taking her back to the same
station in time to catch the last train to Rye. On Saturdays and
Sundays she was occupied all day in typing her mother's manuscript.

Of Tietjens, then, she saw almost nothing. She knew that his
poor mind was empty of facts and of names; but her mother said
he was a great help to her. Once provided with facts his mind
worked out sound Tory conclusions—or quite startling and
attractive theories—with extreme rapidity. This Mrs. Wannop
found of the greatest use to her whenever—though it wasn't now
very often—she had an article to write for an excitable newspaper. She still, however, contributed to her failing organ of
opinion, though it paid her nothing. . . . [46]

Mrs. Duchemin, then, Valentine Wannop still chaperoned,
though there was no bond any more between them. Valentine
knew, for instance, perfectly well that Mrs. Duchemin, after she
had been seen off by train from Charing Cross, got out at
Clapham Junction, took a taxi-cab back to Gray's Inn after dark
and spent the night with Macmaster, and Mrs. Duchemin knew
quite well that Valentine knew. It was a sort of parade of circumspection and rightness, and they kept it up even after, at a sinister
registry office, the wedding had taken place, Valentine being the
one witness and an obscure-looking substitute for the usual pew
opener[*] another. There seemed to be, by then, no very obvious
reason why Valentine should support[47] Mrs. Macmaster any more
on these rather dreary occasions, but Mrs. Macmaster said she
might just as well, until they saw fit to make the marriage public.
There were, Mrs. Macmaster said, censorious tongues, and even
if these were confuted afterwards it is difficult, if not impossible,
to outrun scandal. Besides, Mrs. Macmaster was of opinion that
the Macmaster afternoons with their[48] geniuses must be a liberal
education for Valentine. But, as Valentine sat most of the time
at the tea-table near the door, it was the backs and side faces of
the distinguished[49] rather than their intellects with which she
was most acquainted. Occasionally, however, Mrs. Duchemin
would show Valentine, as an enormous privilege, one of the
letters to herself from men of genius: usually North British,

* Usher.

written, as a rule, from the Continent or more distant and peaceful climates, for most of them believed it their duty in these hideous times to keep alive in the world the only glimmering spark of beauty. Couched in terms so eulogistic as to resemble those used in passionate love-letters by men more profane, these epistles recounted, or consulted Mrs. Duchemin as to, their love affairs with foreign princesses, the progress of their ailments or the progresses of their souls towards those higher regions of morality in which floated their so beautiful-souled correspondent.[50]

The letters entertained Valentine and, indeed, she was entertained by that whole mirage. It was only the Macmasters'[51] treatment of her mother that finally decided Valentine that this friendship had died; for the friendships of women are very tenacious things, surviving astonishing disillusionments, and Valentine Wannop was a woman of more than usual loyalty. Indeed, if she couldn't respect Mrs. Duchemin on the old grounds, she could very really respect her for her tenacity of purpose, her determination to advance Macmaster and for the sort of ruthlessness that she put into these pursuits.

Valentine's affection had, indeed, survived even Edith Ethel's continued denigrations of Tietjens—for Edith Ethel regarded Tietjens as a clog round her husband's neck, if only because he was a very unpopular man, grown personally rather unpresentable and always extremely rude to the geniuses on Fridays. Edith Ethel, however, never made these complaints that grew more and more frequent as more and more the distinguished flocked to the Fridays, before Macmaster. And they ceased very suddenly and in a way that struck Valentine as odd.

Mrs. Duchemin's grievance against Tietjens[52] was that, Macmaster being a weak man, Tietjens had acted as his banker until, what with interest and the rest of it, Macmaster owed Tietjens a great sum: several thousand pounds. And there had been no real reason: Macmaster had spent most of the money either on costly furnishings for his rooms or on his costly journeys to Rye. On the one hand Mrs. Duchemin could have found Macmaster all the bric-a-brac he could possibly have wanted from amongst the things at the rectory, where no one would have missed them and, on the other, she, Mrs. Duchemin, would have paid all Macmaster's travelling expenses. She had had unlimited money from her husband, who never asked for accounts. But, whilst Tietjens still had influence with Macmaster, he had used it uncompromisingly against this course, giving him the delusion —it enraged Mrs. Duchemin to think!—that it would have been dishonourable. So that Macmaster had continued to draw upon him.

And, most enraging of all, at a period when she had had a power of attorney over all Mr. Duchemin's fortune and could, perfectly easily, have sold out something that no one would have missed for the couple of thousand or so that Macmaster owed, Tietjens had very forcibly refused to allow Macmaster to agree to anything of the sort. He had again put into Macmaster's weak head that it would be dishonourable. But Mrs. Duchemin—and she closed her lips determinedly after she had said it—knew perfectly well Tietjens'[53] motive. So long as Macmaster owed him money he imagined that they couldn't close their doors upon him. And their establishment was beginning to be a place where you met[54] people of great influence who might well get for a person as lazy as Tietjens a sinecure that would suit him. Tietjens, in fact, knew which side his bread was buttered.

For what, Mrs. Duchemin asked, could there have been dishonourable about the arrangement she had proposed?[55] Practically the whole of Mr. Duchemin's money was to come to her: he was by then insane; it was therefore, morally, her own. But immediately after that, Mr. Duchemin having been certified,[56] the estate had fallen into the hands of the Lunacy Commissioners and there had been no further hope of taking the capital. Now, her husband being dead, it was in the hands of trustees, Mr. Duchemin having left the whole of his property to Magdalen College and merely the income to his widow. The income was very large; but where, with their expenses, with the death duties and taxation, which were by then merciless, was Mrs. Duchemin to find the money? She was to be allowed, under her husband's will, enough capital to buy a pleasant little place in Surrey, with rather a nice lot of land—enough to let Macmaster know some of the leisures of a country gentleman's lot. They were going in for shorthorns, and there was enough land to give them a small golf-course and, in the autumn, a little—oh, mostly rough!— shooting for Macmaster to bring his friends down to. It would just run to that. Oh, no ostentation. Merely a nice little place. As an amusing detail the villagers there already called Macmaster "squire" and the women curtsied to him. But Valentine Wannop would understand that, with all these expenses, they couldn't find the money to pay off Tietjens. Besides, Mrs. Macmaster said she wasn't going to pay off Tietjens. He had had his chance once: now he could go without, for her. Macmaster would have to pay it himself and he would never be able to, his contribution to their housekeeping being what it was. And there were going to be complications. Macmaster wandered[57] about their little place in Surrey, saying that he would consult Tietjens about this and that alteration. But over the doorsill of that place the foot of Tietjens was never going to go! Never! It would mean a good deal of unpleasantness; or rather it would mean one sharp: "C-r-r-unch!" And then: Napoo finny!* Mrs. Duchemin sometimes, and with great effect, condescended to use one of the more picturesque phrases of the day.

To all these diatribes Valentine Wannop answered hardly anything.[58] It was no particular concern of hers;[59] even if, for a moment, she felt proprietarily towards Christopher as she did now and then, she felt no particular desire that his intimacy with the Macmasters should be prolonged, because she knew he could have no particular desire for its prolongation. She imagined him turning them down with an unspoken and good-humoured gibe. And, indeed, she agreed on the whole with Edith Ethel. It *was* demoralising for a weak little man like Vincent to have a friend[60] with an ever-open purse beside him. Tietjens ought not to have been princely: it was a defect, a quality that she did not personally admire in him.† As to[61] whether it would or wouldn't have been dishonourable for Mrs. Duchemin to take her husband's money and give it to Macmaster,[62] she kept an open mind. To all intents and purposes the money *was* Mrs. Duchemin's, and if Mrs. Duchemin had then paid Christopher off it would have been sensible. She could see that later it had become very inconven-

---

* British soldiers' slang version of the French 'il n'y en a plus; fini' meaning 'no more, finished'.
† Ford often quoted the expression 'the defect of his qualities', from the proverb, said to be French, and used in English by writers such as Benjamin Disraeli, Henry James, and Arthur Symons, that 'No man is without the defect of his qualities.'

ient. There were, however, male standards to be considered, and Macmaster at least[63] passed for a man. Tietjens, who was wise enough in the affairs of others, had, in that, probably been wise; for there might have been great disagreeablenesses with trustees and heirs-at-law had Mrs. Duchemin's subtraction of a couple of thousand pounds from the Duchemin estate afterwards come to light. The Wannops had never been large property owners as a family, but Valentine had heard enough of collateral wranglings over small family dishonesties to know how very disagreeable these could be.

So she had made little or no comment; sometimes she had even faintly agreed as to the demoralisation of Macmaster and that had sufficed. For Mrs. Duchemin had been certain of her rightness and cared nothing at all for the opinion of Valentine Wannop, or else took it for granted.

And when Tietjens had been gone to France for a little time Mrs. Duchemin seemed to forget the matter, contenting herself with saying that he might very likely not come back. He was the sort of clumsy man who generally got killed. In that case, since no I.O.U.s or paper had passed, Mrs. Tietjens would have no claim. So that would be all right.

But two days after the return of Christopher[64]—and that was how Valentine knew he had come back!—Mrs. Duchemin[65] with a lowering brow exclaimed:

"That oaf, Tietjens, is in England, perfectly safe and sound.[66] And now the whole miserable business of Vincent's indebtedness ... Oh!"

She had[67] stopped so suddenly and so markedly that even the[68] stoppage of Valentine's own heart couldn't conceal the oddness from her. Indeed it was as if there were an interval before she completely realised what the news was and as if, during that interval, she said to herself:

"It's very queer. It's exactly as if Edith Ethel has stopped abusing him on my account ... [69] As if she *knew*!" But how could Edith Ethel know that she loved the man who had returned? It was impossible! She hardly knew herself. Then the great wave of relief rolled over her: he was in England. One day she would see him, there: in the great room. For these colloquies with Edith Ethel always took place in the great room where she had last seen

Tietjens. It looked suddenly beautiful and she was resigned to sitting there, waiting for the distinguished.

It was indeed a beautiful room: it had become so during the years. It was long and high—matching the Tietjens'. A great cut-glass chandelier from the rectory hung dimly coruscating in the centre, reflected and re-reflected in convex gilt mirrors, topped by eagles. A great number of books had gone to make place on the white panelled walls for the mirrors, and for the four[70] orange and brown pictures by Turner, also from the rectory. From the rectory had come the immense scarlet and lapis lazuli carpet, the great brass fire-basket and appendages, the[71] great curtains that, in the three long windows, on their peacock blue Chinese silk showed parti-coloured cranes ascending in long flights—and all the polished Chippendale arm-chairs. Amongst all these, gracious, trailing, stopping with a tender gesture to rearrange very slightly the crimson roses in the famous silver bowls, still in dark blue silks,[*] with an amber necklace and her elaborate black hair, waved exactly like that of Julia Domna in the Musée Lapidaire at Arles,[†] moved Mrs. Macmaster—also from the rectory. Macmaster had achieved his desire: even to the shortbread cakes and the peculiarly scented tea that came every Friday morning from Princes Street.[‡] And, if Mrs. Macmaster hadn't the pawky, relishing humour of the great Scots ladies of past days, she had in exchange her deep aspect of comprehension and tenderness. An astonishingly beautiful and impressive woman: dark hair; dark, straight eyebrows; a straight nose; dark blue eyes in the shadows of her hair[§] and bowed, pomegranate lips in a chin curved like the bow of a Greek boat. . . .

The etiquette of the place on Fridays[72] was regulated as if by a royal protocol. The most distinguished and, if possible, titled person was led to a great walnut wood fluted chair that stood

[*]  Rossetti's 1868 portrait of Jane Morris is also known as *The Blue Silk Dress* (oil on canvas, the Society of Antiquaries of London, Kelmscott Manor).
[†]  Julia Domna was empress and wife of the Roman emperor Lucius Septimius Severus. The 'Musée Lapidaire' at Arles is a museum of pagan sculpture.
[‡]  Though there are two Princes Streets in London (in the West End and the City), this more probably refers to Edinburgh's main shopping street, with several well-known tea rooms, such as the one in J. W. Mackie's, which supplied shortbread to Queen Victoria, and which once had a letter delivered addressed simply to 'To the makers of finest shortbread in Scotland, Princes Street'.
[§]  Cf. 69.

askew by the fire-place, its back and seat of blue velvet, heaven knows how old. Over him would hover Mrs. Duchemin: or, if he were *very* distinguished, both Mr. and Mrs. Macmaster. The not so distinguished were led up by turns to be presented to the celebrity and would then arrange themselves in a half-circle in the beautiful arm-chairs; the less distinguished still, in outer groups in chairs that had no arms: the almost undistinguished stood, also in groups or languished, awe-struck on the scarlet leather window seats. When all were there Macmaster would establish himself on the incredibly unique hearthrug and would address wise sayings to the celebrity; occasionally, however, saying a kind thing to the youngest man present—to give him a chance of distinguishing himself. Macmaster's hair, at that date, was still black, but not quite so stiff or so well brushed; his beard had in it greyish streaks, and his teeth, not being quite so white, looked less strong. He wore also a single eyeglass, the retaining of which in his right eye gave him a slightly agonised expression. It gave him, however, the privilege of putting his face very close to the face of anyone upon whom he wished to make a deep impression.* He had lately become much interested in the drama, so that there were usually several large—and, of course, very reputable and serious actresses in the room. On rare occasions Mrs. Duchemin would say across the room in her deep voice:

"Valentine, a cup of tea for his highness," or "Sir Thomas," as the case might be, and when Valentine had threaded her way through the chairs with a cup of tea Mrs. Duchemin, with a kind, aloof smile, would say: "Your highness, this is my little brown bird." But as a rule Valentine sat alone at the tea-table, the guests fetching from her what they wanted.

Tietjens came to the Fridays twice during the five months of his stay at Ealing. On each occasion he accompanied Mrs. Wannop.

In earlier days—during the earliest Fridays—Mrs. Wannop, if she ever came, had always been installed, with her flowing black, in the throne and, like an enlarged Queen Victoria, had sat there

---

* Ford wrote of Conrad: 'When you had really secured his attention he would insert a monocle into his right eye and scrutinise your face from very near as a watchmaker looks into the works of a watch': *Joseph Conrad* 11.

whilst suppliants were led up to this great writer. But now: on the
first occasion Mrs. Wannop got a chair without arms in the outer
ring, whilst a general officer commanding lately in chief somewhere in the East, whose military success had not been
considerable, but whose despatches were considered very literary,
occupied, rather blazingly, the throne. But Mrs. Wannop had
chatted very contentedly all the afternoon with Tietjens, and it
had been comforting to Valentine[73] to see Tietjens' large,
uncouth, but quite collected figure, and to observe the affection
that these two had for each other.

But, on the second occasion, the throne was occupied by a
very young woman who talked a great deal and with great assurance. Valentine didn't know who she was. Mrs. Wannop, very
grey[74] and distracted, stood nearly the whole afternoon by a
window. And even at that, Valentine was contented, quite a
number of young men crowding round the old lady and leaving
the younger one's circle rather bare.

There came in a very tall, clean run and beautiful, fair woman,
dressed in nothing in particular. She stood with extreme—with
noticeable—unconcern near the doorway. She let her eyes rest
on Valentine, but looked away before Valentine could speak. She
must have had an enormous quantity of fair tawny hair, for it was
coiled in a great surface over her ears. She had in her hand several
visiting cards which she looked at with a puzzled expression and
then laid on a card table. She was no one who had ever been there
before.

Edith Ethel—it was for the second time!—had just broken up
the ring that surrounded Mrs. Wannop, bearing the young men
tributary to the young woman[75] in the walnut chair and leaving
Tietjens and the older woman high and dry in a window: thus
Tietjens saw the stranger, and there was no doubt left in Valentine's mind. He came, diagonally, right down the room to his wife
and marched her straight up to Edith Ethel. His face was perfectly
without expression.

Macmaster, perched on the centre of the hearthrug, had an[76]
emotion that was extraordinarily comic to witness, but that
Valentine was quite unable to analyse. He jumped two paces
forward to meet Mrs. Tietjens, held out a little hand, half with-
drew it, retreated half a step. The eyeglass fell from his perturbed

eye: this gave him actually an expression less perturbed, but, in revenge, the hairs on the back of his scalp grew suddenly untidy. Sylvia, wavering along beside her husband, held out her long arm and careless hand. Macmaster winced almost at the contact, as if his fingers had been pinched in a vice. Sylvia wavered desultorily towards Edith Ethel, who was suddenly small, insignificant and relatively coarse. As for the young woman celebrity in the arm-chair, she appeared to be about the size of a white rabbit.

A complete silence had fallen on the room. Every woman in it was counting the pleats of Sylvia's skirt and the amount of material in it. Valentine Wannop knew that because she was doing it herself. If one had that amount of material and that number of pleats one's skirt might hang like that.... For it was extraordinary: it fitted close round the hips, and gave an effect of length and swing—yet it did not descend as low as the ankles. It was, no doubt, the amount of material that did that, like the Highlander's kilt that takes twelve yards to make. And from the silence Valentine could tell that every woman and most of the men[77]—if they didn't know that this was Mrs. Christopher Tietjens—knew that this was a personage of *Illustrated Weekly*,* as who should say of county family, rank. Little Mrs. Swan, lately married, actually got up, crossed the room and sat down beside her bridegroom. It was a movement with which[78] Valentine could sympathise.

And Sylvia, having just faintly greeted Mrs. Duchemin, and completely ignored the celebrity in the arm-chair—in spite of the fact that Mrs. Duchemin had tried half-heartedly to effect an introduction—stood still, looking round her. She gave the effect of a lady in a nurseryman's hothouse considering what flower should interest her, collectedly ignoring the nurserymen who bowed round her. She had just dropped her eyelashes, twice, in recognition of two staff officers with a good deal of scarlet streak about them who were tentatively rising from their chairs. The staff officers who came to the Tietjens[79] were not of the first vintages; still they had the labels and passed as such.

---

\* A generic rather than specific title. Sylvia is the kind of glamorous socialite to figure in any of the illustrated weeklies, such as *The Gentlewoman: An Illustrated Weekly Journal for Gentlewomen*; *The Graphic: An Illustrated Weekly Magazine*; *The Illustrated London News*; or *The Sphere: An Illustrated Newspaper for the Home*.

Valentine was by that time beside her mother, who had been[80] standing all alone between two windows. She had dispossessed, in hot indignation, a stout musical critic of his chair and had sat her mother in it. And, just as Mrs. Duchemin's deep voice sounded, yet a little waveringly:

"Valentine . . . a cup of tea for . . ." Valentine was carrying a cup of tea to her mother.

Her indignation had conquered her despairing jealousy, if you could call it jealousy. For what was the good of living or loving when Tietjens had beside him, for ever, this[81] radiant, kind and gracious perfection. On the other hand, of her two deep passions, the second was for her mother.

Rightly or wrongly, Valentine regarded Mrs. Wannop as a great, an august figure: a great brain, a high and generous intelligence. She had written, at least, one great book, and if the rest of her time had been frittered away in the desperate struggle to live that had taken both their lives, that could not detract from that one achievement that should last and for ever take her mother's name down time.* That this greatness should not weigh with the Macmasters had hitherto neither astonished nor irritated Valentine. The Macmasters had their game to play and, for the matter of that, they had their predilections. Their game kept them amongst the officially influential, the semi-official and the officially accredited. They moved with such C.B.s, knights, presidents and the rest as dabbled in writing or the arts: they went upwards with such reviewers, art critics, musical writers and archæologists as had posts in, if possible, first-class public offices or permanent positions on the more august periodicals. If an imaginative author seemed assured of position and lasting popularity Macmaster would send out feelers towards him, would make himself humbly useful, and sooner or later either Mrs. Duchemin

---

* In the 'Dedicatory Letter to Stella Ford' added to the 1927 edition of *The Good Soldier*, Ford wrote: 'I used to think – and I do not know that I do not think the same now – that one book was enough for any man to write, and, at the date when *The Good Soldier* was finished, London at least and possibly the world appeared to be passing under the dominion of writers newer and much more vivid. Those were the passionate days of the literary Cubists, Vorticists, Imagistes and the rest of the tapageux [French: boisterous] and riotous *Jeunes* of that young decade. So I regarded myself as the Eel which, having reached the deep sea, brings forth its young and dies – or as the Great Auk I considered that, having reached my allotted, I had laid my one egg and might as well die': 3–4. And in *Return* 325 he referred to *The Good Soldier* as 'my one novel'.

would be carrying on with him one of her high-souled[82] correspondences—or she wouldn't.

Mrs. Wannop they had formerly accepted as permanent leader
writer and chief critic of a great organ, but the great organ having
dwindled and now disappeared the Macmasters[83] no longer
wanted her at their parties. That was the game—and Valentine
accepted it. But that it should have been done with such insolence, so obviously meant to be noted—for in twice breaking up
Mrs. Wannop's little circle Mrs. Duchemin had not even once so
much as said: "How d'ye do?" to the elder lady!—that was almost
more than Valentine could, for the moment, bear, and she would
have taken her mother away at once and would never have re-
entered the house, but for the compensations.

Her mother had lately written and even found a publisher for
a book—and the book had showed no signs of failing powers. On
the contrary, having been perforce stopped off the perpetual jour-
nalism that had dissipated her energies, Mrs. Wannop had turned
out something that Valentine knew was sound, sane and well
done. Abstractions and[84] failing attention to the outside world
are not necessarily in a writer signs of failing, as a writer. It may
mean merely that she is giving so much thought to her work that
her outside contacts suffer. If that is the case her work will gain.
That this might be the case with her mother was Valentine's great
and secret hope. Her mother was barely sixty: many great works
have been written by writers aged between sixty and seventy. . . .

And the crowding of youngish men round the old lady had
given Valentine a little confirmation of that hope. The book
naturally, in the maelstrom[85] flux and reflux[86] of the time, had
attracted no attention, and poor Mrs. Wannop had not succeeded
in extracting a penny for it from her adamantine publisher: she
hadn't, indeed, made a penny for several months, and they
existed almost at starvation point in their little den of a villa—
on Valentine's earnings as athletic teacher. . . . But that little bit
of attention in that semi-public place had seemed, at least, as a
confirmation to Valentine: there probably was something sound,
sane and well done in her mother's work. That was almost all she
asked of life.

And, indeed, whilst she stood by her mother's chair, thinking
with a little bitter pathos that if Edith Ethel had left the three or

four young men to her mother the three or four might have done
her poor mother a little good, with innocent puffs and the like—
and heaven knew they needed that little good badly enough!—a
very thin and untidy young man *did* drift back to Mrs. Wannop
and asked, precisely, if he might make a note or two for publication as to what Mrs. Wannop was doing. Her book, he said, had
attracted so much attention. They hadn't known that they had
still writers among them. . . .[87]

A singular, triangular drive had begun through the chairs from
the fireplace. That was how it had seemed to Valentine! Mrs.
Tietjens had looked at them, had asked Christopher a question
and, immediately, as if she were coming[88] through waist-high surf,
had borne down,[89] Macmaster and Mrs. Duchemin, flanking her
obsequiously, setting aside chairs and their[90] occupants, Tietjens
and the two, rather bashfully following staff officers, broadening
out the wedge.

Sylvia, her long arm held out from a yard or so away, was
stretching out her hand to Valentine's mother. With her clear,
high, unembarrassed voice she exclaimed, also from a yard or so
away, so as to be heard by everyone in the room:

"You're Mrs. Wannop. The great writer! I'm Christopher
Tietjens' wife."

The old lady, with her dim eyes, looked up at the younger
woman towering above her.

"You're Christopher's wife!" she said. "I must kiss you for all
the kindness he has shown me."

Valentine felt her eyes filling with tears. She saw her mother
stand up, place both her hands on the other woman's shoulders.
She heard her mother say:

"You're a most beautiful creature. I'm sure you're good!"

Sylvia stood, smiling faintly, bending a little to accept the
embrace. Behind the Macmasters, Tietjens and the staff officers,
a little crowd of goggle eyes had ranged itself.

Valentine was crying. She slipped back behind the tea-urns,
though she could hardly feel the way. Beautiful! The most beautiful woman she had ever seen! And good! Kind! You could see
it in the lovely way she had given her cheek to that poor old
woman's lips. . . . And to live all day, for ever, beside him . . . she,
Valentine, ought to be ready to lay down her life for Sylvia Tiet-

jens. . . .

The voice of Tietjens said, just above her head:

"Your mother seems to be having a regular triumph," and, with his good-natured cynicism, he added, "it seems to have upset some apple-carts!" They were confronted with the spectacle of Macmaster conducting the young celebrity from her deserted arm-chair across the room to be lost in the horseshoe of crowd that surrounded Mrs. Wannop.

Valentine said:

"You're quite gay to-day. Your voice is[91] different. I suppose you're better?" She did not look at him. His voice came:

"Yes! I'm relatively gay!" It went on: "I thought you might like to know. A little of my mathematical brain seems to have come to life again. I've worked out two or three silly problems. . . . "

She said:

"Mrs. Tietjens will be pleased."

"Oh!" the answer came.[92] "Mathematics don't interest her any more than cock-fighting."[93] With immense swiftness, between word and word, Valentine read into that a hope! This splendid creature did not sympathise with her husband's activities. But he crushed it heavily by saying: "Why should she? She's so many occupations of her own that she's unrivalled at!"

He began to tell her, rather minutely, of a calculation he had made only that day at lunch. He had gone into the Department of Statistics and had had rather a row with Lord Ingleby of Lincoln. A pretty title the fellow had taken!* They had wanted him to ask to be seconded to his old department for a certain job. But he had said he'd be damned if he would. He detested and despised the work they were doing.

Valentine, for the first time in her life, hardly listened to what he said. Did the fact that Sylvia Tietjens had so many occupations of her own mean that Tietjens found her unsympathetic? Of their relationships she knew nothing. Sylvia had been so much of a mystery as hardly to exist as a problem hitherto. Macmaster, Valentine knew, hated her. She knew that through Mrs. Duchemin; she had heard it ages ago, but she didn't know

---

* Sir Reginald has been made a life-peer since the opening of the novel, and has thus been able to choose the geographical name attached to the title.

why. She had never come to the Macmaster afternoons; but that
was natural. Macmaster passed for a bachelor, and it was excus-
able for a young woman of the highest fashion not to come to
bachelor teas of literary and artistic people. On the other hand,
Macmaster[94] dined at the Tietjens'[95] quite often enough to make
it public that he was a friend of that family. Sylvia, too, had never
come down to see Mrs. Wannop. But then it would, in the old
days, have been a long way to come for a lady of fashion with no
especial literary interests. And no one, in mercy, could have been
expected to call on poor them in their dog kennel in an outer
suburb. They had had to sell almost all their pretty things.

Tietjens was saying that after his tempestuous interview with
Lord Ingleby of Lincoln—she wished he would not be so rude to
powerful people!—he had dropped in on Macmaster in his
private room,[96] and finding him puzzled over a lot of figures had,
in the merest spirit of bravado, taken Macmaster and his papers
out to lunch. And, he said, chancing to look, without any hope
at all, at the figures, he had suddenly worked out an ingenious
mystification. It had just come!

His voice had been so gay and triumphant that she hadn't
been able to resist looking up at him. His cheeks were fresh
coloured, his hair shining; his blue eyes had a little of their old
arrogance—and tenderness! Her heart seemed to sing with joy!
He was, she felt, her man. She imagined the arms of his mind
stretching out to enfold her.

He went on explaining. He had rather, in his recovered self-
confidence, gibed at Macmaster. Between themselves, wasn't it
easy to do what the Department, under orders, wanted done?
They had wanted to rub into our allies[97] that their losses by devas-
tation had been nothing to write home about—so as to avoid
sending reinforcements to their[98] lines! Well, if you took just the
bricks and mortar of the devastated districts,[99] you could prove
that the loss in bricks, tiles, woodwork, and the rest[100] didn't—
and the figures with a little manipulation would prove
it!—amount to more than a normal year's dilapidations spread
over the whole[101] country in peace time. . . . House repairs in a
normal[102] year had cost several million sterling. The enemy had
only destroyed just about so many million sterling in bricks and
mortar. And what was a mere year's dilapidations in house prop-

erty! You just neglected to do them and did them next year.

So, if you ignored the lost harvests of three years, the lost industrial output of the richest industrial region of the country, the smashed machinery, the barked fruit trees, the three years' loss of four and a half-tenths of the coal output for three years— and the loss of life!—we could go to our allies and say:[103]

"All your yappings about losses are the merest bulls.[104]* You can perfectly well afford to reinforce the weak places of your own lines. We intend to send our new troops to the Near East, where lies our true interest!" And, though they[105] might sooner or later point out the fallacy, you would by so much have put off the abhorrent expedient of a single command.

Valentine, though it took her away from her own thoughts, couldn't help saying:

"But weren't you arguing against your own convictions?"

He said:

"Yes, of course I was. In the lightness of my heart! It's always a good thing to formulate the other fellow's objections."

She had turned half round in her chair. They were gazing into each other's eyes, he from above, she from below. She had no doubt of his love: he, she knew, could have no doubt of hers. She said:

"But isn't it dangerous? To show these people how to do it?"

He said:

"Oh, no, no. No! You don't know what a good soul little Vinnie is. I don't think you've ever been quite just to Vincent Macmaster! He'd as soon think of picking my pocket as of picking my brains. The soul of honour!"

Valentine had felt a queer, queer sensation. She was not sure afterwards[106] whether she had felt it before she had realised that Sylvia Tietjens was looking at them. She stood there, very erect, a queer smile on her face. Valentine could not be sure whether it was kind, cruel, or merely distantly ironic; but she was perfectly sure it showed, whatever was behind it, that its wearer knew all that there was to know of her, Valentine's, feelings for Tietjens

---

*    The OED gives a definition of 'bull' as 'an expression containing a manifest contra-
diction in terms or involving a ludicrous inconsistency unperceived by the speaker'.
Yet this may be a publisher's euphemism for the word Ford wrote in the manuscript:
'balls'.

and for Tietjens' feelings for her. . . . It was like being a woman taken[107] in adultery in Trafalgar Square.

Behind Sylvia's back, their mouths agape, were the two staff officers. Their dark hairs were too untidy for them to amount to much, but, such as they were, they were the two most presentable males of the assembly—and Sylvia had snaffled them.

Mrs. Tietjens said:

"Oh, Christopher! I'm going on to the Basils'."[108]

Tietjens said:

"All right. I'll pop Mrs. Wannop into the tube as soon as she's had enough of it, and come along and pick you up!"

Sylvia had just drooped her long eyelashes, in sign of salutation, to Valentine Wannop, and had drifted through the door, followed by her rather unmilitary military escort in khaki and scarlet.

From that moment Valentine Wannop never had any doubt. She knew that Sylvia Tietjens knew that her husband loved her, Valentine Wannop, and that she, Valentine Wannop, loved her husband—with a passion absolute and ineffable. The one thing she, Valentine, didn't know, the one mystery that remained impenetrable, was whether Sylvia Tietjens was good to her husband!

A long time afterwards Edith Ethel had come to her beside the tea-cups and had apologised for not having known, earlier than Sylvia's demonstration, that Mrs. Wannop was in the room. She hoped that they might see Mrs. Wannop much more often.[109] She added after a moment that she hoped Mrs. Wannop wouldn't, in future, find it necessary to come under the escort of Mr. Tietjens. They were too old friends for that, surely.

Valentine said:

"Look here, Ethel, if you think that you can keep friends with mother and turn on Mr. Tietjens after all he's done for you, you're mistaken. You are really. And mother's a great deal of influence. I don't want to see you making any mistakes: just at this juncture. It's a mistake to make nasty rows. And you'd make a very nasty one if you said anything against Mr. Tietjens to mother. She knows a great deal. Remember. She lived next door to the rectory for a number of years.[110] And she's got a dreadfully incisive tongue. . . ."

Edith Ethel coiled back on her feet as if her whole body were threaded by a steel spring. Her mouth opened, but she bit her lower lip and then wiped it with a very white handkerchief. She said:

"I hate that man! I detest that man! I shudder when he comes near me."

"I know you do!" Valentine Wannop answered. "But I wouldn't let other people know it if I were you. It doesn't do you any real credit. He's a good man."

Edith Ethel looked at her with a long, calculating glance. Then she went to stand before the fireplace.

That had been five—or at most six—Fridays before Valentine sat with Mark Tietjens in the War Office waiting hall, and, on the Friday immediately before that again, all the guests being gone, Edith Ethel had come to the tea-table and, with her velvet kindness, had placed her right hand on Valentine's left. Admiring the gesture with a deep fervour, Valentine knew that that was the end.

Three days before, on the Monday,* Valentine, in her school uniform, in a great store to which she had gone to buy athletic paraphernalia, had run into Mrs. Duchemin, who was buying flowers. Mrs.[111] Duchemin had been horribly distressed to observe the costume. She had said:

"But do you go *about* in that? It's really dreadful."

Valentine had answered:

"Oh, yes. When I'm doing business for the school in school hours I'm expected to wear it. And I wear it if I'm going anywhere in a hurry after school hours. It saves my dresses. I haven't got too many."

"But *any* one might meet you," Edith Ethel said in a note of agony. "It's very inconsiderate. Don't you *think* you've been[112] very inconsiderate? You might meet any of the people who come to our Fridays!"

"I frequently do," Valentine said. "But they don't seem to

---

* There are some inconsistencies in the time-scheme of Part II. Most references place the action as running from Friday afternoon (when Macmaster has his salon) to Saturday morning. But Port Scatho says 'To-day's Monday' on 242. Here, whether the 'before' means before the Friday Edith Ethel places her hand on Valentine's arm, or before the day Valentine is sitting at the War Office with Mark, the day should be Tuesday, not Monday.

mind. Perhaps they think I'm a Waac officer. That would be quite respectable...."

Mrs. Duchemin drifted away, her arms full of flowers and real agony upon her face.

Now, beside the tea-table she said, very softly:

"My dear, we've decided not to have our usual Friday afternoon next week." Valentine wondered whether this was merely a lie to get rid of her. But Edith Ethel went on: "We've decided to have a little evening festivity. After a great deal of thought we've come to the conclusion that we ought, now, to make our union public." She paused to await comment, but Valentine making none she went on: "It coincides very happily—I can't help feeling it coincides very happily!—with another event. Not that *we* set much store by these things.... But it has been whispered to Vincent that next Friday.... Perhaps, my dear Valentine, you, too, will have heard ..."

Valentine said:

"No, I haven't. I suppose he's got the O.B.E. I'm very glad."

"The Sovereign," Mrs. Duchemin said, "is seeing fit to confer[113] the honour of knighthood on him."

"Well!" Valentine said. "He's had a quick career. I've no doubt he deserves it. He's worked very hard. I do sincerely congratulate you. It'll be a great help to you."

"It's," Mrs. Duchemin said, "not for mere plodding. That's what makes it so gratifying. It's for a special piece of brilliance, that has marked him out. It's, of course, a secret. But ..."

"Oh, I know!" Valentine said. "He's worked out some calculations to prove that[114] losses in the devastated districts, if you ignore machinery, coal output, orchard trees, harvests, industrial products and so on, don't amount to more than a year's household dilapidations for the ..."

Mrs. Duchemin said with real horror:

"But how did you know? How on *earth* did you know? ..." She paused. "It's such a *dead* secret.... That fellow must have told you.... But how on earth could *he* know?"

"I haven't seen Mr. Tietjens to speak to since the last time he was here," Valentine said. She saw, from Edith Ethel's bewilderment, the whole situation. The miserable Macmaster hadn't even confided to his wife that the practically stolen figures weren't his own. He desired to have a little prestige in the family circle; for once a little prestige! Well! Why shouldn't he have it? Tietjens, she knew, would wish him to have all he could get. She said therefore:

"Oh, it's probably in the air.... It's known the Government want to burke[115*] their claims to the higher command. And anyone who could help them to that would get a knighthood...."

Mrs. Duchemin was more calm.

"It's certainly," she said, "Burke'd, as you call it, those beastly people."[116] She reflected for a moment. "It's probably that," she went on. "It's in the air. Anything that can help to influence public opinion[117] against those horrible people is to be welcomed.[118] That's known pretty widely.... No! It could hardly be Christopher Tietjens who thought of it and told you. It wouldn't enter his head. He's their friend![119] He would be ..."

"He's certainly," Valentine said, "not a friend of his country's enemies. I'm not, myself."

Mrs. Duchemin exclaimed sharply, her eyes dilated:[120]

"What do you mean? What on earth do you dare to mean? I thought you were a pro-German!"

Valentine said:

"I'm not! I'm not! ... I hate men's deaths.... I hate any men's deaths.... Any men ..." She calmed herself by main force. "Mr. Tietjens says that the more we hinder[121] our allies the more we drag the war on and the more lives are lost.... More lives, do you understand? ..."

Mrs. Duchemin assumed her most aloof, tender, and high air:[122]

"My poor child," she said, "what possible concern can the opinions of that broken fellow cause anyone? You can warn him from me that he does himself[123] no good by going on uttering these discredited opinions. He's a marked man. Finished! It's no good Guggums, my husband, trying to stand up for him."

"He *does* stand up for him?" Valentine asked. "Though I don't

---

\* 'Burke' derives from Edinburgh murderers Burke and Hare, who smothered their victims; hence 'To smother, "hush up", suppress quietly': OED. By 'those beastly people' Edith Ethel means the French (originally identified in the manuscript: see 'A Note on the Text of *Some Do Not* ...' lxxxvi).

see why it's needed. Mr. Tietjens is surely able to take care of himself."

"My good child," Edith Ethel said, "you may as well know the worst. There's not a more discredited man in London than Christopher Tietjens, and my husband does himself infinite harm in standing up for him. It's our one quarrel."

She went on again:

"It was all very well whilst that fellow had brains. He was said to have some intellect, though I could never see it. But now that, with his drunkenness and debaucheries, he has got himself into the state he is in; for there's no other way of accounting for his condition! They're striking[124] him, I don't mind telling you, off the roll of his office. . . . "

It was then[125] that, for the first time, the thought went through Valentine Wannop's mind, like a mad inspiration: this woman must at one time have been in love with Tietjens. It was possible, men being what they were, that she had even once been Tietjens' mistress. For it was impossible otherwise to account for this spite, which to Valentine seemed almost meaningless. She had, on the other hand, no impulse to defend Tietjens against accusations that could not have any possible grounds.

Mrs. Duchemin was going on with her kind loftiness:

"Of course a fellow like that—in that condition!—could not understand matters of high policy. It is imperative that these fellows[126] should not have the higher command. It would pander to their insane spirit of militarism. They *must* be hindered. I'm talking, of course, between ourselves, but my husband says that that is the conviction in the very highest circles. To let them have their way, even if it led to earlier success, would be to establish a precedent—so my husband says!—compared with which the loss of a few lives. . . . "

Valentine sprang up, her face distorted.

"For the sake of Christ," she cried out, "as you believe that Christ died for you, try to understand that millions of men's lives are at stake. . . . "[127]

Mrs. Duchemin smiled.

"My poor child," she said, "if you moved in the higher circles you would look at these things with more aloofness. . . . "

Valentine leant on the back of a high chair for support.

"You don't move in the higher circles," she said. "For Heaven's sake—for your own—remember that you are a woman, not for ever and for always a snob.[128] You were a good woman once. You stuck to your husband for quite a long time...."

Mrs. Duchemin, in her chair, had thrown herself back.

"My good girl," she said, "have you gone mad?"

Valentine said:

"Yes, very nearly. I've got a brother at sea; I've had a man I loved out there for an infinite time. You can understand that, I suppose, even if you can't understand how one can go mad merely at the thought[129] of suffering at all.... And I know, Edith Ethel, that you are afraid of my opinion of you, or you wouldn't have put up all the subterfuges and concealments of all these years...."

Mrs. Duchemin said quickly:

"Oh, my good girl.... If you've got personal interests at stake you can't be expected to take abstract views of the higher matters. We had better change the subject."

Valentine said:

"Yes, do. Get on with your excuses for not asking me and mother to your knighthood party."

Mrs. Duchemin, too, rose at that. She felt at her amber beads with long fingers that turned very slightly at the tips. She had behind her all her mirrors, the drops of her lustres,* shining points of gilt and of the polish of dark woods. Valentine thought that she had never seen anyone so absolutely impersonate kindness,[130] tenderness and dignity. She said:

"My dear, I was going to suggest that it was the sort of party to which you might not care to come.... The people will be stiff and formal and you probably haven't got a frock."

Valentine said:

"Oh, I've got a frock all right. But there's a Jacob's ladder in my party stockings and that's the sort of ladder you can't kick down." She couldn't help saying that.

Mrs. Duchemin stood motionless and very slowly redness mounted into her face. It was most curious to see[131] against that scarlet background the vivid white of the eyes and the dark, straight eyebrows that nearly met. And, slowly again her face

---

* The prismatic glass pendants from her chandeliers.

went perfectly white; then her dark blue eyes became marked. She seemed to wipe her long, white hands one in the other, inserting her right hand into her left and drawing it out again.

"I'm sorry," she said in a dead voice. "We had hoped that, if that man went to France—or if other things happened—we might have continued on the old friendly footing. But you yourself must see that, with our official position, we can't be expected to connive ..."

Valentine said:

"I don't understand!"

"Perhaps you'd rather I didn't go on!" Mrs. Duchemin retorted. "I'd much rather not go on."

"You'd probably better," Valentine answered.

"We had meant," the elder woman said, "to have a quiet little dinner—we two and you, before the party—for auld lang syne.[132] But that fellow has forced himself in, and you see for yourself that we can't have you as well."

Valentine said:

"I don't see why not. I always like to see Mr. Tietjens!" Mrs. Duchemin looked hard at her.

"I don't see the use," she said, "of your keeping on that mask. It is surely bad enough that your mother should go about with that man and that terrible scenes like that of the other Friday should occur. Mrs. Tietjens was heroic; nothing less than heroic. But you have no right to subject us, your friends, to such ordeals."

Valentine said:

"You mean ... Mrs. Christopher Tietjens ..."

Mrs. Duchemin went on:

"My husband insists that I should ask you. But I will not. I simply will not. I invented for you the excuse of the frock. Of course we could have given you a frock if that man is so mean or so penniless as not to keep you decent. But I repeat, with our official position we cannot—we cannot; it would be madness!— connive at this intrigue. And all the more as the wife appears likely to be friendly with us. She has been once: she may well come again." She paused and went on solemnly: "And I warn you, if the split comes—as it must, for what woman could stand it!—it is Mrs. Tietjens we shall support. She will always find a home here."

An extraordinary picture of Sylvia Tietjens standing beside

Edith Ethel and dwarfing her as a giraffe dwarfs an emu, came into Valentine's head. She said:

"Ethel! Have I gone mad? Or is it you? Upon my word I can't understand...."

Mrs. Duchemin exclaimed:

"For God's sake hold your tongue, you shameless thing! You've had a child by the man, haven't you?"

Valentine saw suddenly the tall silver candlesticks, the dark polished panels of the rectory and Edith Ethel's mad face and mad hair whirling before them.

She said:

"No! I certainly haven't. Can you get that into your head? I certainly haven't." She made a further effort over immense fatigue. "I assure you—I beg you to believe if it will give you any ease—that Mr. Tietjens has never addressed a word of love to me in his life. Nor have I to him. We have hardly talked to each other in all the time we have known each other."

Mrs. Duchemin said in a harsh voice:

"Seven people in the last five weeks have told me you have had a child by that brute beast: he's ruined because he has to keep you and your mother and the child. You won't deny that he has a child somewhere hidden away? ..."[133]

Valentine exclaimed suddenly:

"Oh, Ethel, you mustn't ... you *mustn't* be jealous of me! If you only knew you wouldn't be jealous of me.... I suppose the child you were going to have was by Christopher? Men are like that.... But not of me! You need never, never. I've been the best friend you can ever have had...."

Mrs. Duchemin exclaimed harshly, as if she were being strangled:[134]

"A sort of blackmail! I knew it would come to that! It always does with your sort. Then do your damnedest, you harlot. You never set foot in this house again! Go you and rot...." Her face suddenly expressed extreme fear and with great swiftness she ran up the room. Immediately afterwards she was tenderly bending over a great bowl of roses beneath the lustre. The voice of Vincent Macmaster from the door had said:

"Come in, old man. Of course I've got ten minutes. The book's in here somewhere...."

Macmaster was beside her, rubbing his hands, bending with his curious, rather abject manner, and surveying her agonisedly with his eyeglass, which enormously magnified his lashes, his red lower lid and the veins on his cornea.

"Valentine!" he said, "my dear Valentine . . . . You've heard? We've decided to make it public. . . . Guggums will have invited you to our little feast. And there will be a surprise, I believe. . . ."

Edith Ethel looked, as she bent, lamentably and sharply, over her shoulder at Valentine.

"Yes," she said bravely, aiming her voice at Edith Ethel, "Ethel has invited me. I'll try to come. . . ."

"Oh, but you must," Macmaster said, "just you and Christopher, who've been so kind to us. For old time's sake. You couldn't[135] not . . ."

Christopher Tietjens was ballooning slowly from the door, his hand tentatively held out to her. As they practically never shook hands at home it was easy to avoid his hand. She said to herself: "Oh! How is it possible! How could he have . . ." And the terrible situation poured itself over her mind: the miserable little husband, the desperately nonchalant lover—and Edith Ethel mad with jealousy! A doomed household. She hoped Edith Ethel had seen her refuse her hand to Christopher.

But Edith Ethel, bent over her rose bowl, was burying her beautiful face in flower after flower. She was accustomed to do this for many minutes on end: she thought that, so, she resembled a picture by the subject of her husband's first[136] little monograph.* And so, Valentine thought, she did. She was trying to tell Macmaster that Friday evenings were difficult times for her to get away. But her throat ached too much. That, she knew, was her last sight of Edith Ethel, whom she had[137] loved very much. That also, she hoped, would be her last sight of Christopher Tietjens—whom also she had loved very much. . . . He was browsing along a bookshelf, very big and very clumsy.

Macmaster pursued her into the stony hall with clamorous repetitions of his invitation. She couldn't speak. At the great[138]

---

\*   Many of Rossetti's celebrated pictures of women have floral backgrounds. Edith Ethel is perhaps thinking of *The Beloved* (*The Bride*) of 1865–6, in which (in the version in Tate Britain) an African servant girl holds up to the bride a golden pot full of roses. Ford had used a slightly different version as frontispiece to his small monograph on Rossetti.

iron-lined door he held her hand for an eternity, gazing lamentably, his face close up against hers. He exclaimed in accents of great fear:

"Has Guggums? ... She *hasn't* ..."[139] His face, which when you saw it so closely was a little blotched, distorted itself with anxiety: he glanced aside with panic at the drawing-room door.

Valentine burst a voice through her agonised throat.

"Ethel," she said, "has told me she's to be Lady Macmaster. I'm so glad. I'm so truly glad for you. You've got what you wanted, haven't you?"

His relief let him get out distractedly, yet as if he were too tired to be any more agitated:

"Yes! yes! ... It's, of course, a secret. ... I don't want *him* told till Friday next ... so as to be a sort of *bonne bouche*\* ... He's practically certain to go out again on Saturday. ...[140] They're sending out a great batch of them ... for the big push. ..." At that she tried to draw her hand from his: she missed what he was saying. It was something to the effect that he would give it all for a happy little party. She caught the rather astonishing words: "*Wie im alten schoenen Zeit.*"† She couldn't tell whether it was his or her eyes that were full of tears. She said:

"I believe ... I believe you're a kind[141] man!"

In the great stone hall, hung with long Japanese paintings on silk, the electric light suddenly jumped; it was at best a sad, brown place.

He exclaimed:

"I, too, beg you to believe that I will never abandon ..." He glanced again at the inner door and added: "You both ... I will never abandon ... you both!" he repeated.

He let go her hand: she was on the stone stairs in the damp air. The great door closed irresistibly behind her, sending a whisper of air downwards.

---

\*   A titbit, delicacy (French). Cf. *The Good Soldier* 30.

†   The phrase 'der alten, schönen Zeit' appears in several poems by Josef Karl Benedikt von Eichendorff (1788–1857): 'In der Fremde' ('In Foreign Lands'), set by Schumann in his *Liederkreis*, Op. 39 (1840), including the quatrain, 'Die Nachtigallen schlagen / Hier in der Einsamkeit, / Als wollten sie was sagen / Von der alten, schönen Zeit' ('The nightingales speak here in the solitude, as if they wanted to talk of the lovely old days'); 'Heimweh', set by Hugo Wolf in 1886–8, including the lines, 'Was wisset ihr, dunkle Wipfel, / von der alten, schönen Zeit?' ('What do you know, dark treetops, of the old, beautiful times?'); and also in 'Lockung' ('Allure'). Ford had used the phrase in *The Cinque Ports* 158 and 112.

# V

MARK TIETJENS' announcement that his father had after all carried out his long-standing promise to provide for Mrs. Wannop in such a way as to allow her to write for the rest of her life only the more lasting kind of work, delivered Valentine Wannop of all her problems except one. That one loomed, naturally and immediately, immensely large.

She had passed a queer, unnatural week, the feeling dominating its numbness having been, oddly, that she would have nothing to do on Friday! This feeling recurred to her whilst she was casting her eyes over a hundred girls all in their cloth jumpers and men's black ties,[1] aligned upon asphalte; whilst she was jumping on trams; whilst she was purchasing the tinned or dried fish that formed the staple diet of herself and her mother;[2] whilst she was washing-up the dinner-things; upbraiding the house agent for the state of the bath, or bending closely over the large but merciless handwriting of the novel of her mother's that she was typing. It came, half as a joy, half mournfully across her familiar businesses; she felt as a man might feel who, luxuriating in the anticipation of leisure, knew that it was obtained by being compulsorily retired from some laborious but engrossing job. There would be nothing to do on Fridays!

It was, too, as if a novel had been snatched out of her hand so that she would never know the end. Of the fairy-tale she knew the end: the fortunate and adventurous tailor had married his beautiful and be-princessed goose girl, and was well on the way to burial in Westminster Abbey—or at any rate to a memorial service, the squire being actually buried amongst his faithful villagers.* But she would never know whether they, in the end,

---

\* Valentine combines two stories by the Brothers Grimm. In 'The Valiant Little Tailor' the resourceful tailor marries a princess. If this suggests an allegory for Macmaster's upward mobility, the relevance of the other story is more ambiguous. In 'The Goose Girl' the princess is forced to swap places with her maid. Valentine's vision of Edith Ethel's underlying coarseness casts her as the impostor, whose gentility is merely a

got together all the blue Dutch tiles they wanted to line their bathroom.[3]... She would never know. Yet witnessing similar ambitions had made up a great deal of her life.

And, she said to herself, there was another tale ended. On the surface[4] the story of her love for Tietjens had been static enough. It had begun in nothing and[5] in nothing it had ended. But, deep down in her being—ah! it had progressed enough. Through the agency of two women! Before the scene with Mrs. Duchemin there could, she thought, have been few young women less pre-occupied than she with the sexual substrata, either of passion or of life. Her months as a domestic servant had accounted for that, sex, as she had seen it from a back kitchen, having been a repulsive affair, whilst the knowledge of its manifestations that she had thus attained had robbed it of the mystery which caused most[6] of the young women whom she knew to brood upon these subjects.

Her convictions[7] as to the moral incidence of sex were, she knew, quite opportunist. Brought up amongst rather "advanced" young people, had she been publicly challenged to pronounce her views she would probably, out of loyalty to her comrades, have declared that neither morality nor any ethical aspects were concerned in the matter. Like most of her young friends, influenced by the advanced teachers and tendential novelists of the day, she would have stated herself to advocate an—of course, enlightened!—promiscuity. That, before the revelations of Mrs. Duchemin! Actually she had thought very little about the matter.

Nevertheless, even before that date, had her deeper feelings been questioned she would have reacted[8] with the idea that sexual incontinence was extremely ugly and chastity to be prized[9] in the egg and spoon race that life was. She had been brought up by her father—who, perhaps, was wiser than appeared on the surface—to admire athleticism, and she was aware that profi-ciency of the body calls for chastity, sobriety, cleanliness and the various qualities that group themselves under the heading of

---

disguise. But by the same token it casts Valentine, who has been forced to work as a servant, as the true princess, now unsure whether Tietjens can be her fairy-tale prince (despite what she thinks in the next paragraph about their fairy-tale having already ended unhappily).

abnegation. She couldn't have lived amongst the Ealing servant-class—the eldest son of the house[10] in which she had been employed had been the defendant in a peculiarly scabrous breach of promise case, and the comments of the drunken cook on this and similar affairs had run the whole gamut from the sentimentally reticent to the extreme of coarseness according to the state of her alcoholic barometer—she couldn't then have lived among the Ealing servant-class and come to any other subliminal conclusion. So that, dividing the world into bright beings on the one hand and, on the other, into the mere stuff to fill graveyards whose actions during life couldn't matter, she had considered that the bright beings must be people whose public advocating of enlightened[11] promiscuity went along with an absolute continence. She was aware that enlightened beings occasionally fell away from these standards in order to become portentous Egerias; but the Mary Wollstonecrafts, the Mrs. Taylors, and the George Eliots[12] of the last century she had regarded humorously as rather priggish nuisances.* Indeed, being very healthy and very hard worked, she had been in the habit of regarding the whole matter, if not humorously, then at least good-humouredly, as a nuisance.

But being brought right up against the sexual necessities of a first-class Egeria had been for her a horrible affair. For Mrs. Duchemin had revealed the fact that her circumspect, continent and suavely æsthetic personality was doubled by another at least as coarse as, and infinitely more incisive in expression than, that of the drunken cook.[13] The language that she had used about her lover—calling him always "that oaf" or "that beast"!—had seemed literally to pain the girl internally, as if it had caused so many fallings away of internal supports at each two or three words. She had hardly been able to walk home[14] through the darkness from the rectory.

---

* The author and feminist Mary Wollstonecraft (1759–97) defied convention, having a daughter by one of her lovers before she married the philosopher William Godwin. She died ten days after the birth of their daughter Mary (later Mary Shelley, the author of *Frankenstein*). Harriet Taylor (1807–58) conducted a public but unconsummated relationship with John Stuart Mill, until her first husband died in 1849 and she was able to marry Mill two years later. Mary Ann Evans (1819–80) used 'George Eliot' as a pen-name. She lived openly with George Henry Lewes, who was unable to divorce his wife Agnes Jervis.

And she had never heard what had become of Mrs. Duchemin's baby. Next day Mrs. Duchemin had been as suave, as circumspect, and as collected as ever. Never a word more had passed between them on the subject. This left in Valentine Wannop's mind[15] a dark patch—as it were of murder—at which she must never look. And across the darkened world of her sexual tumult there flitted continually the[16] quick suspicion that Tietjens might have been the lover of her friend. It was a matter of the simplest analogy. Mrs. Duchemin had appeared a bright being: so had Tietjens. But Mrs. Duchemin was a foul whore.... How much more then must Tietjens, who was a man, with the larger sexual necessities of the male ... Her mind always refused to complete the thought.

Its suggestion wasn't to be combated by the idea of Vincent Macmaster himself: he was, she felt, the sort of man that it was almost a necessity for either mistress or comrade to betray. He seemed to ask for it. Besides, she once put it to herself, how could any woman, given the choice and the opportunity—and God knows there was opportunity enough—choose that shadowy, dried leaf, if there were the splendid masculinity of Tietjens in whose arms to lie. She so regarded these two men. And that shadowy conviction was at once fortified and appeased when, a little later, Mrs. Duchemin herself began to apply to Tietjens the epithets of "oaf" and "beast"—the very ones that she had used to designate the father of her putative child!

But then Tietjens must have abandoned Mrs. Duchemin; and, if he had abandoned Mrs. Duchemin, he must be available for her, Valentine Wannop! The feeling, she considered,[17] made her ignoble; but it came from depths of her being that she could not control and, existing, it soothed her. Then, with the coming of the war, the whole problem died out, and between the opening of hostilities and what she had known to be the inevitable departure of her lover, she had surrendered herself to what she thought to be the pure physical desire for him. Amongst the terrible, crashing anguishes of that time, there had been nothing for it but surrender! With the unceasing—the never ceasing—thought of suffering; with the never ceasing idea that her lover, too, must soon be so suffering, there was in the world no other refuge. No other!

She surrendered. She waited for him to speak the word, or look the look that should unite them. She was finished. Chastity: napoo finny! Like everything else!

Of the physical side of love she had neither image nor conception. In the old days when she had been with him, if he had come into the room in which she was, or if he had merely been known to be coming down to the village, she had hummed all day under her breath and had felt warmer, little currents passing along her skin. She had read somewhere that to take alcohol was to send the blood into the surface vessels of the body, thus engendering a feeling of warmth. She had never taken alcohol, or not enough to produce recognisably that effect; but she imagined that it was thus love worked upon the body—and that it would stop for ever at that!

But, in these later days, much greater convulsions had[18] overwhelmed her. It sufficed for Tietjens to approach her to make her feel as if her whole body was drawn towards him as, being near a terrible height, you are drawn towards it. Great waves of blood rushed across her being as if physical forces as yet undiscovered or invented attracted the very fluid itself. The moon so draws the tides.

Once before, for a fraction of a second, after the long, warm night[19] of their drive, she had felt that impulsion. Now, years after, she was to know it all the time, waking or half waking; and it would drive her from her bed. She would stand all night at the open window till the stars paled above a world turned grey.* It could convulse her with joy; it could shake her with sobs and cut through her breast like a knife.

The day of her long interview with Tietjens, amongst the amassed beauties of Macmaster furnishings, she marked in the calendar of her mind as her great love scene. That had been two years ago: he had been going into the army. Now he was going out again. From that she knew what a love scene was. It passed without any mention of the word "love"; it passed in impulses; warmths; rigors of the skin. Yet with every word they had said to each other they had confessed their love; in that way, when you listen to the nightingale you hear the expressed craving of your lover beating upon your heart.

---

* In *The Good Soldier* 159 Edward Ashburnham quotes from Swinburne's 'Hymn to Proserpine': 'Thou hast conquered, O pale Galilean'. The line continues 'the world has grown grey from thy breath'.

Every word that he had spoken amongst the amassed beauties of Macmaster furnishings had been a link in a love-speech. It was not merely that he had confessed to her as he would have to no other soul in the world—"To no other soul in the world," he had said!—his doubts, his misgivings and his fears: it was that every word he uttered and that came to her, during the lasting of that magic, had sung of passion. If he had uttered the word "Come" she would have followed him to the bitter ends of the earth; if he had said, "There is no hope," she would have known the finality of despair. Having said neither he said, she knew: "This is our condition; so we must continue!" And she knew, too, that he was telling her that he, like her, was ... oh, say on the side of the angels. She was then, she knew, so nicely balanced that, had he said, "Will you to-night be my mistress?" she would have said "Yes"; for it was as if they had been, really, at the end of the world.

But his abstention not only strengthened her in her predilection for chastity; it restored to her her image of the world as a place of virtues and endeavours. For a time at least she[20] again hummed beneath her breath upon occasion, for it seemed as if her heart sang within her. And there was restored to her her image of her lover as a beautiful spirit. She had been able to look at him across the tea-table of their dog kennel in Bedford Park, during the last months, almost as she had looked across the more shining table of the cottage near the rectory. The deterioration that she knew Mrs. Duchemin to have worked in her mind was assuaged. It could even occur to her that Mrs. Duchemin's madness had been no more than a scare to be followed by no necessary crime. Valentine Wannop had re-become her confident self in a world of at least straight problems.

But Mrs. Duchemin's outbreak of a week ago had driven the old phantoms across her mind. For Mrs. Duchemin she had still had a great respect. She could not regard her Edith Ethel as merely a hypocrite; or, indeed, as a hypocrite at all. There was her great achievement of making something like a man of that miserable little creature—as there had been her other great achievement of keeping her unfortunate husband for so long out of a lunatic asylum. That had been no mean feat; neither feat had been mean. And Valentine knew that Edith Ethel really loved beauty, circumspection, urbanity. It was no hypocrisy that made her advocate the Atalanta race of chastity. But, also, as Valentine Wannop saw it, humanity has these doublings of strong natures; just as the urbane and grave Spanish nation must find its outlet in the shrieking lusts of the bull-ring or the circumspect, laborious and admirable city typist must find her derivative in the cruder[21] lusts of certain novelists, so Edith Ethel must break down into physical sexualities—and into[22] shrieked coarseness of fish-wives. How else, indeed, do we have saints? Surely, alone, by the ultimate victory of the one tendency over the other!

But now[23] after her farewell scene with Edith Ethel a simple re-arrangement of the pattern had brought many of the old doubts at least temporarily back. Valentine said to herself that, just because of the very strength of her character, Edith Ethel couldn't have been brought down to uttering her fantastic denunciation of Tietjens, the merely mad charges of debauchery and excesses and finally the sexually lunatic charge against herself, except under the sting of some such passion as jealousy.[24] She, Valentine, couldn't arrive at any other conclusion. And, viewing the matter as she believed she now did, more composedly, she considered with seriousness that, men being what they are, her lover respecting, or despairing of, herself had relieved the grosser necessities of his being—at the expense of Mrs. Duchemin, who had, no doubt, been only too ready.

And in certain moods during the past week she had accepted this suspicion; in certain other moods she had put it from her. Towards the Thursday it had no longer seemed to matter. Her lover was going from her; the long pull of the war was on; the hard necessities of life stretched out; what could an infidelity more or less matter in the long, hard thing that life is. And on the Thursday two minor, or major, worries came to disturb her level. Her brother announced himself as coming home for several days' leave, and she had the trouble of thinking that she would have forced upon her a companionship and a point of view that would be coarsely and uproariously opposed to anything that Tietjens stood for—or for which he was ready to sacrifice himself. Moreover she would have to accompany her brother to a number of[25] riotous festivities whilst all the time she would have to think of Tietjens as getting hour by hour nearer to the horrible circumstances of troops in contact with enemy forces. In addition her mother had received an enviably paid for commission from one of the more excitable Sunday papers to write a series of articles on extravagant matters connected with the hostilities. They had wanted the money so dreadfully—more particularly as Edward was coming home—that Valentine Wannop had conquered her natural aversion from the waste of time of her mother.... It would have meant very little waste of time, and the £60 that it would have brought in would have made all the difference to them for months and months.

But Tietjens,[26] whom Mrs. Wannop had come to rely on as her right hand man in these matters, had, it appeared, shown an unexpected recalcitrancy. He had, Mrs. Wannop said, hardly seemed himself and had gibed at the two first subjects proposed— that of "war babies" and the fact that the Germans were reduced to eating their own corpses—as being below the treatment of any decent pen. The illegitimacy rate, he had said, had shown very little increase; the French-derived German word "*Cadaver*" meant bodies of horses or cattle; *Leichnam* being the German for the word "corpse." He had practically refused to have anything to do with the affair.

As to the *Cadaver* business Valentine agreed with him, as to the "war babies" she kept a more open mind. If there weren't any war babies it couldn't, as far as she could see, matter whether one wrote about them; it couldn't certainly matter as much as to write about them, supposing the poor little things to exist. She was aware that this was immoral, but[27] her mother needed the money desperately and her mother came first.

There was nothing for it, therefore, but to plead with Tietjens, for Valentine knew that without so much of moral support from him as would be implied by a good-natured, or an enforced sanction of the article, Mrs. Wannop would drop the matter and so would lose her connection with the excitable paper which paid well. It happened that on the Friday morning Mrs. Wannop received a request that she would write for a Swiss review* a prop-

---

* Ford had written at least two propaganda pieces for Swiss reviews during the war: 'Une partie de cricket', *Bibliothèque universelle et revue suisse*, 85 (Jan. 1917), 117–26, was reprinted as the envoi to *No Enemy*, 293–302. 'Pon... ti... pri... ith' was published in the Geneva periodical *La Revue des Idées* (Nov. 1918), 233–8; translated in *War Prose*, 30–5. *Nightingale*, 4–6, recounts writing a controversial article on peace terms for Arnold Bennett, which Ford was told got lost in the post.

aganda article about some historical matter connected with the peace after Waterloo. The pay would be practically nothing, but the employment was at least relatively dignified, and Mrs. Wannop—which was quite in the ordinary course of things!— told Valentine to ring Tietjens up and ask him for some details about the Congress of Vienna at which, before and after Waterloo, the peace terms had been wrangled out.

Valentine rang up—as she had done hundreds of times; it was to her a great satisfaction that she was[28] going to hear Tietjens speak once more at least. The telephone was answered from the other end, and Valentine gave her two messages, the one as to the Congress of Vienna, the other as to war babies. The appalling speech came back:

"Young woman! You'd better keep off the grass. Mrs. Duchemin is already my husband's mistress. You keep off." There was about the voice no human quality; it was as if from an immense darkness the immense machine had spoken words that dealt blows. She answered; and it was as if a substratum of her mind of[29] which she knew nothing must have been prepared for that very speech; so that it was not her own "she" that answered levelly and coolly:

"You have[30] probably mistaken the person you are speaking to.[31] Perhaps you will ask Mr. Tietjens to ring up Mrs. Wannop when he is at liberty."

The voice said:

"My husband will be at the War Office at 4.15. He will speak to you there—about your war babies. But I'd keep off the grass if I were you!" The receiver at the other end was hung up.

She went about her daily duties. She had heard of a kind of pine kernel that was very cheap and very nourishing, or at least very filling. They had come to it that it was a matter of pennies balanced against the feeling of satiety, and she visited[32] several shops in search of this food. When she had found it she returned to the dog kennel; her brother Edward had arrived. He was rather subdued. He brought with him a piece of meat which was part of his leave ration. He occupied himself with polishing up his sailor's uniform for a rag-time[33] party to which they were to go that evening. They were to meet plenty of conchies,[34*] he said.

* Conscientious Objectors.

Valentine put the meat—it was a Godsend, though very stringy!—on to stew with a number of chopped vegetables. She went up to her room to do some typing for her mother.

The nature of Tietjens' wife occupied her mind. Before, she had barely[35] thought about her: she had seemed unreal; so mysterious as to be a myth! Radiant and high-stepping: like a great stag! But she must be cruel![36] She must be vindictively cruel to Tietjens himself, or she could not have revealed his private affairs! Just broadcast; for she could not, bluff it how she might, have been certain of to whom she was speaking! A thing that wasn't done! But she had delivered her cheek to Mrs. Wannop; a thing, too, that wasn't done! Yet so kindly! The telephone bell rang several times during the morning. She let her mother answer it.

She had to get the dinner, which took three-quarters of an hour. It was a pleasure to see her mother eat so well; a good stew, rich and heavy with haricot beans. She herself couldn't eat, but no one noticed, which was a good thing. Her mother said that Tietjens had not yet telephoned, which was very inconsiderate. Edward said: "What! The Huns haven't killed old Feather Bolster yet? But of course he's been found a safe job." The telephone on the sideboard became a terror to Valentine; at any moment his voice might . . . Edward went on telling anecdotes of how they bamboozled petty officers on mine-sweepers. Mrs. Wannop listened to him with the courteous, distant interest of the great listening to commercial travellers. Edward desired draught ale and produced a two shilling piece. He seemed very much coarsened; it was, no doubt, only on the surface. In those[37] days everyone was very much coarsened on the surface.

She went with a quart jug to the jug and bottle department* of the nearest public-house—a thing she had never done before. Even at Ealing the mistress hadn't allowed her to be sent to a public-house; the cook had had to fetch her dinner beer herself or have it sent in. Perhaps the Ealing mistress had exercised more surveillance than Valentine had believed; a kind woman, but an invalid. Nearly all day in bed. Blind passion overcame Valentine at the thought of Edith Ethel in Tietjens' arms. Hadn't she got her own eunuch? Mrs. Tietjens had said: "Mrs. Duchemin is his

---

* The pubs competed with off-licences by selling people drink to take home.

mistress!" *Is!* Then she might be there now!

In the contemplation of that image she missed the thrills of buying beer in a bottle and jug department. Apparently it was like buying anything else, except for the smell of beer on the sawdust. You said: "A quart of the best bitter!"[38] and a fat, quite polite man, with an oily head and a white apron, took your money and filled your jug. . . . But Edith Ethel had abused Tietjens so foully! The more foully the more certain it made it! . . . Draught beer in a jug had little marblings of burst foam on its brown surface. It mustn't be spilt at the kerbs of crossings!—the more certain it made it! Some women did so abuse their lovers after sleeping with them, and the more violent the transports the more frantic the abuse. It was the "*post-dash-tristia*" of the Rev. Duchemin! Poor devil! Tristia! Tristia!

*Terra tribus scopulis vastum . . . Not* longum!*

Brother Edward began communing with himself, long and unintelligibly, as to where he should meet his sister at 19.30[39] and give her a blow-out! The names of restaurants fell from his lips into her panic. He decided hilariously and not quite steadily—a quart is a lot to a fellow from a mine-sweeper carrying no booze[40] at all!—on meeting her at 7.20[41] at High Street and going to a pub. he knew; they would go on to the dance afterwards. In a studio. "Oh, God!" her heart said, "if Tietjens should want her then!" To be his; on his last night. He might! Everybody was coarsened then; on the surface. Her brother rolled out of the house, slamming the door so that every tile on the jerry-built dog kennel rose and sat down again.

She went upstairs and began to look over her frocks. She couldn't tell what frocks she looked over; they lay like aligned[42] rags on the bed, the telephone bell ringing madly. She heard her mother's voice, suddenly assuaged: "Oh! oh! . . . It's you!" She shut her door and began to pull open and to close drawer after drawer.[43] As soon as she ceased that exercise her mother's voice became half audible; quite audible when she raised it to ask a question. She heard her say: "Not get her into trouble . . . Of *course!*" then it died away into mere high sounds.

She heard her mother calling:

* See notes on 117 and 165.

"Valentine! Valentine! Come down.... Don't you want to speak to Christopher? ... Valentine! Valentine! ..." And then another burst: "Valentine ... Valentine ... *Valentine* ..." As if she had been a puppy dog![44] Mrs. Wannop, thank God, was on the lowest step of the creaky stairs. She had left the telephone. She called up:

"Come down. I want to tell you! The dear boy has saved me! He always saves me! What shall I do now he's gone?"

"He saved others: himself he could not save!" Valentine quoted bitterly.* She caught up her wide-awake.[45] She wasn't going to prink herself for him. He must take her as she was.... Himself he could not save! But he did himself proud! With women! ... Coarsened! But perhaps only on the surface! She herself! ... She was running downstairs!

Her mother had retreated into the little parlour: nine feet by nine; in consequence, at ten feet it was too tall for its size. But there was in it a sofa with cushions.... With her head upon those cushions, perhaps.... If he came home with her! Late! ...

Her mother was saying: He's a splendid fellow.... A root idea for a war baby article.... If a Tommy was a decent fellow he abstained because he didn't want to leave his girl in trouble.... If he wasn't he chanced it because it might be his last chance....

"A message to me!" Valentine[46] said to herself. "But *which* sentence...."[47] She moved, absently, all the cushions to one end of the sofa. Her mother exclaimed:

"He sent his love! His mother was lucky to have such a son!" and turned into her tiny hole of a study.

Valentine ran down over the broken tiles of the garden path, pulling her wide-awake firmly on. She had looked at her wrist watch: it was two and twelve: 14.45. If she was to walk to the War Office by 4.15—16.15—a sensible innovation!—she must step out. Five miles to Whitehall. God knows what, then! Five miles back! Two and a half diagonally, to High Street Station by half-past 19! Twelve and a half miles in five hours or less. And three hours dancing on the top of it. And to dress! ... She needed to be fit ... And, with violent bitterness, she said:

"Well! I'm fit...." She had an image of the aligned hundred

* *Matthew* 27.41–2: see note on 18 above.

of girls in blue jumpers and men's ties keeping whom fit had kept her super-fit. She wondered how many of *them*[48] would be men's mistresses before the year was out. It was August then. But perhaps none! Because she had kept them fit. . . .

"Ah!" she said, "if I had been a loose woman, with flaccid breasts and a soft body. All perfumed!" . . . But neither Sylvia Tietjens nor Ethel Duchemin were soft. They might be scented on occasion! But they could not contemplate with equanimity doing a twelve mile walk to save a few pence and dancing all night on top of it! She could! And perhaps the price she paid was just that; she was in such hard condition she hadn't moved him to . . . She perhaps exhaled such an aura of sobriety, chastity and abstinence as to suggest to him that . . . that a decent fellow didn't get his girl into trouble before going to be killed. . . . Yet if he were such a town bull!* . . . She wondered how she knew such phrases. . . .

The sordid and aligned houses seemed to rush past her in the mean August sunshine. That was because if you thought hard time went quicker; or because after you noticed the paper shop at this corner you would be up to the boxes of onions outside the shop of the next corner before you noticed anything else.

She was in Kensington Gardens, on the north side; she had left the poor shops behind. . . . In sham country, with sham lawns, sham avenues, sham streams. Sham people pursuing their ways across the sham grass. Or no! Not sham! In a vacuum! No! "Pasteurised" was the word! Like dead milk. Robbed of their vitamines.† . . .

If she saved a few coppers by walking it would make a larger pile to put into the leering—or compassionate—taxi-cabman's hand after he had helped her support her brother into the dog kennel door. Edward would be dead drunk. She had fifteen shillings for the taxi.[49] . . . If she gave a few coppers more it seemed generous. . . . What a day to look forward to still! Some days were lifetimes!

She would rather die than let Tietjens pay for the cab!

---

* OED: 'a bull formerly kept in turn by the cow-keepers of a village; hence *fig.* of a man'.
† 'Vitamine' was still the standard spelling in the 1920s; it was later changed on the grounds that 'the termination "-ine" is one strictly employed in chemical nomenclature to denote substances of a basic character': OED.

Why? Once a taximan had refused payment for driving her and Edward all the way to Chiswick, and she hadn't felt insulted. She had paid him; but she hadn't felt insulted! A sentimental fellow; touched at the heart by the pretty sister—or perhaps he didn't really believe it was a sister—and her incapable bluejacket brother! Tietjens was a sentimental fellow too.... What was the difference? ... And then! The mother a dead, heavy sleeper; the brother dead drunk. One in the morning! He couldn't refuse her! Blackness: cushions! She had arranged the cushions, she remembered. Arranged them subconsciously! Blackness! Heavy sleep; dead drunkenness! ... Horrible! ... A disgusting affair! An affair of Ealing.... It shall make her one with all the stuff to fill graveyards.... Well, what else was she, Valentine Wannop: daughter of her father? And of her mother? Yes! But she herself ... Just a little nobody!

They were no doubt wirelessing from the Admiralty.... But her brother was at home, or getting a little more intoxicated and talking treason. At any rate the[50] flickering intermittences over the bitter seas couldn't for the moment concern him.... That 'bus touched her skirt as she ran for the island.[51] ... It might[52] have been better.... But one hadn't the courage!

She was looking at patterned deaths under a little green roof, such as they put over bird shelters. Her heart stopped! Before, she had been breathless! She was going mad. She was dying ... All these deaths! And not merely the deaths.... The waiting for the approach of death; the contemplation of the parting from life! This minute you were; that, and you weren't! What was it like? Oh heaven, she knew.... She stood there contemplating parting from ... One minute you were; the next ... Her breath fluttered in her chest.... Perhaps he wouldn't come ...

He was immediately framed by the sordid stones. She ran upon him and said something; with a mad hatred. All these deaths and he and his like responsible! ... He had apparently a brother,[53] a responsible one too! Browner complexioned! ... But he! He! He! He! completely calm; with direct eyes.... It wasn't possible. "*Holde Lippen: klaare*[54] *Augen: heller Sinn....*"* Oh, a little bit

---

\* The words are from Adelbert von Chamisso's *Frauenliebe*, best known from Robert Schumann's 1840 setting in his cycle *Frauenliebe und -leben*, Op. 42, ('Woman's Love and Life'): the second song, 'Er, der Herrlichste von allein' ('He, the Most Glorious

wilted, the clear intellect! And the lips? No doubt too. But he couldn't look at you so, unless . . .

She caught him fiercely by the arm; for the moment he belonged—more than to any browner, mere civilian, brother!—to her! She was going to ask him! If he answered: "Yes! I am such a man!" she was going to say: "Then you must take me too! If them, why not me? I must have a child. I too!" She desired a child. She would overwhelm this hateful lodestone[55] with a flood of argument; she imagined—she felt—the[56] words going between her lips. . . . She imagined her fainting mind; her consenting limbs. . . .

His looks[57] were wandering round the cornice of these stone buildings. Immediately she was Valentine Wannop again; it needed no word from him. Words passed, but words could no more prove an established innocence than[58] words can enhance a love that exists. He might as well have recited the names of railway stations. His eyes, his unconcerned face, his tranquil shoulders; they were what acquitted him. The greatest love speech he had ever and could ever make her was when, harshly and angrily, he said something like:

"Certainly not. I imagined you knew me better"—brushing her aside as if she had been a midge. And, thank God, he had hardly listened to her!

She was Valentine Wannop again; in the sunlight the chaffinches said "Pink! pink!" The seed-heads of the tall grasses were brushing against her skirt. She was clean-limbed, clear-headed. . . . It was just a problem whether Sylvia Tietjens was good to him. . . . Good *for* him was, perhaps, the more exact way of putting it. Her mind cleared, like water that goes off the boil. . . . "Waters stilled at even."* Nonsense. It was sunlight, and he had an adorable brother! He could save *his* brother. . . . Transport! There was another meaning to the word. A warm feeling

of All'); though Valentine (or perhaps Ford) turns Chamisso's 'clear eye' into a plural: 'Er, der Herrlichste von allen, / Wie so milde, wie so gut! / Holde Lippen, klares Auge, Heller Sinn und fester Mut' ('He, the most glorious of all, / O how mild, so good! / lovely lips, clear eyes, / bright mind and steadfast courage').

\*   From Dante Gabriel Rossetti's 'The Blessed Damozel', which begins: 'The blessed damozel leaned out / From the gold bar of Heaven; / Her eyes were deeper than the depth / Of waters stilled at even'.

settled down upon her; this was *her* brother; the next to the best ever! It was as if you had matched a piece of stuff so nearly with another piece of stuff as to make no odds. Yet just not the real stuff! She must be grateful to this relative for all he did for her; yet, ah, never so grateful as to the other—who had done nothing!

Providence is kind in great batches! She heard mounting the steps the blessed word Transport! "They," so Mark said: he and she—the family feeling again—were going to get Christopher into the Transport.... By the kindness of God the First Line Transport was the only branch of the services of which Valentine knew anything. Their charwoman, who could not read and write, had a son, a sergeant in a line regiment. "Hooray!" he had written to his mother, "I've been off my feed; recommended for the D.C.M.* too. So they're putting me senior N.C.O.† of First Line Transport[59]‡ for a rest; the safest soft job of the whole bally front line caboodle!" Valentine had had to read this letter in the scullery amongst black-beetles. Aloud! She had hated reading it as she had hated reading anything that gave details of the front line. But charity begins surely with the char!§ She had had to. Now she could thank God. The sergeant, in direct, perfectly sincere language, to comfort his mother, had described his daily work, detailing horses and G.S. limber wagons** for jobs and superintending the horse-standings. "Why," one sentence ran, "our O.C.†† Transport is one of those fishing lunatics. Wherever

---

* Distinguished Conduct Medal, the second-rank medal for gallantry after the Victoria Cross.
† Non-Commissioned Officer: an enlisted man given a rank of authority over other enlisted men.
‡ Ford and his fellow members of the Welch Regiment were attached to the 9th Battalion, and left the base camp at Rouen on 18 July 1916 to join their units in the Battle of the Somme, which had begun on 1 July with notoriously heavy casualties. He was stationed with the battalion transport, near Bécourt Wood, just behind the front line near Albert, and wrote to Lucy Masterman on the 28th: 'We are right up in the middle of the strafe, but only with the 1st line transport. We get shelled two or three times a day, otherwise it is fairly dull [...]': Saunders, *Dual Life* II 2.
§ Puns on the proverb 'Charity begins at home', and the domestic cleaner – 'charwoman' or 'charlady'.
** The *OED* defines a limber as 'The detachable fore part of a gun-carriage, consisting of two wheels and an axle, a pole for the horses, and a frame which holds one or two ammunition-chests'. G.S. ('General Service') limbers were used to transport other logistical supplies.
†† Officer Commanding.

we go he has a space of grass cleared out and pegged and b——y hell to the man who walks across it!" There the O.C. practised casting with trout and salmon rods by the hour together. "That'll show you what a soft job it is!" the sergeant had finished triumphantly. . . .

So that there she, Valentine Wannop, sat on a hard bench against a wall; downright, healthy middle-class—or perhaps upper middle-class—for the Wannops were, if impoverished, yet of ancient family! Over her sensible, moccasined[60] shoes the tide of humanity flowed before her hard bench. There were two commissionaires, the one always benevolent, the other perpetually querulous, in a pulpit on one side of her; on the other, a brown-visaged sort of brother-in-law with bulging eyes, who in his[61] shy efforts to conciliate her was continually trying to thrust into his mouth the crook of his umbrella. As if it had been a knob. She could not, at the moment, imagine why he should want to conciliate her; but she knew she would know in a minute.

For just then she was occupied with a curious pattern; almost mathematically symmetrical. *Now* she was an English middle-class girl—whose mother had a sufficient income—in blue cloth, a wide-awake[62] hat, a black silk tie; without a thought in her head that she shouldn't have. And with a man who loved her: of crystal purity. Not ten, not five minutes ago, she had been . . . She could not even remember what she had been! And he had been, he had assuredly appeared a town . . . No, she could not think the words. . . . A raging stallion then!* If now he should approach her, by the mere movement of a hand along the table,[63] she would retreat.

It was a Godsend;[64] yet it was absurd. Like the weather machine of the old man and the old woman on opposite ends of the stick. . . . When the old man came out the old woman went in and it would rain; when the old woman came out . . . It was exactly like that! She hadn't time to work out the analogy. But it was like that. . . . In rainy weather the whole world altered. Darkened! . . . The cat-gut that turned them slackened . . . slackened. . . . But, always, they remained at opposite ends of the stick!

Mark was saying, the umbrella crook hindering his utterance:

* Cf. *The Good Soldier* 15; see note on 281 above.

"We buy then an annuity of five hundred for your mother...."

It was astonishing, though it spread tranquillity through her, how little this astonished her. It was the merely retarded expected. Mr. Tietjens senior, an honourable man, had promised as much years ago. Her mother, an august genius, was to wear herself out putting, Mr. Tietjens alive, his political views in his paper. He was to make it up to her. He was making it up. In no princely fashion, but adequately, as a gentleman.

Mark Tietjens, bending over, held a piece of paper. A bell-boy came up to him and said: "Mr. Riccardo?"[65] Mark Tietjens said: "No! He's gone!" He continued:

"Your brother.... Shelved for the moment. But enough to buy a practice, a good practice! When he's a full-fledged sawbones." He stopped, he directed upon her his atrabilarian* eyes, biting his umbrella handle; he was extremely nervous.

"Now you!" he said. "Two or three hundred. A year of course! The capital absolutely your own...." He paused: "But I warn you! Christopher won't like it. He's got his knife into me. I wouldn't grudge you ... oh, any sum!"... He waved his hand to indicate an amount boundless in its figures. "I know you keep Christopher straight," he said. "The only person that could!" He added: "Poor devil!"

She said:

"He's got his knife into you? Why?"

He answered vaguely:

"Oh, there's been all this talk.... Untrue, of course."

She said:

"People have been saying things against you? To him? Perhaps because there's been delay in settling the estate."

He said:

"Oh, no! The other way round, in fact!"

"Then they have been saying," she exclaimed, "things against ... against me. And him!"

He exclaimed in anguish:

"Oh, but I ask you to believe ... I beg you to believe that I believe ... you! Miss Wannop!" He added grotesquely: "As pure

* 'Atrabilious, melancholy, hypochondriacal': *OED*.

as dew that lies within Aurora's sun-tipped ..."* His eyes stuck
out like those of a suffocating fish. He said: "I beg you not on that
account to hand the giddy mitten to ..."† He writhed in his tight
double collar. "His wife!" he said ... "She's no good to ... *for*
him! ... She's soppily in love with him. But no *good* ..." He very
nearly sobbed. "You're the only ..." he said, "I *know* ..."

It came into her head that she was losing too much time in
this Salle des Pas Perdus!‡ She would have to take the train home!
Fivepence! But what did it matter. Her mother had five hundred
a year.... Two hundred and forty times five....

Mark said brightly:

"If now we bought your mother an annuity of five hundred....
You say that's ample to give Christopher his chop.... And
settled on her three ... four ... I like to be exact ... hundred a
year.... The capital of it: with remainder to you ..." His inter-
rogative face beamed.

She saw now the whole situation with perfect plainness. She
understood Mrs. Duchemin's:

"You couldn't expect us, with our official position ... to
connive ..." Edith Ethel had been perfectly right. She *couldn't*
be expected.... She had worked too hard to appear circumspect
and right! You can't ask people to lay down their whole lives for

---

* 'As radiant as that matchless rose / Which poet-artists fancy; / As fair as whitest lily-
blows, / As modest as the pansy; / As pure as dew which hides within / Aurora's
sun-kissed chalice; / As tender as the primrose sweet– / All this, and more, is Alice':
from John Habberton, *Helen's Babies*, first published anonymously (Boston: Loring,
1876), which became a humorous children's classic. Habberton (1842–1921) was
best-known for his tales of life in early California, collected in *Romance of California
Life; Illustrated by Pacific Slope Stories, Thrilling, Pathetic and Humorous* (New York:
Baker, Pratt & Co., 1880).
† Brewer's *Dictionary of Phrase and Fable* glosses 'To give one the mitten' as 'To reject a
sweetheart; to jilt'; possible derived from the Latin *mittere*, to send (New York: Avenel
Books, 1978). Conrad Cork, Letters, *LRB*, 22:12 (22 June 2000) explains that in this
case the 'giddy' just adds emphasis, as in 'the giddy limit'. Mark is thus urging Valentine not to abandon Christopher on account of the malicious gossip about them. In
Ford's 1913 novel *Mr Fleight* (London: Howard Latimer, 1913), the Marwoodian character 'Mr. Blood' advises the German-bred Augusta Macphail: 'I should advise you, if
you want to appear really English, to say not "the chug," [i.e. 'the chuck'] but the "giddy
mitten." It sounds so much more English to be thoroughly American' (37). Partridge
agrees that the phrase to get or give the mitten was originally American, but Angli-
cised c. 1870, with further sense, to dismiss.
‡ 'Hall of Lost Steps' (French). A large vestibule in public buildings; in particular, the
room in the Palais de Justice in Paris where prisoners can walk off their anxiety while
awaiting a verdict.

their friends! . . . It was only of Tietjens you could ask that! She said—to Mark:

"It's as if the whole world had conspired . . . like a carpenter's vice[66]—to force us . . ." she was going to say "together. . . ." But he burst in, astonishingly:[67]

"He must have his buttered toast . . . and his mutton chop . . . and Rhum. St James!"* He said: "Damn it all. . . . You were made for him. . . . You can't blame people for coupling you. . . .[68] They're forced to it. . . . If you hadn't existed they'd have had to invent you . . . Like Dante for . . . who was it? . . . Beatrice? There *are* couples like that."[69]

She said:

"Like a carpenter's vice. . . . Pushed together. Irresistibly. Haven't we resisted?"

His face became panic-stricken; his bulging eyes pushed away towards the pulpit of the two commissionaires. He whispered:

"You won't . . . because of my ox's hoof† . . . desert.[70] . . ."

She said:—she heard Macmaster whispering it hoarsely.[71]

"I ask you to believe that I will never . . . abandon . . ."

It was what Macmaster had said. He must have got it from Mrs. Micawber!‡

Christopher Tietjens[72]—in his shabby khaki, for his wife had spoilt his best uniform—said suddenly from behind her back, since he had approached her from beyond the pulpit of the two commissionaires and she had been turned towards Mark on his bench:

"Come along! Let's get out of this!" He was, she asked herself, getting out of this! Towards what?[73]

Like mutes from a funeral—or as if she had been, between the brothers, a prisoner under escort—they walked down steps; half righted towards the exit arch; one and a half righted§ to face

---

* Rhum Saint James, from the French Caribbean island of Martinique, is a type of sipping rum dating back to 1765, fermented from pure sugar cane juice (rather than the molasses used for most rums) in a continuous single distillation process like that used for Armagnac.

† i.e. because he put his foot in it.

‡ Mrs Micawber in Dickens' *Nicholas Nickleby* (1838–9) protests several times that she never will desert her husband.

§ A half-right turn is a drill command ordering a turn of half a right-angle, or 45°; one and a half right would thus be a right angle plus 45°.

Whitehall. The brothers grunted inaudible but satisfied sounds over her head. They crossed, by the island,[74] Whitehall, where the 'bus had brushed her skirt. Under an archway.... [75]

In a stony, gravelled majestic[76] space* the brothers faced each other. Mark said:

"I suppose you won't shake hands!"

Christopher said:

"No! Why should I?" She herself had cried out to Christopher: "Oh, *do!*" (The wireless squares[†] overhead no longer concerned her. Her brother was, no doubt,[77] getting drunk in a bar in Piccadilly.... A surface coarseness!)

Mark said:

"Hadn't you better? You might get killed! A fellow just getting killed would not like to think he had refused to shake his brother by the hand!"

Christopher had said: "Oh ... well!"

During her happiness over this hyperborean sentimentality he had gripped her thin upper arm. He had led her past swans—or possibly huts; she never remembered which—to a seat that had over it, or near it, a weeping willow. He had said, gasping, too, like a fish:

"Will you be my mistress to-night? I am going out to-morrow at 8.30 from Waterloo."

She had answered:

"Yes! Be at such and such a studio[‡] just before twelve.... I have to see my brother home.... He will be drunk...." She meant to say: "Oh, my darling, I[78] have wanted you so much...."

She said instead:

"I have arranged the cushions...."

She said to herself:

"Now whatever made me say that? It's as if I had said: 'You'll find the ham in the larder under a plate....' No tenderness about it...."

---

* Presumably Horse Guards Parade.
† 'Loop antennae' were coils sometimes made into large square or diamond shapes.
‡ Probably a nod to Stella Bowen, who had come to London to study painting under Walter Sickert. She had a younger brother, Tom, who had been in the army in France, and from whom she wanted to keep her affair with Ford hidden at first.

She went away, up a cockle-shelled path, between ankle-high[79] railings, crying bitterly. An old tramp, with red weeping eyes and a thin white beard, regarded her curiously from where he lay on the grass. He imagined himself the monarch of that landscape.

"That's women!" he said with the apparently imbecile enigmaticality of the old and the hardened. "Some do!" He spat into the grass; said "'Ah!" then added: "Some do not!"

# VI

HE let himself in at the heavy door; when he closed it behind him, in the darkness, the heaviness of the door sent long surreptitious whisperings up the great stone stairs. These sounds irritated him. If you shut a heavy door on an enclosed space it will push air in front of it and there will be whisperings; the atmosphere of mystery was absurd. He was just a man, returning after a night out.... Two-thirds, say, of a night out! It must be half-past three. But what the night had lacked in length it had made up in fantastic aspects....

He laid his cane down on the invisible oak chest and, through the tangible and velvety darkness that had always in it the chill of the stone of walls and stairs, he felt for the handle of the break-fast-room door.

Three long parallelograms existed: pale glimmerings above,[1] cut two-thirds of the way down by the serrations of chimney pot and roof-shadows! Nine full paces across the heavy piled carpet; then he ought to reach his round-backed chair, by the left-hand window.[2] He sank into it; it fitted exactly his back. He imagined that no man had ever been so tired and that no man had ever been so alone! A small, alive sound existed at the other end of the room; in front of him existed one and a half pale parallelo-grams. They were the reflection of the windows of the mirror; the sound was no doubt Calton, the cat. Something alive, at any rate! Possibly Sylvia at the other end of the room, waiting for him, to see what he looked like.* Most likely! It didn't matter!

His mind stopped! Sheer weariness!

When it went on again it was saying:

"Naked shingles and surges drear ..." and, "On these debat-able borders of the world!" He said sharply: "Nonsense!" The one was either *Calais beach* or *Dover sands* of the whiskered man:[3]

---

* This is confirmed by the variant ending and by Tietjens' thinking back on the scene in *No More Parades*: see Appendix.

Arnold.* . . . He would be seeing them both within the twenty-
four hours. . . . But no! He was going from Waterloo.
Southampton, Havre, therefore! . . . The other was by that
detestable fellow: "the subject of our little monograph!"† . . .
What a long time ago! . . . He saw a pile of shining despatch cases:
the inscription *This rack is reserved for . . .*": a coloured—pink
and blue!—photograph‡ of Boulogne sands and the held up
squares,⁴ the proofs of "our little. . ." What a long time ago! He
heard his own voice saying in the new railway carriage, proudly,
clearly and with male hardness:

"*I stand for monogamy and chastity. And for no talking about it.
Of course if a man who's a man wants to have a woman he has her.
And again no talking about it. . . .*" His voice—his own voice—
came to him as if from the other end of a long-distance telephone.
A damn long-distance one! Ten years . . .

If then a man who's a man wants to have a woman. . . . Damn
it, he doesn't! In ten years he had learnt that a Tommie who's a
decent fellow. . . . His mind said at one and the same moment,
the two lines running one over the other like the two subjects of
a fugue:

"Some beguiling virgins with the broken seals of perjury,"§
and:

"Since when we stand side by side, only hands may meet!"**
He said:

"But damn it, damn it again! The beastly fellow was wrong!

---

* Matthew Arnold's 'Dover Beach' (1867), contemplates 'the vast edges drear / And
  naked shingles of the world'. He also wrote 'Calais Sands'. See *The Poems of Matthew
  Arnold*, second edition, ed. Kenneth Allott and Miriam Allott (London: Longman,
  1979), 253–7 and 247–8.
† i.e. Dante Gabriel Rossetti, the subject of the monograph Macmaster is proofreading
  in I.i. In Rossetti's sonnet-sequence, 'The House of Life', Sonnet XIV in Part I,
  'Youth's Spring-Tribute' (1881), includes the lines: 'On these debateable borders of
  the year / Spring's foot half falters' (www.rossettiarchive.org).
‡ Though there were experimental technologies for coloured photography, such as the
  Autochrome method patented by the Lumière brothers in 1903, they involved glass
  plates and required projection. Until the advent of Kodachrome in 1935 black-and-
  white prints were often hand-coloured.
§ Shakespeare, *Henry V*, IV.i.160–2; King Harry, disguised, debating with his soldiers
  that the king can't be responsible for the sins of his soldiers that might weigh on their
  souls should they die in battle: 'Some, peradventure, have on them the guilt of premed-
  itated and contrived murder; some, of beguiling virgins with the broken seals of
  perjury.'
** See note on 22.

Our hands didn't meet.... I don't believe I've shaken hands....
I don't believe I've touched the girl ... in my life.... Never
once! ... Not the hand-shaking sort.... A nod! ... At[5] meeting
and parting! ... English, you know ... But yes, she put her arm
over my shoulders.... On the bank! ... *On such short acquaintance!* I said to myself then ... Well, we've made up for it since
then. Or no! Not made up! ... Atoned.... As Sylvia so aptly
put it;[6] at that moment mother was dying...."

He, his conscious self, said:

"But it was probably the drunken brother.... You don't
beguile virgins with the broken seals of perjury in Kensington
High Street at two at night supporting, one on each side, a
drunken bluejacket with intermittent legs...."

"Intermittent!" was the word. "Intermittently functioning!"

At one point the boy had broken from them and run with
astonishing velocity along the dull wood paving of an immense
empty street. When they had caught him up he had been
haranguing under black hanging trees, with an Oxford voice, an
immobile policeman:

"You're the fellows!" he'd been exclaiming, "who make old
England what she is! You keep the peace in our homes! You save
us from the vile excesses...."

Tietjens himself he had always addressed with the voice and
accent of a common seaman; with his coarsened surface voice!

He had the two personalities. Two or three times he had said:

"Why don't you kiss the girl? She's a *nice* girl, isn't she? You're
a poor b——y Tommie, ain't cher?[*] Well, the poor b——y
Tommies ought to have all the nice girls they want! That's
straight, isn't it? ..."

And, even at that time they hadn't known what was going to
happen.... There are certain cruelties.... They had got a four-
wheel cab at last. The drunken boy had sat beside the driver; he
had insisted.... Her little, pale, shrunken face had gazed straight
before her.... It hadn't been possible to speak; the cab, rattling
all over the road had been pulled up with frightful jerks when the
boy had grabbed at the reins.... The old driver hadn't seemed
to mind; but they had had to subscribe all the money in their

---

[*]   Faux Cockney: 'Aren't you?'

pockets to pay him after they had carried[7] the boy into the black house....

Tietjens' mind said to him:

"Now when they came to her father's house so nimbly she slipped in,
And said: 'There is a fool without and there is a maid within....'"[8*]

He answered dully:

"Perhaps that's what it really amounts to...." He had stood at the hall door, she looking out at him with a pitiful face. Then from the sofa within the brother had begun to snore; enormous, grotesque sounds, like the laughter of unknown races from darkness.[†] He had turned and walked down the path, she following him. He had exclaimed:

"It's perhaps too ... untidy ... "

She had said:

"Yes! Yes ... Ugly ... Too ... oh ... *private!*"[9]

He said, he remembered:

"But ... for ever ... "

She said, in a great hurry:

"But when you come back ... Permanently. And ... oh, as if it were in public." ... "I don't know," she had added. "*Ought* we? ... I'd be ready ... " She added: "I will be ready for anything you ask."

He had said at some time: "But obviously.... Not under *this*

---

\* 'Blow Away the Morning Dew', a ballad existing in many versions in many regions since at least the seventeenth century. No. 112 in vol. 2 of Francis J. Child's five-volume work, *The English and Scottish Popular Ballads* (Boston: Houghton Mifflin, 1882–98): 'When she came to her father's gate, she tirled at the pin / And ready stood the porter there to let this fair maid in / / And when the gate was opened, so nimbly's she whipped in / Pough, You're a fool without, she says, and I'm a maid within.' Alternative titles are 'The Overcurteous Knight' and 'The Disappointed Lover'. Because he doesn't make love to her when he has the chance to, she decides not to give him another chance. The ballad ends: 'There is a flower in our garden, we call it marigold / He that would not when he might, he should not when he would.' Ford gave a different version as the epigraph to *A Call* (1910), where it is attributed to *Folk Songs from Somerset*. Tietjens' wry point is that Valentine is still a maid despite both their intentions.

† This detail in the scene perhaps alludes to one of Ford's favourite novels, Flaubert's *Sentimental Education*, when, at the end of Chapter 4, Frédéric returns home puffed up with his fantasy vocation as a painter, and hears the snoring of his friend Deslauriers, whom he had forgotten about in his excitement. However, the vocabulary of the sentence is markedly Conradian.

roof. . . ." And he had added: "We're the sort that . . . *do not!*"

She had answered, quickly too:

"Yes—that's it. We're that sort!" And then she had asked: "And Ethel's party? Was it a great success?" It hadn't, she knew, been an inconsequence. He had answered:

"Ah . . . *That's* permanent. . . . *That's* public. . . . There was Rugeley. The Duke . . . Sylvia brought him. She'll be a great friend! . . . And the President of the . . . Local Government Board, I think . . . And a Belgian . . . equivalent to Lord Chief Justice . . . and, of course, Claudine Sandbach. . . . Two hundred and seventy; all of the best, the modestly-elated Guggumses said as I left![10] And Mr. Ruggles . . . Yes! . . . They're established. . . . No place for me!"

"Nor for *me!*" she had answered. She added: "But I'm glad!"

Patches of silence ran between them: they hadn't yet got out of the habit of thinking they had to hold up the drunken brother. That had seemed to last for a thousand[11] painful months. . . . Long enough to acquire a habit. The brother seemed to roar: "Haw—Haw—Kuryasch. . . ." And after two minutes: "Haw—Haw—Kuryasch. . . ." Hungarian, no doubt!*

He said:

"It was splendid to see Vincent standing beside the Duke. Showing him a first edition! Not of course *quite* the thing for a, after all, wedding party! But how was Rugeley to know that? . . . And Vincent not in the least servile! He even corrected cousin Rugeley over the meaning of the word *colophon!*† The first time he ever corrected a superior! . . . Established, you see! . . . And *practically* cousin Rugeley. . . . Dear Sylvia Tietjens' cousin, so the next to nearest thing! Wife of Lady Macmaster's *oldest* friend. . . . Sylvia going to them in their—quite modest!—little place in

---

*   More probably Russian; in which the word **КОРЕШ**, transliterated as 'Koresch' or 'Koryesch' (which, with the vowels neutralised in unstressed syllables, could sound like 'Kuryasch') is a colloquial form of address often used among the working-class and in the army and navy, and corresponds to 'mate', 'chum', or the American 'buddy'. Alternatively, it might be a corrupt form of 'Kurish': the second person singular of the verb 'smoke'. The participle – **КУРЯЩИЙ**; 'smoking' – is 'Kuryashchi', but would be unlikely to be used on its own.

†   From Greek, 'finishing touch': tailpiece, often ornamental, in old manuscript or book, giving writer's or printer's name and the date; also the publisher's device on the title-page.

Surrey.... As for us," he had concluded, "they also serve who only stand and wait...."*

She said:

"I suppose the rooms looked lovely."

He had answered:

"Lovely.... They'd got all the pictures by that beastly fellow up from the rectory study in the dining-room on dark oak panelling.... A fair blaze of bosoms and nipples and lips and pomegranates....[12] The tallest silver candlesticks of course.... You remember, silver candlesticks and dark oak...."

She said:

"Oh, my dear ... Don't ... *Don't!*"

He had just touched the rim of his helmet with his folded gloves.

"So we just wash out!"† he had said.

She said:

"Would you take this[13] bit of parchment.... I got a little Jew girl to write on it in Hebrew: It's 'God bless you and keep you: God watch over you at your[14] goings out and at ...'"[15]‡

He tucked it into his breast pocket.[16]

"The talismanic passage," he said. "Of course I'll wear it...."

She said:

"If we *could* wash out this afternoon.[17]... It would make it easier to bear.... Your poor mother, you know, she was dying when we last ..."

---

* The last line of Milton's sonnet 'On his Blindness'.

† Tietjens' phrase is ambiguous: it could mean clean or flush or rinse out, suggesting figuratively that they stick to the path of clean living and integrity, unlike those around them. As it recurs, it seems more likely to mean that by their actions they can erase the blot on their chastity of his asking her to be his mistress, and her consenting. Alternatively (and more slangily), it could mean they fail (by comparison with the success of the Macmasters' scheming). This is closer to the sense when Tietjens says (in *No More Parades* III.ii) that a complaint against him is 'a washout'; i.e. a non-starter.

‡ From Psalm 121; in the Authorised Version: 'The Lord shall preserve thee from all evil: he shall preserve thy soul. / The Lord shall preserve thy going out and thy coming in from this time forth, and even for evermore.' Printed talismans usually took their texts from this Psalm or Psalm 91. Writing his painful farewell to Elizabeth Cheatham, Ford said: 'All through the war I carried a talisman given me by Dr Wallis Budge of the British Museum – the valedictory psalm in Hebrew: The Lord guide thee, the Lord guard thee, the Lord watch over thee at thy goings out and at thy comings in from the same...': Saunders, *Dual Life* II 352.

He said:

"You remember *that* . . . Even then you . . . And if I hadn't gone to Lobscheid. . . ."

She said:

"From the first moment I set eyes on you. . . ."

He said:

"And I . . . from the first moment . . . I'll tell you . . . If I looked out of a door . . . It was all like sand. . . . But to the half left a little bubbling up of water. That could be trusted.[18] To keep on for ever. . . . You, perhaps, won't understand."

She said:

"Yes! I know!"

They were seeing landscapes. . . .* Sand dunes; close-cropped. . . . Some negligible shipping; a stump-masted brig from Archangel. . . .[19]

"From the first moment," he repeated.

She said:

"If we *could* wash out . . ."

He said, and for the first moment felt grand, tender, protective:

"Yes, you *can*," he said. "You cut out from this afternoon, just before 4.58 it was[20] when I said that to you and you consented . . . I heard the Horse Guards clock. . . . To now. . . . Cut it out; and join time up. . . . It *can* be done. . . . You know they do it surgically; for some illness; cut out a great length of the bowel and join the tube up. . . . For colitis, I think. . . ."

She said:

"But I *wouldn't* cut it out. . . . It was the first spoken sign."[21]

He said:

"No it wasn't. . . . From the very beginning . . . with every[22] word. . . ."

She exclaimed:

---

* Compare *No Enemy*. The narrator explains how the war shattered Gringoire's sense of the landscape as a sanctuary, and that under its strain 'aspects of the earth no longer existed for him' (13). The first part of *No Enemy* is structured in terms of the 'Four Landscapes' that did make an impression on him, and 'which represent four moments in four years when, for very short intervals, the strain of the war lifted itself from the mind. They were, those intermissions of the spirit, exactly like gazing through rifts in a mist' (14).

"You felt that.... Too!... We've been pushed, as in a carpenter's vice.... We couldn't have got away...."

He said:[23]

"By God! That's it...."

He suddenly saw a weeping willow in St James's Park; 4.59! He had just said: "Will you be my mistress to-night?" She had gone away, half left,[24] her hands to her face.... A small fountain; half left. That could be trusted to keep on for ever....

Along the lake side, sauntering, swinging his crooked stick, his incredibly shiny top-hat perched sideways, his claw-hammer coat tails, very long, flapping out behind, in dusty sunlight, his magpie pince-nez gleaming, had come, naturally, Mr. Ruggles. He had looked at the girl; then down at Tietjens, sprawled on his bench. He had just touched the brim of his shiny hat. He said:

"Dining at the club to-night? ..."

Tietjens said: "No; I've resigned."

With the aspect of a long-billed bird chewing a bit of putridity, Ruggles said:

"Oh, but we've had an emergency meeting of the committee ... the committee was sitting ... and sent you a letter asking you to reconsider...."

Tietjens said:

"I know.... I shall withdraw my resignation to-night.... And resign again to-morrow morning."

Ruggles' muscles had relaxed for a quick second, then they stiffened.

"Oh, I say!" he had said. "Not that.... You couldn't do that.... Not to the *club*!... It's never been done.... It's an insult...."

"It's meant to be," Tietjens said. "Gentlemen shouldn't be expected to belong to a club that has certain members on its committee."

Ruggles' deepish voice suddenly grew very high.

"Eh, I say, you know!" he squeaked.

Tietjens had said:[25]

"I'm not vindictive.... But I *am* deadly tired: of all old women and their chatter."

Ruggles had said:

"I don't ..." His face had become suddenly dark brown,

scarlet and then brownish purple. He stood droopingly looking at
Tietjens' boots.

"Oh! Ah! Well!" he said at last. "See you at Macmaster's to-
night.... A great thing his knighthood. First-class man...."

That had been the first Tietjens had heard of Macmaster's
knighthood; he had missed looking at the honours' list of that
morning. Afterwards, dining alone with Sir Vincent and Lady
Macmaster, he had seen, pinned up, a back view of the Sovereign
doing something to Vincent; a photo for next morning's papers.
From Macmaster's embarrassed hushings of Edith Ethel's explanation that the honour was for special services[26] of a specific kind
Tietjens guessed both the nature of Macmaster's service and the
fact that the little man hadn't told Edith Ethel who, originally,
had done the work. And—just like his girl—Tietjens had let it
go at that. He didn't see why poor Vincent shouldn't have that
little bit of prestige at home—under all the monuments! But he
hadn't—though through all the evening Macmaster, with the
solicitude and affection of a cringing Italian greyhound, had
hastened from celebrity to celebrity to hang over Tietjens, and
although Tietjens knew that his friend was grieved and appalled,
like any woman, at his, Tietjens', going out again to France—
Tietjens hadn't been able to look Macmaster again in the
face.... He had felt ashamed. He had felt, for the first time in his
life, ashamed!

Even when he, Tietjens, had slipped away from the party—to
go to his good fortune!—Macmaster had come panting down the
stairs, running after him, through guests coming up. He had said:
"Wait ... You're not going.... I want to ..." With a miserable and appalled glance he had looked up the stairs; Lady
Macmaster might have come out too. With his black, short beard
quivering and his wretched eyes turned down, he had said:
"I wanted to explain.... This miserable knighthood...."[27]

Tietjens patted him on the shoulder, Macmaster being on the
stairs above him.

"It's all right, old man," he had said—and with real affection:
"We've powlered* up and down enough for a little thing like that
not to ... I'm very glad...."

* Not in the *OED*, but Frederic Harrison, *Studies in Early Victorian Literature* (London:
Edward Arnold, 1895), 37, gives the gist and the allusion: 'The England of Fielding

Macmaster had whispered:

"And Valentine.... She's not here to-night...."

He had exclaimed:

"By God! ... If I thought ... " Tietjens had said: "It's all right. It's all right. She's at[28] another party.... I'm going on ... "

Macmaster had looked at him doubtingly and with misery, leaning over and clutching the clammy banisters.

"Tell her ... " he said ... "Good God! You may be killed.... I beg you ... I beg you to believe ... I will ... Like the apple of my eye...." In the swift glance that Tietjens took of his face he could see that Macmaster's eyes were full of tears.

They both stood looking down at the stone stairs for a long time.

Then Macmaster had said: "Well ... "

Tietjens had said: "Well ... " But he hadn't been able to look at Macmaster's eyes,[29] though he had felt his friend's eyes pitiably exploring his own face.... "A backstairs way out of it," he had thought; a queer thing[30] that you couldn't look in the face of a man you were never going to see again!

"But by God," he said to himself fiercely, when[31] his mind came back again to the girl in front of him, "this isn't going to be another backstairs exit.... I must tell her....[32] I'm damned if I don't make an effort...."

She had her handkerchief to her face.

"I'm always crying," she said.... "A little bubbling spring that can be trusted to keep on...."[33]

He looked to the right and to the left. Ruggles or General Someone with false teeth that didn't fit *must* be coming along. The street with its sooty boskage was clean empty and silent. She was looking at him. He didn't know how long he had been silent, he didn't know where he had been; intolerable waves urged him towards her.

After a long time he said:

---

and the Scotland of Scott were breezy, boisterous, disorderly, picturesque, and jolly worlds, where gay and hot spirits got into mischief and played mad pranks as, in the words of the old song, "They powlered up and down a bit and had a rattling day.'" The song is known as 'Three Jolly Huntsmen', or – in a popular illustrated version appearing in R[andolph]. Caldecott's *Collection of Pictures and Songs* (London: Rout-ledge, 1881) – 'The Three Jovial Huntsmen'.

"Well . . ."

She moved back. She said:

"I won't watch you out of sight. . . . It is unlucky to watch anyone out of sight. . . . But I will never . . . I will never cut[34] what you said then out of my memory . . . " She was gone; the door shut. He had wondered what she would never cut out of her memory. That he had asked her that afternoon to be his mistress? . . .

He had caught, outside the gates of his old office, a transport lorry that had given him a lift to Holborn. . . .

**THE END**[35]

# TEXTUAL NOTES

## Conventions used in the Textual Notes

The textual endnotes use the following abbreviations and symbols:

**UK** First United Kingdom edition of *Some Do Not* ... (London: Duckworth and Company, 1924)
**MS** Manuscript of *Some Do Not* ...
**PP** Princeton proofs of UK I.i only, with autograph corrections
**TR** *transatlantic review*
**US** First American edition of *Some Do Not* ... (New York: Thomas Seltzer, 1924)
**Ed** Editor
**< >** Deleted passages
**[ ]** Conjectural reading (or editorial comment that a passage is illegible)
↑ Passage inserted above a line; often to replace a deleted passage
↓ Passage inserted below a line; often to replace a deleted passage

Most of the textual notes compare a passage from UK with the corresponding passage from MS, and where appropriate, with other witnesses. In these notes the abbreviation for the witness is given in bold typeface. Where witnesses agree, their abbreviations are listed, separated by commas. Semi-colons are used to separate the different quotations. The first quotation is always from UK; it is followed by the corresponding segment(s) from the manuscript and/or other witness(es). With segments longer than a single word in UK, the first and last words are identical in all versions, to enable ready comparison. In the example:

**UK, MS, US** a tobacco shop; **TR** a sweet shop

the UK and US texts both print 'a tobacco shop', following the manuscript; but the *transatlantic review* version prints 'a sweet shop'.

Deletions in the manuscript are quoted within angled brackets; insertions are recorded between vertical arrows, beginning with an up-arrow if the word is inserted from above the line; or with a down-arrow if inserted from below. Thus:

**UK** had taken a cab from; **MS** had <marched> ↑taken a cab↓ from

indicates that where UK prints 'had taken a cab from', in the corresponding passage in the manuscript, the word 'marched' has been deleted, and the phrase 'taken a cab' inscribed above.

The abbreviation **Ed** is only used where the editor adopts a reading different from all the witnesses. This is mainly used only for grammatical corrections.

Discursive notes (which don't compare versions) are differentiated by not using bold face for the witness abbreviations.

The symbol ¶ is used to indicate a paragraph break in a variant quoted in the textual endnotes. For verse quoted in the footnotes, a line break is indicated by '/'.

## Textual Note for Title-Page

1   The first page of I.i in MS is headed with the title: 'Some Do Not.' with single full stop (as in the first instalment of the TR serialisation) instead of suspension dots. This differs from the form on MS's title-page, which reads (with four suspension dots – not the three given in UK, US, and subsequent editions): 'Some do Not.... / A Novel / by / Ford Madox Ford / Author of "The <u>Marsden Case</u>, "<u>Mister</u> / <u>Bosphorus & the Muses</u>" / etc etc'. Of the chapters of MS that are headed with the title and not just the Part and Chapter number, some use the suspension dots (as early as I.ii), and some – do not.
        Though Ford had changed his name in 1919, he continued to publish as 'Hueffer' until 1923. The other two works he cites here were two of his first three as 'Ford'; they were also his first two books for Duckworth after returning to them after the war. The last book he wrote for them was *The Pre-Raphaelite Brotherhood* (1907), but they had acquired the rights to and reissued his trilogy of books known collectively as *England and the English*, publishing *The Soul of London* in 1911, and *The Heart of the Country* and *The Spirit of the People* in 1915 (perhaps as a patriotic wartime gesture). The citation of *The Marsden Case* and *Mister Bosphorus* is followed exactly in UK, either to emphasise a change of direction in the author's literary career or to publicise his Duckworth books. The third book published under the name 'Ford' by 1924 was *Women & Men*, published in a limited edition in Paris by the Three Mountains Press in 1923. These three all added '(Ford Madox Hueffer)' under his new name, as did all four Duckworth volumes of *Parade's End*, on the front covers, spines, and jackets. The US first editions didn't carry the Hueffer name on the books, but the first two volumes only added it on their jackets.

## Textual Notes for I.i

1   **UK** PART ONE; **US** PART I
        Emended for consistency between all four volumes. *Some Do Not . . .* was the only Duckworth edition not to use large roman numerals for any Part number. *Last Post* is inconsistent, having 'PART ONE' but 'PART II'. The other volumes use large roman numerals throughout. In the MS of *Some Do Not . . .* the chapters of the second part are headed 'Part II' (those of Part I carrying no Part number), though there the chapter numbers switch from

the Roman numerals of Part I to Arabic numbers for Part II!

2 **UK** perfectly appointed railway carriage; **MS** perfectly appointed <first class> railway carriage

3 **UK** design of a geometrician in Cologne; **MS** design of a<n [artist in]> ↑geometrician in↓ Cologne

4 **UK** compartment smelt; **MS** compartment <– that symbol [of] English [illegible] [desire] for isolation>, smelt

5 **UK** had taken a cab from; **MS** had <marched> ↑taken a cab↓ from

6 **UK, US** tailored; **MS, TR** tweed

    Confirmed by 20: 'in his grey tweeds'. The corrector of the Princeton proofs has underlined 'tailored' but not emended it.

7 **UK, US** that; **MS, TR** their

8 **UK, TR, US** could; **MS** would

9 **UK** had married a woman; **MS** had married <[– too early his People said – ]> a woman

10 **UK** would murmur: "You're; **MS** would <say> ↑murmur↓: "You're

11 **UK, TR, US** deep affection; **MS** deep, slow affection; **PP** deep, dear affection

12 **UK, TR, US** many; **MS** very

13 **UK, TR, US** the Tietjens' family; **MS** the Tietjens family

14 **UK** that fellow Macmaster; **MS** that fellow <Tietjens> Macmaster

15 **UK, PP, TR, US** would; **MS** [could]

    MS's reading picks up the idea of its being 'perfectly possible' for the Tietjens family to help, and that Christopher 'had been able' to ask his mother. The money is a 'small sum' so it's unlikely Tietjens would have had to make the request repeatedly, as 'would' implies.

16 **UK** How much?" ¶ With an English; **MS** How much?" ¶ <"A hundred this year and a hundred next" ¶ "Yes, my dear. I will speak to your father."> ¶ With an English

17 **UK** lower orders that would have; **MS** lower <[classes]> ↑orders↓ that <would not have been possible – [or] at least it> would have

18 This sentence is written in a more constricted hand, suggesting a later addition.

19 **UK** filled a place that; **MS** filled a place <in the young man's life> that

20 **UK** emotions. As Tietjens; **MS** emotions. <That was no doubt why, after [three[?]] years, his wife had left him. For> As Tietjens

21 **UK** suggested; **MS, TR, US** digested

    PP has been corrected to 'digested', suggesting that – for this chapter at least – TR was being set up from these Duckworth proofs. However, though US here agrees with TR and not UK, I assume in general that US was set from UK; in which case, Ford or another proofreader must have made the correction for US.

22 **UK** ffolliott; **MS, PP** Ffolliott; **TR** Flolliott

    The name is sometimes spelt with lower-case 'ff', like 'ffrench'.

23 **UK** second him. He'd better; **MS** second him. <That will [make him safe].> He'd better

24 Replaces a heavily deleted word that probably begins with an 'f'; perhaps 'five' for the total number of other children; or 'four', which Ford then decided to change.

25 There's a blank line in the MS here but no instruction to drop a line, which

Ford sometimes includes. In Duckworth this falls on the break between 14 and 15, so it's unclear whether there's a blank line. Neither TR nor US has one.

26 **UK, MS, US** looking; **TR** staring
   Perhaps TR was emended to avoid the echo of 'Tietjens looked' in the previous sentence?

27 **UK, US** agitated; **MS, TR** crepitated
   In PP 'agitated' has been corrected to read 'crepitated', but the correction was not carried over to the book editions.

28 **UK** the glass; **MS** the <liqueur> glass

29 Written above a deleted name, which appears to begin with 'B' and end with 't'.

30 **UK** of yours. If we; **MS** of yours <by the bye>. If we

31 **UK** Then British North America can go to the printers. It's; **MS** Then <Canada can go to the> British North America can go to the printers <while we're away>. It's

32 **UK** all right with Sir Reginald," Tietjens said. ¶ "Oh, yes I can; **MS** all right ↑with Sir Reginald.↓" ¶ Tietjens said: ¶ "Oh, yes I can; **US** all right with Sir Reginald." Tietjens said: ¶ "Oh, yes I can
   PP had a comma after 'Reginald', which was corrected to a full stop, and had a full stop after 'Tietjens said', which was corrected to a colon. Presumably the need for these corrections, together with the manuscript insertion, distracted the corrector from the need for a new paragraph (without which Macmaster's speech appears to be assigned to Tietjens as well).

33 **UK, PP, TR, US** pleased; **MS** pleaseder

34 **UK** finished. I'll have them; **MS** finished. <He [didn't hope] for them for three days yet> I'll have them

35 **UK** ten." ¶ Macmaster; **MS** ten." <He'll be as pleased as punch>." ¶ Macmaster

36 There appears to be a blank line in the MS after this paragraph, but not in the printed texts.

37 UK and US both use four dots with a preceding space here, as opposed to their normal convention of three dots with preceding space for incomplete sentences. This has not been standardised here, as it corresponds to Macmaster's evident difficulty in making his comment.

38 **UK** abroad to cover up Sylvia's retreat. She's; **MS** abroad ↑to cover up Sylvia's retreat↓. She's

39 **UK, PP, TR, US** few; **MS** four
   This appears more likely to be a compositor's misreading, but one too unobtrusive to have been corrected. The correction is warranted because 'four months', tallying with pp. 8, 10, 53 and 152, makes it clearer that Tietjens has adopted this exercise with the encylopaedia as a form of mental anaesthetic (see 152).

40 **UK** tabulating from memory the errors; **MS** tabulating ↑from memory↓ the errors

41 **UK, MS, PP, US** I remember Clifton hated it; **TR** I remember the School hated it
   TR's variant indicates a further stage of proofreading – after the correcting of PP – for the serialisation.

42 Again there appears to have been a change of name; 'Conder' is inscribed

above the deleted name 'Lowndes' here and in the next two occurrences later in the same paragraph. Ford probably changed the name because of the placing of the Tietjens' London house in Lowndes Street. See 14.

43 **UK** were unsafe. It was; **MS** were <[disgraced]. And> ↑unsafe.↓ It was

44 **UK, TR, US** Conder; **MS, PP** Lowndes
Another indication of further correction for TR after the correcting of PP.

45 **UK** accept them, and it gets; **MS** accept them <. You seem to have> and it gets

46 **UK, US** get's; **MS, PP, TR** gets.

47 MS has an instruction here to '(drop a line)'. Followed by UK and TR, but not evidently in US because it falls at the foot of 12.

48 **UK** Tietjens had thrown; **MS** Tietjens <looked up from his> had thrown

49 **UK** his position. In the office; **MS** his position. <Not only must it [immensely] strengthen his position in the long-curtained drawing-rooms of Mrs. Leamington, Mrs. Cressy and the Hon. Mrs. de Limoux but it would [give], in the office of the Department of Statistics, a finishing touch to the cachet he needed. The drawing-rooms were only a step in a direction.> In the Office

50 **UK, PP, TR, US** adverse from; **MS** averse from

51 **UK** the promotion of the distinguished are not objected to; **MS** the promotions of the distinguished are not objected to; **TR, US** the promotion of the distinguished is not objected to
PP corrects 'are' to 'is' but this change was not made in UK.

52 **UK** Sir Reginald Ingleby; **MS** Sir <Robert> ↑Reginald↓ Ingleby

53 The rest of this sentence, and the next, are inserted in a text box in the left-hand margin of the MS.

54 **UK, PP, TR, US** every one; **MS** everyone

55 **UK, MS, US** a tobacco shop; **TR** a sweet shop
As with 'crepitated' above (note 27), the revision from 'tobacco' to 'sweet' was made in PP for TR but was not carried into UK or US. This confirms the hypothesis that the PP of I.i were used to set TR, but neither they nor TR were used by Duckworth. There is some evidence (see the correction from 'change' to 'charge' below, for example) that – as one would expect – there was a further stage of correction when the proofs for the TR instalments were checked. Though TR's version counts as a prior publication to UK, the UK version has been allowed to stand here, since it is not an error, and we can't be sure that Ford didn't change it back in correcting the UK proofs for Duckworth.

56 **UK** manipulator of sonorous, rolling; **MS** manipulator of ↑sonorous,↓ rolling

57 **UK** the outward aspects; **MS** the <aspects> outward aspects

58 **UK** Tietjens' face. . . . ¶ He could still feel the blow; **MS** Tietjens' face. . . . ¶ <He had made [one] spring for the brandy.> He could still feel the <remember the feeling as if of a> blow
The words 'feel the' occur at the end of the line and were presumably added later when this second deletion was made. In which case the original version would have read 'He could still remember the feeling as if of a blow'; subsequently revised to make it more direct: 'He could still feel the blow'.

59 **UK** At the office, but later, he; **MS** At the office, ↑but later,↓ he

60 **UK, PP, US** correct those fellows by; **MS** correct <them> ↑those fellows↓ by; **TR** correct those fellows by

61 **UK, MS, US** lumpish; **PP, TR** limpish

62 **UK** without appeals; **MS** without <agonised> appeals

63 **UK, TR, US** was; **MS** were

64 **UK** very little. Yorkshire men of; **MS** very little: <But Macmaster's mind taking appalled charge> Yorkshiremen of

65 **UK, PP, US** change; **MS, TR** charge

66 **UK** have introduced; **MS** have <[brought] up> introduced

67 **MS** lays out without indentations for alternate lines, and whole poem lined up with 'Since', so that the first line doesn't separate from the rest of the stanza.

68 **UK, MS, TR** Mill's; **US** Mills

69 **UK, TR** Eliot's for the; **US** Eliots for the; **MS** Eliot's <and your Carlyle's> for the

70 **UK** oily man; **MS** oily <greasy> man

71 **UK** in a grease-spotted dressing-gown; **MS** in a <spotted dre> grease-spotted dressing-gown

72 **UK** *Precicuses Ridicules*; **MS** *Précieuses Ridicules*; **PP, TR** *Preciurses Verdecules*; **US** *Precieuses Ridicules*

73 **MS** has no dash but Ford's characteristic ampersand (which resembles a '+' with the top and left-hand arm joined), which here looks like a dash.

74 The next line in **MS** consists of a deleted fragment – "'I'll admit," Macmaster' – which oddly interrupts this sentence. It is repeated as the opening of the next paragraph.

75 **UK, PP, TR, US** coincided; **MS** conceded

76 In **MS**, the phrase 'except by a woman' is inserted in the left-hand margin suggesting a revision prompted by thinking of the character of Mrs Wannop.

77 **UK** a healthy, human desire; **MS** a <natural> healthy, human desire

78 **UK** agreeable with talk of Tasso; **MS** agreeable <talking of> ↑with talk of↓ Tasso

79 **UK** to have bathrooms **MS** to have <white enamel and> bathrooms

80 **UK** to go round to satisfy; **MS** to go round <. Just as there aren't [. . .]> to satisfy

81 **UK** nodded to Tietjens. ¶ Macmaster considered; **MS** nodded to Tietjens <[who didn't much] notice them>. ¶ Macmaster considered

82 **UK** a bone tonight if you're going; **MS** a bone to-<morrow> ↑night↓ if you're going

83 **UK TR, US** Lobscheid; **MS** Lobschied
      MS uses the correct spelling at the start of the next chapter.

84 **UK** Paul Sandbach is down. He's; **MS** <There's [illegible name] with our lot > ↑Paul Sandbach is down.↓ He's

85 **UK** will you?" He jumped; **MS** will you?" <They've got my beastly bag under all the luggage for Folkestone.> He jumped

86 **UK** dinner to-night. You'll come; **MS** dinner to-<morrow> ↑nigh [*sic*]↓. You'll come

87 **UK** offices. Tietjens only; **MS** offices. <Macmaster> ↑Tietjens↓ only

88 **UK, US** part; **MS, TR** pant

89 **UK** quoted to himself; **MS** quoted <from something> to himself

90 In **MS** this ending is followed by a deleted four-line paragraph:
      '<And he fell into a musing as to whether that were or were not the same thing as saying: To-day to me; to-morrow to them. He had a mind that stiffened and sustained itself by quotation from the poets[.] Tietjens said that was a bad habit: it induced mental atrophy[.]>'

## Textual Notes for I.ii

1 **UK, TR, US** their; **MS** them
Emended to restore the idiom.

2 **UK** tuberculosis, was; **MS** tuberculosis, <& [illegible word]>, was

3 **UK, US** a perpetual laugh, like; **MS** a ↑perpetual↓ laugh too, like; **TR** a perpetual laugh like

4 **UK** the financial assistance; **MS** the ↑financial↓ assistance

5 **UK** tremendous love affair with; **MS** tremendous <flirtation> ↑love affair↓ with

6 **UK** young fellow, who included a gun; **MS** young fellow, ↑who included↓ <with> a gun

7 **UK, US** young Förster tried; **MS** young <fellow tried to> Förster tried; **TR** young Forster tried

8 **UK** young blonde sub-lieutenant; **MS** young ↑blonde↓ sub-lieutenant

9 **UK** Consett, breathing heavily and looking; **MS** Consett, <panting a good deal> ↑breathing heavily↓ and looking

10 **UK** She wore; **MS** She <always> wore

11 **UK, TR, US** silk that might have been thrown; **MS** silk that appeared to have been thrown

12 **MS, TR, UK, US** mat
Alternative spelling of 'matt'.

13 **UK** ribbon stuck here; **MS** ribbon ↓stuck↑ here

14 **UK, TR, US** to show she; **MS** to show that she
The 'that' in MS has a long horizontal bar on the initial 't' that might indicate deletion, or might have been misread as a deletion by the printer.

15 **UK, TR, US** rests; **MS** [seats]
The 'rests' might be arm- or foot-rests, and could be an authorial correction in the proofs, so MS's reading (which is anyway unclear) has not been restored. MS possibly referred to the simple sofa design with an upholstered seat and cushions that provide the back and arm-rests.

16 **UK** bath-rooms, verandahs, and; **MS** bath-rooms, ↑verandahs,↓ and

17 **UK, TR** contemplation; **MS** contemplations

18 **UK** He is; **MS** He <says he> is

19 **UK** wicked place. But never; **MS** wicked <thing> ↑place↓. But never

20 **UK** neck. It was; **MS** neck. <And I couldn't [go away]> It was

21 **UK** have no such feelings; **MS** have <none of these> ↑no such↓ feelings

22 **UK, MS, TR** practises; **US** practices

23 **UK, TR, US** interlocutress; **MS** interlocutrix

24 **UK** It was probably Drake's; **MS** It was <certainly> ↑probably↓ Drake's

25 **UK** my daughter appearing in trouble; **MS** my daughter ↑appearing↓ in trouble
At this stage she wouldn't have been able to be sure Sylvia actually was pregnant, though as it turned out she was.

26 **UK** she was a tiny. And I thank; **MS** she was a tiny < – for your goodness to me and [my poor flock]>. And I thank

27 **UK** all men at her feet; **MS** all <the> men <of everywhere> at her feet

28 **TR, UK, US** Gosingeux; **MS** Yssingeux
The place Sylvia has been with Perowne in Brittany, given the full name of 'Yssingueux-les-Pervenches' in *No More Parades*.

29 **UK** been renewing his; **MS** been <[widening]> ↑renewing↓ his
30 **UK, TR** Accept; **MS** accept
   Emended as consonant with the repetition of the quotation on the same
   page.
31 **UK** he muttered. He made a sound like "Umbleumbleumble; **MS** he
   muttered. ↑He made a sound like↓ "Umbleumbleumble
32 **UK** *for you and mother reflect upon*; **MS** *for you*<r reflection> *and mother reflect
   upon*
33 **UK, US** task; **MS, TR** tack
34 **UK** *solely comma*; **MS** *solely* <*emphasised to affairs*> *comma*
35 UK and US fail to close the double inverted commas of Father Consett's
   speech. MS is unclear: there's one large mark that might be two inverted
   commas that have blotted into one, but it's more likely Ford forgot to close
   the outer set.
36 **UK, US** take it . . . ." Father; **MS** take it . . ." Father
   Emended because Duckworth violates its normal rule of using three dots
   (with preceding space) for incomplete sentences.
37 **UK** He broke off. Walking slowly; **MS** He broke off. <Sylvia> Walking slowly
   The 'w' of 'walking' has been extended into a capital when Ford decided to
   delay the subject of the sentence to the final clause.
38 **UK, US** bitter; **MS** [better]; **TR** better
   The second letter is ambiguous in MS, with neither loop nor dot. It's possible
   Ford meant 'bitter', which was misread for TR then corrected for UK.
   However, the revision of 'better' to 'more virtuous' later in the sentence,
   suggests that the earlier word was also 'better', and that the later was revised
   avoid repetition. In which case the first word would have been misread as
   'bitter' in Duckworth's proofs, and corrected when revised for TR.
39 **UK** looked more virtuous than you; **MS** looked <better> ↑more virtuous↓
   than you
40 **UK** I'll tell you," she said, "why; **MS** I↑'ll↓ tell you," <said> she said, "why.
41 **UK, TR, US** that dull; **MS** that oaf's dull
42 **UK** He sent it out of; **MS** He sent it <[purely]> out of
43 Double inverted commas in MS and UK, but UK 43 uses single for embedded
   quotations, as does the rest of this paragraph, so standardised here.
44 **UK** in my cogitation; **MS** in my <[cal]> cogitation
45 **UK** delights to lurk in the shadow; **MS** delights <lurking> ↑to lurk↓ in the
   shadow
46 **UK, TR, US** It's a great handicap we; **MS** It's great handicaps we
   MS's reading restored to match the repetition in Consett's next speech.
47 **UK** him," Father Consett went on, "yet; **MS** him," <I'm here [on my]
   holiday, making> ↑Father Consett went on↓ "yet
48 **UK, TR** Sylvia said, "if the nuns; **MS, US** Sylvia said. "If the nuns
   The punctution is ambiguous: an elongated full stop or a comma, but Ford's
   capital 'I' is clear.
49 **UK, MS, TR, US** husband's; **Ed** husbands'
50 **UK** with her; **MS** with <me> her
51 **UK** wit to give; **MS** wit <at [least] to> ↑to↓ give
52 **UK, TR, US** more; **MS** [now]
   Though the word isn't unambiguous in MS, 'more' doesn't make sense: 'more
   suddenly' than what? – she's been dozing! It looks more like 'now', and is a

reasonably close match to other examples of 'now' in the chapter.

53 **UK** men if you could not find the young; **MS** men <[except]> ↑if you could not find↓ the young

54 **UK, US** "There's some of them said to be rather good," Sylvia said. "Di Wilson's told me about one. She said; **MS, TR** "There's one of them said to be rather good," Sylvia said. "Di Wilson's told me about her. She said
The MS/TR reading has been restored because (a) the small gap in MS between the 's' of 'There's' and 'one' is easily misreadable as 'some'; (b) though the ungrammatical 'There's some' might be slangy, Sylvia's language is generally more correct; and (c) TR represents a prior publication, under Ford's editorship.

55 **UK, US** will. . . ."; **MS** will."; **TR** will. . ."
The full stop followed by low double quotation marks in MS may have been misread as suspension dots, and quotation marks may have been added as a correction. As the dots appear in TR as well as UK, they have been retained.

56 **UK, TR, US** any; **MS** my
As the maid is on loan to Mrs Satterthwaite, it's possible she says 'any maid' meaning 'even someone else's'. But the phrase's awkwardness suggests 'my' as a preferable reading of the (admittedly ambiguous) handwriting. There's little difference between the ways Ford writes 'any' or 'my' in this chapter, and the latter fits better with Sylvia's reference to 'that Marie of yours' and with her previous question: 'Why don't you keep your maid up?'

57 **UK, TR** of your's arms; **MS, US** of yours' arms

58 **UK** your hearts." ¶ Sylvia; **MS** your hearts." <only I never got down [to it]>" ¶ Sylvia

59 **UK** the future mothers; **MS** the ↑future↓ mothers

60 **UK, TR, US** mother or grandmother; **MS** mothers or grandmothers
MS restored on the ground that the 's's are indistinct so easily overlooked, and that the plurals are consistent with Sylvia's first-person plural and Consett's other plural nouns.

61 **UK, US** to Mrs. Vanderdecken. And, of course, Freud."; **MS** to Mrs. Vanderdecken. And of course Freud."; **TR** to Mrs. Freud Vanderdecken. And, of course,"

62 **UK** Mrs. Satterthwaite answered. ¶ The Father; **MS** Mrs. Satterthwaite answered. ¶ <It [can't] be> The Father

63 In MS instead of following the usual convention of starting a new paragraph for 'Sylvia said', the words appear to have been inserted at the end of the previous line as an afterthought. Neither UK nor US noticed the need for the new paragraph.

64 **UK** then there is the boredom; **MS** then <[illegible] ↑there is the↓ boredom

65 **UK, TR, US** hate; **MS** *hate*
Emended since the extra emphasis justifies the repetition.

66 **UK, US** you're a priest and mother's mother; **MS, TR** you're a priest and mother
Presumably corrected to avoid suggestion of the priest being a mother!

67 **UK** utte s; **MS, TR, US** utters

68 **UK, TR, US** even in these I don't know that we differed so much—I found; **MS** even in these <I> we don't know that I differed so much—I found
It appears that Ford emended the first 'I' within the parenthesis instead of the second by mistake.

69 **UK** him. That's an end; **MS** him. <Let that be> ↑That's↓ an end

70 **UK, MS, US** it; **TR** them

71 Christopher's comments appear within double inverted commas in UK (following MS), despite being embedded within Sylvia's speech; emended here to single, following US.

72 **UK, TR, US** everything!; **MS** *everything!*
MS reading restored on the grounds that the line under 'every' in MS is close enough to the line below to be easily missed by a compositor.

73 **UK, TR, US** that; **MS** the

74 UK has three dots; emended since it's a pause after a completed sentence.

75 **UK** for a month or two; **MS** for a <week> ↑month↓ or two

76 **UK** Birkenhead, many ladies go there," the Father; **MS** Birkenhead, ↑many ladies go there,"↓ the Father

77 **UK** if only for a month; **MS** if only for a <[week]> month

78 **UK, TR, US** nauseated; **MS** nausea

79 MS and TR include suspension dots after the exclamation mark (perhaps to correspond to Sylvia's panting). Omitted by UK and US.

80 **UK** my pistol pocket; **MS** my ↑pistol↓ pocket

81 **UK** occasions. What if I was; **MS** occasions. <If> ↑What if↓ I was

82 UK TR, and US fail to close inverted commas; correct in MS.

83 **UK, TR, US** feet; **MS** legs

84 **UK** shouldn't have ..." ¶ Her; **MS** shouldn't have .... I'm ...." ¶ Her

85 **UK, MS, TR, US** who's; **Ed** whose

86 **UK, TR** it's; **MS, US** its

87 The passage above, from 'It's not much more than palmistry [...] black or white' appears here in MS, is ringed around, and inserted above after 'idle girls'.

88 Long deleted passage here:

> 'Mrs. Satterthwaite said:
> "Oh dear! Oh dear!" with such [evident real] distress that the father said: "It won't kill me. It's a warm night and a walk will do me no harm...."
> Mrs. Satterthwaite stood up.
> "I'll go with you," she said, "I won't have you go alone through the forest...."
> The father stood amazed and touched.
> "I'll not have you go alone," Mrs. Satterthwaite said. "I'll *not*"
> A shrill sound pierced the darkness. The father gave an immense laugh that went on and on:
> "Listen!" he said. "That's cockcrow... They'll be going to their beds. And do you go to yours." He said: "I'll take one of your candles to light me downstairs. It'll be the grey dawn outside."'

The 'They' who'll be going to their beds are presumably the devils the superstitious Mrs Satterthwaite is afraid of. In some ways the deleted passage indicates the tightness of Ford's architecture of motifs: Consett's 'immense laugh' echoes the description of his 'perpetual laugh' at the start of the chapter; the piercing sound of the cock-crow, which appears ominous before they grasp what it was, offers an antithesis to the sinister scratching noise at the window. But Ford was prepared to sacrifice these formal satisfactions to achieve the kind of off-beat ending he prizes.

## Textual Notes for I.iii

1   **UK** door, Tietjens started; **MS** door, <Macmaster> ↑Tietjens↓ started
2   **UK** which cut into squares; **MS** which <[also] made> ↑cut into↓ squares
3   **UK** planking. Tietjens, who; **MS** planking. <Macmaster>, ↑Tietjens↓ who
4   **UK** was one of those restored; **MS** was <a restored> one of those restored
5   **UK** the inspiration; **MS** the <[culture] and> inspiration
6   **UK** professional dealers; **MS** professional <and [more trusted]> dealers
7   **UK** as at; **MS** as <[?] to be consulted upon certain pieces by Government [on occasion] and> at
8   **UK** value great properties; **MS** value <distinguished> ↑great↓ properties
9   **UK, US** said, General; **MS** said the General; **TR** said, the General
10  **UK** a Cabinet Minister; **MS** a ↑Cabinet↓ Minister
11  **UK** Town! It probably won't; **MS** Town! <In any case it>, It probably won't
12  A further sign of confusion over names here, with a deleted 'Mac' before 'Tietjens' in MS.
13  **UK** the late; **MS** the <novelist> late
14  **UK, TR, US** she's housemaid for her; **MS** she <[works] with> ↑housemaids for↓ her
15  **UK, TR, US** squeaked—is a stranger; **MS** squeaked and fell in—is a stranger
    In MS the 'and' is Ford's characteristic ampersand, more like a '+' with the horizontal bar more pronounced. I assume the compositor's eye misread it as a dash and jumped to the dash after 'fell in'. As it's unlikely that exactly the same error would have occurred twice, this suggests that TR was set from UK or UK proofs (as with I.i), or vice-versa, rather than both being set from MS. See 'A Note on the Text' xcii–xciii.
16  There is considerable alteration in Waterhouse's names. Ford's different versions of the surname are noted below. His first name is given as 'Edward' below (65), where his middle name is spelt 'Fenwick', as it is in the only other instance in the book, on 73. So though all witnesses give 'Fenick' here, I have emended for consistency. 'Stephen' is used again on 73, so is allowed to stand here.
17  **UK, TR, US** Stephen Fenick Waterhouse's compliments; **MS** Fenick <Waterman> ↑Waterhouse↓'s compliments; **Ed** Stephen Fenwick Waterhouse's compliments
    The earlier version of the name confirms the suggestion that Ford was modelling Waterhouse closely on Masterman. There's another small deletion above the 'man' of 'Waterman' – possibly <field>; then a marginal insertion reading 'Waterhouse's'. It was perhaps Ford's concentration over changes in the surname that caused him to miss the error over the first names.
18  **UK, TR, US** didn't; **MS** *didn't*
    The underlining in MS could have been misread as a continuation of the line indicating the insertion of a marginal addition above the next line.
19  In MS <him> has been replaced by marginal insertion 'Mr. Waterhouse'.
20  This entire sentence added in the margin.
21  Again Ford seems to have confused the names, writing then deleting what appears to be <Mac> before 'Tietjens'.
22  **UK** earth! I wanted; **MS** earth! <tonight.> I wanted
    The deletion of 'tonight.' indicates the exclamation mark was added as an afterthought.

23 **UK** the calculation. They only asked you to work it out; **MS** the <figures>. ↑calculation↓ They ↑only↓ asked you to work <them> ↑it↓ out

24 Again MS originally read 'Waterman'; <man> deleted; <field> above also deleted; 'house' inserted above that.

25 This speech within a speech is given double inverted commas in UK and US, but is emended here for consistency with UK's general practice.

26 **UK** by up; **MS, TR, US** up by

27 Revised twice, as in note 24 above.

28 **UK, US** But these are the actuarial variations; **MS** But [there] are the ↑actuarial↓ variations; **TR** But there are the acturial [*sic*] variations

29 **UK** them." Tietjens; **MS** them." ¶ < "Oh, I'd help you,"> Tietjens

30 MS clearly leaves a blank after this paragraph, but it is omitted by UK, TR, US; also here, since the syntax connects the paragraphs.

31 **UK** beastly placard like Senior Wrangler hung; **MS** beastly <label> placard like <that> ↑Senior Wrangler↓ hung

32 **UK, TR, US** at the club all these, in; **MS** at [illegible deletion] The Club all these and more, in

33 **UK** And he; **MS** And <for all his [safeness &] [illegible] [of making mental exertions]> he

34 **UK, MS, TR, US** Duchemin's; **Ed** Duchemins'

35 **UK, MS, TR, US** Mountsby; **Ed** Mountby
The first instance of a widespread confusion in MS over this name. See note 40 below.

36 **UK** can. Had; **MS** can. <They've> Had

37 **UK** serious? Chrissie; **MS** serious? <Well then.> Chrissie
Perhaps deleted because repeated at the end of this speech.

38 **UK, TR, US** fearless.—She'd; **MS** fearless . . . She'd
The last two dots have run together but are on the same level as the first; clearly not intended in MS as a dash.

39 **UK** rage. You should have seen her; **MS** rage. <I've seen> ↑You should have seen↓ her

40 **UK, TR, US** Mountby; **MS** Mountsby
The small 's' in MS perhaps caused the compositor to miss it. The spelling of the name is inconsistent in MS, whereas UK and US opt fairly consistently for 'Mountby', so that spelling has been used for this edition. For further discussion see note 84 to I.vii.

41 In MS 'Waterhouse' is written above two deletions – the first illegible, but presumably again <Waterman> and the second <Waterfield>. His first name appears as 'Edward' at this point in all witnesses; but he is 'Stephen' above (61) and below (73). While it's possible the hesitation over the surname may have distracted Ford's attention away from spotting an error of his own, it's equally possible that he intended the confusion as Macmaster's (who doesn't recognise Waterhouse in the clubhouse on 73) and that the passage is in free indirect style; thus the name has been allowed to stand.

42 **UK** Liberal down for a week-end of golf, preferred; **MS** Liberal ↑down for a week-end of golf↓, preferred

43 **UK** men. ¶ Macmaster; **MS** men <¶ They were worried. A couple of Suffragettes – the woman's movement> ¶ Macmaster

44 **UK** disagreeable scene; **MS** disagreeable <a [most unsavoury]> scene

45 **UK** have written if she wanted to be taken back; for, had; **MS** have written

↑if she wanted to be taken back↓; for, had

46 **UK** of very old red brick; **MS** of ↑very old↓ red brick

47 **UK** a peasant's; **MS** a <farmhouse or> peasant's

48 **UK** he could afterwards remember; **MS** he could ↑afterwards↓ remember

49 **UK** the quiet; **MS** the <absolutely> quiet

50 **UK** Duchemin at; **MS** Duchemin <and to stamp him> at

51 **UK** came down; **MS** came <low> down

52 **UK** mediæval saint's; **MS** mediæval <sculpture of [some]> saint's

53 **UK** Duchemin. Mrs. Duchemin; **MS** Duchemin. <With this [new] bond> Mrs. Duchemin

54 **UK** word. There; **MS** word <for a quality that [illegible doubly deleted word] he had always considered delectable. For>. There

55 **UK, TR, US** Delawnay; **MS** Delaunay
Though the fourth letter isn't clear, 'Delaunay' is confirmed by the long dele-tion in note 59 below. Ford would have known the name by 1923–4 from the avant-garde artists Robert and Sonia Delaunay.

56 **UK** Her assured; **MS** Her <mysterious ↑enigmatic↓> assured

57 **UK, TR, US** as of a; **MS** as if a

58 **UK** once artistic—absolutely; **MS** once <authentic> ↑artistic↓ — absolutely

59 **UK** fit. She had; **MS** fit. <↑Mrs↓ Tietjens always objected to at least one half of the ladies in the drawing rooms of Mrs. Cressy, the Hon. Mrs. Limoux and Mrs. Delaunay, that their clothers appeared to have been cut out of sage green sacking with garden shears and machined together with parcel string. She couldn't say that of Mrs. Tietjens Duchemin. Mrs. Duchemin> ↑She↓ had

60 **UK** thought! ¶ Suddenly; **MS** thought! <But otherwise she had not seemed very overwhelmingly intellectual. He did not ask for that. The genuine, pur [sang], women of the Aesthetic Movement had been described as odalisques and, if he did not absolutely want that> ¶ Suddenly

61 **UK** Influence!" ¶ A vista; **MS** Influence!" ¶ <In a daydream> A vista

62 **UK, US** accepted the invitation; **MS, TR** accepted an invitation

63 **UK, TR, US** Claudine; **MS** Claude

64 **UK** kedgeree Claudine gives; **MS** kedgeree <Geraldine> ↑Claudine↓ gives

65 **UK** cook. Claudine has; **MS** cook. <Geraldine> ↑Claudine↓ has

66 In **MS** this originally read 'carriage accident'. This was deleted and replaced with 'motor accident', and the following sentence (to 'met with frequent accidents') inserted in the margin: presumably to prepare for, or in Ford's and Conrad's term 'justify', the accident in I.vii when Campion crashes his car into the dog-cart Tietjens is in with Valentine.

67 **UK** from his; **MS** from <attendance at> his

68 **UK** epethet; **MS, TR, US**, epithet

69 **UK** lying attorney; **MS** lying <[swine]> attorney
The following clause concluding the sentence (from 'and') is inserted at the foot of the page in MS.

70 **UK, TR, US** Tietjens' table; **MS** Tietjens table

71 In **MS** this last sentence is in a tighter, neater version of Ford's hand, and the 'W' overwrites the original closing inverted commas, showing that it was a later addition.

72 The three occurrences of 'Mountby' here, in the next paragraph, and seven paragraphs below appear to be spelt without the 's' in MS. UK, TR, and US

all read 'Mountby'.
73 **UK** Minister's features were distorted; **MS** Minister's <face was> ↑features were↓ distorted
74 **UK** words in; **MS** words: <[impressed]> in
75 **UK** writing. *Not;* **MS** writing, <in little squares>. *Not*
76 **UK, US, MS** sister; **TR** sister's
77 **UK, TR, US** pity!; **MS** *pity!*
78 **UK** and there; **MS** and <in his [careful] way, he knew that> there
79 **UK** to dinner; **MS** to <the cold> dinner
80 **UK, US** Oh!; **MS, TR** Oo!
    This supports the evidence in I.ii that TR was being set from MS and not from UK proofs as in I.i.
81 **UK** isn't wise to; **MS** isn't <usual> ↑wise↓ to
82 **UK** eh . . . domestic circumstances; **MS** eh . . . <[private]> domestic circumstances
83 **UK, TR, US** oily; **MS** oiled
84 **UK, TR, US** last; **MS** Last
85 **UK, TR, US** these; **MS** those
86 **UK, TR, US** Waterslop; **MS** Waterslops
    The terminal 's' is indistinct in MS, but the other two instances of Sandbach's nickname for Waterhouse on 81 and 82 clearly include it.
87 **UK, TR, US** friendly; **MS** friendlily
88 **UK** tired. A; **MS** tired. <[The] moment after> A
89 **UK** actuarially sound; **MS** actuarially <[sound] for the country> sound
90 **MS** starts a new line for the General's speech; TR, UK, US don't.
91 The words 'in principle' were added in the left-hand margin of MS.
92 In MS, 'Sir' is inserted as an afterthought, presumably to emphasise how far Macmaster is straining his habitual deference in defence of his friend.
93 **UK, US, TR** disappointing; **MS** disapproving
94 **UK** did? ¶ Sandbach; **MS** did?" <¶ Tietjens said: ¶ But [Sir] . . ." ¶> Sandbach
95 **UK** I'm receiving this; **MS** I'm <taking> ↑receiving↓ this
96 **UK** competition wallah head clerks; **MS** competition <wallahs of> wallah head clerks
97 **UK** your mind!; **MS** your <head> mind!
    Again a small change, but one that shows Ford's care with these social registers, as Tietjens treads such a fine line between directness and respect.
98 **UK, US, TR** these; **MS** those
    Emended to be consistent with emendation above and because the two city men are outside, whereas 'these' would imply Campion and Macmaster.
99 **UK** plus one at; **MS** plus <[two]>↓one↑ at
100 **UK** plus two anywhere; **MS** plus <four> ↑two↓ anywhere

## Textual Notes for I.iv

1 **UK** distinct prismatic outlines; **MS** distinct ↑prismatic↓ outlines
2 **UK** road that; **MS** road <,. Ahead of them, on the next hole the two city men with their two caddies were [illegible]> that
3 **UK, US** Middlebrough, seven; **MS** Middlesborough, <which was> seven;

TR Middle orough [*sic*], seven; **Ed** Middlesbrough

4  **UK** The financial operations connected with the amalgamating; **MS** the ↑financial operations connected with the↓ amalgamating

5  **UK** of odium in; **MS** of <unpopularity> ↑odium↓ in

6  **UK** friend undisputably excelled; **MS** friend indisputably <[& consistently]> excelled; **TR, US** friend indisputably excelled
   In TR the initial 'i' of 'indisputably' is fainter and has a broader space before it than elsewhere on the line, suggesting a correction, probably from a 'u', and if so, supporting the possibility that TR was still being set from Duckworth proofs.

7  In MS the phrase 'when they golfed' is an addition in the left margin.

8  **UK** calculations as; **MS** calculations <when he had to play > as

9  In MS the words 'accounted for' are a marginal addition replacing a deleted word, possibly 'left'.

10 **UK, MS, US** fixed scowl was; **TR** fixed search was

11 **UK** a striped cotton; **MS** a <[pink]> striped cotton
   The deleted word is unclear, and might be 'print' (indicating a cheap fabric, contrasting with the tweed skirt). Nor is it unequivocally deleted; it may just have been over-written to change it or make it less illegible. But the uncertainties (about what the word is and what its status is) preclude restoring it. Cf. 370 n. 31.

12 **UK, MS, US** me I; **TR** me: I
   The 1948 Penguin and Bodley Head editors also felt punctuation was needed here, inserting a comma.

13 **UK** gesticulating. His; **MS** gesticulating <like the [mournful] King of boy's books>. His

14 **UK** open country. It; **MS** open country <, upon a sandhill>. It

15 **UK, TR, US** his clubs off; **MS** his <golf-bag> club [*sic*] off

16 **UK** companion's hat; **MS** companion's <flat, nondescript> hat

17 **UK** off." ¶ The Rt.; **MS** off." ¶ <Tietjens thought that> the Rt.

18 **UK** jump: up; **MS** jump: <It gave Tietjens a [painful] feeling>: up

19 **UK** land. Not; **MS** land <It was hopeless to follow [illegible] across the [intricacies] of the dyke.> Not
   The sentence 'Not one of them [. . .] bottom of the dyke' is a later marginal insertion.

20 **UK, TR, US** deviated; **MS** divagated

21 **UK** calmly; the heat; **MS** calmly; <he felt himself to be stronger in health. He observed on> the <the flanks> heat

22 **UK** Lowestoft fleet; **MS** Lowestoft <fishing> fleet

23 **UK** Archangel vessel; **MS** Archangel <boat> ↓vessel↑

24 **UK** stoneware, washing; **MS** stone-ware washing

25 Here all witnesses read 'Mountby'.

26 **UK** General's superior age and; **MS** General's <white hair> ↑superior age↓ and

27 **UK, MS** Macmaster; **TR, US** Tietjens

28 **UK, US** brilliant fellow. . . . I only want, my dear boy, to hint that . . . ; **MS** brilliant fellows . . <It isn't as if I were admonishing a young subaltern for his good. About women no doubt. . . >. I only want, my dear boy, to hint . . . . ; **TR** brilliant fellows. . . . I only want, my dear boy, to hint. . .

29 **UK** friend" ¶ "Then"; **MS** friend" <and I've played with your children and

you've [hammered?] into us all with a razor strap.>" ¶ "Then

30 **UK** a bookmaker's secretary," Tietjens; **MS** a <tea shop waitress> ↑bookmaker's secretary↓," Tietjens

31 **UK, US** discreditable."; **MS** discreditable ...."; **TR** discreditable..."; **Ed** discreditable ..."

It's clear from 'The General interrupted' that Tietjens doesn't complete the sentence, which makes the US/UK punctuation inconsistent.

32 **UK** believe you; **MS** believe him

33 **UK** glory! Through; **MS** glory! <and guided the [trollops]> Through

34 **UK** Haymarket, of; **MS** Haymarket <with your hand under her elbow as if she'd been the Duchess of Rutland. That's what Sandbach said .... > of

35 **UK** said: ¶ "I was; **MS** said: ¶ "<I don't consider," he began resolutely, "that anyone but you would have a right to an explanation.> " I was

36 The passage from 'one to be seen [...] public official' is added in the left-hand margin, replacing the deleted passage: 'a female of the first [water], at any rate in the matter of ["his"]'

37 **UK** Army. I leave; **MS** Army. <That's the general opinion and I know it is right... So > I leave

38 **UK** did...." He had told the exact truth, but he was not; **MS** did...." <He was [certainly]> ↑He had told the exact truth, but he was↓ not

39 There is a heavily scored illegible deletion of several words here in MS.

40 **UK** now. You've; **MS** now. <And that's what you've got to do.... That> You've

Deletion replaced by insertion in left-hand margin: 'You've told me the story you want told and it's the story I'll tell for you! But that'

41 **UK, US** girl who demonstrates?" ¶ "Sandbach; **MS** girl on the ...." ¶ "<[Yes]> Sandbach; **TR** girl on the..." ¶ "Sandbach

42 **UK** women." ¶ "I say; **MS** women." <But ....">¶ "I say

43 The phrase 'the only novel worth reading since the eighteenth century' was a later insertion in the left-hand margin.

44 **UK** courting in; **MS** courting <behind the shop> in

45 **UK** Lady Claudine; **MS** Lady <Paul> Claudine

46 **UK, US** as that, but you; **MS, TR** as that, you

47 **UK** would be." ¶ "What; **MS** would be." ¶ "<I know you aren't," Tietjens said. "You're being of the greatest use to me>. "What

This deleted passage begins what appears to be a supplementary page, numbered '85a', written to replace the long deletion at the top of the following MS page. See note 50 below. It ends with 'But I may tell you that but for your', with the remaining blank page filled with a vertical squiggle to indicated that this passage is continued on the next page.

48 The passage 'And, of course [...] track! ...' is an addition in the left-hand margin.

49 **UK, US** shyness—pain; **MS, TR** shyness and pain

Ford's characteristic ampersand, looking more like a '+' with a short vertical, has misled the compositor here.

50 Long deleted passage at the top of **MS** leaf 86:

**UK** but for your mother-in-law; **MS** but for your

<"I know you aren't," Tietjens said, "you're being of the greatest use to me. "What does it amount to?"

"Only," the General said, "that you ... your views are immoral. And that

you're extravagant... Oh, hang it. Eternal hansoms and taxis and telegrams... You know my boy times aren't what they were when your father and I married. You could do it on five hundred a year, then.... But now ... and then that girl too.... Of course Mrs. Satterthwaite backs you through thick and thin ... But you know what women are with a handsome son in law. And Mrs. Satterthwaite never did justice to Sylvia. . But I may tell you that but for your>
mother-in-law

51 **UK** said ..." ¶ "I'll wash; **MS** said"... <I'll see if I want to answer anything.> ¶ "I'll wash

52 **MS** drops a line here. That Ford saw this point as a pause is supported by the fact that it also served as the end of the TR April instalment – the last part we can be certain was set before the publication of UK. See 'A Note on the Text', xci.

53 **UK** problems. The fly; **MS** problems. <They buzzed at the back of his mind, past landscapes and behind discussions like a dull ache that, in periods of silence became the buzz of a mechanical saw. The fly went with the slow pomp of a> The fly
The passage in UK 'The fly [...] pomp of a' is an insertion in the left-hand margin. Presumably the repeated 'buzz' here introduced unwanted associations with 'fly'!

54 **UK, US** soundness! ¶ Two; **TR** soundness! ¶ The two; **MS** soundness! ¶ <It appeared that> The two

55 **UK** police. The; **MS** police. <[illegible deletion: possibly:] [The police, themselves, wouldn't do anything.]> The

56 **UK, US** and guiltily, that; **MS** and quietly, that; **TR** and clearly, that
Campion's dressing down of the two men is too haughty to be described as done 'guiltily'. The 'e' is elongated, making the word look like 'quiltly', accounting for UK's misreading. It's not plausible that TR's compositor misread it as 'clearly', however, which must be a proof correction. If Ford's, it is debatable whether it were made before the publication of UK (see note 52 above). Thus I have preferred MS's reading as what UK should have followed.

57 **UK** about Tietjens. ¶ Tietjens; **MS** about Tietjens. <In the jolting conveyance the General shouted: ¶ "You know you shouldn't act that way"> ¶ Tietjens

58 **UK** that the fault; **MS** that <he supposed [he shouldn't and that the]> fault

59 **UK** gentlemen's company of such social swipes; **MS** gentlemen's <society of such [illegible]> ↑company of such social↓ swipes

60 **UK** politics. A bit; **MS** politics. <They couldn't ask for everything in those days.> A bit

61 **UK** everything! And; **MS** everything! <in those days.> And

62 **UK** mind. To; **MS** mind. <so that it would not crop up again until he let it.> To

63 **UK** listened. The; **MS** listened. <He was examining his own position.> The

64 In **MS** the phrase 'could usually ignore allegations against himself and' is inserted in the left-hand margin.

65 **UK** more. And; **MS** more. <and he considered himself to be fairly indifferent to what was said of himself as long as he didn't hear what was said.> And

66 **UK** the strumpet. That; **MS** the <whore> ↑strumpet↓. That

67  **UK** But he; **MS** But <[he considered that]> he
68  In **MS** the following passage is inserted in the left-hand margin: 'more vigor-
    ously. For he imagined that, had he really tried, he could have made the
    General believe him. But he had behaved rightly! It was not mere vanity.'
    It replaces the deletion: <And [illegible] rightly! [Gallantly]!>
69  **UK** mother! ¶ The General; **MS** mother! <He considered then that he had
    acted rightly, put the subject away and had done with it till he chose to re-
    consider it in the light of his future life with his wife.> ¶ The General
70  **UK, TR** Henry VIII. built; **MS, US** Henry VIII built
71  **UK, US** that the tide floated here, and; **MS** that he tide-floated here <from
    Normandy>, and; **TR** that was tide-floated here, and
    The US/UK reading is disconcertingly without human agency, whereas MS
    has a clear dot serving as a hyphen, making 'tide' part of the verb, not its
    subject. That TR also has 'tide-floated' indicates that Ford (if he proofread
    the May issue) either let it stand as what he had written in MS, or (if this
    instalment was being set from Duckworth proofs) corrected it back. (That
    alternative may seem less likely given that he didn't make the correction in
    the Duckworth proofs themselves, but see the following note for a clearer
    example of TR reading correctly what UK gets wrong – suggesting that UK
    was in press and no longer correctable when the May TR issue was being
    typeset.)
72  **UK, US** your tiny pet things; **MS** your tin pot things; **TR** your tin-pot things
73  **UK, TR** Henry VIII. as; **MS, US** Henry VIII as
74  **UK** listening. He; **MS** listening. <The General was off on a long tale of mili-
    tary grievances against an indifferent public and a government of traitors.
    On Tietjens the [cloud] had settled down again.> He
75  **UK** women with; **MS** women <he was thinking> with
76  **UK** just groaning at the thought of the; **MS** just <denouncing> ↑groaning
    at the thought of↓ the
77  **UK** himself. . . . ¶ In; **MS** himself. . . . <It felt like one of those dreams when,
    for a second, you dream that you are falling.> ¶ In
78  **UK, US** was aware that; **MS, TR** was anxious that
79  **UK** but a five; **MS** but <[he hated to be made to look a fool]> a five
80  **UK** cream of; **MS** cream <for all the world those> of
81  **UK** with gratitude; **MS** with <interest and even> with gratitude
82  **UK, US** You look at a; **MS, TR** You took a
83  **UK, TR, US** some Russian; **MS** some depressed Russian
84  **TR** omits the last two paragraphs of I.iv.

## Textual Notes for I.v

1   **UK** at school of course; **MS** at <Eton> ↑school↓ of course
2   **UK** said: ¶ "Let's; **MS** said: ¶ <"Look here Edie . . . > "Let's
3   **UK** months. I; **MS** months. <I don't know why. Or I do.> I
4   **UK** pride. And; **MS** pride. <Besides I was only seventeen> And
    The passage including this deletion, from 'But if we've inherited [. . .] after
    the sale', is written on the last three lines of leaf 93 of MS, but is ringed round
    and moved two lines up.
5   **UK, US** an athletic; **MS, TR** an athlete

6  **UK** tic ...; **MS** tic, <but he did> ....
7  **UK, TR, US** me; that it's said; **MS** me; <I've been a slavey>. That <they're> ↑it's↓ said
   While it looks possible that the compositors missed the capital 'T', since Ford had left both the semi-colon and full stop standing, I have not emended UK since the reading is shared with TR.
8  **UK** Gilbert as soon as we talked at all....; **MS** Gilbert <almost> as soon as we talked <English> ↑at all↓ ....
9  **UK** virtuous." ¶ Mrs. Duchemin; **MS** virtuous." ¶ <Miss Wannop had tears in her eyes. She said quickly: ¶ "Now don't [run/rush? upon] me just yet. It's difficult to [talk like] that. It upsets me. But it had to be done." ¶> Mrs. Duchemin
10 **UK** too. Because; **MS** too <, if you want to know>. Because
11 **UK** only twenty-two!; **MS** only <nineteen> ↑twenty-two↓!
12 **UK** anti. Don't; **MS** anti. < – let it go at that.> Don't
13 **UK, MS, TR, US** Cliquot; **Ed** Clicquot
14 **UK, US** Then; **MS, TR** When
   'When' makes the paper's threat an example of the 'tight places' he has rescued her from; but it's possible Ford emended it to 'Then' to emphasise the sequence of events.
15 **UK** tortured, body; **MS** tortured, <that we ...> body
16 **UK, TR** Censorious!; **MS, US** Censorious!
17 **UK** said. ¶ "It; **MS** said. <You've got to keep the spoon level and your mind on the egg past all sorts of obstacles and all sorts of temptations to look up."> ¶ "It
   Did Ford cut this because it didn't work dramatically – since Mrs Duchemin doesn't need the rules explained to her? Or because English readers didn't? Or was it because Valentine's harping on her analogy began to make it sound (too salaciously for the character Ford had in mind for her) like she was punning between 'egg' and ovum, and 'spoon' and 'spooning'?
18 **UK** not turning; **MS** not <dropping the golden> turning
19 **UK** real truth hidden in the; **MS** real <symbolic meaning of> ↑truth hidden in↓ the
20 **UK** them, for; **MS** them <↑[illegible]↓ [&]it was observed that they were all> for
21 **UK** voice. He **MS** voice. <which he modified [purposely] by an [infantine titter]>. He
22 **UK** him, because; **MS** him, <not so much because he was rude as> because
23 **UK** success.... ¶ "A STATE; **MS** success.... <Mr. Horsley from reading the papers as to the distressing conditions of North and South embattled one against another in Ireland, had got hold of the phrase, not then very usual in the world: a state of siege. And, his hollow eyes dancing with excitement, he used it to death.> ¶ "A STATE
24 **UK, MS, US** Mountby; **TR** Mounby
25 **UK** arms. ¶ As; **MS** arms. <Effie Marsh had had a recurrence of her epileptic fits, old Mrs. Hogben of Nobey one of her bad heart attacks; two of the motor bicycles had collided at [Iden] corner ...> ¶ As
26 **UK** and afforded; **MS** and, <the others having to be perforce silent, it> afforded
27 **UK** other. Miss; **MS** other, <their mouths and eyes wide open>. Miss

28 **UK** Gertie; **MS** <Effie> ↑Gertie↓
29 **UK, US** masked; **MS, TR** marked
30 **UK** perturbations. of; **MS, TR** perturbations of; **US** perturbations, of
   The full stop in UK is clearly an error. US's comma confuses the sense.
   Valentine is not thinking of a criminal, she's having the perturbations of
   one, fearing the police are after her.
31 **UK** that. ¶ In every; **MS** that. ¶ <The << sup suppression>> suppression of
   his feelings to which Tietjens disciplined himself did not extend to the
   suppression of <<feelings>> ↑emotions↓ of agreeable surprise on meeting
   individuals. If he felt pleasurable surprise he just showed it: he couldn't see
   why he shouldn't. And he was surprised. He hadn't been able to understand
   the General's last night's emotions over what he remembered as a frowning
   girl ↑who confessed to having been in domestic service↓: very pale, though
   she should have been red with running; in a cheap [cottager's] pink blouse:
   cheap boy's running shoes and a cheap white hat. The skirt had been all
   right. He saw now that the General hadn't been such an ass as he had
   supposed. ¶ Tietjens, in fact, was critical of women's dress – as an indication
   of social or moral appropriatenesses. He saw at once that the pink blouse had
   enhanced the girl's paleness: he knew too at once that the girl must have put
   on those cheap things to keep in countenance the poor, shabby, London
   Gertie. She was now all right. The skirt was the same: well cut and hanging
   well. She had the proper colour for a girl who could run, jump quite neatly
   and call out well from good lungs. The silk blouse was well cut too and the
   cream colour did not take away from her complexion. Her hair now visible
   because she was bare-headed, was healthily gold, [short] and plaited round
   her head ... a style Tietjens liked in youngish girls because it revealed the
   youthful nape of the neck and the slight <<suggestion>> hint of round
   shoulderdedness [sic] that suggests humility. The shoes were good, sensible,
   well-cleaned brown brogues with moccasin, shredded leather bunches over
   the [insteps]. Tietjens did not consider the moccasin bunches sensible.
   <<But>> Yet something must be offered for coquetry.... > ¶ <[Neverthe-
   less]> In every

   This long passage underwent minor revisions, before being deleted *in toto*
   with a light grid of vertical and horizontal lines (leaving it clearer to transcribe than many of the shorter deletions). These minor revision are
   indicated above with double angled brackets.
32 The long passage from here to the end of the next paragraph ('[...] club
   gossip!') is written on a supplementary leaf, numbered 99a, and replaces the
   following paragraph deleted from the top of leaf 100 (again with minor deletions and revisions, then overall cancelling:

   side, the one correcting the other: emotion against reason, intellect correcting passion, first impressions acting simultaneously with quick reflection.
   Yet first impressions have always a bias in their favour and quiet reflection
   has often a job to efface them. Quite naturally, the night before Tietjens had
   given several thoughts to this young woman whom General Campion had
   assigned to him as *maîtresse en titre*. <[Obviously] *en titre* because> He was
   supposed to have ruined himself, and broken up his home, over her. That
   was in itself <as a matter of fact unremarkable,> silly gossip. He couldn't
   remember having spent since his marriage one penny of his own, let alone

Sylvia's, on any woman. [But] that he should have ruined himself over an unpresentable young female of the servant class! That went beyond anything in sheer imbecility....

33 **UK** *maîtresse du titre*; **MS, TR, US** *maîtresse en titre*
34 **UK** For Tietjens; **MS** For <And that made a strong [case] for Miss Wannop [since]> Tietjens
35 **UK** was of; **MS** was <it was true [the] daughter of a very brilliant man; of a [very brilliant man]> of
36 **UK** to. ¶ But; **MS** to. ¶ <And that was what Tietjens' reflections, as far as they had gone and as far as they concerned Miss Wannop, had got to at the time of their meeting.... ¶ He found himself now thinking her suddenly, quite marriageable for some one not very brilliant.... It was probably the ecclesiastical calibre of Mr. Horsley's voice, booming on, that suggested a definite [putting] in words of the thought. Half the courtships in England are conducted by glances in country churches: marriages take place to those intonations; the church is in any case an [oversexed] affair; and wasn't it from behind a pillar, to nasal boomings and reed-stopped tones, that Faust watched Gretchen? Miss Wannop, if she could sing, would make a good Gretchen at a country house rendering of Gounod's *Faust*. Her eyes when they were not diminished by a frown were a remarkable spinning blue.> ¶ But

This long deleted passage was replaced by the two paragraphs from 'But, brightened up [. . .] pressure of suggestion!', which are written on a supplementary leaf, numbered 100a.

37 **UK** and considered; **MS** and <a glance was enough to let him> considered
38 **UK, US** turret; **MS** [throat]; **TR** throat
The word looks extraordinarily like 'turret' in MS; but the emendation is warranted not only by TR's reading, and the need to make better sense, but by the close match with later occurrences of the word 'throat', as on leaf 258 (p. 316 here) and especially leaf 259 (p. 317). Mrs. Duchemin's voice is described as 'deep' on 299 and 302.
39 **UK, TR, US** Haglen; **MS** Hogben
The name at this point in MS is easily read as 'Haglen' but in the deleted passage on leaf 98 (see note 25 above) it is clearly 'Hogben', a name Ford knew from the farmhouse at Aldington which the Conrads had rented in 1908: Hogben House.
40 **UK** to Macmaster and the extinction of her interest in himself had been; **MS** to Macmaster ↑and the extinction of her interest in himself↓ had been
41 **UK** said: ¶ "What have you done with Gertie?" ¶ "Gertie!"; **MS** said: ¶ <"But mother!> "What have you done with <Effie> ↑Gertie↓ "? ¶ "<Effie> Gertie!"
42 **UK** to-day. So we had!" She; **MS** to-day. ↑So we had!↓" She
43 **UK** then went on brightly: "Of course; **MS** then <said> ↑went on↓ brightly: <to Macmaster> "Of course
44 **UK** look at Gertie Wilson; **MS** look at <Effie> ↑Gertie↓ Wilson
45 **UK** eleven; **MS** <twelve> eleven
This correction shows Ford's care with the time-scheme. The breakfast begins at about ten (see 69, where Mrs Duchemin tells Macmaster her car will call at quarter to ten to pick him and Tietjens up; and 116, where she

says it's hard to give a breakfast before ten).

46 **UK** morning. If she did, the news would; **MS** morning. <It> ↑If she did the news↓ would

47 **UK** present. The; **MS** present. <On this occasion>, the

48 This sentence appears to have been an afterthought in MS. Though the first five words complete the first paragraph on leaf 103, the nib was drier, suggesting a later addition; anyway, the continuation of the sentence is inserted at the head of the leaf.

49 **UK** Her arrival worried; **MS** <This> ↑Her arrival↓ worried
A revision necessitated by the addition of the preceding sentence.

50 **UK** easy. Mrs. Wannop, who was uninvited, refused; **MS** easy; <the arrival of> Mrs. <Duchemin> ↑Wannop↓, who was uninvited <having upset the balance of their table. And Mrs. Wannop> refused

51 **UK** window. It; **MS** window. <And indeed> It

52 **UK** Mrs.; **MS**, **TR**, **US** Mr.

53 **UK** lady with; **MS** lady <and accomplished it> with

54 **UK** reserved for Miss Gertie Wilson; **MS** reserved for <her, or rather> for [*sic*] Miss Gertie Wilson
The chair couldn't have been reserved for Mrs Wannop since she was uninvited.

55 **UK** Macmaster, her eyes; **MS** Macmaster, <Mrs Duchemin> her eyes

56 **UK** sufferings, he might; **MS** sufferings <and her [perturbations]>, he might

57 **UK** lovely; their scent; **MS** lovely <beyond belief>; their scent

58 **UK** was setting up; **MS** was <[obviously]> setting up

59 **UK**, **TR** Sevres; **MS**, **US** Sèvres

60 **UK** Caliban. ¶ She buckled; **MS** Caliban. <Now she had to pay for it. . . .> She buckled

61 **UK** he asked. ¶ "Oh!"; **MS** he asked. <"In summer!"> ¶ "Oh!"

62 **UK**, **TR**, **US** salmon, and red mullet, this; **MS** salmon, red mullet, this
The comma after 'salmon' is larger than usual, and was perhaps misread as an ampersand. The version in MS avoids the awkwardness of using 'and' there but not before 'this'; 'this' presumably refers to the caviare.

63 **UK** careful sentences on; **MS** careful <phrases> ↑sentences↓ on

64 **UK** fellow; she couldn't; **MS** fellow; <he seemed however to force her>: she couldn't

65 **UK** moods her husband had told; **MS** moods <Ruskin> ↑her husband↓ had told

66 **UK** monstrous, and; **MS** monstrous, <in her eyes> and

67 **UK**, **TR**, **US** if ever—" For; **MS** if ever . . . ." For; **Ed** if ever . . ." For
In MS two pairs of suspension dots have smudged together. It appears the compositor misread these as dashes, and took the punctuation to be an em dash despite the dots being on the bottom of the line.

68 **UK** the man on her other side. He was the male; **MS** the <[other man . . . of]> ↑man on her other side. He was↓ the male

69 **UK** feelings. . . . ¶ She; **MS** feelings. . . . <That was a bad moment for the friendship [of] Tietjens and Macmaster>. . . . ¶ She

70 **UK**, **MS**, **TR**, **US** *tristia*

71 Unclear sequence of revisions here; partly legible deletions might read: '<But it seemed> sardonically <to [her that her every framing] of the inevitable [illegible]>'. The word 'sardonically' has been ringed and moved to the previous sentence.

72 **UK** familiarity of; **MS** familiarity <as it were> of

73 **UK** that already; **MS** that <there were> already
The words 'were developing' appear to be a later addition with a drier or finer nib.

74 **UK** gloating, cruel tones that had asked; **MS** gloating, <as if> cruel tones <asking> that had asked

75 **UK, TR, US** that; **MS** *that*

76 **UK** Parry! the Bermondsey light middle-weight! He's there to carry Duchemin off if he becomes violent!" ¶ During the quick look; **MS** Parry! the ↓Bermondsey↑ light middle-weight! <They do these things in style!> He's there to carry Duchemin off if he becomes violent!" ¶ During <In the course of> the quick look

77 Sentence inserted in left-hand margin.

78 **UK** was settled; **MS** was <at last> settled

79 **UK** Tietjens said; **MS** Tietjens <, [coming] back to her, from his glance round the table>, said

80 **UK** with your husband's tendencies; **MS** with <those> ↑your husband's↓ tendencies

81 **UK** morale. Macmaster; **MS** morale. <She *knew* that, as far as such a thing could be done, this had been well done. And> Macmaster

82 **UK, US** snuffingly; **MS** snufflingly

83 **UK** *Trimaldrian*; **MS, TR, US** *Trimalchion*

84 **UK, MS** snuffling; **US** snuffing

85 **UK** *Froturianas*; **MS** Festinamus; **TR, US** *Festinans*
'callidus' means skilful or crafty; 'calidus' (which the Knopf edition assumes, emending to 'calide') means 'warm'.

86 **UK** have guessed!; **MS** have <argued out> ↑guessed↓!

87 **UK** here. One; **MS** here. <She said it [of course] gently; but with firmness. She was going to make her [move] against this minatory being. She knew that *he* knew that women can influence even the relationships of one's best man friend. She was going to convey to him that she would not [take him lying down] She added: > One

88 **UK** of bounders get; **MS** of <people> ↑bounders↓ get

89 **UK** Macmaster four minutes before had; **MS** Macmaster ↑four minutes before↓ had

90 **UK** had moved a hand; **MS** had <motioned> moved a hand
The phrase 'moved a hand' is inserted in left-hand margin.

91 This sentence is an addition in MS, inserted in a gap after the following sentence.

92 **UK, US** words. Mrs.; **TR** words Mrs.
TR has a blemish just below the line, which the compositor of UK possibly misread as a full stop. But in MS the phrase 'Mrs. Duchemin—and Tietjens!—had heard.' is inserted at the foot of the page, with a caret next to but not quite deleting the original full stop.

93 The second half of this sentence (after 'enough') is a later left-hand marginal insertion in MS.

94 In MS the friend's name appears originally to have been 'Smith' at these first two references to him.

95 **UK** prestige in; **MS** prestige <or gratitude> in

96 **UK** to an intimacy; **MS** to <a certain> ↑an↓ intimacy

97 **UK** Willanrovitz Möllendorf; **MS, TR, US** Willamovitz Möllendorf
*When Blood* xvi–xvii gives the name as Willamovitz-Moellerndorff. In MS the next paragraph began with the following deleted passage: '<Mr. Duchemin put his thin hand ↑on Macmaster's arm↓– it had a great cornelian seal set in red gold on the third finger. He went on quoting in ecstasy>'.

98 **UK** quickly back; **MS** quickly <away and> back

99 **UK** himself, partly; **MS** himself, <observing Mr. Duchemin as a phenomenon>; partly

100 **UK** feeling admiration; **MS** feeling <gratitude and> admiration

101 **UK** agony. Macmaster; **MS** agony. <She imagined> Macmaster

102 **UK** a position; **MS** a <situation> position

103 **TR** muddles the sequence here. At this point (the middle of 457 of the June instalment) it drops the following page and two-fifths of UK, resuming with 'Suddenly, from behind Macmaster's back [. . .]'. The missing passage reappears on 458–9 of TR, absurdly interrupting Macmaster's whispering to Parry with his response to being touched by Mrs Duchemin.

104 **UK** Mrs. Duchemin; her; **MS** Mrs. <Macmaster> ↑Duchemin↓: her

105 **UK, US** *duma casta et sola*; **MS, TR** *dum casta et sola*

106 **UK** grew slowly crimson; **MS** grew <suddenly> ↑slowly↓ crimson

107 This clause is an insertion in the left-hand margin in MS.

108 **UK** for you from; **MS** for you <by the bye> from

109 The final three-and-a-half lines after this point at the foot of leaf 111 of MS (up to 'could get Mr.') are written with a finer/drier nib. They appear to be a later revision, replacing the following deleted passage at the top of leaf 112: '<Macmaster had been whispering swiftly to Parry the prize-fighter who had twice touched his master on the arm and shouted: ¶ "Your breakfast's getting cold!" Parry whispered that he ↑and the Rev. Horsley↓ could get Mr.>'. The superscript insertion replaces the deleted sentence coming after the end of this one: '<[Him] and the Rev. Horsley could do it.>'.

110 **UK** face. Mrs. Duchemin; **MS** face. <for the sake of effect.> Mrs. Duchemin

111 **UK** Duchemin thought that the arrow of God struck; **MS** Duchemin <imagined> ↑thought↓ that the arrow of God <had> struck

112 **UK** "Forgive!" with; **MS** "Forgive!" <and passing the smallest handkerchief in her palm across her eyes> ↑<[illegible word]>↓ with

113 **UK** cravings, can; **MS** cravings <for [illegible] [and the letting forth] of words>, can

114 **UK, TR, US** ensue; **MS** [ensue]
It is possible MS reads 'ensure'. The Bodley Head text's emendation to 'endure' is more idiomatic, but is not warranted by MS. The OED records an archaic sense of 'ensue' as 'To follow or seek after, strive to obtain, aim at', and gives a citation from 1874.

115 **UK** pressure. But; **MS** pressure. <that should have said many things to him.> But

116 **UK, TR, US** asked; **MS** said
Emended because the speech is not a question.

117 **UK** friend ¶ Mrs. Wannop; **MS** friend ¶ <Suddenly> Mrs. Wannop

118 **UK, TR, US** talking; **MS** booming

119 **UK** The *Mosella* of Ausonius; the subject of the essay he was writing is

mostly about fish. . . . ; **MS** The *Mosella* of Ausonius: the subject of the essay he was writing, is mostly about fish. . . ; **TR** The *Mosella* of Ausonius, the subject of the essay he was writing is mostly about fish.; **US** The *Mosella* of Ausonius, the subject of the essay he was writing, is mostly about fish. . . . The Bodley Head edition (130) drops the 'about', presumably on the grounds that it would be a solecism to write 'the subject [. . .] is about fish'. But that construction was made possible by the dropping of MS's comma after 'writing'. Ford's use of the colon (or perhaps semi-colon) after 'Ausonius' is confusing (it was emended in TR to a comma), and perhaps suggests a change of mind during the course of the sentence. But US's punctuation is both closest to MS and makes the best sense.

120 There are spurious opening double inverted commas before *Vannulis* in all witnesses. Presumably Ford wanted the quotation in inverted commas, but forgot to close them, so single inverted commas have been supplied here.

121 **UK, US** horse; **TR** house; MS could support either reading.

122 **UK** parents. In her; **MS** parents. <Mr. Horsley with [discreet] farewells, and Miss Fox without any, had disappeared through the panelled door.> In her

123 **UK** there. . . . ¶ The echoes; **MS** there. . . . <And they had all said: "Certainly!" and "Oh [surely . . . .]>" ¶ The echoes

124 **UK** didn't know. . . . Almost harshly she exclaimed; **MS** didn't know. . . . <She exclaimed> Almost harshly <almost beginning with: "Before you go any further>," she exclaimed

125 **UK, TR, US** abstractly; **MS** abstractedly

126 **UK, US** He's making calculations now. For the Government that no other man in England could make.; **MS** He's making calculations now. For the Government. That no other man in England could make.; **TR** He's making calculations now for the Government that no other man in England could make.

The punctuation in UK and US summons up the unwanted meaning that it is the Government rather than the calculations Tietjens is making. The breathless parataxis of MS goes better with the following fragmentary clause. If TR was being set from UK the compositor may have compounded the error by removing the full stop after 'now' in addition to that (in MS) after Government.

## Textual Notes for I.vi

1 In MS this is mis-numbered as a second chapter V, a slip which was replicated in TR, UK, US, and even the 1948 Penguin edition. It was corrected for the 1950 Knopf first omnibus edition.

2 **UK** a ten foot; **MS** a <high> ten foot

3 **UK, TR, US** chaffinchs; **MS** chaffinches

4 **UK** *amonrer*; **MS, TR, US** *ammer*

5 **UK, US** coltsfoot; **MS, TR** cocksfoot
Cocksfoot, or *Dactylis glomerata* is found in rough grassland: 'This dense, tufted perennial grass has bluish-green leaves that are flattened at the base and are sharply pointed. The long flowering stems are topped with pyramidal, branched, densely packed, purplish flower spikelets vaguely reminiscent

of a chicken's foot, hence the name.' http://www.plantpress.com/wildlife/
o1058-cocksfoot.php
Coltsfoot, or *Tussilago farfara*, is a small yellow flower of the sunflower family,
and most amongst 'the best grass mixture for pemanent pasture'.

6   **UK, TR, US** my dear): So interesting!; **MS** my dear: So interesting!)
The phrase 'So interesting!' is clearly within the parenthesis in MS, and sits
better there as coming from the imagined voices of the 'best people', rather
than from the interior monologue of Tietjens, who is soon shown to be too
scathing of 'imbecile epithets' to make such a comment. The emendation is
also supported by analogy with 'So racy of the soil!' later in the paragraph.

7   **UK** poigle; **MS** Paigle; **TR**, **US** paigle

8   **UK, US** but; **MS, TR** let
MS repeats 'thrive', which is corrected to 'wive' in TR, UK, and US.

9   **UK, MS, TR, UK** maid's; **Ed** [and Shakespeare] maids

10 **UK, TR, US** literal; **MS** liberal
When Tietjens recalls this moment on 290, both MS and UK agree on
'liberal'.

11 **UK, TR** quotation; **MS, US** quotations

12 The words 'bad lunch. The young woman, so the young man is duly warned'
were dropped from TR.

13 **UK** pain; pickles, also preserved in wood-vinegar; two; **MS** pain; ↑pickles,
also preserved in wood-vinegar↓; two

14 **UK** himself in high good humour. "'Land; **MS** himself ↑in high good
humour↓. "'Land

15 **UK** all wood wind; **MS** all <strings> wood wind

16 The following passage, from 'Pipe exactly right' to 'may not go abroad', was
written at the end of this paragraph in MS, ringed and moved up to its
current position.

17 **UK, TR, US** however else; **MS** how else

18 **UK** long! . . Why; **MS, TR, US** long! . . . Why

19 **UK, US** sung: 'Highland Mary' a better tune than 'This; **MS** sung: "Highland Mary", a better tune than: "This; **TR** sung: 'Highland Mary' a better
tune than 'This; **Ed** sung 'Highland Mary', a better tune than 'This
The comma after "'Highland Mary'" in MS is faint, but seems required. MS
uses colons before both song titles. The other witnesses inconsistently drop
the second (perhaps because TR's compositor seems to have been having
trouble with inverted commas, and got distracted). I've removed both on the
grounds that UK's punctuation is generally lighter than MS's.

20 **UK, TR, US** steps; **MS** step
Though Kentish stiles can have either one or two steps on each side, Ford
only mentions one on the first side. And, athletic though Valentine is, it's
hard to see how she could use two steps on the other side with the same foot.

21 **UK** infinitely pathetic. To let scandal attach to her; **MS** infinitely <attrac-
tive> pathetic. To let <[muddy be thrown at]> ↓scandal attach to↑ her

22 **UK** them?; **MS** then!; **TR** them!; **US** then?

23 **UK** Administraton; **MS, TR, US** Administration

24 Small illegible deletion after this in MS.

25 **UK, TR, US** settle; **MS** [nail]
The word in MS is certainly not 'settle'. It appears to end in a 't' (in which
case it might conceivably be 'rivet'), but the cross could be a near miss when

dotting the 'i'.

26 In MS the phrase 'along the opposite hedgerow' was written as the following line, and inserted here. The revision appears to have been made before the writing of the next paragraph (unless Ford had left a blank line between paragraphs and filled it later, which is unlikely since the action continues in the next paragraph). It is thus characteristic of his tendency to make minor revisions to recently composed passages.

27 **UK** she said; **MS** she <exclaimed> said

28 **UK, MS, TR, US** Mountby
See I.vii, endnote 63, where MS reverts to 'Mountsby'.

29 **UK** mad bullock; **MS** mad <[ox]> bullock
The revision was made immediately, suggesting the pun on Ford's name was unwelcome. Yet its appearance perhaps indicates the depth of identification with the character.

30 **UK** The voice of Mrs. Wannop—of course it was only mother! Twenty feet on high or so behind the kicking mare, with a good, round face like a peony—said; **MS** The voice of Mrs. Wannop said: (of course it was only mother! Twenty feet on high or so behind the kicking mare: with a good round face like a peony.) The voice said

31 **UK** from beside; **MS** from <behind> beside

32 **UK, TR, US** Stephen; **MS** Stop her
By the July instalment TR would probably have been set from UK, as would US in September/October; and Ford is unlikely to have been as attentive to proofs of either once the entire novel was already published. Thus any misreadings of MS made in UK are (arguably) more likely to stand in the other witnesses (so the fact they all agree carries less weight from the May or June issues onwards). The case for emending here is based not only on the difference between the form(s) here and the form of 'Stephen' (Waterhouse) on 67 of MS, but on the implausibility of Mrs Wannop's using Joel's full name – elsewhere he's only referred to as 'Joel' – while her horse is out of control. It's possible the manuscript was misread because the nearby male pronouns referring to the horse (see next note) may have made it harder to read this as 'her' – though it could indicate that the characteristically inaccurate Mrs Wannop is still under the impression the horse is a mare.

33 **UK, MS, TR, US** his bit: his mouth's
The Penguin (121) and Bodley Head (140) texts emend to 'her bit: her mouth's', presumably on the grounds that the horse has already been described as a 'mare'. But see the footnote to this paragraph, which shows Ford's exactness about how Tietjens is able to show how the horse has been mistakenly passed off as a mare.

34 **UK** knife like a schoolboy's. He; **MS** knife ↑like a schoolboy's↓. He

35 **UK, TR, US** no Yorkshireman; **MS** no horse coper and Yorkshireman

36 **UK** got you deuced good value; **MS** got you ↑deuced good↓ value

37 **UK** kept it in the sun; **MS** kept it <waiting> in the sun

38 **UK** her. She could have her husband put in a lunatic asylum to-morrow; **MS** her. <The cart went off at a gentle, regular trot.> She could have <that> her husband put in a lunatic asylum to-morrow.

39 **UK** poor, weak women; **MS** poor ↑weak↓ women

40 **UK** "I wasn't; **MS** "<Of course> I wasn't

41 MS has a deleted line here at the top of leaf 125: '<turning up from nowhere

in the nick of time>'.

42 **UK, TR, US** immensely, strongly; **MS** immensely strongly
Emended because in MS the 's' is detached from the rest of 'strongly', and appears to have been misread as a comma.

43 **UK** she's an anti; **MS** she's <really> an Anti

44 **UK** want. Women; **MS** want. <and he said drily [—] for> Women

45 **UK, TR, US** explained; **MS** exclaimed

46 MS has a mostly illegible deleted line here: '<They [continued thus] [illegible] >'

47 MS drops a line here, but this isn't followed in UK (where the break coincides with the end of 145) or the other witnesses. Reinstated for consistency with Ford's practice of dropping a line for changes of scene.

48 **UK** who, a few years ago; **MS** who, <five> a few years ago
The word 'few' is inserted in the left-hand margin, suggesting a later correction, probably to remove the inconsistency with 'four years' in the next paragraph.

49 **UK** the acuteness of that pang; **MS** the <sharpness> ↑acuteness↓ of that pang

50 **UK** feeling... Now; **US** feeling.... Now
Emended because UK departs from its usual practice of four dots after a completed sentence.

51 **UK, MS, TR** Tietjen's; **US** Tietjens'

52 **UK** said... And; **US** said.... And
Again emended following US to conform to UK's usual practice. Though MS uses three dots here, its handling of ellipses is erratic. It uses four after this 'And', corrected in both UK and US to three as an incomplete sentence.

53 **UK, TR**, sublimal; **MS, US** subliminal

54 **UK, MS, TR** log!" He's; **US** log!' He's

55 **UK, TR, US** clever stupidities; **MS** clever-stupidities
The hyphen, typically of Ford's practice here, is a dot near the left-hand word, rather than a dash filling up the space between the words. Restored here because easily missed by a compositor, though clear enough when looked for, it is needed to stop 'ingenious clever' from reading like a tautology unworthy of Valentine. The phrase 'clever stupidity' evidently already had some currency. See for example George Eliot's *The Mill on the Floss*, Chapter III: 'It always seemed to me a sort of clever stupidity only to have one sort of talent,– almost like a carrier-pigeon'. The *OED* gives a citation from 1911 for the hyphenated compound 'clever-stupid'.

56 **UK** the girl who always; **MS** the <fellow> ↑girl↓ who always
In MS 'always' is inserted in the left-hand margin. Presumably Ford realised he needed to change the gender of the telegraphist (to fit 'Sylvia Hopside') and then wanted to emphasise that Valentine had previously received many telegrams from 'Hopside', so this was an understandable confusion.

57 **UK** Luxemburg." She went; **MS** Luxemburg." <She lifted up her tray and said: "So we're not going to war with Germany. I quite thought it was a code message from the paper. Mother moves in an atmosphere of these awfulnesses. and the German Emperor's interview *has* made a muddle of things.>" She <said she would leave them to finish their nap and> went
The *Daily Telegraph* had published an interview with Emperor Wilhelm II on 28 October 1908. His attempt to advance Anglo-German friendship went

disastrously wrong, since his outbursts alienated British readers, who took offence at reading comments like: 'You English are mad, mad, mad as March hares.'

58 **UK** taken twice the time, and would; **MS** taken <half> ↑twice↓ the time, <spilt half the crumbs on the carpet> and would

59 **UK** uses toys like fireworks; **MS** uses ↑toys like↓ fireworks

60 **UK, TR, US** usually; **MS** cruelly

61 **UK, MS, TR** sit putt; **US** sit put

62 **UK, TR, US** he said within himself, "if; **MS** he said, "if

63 This sentence appears within square brackets in MS, but without in UK, TR, and US.

64 **UK** for, in his mind, he felt; **MS** for, <[with]> ↑in↓ his mind, <Tietjens> he felt

65 **UK, TR, US** roof; **MS** roofs

66 **UK, TR, US** air. Tietjens; **MS** air: Tietjens
MS punctuation restored to restore the sense: 'Straining his intelligence, [...] Tietjens said'.

67 **UK** told you all that already. I can't go over it again; **MS** told you ↑all↓ that already. I can't go over it <all> again

68 **UK, MS, TR, US** Mountby

69 In MS '*you* won't repeat them' appears as a separate sentence in square brackets, preceded by a full stop instead of a dash.

## Textual Notes for I.vii

1 **UK, MS, TR, US** VI; **Ed** VII
See note 1 for previous chapter.

2 **UK** step of the dog-cart the girl; **MS** step ↑of the dog-cart↓ the girl

3 **UK, TR, US** completely disappeared; **MS** disappeared completely

4 **UK** more completely than if she had dropped into deep water, into snow—or; **MS** more completely <than if she had dropped into the blackness of [a cave]>: than if she had dropped into deep water, ↑into snow↓—or

5 **UK, MS, US** constation; **TR** constatation
Like Henry James, Ford was fond of using the French term *constatation* to denote an exact verbalisation. He appears to have made this slip twice in MS, which was duplicated in UK and US ('constation' is recorded neither in the OED nor in *Littré*), but corrected in both instances for TR.

6 **UK** grunts. But; **MS** grunts, <"[Ugh]!"> But

7 **UK** startling: ¶ "Make; **MS** startling: ¶ "<[Keep on]> Make

8 **UK, MS, US** constations; **TR** constatations

9 **UK** the absurd; **MS** the <extravagantly> absurd

10 **UK, TR, US** ken, John Peel at the break; **MS** ken John Peel and at break

11 **UK** at it, the only; **MS** at it, <[it being]> the only

12 **UK** two younger sons; **MS** two ↑younger↓ sons

13 UK and US have erroneous closing inverted commas here, which were left in MS after the deletion of an illegible short quotation.

14 **UK, MS** apopleptic; **US** apoplectic

15 **UK, TR, US** quiet; **MS** queer
Partridge and Beale, *A Dictionary of Slang*, 947, define a 'queer stick' as 'A

very odd, or incomprehensible, fellow'. The word is clear enough in MS. While 'quiet' could be an authorial revision, it seems more probably a misreading that made good enough sense (Mark *is* quiet) to escape detection.

16  **UK, TR, US** bowler-hat; **MS** bowler hat
When the phrase is repeated later in the paragraph, UK and TR omit the hyphen; US adds one. But neither instance is hyphenated in MS.

17  **UK, TR, MS** bowler hat!; **US** bowler-hat!

18  **UK** anyone shaken his head at Mark and; **MS** anyone <slightly> shaken his head ↑at Mark↓ and

19  In MS the clauses 'faulty in reasoning naturally, but quite intelligent' was originally written three sentences further down, after 'on both sides! ...'

20  In MS, the inverted commas indicating Tietjens' speech to himself close here, rather than after 'years.' three sentences above.

21  **UK** mind: remorseless; **MS** mind: <of humankind:> remorseless

22  **UK, TR, US** mirs; **Ed** mir's
MS is ambiguous here. There is a space between 'mir' and 's', but a single mark which appears to serve both as the dot for the 'i' and the apostrophe. In the partial quotation of these lines two pages later, there is an unequivocal apostrophe, so I have restored it here.

23  **UK, US** schwiegsame; **MS** schwiegsames; **TR** schweigsames
TR's reading is the correct German here, but Ford has spelled the word with 'ie' on both occasions in this chapter, and TR reverts to 'ie' on the second; so the question is whether the error is his or meant as Tietjens'. Given Ford's knowledge of German, I've thought it best to let MS stand.

24  **UK, TR, US** could; **MS** would

25  **UK** now. It; **MS** now: <[trusted her]>. It

26  **UK, TR, US** banished; **MS** broken

27  **UK** it being then just after cockcrow; **MS** it being then the [*sic*] <morning> ↑just↓ after cockcrow

28  In MS the clauses 'hoarse by now, of course—in June he changes his tune' appear in brackets (and with a full stop instead of a dash), and thus connect with the comments in brackets at the beginning of the previous chapter, which seem to be voices that Tietjens imagines uttering countryside clichés.

29  **UK, US** *schwiegsame*; **MS, TR** *schwiegsames*
See note 23 above. In MS this word is preceded by an illegible deletion.

30  **UK** From White ... The *Natural History*; **MS** From White ... <White's> The *Natural History*

31  **UK, TR, US** German." ¶ She; **MS** German." <[Caesar = Kaiser]!"> ¶ She

32  **UK, TR, US** unnecessarily; **MS** [unconscion]ably
The word is unclear in MS, but appears to end in '-ably'. It's possible Ford wrote 'unconscionably' and the compositor misread it, or that Ford decided to revise it in proof to a word that sounded less priggish as they become less defensive with each other.

33  **UK, TR, US** know; **MS** *know*

34  **UK** Sad tears mixed with kisses; **MS** Sad <kisses> ↑tears↓ mixed with <tears> ↑kisses↓

35  **UK** ought; **MS** *ought*

36  **UK** learned his Latin; **MS** learned <German> ↑his↓ Latin
The placing of the original closing inverted commas of this speech, which

fall above 'from' in MS, show that the phrase 'from the German' was an afterthought, added after the deletion of the earlier instance of 'German'.
37 **UK** my line!; **MS** my <*forte*> line!
38 **UK** said with the snuffy contempt of a scholar of Trinity College,
Cambridge. But; **MS** said ↑with the snuffy contempt of a scholar of Trinity
College, Cambridge↓ <[piteously]>. But
39 **UK** side-car, it; **MS** side-car <myself>: it
40 **UK** because I *knew*; **MS** because <you're so impossibly self-sufficient;> I
*knew*
41 **UK** side-car than driven with me."; **MS** side-car <if you [heard we had one]
. . . . > than driven with me" <if you [heard we had one]>."
42 **UK** I never drove it in my life. I looked; **MS** I <don't know it a bit> ↑never
drove it in my life↓. I looked
43 **UK** We're thirteen miles; **MS** We're <six miles and a half> thirteen miles
44 **UK** to be interested in; **MS** to ↑be↓ interested <[yourself]> in
Presumably Ford added the 'ed' to change 'interest yourself' to 'be interested'.
45 **UK** pathos," the girl; **MS** pathos, <my dear Watson>" the girl
46 **UK** about the road. The; **MS** about <it> ↓the road↑. The
47 **UK** middle ow [*sic*]; **MS**, Middle Low; **TR** middlelow; **US** middle Low
In his 1912 volume of poems, *High Germany*, Ford capitalises 'High'. Both
terms capitalised here, following MS and for consistency with 131 above.
48 **UK, MS, US** a Nenglish country; **TR** an english country
49 **UK, TR, US** sore; **MS** raw
50 **UK, TR, US** said; **MS** added
51 In MS this sentence was later inserted here, ringed and moved from the
following line, but the process of composition is puzzling. The lineation is
thus:

devoted to a horse-deal in the market-town where he happened to know
the horse-dealer. | – A luxurious, long argument in the atmosphere of
⸻⸻⸻⸻⸻⸻⸻⸻⸻⸻⸻⸻⸻⸻⸻⸻⸻⸻⸻⸻⸻
| The horse-dealer, indeed, was known to every hunting man in England! |
⸻⸻⸻⸻⸻⸻⸻⸻⸻⸻⸻⸻⸻⸻⸻⸻⸻⸻⸻⸻⸻
stable-hartshorn and slow wranglings couched in ostler's epigrams. You

The question is: when did he write the ringed sentence. Was it the start of
a new paragraph, in which case the previous one must originally have ended
with 'happened to know the horse-dealer'; but then immediately after
writing the ringed sentence he must have decided the previous paragraph
needed a different ending, since the sentences preceding and succeeding this
one appear to have been run together previously with a dash; and then, while
adding the new ending, he changed his mind about the new paragraph and
incorporated the ringed sentence into the previous one. Or alternatively
(and less convolutedly) the alignment of the ringed sentence with the page's
other paragraph indentations is coincidental, and it was merely written in as
an insertion into the line above. In which case its positioning indicates it
must have been written while Ford was still composing the previous line. In
this case the most likely conjecture is perhaps that while writing 'A luxurious, long argument in the atmosphere of', Ford decided that he needed to
get in something about the fame of the horse-dealer soon, because the rest
of Tietjens' train of thought was going to be expansive.
52 **UK, US** pub. probably; **MS** pub probably; **TR** pub, probably
53 **UK, TR, US** sudden moonlight. ¶ Before; **MS** sudden [sunlight]. ¶

\<Suddenly\>: Before
As the scene has been moonlit up to this point it's possible a compositor misread 'sunlight' (as often, Ford's hand here is not unequivocal) and the error wasn't caught. However, sunlight would be more likely than moonlight to make Valentine's hair appear 'golden'; and this moment perhaps prepares for the sudden sunrise on the following page. Alternatively, as it's Valentine who notices the sunrise, 'moonlight' might indicate that to Tietjens Valentine's Venus-like birth out of the silver mist is still an affair of romantic night-lighting. That is, we can't be certain Ford didn't revise to 'moonlight', or prefer that reading, so it has been retained.

54 **UK** might as well; **MS** might \<just as\> ↑as↓ well

55 The oddity of the inverted commas closing and opening again here without a change of speaker is explained by the fact that in MS, the passage from "'I've found,'" to 'But I've' was a later revision inscribed at the foot of leaf 147. It replaced an illegible deletion of four or five words ending with 'I've'.

56 This insertion in MS underwent at least two revisions, heavily deleted, but which perhaps read 'she went on, "a \<[milestone ↑stone↓ that had R. D. C. on it &]\> stone that had I. R. D. C. on it'

57 **UK** worked out what; **MS** worked out \<, by the bye,\> what

58 **UK, MS, TR** She said: ¶ "Oh, *gentlemen* do!" she said, "use fallacies; **US** She said: ¶ "Oh, *gentlemen* do use fallacies
The repetition of 'she said' does appear an oversight, but one that was allowed to stand in MS, TR, and UK, and was even repeated by Penguin, Knopf, and the Bodley Head, so has been allowed to stand here. US's solution of deleting the second instance and running Valentine's speeches into one loses the rhythm (clearly indicated by Ford's exclamation mark) with which she counter's Tietjens' comment, then decides to continue the thought.

59 **UK** pulling." ¶ Suddenly; **MS** pulling." ¶ \<Suddenly he said – & he hadn't [an idea] that he was going to say it: ¶ "If you go on like that I shall kiss you!" & his heart stopped beating. The outline of her profile remained to a hair's breadth the same. ¶ "You could [for all I'd care]!" she said\> Suddenly

60 **UK** I'm so glad . . ."; **MS** I'm so glad . . ." \<The day's begun . . ."\>
Presumably Ford first wrote 'I'm so glad . . . The day's begun . . .'", then deleted the last clause and added the first set of closing inverted commas, deciding it'd be better to let Tietjens wonder how she would have finished the thought.

61 **UK** Tietjens asked. ¶ She looked; **MS** Tietjens asked: \<*That* was why . . ." ¶ "It would have spoilt it," she said &\> She looked

62 **UK** shingle tower roof; **MS** shingle ↓tower↑ roof

63 In MS this and the following three instances are again given as 'Mountsby' whereas UK, TR, and US all read 'Mountby'.

64 **UK** it made a right-angle just before coming into the road and the road went away at right-angles across the gate; **MS** it \<came at right angles\> ↑made a right-angle just before coming↓ into the road and the road went away at right-angles \<to its gate: right\> across the gate

65 **UK** the underneath of; **MS** the \<[under] side\> ↑underneath↓ of

66 **UK, TR, US** forward. ¶ The horse; **MS** forward. \<in her seat.\> ¶ The horse

67 In MS this sentence is inserted in the left-hand margin.

68 **UK** gently: up to all; **MS** gently: \<[precisely]:\> ↑up to↓ all

69 **UK** between shaven grass banks!; **MS** between <green> shaven ↑grass↓ banks!
70 **UK, TR, US** Out; **MS** Cut
   'Out' does make sense here, and perhaps the 'O' was just not completely formed. I have not emended to 'Cut' since the cut turns out to be to the horse's shoulder, not head.
71 **UK, TR, US** couldn't; **MS** shouldn't
72 **UK, TR, US** cut!; **MS** cut?
73 **UK** she asked. "Yes!"; **MS** she <said> ↑asked↓: "Yes!"
74 **UK** Tear one half off first; **MS** Tear <it in> ↑one↓ half ↑off↓ first
75 The clause 'with crumpled mud-guards' is inserted in the left-hand margin in MS.
76 **UK** Teitjens; **TR, US** Tietjens
   MS is unclear, with the 'i' and 'e' similar, and the dot over the second, which perhaps accounts for UK's error.
77 **UK, US** for; **MS, TR** of
78 **UK** Tietjens was extending the; **MS** Tietjens was <holding> ↑extending↓ the
79 **UK, TR, US** Buff's; **MS** Buffs'
80 **UK** devil were you doing coming into; **MS** devil <are> ↑were↓ you doing come into
81 **UK** "Look here," the General suddenly; **MS** "Look here," the ↑general↓ suddenly
   MS appears originally to have read 'he suddenly', with a 't' later added to the 'he', and 'general' inserted, when Ford realised the pronoun would be read as referring back to Tietjens.
82 In MS the phrase 'in Duchemin's church at' is a later insertion in the blank half-line after the end of the sentence, ringed and inserted between 'at' and 'Pett'. Following the instruction exactly would have produced 'at in' – an error all the printed witnesses avoid.
83 In MS, 'horse-ambulance' originally read 'horse-<slaughterer's truck>'. There are two deletions above this phrase, the first clearly, and the second probably, '<ambulance>', before 'ambulance' was inserted in the left-hand margin. The revision was necessitated by Tietjens' determination to save the horse's life.
84 As previously (see note 63 above), the three occurrences of this name on leaf 153 of MS are given as 'Mountsby', but in these cases (unlike the previous ones) the 's' appears to have been inserted as an afterthought. All the printed versions continue to read 'Mountby'. What appears to have happened is that Ford began writing the name as 'Mountsby', then from I.iii began dropping the 's' inadvertently until the end of I.vi (see 377 / note 28 to I.vi above). He became aware of the inconsistency and started inserting it, but that at proof stage either he or his copy-editor opted instead for 'Mountby', removing the 's' in all cases but that on UK 65.
85 **UK** moved it two yards; **MS** moved <the horse> ↑it↓ two yards
86 **UK** alter it . . . just; **MS** alter it . . . <You'll> Just
87 **UK** had brooded. Ever; **MS** had brooded <for centuries>. Ever
88 **UK, MS, TR** brother's; **US** brothers
89 In MS these three sentences – from 'It was the dreadful [. . .] smashed it up.' – are a later insertion in the left-hand margin. The addition shows Ford concerned to clarify that it is the strain of the accident that releases Tiet-

jens' self-pity (which is also pity for his family traditions).
90 **UK** but I feel you're the splendidest ..." ¶ He; **MS** but <... oh: I feel I'll
keep single for your sake. You're the splendidest ...>" ↑I feel you're the
splendidest ..."↓ ¶ He
91 **UK** acquaintance." ¶ He felt; **MS** acquaintance." <But ...">  ¶ He felt
92 **UK** blear-eyed driver; **MS** blear-eyed <matutinal> driver
93 MS has two separate deletions here: '<Tietjens stood up to say:>'; then '<Not
a bad old stick, the general, Tietjens thought. He stood up to say:>'. Instead
he simply inserted 'Tietjens said' after the following speech.
94 In MS the phrase 'nor miss my' is inserted above a partially illegible longer
deletion: '<[illegible] miss my>'.
95 **UK** a country—you know; **MS** a <[far away]> ↑country↓—you know
96 **UK** north." ¶ The knacker's cart; **MS** north." At least ... Wo horse ... Keep
still or you'll slip that bandage> ...." ¶ The knacker's cart

## Textual Notes for II.i

1  **UK** PART TWO; **US** PART II
Emended for consistency between all four volumes. *Some Do Not ...* was the
only Duckworth edition not to use large Roman numerals for any Part
number. *Last Post* is inconsistent, having 'PART ONE' but 'PART II'. The
other volumes use large Roman numerals throughout.
2  **UK** room, all the women in it realised with mortification; **MS** room, <every
woman realised with mortification> all the women in it realised with mortification
3  **UK** come above; **MS** come <to the edge> above
4  **UK** face, screaming; **MS** face <below>; screaming
5  In MS the phrase 'was a bird' was inserted in the left-hand margin.
6  **UK** the gulls; **MS** the <herring> gulls
7  **UK** conviction that all women in that lurid carnival had become common
property, had burst; **MS** conviction that all <morality had gone to pot in that
lurid carnival> ↑<womankind had become common property in>↓ women
in that lurid carnival had become common property, had burst
The eventual clause 'women in that lurid carnival had become common
property' is inserted in the left-hand margin of MS.
8  **UK** a frozen marble; **MS** a ↑frozen↓ marble
9  **UK** could, she flattered; **MS** could, <she knew,> she flattered
10 **UK** after-breakfast mirrors; **MS** after-<dinner> breakfast mirrors
11 **UK** their eligibilities; **MS** their <[social] positions & fit> eligibilities
12 **UK** and yet how unlike; **MS** and yet *how* unlike
In MS this clause, like others in this paragraph listed below, is enclosed
within square brackets that have been deleted:
'though to be sure no one *wore* feather boas'
'which *does* give, oh, you know ... a *certain* ...'
'And one reads in police court reports of raids what *those* are!'
'*that* she had from Tietjens'
Apart from the last, they are all mimicking the mannered speech-style of
Sylvia's set. What's less clear is whether they represent her own thoughts or
her mockery of her friends' talk (as when Tietjens' interior monologue is

punctuated by his imagining of conversational clichés in I.vi).

13 **UK** *maîtresseen tître*; **MS**, **US** *maîtresse en tître*
14 **UK**, **US** amorous; **MS** amours
15 **UK**, **US** rather; **MS** matter

The singular is perhaps what caused the misreading; that or eye-slip to 'matter rather' two sentences further on. But that balancing repetition clinches the emendation. *OED* gives this sense of 'matter': 'With *of* and a noun or noun phrase, or qualifying adjective: something, or things collectively, of the kind specified, or involving or related to a particular thing. Now *rare*', citing an example from 1884 ('That it is eminently desirable to attain this end is not now matter of dispute') but also from Gilbert White ('This must have been matter of mere accident'). It is possible that the old-fashioned usage is a kind of free indirect style, mimicking the register of the great and good (or not) being discussed.

16 **UK**, **US** terribly, badly; **MS** terribly badly
17 **UK** for fifty years; **MS** for <twenty> ↑fifty↓ years
18 **UK** the country houses; **MS** the <houses> country houses
19 **UK** heard of such country houses; **MS** heard <that> ↑of↓ such country houses
20 **UK** passion or temperimental [*sic*] lewdness; **MS** passion or ↓temperamental↑ lewdness
21 **UK** whom she had seen; **MS** whom <[latterly]> she had seen
22 **UK** her rides; **MS** her <morning> rides
23 **UK** afterwards, and; **MS** afterwards, <Indeed the two sides of life were, in her view, intimately connected> and
24 **UK** life. She; **MS** life. <She kept herself in fact in a state of nearly perfect balance>. [She

The square bracket in MS is not closed.

25 In MS the words 'absolutely continent. And' are inserted in the left-hand margin. The word 'years' is followed by a horizontal line that appears to be deleting a series of suspension dots.
26 **UK** a light vapour; **MS** a ↑light↓ vapour
27 **UK** fashionable doings would transfer; **MS** fashionable <attendances> ↓doings↑ would transfer
28 **UK** and two; **MS** and <one or> two
29 **UK**, **US** dutiable; **MS** *undutied*
30 **UK** were less worn; **MS** were <more valuable or> less worn

Presumably Sylvia would have thought it beneath herself to lie about the cost of the clothes. Passing them off as 'less worn' would not have been to conceal wear and tear, but to reassure potential buyers that she had not been seen (and photographed) in them so often that they would be recognised as second-hand.

31 **UK** They had two floors; **MS** They had <however> two floors
32 **UK** great deal of space, the breakfast-room; **MS** great deal of room the breakfast-room
33 **UK** for you." ¶ Taking a look; **MS** for you." ¶ <Lady Moira>, Taking a look
34 **UK** that if only; **MS** that <her drawing room>, if only
35 **UK** the green halfpenny stamp; **MS** the ↑green halfpenny↓ stamp
36 **UK**, **US** Sir William Heathly; **MS** Sir <Heathly> Wilmot Heathly
37 **UK** Tietjens would listen without talking. Sir John; **MS** Tietjens would

listen <. He would listen by the hour> without talking. <[illegible words; perhaps '—for she' or 'as if he'] knew nothing about it.> Sir John

38 **UK** rather caressing; **MS** rather <[worldly]>, caressing

39 **UK** she abandoned; **MS** she <gradually> abandoned

40 **UK, US** and she was convinced; **MS** and he was convinced
In MS the pronoun is unequivocally 'he', and the next paragraph makes it clear that Sylvia has *not* been convinced by his assurances.

41 **UK** hadn't much; **MS** hadn't <really> much

42 **UK** footmen and milliners. The Tietjens; **MS** footmen, milliners <and [that class]>. The Tietjens

43 **UK** tell him that; **MS** tell him <, or to [make any occasion] for telling him> that

44 In MS the phrase 'that they had done it' was inserted in the left-hand margin.

45 **UK** if; **MS, US** of

46 **UK** the cutlets; **MS** the <[mutton]> cutlets

47 In MS the comments here between parenthetic dashes – 'but that was mostly the mirror's doing' and 'what man's forehead wouldn't long for them?' – appear in square brackets; as before, perhaps suggesting an interior dialogue.

48 Originally MS read 'She went' here, but 'She' was deleted and 'Sylvia' inscribed to the left, to avoid a confusing anaphoric reference back to 'Hullo Central' instead of Sylvia.

49 **UK, US** *Vitare*; **MS** *Vitae*

50 **UK, MS, US** Bishop's Auckland; **Ed** Bishop Auckland
The error (not uncommon, even in standard works such as the *Dictionary of National Biography*) is repeated in II.iii in the narrator's voice, so cannot be attributed solely to Sylvia's character.

51 In MS 'Claudine's' is inscribed above an illegible deletion. It appears to begin with a 'D' and might have been 'Duns', where Mary Borden had the country house party Ford had been at just before the war.

52 **UK** or only Macmaster's; **MS** or ↑only↓ Macmaster's

53 **UK** have a mistress; **MS** have <the same> ↑a↓ mistress

54 **UK** Tietjens said; **MS** <Macm> Tietjens said

55 **UK** Sylvia checked; **MS** Sylvia <who was perfectly aware that Tietjens [never lied]> checked

56 **UK, US** questions; **MS** question

57 In MS, the following passage, from 'And I suppose' to 'I don't think much of your taste', is an insertion in the left-hand margin. There, the phrase 'the woman' was originally 'the <other> woman'.

58 **UK** identification of the party," Tietjens said; **MS** identification ↑of the party↓," Tietjens said

59 **UK** for years. Mrs. Macmaster; **MS** for years. <That's why> Mrs. Macmaster

60 **UK, US** every Friday! to croodle; **MS** every Friday: to croodle

61 **UK** Put her back. She's too young; **MS** Put her back. <Besides>: She's too young

62 **UK** anything . . . except; **MS** anything . . . <'They save ↑have saved↓ others: themselves they cannot save.' . . . > except
The allusion in the deletion is to *Matthew* 27.42; the Pharisees watching Christ die say: 'He saved others; himself he cannot save.'

63 **UK** or discreditably; **MS** or <in the least> discreditably

64 **UK** You're not fit; **MS** You're certainly not fit

The emendation must have been made in the proofs to avoid the repetition of 'certainly' from the preceding sentence.

65  **UK** old Campion." ¶; **MS** old Campion." <to-morrow.">¶

66  **UK, US** woodenly. "Mrs. Macmaster; **MS** woodenly: "Mrs. Macmaster
As Tietjens is clearly correcting himself in mid-sentence MS's punctuation has been restored.

67  **UK** Tremendously respected; **MS** Tremendously <efficient> respected

68  **UK** writes superior; **MS** writes <really> superior

69  **UK, US** snatches; **MS** [chronicles]

70  **UK, MS** "Why," Sylvia said, "did you lend Macmaster all that money?" Sylvia asked.... ¶ "Mind; **US** Sylvia asked: ¶"Why did you lend Macmaster all that money?" ¶ "Mind
The repeated attribution of the speech is awkward. It's possible that Ford added 'Sylvia asked', feeling that form better suited her question, and meant to delete 'Sylvia said'. But he didn't, and UK follows the repetition. To delete it here would be to produce an unprecedented variant; so I follow US on the assumption that even if the correction wasn't Ford's own, he assented to it in proof. For a comparable correction that was implemented in UK as well as US see below, note 95.

71  **UK, US** I told him very emphatically it wouldn't please me ... But; **MS** I told him it very emphatically wouldn't please me ... <He knows all about my money affairs of course. He's managed them for me since you went to France>. But

72  **UK** on which she; **MS** on which <, [against] the light,> she

73  **UK** impluse [*sic*]; **MS** Impulse; **US** impulse

74  **UK, US** "You know then," Sylvia exclaimed almost shrilly. "You know that they; **MS** "You know then," Sylvia exclaimed almost shrilly. "You *know* that they
<that they won't have you back in the office if>

75  **UK** his active brain; **MS** his ↑active↓ brain

76  **UK** A provincial miniature; **MS** A ↑provincial↓ miniature

77  **UK** had been miniature; **MS** had <been [little]> ↑been↓ miniature

78  **UK** he had said, "because; **MS** he <was continuing> ↑had said↓, "because

79  **UK, US** pretence; **MS** picture

80  **UK** squits won't stay; **MS** squits <[illegible phrase]> won't stay

81  **UK** been the first evil effects of; **MS** been <one of the> ↑the first↓ evil effects of
This whole sentence appears within square brackets (instead of the parenthetic dash) in MS.

82  In MS 'remorselessly' was written immediately after 'practical', then ringed and inserted before it.

83  **UK** Sylvia interjected violently; **MS** Sylvia <almost screamed> interjected violently

84  **UK** the Austrian; **MS** the <German> Austrian

85  **UK** the lunch-table; **MS** the <breakfast> ↓lunch↑ table

86  **UK** seeing a quite different figure and other books; **MS** seeing ↓a quite different figure and↑ other books

87  **UK** names, accents or antecedents; **MS** names ↑accents↓ or antecedents

88  **UK** of gloating curiosity; **MS** of <unholy> ↑gloating↓ curiosity

89  **UK** by foul and baseless rumours?; **MS** by <such foulness> ↑foul and baseless rumours↓?

90 **UK** Met . . . Met . . . It's Met; **MS** Met . . . Met . . . <Oh God> . . . It's Met

91 **UK** floor and pulled out; **MS** floor and <took> pulled out

92 **UK** unusually has five suspension dots here.

93 **UK** was cynically laughed at; **MS** was <well [-known]> ↑cynically↓ laughed at

94 **UK** Something burst—or; **MS** Something <bursting;> ↑burst;↓ or

95 **UK, US** Tietjens said: ¶ "I beg your pardon. One gets; **MS** Tietjens said: ¶ "I beg your pardon," Tietjens said: "One gets
The first 'Tietjens' is underlined in MS, perhaps indicating that someone noticed the repetition.

96 **UK** a little awkward to write; **MS** a little <worrying> ↑awkward↓ to write

97 In MS this sentence is an insertion in the left-hand margin.

98 **UK, US** the Germans' bombs; **MS** the German bombs

99 **MS** has an illegible deletion after 'blood', possibly '<& stuff>'.

100 **UK** believe it. . . . You were an officer: they; **MS** believe it. . . . <They knew> You were an officer <I suppose>: they

101 **UK** Tietjens said; "but; **MS** Tietjens said; "<Curly> But

102 **UK** But I remember; **MS** But <of course> I remember

103 **UK** because of me she died; **MS** because of <that> ↑me↓ she died

104 In MS the remainder of this paragraph is inserted in the left-hand margin. The beginning of this sentence was presumably also part of Ford's afterthought: it is in a slightly smaller hand than the rest of the page, suggesting that he filled in the blank space at the end of the paragraph and continued into the margin.

105 **UK, US** I killed; **MS** I had killed

106 **UK** the Almighty, that; **MS** the Almighty, <against yourself> that

107 **UK, US** magpie; **MS** myopic

108 **UK** and you've told me; **MS** and <told him> you've told me

109 **UK, US** *Neither I condemn*; **MS** [and Authorised Version] *Neither do I condemn*

110 **UK** play acting. I shall; **MS** play acting <again>. I shall

111 **UK** anyone is justified in doing anything; **MS** any one <can> ↑is justified in↓ <do> ↑doing↓ anything

112 **UK** raise a hundred pounds between; **MS** raise <two farthings> a hundred between
The words 'a hundred' are inserted in the left-hand margin. The word 'pounds' appears to have been a later addition, presumably in proof.

113 **UK** Sylvia was saying:; **MS** Sylvia <said> was saying:

114 **UK** It hasn't, perhaps, struck you; **MS** It hasn't <of course> ↑perhaps↓, struck you

115 In MS the original name is deleted and illegible (though it possibly began with S and ended in 'en'), with 'Spelden' inserted in the left-hand margin. When repeated on the next leaf it is written clearly as 'Spelden'.

116 **UK, US** suffers; **MS** muffs
Though MS isn't unambiguous here, there are too many vertical strokes before the 'f's and too few after to support the UK/US reading. The sense doesn't support it either, since the man would be suffering the begetting of someone else's child, not 'his'. The *OED* gives the following definition of the verb to 'muff': '*Sport.* To miss (a catch, a ball), esp. in cricket; to play (a shot, a game, etc.) badly.'

117 **UK, US** secret; **MS** surest
118 **UK** tell her; **MS** tell <him> her
119 **UK, UK** gloom; **MS** glooms
120 **UK** Speldon; **MS, US** Spelden
121 **UK, MS, US** Roby
   Though this might look like an error, MS is clear. Presumably Ford meant to give the place name 'Groby' a history, with 'Roby' as an antecedent form.
122 **UK** said. She spoke with intense bitterness.... "Chaste; **MS** said. ↑She spoke with intense bitterness↓.... "Chaste
123 **UK** father...." ¶ Sylvia said; **MS** father...." ¶ <Tietjens> ↑Sylvia↓ said

## Textual Notes for II.ii

1 **UK** moments of unusual stresses; **MS** moments of <great> unusual stresses
2 **UK** love, public dishonour; **MS** love, ↑public↓ dishonour
3 **UK** the hushing up power of the ruling class and the; **MS** the hushing up power of the <[organisations] of the> Ruling Class, <was almost unknown> and the
4 **UK, US** comings; **Ed** coming
   MS is ambiguous. The ending looks more like 'gs' and more like other nearby examples of words ending in 'gs' than a terminal 'g', a view supported by the fact that the tail of the 'g' is looped (something Ford generally wasn't doing with terminal 'g's). Yet the singular verb 'was' doesn't agree with the plural 'comings'. If what Ford meant to write was 'comings', the number of the verb is an error. Alternatively, the mark at the end of the word could be a smudged tail of the 'g' instead of an 's', and UK and US are in error. The editor must choose which to correct and in this case prefers the latter, correcting the noun to the singular.
5 **UK** lacking in constructive intelligence; **MS** lacking in <benevolence> constructive intelligence
6 **UK** London banks, so that; **MS** London banks <: he was forty-five> so that
7 **MS** originally read 'a gloomy and deep passion for Sylvia Tietjens'. Ford then circled 'for Sylvia Tietjens' and inserted it in front of the preceding phrase, reversing the order so he could continue to describe Brownlie's thoughts about his passion.
8 **UK, US** felt on entering the room and finding himself; **MS** felt on entering the distress at finding himself; **Ed** felt on entering the room the distress at finding himself
   In MS the words 'distress at' have a box drawn round them but are otherwise unrevised. Perhaps Ford or his editor felt 'entering the distress' was distractingly ambiguous. But the resultant text isn't coherent. The distress Port Scatho felt on entering was caused by having to deal with Sylvia's letter. '[F]inding himself in the midst of what he took to be a highly emotional family parting' is the cause of his second distress, which affects him only after he has come in and talked to the couple. The 'and' in the UK/US version grants him awareness of the parting as he enters the room; whereas the previous paragraph has shown him only gradually realising it while there; and the rest of this paragraph expands on why he is distressed by a wartime family parting. I assume the addition of the word 'room' to be an authorial

revision (it isn't explicable as a compositor's error); but that the deletion of the marked words 'distress at' was a mistake, which garbled the sentence, motivating someone to repair the grammar with an 'and' that garbled the paragraph. Without the evidence of the proofs the emendation is a speculative conflation, but one which rescues the sense of the narrative while doing least damage to any of the witnesses, losing only the 'and' (which may arguably anyway have been a compositor's misreading of a blot or correction mark as a Fordian ampersand).

9   In MS Ford originally wrote 'emotional parting', then wrote the word 'family' afterwards, ringed it and inserted it before 'parting' (presumably so as to minimise the suggestion of a romantic parting).

10  **UK** Tietjens knew that; **MS** Tietjens knew <that the odds [as to]> that

11  **UK** sentences of praise; **MS** sentences of embarrassed praise

12  **UK** his skin became a shade paler; **MS** his skin became <[slowly]> a shade paler

13  **UK** cloth, from there; **MS** cloth: from there; **US** cloth; from there
    UK frequently converts MS's colons into semi-colons but it hardly ever lightens the punctuation, as here, suggesting an inconsistency, which makes US's reading preferable.

14  **UK, US** filled; **MS** fell

15  **UK, US** Scatho cried: ¶ "But; **MS** Scatho <[exclaimed]> cried: ¶ "But

16  **UK** he said. "God forbid; **MS** he said <agitatedly>. "God forbid

17  UK has a mark resembling a small comma after 'seen', but this appears to be a flaw. It is much smaller than the standard Duckworth commas, and there is no co-ordinating comma later in the sentence. MS and US have no punctuation.

18  **UK** left. . . . ; **MS** left <a great junction> . . .

19  In MS '& dates' appears to be an afterthought: the ampersand at the end of one line and 'dates' inserted in the margin at the beginning of the next.

20  **UK** neutrality. And; **MS** neutrality, <according as the cat jumped>. And

21  **UK** conduce to the standard of comfort of hogs; **MS** conduce to <hoggish comforts> the standard of comfort of hogs

22  **UK, US** hurtled; **MS** hurled
    In MS the loop forming the head of the 'd', characteristically leaning to the left, crosses the top of the 'l', perhaps causing the compositor to misread it as 't'.

23  **UK, US** asked for soft; **MS** asked for <it [& now]> soft

24  UK only has three suspension dots here, which is inconsistent for a completed sentence. But there is also an anomalous blank space after them, suggesting a fourth was intended. It is indeed supplied by US.

25  **UK** and Macmaster; **MS** and <Tie> Macmaster

26  **UK, US** Sadix; **MS** [Sadic]; **Ed** Sadic
    'Sadix' appears otherwise unknown. UK second impression emends to 'Sadic', which was current at the time. The *OED* cites an instance in T. E. Lawrence's *Seven Pillars of Wisdom* from 1926, for example.

27  **UK** From what Tietjens; **MS** From what <M[a]> Tietjens

28  **UK** Lady Port Scatho had been as motherly as possible; **MS** Lady Port Scatho <– who was really more motherly than she was after they had received their title –> had been as motherly as possible

29  **UK** civil to Macmaster, whom he knew; **MS** civil to <Brownlie>

↓Macmaster↑ whom he knew
30 **UK** Macmaster, anyhow; **MS** <Tiet> Macmaster, anyhow
31 **UK** her condition. They; **MS** her <position> ↑condition.↓. They
32 **UK** to town with Mrs. Duchemin, who was certainly; **MS** to town with Mrs. Duchemin, <He wanted also to borrow £50 [as it was impossible during those few days to get cheques cashed.] Tietjens found the money with difficulty [– thanks to Marchant –] his old nurse> who was certainly
33 **UK** trustees in lunacy, and; **MS** trustees ↑in lunacy↓ and
34 **UK** the famous Friday parties; **MS** the famous <Saturday> ↓Friday↑ parties
35 In MS 'at King's Cross' is added in the left-hand margin.
36 **UK** Tietjens; **MS** <Macm> Tietjens
37 **UK, US** she would, no doubt, have done so; **MS** she would, no doubt, not have done so
38 **UK, US** scatological; **MS** scathological
39 **UK** the craving for drink; **MS** the <habit> craving for drink
40 **UK** abroad, wedding feasts; **MS** abroad, <[feasting] and> wedding feasts
41 **UK** Jedburgh? ....; **US** Jedburgh? ...; **MS** Jedburgh ....
The question mark makes Tietjens' answer sound like he's confirming that Macmaster slept apart from Mrs Duchemin, whereas in MS his 'Yes' appears rather to agree that they almost exaggerated their parade of circumspection. I've followed US's punctuation on the grounds that UK breaks its convention of following a question mark by only three dots instead of four.
42 **UK** full of enthusiasm at the thought; **MS** full of ↓enthusiasm at↑ the thought
43 In MS Ford first wrote 'a thousand pounds'. There are two revisions above the 'a', which has been overwritten with a caret: a deleted 'ten' and a second 'a'. When the amount is repeated later in the sentence, Ford first wrote 'ten thousand', having decided to increase the figure and revise the first instance accordingly. He then changed both back to 'a thousand' again.
44 **UK** now and then; **MS** now<adays> and then
45 **UK** erroneously uses double inverted commas here.
46 **UK** friend. She said; **MS** friend. <He said> She said
47 **UK** think fit. Ten days ago I got; **MS** think fit. <The day before yesterday> ↑Ten days ago↓ I got
The adjustment of the chronology appears to have been required by the twelve-day delay in receiving his pay, detailed in the following paragraph.
48 **UK** The total, in fact, amounted to an overdraft; **MS** The total <would have> amounted, in fact, to an overdraft
49 **UK** Do what you like. You'd better; **MS** Do what you like! <I've already resigned from the Club.> You'd better
50 In MS this paragraph appears at the foot of leaf 201, two paragraphs later, where it is circled and moved upwards. There's no indication of its being a later addition. More probably, Ford simply decided to re-order the sequence.
51 **UK** and **US** read 'She' instead of 'and he'. In MS the 'and' is Ford's characteristic ampersand, characteristically joined to the subsequent word. Anyhow, 'he' makes better sense given Port Scatho's comments on the letter and the receipt.
52 In MS this sentence is an insertion in the left-hand margin.
53 **UK** slung across him; **MS** slung <[around] him> across him
54 **UK** in his collection; **MS** in his <museum> collection

55 **UK** Mark said. "I want; **MS** Mark said. "I < ¶ Christopher answered> "want
In MS 'Mark said.' appears originally to have been the the end of the line
and paragraph. The words '<Christopher answered> were written as a new
paragraph. Ford appears then to have deleted them, and added the "'I' that
continues Mark's speech, at the end of the previous line, completing the
sentence on a new line below the deletion.

56 **UK** in any one year." ¶ Port Scatho said: ¶ "Write a letter to the bank. I
don't look after; **MS** in any one year." ¶ <"I don't,"> Port Scatho said:
<look> ¶ "Write a letter to the bank. I don't look after

57 **UK** I only wanted to avoid; **MS** I only wanted to <withdraw my account in
order to> avoid

## Textual Notes for II.iii

1  **UK** the churchyard and; **MS** the <funeral> ↑churchyard↓ and
2  **UK** lunch and paid for their cabs. Perhaps; **MS** lunch ↑and paid for their
cabs.↓ Perhaps
3  **UK, US** matched; **MS** marched
4  **UK** smooking-room; **MS** smoking room; **US** smoking-room
5  **UK, US** you won't marry?" and Mark; **MS** you won't marry?" Mark
6  In MS, 'unusual' is preceded by an illegible deleted word, possibly 'immense'.
7  **UK** to support Mrs. Wannop, Miss Wannop and her child, and to maintain;
**MS** to support Mrs. Wannop, <and her daughter> ↑Miss Wannop and her
child↓ and to maintain
8  **UK** solution. It; **MS** solution <for [these questions]>. It
9  **UK, US** to ascertain that that he had called; **MS** to ascertain that, he had
called
10 **UK** the brother; **MS** the <[room-mate]> brother
11 In MS the phrase 'Glorvina said she could do nothing because' is inserted in
the left-hand margin.
12 **UK** peppered over with hieroglyphics; **MS** peppered over, <even at that>,
with hieroglyphics
13 **UK** Waterhouse's; **MS** Waterfield's
The earlier instance of the name in the same sentence appears originally to
have begun with 'Waterfi', but was then over-written to read 'Waterhouse'.
14 **UK** A person in a relatively; **MS** A ↑person in a↓ relatively
15 **UK** Mark was not yet used to thinking; **MS** Mark <still> was not ↑yet↓ used
to thinking
16 **UK** and—with to give; **MS** and <the next day [at tea] Ruggles had told Mr
Tietjens [senior]>—with to give
17 **UK** married her; he had hushed up; **MS** married her, had hushed up
18 In MS this sentence is a later addition in the left-hand margin.
19 **UK** tenderness. His wife; **MS** tenderness, <if only because> His wife
20 **UK** unusually wrapped up in Christopher, because; **MS** unusually
<devoted> ↑wrapped up in Christopher↓, because
21 **UK** very nearly asked; **MS** very nearly <yielded to the temptation to> asked
22 **UK** in order to atone for; **MS** in order to <make up> ↑atone↓ for
23 **UK** to his other children had prevented; **MS** to his other <sons had pre>
children had prevented

24 **UK, US** him; **MS** his
25 **UK** Mr. Tietjens. Mr. Tietjens; **MS** Mr. Tietjens. <Moreover> Mr. Tietjens
26 **UK** to the son. He had even; **MS** to the son. <Indeed> He had even
27 **UK, US** boy; **MS** oaf
28 **UK, MS** trollops; **US** trollop
   The *OED* cites 'trollops' as a variant of 'trollop'.
29 **UK** broken heart. ¶ A soberly; **MS** broken heart. <And – once again –> A
   soberly
30 **UK, MS, US** Bishop's Auckland; **Ed** Bishop Auckland
31 This sentence appears to be a later insertion in MS, written in a slightly
   smaller and shakier hand, squeezed in at the end of the paragraph.
32 In MS the clause 'for his father's estate was by no means wound up' was an
   afterthought, written on the line below.
33 **UK** I am to let; **MS** I <can> ↑am to↓ let
34 **UK, US** girl who had a child by you. I'm; **MS** girl you had a child by. I'm
35 **UK** I suppose the girl is; **MS** I suppose <she> ↓the girl↑'s
36 **UK** answer. Mark leaned; **MS** answer. <Then> Mark leaned
37 **UK** that night; **MS** that <[very]> night
38 **UK, MS, US** envelopes
   Though the *OED* doesn't include this as a possible spelling of the verb
   'envelop', several of its historical examples from the late eighteenth and
   nineteenth centuries use it.
39 In MS the last two sentences of this paragraph are inserted in the left-hand
   margin.
40 **UK** an account. This discussion; **MS** an account. <if you like.> This discussion
41 In MS there is only a slight indentation for 'Christopher said:', which UK
   and US interpret by not starting a new paragraph. But normally the convention of using a new paragraph for the introduction of a new speaker is only
   (and only sometimes) suspended in UK during stichomythic conversations.
42 **UK** the motives of a gentleman; **MS** the motives of a <North Country>
   gentleman
43 **UK** shrewd. ¶ But, of course; **MS** shrewd. <But of course he *would* be shrewd.
   Indispensable to a great department [illegible]. ¶ "We must move on or I
   shall have to take a cab." Mark [abandoned] his [post]. ¶ "What did you do
   with the other three thousand? he asked. "Three thousand is a hell of a big
   sum for a youngest son to chuck about." ¶ "Except for some furniture I bought
   for my wife's rooms," Christopher said, "they were nearly all loans." ¶
   "Loans! Mark exclaimed. "To that fellow Macmaster?"> But, of course
   This substantial deletion was slightly redrafted in the following paragraph.
44 **UK** indispensible; **MS, US** indispensable
   The *OED* recognises the '-ible' spelling, but as obscure. Emended for consistency with the other instances of the word in UK.
45 **UK, US** younger; **MS** youngest
46 In MS this speech appears to be an afterthought. There is a deleted speech
   – "Pretty warm" – which was presumably Christopher responding to Mark's
   'a pretty warm man now'.
47 **UK** Ruggles' and ffolliot's; **MS** Ruggles's and ffolliots; **US** Ruggles and ffolliot
   The possessives in UK don't make sense, especially since not used for 'our
   father'. MS suggests Ford intended 'Ruggles's' as a plural (as in 'Ruggleses')

– signifying the crowd of people full of types like Ruggles and ffolliott; so it has been restored here.

48 **UK** in the endeavour to imagine the embraces; **MS** in the <contemplation of the> ↑endeavour to imagine the↓ embraces
The original wording 'contemplation of the embraces' might have suggested they had already occurred, which they haven't.

49 **UK** in all probability that would; **MS** in all probability <you> ↑that↓ would

50 **UK** proved the estate at; **MS** proved the <will> ↑estate↓ at

51 In MS Ford originally wrote '[five] times', deleted it and inscribed something above, now illegibly deleted, then followed it with 'twice that'.

52 **UK** old race-glasses; **MS** old <field> race-glasses

53 **UK, US** neat; **MS** new

54 **UK** embankment; **MS** Embankment

55 In MS 'then' is a later insertion in the left-hand margin.

56 **UK** consent now?" Mark asked; **MS** consent <then> ↑now↓?" Mark <said> asked

57 **UK** returned to the club; **MS** returned <from> to the Club

58 **UK** I put it off. I didn't; **MS** I put it off. <[Besides:]> I didn't

59 **UK** Christopher said. ¶ They strolled; **MS** Christopher said, <Whether I'm killed or not. He's a damned fine little pup." ¶ "Good luck to him." Mark said. "I'll see he has the best of everything." ¶ "Thanks," Christopher answered.> ¶ ¶> They strolled

60 **UK** they stopped to look at; **MS** they <looked> ↓stopped to look↑ at

61 In UK there is a single word deleted here, possibly '<little>'.

62 **UK** each line; **MS** each <serrated line> line

63 **UK, US, MS** curb; **Ed** kerb
Since Ford uses the more common British spelling, 'kerb', on the following page, I have emended here for the sake of consistency.

64 **UK** grinned feebly, exhibiting; **MS** grinned feebly <and [faintly]>, exhibiting

65 **UK** of Christopher's khaki sleeve; **MS** of <his> ↓Christopher's↑ khaki sleeve

66 **UK** the mean, grey stoniness of that cold heart; **MS** the ↑mean↓ grey stoninesses of that ↓cold↑ heart

67 **UK, US** hook; **MS** crook

68 **UK** such a tomfool question? *You!*; **MS** such ↑a↓ tomfool question<s>? *You!*

69 **UK, US** know; **MS** knew

70 **UK** cry." He added: "Besides; **MS** cry." ↑He added:↓ "Besides

71 In MS this sentence is in slightly smaller characters, suggesting that it might have been squeezed into the mostly blank line at the end of the paragraph as an afterthought.

72 **UK** the rotten old colonels; **MS** the <damn> ↑rotten↓ old colonels

73 **UK** the rotten old colonels; **MS** the <beastly> ↓rotten↑ old colonels

74 **UK** M.O.s." the; **MS** M O's," the; **US** M.O.'s," the; **Ed** M.O.s," the

75 **UK, US** For the moment he had felt temptation to stay; **MS** For that moment he had felt the temptation to stay

76 **UK** the lines; **MS** the <word> lines

77 **UK** you can. And get; **MS** you can. <and get home to your girl. I suppose it is a girl, God help [us].> And get

78 In MS 'Enquiry' is written above an illegible deleted word.

79 In MS this word is a later insertion above the line, but appears to read 'their'

not 'the'.

80 **UK** down, I suppose. Nine; **MS** down, ↑I suppose↓. Nine
81 **UK** or Welshmen; **MS** or <stinking> Welshmen
82 **UK** doing work; **MS** doing <good in> work

## Textual Notes for II.iv

1 Though UK only has three full stops here, US supplies the fourth.
2 **UK** blue cloth coat. He said; **MS** blue cloth <jumper> ↑coat↓. He said
3 **UK** serging; **US** surging
   The word does look like 'serging' in MS.
4 **UK** believe. He; **MS** believe. <And whe> He
5 **UK** He asked; **MS** He <added> asked
6 **UK** since the day; **MS** since <[two days]> the day
7 **UK, US** stocks; **Ed** sticks
   The word does look like 'stocks' in MS, but the OED records no usage of
   'stock' as a candle-holder (except for one example from Wyclif's translation
   of the Vulgate in 1382). Whereas Ford writes 'tall candles in silver sticks' on
   the following page when Valentine wonders 'What, then, were tall candles
   in silver sticks for?'; and (two pages from the end of the chapter) she 'saw
   suddenly the tall silver candlesticks'. This makes it probable that Ford wrote
   'sticks', but when dotting the 'i' not uncharacteristically missed it and placed
   it to the right (in the following word in MS, 'against', the dot is over the
   right-hand side of the 'n'; two lines above, in 'Mrs. Duchemin', it is again
   over the 'n'), the dot appearing to turn the 'i' into an 'o', the slight smudge
   strengthening the effect.
8 **UK** of renunciations, of; **MS** of renunciations, <and indeed> of
9 **UK** original; when; **MS** original; <or striking:> when
10 **UK** without acquiring a considerable knowledge; **MS** without ↑acquiring↓
    a <great> considerable knowledge
11 In MS a small illegible deletion (presumably 'and') is substituted by the
    words 'on the one hand and on the other of', inserted in the left-hand
    margin.
12 **UK** The tiger; **MS** The <underlying underlying Tiger> tiger
13 **UK** that Edith Ethel had done her; **MS** that <Mrs. Tietjens had done her>
    Edith Ethel had done her
14 **UK** friend..... ¶ On; **MS** friend .... ¶ <And> On; **US** friend.... ¶ On
    The five dots in UK aren't warranted by MS, and are standardised to four in
    US.
15 **UK** Communist Summer School; **MS** Communist <School> Summer
    School
16 In MS 'shouted' is inserted in the left-hand margin, replacing a deleted word,
    probably '<shouting>'.
17 **UK, US** Kaiser; **MS** Kayzer
    The spelling in MS is certainly not Ford's error ('Kaiser' appears repeatedly
    in his propaganda books, as well as later in this chapter); it presumably mimics
    English (and perhaps contemptuous) pronunciation of the German term.
18 **UK, US** isn't exact! She; **MS** isn't <fair> ↑exact↓! She
19 **UK** at Macmaster's; **MS** at <[Mrs.] Duchemin's> Macmaster's

20 **UK, MS, US** chilly, wet; **Ed** chilly wet
   Both the Bodley Head and 1948 Penguin editions remove the comma,
   turning 'wet' from an adjective to a noun. Though the comma is clear in MS,
   this seems the least intrusive way of rescuing coherence. Perhaps Ford had
   first thought to add a noun such as 'weather', then, having written 'wet',
   thought it would do as well. The Knopf/Vintage edition emends differently,
   deleting the 'of' and replacing it with a comma to give: 'a November day,
   very chilly, wet'; also an elegant solution, but even less warranted by MS.

21 **UK** an architect; **MS** an <artist> architect

22 **UK** came to her; **MS** came <over> to her

23 **UK, US** loathesome; **MS** loathsome

24 **UK** by the pacifist friends; **MS** by <her> ↑the↓ pacifist friends

25 **UK** radism; **MS, US** sadism
   The second impression of UK corrects to 'sadism'.

26 **UK, US** these; **MS** those

27 **UK** inflexion of a verb; **MS** inflexion of <the verb> a verb

28 **UK** talk out," Mr. Jegg said; **MS** talk out," <he> ↑Mr. Jegg↓ said

29 **UK** one's sole duty; **MS** one's <[small]> sole duty

30 **UK** the business; **MS** the <agreeable> business

31 **UK** queer, dear; **MS** queer, <my> dear

32 **UK** doing. But don't you see; **MS** doing. ↑But↓ don't you see

33 **UK** probably impolitic to fake; **MS** probably <wrong> ↑impolitic↓ to fake

34 **UK** with clouds of blood; **MS** with <infinite> clouds of blood

35 **UK** helping them means; **MS** helping ↑them↓ means

36 **UK, US** All, you; **MS** And you

37 **UK, US** order; **MS** orders

38 **UK** against our allies with; **MS** against <the French> ↑our allies↓ with

39 **UK** snaffled other peoples' colonies; **MS** snaffled <the French> ↓other
   peoples'↑ colonies

40 **UK** brother and his friends; **MS** brother <and their> and his friends

41 **UK, US** former; **MS** farm-

42 **UK** It was imperative; **MS** It <became> ↑was↓ imperative

43 **UK** to London. ¶ The marsh; **MS** to London. ¶ The <Just then Tietjens
   came back, very heavy, aged and dull. His being quartered in the neighbourhood of> marsh

44 **UK** dull. It was; **MS** dull. <On hearing that he was> It was

45 **UK** house in Bedford Park; **MS** house in <Regents Park> Bedford Park

46 **UK** ends with five dots, standardised to four in US and here.

47 **UK** Valentine should support Mrs. Macmaster; **MS** Valentine should
   <accompany> ↑support↓ Mrs. <Duchemin> Macmaster

48 **UK, US** these; **MS** their

49 **UK** distinguished rather; **MS** distinguished <with which she> rather

50 **UK** their so beautiful-souled correspondent; **MS** their ↑so beautiful-souled↓
   correspondent

51 **UK, US** only the Macmaster's treatment; **MS** only <, at last,> the
   Macmaster's treatment; **Ed** only the Macmasters' treatment

52 **UK, US** Mrs. Duchemin's grievance against Tietjens was; **MS** Mrs.
   Duchemin's grievance against Tietjens – her chief grievance – was

53 **UK** Tietjen's motive; **MS, US** Tietjens' motive

54 **UK, US** meet; **MS** met

55 **UK** arrangement she had proposed? Practically; **MS** arrangement ↑she had proposed?↓. Practically

56 **UK** having been certified, the estate; **MS** having <become a lunatic> ↑been certified↓, the estate

57 **UK, US** wondered; **MS** wandered

58 **UK** Valentine Wannop answered hardly anything; **MS** Valentine Wannop <never> answered ↑hardly↓ anything

59 **UK, US** concern of her's; even; **MS** concern of hers; <she certainly,> even

60 **UK** a friend with; **MS** a <man> ↑friend↓ with

61 **UK, US** to; **MS** for

62 **UK** to Macmaster; **MS** to <Tietjens> Macmaster

63 **UK, US** Macmaster, at least, passed for a man; **MS** Macmaster at least passed for a man
Normally UK's changes in the punctuation have been allowed to stand, but the UK/US reading changes the sense – from suggesting Macmaster is less of a man (with the emphasis on 'passed') to suggesting he is more of one (with the emphasis on 'Macmaster') – so MS's version has been restored.

64 **UK** return of Christopher—and; **MS** return of <Tietjens> ↑Christopher↓—and

65 **UK, US** Duchemin; **MS** Tietjens
There is no space between 'Mrs.' and 'Duchemin' in UK, suggesting that the correction was made at proof stage and the correct name had to be squeezed into the available space.

66 Both UK and US insert a spurious set of closing inverted commas here, unwarranted by MS.

67 **UK** She had stopped; **MS** She ↑had↓ stopped

68 **UK** even the stoppage; **MS** even the <sudden> stoppage

69 There are only three dots in UK, but the space before the first is ambiguous: greater than for a full stop and less than for a first suspension dot according to Duckworth's usual practice. US supplies a fourth dot. But the next clause continues the syntax, indicating a three-dot pause.

70 **UK, US** fair; **MS** four
The description of the rectory dining room on 102 mentions one on each of the four panels.

71 **UK** the great curtains; **MS** the <[trailing]> great curtains

72 **UK** the place on Fridays was; **MS** the place ↑on Fridays↓ was

73 **UK** comforting to Valentine to see; **MS** comforting to <[Christopher]> ↑Valentine↓ to see

74 **UK, US** gay; **MS** [grey]
Though the vowel in MS is ambiguous, there does seem to be an 'r' between it and the 'g'; and the word doesn't resemble the instances of 'gay' on leaf 250 and 251 (pp. 305 and 306 here). This passage is from Valentine's point of view, and it sorts better with her outrage at the slight to her mother (and the balance of the rest of the paragraph) that she thinks of her as deserving greater respect on account of her age, rather than as in high spirits regardless.

75 **UK, US** women; **MS** woman

76 **UK** had an emotion; **MS** had an <extraordinarily comic emotion that it was impossible to analyse> emotion

77 **UK** the men—if they didn't; **MS** the men <there knew> —if they didn't

78 **UK** movement with which Valentine; **MS** movement <that> ↓with which↑ Valentine
79 **UK, MS, US** Tietjens
But given the comment later in the chapter about how their 'dark hairs were too untidy for them to amount to much, but, such as they were, they were the two most presentable males of the assembly', it's possible Ford meant 'Macmasters'.
80 **UK** who had been standing; **MS** who <was> ↑had been↓ standing
81 **UK, US** the; **MS** this
82 **UK** high-souled correspondences; **MS** high-souled <[conversations]> correspondences
83 **UK** Macmasters no longer; **MS** Macmasters now no longer
It is possible that in MS the 'now' has been lightly deleted.
84 **UK, US** Abstractions of failing attention; **MS** Abstractions & failing attention
85 **UK, US** maelstrom; **MS** monstrous
'Maelstrom' is a very creative reading of the word in MS, strengthening the context and convincing apart from the lack of a plausible 'l'. Yet it seems too striking a word to slip past even a lackadaisical proofreader, so has been allowed to stand here as likely on balance to have been accepted (if not actually revised) by Ford.
86 **UK** reflux of the time; **MS** reflux <of the [illegible]> of the time
87 **UK, US** "Her book," he said, "had attracted so much attention. They hadn't known that they had still writers among them. . . ."; **MS** Her book, he said, had attracted so much attention. They hadn't known that they had still writing among them. . . :
In MS the last of the suspension dots at the end of the paragraph looks oddly like a colon. Perhaps the compositor took that for closing inverted commas, and thus thought the rest of the comment needed to be in inverted commas. But as the young man is supposed to be talking to Mrs Wannop, it can't be direct speech. The change from 'writing' to 'writers' might have been an error missed because of distraction over the inverted commas, but it has been retained here as more likely an authorial revision to ease intelligibility.
88 **UK, US** coming; **MS** [coursing]
89 **UK, US** borne down Macmaster; **MS** borne down, Macmaster
The version in UK and US without Ford's clear comma is incoherent.
90 Deleted word in MS here appears to be '<dogding>, perhaps intended for 'dodging'?
91 **UK** voice is different; **MS** voice is <quite> different
92 **UK** answer came. "Mathematics; **MS** answer came. <She wouldn't [be in] the least interested>. "Mathematics
93 **UK** cock-fighting." With; **MS** cock-fighting." <Why should they>? With
94 **UK** Macmaster dined; **MS** Macmaster <had certainly> dined
95 **UK, US** Tietjens quite; **MS** Tietjens' quite
96 **UK** Macmaster in his private room, and; **MS** Macmaster ↓in his private room↑ and,
97 **UK** rub into our allies that; **MS** rub into <the French> ↑our allies↓ that
98 **UK** to their lines; **MS** to their <French> lines
In MS 'their' was originally 'the'.
99 **UK** districts, you could; **MS** districts <and their yearly output of coal> you

could

100 **UK** the rest didn't; **MS** the rest <and the non-produced coal> didn't

101 **UK** whole country in peace; **MS** whole <of [illegible] in> ↑country in↓ peace

102 **UK** normal year had cost several; **MS** normal <French> year had <amounted to> ↓cost↑ several

103 **UK** life!—we could go to our allies and say; **MS** life!—you ↑we↓ could go to <the French and say> our allies and say

104 **UK, US** bulls; **MS** balls

105 **UK** though they might; **MS** though they <French> might
The 'y' was evidently added to the 'the' when 'French' was deleted.

106 **UK** not sure afterwards whether; **MS** not sure ↑afterwards↓ whether

107 **UK, US** woman and man in adultery; **MS** woman taken in adultery
The 't' in MS's 'taken' is not unlike Ford's ampersand, so an understandable compositor's error. But the form closely matches 'taken' on the previous leaf (on p. 306 here). The emendation is also warranted not only by the biblical reference to the story in *John* 7:53-8:11 (quoted on 213), and the unidiomatic nature of the phrase 'a woman and man in adultery', but by the fact that Valentine's feeling is not of committing adultery but of being identified in public as in an adulterous situation. 'Trafalgar Square may also suggest the National Gallery, which acquired Rembrandt's 'The Woman Taken in Adultery' in 1824.

108 **UK, US** the Basil's" ¶ Tietjens; **MS** the Basil's <Zaharoff's>." ¶ Tietjens
Basil Zaharoff (1849–1936) was the controversial director and chairman of the arms firm Vickers Ltd during the war. Zaharoff appears as 'Metevsky' in Pound's *Cantos* XVIII and XXXVIII.

109 **UK** often. She added; **MS** often. <in future>. She added

110 **UK** deal. Remember. She lived next door to the rectory for a number of years. And; **MS** deal. ↓Remember. She lived next door to the rectory for a number of years.↑ And

111 **UK** Mr.; **US** Mrs.
MS is ambiguous, but no more so than in the 'Mrs. Duchemin' in the previous sentence.

112 **UK** *think* you've been very; **MS** *think* <it's> ↓you've been↑ very

113 There is an illegible deletion here in MS.

114 **UK** that losses; **MS** that <the [French] [illegible]> losses

115 **UK, US** to break their claims; **MS** to burke their <French> claims
The emendation to 'burke' is required for Edith Ethel's response to make sense. In MS 'their' was presumably revised from 'the' when 'French' was deleted.

116 **UK** beastly people." She; **MS** beastly <French> ↑people↓." She

117 **UK** opinion against; **MS** opinion <is to be welcomed ag> against

118 **UK** welcomed. That's; **MS** welcomed. <And it is known> That's

119 **UK** He's their friend! He; **MS** He's <a friend of the French> ↓their friend!↑ He

120 Full stop in UK; colon in MS and US.

121 **UK** hinder our allies; **MS** hinder <the [war]> our allies

122 **UK** and US omit to start a new paragraph (and thus violate their conventions), though it is indicated in MS.

123 **UK** does himself no good; **MS** does ↓himself↑ no good

124 **UK** They're striking him; **MS** They're <[throwing] him> striking him
125 **UK** It was there that, for the first time, the thought went; **MS** It ↑<was then that the>↓ ↑was then that, for the first time, the thought↓ went
There are two separate marginal insertions in MS here, the first deleted.
126 **UK** these fellows should not; **MS** these fellows <French> should not
The word 'fellows' is at the end of the line, and its positioning to the far right suggests it was added after the deletion of 'French'.
127 **UK** stake. . . ." ¶ Mrs. Duchemin; **MS** stake. . . ." <What you are saying is too horrible>." ¶ Mrs. Duchemin
128 **UK** a snob; **MS** a <damned> snob
129 **UK, US** thoughts; **MS** thought
130 **UK** kindness, tenderness; **MS** kindness <itself>, tenderness
131 **UK** see against that scarlet background the vivid; **MS** see ↓against that scarlet background↑ the vivid
132 **UK** for auld lang syne; **MS** for <the sake of old times> auld lang syne
133 **UK** hidden away? . . ." ¶ Valentine exclaimed; **MS** hidden away? . . ." ¶ <He's got his son>," Valentine <said, "who lives with his sister in Yorkshire. . . There's no secret about that . . ." She> exclaimed
134 **UK** exclaimed harshly, as if she were being strangled; **MS** exclaimed: harshly, as if she were being strangled
The colon after 'exclaimed' in MS, and the fact that the rest of the sentence is written small to fit between the lines above and below, indicate that 'harshly, as if she were being strangled' is a later addition.
135 **UK, US** You could not; **MS** You couldn't not
136 **UK** husband's first little; **MS** husband's ↑first↓ little
137 **UK** she had loved; **MS** she ↑had↓ loved
138 **UK** great iron-lined door; **MS** great <[open]> iron-lined door
139 In MS the line 'Valentine burst a voice through her agonised throat.' was first written below this line, as a new paragraph, then deleted, and the line above continued. The deleted line was then rewritten as the following paragraph.
140 **UK** Saturday. . . . They're sending; **MS** Saturday. . . .<" At that she tried hard to draw her hand away: she missed what he was saying> They're sending
141 **UK** a kind man; **MS** a <good> ↑kind↓ man

## Textual Notes for II.v

1 **UK** and men's black ties; **MS** and black men's ties
2 **UK** mother; whilst; **MS** mother; < – upbraid> whilst
3 Though MS uses four dots here, both UK and US have only three; but in UK 'bathroom', the last word on 322, is not quite right-justified; the second impression of UK supplies the missing dot.
4 **UK** surface the story of her love; **MS** surface ↓the story of↑ her love
5 **UK** and in nothing; **MS** and <had ended> in nothing
6 **UK** most of the young; **MS** most <young women of [her class] to brood upon these subjects.> of the young
7 **UK** Her conviction as to the moral incidence of sex were; **MS** Her <views upon> ↑convictions as to↓ the moral incidence of sex were

8  **UK** would have reacted; **MS** would have <said> reacted
9  **UK** to be prized; **MS** to be <desired> prized
10 **UK** the house in which she had been employed had; **MS** the house ↓in which she had been employed↑ had
11 **UK** advocating of enlightened promiscuity; **MS** advocating of ↓enlightened↑ promiscuity
12 **UK** George Eliots of the last; **MS** George Eliots <and [even] the George Sands> of the last
13 **UK** drunken cook; **MS** drunken <English> cook
14 **UK** able to walk home; **MS** able to direct her feet in walking home
15 **UK** mind a dark patch; **MS** mind <[a] feeling> a dark patch
16 **UK** the quick suspicion; **MS** the <thought> quick suspicion
17 **UK** she considered, made; **MS** she <knew> ↑considered↓, made
18 **UK** convulsions had overwhelmed; **MS** convulsions ↑had↓ overwhelmed
19 The rest of this paragraph (from 'of their drive') to the middle of the next (to 'love scene was. It') was re-drafted in MS onto a separate leaf, numbered 263, to replace the following cancelled passage at the top of the original leaf 263, which was renumbered as 263a:

warm night <of their drive, she had felt that impulsion, and had known that, towards her, he too was feeling it. Now she was to know this emotion all the time: waking and half-waking: and it would drive her from her bed to stand all night at an open window till the stars paled and the world turned grey. It could convulse her with joy; it could [also] shake her with sobs and cut through her breath [sic] as with a knife.

The day of her long interview – for she named to herself the occasions of all their intercourse: The Walk; the Drive; the Long Interview; the Short Talk – that day then, she marked as the day of her great love scene. From that she knew – and she knew that she knew it better than any of the Poets – what a love scene was. It> passed without

The following leaf was renumbered from 264 to 265; the fact that from leaf 266 onwards no renumbering was necessary suggests the insertion was made before Ford had got further than 266 in the writing.
20 **UK** she again hummed; **MS** she <still hum> again hummed
21 **UK, US** cruder; **MS** sadic
22 **UK, US** into shrieked; **MS** into the <[shrieked]> shrieked
23 **UK** But now after her farewell scene with Edith Ethel a simple; **MS** But ↑now after her farewell scene with Edith Ethel↓ a simple
24 **UK** some such passion as jealousy; **MS** some such <[lunatic]> passion as <very precisely,> jealousy
25 **UK** of riotous; **MS** of <[illegible]> riotous
26 **UK** Tietjens, whom; **MS** Tietjens, <it appeared> whom
27 **UK, US** was immoral, and her; **MS** was <an> immoral <[attitude to take] up>, but her; **Ed** was immoral, but her
28 **UK** was going; **MS** was <at least> going
29 **UK** mind of which she knew; **MS** mind <with which she> of which she knew
30 **UK** You have probably mistaken; **MS** You <are> ↑have↓ probably mistaken
31 There is an illegible deletion of three words here in MS, beginning with 'I' and probably continuing 'am Valenti'.
32 **UK** she visited several shops; **MS** she <[searched]> ↑visited↓ several shops

33 **UK** a rag-time party; **MS** a ↓rag-time↑ party
34 **UK** plenty of conchies; **MS** plenty Conchies
35 **UK, US** barely; **MS** hardly
36 **UK** must be cruel! She must be vindictively cruel; **MS** must be cruel! <She must be [brutal]> She must be vindictively cruel
37 **UK, US** these; **MS** those
The word in MS is clear. The other reason for emending is Ford's use of the phrase elsewhere for war-memories. Compare *The Marsden Case* 196: 'I had – who in those days hadn't! – a sense that black shapes hung over that building'; and *Nightingale* 48: 'In those days you saw objects that the earlier mind labelled as *houses*'.
38 **UK** the best bitter!" and; **MS** the best ↑bitter!↓!" and
39 **UK** at 19.30 and give; **MS** at <seven thirty and giv> nineteen thirty and give
40 **UK, US** booze; **MS** hooch
41 **UK, US** 7.20; **MS** seven thirty
42 **UK, US** aligned; **MS** arranged
43 **UK** close drawer after drawer; **MS** close <door after door> drawer after drawer
44 **UK, US** puppy dog! Mrs. Wannop; **MS** puppy dog! She opened her door. Mrs. Wannop
45 **UK, US** wideawake; **MS** wide awake; **Ed** wide-awake
Emended for consistency with other instances in the book.
46 **UK** me!" Valentine said; **MS** me!" <Sylvia> Valentine said
47 **UK** *which* sentence. . . ." She moved; **MS** *which* sentence. . . ." <Her mother said> She moved
The sentences 'She moved, absently, all the cushions to one end of the sofa. Her mother exclaimed:' are later additions, squeezed into the space after the deleted '<Her mother said>'. They are followed by an illegible deletion of about three words.
48 **UK, US** them; **MS** *them*
49 **UK** has a space before the first of the four dots, which is inconsistent with its general practice. US corrects by removing the space.
50 **UK** the flickering; **MS** the <[infinite,]> flickering
51 **UK** sland; **MS, US** island
52 **UK** It might have; **MS** It <would> ↑might↑ have
53 **UK** brother, a responsible one too! Browner; **MS** brother. ↑a responsible one too! ↓ Browner
54 **UK, MS** klaare; **US** klare
55 **UK, US** these hateful lodestones; **MS** [this] hateful lodestone
In MS 'lodestone' is clearly singular. Presumably the compositor was misled by the ambiguous word before 'hateful' into assuming the plural (it might be 'the', 'this', or 'these'). A lodestone is 'Magnetic oxide of iron; also, a piece of this used as a magnet'; hence '*fig.* Something which attracts': *OED*. The plural aligns the lodestones with the 'the sordid stones' of 'these stone buildings' of the Admiralty and War Office. But in the singular it appears to refer to Christopher, who is attracting Valentine despite her anger (or rather, her attraction towards whom is making her scared and angry).
56 **UK** the words; **MS** the <flood of> words
57 **UK** His looks were; **MS** His <eyes> ↑looks↓ were

58 **UK** than words; **MS** than <, in a love scene> words
59 **UK** Transport for a rest; the safest; **MS** Transport ↑for a rest↓; the safest
60 **UK** mocassined; **MS, US** moccasined
61 **UK** his shy efforts; **MS** his <[nervous &]> shy efforts
62 **UK, US** wideawake; **MS** wide-awake
   Emended for consistency with previous usage.
63 **UK, US** sable; **MS** table
64 **UK, US** was a Godsend; yet; **MS** was God sent; yet
65 **UK, US** Riccardo!" Mark; **MS** Riccardo?" Mark
66 **UK, MS** vice; **US** vise
67 The last nine lines of this leaf (273) have been deleted, and replaced with a
   supplementary leaf (273a), running from "'He must have his buttered toast
   [. . .]'" to 'Mrs. Micawber'. The deleted passage is as follows:

> "He must have his buttered toast . . . and his mutton chop . . . and Rhum.
> St James . . ." He said: "Damn it all! You're the poor dear fellow's Charlotte
> . . . His face became panic-stricken; his eyes gazed on the pulpit of the two
> commissionaires. He whispered:
> "You won't . . . because of my clumsy ox's hoof . . . desert. . . ."
>   She said:
> "I ask you to believe . . . To believe that I will never . . . abandon . . . ."

68 **UK** coupling you. . . . They're; **MS** coupling you. . . . <[They've come to it]>
   They're
69 **UK** Beatrice? There are couples like that." ¶ She; **MS** Beatrice? ↓There are
   couples like that."↑ ¶ She
70 **UK** desert[ / ]. . . .; **US** desert. . . .
   The line ending after 'desert' in the UK implies (perhaps inadvertently) a
   space before the first of the four dots, removed here for consistency.
71 **UK** hoarsely. "I ask; **MS** hoarsely: she said: "I ask
72 **UK** Tietjens—in his; **MS** Tietjens <said suddenly>—in his
73 **UK** Towards what? ¶ Like mutes; **MS** Towards what? ¶ <They walked>,
   Like mutes
74 **UK, US** islands; **MS** island
   Emended also for consistency with the previous mention (on 331), where
   MS even more decisively reads 'island'.
75 Both UK and US end this paragraph with an em dash; an uncharacteristic
   usage here. MS is ambiguous, but has a dot followed by an uneven dash. Both
   are at the bottom of the line, whereas the dash after 'escort' earlier in the
   paragraph (the preceding dash for that parenthesis was added in proof) is in
   the middle of the line, and is much shorter. Ford appears to have written four
   dots here, but to have smudged several together, as he often did.
76 **UK** gravelled majestic space; **MS** gravelled ↑majestic↓ space
77 **UK** was, no doubt, getting drunk; **MS** was ↑no doubt↓ getting drunk
78 **UK** I have wanted; **MS** I <wanted> have wanted
79 **UK** ankle-nigh; **MS, US** ankle-high

## Textual Notes for II.vi

1  **UK** glimmerings above, cut; **MS** glimmerings <at the tops> ↑above↓, cut

2  **UK** ought to reach his round-backed chair, by the left-hand window. He
   sank; **MS** ought to reach his round backed chair, by the left-hand window.
   He reached his round backed chair by the left-hand window. He sank
   The sentence dropped from MS could be a case of compositor's eye-slip due
   to the repetition, but it has not been restored on the grounds that it could
   equally have been an authorial deletion for the same reason.
3  **UK** whiskered man: Arnold; **MS** whiskered <fellow> ↑man↓: Arnold
4  **UK** held up squares; **MS** held up <[illegible] photograph> squares
5  **UK, US** A meeting; **MS** At meeting
6  **UK** aptly put it; **MS** aptly <reminded> put it
7  **UK** they had carried the boy; **MS** they had <walked> carried the boy
8  In UK and US the lines are printed as prose, and the 'And' at the start of the
   second is not capitalised. MS clearly writes the lines as verse, capitalised and
   indented.
9  **UK** Ugly . . . Too . . . oh . . . *private!*" ¶ He said; **MS** Ugly . . . <Too [priv]>
   Too . . . oh . . . *private!*" <[Something]>!" ¶ He said
10 This sentence is a marginal insertion in MS.
11 **UK** thousand painful months; **MS** thousand <yet more> painful months
12 **UK** pomegranates. . . The; **US** pomegranates. . . . The
13 **UK** this bit; **MS** this <little> bit
14 **UK** at your goings out; **MS** at your <comings out and your goings in>" goings
   out
15 Both UK and US garble the punctuation here, using double inverted
   commas for the quotation, forgetting that it's within Valentine's speech and
   thus forgetting the closing inverted commas for that speech.
16 **UK** pocket. ¶ "The talismanic; **MS** pocket. ¶ "<A talisman> The talismanic
17 **UK, US** wash out this afternoon . . . . It; **MS** wash out . . . . It
   The addition (presumably in proofs) of the words 'this afternoon' suggests
   that, whatever Ford meant Tietjens to mean by the phrase 'wash out', Valentine uses it transitively, with a sense of washing away: either suppressing the
   afternoon's meeting altogether, or removing a stain from it.
18 **UK** be trusted. To keep on for ever. . . . You; **MS** be trusted. ↓To keep on
   for ever↑. . . . You
19 UK and US have spurious closing inverted commas here, which are not in
   MS.
20 **UK** just before 4.58 it was when I said that to you and you consented . . . I
   heard; **MS** just before 4.58 it was . . . I heard
   This is an unusual example of a significant addition being made between MS
   and UK, and which was perhaps again made to clarify what they meant by
   'wash out'.
21 **UK** first spoken sign." ¶ He; **MS** first <time ever> ↑spoken↓ . . ." ¶ He
22 **UK** every word; **MS** every spoken word
23 UK and US omit the requisite new paragraph here, though it's clearly indicated in MS.
24 MS has a colon here, which UK and US would normally soften to a semi-
   colon or comma. UK has a blank space where the punctuation should be.
   US merely closes up the gap and uses no punctuation but the rest of the
   sentence implies it.
25 **UK** Tietjens had said: ¶ "I'm not; **MS** Tietjens had said: ¶ "<You drop it,
   [sonny].> "I'm not

26 **UK** services of a specific kind Tietjens; **MS** services <against the French>
   ↑<Allies>↓ ↑of a specific kind↓ Tietjens
27 **UK** unusually has five dots here, MS and US four.
28 **UK, US** She's at another; **MS** She's another
29 **UK** Macmaster's eyes, though; **MS** Macmaster's <face> ↑eyes↓ tho
30 **UK** queer thing that you; **MS** queer thing: <to think> that you
31 **UK** fiercely, when his; **MS** fiercely <now that> ↑when↓ his
32 Again UK has five dots here, US four. MS has only three.
33 **UK** that can be trusted to keep on. . . ."; **MS** that can be trusted. . . ."
34 **UK** I will never cut what you said then out of my memory; **MS** I will never
   cut out of my memory
35 After the single word, 'End', MS is dated 'Paris 22.9.23.'.

# APPENDIX

## Reconstruction of the Original Ending

This appendix contains the only additional known manuscript material for *Some Do Not* . . . : a single torn and crumpled leaf of autograph manuscript and a three-page fragment of typescript, two-thirds of which was typeset and proofed for a dummy copy of the *transatlantic review*. The typescript and proofs belonged to the Ford collector Edward Naumburg, Jr, who published the text in his essay 'A Collector Looks at Ford Again', in *The Presence of Ford Madox Ford*, ed. Sondra J. Stang.* Stang claimed that though 'This chapter was heretofore believed to be the alternate ending of *Some Do Not* . . . It appears to be a draft of the first chapter of Part Two' (xvi). In fact the typescript is only a fragment of a chapter. And though it certainly relates to the end of II.ii (not II.i), since in it Tietjens remembers more of the Christina Rossetti poem he was struggling to recall then, it is clearly located at the end of the narrative. It describes a scene between Christopher and Sylvia, after he has come back from the Wannops' house (in the book's final chapter) the night before his departure for France. Sylvia has been waiting for him in the dark (which develops the moment when he hears something move, and thinks it's probably the cat, then wonders if it's Sylvia). She attempts to seduce him before he leaves, with the threat that he will probably never see her again. Instead of responding sexually, Tietjens quotes the Rossetti poem to her, and she hits him in the face and leaves the room. A couple of hours before he is due to catch his train to Waterloo for France, he hears her say 'Paddington' to the cabman who has come to drive her to the station, on her journey

* Stang, *Presence* 180–2.

to the convent where she is planning to go into retreat. (In the book Tietjens thinks it must be 3.30 when he lets himself in. The time in the typescript here must be about 5.30, since Sylvia has to leave to catch the 6.15 train, and Tietjens thinks of meeting his fellow officers on the train in three hours' time: in the book his train leaves at 8.30 or 9.00.)

The typescript and both sets of proofs identify the extract as for 'Some do Not' (without the suspension dots) and conclude with the words 'The End', making it fairly clear they were indeed intended as the conclusion to that novel. However, Ford recast the material and used the episode in *No More Parades*, presenting it through Tietjens' recollections from France (see below).

Each set of proofs – one corrected by hand, the other revised according to these corrections – consists of just two pages, which omit the central section of the three-page typescript (from '"We might as well not quarrel now"' to the end of the indented song quotation: '""Made answer to my . . . [']"'). The first (hand-revised) proofs quote at the top the last two lines of the song, which suggests that a page is missing.* But these two lines have been deleted and replaced with a line of dots. The revises just include these dots, to indicate an ellipsis or lapse of time, as if no text were actually missing. It is unclear whether Ford meant to delete this section from the novel at this stage, or whether he (or a sub-editor) was simply concealing the lack of continuity in what was, after all, only a dummy issue to give investors a taste of the magazine's contents. The text here is thus taken from the typescript, but incorporating corrections made to those parts existing in proof.

The single autograph page was mistakenly assumed to be a fragment from *No More Parades* when it was first catalogued at Cornell University Library, reasonably enough since it includes a passage that corresponds to one towards the end of the first chapter of that novel, in which Tietjens tells McKenzie/McKechnie about his encounter in the War Office with a man

---

* What can be made out of the original page numbering confirms this. On the first leaf the printed number '10' has been emended by hand to '11', whereas the second appears originally to have borne the printed number '12', which has been deleted, and emended by hand first to '13' then '12'. Thus it appears that there was a page with the printed number 11 that contained the omitted text.

'devising the ceremonial for the disbanding of a Kitchener battalion' after the war, and says that 'the adjutant would say: *There will be no more parades. . . .*' – which of course gave Ford the title for the second novel. In the autograph fragment, Tietjens recalls this scene to himself. When it was originally catalogued, the existence or whereabouts of the manuscript of *No More Parades* was unknown, so it couldn't be compared against that. However, there is no correspondence with that typescript, or the published novel, other than with that scene at the War Office. On the other hand, taken together with the autograph manuscript and the typed variant ending of *Some Do Not . . .*, both at Princeton, the correspondence is compelling.

Essentially, the autograph fragment follows on from the situation described at the beginning of the last chapter in MS and the published version. There, II.vi starts with Tietjens returning to his Holborn flat, sitting in the dark, ruminating on the events of the night, and wondering if a noise at the far end of the room means that Sylvia has been waiting there for him. It ends with his memories of his farewell to Valentine, and concludes with the sentence about the transport lorry giving him a lift back to Holborn; this at the foot of MS's last leaf, 281. That returns the narrative to the flat. The Cornell autograph leaf is numbered 282, and continues the narrative as well as the number sequence. In it, Tietjens is sitting in the flat deep in thought as dawn begins to break. It becomes light enough for him to be able to make out something white on the chair across the room; then suddenly he sees it is indeed Sylvia. She quizzes him about his meeting with his 'girl'. Unfortunately the bottom right-hand corner of the leaf has been torn off, with the loss of some twenty to thirty words.

The two fragments transcribed here are given in the sequence indicated by the plot. Their juxtaposition brings out the extent to which the second follows on directly from the first. In the passage near the beginning of the typed fragment:

> She said at last:
> "Then"—he wondered why she said: "then!"—"you understand that you will in all probability never see me again.

the 'at last' indicates Sylvia finally breaking a silence which could be the one begun at the end of the autograph leaf ('she did not speak'). More to the point, though Tietjens is baffled by her breaking the silence with 'Then', what she says could be understood as following on from (what the tear allows us to see of) their conversation at the end of the autograph leaf. That is, Sylvia hears that Valentine hasn't become Tietjens' mistress, she realises that her plan to seduce him afterwards has been frustrated, and that his love for Valentine is as strong as ever. That is why Sylvia decides to go into retreat: to escape the humiliation of her unreciprocated passion for him. This continuity between the autograph and typed fragments is strongly supported by the page numbering of the latter, which runs from 283 to 285, suggesting that these typed pages were the original ending of MS, and that Ford switched to the typewriter for the last three pages.*

The redescription of this autograph leaf as a fragment from *Some Do Not ...* offers a new understanding of the relation between MS and the typed variant ending, since the autograph fragment proves the bridge between them. This in turn enables us to redescribe the typed variant, not as an early version of a chapter or passage published in the novel, but as additional material to the published text; an earlier ending that Ford simply excised, deciding to cut off the narrative at leaf 281 of MS instead. (It is possible that he rewrote that last leaf once he had cancelled the earlier ending, so as to bring the novel to a close; but we have no evidence there of any revision – other than the word 'End', which must have been a later addition according to this scenario.)

If there is no lacuna between the end of UK and the start of

---

* While it is possible these three typed pages were copy-typed from a lost autograph ending, that seems improbable, since the typist would have been unlikely to transcribe the page numbering from MS (and the numbering is far too high for an issue of the magazine, the first three issues of which didn't exceed 120 pages). Besides, the typing continues to the foot of each page, which would be unlikely were the typist trying to preserve the pagination of a conjectural autograph. Thus the most likely scenario is that these pages were typed as the ending of the novel, but then chosen as material for the *transatlantic* dummy, at which point the words 'Serial' and 'From SOME do NOT' were added to leaf 283. However, the evidence is inconclusive here: while the words 'From SOME do NOT' do not align with the typed number 283, suggesting that the page was reinserted into the machine to add them, the word 'Serial' is on the same line as the '283' (which might mean the typescript was labelled as 'Serial' from the start, which in turn might support its having been copied from a previous version, but doesn't prove it).

Cornell leaf 282 and, as argued above, there is also a continuity between this fragment and the typed fragment, then what we almost certainly have – assembled together here for the first time – is a complete text (bar the words lost on the torn corner) of a cancelled original ending, and probably in its first version, which would also complete the entire original manuscript.* However, we cannot be sure that both fragments are from the same version (which is why they are not conflated here). The fact that they appear to dovetail, and are the only pieces of the jigsaw we have, suggests that they might be; the facts that one is autograph but the other typed, and that they have been separated since 1923, suggests they could equally be from different versions. (It's possible, that is to say, that the cancelled ending existed entirely in autograph, but that some or all of it was then typed up, and possibly revised, for the *review*. However, the manuscripts for the other volumes all mix typescript and autograph; so the fact that what survives of this ending is such a hybrid doesn't prove anything about the number of versions.) Either way, their conti-nuities, as well as their correspondences with the reworked accounts of this episode in *No More Parades*, mean that they give as clear an idea as we're likely to get of how Ford's original ending went.

---

\* A further but more fanciful possibility is that it that it was written purely for the dummy, as a later variation on, or continuation of, the ending in MS, perhaps written more sensationally so as to entice potential backers, but that Ford had never thought of it as part of the published novel. However, it's hard to see why Ford would have numbered it so as to connect it with MS if he meant to disconnect it. Both fragments are discussed further in 'A Note on the Text': see lxxix–lxxxii.

## a) Autograph fragment: leaf 282*

It had grown grey† in the room: the flowers on the breakfast
table shewed white. In the companion arm chair to his own,
thirty feet away beside the other [end] window, there was something white: as if Hullo Central had thrown a table-cloth into it:
or bed-clothes . . .

His mind said to him:

"Well!" as if it asked: "What do we do next?" He seemed to
hear an infantry bugle say faintly: "There's no parade to-day . . . ."
Or rather: At the very beginning of the War he had gone into the
War Office & found a man – they are so careful! – devising the
Ceremonial for disbanding the Kitchener Battalions that were
not yet raised! The Colonel was to say: "Stand Easy": the band to
play: "Land of Hope & Glory." Then: clearly: the Adjutant was
to exclaim:

"There . . . will . . . be . . . no . . . more . . . Parades!" . . . .

He said to his mind:

"There will be no more parades!"

. . . There would be no more parades! No girl:‡ no Club: no
Bank: no Office . . . . Even that poor fool, Father Consett was
killed. . . . Nothing to face but out there, at railheads in the dawn
the great – oh appalling! – bubbling of that distant saucepan.§ He
saw the bonnets** of desultory Highlanders: as he stood on the
step of the train: from above: pale, round disks, catching the
dawn. He forced his mind back to the room. It had become
daylight: by an absurd trick of Providence! As when, on the stage,
a fellow lights a match &, heigh presto, you see every detail of
the plush furniture in a welling blaze of light.

---

* Published with the kind permission of Michael Schmidt and the Carl A. Kroch
  Library, Cornell University.
† See note on 322. The echo of the Swinburne suggests an ambiguity with which Ford
  appears to frame this ending: is Tietjens conceding that he is conquered by his love
  for Valentine, or that the victory is Sylvia's?
‡ This passage is revealing about the semantic range Ford gives the term 'parade', since
  the inclusion of 'the girl' here adds a sense of celebration and exuberance to that of
  pre-war ceremonials and formalities outmoded by the war.
§ This word might seem an implausible transcription, but it picks up the image from
  II.iii, just after Tietjens has recalled some of the Christina Rossetti poem: 'For a
  moment Tietjens saw the grey dawn at rail-head with the distant sound of a ceaselessly boiling pot, from miles away!'
** The caps of the Highlander regiments are referred to as 'bonnets'.

Sylvia: the white mass in the other armchair was of course Sylvia: was looking at him with unwinking eyes.... Marble!

She said:

"Well! Have you had your girl? Did you like her?"

He said:

"No! I haven't."

She had been sitting coiled up: she let her feet slowly to the ground & wavered over to him. She was all in white: a peignoir over a night gown. She looked him [torn]

the eyes. It could not have been so very lig[ht] [torn]

misty.

"You love her so much!" she sa[torn]

much!"

He said:

"We decided that we w [torn]

she said: "Oh God!" She certa[inly?] [torn]

she did not speak.

### b) Typescript fragment found with material for the *transatlantic review**

Serial                              *From* SOME do NOT by F. M. Ford

It was certainly grown lighter. He could see that she had, moving between her breasts, on a little gold chain, a little gold coin that shewed the image; certainly of St. Michael. He wondered whom she had at the front. Catholics wear little gold coins with St. Michael on them when they have lovers at the front, the patron saint of soldier men. She said at last:

"Then" – he wondered why she said: "then!" – "you understand that you will in all probability never see me again. I am going into practically permanent retreat with the female Premonstratensians[†] at Slough.[‡]

He asked:

* Published with the kind permission of Michael Schmidt and Princeton University Library.
† See note to p. 53 above.
‡ In II.i Father Consett recommends Sylvia a Premonstratensian convent near Birkenhead.

"You'll be able to look after the boy?" He was glad she was going to Papist nuns.

She said:

"Yes! He'll go to Eton and to Mother's in the holidays. Perhaps your brother will let us have Groby now and again . . ."

He said:

"He probably will!"

She said:

"You understand that, if you ever go near that girl again, ever even into her mother's house, I'll raise such Cain she'll wish she was never born."

He stood up.

"We might as well not quarrel now," he said.

She exclaimed:

"You oaf!"

He said dully: for he was determined not to quarrel:

"I'd like you to give my really dear love to your mother."

She said:

"She's coming to see you off. She doesn't mind risking meeting your girl . . . That's part of the mischief you've done . . ." He felt a sudden pleasure at the idea of Mrs. Satterthwaite's distracted figure amongst groups of subalterns on a long platform. She said:

"Oh God! How could you be such a skunk! The girl was waiting to drop into your mouth like a grape. Couldn't you bring yourself to seduce a . . . a little kitchen maid? Are they so rare!"

He was wondering by what queer morality a man was a skunk because he wouldn't seduce. Because of the girl's disappointment? That surely was too altruistic.

"Then there'd have been a chance . . ." Sylvia said. She had[1] shaken off her outer garment: the whole of her figure was visible under a film that glistened a little. He felt undoubtedly a desire for her. She, he knew, knew that she could calculate on that. She said, her voice trembling:

"I'm going by the 6.15, if I go. If I go I must go and dress at once . . . No: you won't have to see to the luggage. It has gone: except my dress. If I go you never see me again . . ." The muscles of all her body worked under the thin film that was like the covering of a meringue. He said to himself:

"It must be queer to play Potiphar's wife[*] to your own husband!" The idea of the long hours she had spent crouched in the chair overwhelmed him. She was standing so near him that he could almost feel the warmth. He could quite ...

He said suddenly:

"I've remembered the words of the song you wanted, my memory's suddenly extraordinarily better."

She recoiled the whole of her body from him, though her bare feet remained where they had been in their red leather mules.[2]

He said:

"'Somewhere or other there must surely be
The face not seen: the voice not ever heard:
The voice that never yet: that never yet, ah me,
Made answer to my ... [']"[†]

Whiteness arose before him: there was a peculiar sound: like air escaping from a tyre-valve. He felt great pain on each side of his face. With her fists clenched, downwards, she had struck him with the hams of her hands, using all her strength, on his two cheekbones. There was a tearing sound. She was gone. Her white peignoir lay at his feet as he sank down into his chair again.

"By God!" he said, "I probably am a skunk! ... I probably am!"

He wondered how he would explain two contused eyes to a trainload of brother officers in three hours time. You couldn't invent an accident fantastic enough. They would certainly say it had been a woman.

The fear of the dreadful war dropped down on him and he began to count his chances of escape. What else was there to do? He couldn't in decency, at that moment think of his girl, impregnable. That was to be for tomorrow. Today: it would be like thinking of a new bride over a wife's unfilled grave.

There was no doubt that, by then, it was broad day.

The door just opened itself: a small gold object fell into the room and lay on the carpet, near the door. It was the medallion of St. Michael that had been between his wife's breasts. He wondered if that meant that she cast him off—or that she sent it

---

[*] In the book of *Genesis*, Potiphar is the Egyptian to whom Joseph is sold as a household slave. Potiphar's wife is angry that Joseph resists her attempts to seduce him, so she accuses him of rape and Potiphar sends him to prison.

[†] The correct version of these lines is given in the note to 202.

to him to wear and be safe. It had certainly been blessed by the Pope! He heard down below the great door close. Afterwards he heard, from the street Sylvia's clear, unconcerned voice say: "Paddington!"

—THE END—

### c) Comparable passages in *No More Parades*

The episode was recast into the following passages from *No More Parades*, in which it is pieced together retrospectively, mainly by Tietjens, but in the last quotation by Sylvia, who confirms that it was she who said the word 'Paddington', intending it as significant:

> In the complete stillness of dawn he had heard her voice say very clearly "Paddington" to the chauffeur, and then all the sparrows in the inn waking up in chorus.... Suddenly and appallingly it came into his head that it might not have been his wife's voice that had said "Paddington," but her maid's.... (I.ii)

> Obviously his mind until now had regarded his wife's "*Paddington*" as the definite farewell between his life and hers [...] And of course it might have been only the maid that had spoken.... She too had a remarkably clear voice. So that the mystic word "Paddington" might perfectly well be no symbol at all, and Mrs. Sylvia Tietjens, far from being faint and pale, might perfectly well be playing the very devil with half the general officers commanding in chief from Whitehall to Alaska.
> (I.ii)

> What, in the eyes of God, severed a union? ... Certainly he had imagined—until that very afternoon—that their union had been cut, as the tendon of Achilles is cut in a hamstringing, by Sylvia's clear voice, outside his house, saying in the dawn to a cabman, "Paddington!".... He tried to go with

extreme care through every detail of their last interview in his still nearly dark drawing-room at the other end of which she had seemed a mere white phosphorescence. . . .

They had, then, parted for good on that day. He was going out to France; she into retreat in a convent near Birkenhead—to which place you go from Paddington. Well then, that was one parting. That, surely, set him free for the girl! (I.iii)

"I got home towards two in the morning and went into the dining-room in the dark. I did not need a light. I sat thinking for a long time. Then Sylvia spoke from the other end of the room. There was thus an abominable situation. I have never been spoken to with such hatred. She went, perhaps, mad. She had apparently been banking on the idea that if I had physical contact with Miss Wannop I might satisfy my affection for the girl. . . . And feel physical desires for *her*. . . . But she knew, without my speaking, that I had not had physical contact with the girl. She threatened to ruin me; to ruin me in the Army; to drag my name through the mud. . . . I never spoke. I am damn good at not speaking. She struck me in the face. And went away. Afterwards she threw into the room, through the half-open doorway, a gold medallion of St. Michael, the R.C. patron of soldiers in action that she had worn between her breasts. I took it to mean the final act of parting. As if by no longer wearing it she abandoned all prayer for my safety. . . . It might just as well mean that she wished me to wear it myself for my personal protection. . . . I heard her go down the stairs with her maid. The dawn was just showing through the chimney-pots opposite. I heard her say: *Paddington*. Clear, high syllables! And a motor drove off.["]
(I.iii)

and in Part II from Sylvia's point of view:

But he *had* noticed the word Paddington. . . . Ninety-eight days before. . . . She had counted every day since. . . . She had got that much information. . . . She had said *Paddington* outside the house at dawn and he had taken it as a farewell. He

*had* . . . He had imagined himself free to do what he liked with the girl. . . . Well, he wasn't. . . . That was why he was white about the gills. . . .
(II.ii)

There are various possible conjectures as to why the variant ending was not used in *Some Do Not* . . . . It may be that Ford submitted the book with this ending, but that (as with the expletives in *No More Parades*) the publisher thought Sylvia's interrogation, especially 'Have you had your girl? Did you like her?', and her attempt to seduce Tietjens were too risqué and required the change. But no record of any such negotiation has survived. Or there may have been a more personal reason. Stella Bowen might have been uneasy (or Ford might have been concerned that she would be) about the possible inference that Ford and Violet Hunt had had such conversations about her.

Alternatively, the reason may have been primarily a critical one. Ford may have decided that it would have given the novel too cynical an ending, closing on Sylvia's violence rather than the pathos of Tietjens' and Valentine's renunciation, contrasted with the Macmasters' keeping a secret of their relationship and marriage.

Or he may simply have felt that he hadn't brought it off. The dialogue is perhaps a little too flat to achieve the desired intensity. Perhaps he thought the episode could be more effective filtered through Tietjens' memories of it while at the Front, where it does the extra and recurrent work of magnifying his anxieties there. Ford was reading passages from the novel to friends such as Ezra Pound and Douglas Goldring in Paris.* That might bespeak uncertainty about its effect, and some revisions may have been made in response to his audience's comments.

In a sense, the excision helps explain the reaction of those reviewers who found the novel inconclusive. In his study of Henry James, Ford writes of 'the economically worded, carefully progressing set of apparently discursive episodes, all resolved, as it were, in the *coup de* [*canon*] of the last sentence, that are found

---

* Saunders, *Dual Life* II 134.

in one of the *contes* of Maupassant'.* Sylvia's hitting Tietjens in the face, and her uttering 'Paddington' as a parting shot, would have provided just that pyrotechnic flourish. One can see how, perhaps with some revision, it could have been a highly effective ending; snapping the story shut in terms both of narrative and form, and resulting in a more modern and more satisfyingly complete novel, with Sylvia's explosion of rage recapitulating the shell-blast that Tietjens suffered at the Front. But that may have been exactly what Ford didn't want, either because it would check the forward momentum of the series, or because it would simply be too flashy. After all, his point in *Henry James* is that James is the kind of writer and his stories (which are expansive enough to count as novellas) the kind of writing that don't give us such bravura flourishes. Ford may have wanted to make the ending seem less final. The other volumes have his more characteristic throw-away endings (as in *The Good Soldier*). Closing on Tietjens' meditations about Valentine rather than Sylvia's departure might be a signal that the story was to be continued, leaving a poignant sense of frustrated hope, and an even less resolved situation, that the narrative could return to from different angles and elaborate later on. In the published text Ford tones down the ending even further, leaving us not with Tietjens' ruminations, but the one-sentence paragraph: 'He had caught, outside the gates of his old office, a transport lorry that had given him a lift to Holborn. . . .' This provides a sense of formal completeness to set against the emotional and narrative incompleteness, with, as Paul Skinner notes, 'the balance of that lift in a transport lorry, starting him on his way, off to the slaughterhouse, set against the close of Part I: the knacker's cart coming round the corner'.[†]

Whether or not these fragments should be considered part of the pre-publication material for *Some Do Not . . .*, the fact that so much of the episode is reworked in *No More Parades* might be thought to turn them into working notes towards that novel. However, although the completion date for the manuscript of *Some Do Not . . .*, 22 September, means Ford could have begun the next novel in late 1923, the composition dates given in the

* *Henry James* 129–30 (where '*canon*' has acquired a superfluous extra 'n').
† Paul Skinner to Max Saunders, pers. comm. 15 February 2010.

dedication to *No More Parades* have it started a year later, on 31 October 1924. If the variant ending effectively became a draft of material to be reworked in the sequel, that decision was made later. In the typescript for the *transatlantic* it is still clearly marked as the ending of *Some Do Not . . . .* But it may be that, as Ford's thoughts turned towards the continuation of the story, he simply decided that the material would sit better in *No More Parades* – especially if he had already settled on its title by then.

What the original but abandoned ending reveals is that Ford had already imagined in detail this confrontation between Sylvia and Christopher when he was writing *Some Do Not . . .*; and that though he excluded it from that novel, he didn't exclude it from the story. It thus retained a limbo-like existence, neither quite in nor out of the work, until the completion of *No More Parades*, where the scene, though presented differently, remained much the same. That says much about his working methods, evoking a practice of imagining full lives for the characters even beyond the confines of the book. Of course some aspects of these lives may have come from his own life, as this confrontation perhaps drew on his fraught scenes with Violet Hunt in 1917.* But from another point of view, the uncertain status of such pre-publication variants corresponds to the uncertainty thematised in relation to this episode, when Tietjens isn't sure whether it was actually Sylvia's voice uttering the word he took to be final.

## Textual Notes on the Variant Ending

1 **Typescript** She had She had shaken; **Ed** She had shaken
2 **Typescript** mueles; **Ed** mules

---

* See Saunders, *A Dual Life* II 28–30, 37–8.

# SELECT BIBLIOGRAPHY

## Works by Ford (whether as 'Hueffer' or 'Ford')

*Ancient Lights and Certain New Reflections: Being the Memories of a Young Man* (London: Chapman & Hall, 1911); published as *Memories and Impressions* (New York: Harper, 1911)

*The Benefactor* (London: Brown, Langham, 1905)

*A Call* (London: Chatto and Windus, 1910)

*The Cinque Ports* (Edinburgh and London: William Blackwood and Sons, 1900)

*The Correspondence of Ford Madox Ford and Stella Bowen*, ed. Sondra Stang and Karen Cochran (Bloomington and Indianapolis: Indiana University Press, 1994)

*The Critical Attitude* (London: Duckworth, 1911)

*Critical Essays*, ed. Max Saunders and Richard Stang (Manchester: Carcanet, 2002)

*England and the English*, ed. Sara Haslam (Manchester: Carcanet, 2003) (collecting Ford's trilogy on Englishness: *The Soul of London*, *The Heart of the Country* and *The Spirit of the People*)

*The Fifth Queen* (London: Alston Rivers, 1906)

*The Fifth Queen Crowned* (Eveleigh Nash, 1908)

*The Ford Madox Ford Reader*, with Foreword by Graham Greene; ed. Sondra J. Stang (Manchester: Carcanet, 1986)

*The Good Soldier*, ed. Martin Stannard (Norton Critical Edition; New York and London: W. W. Norton & Company, 1995)

*The Heart of the Country* (London: Alston Rivers, 1906)

*It Was the Nightingale* (1933), ed. John Coyle (Manchester: Carcanet, 2007)

*Joseph Conrad: A Personal Remembrance* (London: Duckworth, 1924; Boston: Little, Brown, 1924)

*Last Post* (London: Duckworth, 1928) – the fourth and final novel of *Parade's End*

*Letters of Ford Madox Ford*, ed. Richard M. Ludwig (Princeton, NJ: Princeton University Press, 1965)

*A Man Could Stand Up* (London: Duckworth, 1926) – the third novel
   of *Parade's End*

*The March of Literature* (London: Allen & Unwin, 1939)

*The Marsden Case* (London: Duckworth, 1923)

*Mightier Than the Sword* (London: Allen & Unwin, 1938)

*Mister Bosphorus and the Muses or a Short History of Poetry in Britain.
   Variety Entertainment in Four Acts... with Harlequinade, Transforma-
   tion Scene, Cinematograph Effects, and Many Other Novelties,* as well
   as *Old and Tried Favourites,* illustrated by Paul Nash (London: Duckworth, 1923)

*No More Parades* (London: Duckworth, 1925) – the second novel of
   *Parade's End*

*No Enemy* (1929), ed. Paul Skinner (Manchester: Carcanet, 2002)

*Pound/Ford: the Story of a Literary Friendship: the Correspondence between
   Ezra Pound and Ford Madox Ford and Their Writings About Each Other,*
   ed. Brita Lindberg-Seyersted (London: Faber & Faber, 1982)

*Privy Seal* (London: Alston Rivers, 1907)

*Provence* (1935), ed. John Coyle (Manchester: Carcanet, 2009)

*Return to Yesterday* (1931), ed. Bill Hutchings (Manchester: Carcanet,
   1999)

*Some Do Not ...* (London: Duckworth, 1924)

*The Spirit of the People* (London: Alston Rivers, 1907)

*Thus to Revisit* (London: Chapman and Hall, 1921)

*War Prose,* ed. Max Saunders (Manchester: Carcanet, 1999)

*When Blood is Their Argument* (London: Hodder & Stoughton, 1915)

## Other Works

Harvey, David Dow, *Ford Madox Ford: 1873–1939: A Bibliography of
   Works and Criticism* (Princeton, NJ: Princeton University Press,
   1962)

Saunders, Max, *Ford Madox Ford: A Dual Life,* 2 vols (Oxford: Oxford
   University Press, 1996)

Stang, Sondra J., ed., *The Presence of Ford Madox Ford* (Philadelphia:
   University of Pennsylvania Press, 1981)

## Further Critical Reading on *Parade's End*

Armstrong, Paul, *The Challenge of Bewilderment: Understanding and
   Representation in James, Conrad, and Ford* (Ithaca, NY, and London:

Cornell University Press, 1987)

Attridge, John, "'I Don't Read Novels ... I Know What's in 'em": Impersonality, Impressionism and Responsibility in *Parade's End*', in *Impersonality and Emotion in Twentieth-Century British Literature*, ed. Christine Reynier and Jean-Michel Ganteau (Montpellier: Université Montpellier III, 2005)

Auden, W. H., 'Il Faut Payer', *Mid-Century*, 22 (Feb. 1961), 3–10

Becquet, Alexandra, 'Modernity, Shock and Cinema: The Visual Aesthetics of Ford Madox Ford's *Parade's End*', in *Ford Madox Ford and Visual Culture*, ed. Laura Colombino, International Ford Madox Ford Studies, 8 (Amsterdam and New York: Rodopi, 2009), 191–204

Bergonzi, Bernard, *Heroes' Twilight: A Study of the Literature of the Great War* (Manchester: Carcanet, 3rd edn, 1996)

Bradbury, Malcolm, 'The Denuded Place: War and Ford in *Parade's End* and *U. S. A.*', in *The First World War in Fiction*, ed. Holger Klein (London and Basingstoke: Macmillan, rev. edn, 1978), 193–209

—'Introduction', *Parade's End* (London: Everyman's Library, 1992)

Brasme, Isabelle, 'Between Impressionism and Modernism: *Some Do Not ...*, a poetics of the *Entre-deux*', in *Ford Madox Ford: Literary Networks and Cultural Transformations*, ed. Andrzej Gasiorek and Daniel Moore, International Ford Madox Ford Studies, 7 (Amsterdam and New York: Rodopi, 2008), 189–99

Brown, Dennis, 'Remains of the Day: Tietjens the Englishman', in *Ford Madox Ford's Modernity*, ed. Robert Hampson and Max Saunders, International Ford Madox Ford Studies, 2 (Amsterdam and Atlanta, GA: Rodopi, 2003), 161–74

Brown, Nicholas, *Utopian Generations: The Political Horizon of Twentieth-Century Literature* (Princeton, NJ: Princeton University Press, 2005)

Buitenhuis, Peter, *The Great War of Words: British, American and Canadian Propaganda and Fiction, 1914–1933* (Vancouver: University of British Columbia Press, 1987)

Calderaro, Michela A., *A Silent New World: Ford Madox Ford's Parade's End* (Bologna: Editrice CLUEB [Cooperativa Libraria Universitaria, Editrice Bologna], 1993)

Caserio, Robert L., 'Ford's and Kipling's Modernist Imagination of Public Virtue', in *Ford Madox Ford's Modernity*, ed. Robert Hampson and Max Saunders, International Ford Madox Ford Studies, 2 (Amsterdam and Atlanta, GA: Rodopi, 2003), 175–90

Cassell, Richard A., *Ford Madox Ford: A Study of his Novels* (Baltimore: Johns Hopkins University Press, 1962)

—*Ford Madox Ford: Modern Judgements* (London: Macmillan, 1972)

—*Critical Essays on Ford Madox Ford* (Boston: G. K. Hall, 1987)

Colombino, Laura, *Ford Madox Ford: Vision, Visuality and Writing* (Oxford: Peter Lang, 2008)

Conroy, Mark, 'A Map of Tory Misreading in *Parade's End*', in *Ford Madox Ford and Visual Culture*, ed. Laura Colombino, International Ford Madox Ford Studies, 8 (Amsterdam and New York: Rodopi, 2009), 175–90.

Cook, Cornelia, 'Last Post', *Agenda*, 27:4–28:1, Ford Madox Ford special double issue (winter 1989–spring 1990), 23–30

Davis, Philip, 'The Saving Remnant', in *Ford Madox Ford and English-ness*, ed. Dennis Brown and Jenny Plastow, International Ford Madox Ford Studies, 5 (Amsterdam and New York: Rodopi, 2006), 21–35

Deer, Patrick, *Culture in Camouflage: War, Empire, and Modern British Literature* (Oxford: Oxford University Press, 2009)

DeKoven, Marianne, 'Valentine Wannop and Thematic Structure in Ford Madox Ford's *Parade's End*', *English Literature in Transition (1880–1920)*, 20:2 (1977), 56–68

Erskine-Hill, Howard, 'Ford's Novel Sequence: An Essay in Retrospection', *Agenda*, 27:4–28:1, Ford Madox Ford special double issue (winter 1989–spring 1990), 46–55

Frayn, Andrew, '"This Battle Was not Over": *Parade's End* as a Transitional Text in the Development of "Disenchanted" First World War Literature', in *Ford Madox Ford: Literary Networks and Cultural Transformations*, ed. Andrzej Gasiorek and Daniel Moore, International Ford Madox Ford Studies, 7 (Amsterdam and New York: Rodopi, 2008), 201–16

Gasiorek, Andrzej, 'The Politics of Cultural Nostalgia: History and Tradition in Ford Madox Ford's *Parade's End*', *Literature & History*, 11:2 (third series) (autumn 2002), 52–77

Gordon, Ambrose, Jr, *The Invisible Tent: The War Novels of Ford Madox Ford* (Austin, TX: University of Texas Press, 1964)

Green, Robert, *Ford Madox Ford: Prose and Politics* (Cambridge: Cambridge University Press, 1981)

Haslam, Sara, *Fragmenting Modernism: Ford Madox Ford, the Novel, and the Great War* (Manchester: Manchester University Press, 2002)

Heldman, J. M., 'The Last Victorian Novel: Technique and Theme in *Parade's End*', *Twentieth Century Literature*, 18 (Oct. 1972), 271–84

Hoffmann, Charles G., *Ford Madox Ford: Updated Edition* (Boston: Twayne Publishers, 1990)

Holton, Robert. *Jarring Witnesses: Modern Fiction and the Representation of History* (Hemel Hempstead: Harvester Wheatsheaf, 1994)

Hynes, Samuel, 'Ford Madox Ford: Three Dedicatory Letters to *Parade's End*, with Commentary and Notes', *Modern Fiction Studies*, 16:4 (1970), 515–28

—*A War Imagined: The First World War and English Culture* (London: The Bodley Head, 1990)

Judd, Alan, *Ford Madox Ford* (London: Collins, 1990)

Kashner, Rita, 'Tietjens' Education: Ford Madox Ford's Tetralogy', *Critical Quarterly*, 8 (1966), 150–63

MacShane, Frank, *The Life and Work of Ford Madox Ford* (New York: Horizon; London: Routledge & Kegan Paul, 1965)

— ed., *Ford Madox Ford: The Critical Heritage* (London: Routledge, 1972)

Meixner, John A., *Ford Madox Ford's Novels: A Critical Study* (Minneapolis: University of Minnesota Press; London: Oxford University Press, 1962)

Mizener, Arthur, *The Saddest Story: A Biography of Ford Madox Ford* (New York: World, 1971; London: The Bodley Head, 1972)

Monta, Anthony P., '*Parade's End* in the Context of National Efficiency', in *History and Representation in Ford Madox Ford's Writings*, ed. Joseph Wiesenfarth, International Ford Madox Ford Studies, 3 (Amsterdam and New York: Rodopi, 2004), 41–51

Moore, Gene, 'The Tory in a Time of Change: Social Aspects of Ford Madox Ford's *Parade's End*', *Twentieth Century Literature*, 28:1 (spring 1982), 49–68

Moser, Thomas C., *The Life in the Fiction of Ford Madox Ford* (Princeton, NJ: Princeton University Press, 1980)

Munton, Alan, 'The Insane Subject: Ford and Wyndham Lewis in the War and Post-War', in *Ford Madox Ford: Literary Networks and Cultural Transformations*, ed. Andrzej Gasiorek and Daniel Moore, International Ford Madox Ford Studies, 7 (Amsterdam and New York: Rodopi, 2008), 105–30

Parfitt, George, *Fiction of the First World War: A Study* (London: Faber & Faber, 1988)

Radford, Andrew, 'The Gentleman's Estate in Ford's *Parade's End*', *Essays in Criticism* 52:4 (Oct. 2002), 314–32

Saunders, Max, 'Ford and European Modernism: War, Time, and *Parade's End*', in *Ford Madox Ford and 'The Republic of Letters'*, ed. Vita Fortunati and Elena Lamberti (Bologna: Editrice CLUEB [Cooperativa Libraria Universitaria, Editrice Bologna], 2002), 3–21

—'Introduction', Ford Madox Ford, *Parade's End* (Harmondsworth: Penguin, 2002), vii–xvii

Seiden, Melvin, 'Persecution and Paranoia in *Parade's End*', *Criticism*,

8:3 (summer 1966), 246–62

Skinner, Paul, '"Not the Stuff to Fill Graveyards": Joseph Conrad and *Parade's End*', in *Inter-relations: Conrad, James, Ford, and Others*, ed. Keith Carabine and Max Saunders (Lublin: Columbia University Press, 2003), 161–76.

—'The Painful Processes of Reconstruction: History in *No Enemy* and *Last Post*', in *History and Representation in Ford Madox Ford's Writings*, ed. Joseph Wiesenfarth, International Ford Madox Ford Studies, 3 (Amsterdam and New York: Rodopi, 2004), 65–75

Snitow, Ann Barr, *Ford Madox Ford and the Voice of Uncertainty* (Baton Rouge: Louisiana State University Press, 1984)

Sorum, Eve, 'Mourning and Moving On: Life after War in Ford Madox Ford's *The Last Post*', in *Modernism and Mourning*, ed. Patricia Rae (Lewisburg, PA: Bucknell University Press, 2007), 154–67

Stang, Sondra J., *Ford Madox Ford* (New York: Ungar, 1977)

Tate, Trudi, 'Rumour, Propaganda, and *Parade's End*', *Essays in Criticism*, 47:4 (Oct. 1997), 332–53

—*Modernism, History and the First World War* (Manchester: Manchester University Press, 1998)

Trotter David, 'Ford Against Lewis and Joyce', in *Ford Madox Ford: Literary Networks and Cultural Transformations*, ed. Andrzej Gasiorek and Daniel Moore, International Ford Madox Ford Studies, 7 (Amsterdam and New York: Rodopi, 2008), 131–49

Weiss, Timothy, *Fairy Tale and Romance in Works of Ford Madox Ford* (Lanham, MD: University Press of America, 1984)

Wiesenfarth, Joseph, *Gothic Manners and the Classic English Novel* (Madison: University of Wisconsin Press, 1988)

Wiley, Paul L., *Novelist of Three Worlds: Ford Madox Ford* (Syracuse, NY: Syracuse University Press, 1962)

# THE FORD MADOX FORD SOCIETY

**Ford c. 1915    ©Alfred Cohen, 2000    Registered Charity No. 1084040**

This international society was founded in 1997 to promote knowledge of and interest in Ford. Honorary Members include Julian Barnes, A. S. Byatt, Hans-Magnus Enzensberger, Samuel Hynes, Alan Judd, Bill Nighy, Ruth Rendell, Michael Schmidt, John Sutherland, and Gore Vidal. There are currently over one hundred members, from more than ten countries. Besides regular meetings in Britain, we have held conferences in Italy, Germany, the U.S.A, and France. Since 2002 we have published International Ford Madox Ford Studies; a series of substantial annual volumes distributed free to members. *Ford Madox Ford: A Reappraisal* (2002), *Ford Madox Ford's Modernity* (2003), *History and Representation in Ford Madox Ford's Writings* (2004), *Ford Madox Ford and the City* (2005), *Ford Madox Ford and Englishness* (2006), *Ford Madox Ford's Literary Contacts* (2007), *Ford Madox Ford: Literary Networks and Cultural Transformations* (2008), *Ford Madox Ford and Visual Culture* (2009), and *Ford Madox Ford, Modernist Magazines and Editing* (2010) are all still available. Future volumes are planned on Ford and France, on his pre-war work, and on *Parade's End* and the First World War. If you are an admirer, an enthusiast, a reader, a scholar, or a student of anything Fordian, then this Society would welcome your involvement.

The Ford Madox Ford Society normally organises events and publishes Newsletters each year. Future meetings are planned in Glasgow, London and Germany. The Society also inaugurated a series of Ford Lectures. Speakers have included Alan Judd, Nicholas Delbanco, Zinovy Zinik, A. S. Byatt, Colm Tóibín, and Hermione Lee. To join, please see the website for details; or send your name and address (including an e-mail address if possible), and a cheque made payable to 'The Ford Madox Ford Society', to:

Dr Paul Skinner, 7 Maidstone Street, Victoria Park, Bristol BS3 4SW, UK.
Telephone: 0117 9715008; Fax: 0117 9020294 Email: p.skinner370@btinternet.com

Annual rates: **Sterling:** Individuals: £12 (by standing order; otherwise £15); Concessions £8; **Euros:** €15.00 (by standing order; otherwise €20.00); Concessions €8.50. **US Dollars:** Any category: $25

For further information, either contact Paul Skinner (Treasurer) at the above address, or Sara Haslam (Chair) by e-mail at: s.j.haslam@open.ac.uk
The Society's Website is at: **http://open.ac.uk/Arts/fordmadoxford-society**